THE SAXON SHORE

THE CAMULOD CHRONICLES

JACK WHYTE

A TOM DOHERTY ASSOCIATES BOOK

NEW YORK

THE SAXON SHORE

Copyright © 1998 by Jack Whyte

This book is printed on acid-free paper.

Map by Ellisa Mitchell

A Forge Book
Published by Tom Doherty Associates, LLC.
175 Fifth Avenue
New York, NY 10010

Forge® is a registered trademark of Tom Doherty Associates, LLC.

Library of Congress Cataloging-in-Publication Data

Whyte, Jack.
    The Saxon shore / Jack Whyte.—1st trade pbk. ed.
      p. cm.
    "A Forge Book"—T.p. verso.
    ISBN 0-765-30650-6
    1. Arthur, King—Fiction. 2. Merlin (Legendary character)—
Fiction. 3. Great Britain—History—To 1066—Fiction.
    4. Arthurian romances—Adaptations. 5. Kings and rulers—Fiction.
    6. Britons—Fiction. I. Title.

    PR9199.3.W4589S39 2003
    813'.54—dc21

    OL671   2003049140

Printed in the United States of America

D 10 9 8 7

THE
SAXON
SHORE

By Jack Whyte from Tom Doherty Associates

THE CAMULOD CHRONICLES
The Skystone
The Singing Sword
The Eagles' Brood
The Saxon Shore
The Fort at River's Bend
The Sorcerer: Metamorphosis
Uther

To my wife, Beverley, with gratitude for twenty-five years
of long-suffering patience, support and encouragement.

THE LEGEND OF THE SKYSTONE

Out of the night sky there will fall a stone
That hides a maiden born of murky deeps,
A maid whose fire-fed, female mysteries
Shall give life to a lambent, gleaming blade,
A blazing, shining sword whose potency
Breeds warriors. More than that,
This weapon will contain a woman's wiles
And draw dire deeds of men; shall name an age;
Shall crown a king, called of a mountain clan
Who dream of being drawn from dragon's seed;
Fell, forceful men, heroic, proud and strong,
With greatness in their souls.
This king, this monarch, mighty beyond ken,
Fashioned of glory, singing a song of swords,
Misting with magic madness mortal men,
Shall sire a legend, yet leave none to lead
His host to triumph after he be lost.
But death shall ne'er demean his destiny who,
Dying not, shall ever live and wait to be recalled.

THE CELTS

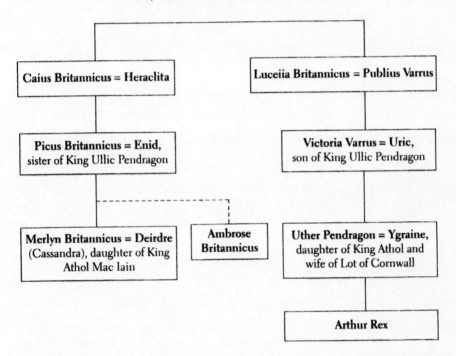

Ullic Pendragon, King of the Pendragon people of Cambria (Modern Wales)

Athol Mac Iain, King of the Scots people of Eire (the Roman *Scotii* of Hibernia)

THE ROMANO-BRITISH

Caius Britannicus = Heraclita

Luceiia Britannicus = Publius Varrus

Picus Britannicus = Enid, sister of King Ullic Pendragon

Victoria Varrus = Uric, son of King Ullic Pendragon

Merlyn Britannicus = Deirdre (Cassandra), daughter of King Athol Mac Iain

Ambrose Britannicus

Uther Pendragon = Ygraine, daughter of King Athol and wife of Lot of Cornwall

Arthur Rex

THE GENEALOGY OF ARTHUR PENDRAGON

PROLOGUE

THERE IS A traditional belief, seldom spoken of but widely held, that age brings wisdom, and that wisdom, once achieved through some arcane epiphany, continues to grow inexorably with increasing age. Like most people, I accepted that throughout my life, until the day I found that I had somehow grown old enough to be considered wise by others. The discovery frightened me badly and shook my faith in most of my other beliefs.

Now that I have survived everyone I once knew, I grow more aware each day of how unwise I have been throughout my life. Unwise might even be too mild a word for this folly of persistence I betray in clinging to a life of solitude and pain. The pain is unimportant, and in a total absence of sympathy it has become a form of penance I gladly accept and endure in expiation of my sins of omission and unpreparedness. The solitude, however, grows unbearable at times and I am now accustomed to talking to myself merely to hear the sound of a human voice. Sometimes I argue with myself. Sometimes I read aloud what I have written. Sometimes I speak my unformed thoughts, shaping them audibly to light a beacon in the darkness in my efforts to write down a clean, coherent chronicle of what once flourished proudly in this land but has now ceased to be.

I find it strange nowadays to think that I may be the only one alive in all this land who knows how to write words down, and because of that may be the only one who knows that words, unwritten, have no value. Set down in writing, words are real; legible, memorable, exact and permitting recollection, imaginings and wonder. Otherwise, sung or spoken, whispered to oneself or shouted to the winds, words are ephemeral, perishing as they are uttered. That, at least, I have learned in my extreme age.

And so I write my chronicle, and in the writing of it I maintain the life in my old bones, unable to consider death while yet the task remains unfinished. For I believe this story must survive. Empires have risen in this world and fallen, and history takes note of few of them. Those that survive in the memories of men do so by virtue of the faults that flawed their greatness. But here in Britain, in my own lifetime, a spark ignited in the breast of one strong man and became a clean, pure flame to light the world, a beacon that might have outshone the great lighthouse of Pharos, had a sudden gust of willful wind not extinguished it prematurely. In the space of a few, bright years, something new stirred in this land; something unprecedented; something wonderful; and men, being men, perceived it with stunned awe and then, being men, destroyed it without thought, for being new and strange.

When it was over, when the light was snuffed out like a candle flame, a young man, full of hurt and bewilderment, asked me to explain how everything had happened. He expected me to know, for I was Merlyn, the Sorcerer, Fount of all Wisdom. And in my folly, feeling for the youth, I sought to tell him. But I was too young, at sixty-four, to understand what had occurred and why it had been inevitable. That was a decade and a half ago. Even now, after years of solitary thought and questioning, I only know that, at the start of Arthur's life, I had no thought of being who I am today, nor of how I could presume to teach a child to be the man, the King, the potent Champion he would become. In those years, I had far too much to learn, myself, to have had time for thoughts on teaching.

I know that by the rules of random chance Arthur should never have been born, but was; and then, being born, he should have died in infancy, yet lived. Feared and despised by men who had no knowledge of his nature, he should not have survived his early boyhood, yet escaped to grow. I know that, reared by men who scarcely knew the name or the meaning of kingship, he should never have emerged to be the High King he became, the culmination of a dream dreamed long before, by men dead long before his birth. I know he was my challenge and my pride, my pupil and my life's sole, crowned success. And I know the dream he fostered and made real deserves to live forever; hence this task of mine.

BOOK ONE

CORNWALL

I

I COULD NOT identify the clattering noise that woke me, and for a space of heartbeats I lay befuddled, not knowing where I was. The sun was high and hot, and I felt my bed tilt alarmingly. Then I became aware of the warmth of the tiny baby I held cradled in my arm, and I remembered everything.

We were adrift in a small galley or birney that was much too large for me to control alone, even had I known how. The smell of the bearskin pelt on which we lay mingled with the scents of sun-warmed pitch and timber. A heavy, rusted, three-pronged grappling hook had landed on the planking beside me, close to my head. As I focused on it, the thing leapt away from me again, before burying two of its points in the solid timbers of the boat's side. I rolled away from the child and struggled to my feet, throwing myself to the side of the boat and looking up and out.

Above me, towering over and dwarfing our small boat, was a great galley with a single, soaring mast and a rearing, giant, painted dragon's head at the prow. In my first glance I saw a row of long oars, glistening with water, raised vertically to permit the two craft to come together, then a red-bearded warrior standing on the prow behind the dragon's head, leaning backward against the pull as he drew in his rope, hand over hand, dragging my smaller craft towards him. Beside him, another man was in the act of throwing a second grappling hook, and I pulled my head down and out of sight as the metal head landed behind me and was jerked back to thump into the birney's timbers, lodging farther forward, beside the first. As I sprawled away to one side, a roar of surprise told me that my appearance had disconcerted them no less than theirs had me. A third and then a fourth hook clanked aboard and made themselves fast, and I felt our boat being hauled in like a fish, its motion changing as it struck laterally against the waves.

This time I raised my head cautiously and saw that it was the target for a score of bows, all of their arrows pointing at my eyes. I raised my hands high above my head, fingers spread, showing them I had no thought of fight or flight, and immediately slid back down the sloping side before stepping hastily back to the centre of the deck, my hands still high above my head as I fought to keep my footing, waiting for the first arrow to find me. Below me, the child had awakened and begun to howl with hunger, his tiny, angry protests lost amid the noises that now swelled all around us.

I glanced towards him and my eyes were suddenly filled with the bulk and substance of the heavy, golden signet ring with the red dragon crest that hung on a golden chain against his tiny chest. I threw myself towards him and removed the thing from around his neck, stuffing it hastily into my own breechclout and hoping it would remain lodged securely there and not fall out onto the deck. It was the only recourse open to me, and I had no time to improve on the instinct that prompted me to hide the ring there.

Moments later, the first of our "rescuers" leapt aboard from the raised deck of the other ship, closely followed by a half-dozen others. He landed lightly, then stepped towards me, noting that I was unarmed but extending his sword point towards my naked throat and glancing around him in curiosity as he closed the distance between us. He was big, as big as I, and hairy in the way of the Celts, with a full black beard, long hair and moustaches, and thick black chest hair showing through the open front of a sheepskin tunic worn fleece-outward. As I lowered my hands and made to speak to him he drew the point of his sword away from me, then brought it swinging, backhanded, to clout me almost heedlessly across the side of the head with the flat of the blade. I fell sprawling and stunned.

I huddled there, my knees drawn up instinctively to protect the contents of my breechclout, clasping my head in my hands, almost blinded by the pain and waiting for his attack to continue. My assailant, however, had done with me and ignored me completely thereafter. By the time my vision cleared enough to see him again, he had stepped away and was bent over the discarded pile of my armour that lay where I had thrown it on the bottom of the boat. My eyes moved onward, ignoring the others who had come aboard with him, searching frantically for the black bearskin that lay at the foot of the central mast. There, surrounded by three of the newcomers, the baby kicked and squirmed, and even through the racket all around me, I could clearly hear his anguished screams. The three men were looking down at him, arguing among themselves. After a single and dismissive glance towards me, one of them shifted his axe from his right hand to his left, stooped quickly and picked up the child by the ankles, crushing them together carelessly.

My head swam with panic.

Once, twice, he spun the tiny form around his head and then released it to fly into the air, high over the vessel's side.

Afterwards, I was unaware of having moved, let alone risen to my feet, but suddenly I was upon them. I heard my own roar of rage as my shoulder took the big man low in the back, hurling him forward and off balance, and my fingers gripped the shaft of the axe that had hung from his left hand. Still reeling from the momentum of my charge, I swung one foot around hard to kick one of his companions behind the knees, sweeping him off his feet. The third man, caught by surprise, simply stood there, giving me time to shift my weight, grip the shaft of the axe firmly in both hands and spin again to bury it in the killer's shoulder, splitting him from neck to breast bone. Pulling him towards me, his flesh locked around the blade of the axe, I used the dead weight of him for leverage and leapt high onto the edge of the boat's side. I saw a flash of white among the waves and threw myself outward towards it, bringing my hands together above my head to break the water.

The sea was far warmer than I had expected, and after the first shock of my plunging dive my head was cleared of noise and pain. A thousand bubbles hissed all around me, and I opened my eyes, searching frantically for a glimpse of the infant. There was nothing, no matter where I looked, and I kicked my way back to the surface, treading water as I looked around me, shaking the hair and water out of my eyes. I surfaced at the top of a wave and quickly found myself in the trough between it and the next, from where I could see nothing. Allowing myself to relax, I waited to be lifted again to the wave top, and heard a zipping noise as an arrow sliced into the water ahead of me. Now I was high again, and saw the galley, enormous from this vantage point, riding high above and in front of me. More arrows hissed into the sea around me, and I heard a distant chorus of shouts and jeers. I ignored them and tried to turn myself around as I went sliding to the bottom of another trough. Moments later, as I rose to the crest of the next wave, I saw the baby on the surface very close to me, disappearing again as I caught sight of him. I filled my lungs, gulping in air until my chest would hold no more, before folding my body and kicking my feet vertically. In the booming, reverberant silence beneath the surface an arrow dropped in front of me, wobbling harmlessly before falling vertically into the depths below. I strained my eyes towards where I thought to have seen the tiny shape of the child, and there he was, pallid and insubstantial at the limit of my sight, floating beneath the waves. I kicked out strongly towards him, knowing I was too late. The shock of hitting the water alone must have killed him, and with him the hopes of my family.

There are times when the mind of a man performs the most amazing feats; when the speed of thought is so enhanced that lifetimes seem to pass in moments; when the mysteries of life seem crystallized, are clearly understood and then forgotten again in the blinking of an eye. Later, I was able to recall the chaos of my thoughts as I swam towards the baby, and to piece them together into coherent patterns that bore no resemblance to the panic-filled, despairing screams that echoed in my mind during those moments. This was my cousin and my nephew both, this babe of two, three months at most, drifting in the clear, warm water just beyond my reach; the son of Uther Pendragon, my dearest friend whom I had sworn to kill. And now they both were dead; as dead as my own unborn son, denied a chance to live, murdered in the womb, I had once believed, by that same Uther. I felt a swelling, aching, unbearable hardness in my chest that told me I was going to have to breathe very soon, and then saw the baby drifting upwards to the surface, rising away from me to where the waves formed a clear green ceiling streaked with lines of writhing, golden light. I kicked harder, forcing myself through the water, clawing my way towards him and seeing without really noticing the way his tiny arms and legs moved rhythmically, almost as if he himself were swimming. Suddenly my face touched him and I grasped him close, breaking the surface, raising him high above my head as I fought for breath, coughing and spluttering and sinking again as I waited for the arrows to find us, finding some insane satisfaction in the knowledge that we would meet death together, united in our blood. Again I broke surface, and this time was able to breathe and keep myself afloat. The galley loomed above us, very close now. We were an unmissable target. I closed my eyes and hugged the baby close, holding his head above the water.

The arrows did not come. A wave broke over us. I opened my eyes and blinked them free of water, and as I did, a rope came snaking down, uncoiling as it fell, to land across my head. Unknowing and uncaring whence it came or why, I grasped it with my left hand, twisting coils of it around my arm as I went under yet again, mouth open and inhaling. Choking in agony, my lungs revolting against the sea water, I felt myself being dragged forward and up, and hands grasped at me, catching my arm, my tunic and my hair. Someone took the child from me, and I felt myself propelled upward and inward and then lowered, quite gently, to the decking of the ship. I rolled onto my belly, coughing and vomiting the brine I had breathed and swallowed, fighting the searing pains that racked my chest and lungs.

The paroxysm passed eventually, leaving me spent and breathless, and I pushed myself up to lean on my elbows, gazing down at the planking of the deck between them and waiting for whatever would befall me next. I had no thought of avoiding it, whatever it might be, knowing that it would be death in one form or another, blooding and vengeance for the man I had killed with the axe. That was why they had dragged me from the sea. They required blood for blood, and death by water would not suffice. The manner of my death was beyond my control, and beyond my caring. The only matter of import in my mind was the death of the child and what it meant to Camulod. The dreams of many people had perished with that baby boy, and I saw them all there in my mind as I gasped and heaved for breath. Caius Britannicus, my grandfather, and Publius Varrus, his friend, both of whom I had revered throughout my life; Picus Britannicus, my father, and Ullic and Uric Pendragon, father and son, and a host of others who had dared to dream of surviving in the face of conquest by barbarian hordes, the same hordes who had now wiped out their line. My mind filled up with the image of the baby boy I had discovered wrapped in a black bearskin here in this very boat, and I recalled the pride and the passionate, exultant tenderness that had swept over me in realizing who he was, in knowing this was *he*, the one who would arise to call the peoples of our land to action and to unity; the future champion for whose hand Publius Varrus had crafted the sword Excalibur. And as I felt the pain of that memory, I also felt another, sharper, localized pain against my pubis, where the signet of Uther Pendragon was evidently still secure, wedged uncomfortably between my body and the deck of the ship.

My chest constricted and I retched again, moving at the same time to ease the discomfort caused by the ring and gasping against the agony of the convulsion that racked me, and as I gulped for breath another image came into my mind: a tall, young man with long, bright golden hair; a champion who perhaps, even now, would be in Camulod, and into whose hands I had commended Excalibur should I not have returned within the year; Ambrose, my own half-brother, absent from my mind since my discovery of the boy.

A heavy foot kicked my elbow and I snatched it away, falling face downward into the bile I had just voided. I lay helpless as my wrists were snatched and bound together at my back, the rough rope burning my skin. When I reared my head back and tried to look around me I saw only legs. At least a dozen men surrounded me, and I saw now that I was on the big galley, not the birney as I had supposed, and that I was lying at the bottom of the well that held the rowers. They hauled me to my feet again and thrust at me, turning me around and pushing me forward until I saw what they required of me.

There was a lateral bench of some kind at the level of my knee, pressing against me. Above it, a narrow wooden step descended from a planked walkway that ran the length of the galley, front to back. Urged onward by the point of either a spear or a sword at the small of my back, I climbed upward, making heavy going of it with the rocking of the vessel and the awkward weight of my arms, tied tightly as they were behind me. I managed the ascent without falling, nevertheless, and stood swaying on the causeway.

I was somewhere approaching midway along the boat, facing the rear. Below me, ranged in rows on either side, a sea of faces glowered up at me in silence. The men were resting on their oars, evidently waiting. At the end of each row, closest to the centre of the keel and within their owners' reach, were piles of axes, swords and spears. Barbarians. The expressions on those faces I could see varied from wild-eyed hatred to dull disinterest. I ignored them, refusing to acknowledge their presence, although I had time to estimate their strength at close to a hundred. A hundred in one galley! That bespoke great wealth on the part of its owners and great skill on the part of their shipbuilders. I looked straight ahead to where the massive mast reared, thick as a horse's barrel, from the bottom of the ship, beneath the planks of the central causeway, which parted around it, leaving enough room for one man to pass on either side. A great cross-spar, half the thickness of the mast itself, was attached to it about head height, though I could not see how because of the billows of dense, saffron-coloured sailcloth that lay draped across the spar.

Prodded roughly from behind again, I made my way rearwards, passing the mast and dipping my head to avoid the overhead spar. The rearmost part of the ship, I estimated about one sixth of the vessel's total length, was decked over completely at the level of the causeway, fronted by a solid wooden wall with a single doorway leading to the enclosed space below. A group of men huddled on this platform, their backs to me. I counted eight of them as I approached, and their armour, such as I could see of it, was mainly toughened leather of the kind our own Celts wore, bossed with iron and bronze, although one wore overlapped iron strip armour in the Roman fashion and another wore a shirt of ring mail. Three wore long cloaks, so I could see nothing of what they wore beneath. All eight wore helmets; conical iron caps, two of which were horned. Alerted by some signal, they swung around as one to look at me, then stepped back to form an open, wedge-shaped grouping that reflected the taper of the vessel's stern and directed my gaze to the man they had concealed.

I stopped short, trying to absorb what I was seeing, and no one pressed me further. The man himself was, of course, the first thing I perceived, but immediately after that I saw the device in which he hung suspended, and my eyes devoured it, attempting to define what it was and how it operated, disdaining its occupant temporarily despite the fact that he obviously held the order of my dying.

Four thick beams, each a handspan square, had been erected from the body of the ship, mortised into the rail that ran around the deck and cantilevered inward at a uniform angle, supported from the deck by other, smaller struts. I saw instantly where they should have met to form a pyramid, but each had been truncated short of that to provide a corner support for a heavy, rectangular frame that hung thus suspended, level with the deck. I had a vision of the great catapults and siege artillery depicted in the books of Publius Varrus, and as my eye took in the workmanship I knew instantly that the craftsman who built it had been the same man who designed and built the galley. The device was a natural extension of the ship. Below it, suspended by ropes and pulleys from strong hooks attached to each corner of this frame, hung a seat, apparently made from strong leather, stitched and shaped and strung from an open-fronted girdle of iron as thick as my thumb. Thin hempen ropes, three of them, hung from this metal chair rim to the floor, whence they passed through a ring bolted into the deck and separated to three other rings, where they were stoutly knotted, one in the back and one on either side. They looked for all the world like reins, and I realized that they were nothing less. The person seated in that chair might ride the turmoil of the waves in comfort, suspended above the deck and able to master all but the wildest motion of the seat by pulling on these ropes.

All of these thoughts had coursed through my mind in less time than it takes to speak of them, and I grew conscious of the silence that hung around me. I looked then at the leader of this crew.

He sat slouched in his hanging seat, wrapped in a great, long cloak of thick, green wool embellished with red symbols unknown to me. Beneath him, one long, booted leg stretched indolently to the deck; the other jutted out horizontally, seemingly rigid beneath the cloak, pointing at me. I gazed at him, looking square into his eyes, holding my own head high.

He had the look of a Celtic chieftain, saturnine, swarthy, with long, dark, flowing moustaches and a small beard that covered his chin but left his cheeks clean shaven. His nose jutted, fine edged and arrogant over cleanly shaped, narrow nostrils, and great black-browed blue eyes, so bright they seemed to glow, swept me from head to foot, taking my measure. I saw the breadth of his high forehead and the long, dark, curling hair swept back behind his ears, the line of it forming the suggestion of a peak exactly at the centre of his brow. He wore a heavy, ornate golden torc, the collar of a chieftain, about his neck, which was thick and strong, hinting of a deep chest and broad shoulders, although these were concealed in his cloak. We faced each other mutely, neither allowing any trace of emotion to paint his features. I was aware of the tension of the men who surrounded me. A wave smacked against the side of the galley, setting the deck atilt beneath my feet, and hemp ropes creaked in protest.

And then he threw aside the cloak, exposing the baby that lay nestled, sleeping or dead, in the cradle of his right elbow. The sight, the unexpectedness of it, caught me off guard and I sprang forward, uttering a cry that was cut off in my throat by a heavy blow across the neck and shoulder that felled me to the deck. As I lay there, struggling for consciousness against the sudden violence that had clamped my eyes tight shut and the roaring of my own blood that filled my head, I heard their voices speaking the tongue of Donuil, the prince of the Eirish tribe we called the Scotii or Scots, whom I had held hostage against his people's good behaviour. They were discussing me.

"Well? Shall I kill him now? He's an Outlander. You'll get nothing out of him. Can't even speak his language." This was a heavy, growling voice, well on in years, and it was greeted by a chorus of consensual muttering. They all fell silent as the next man spoke, and I knew I was hearing the voice of their chieftain.

"Aye, you may be right, Tearlach, but we won't know until we try, will we? He may have information we can use. I think I want to spare his life for now, from curiosity, if nothing else."

"Why waste your time and ours?" The growling voice was filled with menace or disgust. "The whoreson killed Lachie. An eye for an eye, I say, and be damned to your curiosity. Let's spill his tripes and dump him to the fishes."

"*Arragh*, but why did he kill Lachie, and for what?" There was a ring to the question that made even me wish to hear the answer, and the others fell silent again as the voice went on. "If he's a Saxon, as he would seem to be with that head of yellow hair, then why would he die thus gladly for an alien child? Look at this boy, all of you, and tell me where your eyes are. Look at him! Look at his eyes! Here is no Saxon. This child is pure Gael. Why then, ask yourselves, would this Outlander behave as he did in killing Lachie? Or are you all solid bone clear upward from the necks? Where is your desire to know how such things work—what men will do under dire provocation? Could this be the man's son? Ah! In that case, his anger would be yours, had you seen what he saw . . ."

The child was alive! Even in my pain I felt my flesh tingle with the knowledge of what could only be a miracle. The voice above me pressed on.

"And if this be his son, what then? A Saxon father protective to death of a Gaelic child?" His voice faded, then resumed more loudly, cutting short the man Tearlach's effort to interrupt. "What concerns *me*, my friends, is how this yellow-headed wolf came to be aboard yon birney, and adrift at sea. *Our* birney! That concern is not going to be resolved by killing the creature without trying to discover what he might know. Where are our own men, Red Dougal and Alasdair, Fingal and the others of their crew? And far, far more important, where are the women they were sent to find? I'll tell you, my lads, if we cannot find means to loosen this man's tongue, I for one will take little pleasure in the thought of sailing home with such news as we have to bring my father."

A babble of voices broke out as they began to argue among themselves and I made an attempt to rise. It was a forlorn attempt; the hampering effect of my bound arms allowed me only to kick my legs uselessly, squirming around on the planking. I felt a foot insert itself between me and the decking, at the point of my shoulder, and then the heave of a leg turned me so that I almost rolled over onto my back—to be stopped again by my bound arms, coming to rest with the full weight of my body on my tied wrists and one elbow. In spite of my gritted teeth, I could not stifle an agonized groan. I lay squinting up at them while they all stared back. I ground my teeth against the dementing pain in my arms and managed to draw a deep breath.

"I can tell you what you want to know." I grated out the words painfully in their own tongue, through my locked teeth.

The shock on their faces might have been laughable at any other time, but the humour of the scene escaped me until much later. To hear their own liquid gutturals spill fluently from the lips of one they took to be a Saxon Outlander left all of them floundering. They recovered themselves quickly, nevertheless, led by their leader, at whose word two of them leaned over and hauled me to my feet again, bracing me between them. Behind us, I could hear the shocked muttering of the crew as word of this new development spread quickly from one end of the ship to the other.

The leader had pulled himself out of his slouch, sitting erect now, although his right leg still stretched stiffly before him, shrouded in the folds of his long cloak. He held the baby, which had fallen asleep, casually, yet with the assurance of practice, supported by his bent forearm against his side. He gazed at me now through narrowed eyes.

"You understand our tongue."

I nodded, my breathing still too shallow to allow me to speak strongly.

"How so?"

I tried to answer him, but my tongue failed me. I heaved a breath, shaking my head in a mute plea for patience. Finally, when I felt I could articulate the words without faltering, I said, "I learned it from a friend . . . It is not unlike my own."

"Your friend is Erse?"

I nodded. "He is."

I heard a muttered curse from the largest of the men on my left, and recognized the grumbling tone as Tearlach grunted something about a traitorous dog. I ignored it.

The leader was gazing at me fixedly. "How come you here, adrift in this vessel?"

"By hazard," I responded, shaking my head. The pain in my arms had begun to abate now that I was standing again. "I had no thought to leave the land. I merely sought to save the child."

"Save him? From what?"

I blinked at him, surprised that he should have to ask. "From death," I said. "The boat was drifting on the rising tide, floating away from shore, when I heard his cries. I climbed aboard and found him, then found I was too far away from shore to return." I hesitated, unwilling to show ignorance, but knowing there was no way to conceal it. "I have no knowledge of the sea, or ships, and knew not how to return the craft to land."

"You can swim; you could have swum ashore." His eyes were piercing bright, watching me closely. I shook my head.

"No, I wore armour and had no wish to be without it. So I stayed in the hope we'd drift ashore again. Besides, I might have drowned the child."

His eyes moved aside and I followed his glance to where my discarded armour, ring suit, helmet, sword, dagger and cloak lay piled against the ship's side.

After that one glance, however, he chose not to pursue the matter, apparently accepting the truth of my words. "The child is that important to you? Why?"

I said nothing, but he would not accept that.

"Why did you kill my man Lachie, and why leap overboard after the child?" I merely glared at him and he went on. "You thought to save it?"

I could not respond. His question was too alien.

"Well, did you? Did you think to save the child? Answer me, man!"

"Yes."

"Yes." The single word, repeated in his voice, sounded far different from the word I had said. On his tongue, it dripped scorn. "From what, from death?" He lowered his head again to look at the child before facing me again, his eyes now filled with anger. "What kind of fool are you? It would have been a kindness to the babe to let him drown. Now he will die of thirst and starvation, for there is no food here for him. He is *new-born*, fool, fit only for suckling at his mother's teat! He cannot eat, or drink, or feed himself, and we have no milk here."

His angry scorn confounded me, for I had not thought of any of this. In seeking to rescue the child I had thought only of his life, not of the means required to sustain that life beyond the moment of salvation. Realization of my foolishness removed the sting from his angry words, however, and I nodded in acquiescence.

"That's true," I said. "I had not thought of that."

"Hmm." He changed the subject, looking down at the sleeping baby in his arms and rubbing one fingertip against its tiny cheek, and now his voice was softer. "What of the men who crewed the boat, did you see them?"

"Aye, they were all dead. Slain."

"All of them?" His head came up and I heard disbelief in his voice.

"All of them," I repeated. "The women, too."

He sucked in his breath with a sibilant hiss, and I saw a fleeting expression of pain in his dark eyes. "How many women?"

"Eight. Eight women, twenty-one men."

"And you were left alive?"

"Not *left* alive. I was not with them. I arrived late, too late to help them. Could I have a drink?" My throat was raw.

"Later." He was frowning now, a deep, vertical cleft marring his open brow. "Tell me of this. Who are you, and how came you to arrive there at all, let alone too late to help them? And who was responsible for their deaths? Did you watch from safety until the slaughter had been done and then come forth to plunder the remains, or were you one of the killers?" He paused, watching me closely. "I warn you, think carefully before you speak another word."

I looked back at him, eye to eye, and held myself erect. "I rode in pursuit of the man who killed them, thinking him someone else. I saw them from the top of a distant cliff, clustered upon the sands around their boat, which had been stranded high and dry by the receding tide. Even as I watched, I saw their pursuers close with them, and they seemed well matched, man for man. I rode around and down to overtake them, but my horse was hampered by the sand, so that by the time I arrived the fighting was almost over."

The frown was still etched upon his brow. "And they were all killed, every one, on both sides?" I heard his disbelief.

"No, when I came, six of the attacking force remained alive. They were killing the wounded. It had been a hard-fought fight."

"And?"

"I killed them."

"*All six* of them, you alone?" His disbelief was total.

"Aye, with a bow, from well beyond their reach." I had decided, as I spoke the words, to make no mention of the man I had spared.

Now he looked back at my discarded armour. "I see no bow."

"No," I snapped, knowing I was being reckless, "nor do you see my horse. I left both on the beach."

He pursed his lips and said nothing, and the child in his arm kicked and snuffled.

I felt myself swaying with fatigue, and my bound arms burned with agony. The pain in my head, which had been dulled, took on a new sharpness and located itself, it seemed, right in the middle of my forehead.

The seated chieftain continued to bite thoughtfully at the inside of his lower lip, saying nothing for a spell, then returned to the subject of the women, asking me how they had been killed. I told him haltingly, fumbling for words, reliving the scene in which the attacking force, led, I had thought, by Uther Pendragon, had snatched up the eight women and used them as living shields against the arrows of the defenders. I avoided, however, naming names, either my own or Uther's. My own confusion, watching the affair, had been profound, since I had known neither that the man I thought was Uther wore only Uther's armour, nor that the bowmen facing him were Uther's men. I ended my recital to find myself facing another question.

"You were pursuing one man, thinking him someone else, isn't that what you said? Explain that."

"He was my cousin," I told him, reeling so the men supporting me had to renew their grip. "I thought he had killed my wife, and I had hunted him for many days. He warred against Lot of Cornwall."

That captured his interest, but not, it appeared, in Lot of Cornwall. "You thought he killed your wife? You *thought*? You did not know it?"

"No, I did not know, but I believed he had, and I sought vengeance. I saw him from afar, as I have said, recognizing his armour, but when I caught him, it was someone else, an Outlander who had already killed my cousin and stripped his corpse for his own use."

"So your cousin is dead?"

"Aye."

"When did this take place, this slaughter?"

I squinted up at the sun. "Today, although I don't know how long ago. Shortly before or after noon, I think. We were blown out from land and there was nothing I could do but wait until we were blown in again. I lay down with the child and fell asleep."

The man facing me shook his head in wondering disbelief and his lieutenants burst into guffaws of raucous laughter at my innocence of the ways of the sea.

"You may be fortunate we saw you before you fell beneath the horizon," the leader said. "Where did this happen, do you know?" He read the answer in my eyes and spoke to one of his own men. "Sean, how far would he have drifted with this tide, and from where, in, what, four hours?"

The man addressed leaned over the side of the rail and then looked up at the mast top, to where a banner fluttered. Then he leaned outboard, hawked and spat, watching his spittle fly off with the wind. His voice, when he spoke, was peculiarly high, almost a falsetto, a grotesque sound to issue from so big a man.

"Six leagues? Eight? Perhaps ten. The tide is to the east, so the place lies west, and northward."

"How long to get there? Do we have the time?"

Again the squint up to the masthead. "We have a wind, not much, but it should do. With all men on the oars, we could be off the coast close to the place by nightfall, if we go now."

"So be it." The chieftain looked back at me. "You have until nightfall, if we reach the coast, otherwise till morning. The truth or falsehood of your words will be plain when we find the spot." He paused, his head cocked to one side, looking at me obliquely.

"The resolution lies with you, so I hope you will recognise the place we seek. Failure to do so will prove you have lied, and you will die." He spoke to one of the others. "Cut him loose and find him somewhere to lie down until we sight the coast, and give him some water and a bite to eat." Then to me again, "Rest yourself well, Yellow Head. You will have need of all your faculties."

They cut my bonds and led me to the corresponding platform at the decked-in front part of the boat, where they gave me to eat and drink and threw me a skin to sleep on. I drank the water thirstily but fell into sleep before I could eat the bread.

My body stiffened while I slept, so that by the time someone shook me awake my aches had settled deeply into my bones and I had a hard time rising to my feet, beset with cramps and pains and a head that threatened to burst apart with the clamour of my surging blood. That possibility concerned me, for I had twice in recent years been saved from death by the ministrations of a trusted friend whose skills in medicine had prompted him to drill a hole in my head to relieve the pressure of blood on my brain, what he called *hematoma*. Once upright, I leaned for a spell against the fore part of the ship, close by the great, thrusting dragon's head, allowing the gusting wind to clear my head and ignoring the jostling of the fellow sent to fetch me. I braced myself against the surging deck, stretched myself to my full height, closed my eyes and drew deep, steady breaths, holding each one for a count of three before expelling it completely and filling my lungs again.

The exercise worked, and calmed me to the point that I could tell the present pounding in my skull bore no resemblance to those other, far more ominous headaches I had known. The root of this one lay in the hard, flat metal of the weapon that had hammered me to the deck, bruising my neck and shoulder, both of which ached in concert with my head.

As my various pains died down and I approached mastery of myself once more, I realized that I had awoken to noises that were alien to my ear and offered nothing to appease my aching head: the steady, rhythmic pounding of a deep drum that was not, as I had thought at first, the surging of my own blood in my head; the creaking, grunting, strangely shuffling rhythm of the oarsmen; the groaning of straining ropes and the thin, shrieking whistle of the wind; and among all these, the constant, wailing shriek of a hungry child.

I rubbed the sleep crust from my eyes and followed my escort back along the length of the galley to the stern platform, and the first thing I noticed as I set out was the angle of the great cross-spar on the mast. A strong wind had sprung up, and the spar now slanted right to left from fore to stern to catch its full power. The bellied fabric of a mighty sail swelled out above me, blocking out the sky, angled away from me so that I looked into the cup of it, its heaviness anchored to a second great spar high above that must have overlain the lower one when the sail was lowered. Now I could see that both spars were tethered to the mast by large iron rings bolted firmly to the spars themselves, and held in tension by a bewildering array of tight-stretched ropes that permitted the angle of the spars to be changed to catch the wind. I glanced to my left then and saw the shoreline of Lot's kingdom, and below me the swaying bodies of the oarsmen moved to the steady tempo of the drum, thrusting the vessel forward so that it seemed to skim over the surface.

They rowed two men to an oar, one facing the rear, the other forward so that one pushed while his fellow pulled, and even as I watched, the drum fell silent and the oarsmen changed places, ducking beneath their oars to resume their beat again before the vessel had time to lose way.

No one looked at me as I slowly walked the length of the ship, bracing myself against the heaving of the deck. My presence was of no importance for the time being. The baby's cries grew louder as I approached the stern platform and, although no one indicated anything by look or word, I felt sure that the patience of these men must be close to breaking point. I was surprised, however, to see that the leader, still seated in his swinging chair with leg outstretched, continued to hold the child. The only man with him, the one he had called Tearlach, saw me coming and threw me a withering, disgusted look before swinging himself down to the rowers' level, where he disappeared through the door beneath the deck. The leader watched me as I approached to stand beside him, then indicated the screaming infant with a nod of his head.

"Take note of what I said earlier. You would have done the babe a kindness to let him die. Now he is starving."

I swallowed, clearing a film of mucus from my mouth, not knowing how to respond. "I'm surprised you let him live till now then," I said, my voice no more than a croak.

The man in the chair looked at me sharply, offended, and his response was flat and hard. "We are not all as hard as Lachie," he snapped. "I have children of my own. Your folly was to bring the child aboard at all. Allow me the folly of being unable to kill him out of hand." I saw no benefit in seeking to point out that I had sought, not brought, the child aboard. He kicked off with his foot and the chair swung, while he lowered his head and gazed at the child. Finally he looked up at me and brought the chair to stillness with the guide-rope reins he held in his left hand.

"There's the coastline," he said, indicating the shore. "Do you recognize it?"

I looked, but we were still far out, our beak pointed towards a headland that jutted out from the shore to intersect our path. I shook my head.

"No. We may be too far out, but it looks too flat."

"Aye, that's right, you spoke of cliffs, high cliffs. Well, we'll close presently, and once around the headland there, you'll see cliffs aplenty. There are some bays along the shoreline there. One of them should be yours." His tone of voice added, *if what you say is true.* He lifted the child up, resting it over his shoulder against his breast, and then asked, "Are there cattle there?"

I blinked at him. "Cattle? Where?"

His frown was quick. "Ashore! Cattle, man, cows, or goats or even sheep. This child needs milk."

Again I shook my head, bewildered. "I don't know." And then I remembered. "But there's a woman there, with milk! I found her—saw her there—this morning. She was mad . . . insane with grief, kneeling beside the bodies of her man and children. One was a tiny babe, as small as he. She must have milk."

"Are you sure? And could you find her again?"

I nodded. "Aye, I could. I would have to ride back the way I came, retrace my steps. But she will still be there, I think. The poor creature had nowhere else to go."

"And you would bring her back?" I heard the cynical sharpness in his tone.

Now it was I who was offended. We were alone, the two of us, on the platform. "Think you I'd leave the child with you, after what I've gone through for him?"

In response he moved the child again, holding it up in front of him to peer into its angry red face. I swung away in disgust, looking upward as I did to where the great sail bellied above me, and as I did so, the wind died for a space of moments, then gusted again, so that the fabric emptied and went slack, then filled again with a mighty, cracking sound, stretched and taut, thrusting its emblem into my astonished gaze.

The sight of it sent my mind leaping instantly, back through time, to Camulod and a conversation I had had with a young Erse chief, Donuil, whom I had held hostage. He had warned me, that day, that none of the Hibernian tribes—he called them Eirish tribes—save his would be bound by our bargain. The clans of Eire warred constantly among themselves, he said, and each had its own emblem. His father's emblem, the black galley of his clan, would, Donuil had sworn, stay clear of our seas for the five years of his captivity.

Above me, blazoned on the saffron-coloured sail of this great ship, a huge, black galley swelled against the sky.

The realization of where I was, and the myriad complications thus involved, left my mind reeling for a spell. I was conscious that I stood on a threshold of some kind and that the next few moments might decide my future, for I knew that here, immediately, could lie life or death for me and for my helpless, hungry ward. I turned to the side and gripped the handrail, taking care that the man behind me should not see my face while I tried vainly to recall the rest of that conversation, when Donuil had spoken to me of his brothers and their feuds and jealousies. One of them he had loved, the crippled one. And then I had it.

I turned back to the man in the chair, and he raised his eyes to meet mine, his face expressionless.

"It was a bear that took your leg, Connor, was it not?"

He stiffened, and the colour leached from his face. I felt better at once, but I held my breath, nonetheless, and allowed the silence to stretch until he should break it.

"How could you know that? How do you know my name?"

I allowed myself to breathe again.

"You are Connor, son of Athol, High King of the Scots of Eire."

He was rigid, eyes wide, and then he darted a glance sideways, as though looking for assistance. I held up my hand.

"Peace, I am no magician. The knowledge came to me but now, when I looked up and saw the galley on your sail and remembered it. The Black Galley of Athol. Your brother Donuil told me of you."

"Donuil? You know Donuil?" His voice was tight with tension.

I nodded. "He is the friend I spoke of. I am Merlyn Britannicus. Of Camulod. I am the one who took young Donuil captive and held him hostage."

"You!" The tight-wound tension left him visibly and the colour began to come back into his face. He heaved an enormous sigh, and slouched back in his chair. "Donuil, by the stones of Cuchoulain. You had me going there, for a moment, man. I thought you were a . . ." He allowed the thought to die and I did not pursue it.

I sought to press my advantage. "It should please you to know Donuil is well, or was, when last I saw him less than a month ago. He rode northeast on a mission for me, to the lands of King Vortigern, to find my brother." I smiled. "And now I have found his."

Still he said nothing, staring at me in perplexity, and I realized that well he might. Friendship was a term that normally had little significance between captor and hostage. I spoke into his silence.

"I released Donuil from his bond to me more than three years ago. He won his freedom in my service and is now my good friend, as close as any brother." *Brother-in-law,* my mind added.

One of Connor's captains, Sean the navigator, came striding towards us and Connor stopped him with an upraised palm. "Leave us, Sean," he said. "We're talking."

Sean threw me a speculative look. "Aye," he said, his high-pitched voice offering no opinion on the matter, "I see that, but we're about to round the headland there; it might be rough, and you with that babby in your arms. Will you want me to take it?"

Connor looked at him and smiled, the first time I had seen him do so, and the act transformed his whole face, so that I saw a different man. "No, I'll be just grand, Sean, and so will the babby, now away you go and leave us to our talk." As he said the words, the galley pitched steeply, its nose tilting sharply upward and then falling in a swooping, spiralling lurch to crash jarringly into the first turmoil of the waters surging round the rocky point. Caught off balance and completely unprepared, I staggered sideways, groping frantically for the rail, my eyes sweeping upward, awestruck, to where the top of the huge mast whipped in a dizzying circle. Only now did I notice that two men had climbed the great mast and moved out to the end of the spar, where they now leaned suicidally outward, far above the surface of the sea, clinging to lines and anchored by ropes around their waists, peering down into the shallow waters as they watched for rocks and shoals.

By the time I had recovered my balance, having fallen painfully to one knee and clutched at a handy rope that helped me to regain my footing, the atmosphere aboard the galley had changed completely, urgent with raised voices shouting orders as the oarsmen battled to realign the ship, to point it straight into the waves and keep it thrusting forward amid the sudden turbulence that surrounded it and seemed, to my untrained eye, to be threatening to overwhelm it.

"What's happening?" I yelled above the pandemonium.

Connor's attention was on his crew, but he heard the sudden fear in my voice and glanced back to where I stood clutching the rail.

"Nothing to worry about," he shouted, cradling the baby calmly. "Conflicting currents, that's all. The tide from behind us is meeting the ebb from the other side of the headland, so it will be choppy until we round the point." Even as he spoke, the pitching, crosswise motion eased and the ship slid into smoother water. I waited, nonetheless, until the vessel had resumed its former, sweeping gait, before I released my death grip on the rope and the handrail beneath my hands.

Once in the shelter of the headland, however, the wind died with the leaping waves and the sail above me lost its belly, its fabric settling under its own weight to hang inertly from the upper spar. In response, the rhythm of the oarsmen's drum grew faster, and the boat leapt ahead, gliding parallel to the shore, which now lay less than a longbow-shot from where I stood. I stared ahead, looking along the length of the vessel to where high cliffs now appeared, rising one behind the other in serried banks. I raised my hand and pointed.

"That looks familiar, over there," I said, realizing that I no longer needed to shout.

"Let's hope you're right," Connor answered, quietly. Something in the tone of his voice made me look back at him. He was staring at the shoreline, a look on his face that I could not identify, and I remembered his earlier comment.

"What's wrong?" I asked him. "Am I still to die if I can't find the place?"

He shook his head, dismissing my question, his preoccupied gaze still fixed on the land. I asked the next question, unable to recall what Donuil had told me, unsure of how Connor might respond.

"Were you very fond—" I broke off and cleared my throat. "Were you close to your sister Ygraine?"

This time he showed no surprise. He merely closed his eyes for a moment and then turned to look at me. "Ygraine, too?" he said. "How do you know Ygraine?"

"I didn't," I replied quietly. "I only knew of her. Donuil had told me at the outset, when I first met him, that her betrothal to Lot was part of the price of your father's alliance with Cornwall. That was years ago." He was looking at me passively as I continued. "I had forgotten her thereafter, until I heard her name again several days ago, on a battlefield."

"On a *battlefield*? My sister was discussed in the middle of a battle?" I could not tell from his tone whether he was angry or merely disbelieving.

"No," I said, seeking to explain myself. "The battle was over when I arrived. I met a survivor, one of my own men, who told me Lot's wife had escaped the carnage. That's when I remembered who Lot's wife was."

He shook his head in what might have been commiseration or, again, rueful disbelief.

"It's a Druid you should have been, Yellow Head. You seem to have the great talent for arriving on battlefields after the fighting's all done, wouldn't you say so?"

"Aye," I grunted. "It must seem that way. But—" I broke off abruptly as old Tearlach approached, followed by the navigator and two others. Their expressions were grim, and I hurried to get my next words out before they arrived within hearing distance. "Connor, we must talk more. I have much to say to you."

"*Hmm'ph'mm!*" That was a sound I had heard Donuil make a thousand times, and it had a thousand possible translations. He swung to face the newcomers. "Tearlach, Padraic, our yellow-headed captive here knows much about us."

The older man scowled, his glance sweeping me up and down dismissively. "Aye, do ye tell me?" he growled. "And what could he know about us that would bother us any more than a midge bite through thick cloth?"

My retort was quick, stung by his disdain. "I know you are honour-bound by the word of your High King to stay far from your stinking ally Lot of Cornwall and far from our shores until the release of your prince, Donuil!"

His eyes widened in shock and his head snapped around to look at Connor, who smiled and spoke to all of them. "He speaks the tongue well, does he not? 'Twas Donuil himself, he tells me, who taught him the knack of it, teaching him the Erse out of the crude Gaelic his own people speak. They became friends, rather than captor and captive, it seems, and Donuil earned his freedom."

"And you believe him? Where is Donuil now, then? He never came home." His surprise mastered, Tearlach's scowl returned. The others ignored him, their eyes on Connor, who took his time before answering, swinging his seat back slowly until he faced me.

"Aye," he drawled, finally. "That is true, and it has been five years and more since he was taken. And yet, I think I believe him. Donuil is still here in Britain."

"Dead meat, too, if I'm any judge!"

Tearlach's words went unanswered. Connor sniffed, glancing down at the sleeping babe.

"Here, Sean," he said. "Take the wee boy and place him somewhere where he'll come to no harm."

The navigator moved to take the child and carried it away, disappearing in the direction of the area beneath the deck. Mine were the only eyes that followed him, but a movement from the seated chieftain brought my attention back to him. Slowly, his eyes never leaving me, he reached up and undid the clasp that held his cloak in place, then he reached up above him with both hands and grasped two of the ropes from which his chair was hung. Smoothly, effortlessly, the muscles of his arms bunched and he pulled himself erect, the cloak falling from him unheeded as he moved. When his weight was fully on his left leg, he swung the other and it fell to the deck with a solid thump, revealing a carved, wooden peg that stretched to his knee and was attached there by a large leather socket. The limb was a tapered cylinder, perfectly turned out of some dark, dense wood and polished to a high lustre. Above it he wore a rich, woollen tunic in the Roman style, pale green with a Grecian border in the same deep red as the symbols on his cloak, and the thigh beneath the hem, before it disappeared into the leather socket, was solid and roped with muscle. A breastplate of toughened, polished hide, moulded to his torso in the Roman style, was all the armour that he wore, and from his shoulders hung a crossed pair of belts, one supporting a sword and the other a dagger. I had great difficulty in not staring at the wooden leg, but I judged it wise to ignore it.

Connor stood there, still holding the ropes by which he had pulled himself up, and no one moved or spoke as he dragged his wooden leg back to where it would support his weight. The end of it was capped with several layers of leather, cut and fitted to the shape of the appendage's base. He lodged it firmly and then took time to feel the rhythm of the ship, swaying his body slightly to the motion of it. Finally, when he judged his balance sufficiently secure, he released the ropes and stood unsupported, looking at me.

"I still fall sometimes, but not often and I'm used to it now." He turned and walked to the rail around the deck, crossing the space in four steps, swinging the wooden limb out and around each time he moved it, so that his motion was more of a swagger than a walk. When he reached the rail, he turned back to face me, leaning his buttocks against it and bracing himself with his hands. "Well, Yellow Head, I don't know what to make of you, or what to do with you." He glanced at one of the others. "Padraic, what say you?"

The man addressed hawked loudly and spat over the side without looking at me. "I say Tearlach has the right of it. Donuil did not come home. This one should not go home, either."

The navigator reappeared and joined us, glancing from one to the other of his companions, trying to gauge their temper.

"We are talking still of Donuil and his fate," Connor informed him. "Tearlach and Padraic think this man should die. Do you?"

The navigator shrugged. "The babby's going to die. Donuil has been dead to us all for years. Everybody dies."

"The baby will not die," I interrupted him, addressing myself to Connor. "I told you, I know of a wom—"

"Be silent! You will hold your peace until required to speak." The reprimand was whiplash quick, savage and implacable. I subsided. Connor looked back at the navigator. "Sean?"

The navigator shook his head gently and with finality. "Throw him over the side."

"He can swim, Sean."

Sean sniffed. "Lachie could swim, too, but not after this one clove him with the axe. Could he do any better than Lachie?"

"Diarmid?"

Diarmid was the only one of the four who had so far remained silent, a large, red-faced man with a wild beard and a head of hair to match, judging by the thick, coarse ringlets that hung from beneath his big, horned helmet. Now, addressed directly by his leader, he turned his gaze on me and I saw his eyes, pale blue and cold. "He's an Outlander. Kill 'im."

I followed all of this with disbelief, amazed at the change this Connor had undergone in the space of moments. When I had told him of my friendship with his brother, I had thought he believed me. He himself had said as much. What I was witnessing now, however, gave the lie to all of that. He stood, looking down towards his knees, the fingers of his right hand scratching idly in the hair that swept back behind his ears. He finally withdrew his hand, inspecting the tips of his fingers as he rubbed them pensively with his thumb, then made a tutting sound and heaved a quick, sharp sigh.

"Well, Yellow Head," he said. "You hear the verdict of my trusted friends. They want you dead." He sucked air reflectively between his teeth. "But the decision is mine. And what do I have to guide me in the making of it? You!" He shot out an arm and pointed a long finger in my face. "You tell me that my brother is alive, and well, and living in Britain as your friend. As proof of that, you offer me words that he could have told you at any time, under any kind of duress, and I have said I do believe that he is here in Britain." The arm fell back to his side.

"But Tearlach could have the right of it. Donuil might be dead in Britain. How am I to know?

"And what of the child, the starving babby there? Whose child is he? Not yours, for you said you did not know beyond a doubt your cousin killed your wife. Your wife is dead, but had the child been yours and taken by your cousin, then you would know, beyond a doubt, his guilt. And then the 'cousin' that you found was not your cousin, but someone who had killed him and stripped his armour for his own purpose. Did he take the babby, too, for his own use? Or are we to believe you bore the infant with you, into war, new-born just weeks ago, in all your armour?

"So . . . the child's not yours. And yet you value it enough to risk your life to save it, not once, but twice? Whose child is this? And what could be his value to you, to me, to anyone? Here is a mystery, Yellow Head, and too profound for me. If the babby be not yours, and not your cousin's, then whose can it be, for it must belong to someone? And then I mind me that there were women among the slain whom you arrived too late to help. But who were the women? You say Ygraine, my sister, was one of them. I doubt that, Yellow Head, since you yourself have said you did not know my sister, other than by name. You may be lying, although to what end I could not guess, other than to extend your life, which might be good and ample reason."

"Deck, there!" The hail from above brought every eye sweeping up to the two lookouts on the spar above. "There's a body in the water!"

As everyone thronged to the side, I looked towards the shore and recognized the dunes and the rising hills I had descended earlier that day. Connor stood beside me, staring down, searching the water. I nudged him and pointed towards the land. We were close inshore now.

"This is the place. Look, you can see bodies up there on the sand."

He glanced to where I pointed and swung to the navigator. "Take her ashore, as soon as we have secured that body!"

II

THE BUSINESS WITH the bereaved woman, potential wetnurse for the child, turned out to be quite simply taken care of. Once on shore, escorted by a group of warriors hand-picked by Connor, I had no difficulty finding my horse and my abandoned bow and quiver, after which I retraced my path to the clearing that contained the ruined farmstead and its scattered, pathetic corpses. The woman was still there, although she no longer knelt by her dead baby. Prompted by some motive known to her reeling mind alone, she had moved away and we found her wandering close by, among the bushes surrounding the ruin of her home. She gave no response to our greetings, her maddened, empty eyes betraying no awareness even of our presence, but she responded to the gentle urgings of guiding hands and accompanied us without protest. Only once did she resist, at the point where she was led from the clearing. She tugged her arms free and turned around, staring back, then made as if to return, but she had little fight left in her and quickly submitted to the restraining hands that held her again, after which she went where she was led, in a state of utter, uncaring docility.

Night fell as we made our way back towards Connor's galley, through a war-ravaged landscape that was almost completely alien to me. The moon broke through a gap in the clouds just as we approached the end of the solid, flint-strewn ground, marked by a ragged, eroded edge where the highest of spring tides had penetrated inland. Beyond that edge and less than the height of a tall man below its lip, the domain of the sea began in a flat-bottomed stretch of arid land composed of shale and clay and advancing sand. This barren, pebble-strewn strip, stippled with clumps of hardy grass that fought for life against the saline, briny sourness clogging its roots, extended southward and to the east, its clay and shale quickly giving way to sand and more sand, to where a series of tall, weed-crowned dunes swept up to block all sight or sound of the distant sea.

I drew rein, and my companions stopped with me, grouped around me motionless in that stillness that descends instantly from time to time upon men moving uncertainly in darkness through hostile territory. I ignored them, standing in my stirrups to look about me in the hush of total silence, my ears listening in vain for any sound of waves from the distant shore. Ahead of me and several hundred paces to my right, the first hill began to swell upward, angling southwest to where its steep-soaring might would also be truncated by the hungry sea to become the first of the frowning cliffs that stretched unbroken from there all the way to the farthest tip of the rugged peninsula of Cornwall. The moon was enormous, almost full, and its brightness lit the distant hillside well enough to throw shadows visible from where I sat, but it revealed no glimmer of water, south or east. None of my escort had sought to question me, or to comment on the route I chose to follow. None could, for they were strangers here, more alien than I to these bleak lands that had belonged to Gulrhys Lot, the self-styled Duke, and later King, of Cornwall.

There were fifteen of us, and I the only one astride a horse. The others stood grouped around me, waist deep and deeper in the sturdy, stunted brush that coated the terrain here in wild, haphazard clumps and thickets separated by skeins of stony, lichen-covered ground too inhospitable to accommodate even these bushes' hardy roots. The biggest of the men, their leader Tearlach, glanced up at me.

"Well? Are we close?"

I considered how to respond. "We must be," I said eventually. "Or we ought to be. Can't see a thing from here." I cleared my throat, forcing myself to speak with an authority I did not possess in my present circumstances.

"They'll have a fire, a beacon light to guide us in, but we can't hope to see it from here, with all those dunes between us and the sea." I gestured upward with my chin to where the moonlit hillside reared above us in the southwest. "I'll ride up there and take a look. Wait for me here."

I swung my horse around and rode off at a canter, following the rim of the broken land adjacent to the beach. My horse Germanicus, the eighth of his name, moved with confidence now, far more secure than he had been before the moon had emerged to light his world, and I glanced up at the sky as I went, pleased to see that the clouds were clearing rapidly and that stars were now visible almost everywhere I looked.

Soon the ground began to shelve upward and we were on the hillside proper, above the invisible line that held back the scrubby whins and bushes, and moments later I saw the moonlight reflecting in a silver band across the waters beyond the dunes that now lay below and to my left. Higher we mounted, and with every stride, it seemed, my horse laid ever widening, moonlit vistas open to my gaze. We had almost reached the summit, however, before I saw the glow of distant firelight on the beach, miles to the east. I knew the fire must be a large one, but to my eyes it seemed the merest spark, so distant was it from my present perch, but it was a spark ignited and fed by an enemy, the brother of a friend, and he had in his keeping something more precious to me than life itself. When last I saw him, he had held my honour and my duty, carelessly but unknowingly, in the crook of his bent elbow.

A pounding in my chest told me I had been holding my breath, and I released it in a sibilant gust, sniffing thereafter and shaking my head briefly to clear it of unwelcome thoughts, before reining my mount around again and retracing my path downward to where my escort waited with the woman.

I found it in no way strange that they should have permitted me to ride off thus, alone. Mine was the only mount, and yet they had no fear I might attempt to flee. They knew—at least their leader knew—that I would do what I had set out to do. They had good reason to know how greatly I valued what they held of mine.

They could never have imagined how short of the truth their knowledge fell.

The moon held, lighting our way for the remainder of our journey, but it took us almost three more hours to make our way through the dunes and along the narrow strand to where the fire blazed, and Tearlach strode ahead of me for the last half mile, making better progress over the loose sand than my mount. The tide was far out when we arrived, and the great galley lay high and dry on the beach not far beyond the firelight, lolling on its side, for all the world like some giant sea beast.

One of the men on guard heard or saw our approach while we were still far distant and raised the alarm, but big Tearlach pulled a bull's horn from inside his scrip and blew a long, winding note that informed them who we were. When we arrived at the firelight's edge some time later, I dismounted and walked the last short distance with the others, dropping the ends of my horse's reins on the ground, confident in the training that would keep him standing there until I returned to him.

The galley's entire crew stood silent in the leaping light of the enormous fire, watching our arrival with great interest, ranged in a broad arc behind their commander. He stood alone, slightly ahead of his lieutenants, shadowed by the flickering of the flames beyond his left shoulder, bareheaded and with his arms crossed on his chest beneath his great, ground-sweeping cloak. Only the sound of our feet in the sand, the roaring of the pyre and the thin, incongruous wailing of a child broke the hush that lasted until Connor and I stood face to face beside the great fire. He gazed at me for long moments, his lips pursed beneath the swooping lines of his full moustache, and then his eyes moved to where the woman stood unmoving between two of his men, each of them holding her loosely by one elbow.

"So," he grunted eventually. "You found her. Did you have difficulty?"

"No, none at all. She had hardly moved from where I saw her last."

"Hmm. What tongue does she speak?" His gaze remained fixed on the woman.

I shook my head. "None that I know of. She has made no sound since we picked her up."

He looked at me then, surprise showing in the speed with which his eyes sought mine. "Is she mute?"

"I doubt it. She is demented, unhinged by grief."

"Aye." His eyes swung back to the woman. "Well, we may be able to cure that." He nodded his head in a brief, sideways jerk, and one of his lieutenants, who had been watching him more closely than the others, moved forward immediately and signalled to the men holding the woman's arms. He strode off and they followed him, leading the woman between them. Connor looked back to me.

"Well, Caius Merlyn," he said. "It would appear you have some truthfulness in you, at least. My tent is yonder, and I have some mead. Come you."

I ignored the implied insult and hesitated, torn by a strong desire to follow the woman and her escort, but resigned myself to following him to a smaller fire that burned outside the only tent on the beach, wondering as I went at the easy confidence of his swaying gait as he swung the carved wooden peg that had replaced his right leg. By the fire he waved me towards a wooden stool and disappeared into the tent to reappear moments later carrying a stoppered flask and two horn cups. He seated himself on a second stool and stretched his real leg out towards the fire, then pulled the stopper from the flask and filled a cup, passing it to me before pouring his own.

I sat without speaking, waiting until he had finished, gripping the flask securely between his knees and stoppering it one-handed before allowing it to fall by his feet. He gazed at me then with a trace of ironic amusement, then he raised his cup to his lips. I drank with him, feeling the fiery sweetness of the honeyed mead fill my mouth with a sudden, flowering burst of warmth and flavour, starting the saliva flowing strongly before sliding down my gullet to spread its liquid, energizing heat through my body, which I only now realized was deep chilled by the cold night air.

I shuddered with pleasure, feeling the fire's warmth reach out, as though suddenly to caress me. He drank more deeply than had I, and when he lowered his cup with a satisfied sigh I knew it was empty. And then he was standing again, looming above me.

"Stay here," he said. "Enjoy the fire. I'll be back presently."

I watched him walk away, his ungainly yet strangely graceful gait silhouetted briefly against the larger fire close by, and then I was alone. A few moments longer I sat there, staring into the flames beside me until my eyes teared, and then I swung myself around to face the sea, allowing the flames to heat my back. I was fire-blind at first, and the darkness before me was total, but as my eyes adjusted to the night again, the looming shape of the galley's hull came into focus, its outline leaping up high above me to blot out the star-pricked sky. I leaned backward, craning my neck to see the top of it and remembering how enormous it had seemed the last time I had seen it thus, from beneath, as I floundered helplessly in the waters that bore it so easily.

The sounds of Connor returning brought me back from my recollection and I turned to face him where he stood by the fire, eyeing me with that same, strange expression I had marked before.

"Where did you find the horse?"

I shrugged my shoulders. "Where I left him."

He looked surprised. "The very spot?"

"No, not exactly. I had left him ground-tethered. He is trained to stay where I leave him, but I had been gone for many hours. He's an intelligent beast and had wandered away from the shore to the nearest forage. He stayed there."

"Hmm. And the bow?"

"Where I left it, too, with my arrows. The very spot. It wasn't hungry."

He thrust the tip of his tongue behind his lower lip, digesting that without smiling.

"I have never seen such a large bow. Those others we found on the strand are as long, but differently made."

"Aye," I concurred. "It's different, unique, I think. It came from Africa, many years ago, long before I was born. It belonged to my great-uncle Varrus." I saw no point in adding that the others, the Pendragon longbows as they were becoming known, had been modelled upon my own, for length, at least, since the Pendragon had no means of fashioning the layered, double-arched complexity of the great bow's compound structure of wood, horn and sinew.

"Varrus?" Connor's eyebrow had ridden up on his forehead. "What kind of a name is that?"

"It's Roman. His full name was Gaius Publius Varrus."

"So your uncle was a Roman? And who else had a hand in the making of you? Romans were small, I'm told, and dark of skin. Your yellow hair and the height of you makes me doubt you're purely Roman . . ."

I said nothing in response to this and he considered my silence for long moments before turning away abruptly and jerking his hand in a gesture that meant I should accompany him. I rose and followed him, our path skirting the larger bonfire and plunging into the darkness again to where a glow, shrouded by the massed figures of many men, announced another, smaller fire that could not possibly afford warmth for the hushed throng that surrounded it.

The crowd parted at our approach, allowing us access to the small fire and the sight that had held them all so rapt. The woman we had brought with us knelt there, head down, her milk-swollen udders bare to the night and the eyes of all as she suckled the tiny, gluttonous starveling she held tenderly in her arms, and as I watched them, my throat swollen suddenly with a feeling close to grief, I saw the tears that fell from beneath her hair to land upon the child. Someone among the fierce Eirish warriors surrounding her moved forward and quietly placed a blanket over the woman's shoulders, smoothing it into place and draping it across her to cover the nursing baby, whose eyes were closed now in sleepy, well-fed bliss.

How long I stood there, I cannot recall, but presently I felt Connor's fingers on my arm, and I went back with him to his own fire where we seated ourselves again and he poured another cup of mead for each of us. No one came near us after that, and we sat without talking, he staring into the flames and I staring at him as we sipped at our cups.

We had not found his sister Ygraine on the shore. She and her slaughtered women, with the bodies of the birney's entire crew, had been swept out to sea by the incoming tide that had borne me away in the birney. The sole corpse we had found floating naked in the sea had been one of them, but a stranger to Connor. Where her clothes had gone I could not tell, but deprived of them her body had possessed nothing to signify rank or station. What we had found was merely a dead woman, drifting alone and bereft, as all corpses are, of any human dignity. Ashore, only the corpses of some of Uther's bowmen remained, lying where they had died in their last stand on the dunes above the high tide mark with several of those commanded by Derek of Ravenglass, the man who had killed my cousin Uther Pendragon and stripped him of his armour, donning it himself and thereby causing me to pursue him, mistaking him for Uther.

Connor had refused to believe his sister dead, in spite of my story and of the evidence scattered along the shoreline. That there had been a fight of some sort, he could see; that some women had been involved, and had been killed there, he was prepared to accept, having seen one of them. The death of his own sister, however, the Queen of this wild region of Cornwall, whom he had come to rescue and return to her father's hearth, he simply refused to accept without the evidence of his own senses. He had my own admission that I had never seen Ygraine before that encounter, and that, allied with the fact that the woman found floating in the sea was a stranger to him, cast doubt over the identity of the dead woman I had named Ygraine of Cornwall.

I could have convinced him otherwise, I knew beyond question, simply by telling him of my own wife, Deirdre, his other sister, whom he had thought dead for more than a decade. For Deirdre of the Violet Eyes, as she had been known in childhood, had lived beyond the time of her supposed death, vanishing from Eire and travelling to Britain by unknown means, where, years later, we two had met and loved each other for the space of one short, wonderful year. I had known Ygraine the instant I set eyes upon her, for she could have been twin to my Deirdre, whom I had known as Cassandra. For some inchoate reason, however, one which I remained unable to define even to myself, I had said nothing of any of this. Something, some foreknowledge, some formless but potent *caution*, barred me from speaking these thoughts aloud. Three times I had been on the point of telling him, but on each occasion I had found myself robbed of speech. Bewildered, even slightly panicked by the premonition that seemed to force me to remain silent, each time I had swallowed hard and covered my confusion in silence, refusing to think about it thereafter. Now it had returned, unsought. Perhaps, I thought then, watching him, it had to do with the manner of the dreadful death that had come upon my wife. Deirdre had been murdered, pregnant with our child, while I was far from home on the affairs of Camulod, the colony established by my grandfather Caius Britannicus and his comrade and brother-in-law Publius Varrus.

Connor broke into my thoughts.

"I think I have decided what to do with you, Yellow Head."

I glanced at him, forcing myself to react casually, as though his comment were of minor import. "That's interesting," I heard myself say, and some interior part of me was surprised by the calmness of my own voice. "Do you intend to tell me about it?"

My restraint was rewarded with a bright, amused, slightly surprised grin. "Of course," he answered, the whiteness of his even teeth startling in the reflected light of the leaping flames. "And you can be assured you are the first to know of it."

"Well, my thanks for that, at least. It's pleasant for a man to know that his fate has not been common gossip before he learns of it." He returned his stare to the fire at that, disdaining, I thought, to respond to my ironic tone, and a brief silence fell, quickly dispelled by me. "How long must I wait?"

Connor pursed his lips and ejected a stream of spit into the fire. "My mouth tastes like the floor of a bear's cage," he grunted. "Have you ever seen a caged bear, Yellow Head?"

"Aye, several." My thoughts had leapt back in time to my boyhood and the books of Publius Varrus; to the description of the caged bear he had pitied and then forgotten immediately on the day he met the girl dressed in blue who was to haunt his dreams for years.

"And?"

I blinked at him. "And what?"

"What think you of bears?"

"What should I think of bears? If anything, I should wonder, I suppose, why you would compare a foul taste in your mouth to anything bearish."

"Don't you think there's something unnatural about a caged bear?"

"Aye, there is, but there's nothing unnatural about a bad taste in one's mouth. If you insist on the analogy, however, then I must say that of all the animals I know, the bear least deserves to be caged. It is the most intelligent of beasts I've ever come across."

He smiled now, and there was an element of wistfulness, perhaps of sadness in his smile. "I know what you mean. It was a bear, as you know, that ate my leg."

"Ate it?"

"Well, no, not exactly. It bit me. Severed the muscles of my calf, and they festered. I owe my life to one man in our company at the time who was not afraid to cut off my leg in the face of threats on his own life. He chopped me at the knee, cleanly, with an axe. One blow. Placed the axe in position, and then hammered it home with an iron maul. Drove me into unconsciousness, and almost into dementia afterwards. Thank all the gods of Eire, he had told his assistant what to do after that to cauterize and staunch the wound, because Lachie—the man you slew—struck him dead when I screamed out."

There was not much open to me then in the way of response, but I seized on what he had said about his saviour. "He was a physician, then?"

"Who, the man who saved me? No, he was a Druid."

That really surprised me. "Lachie killed a Druid?"

Connor nodded. "Aye. Stone dead. And lived accursed thereafter."

"Hmm . . ." I paused, collecting my thoughts. When he showed no inclination to speak further, I went on. "So, pardon me for asking, but what has all this of bears to do with your decision regarding my fate?"

"Your fate?" He laughed aloud. "Hardly your fate, Caius Merlyn, in the sense I think you mean it. I have not pondered the death of you."

"Ah! Then what have you pondered, if I might presume to ask?"

"Your life, and the manner of it."

"My life." I stared at him, unable to decipher his expression. "The manner of it." I felt foolish even as I uttered the banality, but he laughed again and reached down between his feet to retrieve the mead flask.

"You're something of a bear yourself, Merlyn. That long black cloak of yours with the big silver emblem on the back marks you as one; a bear, a warrior, a formidable foe"—he pulled the stopper with his teeth and spat it out onto the ground before continuing as he poured for himself—"or a staunch and intelligent ally." He proffered the flask and I leaned forward to take it as he went on. "So, here is what I have decided. I must go home soon to my father's Hall, perhaps without my sister." I held my horn cup on one knee and poured carefully, my eyes on my task, my ears straining for every subtlety of his voice. "If that should come to pass, my father Athol will not be happy to see me back empty-handed, but by then I'll have little option other than to face his wrath. I cannot remain on land here, with a mere hundred or so men, not knowing where to begin to seek Ygraine—not when the land is acrawl with hostile armies. You tell me Lot is dead, and I see no reason to doubt you. Men die in war, and leaders are human, too, and die as men do from time to time. Ygraine is strong. She has her own bodyguard, and they loyal to her to a man, since they are all her own, my father's people. She knows I will be here, waiting for her, and so I shall stay, keeping myself offshore, for as long as I can. A month, at most. She should be here long before that."

"And I?" I turned as I asked the question, to find his gaze fixed steadily on me, his eyes twinkling beneath raised brows.

"You, Yellow Head? You are my surety against returning completely empty-handed. You hold my brother Donuil, whether as prisoner or friend, I neither know nor care. Tearlach and the others think he is dead. I choose to believe you. Donuil was—and is—greatly beloved by my father, the king, and by me, too, let it be said. You shall bring Donuil to me, and I shall take him home with me, and when you do, you may have the child back, safe and sound and in good health now that he has a nurse."

"What? You expect me to ride off and leave the child here with you?"

"You expect me to allow you to ride off, taking the babe with you, and no assurance that you will return, other than your word?"

I had risen to my feet in anger. "My word has been taken before now, and never found lacking!"

He ignored my anger and did not answer for the space of several heart-beats, then in a musing voice he said, "Aye, but by whom? Your friends and equals? I am an Outlander to you, man. No bonds of honour tie a civilized man's word to such, not even in my country." His calm reply chastened me. I sat down again, my mind racing.

"A month, you say?"

"Aye, at most, a month."

"And what if . . . what if trouble befalls you?"

"Trouble? You mean if we are attacked? We won't be on land. We'll sail off and return when it is safe."

"Unless another galley finds you."

He shrugged. "Aye, there is that, in which case we shall fight, and we shall likely win. Mine is a large galley, and a fierce crew."

"A month might not be long enough."

He laughed, half in scorn. "For what? How far must you travel to this home of yours . . . what did you call it?"

"Camulod."

"Aye, Camulod. Is it more than two weeks' journey from here? It can't be."

"No," I agreed. "No more than six days, seven at the most, but Donuil may not be there when I arrive. I told you, he had ridden out to the northeast at my request, at the same time I left Camulod, to search for someone. He may not have returned, may not even have found the man he seeks. It could be months before he returns."

Now it was Connor who rose from his seat, his face set in displeasure. He dropped his cup on the ground by his side and twitched his cloak so that it settled about his body. "In that case, Yellow Head, seek ye the child in Eire, in my father's Hall, for that is where he will be." I moved to protest, but he cut me short with a stabbing gesture of his left hand. "Enough! No more discussion. Be satisfied I choose to trust you thus far. I know how you value the child, although I know not what he is, or means, to you. Suffice it that you are prepared to die for him. I can make use of that, since it means you'll be prepared to live for him as well, and thus return my brother to his father's hearth. A hostage for a hostage, no? You will leave tomorrow, in the light of dawn. You have your horse and your bow. Your armour and the rest of your weapons are there, all of them, inside my tent. Take them, and then find yourself a place to sleep. In the morning you will leave. No one will hinder you and we two shall meet again either here within the month, or in Eire when you arrive there. Until then, farewell."

He turned on his false leg and made his way towards the clustered forms of his lieutenants around the main fire. I watched him leave and then finished the mead in my cup, setting the flask down carefully after replacing the stopper, then I collected the bulky bundle of my weapons, helmet and armour from the darkness inside the doorway of his tent. I thought of searching out the child and his new nurse, but I knew not where to begin looking. Instead, I carried my gear to where I had left Germanicus, unsaddled him, and spent a half hour rubbing him down with coarse sand-grass before leading him away from the firelight to a place beyond the beach where he could graze and I could sleep for the remainder of the night.

Sleep would not come, however, and I lay awake thinking bleak thoughts. Finally, I sat up, lifted my tunic and unwound a long strip of cloth from around my waist where I had tied it the previous day. Secure between its folded layers was a small, leather pouch, and I tipped its contents into the palm of my hand. Two massive golden signets, one of them on a thin gold chain—the red dragon seal of Pendragon and the savage, curl-tushed boar seal of Cornwall—both held in trust for the infant who now lay sleeping somewhere close by, warm and at peace for now in the milk-sweet embrace of his new nurse. I replaced the rings in the pouch, hearing the solid, heavy clink they made in meeting, and retied them securely about my waist, and then I rolled myself in my cloak and sought sleep once more, this time successfully. My last waking thought was of Uther Pendragon, lying cold and long days dead on a riverbank, somewhere to the west of us.

The sound of voices woke me in the darkness before dawn as the camp stirred into life. I rose slowly and sleepily and dressed in my full armour before moving to saddle my horse, tightening the cinches securely before hauling myself up onto his back. It felt good to feel the weight of my swordbelt again and the solid cover of my iron, leather-lined helmet. New fires were springing into life all along the narrow strand that fronted the sea, and I could smell the briny tang and hear the roar of waves washing up as the tide came in, the sound amplified strangely by the ear flaps of my helm. I kicked Germanicus into motion, and rode directly west, recalling clearly the directions of Derek of Ravenglass, and had no difficulty in finding the mouth of the river on whose banks Uther Pendragon lay unburied. The great white stone Derek had described as marking the entrance to the river's channel was visible from far away, and when I reached it I swung inland, moving through the shallows by the riverbank, allowing the big black to pick his own way among the boulders that littered the bed of the stream. The river scarcely merited the status Derek of Ravenglass had accorded it, being no more than a broad, shallow stream, slightly over fifty paces wide at its broadest, where it flowed out to join the sea. Within the channel, cool and tree-covered, it dwindled rapidly in the space of a hundred paces to less than one third that size. It was pleasant there, however, for the day, young as it was, had already grown more than merely warm, and the twelve heavy miles along the sandy beach from the site of Connor's galley had heated both my horse and me uncomfortably. Three miles upstream, the Ravenglass king had told me, I would find the remains of Uther and his men, mixed with a number of Derek's own.

From time to time as my horse carefully picked its way upstream, I came to deep and pleasant-seeming pools trapped behind fallen logs or dug deep-channelled by the fall of water from some minor obstacle higher in the stream bed, which rose steadily as we moved inland. Each of them tempted me to dismount and bathe, for I was itchingly aware of the long passage of time since I had last been truly clean. For all that, however, I had no real desire to yield to the impulse here. Somewhere upstream, I knew, the bodies of a substantial number of slain men lay scattered in and around this stream; mutilated bodies that had been dead for days. I thought of Lucanus and his horror of polluted water, and I recalled my horror—God! had that been mere days ago?—when, just as I stooped to drink from another stream, I had suspected *wrongness*, and had found other slain men, men whom I had known, floating a short way upstream, swollen obscenely, their leaking fluids fouling the water around them.

I rode on, trying to rid my mind of such thoughts by dwelling on other things. Derek of Ravenglass came back into my mind, and I pondered our bizarre encounter days earlier, and the strange lack of ill will I bore him then and now. He had killed my cousin Uther Pendragon, but in so doing he had, in the oddest way, restored to me my faith in Uther himself, a faith that had died the day before I had set out to find him and kill him. For, as I had told Connor, I had believed that Uther, my cousin and dearest friend, had brutally slain my wife and unborn child. Derek of Ravenglass, by killing Uther and despoiling him of his arms and armour, had given me cause to doubt my belief again, based as it was upon logic that I now suspected might have been flawed from the outset.

Confronted that day with Derek where I had expected Uther, since he wore Uther's distinctive armour, I had seen what I might not have seen had I, in fact, met Uther. Hooked to Uther's saddle bow hung an iron-balled flail with a leather-covered handle. Derek had agreed to give it to me, and it hung now from my own saddle bow. The red paint that coated its short chain and the heavy, iron ball on the end of it was chipped and battered from much use. Now, as I rode, I unhooked the weapon and grasped the handle, swinging it up to catch the weighty mass of the ball in my left hand, where I examined it closely. The thing had been the death of many men, but I knew now, almost beyond a doubt, it had not taken the life of my Cassandra. I had believed, before seeing it in Derek's possession, that I had found the self-same flail sunk in the muddy bottom of a shallow mere, close by the spot where my wife had met her death. I had assumed it Uther's, for at that time I knew of only two such weapons and Uther had made them both, one for me and the other for himself. I had been carrying my own, many miles away, when my wife was killed. Uther had vanished from Camulod again, as he used to do, without a word. His guilt, once I had found the flail and recalled other profound suspicions, had been glaringly self-evident to me.

I sighed now, and reslung the weapon from its hook, remembering my father and his startling example, recounted to me at his own expense, of the requirement for moral men to be willing to accord the benefit of doubt when faced with a lack of solid proof, no matter how great the *circumstantial* evidence of wrongdoing.

In the few years that had elapsed since Uther's invention of this fearsome tool, years through which I had remained immured, all memory and knowledge driven from my head by a battle wound, others had copied Uther's design and the weapon had become widely used. I knew that now, but my knowledge was very recent. Someone had used one to murder my wife and the child she carried. Someone, but evidently not Uther. Or was that evident? My memory stirred again with suspicion. Perhaps he made another, identical, to replace the one he had lost. I shook my head violently, attempting to dislodge the thought, and as I did so I heard the crows.

My flesh crawled with revulsion at the familiar sound, the anthem, the very death-watch of war. The discordant cacophony was still far off, but I kicked my horse to a faster gait, dreading what I should shortly face but unable to tolerate the thought of allowing the grisly feast ahead of me to pass uninterrupted for a moment longer than I could help.

The stream bed narrowed dramatically at one point, throwing its waters higher and more strongly, as though to impede my passage, and the banks became suddenly rocky and precipitous, looming high above me as though to shut out the light of day. The channel turned sharply right and then left again, rising steeply, and then I reached the end of the broken water and emerged suddenly into a clearing where the high wall on my left fell away abruptly, leaving an open, thickly treed glade along the river's grassy edge where the water flowed smooth and deep. On the right, the cliff loomed still, harsh and unyielding.

I pulled my mount to a clattering halt, scanning the scene before me. White and black. For long moments my eyes refused to acknowledge what confronted them. The white was naked flesh, bleached and blood-drained, for a chaos of once-fierce warriors lay stripped of everything, including any semblance of humanity. The black was dried blood, torn flesh and flap-winged scavengers. Outraged, I screamed my anguish and sent my mount charging through the shallows, splashing mightily and dislodging the gorging birds from their repast so that they rose in an angry, fluttering cloud, their caws of panicked warning deafening me. I reined in my horse when we reached the bank, hauling him back onto his haunches as I gazed in horror at the scene around me. Corpses, hundreds of them, it seemed, lay sprawled and tangled, piled in confusion, with, here and there, the solitary, lonely-looking, swollen-bellied body of a horse among them. From the trees around me, the crows and magpies chattered and scolded, warning me away from what was now theirs, and above their sound, I slowly became aware of another more pervasive, the buzzing of a million swarming flies.

My stomach churning with the need to vomit, I forced myself to look around me carefully, knowing immediately I had no hope of finding Uther's body. These ravaged corpses had been thoroughly despoiled. No weapons lay abandoned on the ground, no clothes, no armour, no signs of the camp I knew had been here. No order governed the disposition of the bodies, either; friend lay entwined with foe, united, inseparable and indistinguishable. The flies held dominion here; they and the scavenging birds the only living creatures in sight.

Disgusted, and shaking with nausea, I turned my horse around and left that awful place, following the outline of a clearly trampled path, and there, mere paces from my passage, I found Uther Pendragon.

There was no mistaking him, even after three days of death. His size, his hair, and the hideous, gaping, ragged-edged wound in his lower back, just where I had seen, known and felt it in an awful dream, left no room for doubt. He lay where Derek of Ravenglass had left him after stripping him, alone by the base of a great, dead, hollow pine, spread-eagled among a welter of tumbled, rotting boughs so that his right foot stuck grotesquely skyward, his knee caught in a fork of one of them. The green and blue carpet of flies that coated him finally overwhelmed me, and I fell from my saddle to the ground, retching helplessly.

Later, when I was strong enough, I staggered to my feet and covered my mouth and nostrils with a cloth, tying it in place to leave my hands free for the task. It was the work of mere moments to drag some of the dried-out tree limbs to where he lay and pile them over him. Moments more, and I had struck flint to steel and breathed a small flame to life. I tended it carefully and watched it grow to become ravenous, and then I fed its hunger with Uther's pyre. Remounting my horse, I sat and waited until the leaping tongues of flame soared high enough to lick at, then ignite the long-dead wood of the great hollow pine above him. Only when I was sure that the conflagration could not be stopped did I move my horse away. Then a neighbouring tree, another pine, its inner growth dark and dry, flashed into violent, blazing fury, throwing a sudden cloud of flames and whirling sparks into the air, startling me. Grass fires were breaking out already from the flying sparks. The entire glade would burn, and all that it contained. The air had grown thick and black with whirling smoke and departing birds, and the fury of the fire that consumed Uther Pendragon, nurtured by burning pine sap, already hid him from my view.

"Farewell, Cousin," I whispered, feeling a desolation the like of which I had never known. "Your son will think well of you, I swear."

I departed then, quickly, leaving everything behind me to the cleansing flames.

III

I HAD RIDDEN through a war-torn landscape on my journey to Cornwall and the southwest, but the return journey demonstrated to me just how little of it I had really noticed. Then, I had ridden fuelled largely by an outrage kindled by my own, personal anger at Uther and what I believed him to have done, and partly by my shock at the stories of the atrocities committed by my own men, the soldiers of Camulod, under his leadership in the war against Lot. The sights I had seen had been those I wished to see on that stage of my journey, those that would feed my rage against the cousin who had wronged me. I had looked for them diligently and had found them in profusion, but in the seeking of them, I had ridden oblivious of other, more terrible spectacles.

Now, much less than a month later, I returned by the same route, sickened by the carnage I had seen in Cornwall, appalled by the senseless squandering of so many young, healthy men. I rode in full awareness now of the path of war and warriors and the havoc they had wreaked between them. The burned and ruined cottages now gave off a sullen, all-pervading stench of bitter smoke and charred embers that spoke wordlessly of desolation and despair. The sight of hanging corpses that had angered me earlier seemed insignificant now on my homeward ride, the smell of them hardly noteworthy now, the swarms of flies and scavenging birds attracted to the mouldering bodies negligible by comparison with the sheer enormity of the numbers of dead and maimed and crippled soldiers littering the landscape I had newly quit. I rode through all of it in a state of almost total despair.

Only once on the journey did I come across any sign of danger, and it might have been no more than my frame of mind that made it seem thus. Early one bright morning, new-risen from a bed of thick-piled grass that had done little to ease my uneasy wakefulness, I emerged from a dense copse on the banks of a shallow river to find myself confronting four armed and mounted men on the other bank. A single glance told me I knew none of them, nor recognized their style of dress. They were all armoured, after a fashion, in mismatched, bossed leather garments, breastplates and leggings, and they all carried leather-covered shields. On seeing them, a deep and sullen anger overtook me and I stood upright in my stirrups, drawing my long sword and passing it to my left hand and then unhooking Uther's heavy flail from the saddle bow and swinging it around my head, daring them wordlessly to challenge me. They exchanged sullen glances among themselves and then swung about in unison and rode away, kicking their shaggy horses to a gallop that soon bore them from my sight.

I drank from the stream and went on my way, acutely aware for the remainder of the day that they might be waiting somewhere ahead of me, hoping to take me by surprise. I saw no sign of them, however, and by the following day had forgotten them.

Three days later I came again to the hostelry where I had heard the chastening tale of the visitations of the armies of Lot of Cornwall and Uther Pendragon—Uther of Camulod had been the name they gave him, to my angry dismay. The place had been owned by a man called Lars, who had turned out to be the long-lost eldest son of Uncle Varrus's old friend Equus. In the course of a pleasant evening with him and his wife and her brother Eric, a merchant, I discovered not only that Eric made his living largely by trading amicably with the Saxons who had settled the lands to the southeast of Isca, but that the people of the entire region around that city thought more kindly of their recently arrived Saxon neighbours than they did of Uther's armies and the forces of Lot of Cornwall. Those sentiments, outrageous as they had seemed to me upon hearing them, had begun to seem almost acceptable a short time later, when viewed in the context of what these people had suffered at the hands of their fellow countrymen. Now the hostelry lay empty and abandoned, all the doors and windows boarded over. I hoped that they had made their way safely northward to Camulod, as I had urged them to.

It began to rain, as it had rained when last I passed this way, and for the next two days I rode through heavy, intermittent squalls that soaked me to the skin and turned the world into a place of dripping, miserable, lightless shades of grey.

The sun came out again on the third day to reveal to my unprepared eyes a scene untouched by war. From that moment on, I rode through green and pleasant landscapes where men worked peacefully and fearlessly, it seemed, in their own fields, as if the struggles of ambitious warriors had no existence in this land.

I avoided Isca and Ilchester, the desolate town closest to Camulod, keeping my distance from the great Roman road and riding across country now, through heavily wooded land, towards the borders of our Colony, feeling a shapeless joy stirring in me as I began to recognize landmarks. By the time I realized I would not, despite my wishful thinking, arrive home before darkness fell that day, I had reached the beginnings of that area closest to our lands, where the dense forest began to yield to the openness of our fertile valley. I knew exactly where I was now, and remembered a favoured campsite from my youth, a grassy, moss-soft bed beside a rippling stream, concealed from casual view by a screen of thick bushes and a waist-high embankment that once had marked the edge of a much greater stream than flowed there now. Only as I approached within bowshot of the spot, riding almost carelessly in the gathering dusk, did I realize that the site was already occupied.

I drew rein immediately, holding my horse still, wondering if I had been seen moving through the dense shadows beneath the widely spaced trees, and sat there for long moments, every sense alert. I had no idea who was there by the stream, and reason told me that here, on my home lands, it was more likely to be a friend than otherwise, but my recent travels had shown me graphically that nothing in this land today should be taken for granted and that it behoved a cautious man to entrust himself fully to his own instincts for self-preservation.

Germanicus stood stock-still beneath me, his ears pricked forward, as alert as I. He, too, had heard what I had: either a grunt of pain or a bark of laughter from the direction of the hidden bank. Moments passed slowly, and then the sound came again. A man's voice, speaking normally this time, too far away for me to hear the words. The tone, however, told me I was unobserved; I detected no urgency, no warning note. Slowly, taking pains to move in silence, I dismounted and led my horse to the nearest tree, where I tethered him securely with the bole between his bulk and the direction from which the voice had come. I removed my war cloak and folded it across my saddle, then unharnessed my long sword from where it hung against the horse's side and slipped it through the ring at my back between my shoulders, where I could unsheathe it quickly. That done, I retrieved and strung my great bow, slipped my left arm through the sling of my quiver and nocked an arrow before moving forward cautiously towards whatever awaited me.

It took me a long time to cover the hundred and fifty paces to a spot where I could hope to see beyond the protective fringe of bushes that screened the campsite. At the outset, I moved with extreme stealth, hoping to number the group ahead of me by the sound of their voices. As I progressed, however, it became clear that one man was doing all the speaking, and I grew confident that he was alone with perhaps one other. I increased my pace slightly after that, although still moving with great care, until finally I heard a second voice, which was unmistakably feminine. This was an unknown voice, but it was young, and with its utterance came an end to any immediate threat of danger. One man and one young woman together in a secluded spot seldom offered threat to anyone. Unless, I revised, it be to a stealthy stranger creeping up to invade their privacy.

I coughed, as though clearing my throat of phlegm, and a man's head sprang into view directly ahead of me. His eyes met mine and both of us froze for a space of heartbeats. He was bareheaded, not only unarmoured but unarmed, and I saw his eyes fly wide as his mind registered the danger implicit in my helmed and crested head and the high cross-hilt of the cavalry sword slung behind my shoulder. Recognition flared in me and my own shock was as great as his as I took in the thin, aquiline set of his swarthy features and the narrow peak of hair that swept forward to split the expanse of his wide forehead, leaving his greying temples almost bald.

"Cay!" he said, almost conversationally, managing to sound surprised and unruffled at the same time. He had collected himself far more quickly than I. "Where in Hades have you come from? And afoot?"

I was on the point of answering when his companion raised her head above the bushes separating us, confounding me further. She was very young and extremely beautiful, although the height of the intervening shrubbery prevented me from seeing lower than her chin, which, by the angle at which it was stretched, told me she was standing on tiptoe to peer at me. I was aware of straight, black, glossy hair, and large, bright blue eyes that were opened wide as though before an apparition. It occurred to me later that I probably looked as startled as she did, for this bucolic solitude was a situation in which I had never expected to find my good friend Lucanus.

"What's the matter?" Lucanus's head was tilted slightly to one side as it always was when something puzzled him.

"Nothing," I assured him. "Nothing at all. I simply did not expect to find you out here, so far from your Infirmary."

The young woman had disappeared.

"Well, come and join us. We were just about to set off for home."

"To Camulod?" The idea almost made me laugh. "You're too late. You'll never get there before dark."

"Nonsense, Caius. Lots of time. Come, come in."

"Fine," I shrugged. "Let me fetch my horse. I left him beneath the trees back there, since I didn't know who you were."

In the few moments I required for my task I had time to regain my mental composure. I had never know Lucanus to consort with a woman, and I had known him for many years. Never, in all those years, had I seen him alone in the company of a woman other than by casual or accidental circumstance. So it was no more than natural, I told myself, that I should be amazed to find him here, so far from anywhere, alone in the company of an extraordinarily beautiful young woman.

As I moved around the screen of bushes and into the lovely little campsite, my surprise grew. A single blanket lay upon the mossy, grass-covered mound at its centre, and the young woman knelt, head down, wrapping the ends of another blanket around a long, compact bundle. I saw no tent, and only the smallest kind of fire, without cooking stones or utensils. I stopped short, my eyes scanning the clearing.

"By the gods, Luke, you were serious! You intended to return to Camulod today."

"Well of course! Why would you doubt it?"

"But you'll never make it. It's more than twelve miles and it'll be dark in a couple of hours."

"Aye." He looked up at the sky. "Well, we did lose track of the time slightly."

The young woman now rose to her feet, clutching her bundle to her chest. In doing so, however, she somehow managed to step on the skirts of her own clothing, pulling herself sharply off balance so that she lurched and lost her grip on her burden. It sagged and fell apart with a strange series of hollow-sounding noises, and I gaped in disbelief as a cascade of shiny bones clattered to the ground. That they were anything other than human was a possibility dispelled immediately by the shiny skull that rolled towards me and came to rest by my foot, its upper teeth seemingly sunk into the mossy ground and its hollow sockets glaring up at me. Bereft of words, I turned slowly to look at Lucanus. His eyes, too, were on the skull.

"Aye," he muttered after a prolonged moment of silence. "A pretty skull." He stooped and retrieved it, wiping a trace of dirt with reverence from its polished brow before passing it in silence to the young woman, who promptly knelt in front of him, ignoring me completely, and began from the beginning, spreading the blanket wide and piling the large collection of bones—even my unpracticed eye could see arm and leg bones and ribs and a pelvis—in the centre of the square. I was gazing in fascination at a small, blue bag that lay among them.

"What's in the bag?"

"What?" Lucanus, distracted, had to glance to see where I was looking. "Oh! Phalanges, metacarpals, metatarsals, other small bones . . . hands and feet."

I realized I should not have asked, as a vision of the brocaded bag that had held the dismembered hands and feet of Gulrhys Lot flashed into my mind. Lucanus was moving.

"Come, we had best be on our way. No point in losing any more time than we have already."

"No, Luke, wait." He turned to face me, almost in mid stride. I glanced at the girl. "I meant what I said. It's too late. The night will be black as Hades and you'll only be inviting trouble if you insist on trying to win back to Camulod in utter darkness. Better to stay here and head back at dawn. Have you any sleeping mats?"

He shook his head in a mild negative.

I grinned and sighed. "Well, no matter. I have resources to provide bedding for all of us, providing the night is not too cold. And we can build a larger fire. What about food? Is there any?" Again a negative. I sighed again, this time less patiently. "Can you fish?"

"Er . . ."

"I can." This was the young woman. I glanced at her, trying to ignore her beauty and the visions of her and Lucanus that were flickering behind my eyes.

"Good. I have lines and hooks, and I know there's fish aplenty in the stream there. If you don't object to catching some fish for us to eat, I'll go looking for something more meaty, while it's still light enough to shoot. What's your name?"

"Ludmilla." Her great blue eyes looked at me directly as though challenging me. I felt a tiny frown flick at my brow. The name was familiar. Ludmilla. I sought it briefly, but could not place it, then merely shrugged and directed her to my saddlebags, where she would find fishing lines and hooks. While she was doing that, I gave Lucanus my tinderbox and instructed him to light a fire, after which I stripped off my armour thankfully, and clad only in my tunic and sandals, gathered up my bow and quiver.

An hour later I returned with a fine hare that I had taken on the run with a well-flighted arrow. Ludmilla was still fishing, and Lucanus sat alone by the fire, which he had nurtured and bordered with large flat stones for cooking on. My collapsible cooking irons formed a tripod over the flames from which hung my leather boiling bag, the water in it just beginning to steam. Behind Luke, close by the fire but far enough away to leave us room to move around, my leather tent was pitched and a shelter had been rigged over the lower limb of the nearby fir tree. I could see a pile of fresh-cut bracken within my tent, and another between that and the blanket shelter. That gave me pause. I had assumed that he and Ludmilla would share a couch.

"That's a splendid-looking hare."

I grinned at him. "Isn't it? Took him in full flight, too, with one arrow. He was going like the wind." I dropped my bow and quiver and took the hare to the water's edge, where I began to skin it. "Good thing I did, too. It was almost too dark to see by the time I found him, and he was the only living thing I'd seen. Has Ludmilla had any luck?"

"Of course she has. Look." Ludmilla's voice came from behind me, and I turned to see her brandishing a trio of lovely trout, each one a meal in itself.

We ate like courtiers that night, sitting by the fireside long after darkness had fallen. Familiar with the place, I had known exactly where to find wild onions and garlic, since I had planted them myself, with my boyhood mentor, the Legate Titus, many years earlier. With young nettle shoots and a liberal pinch of salt from my cooking supplies, they turned the hare into a stew fit for the gods, and while it simmered, Ludmilla prepared the fish she had caught and I took the opportunity to walk downstream and bathe in the darkness, scrubbing the travels' stains from my skin with icy water, then towelling myself dry afterwards. By the time my teeth had stopped chattering, I had returned to the welcoming fire where we nibbled on fresh trout that had been garnished with onion and sprinkled with salt before being cooked slowly, wrapped in burdock leaves laid on the flat stones at the edge of the fire. We had no bread, but Lucanus, it transpired, carried in his saddlebags a quartet of nested metal bowls, used for many medicinal purposes, none of which included the serving of food therein, although they were perfect for precisely such a use. And from his saddle bow he retrieved a capacious, almost full wineskin, some of which I added to the contents of our stew-pot. As our leisurely meal progressed, I came to understand that there was nothing of the carnal in the relationship between my two companions. What there was, in fact, remained unmentioned, but whatever it was, it lacked sensuality. They behaved towards each other like courteous neighbours, and I soon became convinced that this had nothing to do with my presence.

Reluctant to pry, I avoided the topic of their strange presence in this place by asking Lucanus to bring me up to date on what had been happening in Camulod in the month I had been away. All was well, he told me, although Donuil had not yet returned from his quest to find my brother Ambrose. But Aunt Luceiia was in good health, he said, and everything was as it should be—except for some recent bad tidings. His voice died away, and I could see he was searching for words, looking distinctly uncomfortable. I waited, saying nothing, and finally he cleared his throat decisively and looked me straight in the eye.

"There's ill news of Uther, Cay. A report—several of them, in fact—that he might have been killed in Cornwall. Nothing definite, you understand . . . simply reports, all unconfirmed, and all very recent. His army suffered a massive defeat against Lot, a few weeks ago, somewhere in the southwest. An appalling slaughter. Apparently Uther marched into an elaborate trap. From what we've heard, he came against two armies where he expected only one, and was caught between them. Popilius was there, and survived, but he has been too ill since his return to tell us anything concrete. He has pneumonia, but I have high hopes for his recovery, despite his age and his weakness from his wounds. The main party of survivors has not yet reached Camulod, unless they arrived today. They have a large train of wounded with them, I'm told.

"Anyway, Popilius and his escort, a group of twenty men, arrived two days ago after having spent a week on the road. Several other small groups have drifted in since then. It was from two of these that we heard rumours of Uther's death, but no more than rumours, as I have said. We have had no confirmation."

I had been staring into the fire as he spoke, unwilling to let him see the expression in my eyes. Across the fire from me, the woman Ludmilla sat motionless, and I could feel her eyes upon me. Now I looked up and spoke, hearing the deadness in my voice.

"Uther is dead, Luke. I burned his body myself. He met three armies in that trap, not two. There was one ahead of him that he had been harrying and thought to catch, but Lot's main force was there, too, waiting for him, and a third rabble of Hibernians came up behind him. I was there, but not before it was over. I had been trying to catch up to him, to warn him, but I came too late. The carnage was complete, but Uther had escaped with something less than a thousand men, mainly his own Pendragons, pursued by Lot. I followed the sign of their running fight for days and saw too many corpses of men from Camulod. Then one day I found Gulrhys Lot hanged from a tree. I don't know how he died, or who killed him, but he is dead, nonetheless. I cut him down and burned him, too. Uther was killed the day after that, early in the morning, surprised as he and the remnants of his party were breaking camp."

I stopped suddenly, on the point of telling him about Ygraine of Cornwall and the child, but acutely aware again of the woman sitting listening on the other side of the fire. During the pause that ensued, neither of them showed any awareness of my sudden reticence, or if they had noticed it, they had evidently attributed it to an emotional reaction to the tale I had to tell. Lucanus broke the silence.

"How did you find him?"

"I was told where to look, by the man who killed him." His eyes widened but he said nothing. "Do you remember Derek of Ravenglass?" He nodded, his eyes widening even more. "Well, it was Derek who killed Uther, although at the time, and until I confronted him and told him so, he had no idea the man he had killed was Uther."

"And?" Lucanus was watching me closely. "Did you kill Derek?"

I opened my mouth to answer him, but nothing came out. Finally, I broke his gaze and turned my eyes back to the flames. "No," I grunted. "I did not. I was sick of killing and of death by that time. Ravenglass told me he had killed Uther in battle, not knowing who he was. The killing was impersonal. The only thing that distinguished Uther in his eyes was the size of him. They were both of a size and build, you'll recall. He took Uther's armour for his own use. He was wearing it when I caught up with him. That's how and why I caught up with him."

"You thought he was Uther."

"Aye."

"So the two of you did not even fight?"

"That's what I said."

"No, you said you had not killed him. You might have fought him and shown clemency."

"Aye, you're right, I might. But we did not even fight. The clemency I showed was to myself."

Lucanus eyed me in silence for a time, mulling over what I had said, and then shifted to a more comfortable spot on his mossy bed. "I believe you," he murmured, "and it was merited . . . I have great hopes for you, Caius Merlyn Britannicus. But tell me, what was it that convinced you Derek of Ravenglass spoke the truth—that in fact he had no idea of Uther's identity?"

I glanced at him sharply. "Why would you ask me that?"

"Why would I not? Uther Pendragon was your dearest friend, apart from being close kin, your first cousin. Was he not?" The barest hesitation had prefaced that final question and I knew it related to the friendship rather than the blood kinship. I also knew it portended an awakening suspicion in Luke's questing mind about my reasons for seeking out my cousin, but I chose to ignore it as he went on. "It seems to me you would demand proof of Derek of Ravenglass that this killing was, in fact, a simple battle casualty, rather than the premeditated killing of a notorious enemy leader."

I looked away again. "I needed no such proof. It was there in his face and in his words. I recognized the truth as he spoke it."

"Hmm. How?"

"Damnation, Luke, what do you mean, how? He told me what had happened that morning and I believed him."

"How so? Don't be angry with me, Cay. I'm not trying to vex you. I have no doubt of the truth of what you're telling me, but I must confess I am extremely curious. The Caius Britannicus I've known in the past would have killed his cousin's killer out of hand, merely for wearing Uther's armour, before the fellow had a chance to say a word. Is that not so?"

"Hmmph."

"So? Something must have given you pause. Something stopped you. What was it?"

"Could you bring yourself to believe it might have been the blood through which I had been wading for days? I told you I had seen enough of death and killing by then."

He ignored my sarcasm. "Yes, I could, Cay, had the victim of his killing been anyone else in the world. But not Uther Pendragon."

I tore my gaze away from the fierce centre of the fire and stood up to face the woman across the fire, waiting in silence until my eyes had adjusted to the change in light and I could see her clearly. Finally, the dots in front of my eyes subsided and I gazed into her eyes, clearing my throat uncomfortably. She returned my gaze openly and forthrightly, her face a portrait of dignity and calm serenity.

"Lady Ludmilla, I have no wish to insult you. Lucanus is my closest friend, normally far more astute at sensing the discomfort of others than he has shown himself tonight. But he is being obdurate and inquisitive and so I must be forthright. I simply may not speak of this matter in your presence, or in the presence of any other, and for that I ask your forgiveness. The words I have to say are for his ears alone, to be delivered at another time and in another place. That has nothing to do with you, but solely with me and my need to keep my own counsel on this matter." I knew I sounded pompous and I hated the awareness, but I could think of no other words. I turned back to Lucanus who sat gaping at me in astonishment. "Now, my inquisitive, curiosity-driven persecutor, may we change the topic?"

He jumped as though stung. "Oh, of course, by all means." His eyes went immediately to Ludmilla. "My dear," he said, "I can't begin to say how—"

Ludmilla, however, forestalled him, rising to her feet and leaning forward to look into the leather pot that still bubbled merrily over the fire. "Master Lucanus," she said, "you have done nothing to regret. I understand perfectly what Commander Merlyn means, and I am not offended. But this stew is ready. Now, how do we remove it from the bag into our bowls?"

A simple problem, easily solved: we used the smallest of the four metal bowls as a dipper to fill the others.

We ate thereafter in a suddenly easy, companionable silence, broken only by light exchanges as we replenished our bowls until the boiling bag would yield no more. Ludmilla ate as much as we did, and I watched her closely from time to time, seeing the way her strong, white teeth stripped the hare meat from its bones, and admiring the lines of her neck as she tipped her head back to drain the last delicious broth from her bowl. In all the time it took us to consume the stew, I did not see Lucanus cast as much as a glance in her direction, other than when she replenished his bowl, but my own eyes returned to her constantly. I knew I had never seen her before, yet her name sounded strangely familiar to me, suggesting that I should indeed know who she was. Ludmilla was a common enough name. I had heard it many times. But hard as I tried, I could not remember ever having actually met anyone called Ludmilla.

Finally I could suffer my curiosity no longer. We had finished eating, and Lucanus had stretched out comfortably by the fire. Each of us had scrubbed out our bowls with earth and then gone individually to rinse the vessels clean in the stream. Ludmilla, the last to do so, came back to the fireside and bade us a good night, but I stopped her as she began to turn away towards her shelter beneath the fir bough.

"Ludmilla, before you go, tell me, please, who you are and where you came from. Lucanus treats you with an air of long acquaintance, yet I cannot remember having seen you before today, and I am sure I could not have forgotten you had our paths crossed."

She stopped, looking at me with the beginnings of a smile on her face. "Oh, we have met, Commander Merlyn, many times."

"We have? Where?"

Now her smile broadened and she nodded her head. "In Camulod, in your aunt's house."

"In my . . ." and then my memory stirred. "You are my *aunt's* Ludmilla?"

"Of course, if by that you mean I am part of your aunt's household. She has been very kind to me, considering we are only distantly related."

"Related? How? What do you mean? Are you telling me that we two are kin?"

"No, not you and I. I am second cousin to Uther." Her face darkened for a moment and then cleared again, as though a shadow had passed over it. "I mean I was . . . but you and I are not related."

I had risen to my feet. "But . . . how can that be? How could I not know you? You have been in Camulod, in my aunt's household, for years. I've heard her speak of you many times. But you are too . . . Your youth surprises me. I had thought Ludmilla to be older, much older. Are there two of you?"

"No." Her smile was sweet, mocking, I chose to think. "I am the only one, but otherwise you are correct. I have been with your aunt for more than five years now."

"But how could we never have met, and how would I have been unaware of your relationship to Uther?"

Now she laughed aloud, a sound of tinkling, yet resonant silver bells. "Commander, most of that time you did not even know Uther! You were not yourself."

I glanced at Lucanus, hoping for some assistance there, but he lay silent, hands clasped behind his head, eyes closed, enjoying the warmth of the fire. I waved my arm feebly towards the stump on which she had been seated earlier.

"Please, sit again for a moment and help me to understand this. I feel extremely foolish."

"Without reason." She moved back and sat across from me and for the space of heartbeats I stood gazing down at her, perplexed, until she continued. "Will you not sit, too, Commander Merlyn? You are too tall for me to gaze up at without straining my neck." There was still laughter in her voice, I thought, mockery in her eyes. I looked around me for my seat, feeling awkward. When I was seated, she spoke again, no trace of raillery in her voice.

"My tale is brief, and soon told. My grandmother Riganna was half-sister to Enid, Uther's mother. Riganna was the firstborn female child of her father's first wife and Enid the last of his second wife. Fifteen years separated them. Riganna had a daughter called Bronwynn, who was my mother and first cousin to Uther. When I was fourteen, I visited Camulod with my mother and father. You met me then, but I was a mere child and you had just brought your young wife back to live in your aunt's house. Your aunt liked me because I reminded her of herself at my age, and she persuaded my parents to allow me to remain with her for a time in Camulod when they returned home.

"At that time, everyone in Camulod—you more than any other—was completely involved in preparing the embassage to attend the upcoming debate in Verulamium, and shortly after it had been arranged that I should stay you left the Colony. While you were gone, Lot of Cornwall invaded again, and my father was killed in the fighting. When you yourself came back to Camulod, you were gravely wounded. I helped to tend you, but you were unaware of me, or of anyone else." She smiled again. "In the years since then, you have had more to concern you than the servants of your aunt, and my duties have changed, keeping me far from your sight, so it is quite natural you should be unaware of me."

I gazed at her unspeaking, then asked, "You knew Uther?"

She nodded her head. "Very slightly. Not well at all. He knew who I was, and he treated me kindly, as a kinswoman."

"What about your mother? Is she in Camulod now?"

"No, she died soon after my father—of grief, I think."

"So now Camulod is your home." I turned to look towards Luke's recumbent figure and then returned my eyes to her. "But what are you doing here—tonight, I mean? And what about the bones?"

"She is a student." Luke's eyes were still closed. "We were studying the anatomy of the *corpus humanus*."

"Oh, you're awake, are you? You will admit, at least, Luke, that my curiosity on this subject has been admirably restrained."

"Hmm. I was beginning to wonder if you had even noticed, although you looked shocked to your soul when the skull rolled to your feet." Now he opened his eyes and sat up, shuffling himself into a comfortable position and coming to rest with his elbows on his knees, his face serious. "Much has changed in Camulod in recent years, Merlyn. Particularly in areas that have, I am quite sure, by their very nature escaped your notice."

"Like what?"

He cleared his throat and spat into the fire. "Well, the main one as far as I am concerned is in the treatment of our wounded." I waited for him to continue. "We've been at war now for five years and more. Most of the fighting has been done far from Camulod, thank God, but all of it has demanded much of our young fighting men and, by default, much of the work they used to do is handled now by women. Farming, and labouring, and working in the Infirmary."

"I knew that."

"Certainly you did, but you grew accustomed to it only after your first head injury. You retained no memory of the way things had been before. Your renewed life was one in which women played roles unknown to them prior to your injury." I realised he was right and held my peace. "Ludmilla here began helping in the Infirmary while you were first confined there. She enjoyed the work and became very useful to me, in spite of her extreme youth. As she grew older, she became more and more valuable, and I discerned in her the makings of a natural surgeon. This child is gifted with an awareness of human physiology the like of which I have never encountered, and so, about a year ago, I began to train her as my own assistant. She quickly assimilated an astounding knowledge and understanding of the musculature and organs of the body, and as her knowledge grew, my own awareness of the haphazard nature of the training I had been giving her grew commensurately. So I decided to complete her training properly, beginning anew and more methodically this time. I assembled a complete skeleton, and have been teaching her the entire, shall we say, mechanics of the body. The names and the functions of the individual bones, the major blood vessels and organs, and all the knowledge I have managed to accumulate over the years." He stopped and smiled across the flames at Ludmilla. "She learns more quickly than I am capable of teaching. She is a true descendant of Aesculapius."

I looked at Ludmilla with new respect. Lucanus had never been a man to toss out hollow compliments. He was speaking again.

"Anyway, in the past few weeks, the trickle of wounded returning to Camulod has swollen to a flood and we have been overworked, just as we were approaching a crucial period of Ludmilla's training—a period which, once entered upon, should not be interrupted, but should be completed quickly. I had decreed today a day of study. But it was the fourth consecutive day I had thus designated, and the previous three had been pre-empted by emergencies. The day dawned bright, and Ludmilla suggested we absent ourselves from Camulod, and from interruption, for the day. I remembered having spent a pleasant day with you here some years ago and decided I could find the spot again. We arrived long before noon and began working immediately, and time escaped us. You arrived as we were preparing to leave."

"Well." I found that I was able to smile openly now at the young woman opposite me. "Lady Ludmilla, I am honoured to meet you and to know you now, and I shall certainly never be able to forget you again. I hope you will find it in your heart to forgive me for my lapse of memory."

She smiled again and nodded wordlessly, and I felt better than I had all evening. The fire collapsed upon itself and I leaned forward to replenish it. "It's a warm night," I said. "I think we should sleep well, fed as we are, and rise early for a pre-dawn start. I can't wait to see Camulod again. Lucanus, you take the shelter, I'll sleep outside. Lady Ludmilla, you take the tent."

She would not hear of it, and went directly to the shelter. Lucanus took the tent. Before he retired, he glanced at me again. "About Uther . . ."

"Tomorrow, Luke. Another time, another place. Sleep well."

IV

As it transpired, a regular session of the Council of Camulod was scheduled for the afternoon of the day of my return, and that relieved me of any doubts I might have had about the swiftest and most appropriate means of confirming, officially, the rumours of Uther's death. I had pledged Lucanus and Ludmilla, upon the road that morning, to say nothing until I had made the news known to my Aunt Luceiia and the senior councilors, and it was then that Lucanus told me of the meeting.

On our arrival in Camulod, I had made my way directly to the home of my aunt. She absorbed my tidings of the death of her beloved grandson with self-possession and quiet dignity, surprising me in spite of the fact that I knew she had been prepared for the worst by the rumours. As I had had good reason to observe in the past, my great-aunt Luceiia Britannicus was a woman of extraordinary strength and resilience, and great perspicacity. She had known as soon as I greeted her that I bore ill tidings and had assumed, correctly, that they concerned Uther.

She sat in silence as I told her briefly of my discovery of Uther's body, and the primitive funeral pyre I had set to consume him. As I spoke, her eyes filled with tears, but her face remained calm and no drop spilled beyond her lashes. When I had finished speaking she sat motionless for a spell, then reached out distractedly and touched my hand, patting it tenderly as though to comfort me. I sat there beside her, awkwardly, wanting to put my arm around her to comfort her, yet fearful of intruding upon the reserves of strength that enabled her to bear her grief so stoically. After a time, however, she dabbed her eyes with the end of her shawl, sat up even straighter and cleared her throat.

"So Uther is gone, irrevocably. May God look kindly upon him. I knew the truth of it as soon as I first heard the rumour, although he had always seemed so invulnerable." She looked directly into my eyes now, and her gaze was clear and sharp. "I mourned for him then. Sadly, there is no time to mourn further now. How are you, Nephew? And what prompted you to search for Uther? When you left, you said merely that you had to be alone for a time, to come to terms with yourself, that you had no idea where your wanderings might take you."

There was no censure in her voice, and I knew that she yet harboured no suspicion of the vengeful anger that had driven me in pursuit of my cousin. I saw no need to mention it now and cause her further pain, so I merely shook my head and evaded her question.

"I am well, Auntie, but sickened by what I saw in Cornwall and the south, the appalling waste of life and young men. Lot of Cornwall is dead, too, did you know that?"

"No, but I am glad to hear of it. He was an evil man. Are you sure of his death, or is it a report?"

"No. I found him myself, and cut him down from the tree where he had been hanged. Who hanged him we may never know, but it was effectively done. His hands and feet had been severed and hung in a bag about his neck. A richly worked bag that bore the arms of Pendragon. I would have ascribed the death to Uther personally, but that one of the severed hands yet wore the seal of Cornwall and I cannot see Uther leaving that for the Fates to dispose of. He would have taken it as proof of Lot's death, if for no other reason. So would any of his men who sought to impress Uther with his zeal and loyalty. It is a mystery, I suppose, that will never be solved."

"Did you remove it?"

"Aye. I have it here, with Uther's own." I pulled the small leather bag from my scrip and passed it to her. She untied the drawstring and tipped the contents into her palm, immediately setting aside the seal of Gulrhys Lot with distaste upon a small table and fingering the great gold signet of Pendragon with its dragon crest, holding it close to her face to admire the intricacies of the dragon inscribed deeply into its flat oval crown.

"Who will wear this now?" she mused, and then looked up at me and offered it back. "It must be returned. Uther has no heir, so his crown will be assumed by some other, by acclamation or inheritance. It has probably occurred already. He had many uncles and kinsmen. This should belong to one of them."

I drew a deep breath, and spoke softly and clearly. "No, Auntie, both of those rings belong to Uther's heir." She glanced at me sharply, pain in her eyes now, prepared to reprimand me. "He has one," I continued.

Her face went blank, then her eyes took on a new awareness, an excitement. "Where?"

I grimaced. "In Eire, among the Scots, with Donuil's people. He is their heir, too. His name is Arthur."

"*Their* heir, too?" She paused for the space of three heartbeats, her piercing bright eyes scanning my face. "You have a tale to tell me, Nephew," she said then, glancing around to make sure we were alone. "And I think you have no wish to speak it aloud for other ears. Am I correct?"

I rose and crossed to the double doors of her quarters, leaning out to make sure that no one was near by before I drew them closed and crossed the room swiftly to ensure that the other door was firmly closed and we were quite alone, and then I returned to share her couch and told her the entire tale of Uther, Ygraine and their son, Arthur. She listened closely, making no attempt to interrupt me while I went on to describe my own adventures with Connor and his Ersemen, and my loss of the child. When I had finished speaking, she stood up and moved to a table against the wall, where a white cloth covered a jug of wine and a bowl of fruit. She poured wine for me and brought it back, and as I accepted it she said, "So this child Arthur is related to you both by blood and marriage, the son of your wife's sister, and the son of your own cousin."

"Aye. Nephew and cousin."

"And heir to Pendragon, and to Camulod."

"More than that, Auntie. He is also heir to Cornwall."

She frowned immediately. "How so? Lot was Cornwall's king, and Arthur is Uther's son. His mother was Hibernian. The child has no claim to Cornwall."

"True," I said. "But only we know that. I am splitting hairs, here, being a sophist, I suppose. But to good purpose. Lot acknowledged the child, publicly at least, as his own, according to Popilius, and left no other children. The child has possession of Gulrhys Lot's own seal. Furthermore he is grandson of the king of the Hibernian Scots."

She gazed at me steadfastly for some time, then nodded. "A potent mixture," she murmured eventually, her voice sounding far away, as though she saw great distances ahead of her.

"Aye, the same thought occurred to me when first I saw him. He is a fine, lusty child, Auntie, and his eyes are yellow gold, as were your brother's." I paused, then smiled as I went on. "I could be wrong, of course, but I fancy the resemblance to Caius Britannicus might run even deeper. The boy's nose is large, even for a babe."

"What? He has Cay's eyes and nose? What of his hair? What colour is that?"

I smiled. "His hair is dark, with a baby's darkness that could change as he grows. Not black, though, Auntie, more a deep, dark brown."

"Dark brown plumage, gold eyes and a Roman beak. You describe a golden eagle, Cay." I merely nodded, smiling still. "How will you get him back, Cay, and more to the point, when? I should like to see this child before I die."

I embraced her, slipping one arm around her frail shoulders. "You will, Auntie, I promise. As soon as Donuil returns from Northumbria or wherever he is, we shall leave for Eire. Has there been any news of him?"

"No, not a word. Will you seek him now?"

I shook my head. "Where would I start? He could arrive from a direction other than the obvious route from the northeast. What point in riding off without knowledge of his whereabouts? He could pass unseen within half a mile of me at any time. I have no choice other than to wait here for his return, in the hope that he will come soon, remembering his five-year sentence has elapsed. His uncle promised to come seeking him at the end of that time. I should hate to end one war and plunge directly into another simply because I could not produce my hostage on demand."

My aunt frowned at that. "Is that likely, Caius?"

I grinned at her and shook my head. "No, not at all, Auntie. I told you, Connor holds the child and knows how highly I value its life. He and his people now have a hostage to my good behaviour."

"How, a hostage? You said he was their heir. You think they might harm the boy, their own kin, should you fail to appear with Donuil?"

"They do not know who he is, Auntie. I did not tell Connor the babe was his sister's. Even so, I doubt that they would harm him. Connor is not a cruel man, and he loves children. I could see that from the way he handled the boy and spoke of his own. When we parted, he gave me a month to deliver Donuil home, alive and in good health, in exchange for the child. I told him then that Donuil's absence on my own behalf might make it impossible for me to meet that expectation, and now it looks as though I was correct . . . but I have no fears of Connor's taking vengeance on the child, lacking real proof of Donuil's death. When Donuil returns, we will journey to Eire. The boy will be safe until then."

She was gazing at me strangely now, a trace of troubled shadow in her eyes. "You have not told me everything, I see, Cay. Why would you not tell this Connor who the infant was? Surely, for the child's safety, that would have been prudent?"

I dipped my head, acknowledging the truth of that. "It would, of course, Auntie, but there were other matters to be taken into account, equally important to the child's safety. The matter of his blood, more than any other. As grandson of Athol, King of Scots, they might have taken him and kept him, thinking his place should be in his grandfather's Hall. I see it otherwise. As the son of Uther Pendragon, his place is here in Britain, in his paternal grandfather's Colony and in his own mountains. That is his heritage. To that end he was born."

"What do you mean? To what end?"

"He will fulfill the Dream, Auntie."

She frowned again, perplexed. "What dream?"

"The Dream of Caius Britannicus and of Publius Varrus. The unification of two peoples, Roman and Celt, beneath one Leader."

"Nonsense!" Her voice was sharp with asperity. "My brother and Publius Varrus dreamed of survival, and they dreamed well, but their dream was of this Colony of ours, not of two entire *peoples*. Those two could never be that grandiose. You forget I knew both of them far better than you and for more years than you have yet lived."

"One people, Auntie. The Britons." I had arrived at a decision, without forethought and purely on the spur of the moment. "Among the last things Uncle Varrus told me on his deathbed was that I would be true to my trust and would recognize the one I awaited the moment I saw him. For a time, I thought it might be my brother Ambrose, but now I know I was wrong. It was the child. I knew from the instant I set eyes on him."

She sat staring at me as though I were a stranger, and when she spoke again, her tone was wondering. "Caius," she said, "my beloved nephew, I have no idea what you are talking about, and I find that rather frightening."

I rose to my feet, holding out my hand to her, and she pulled herself up wordlessly and followed where I led.

Moments later, I leaned my back against the closed, bronze-covered doors of the Armoury, watching her as she stood gazing around the walls of the room her husband had built and furnished with such love.

"I seldom come here now," she said. "It hurts to be here. I am reminded too strongly of the man I loved and have lost. And yet it is a wonderful place. It seems filled with the very essence of my husband."

"Far more than you know, Auntie," I said softly.

I seated her in Uncle Varrus's favourite chair, beside his writing table, and she watched silently as I took down the wooden hammer-keys from the wall and used them to unlock the secret hiding-place beneath the boards of the floor. Silent too, I stooped and drew out the long, polished wooden case that lay concealed there, wiping the dust from its surface with my sleeve before carrying it to the table and placing it gently and reverently before her. Wordless still, she stretched out her hand and traced with her fingertips the outlines of the falling star inlaid in gold and silver in the lustrous wood of the case's surface. The case seemed solid, one single block of wood unmarked by seams or joints.

"It's beautiful. What is it, Cay?"

"This case, Auntie, contains the very essence, as you said, of Publius Varrus; the apotheosis of his craft and his love of his work and art. Permit me." I moved behind the table and leaned forward to press with my fingers on the concealed joins and the case swung open, its lid rising easily towards me as I watched her eyes. They sprang wide and her breath caught in her throat and again she reached out in wonder, but this time it was I who was amazed. Her hand, which had been hidden momentarily from my view by the raised lid, came back into view clutching the brightly coloured square of silk that had covered the case's contents since before I was born. Aunt Luceiia had no eyes for what had lain beneath it. As I stared in wonder at her, she raised the bright square slowly to her cheek, pressing its softness gently against her face with both hands, and two great tears trickled down to wet its folds, spreading in dark patches where they touched the material.

"This was mine, Cay, a gift from Publius, given and lost again many, many years ago. I grieved at losing it, but never mentioned it to Publius. He must have taken it—" She broke off suddenly, her words forgotten as her eyes became aware at last of what the silken scarf had covered. The brightly coloured cloth escaped from her suddenly nerveless fingers and slipped unheeded into her lap. I stepped around the table again to stand beside her and for long moments we stared together in awe at the sight before us. It was she who broke the reverent stillness, her voice little more than a whisper. "My husband . . . Publius made this?"

"Aye, who else? Who else could conceive of such beauty, let alone create it, other than Publius Varrus? See, his mark is stamped into the metal, just below the hilt there."

My aunt leaned forward, peering at the tiny "v." " 'Varrus.' Just like the skystone dagger his grandfather made." She jerked her head towards me. "Is this . . . ?"

"Aye, Auntie, it is a skystone sword, made from the metal statue of Coventina, the Lady of the Lake, as Uncle Varrus called her. It's called Excalibur."

"Excalibur . . . Excalibur." Her voice was still a whisper. "Take it out. I want to touch it, to hold it."

I removed the sword from its case, resisting the temptation to swing it and enjoy its superb balance. Instead, I grounded its point between her feet, holding it upright and steady in front of her eyes with the tip of one index finger on the end of the golden cockleshell that formed its pommel. She stared at it for some time before reaching out to touch it, but then I relinquished my fingertip hold and watched as she ran her fingers over the intricate scrollwork of its huge cross-guard and the abrasive texture of its sharkskin-covered hilt bound in its filigreed network of gold and silver wire.

For long moments she said nothing at all, devouring the perfection of the sword with her eyes, but then she glanced up at me. "Caius? Would you mind leaving me alone here for a little while? My thoughts are . . . I want to . . . absorb this, privately."

"Of course, Auntie. I'll be right outside the doors. Call me when you're ready, and I'll put it away again. Take your time; there's no hurry." I stooped and kissed the top of her head and left her alone with her thoughts.

Moments later, Lucanus found me leaning against the wall in the passageway by the side of the great, bronze-covered doors, my arms crossed on my chest. He had come striding from the rear of the house and stopped short, his face reflecting his surprise at seeing me there, apparently lounging aimlessly. I straightened up, standing away from the wall, and he approached me slowly, returning my greeting.

"You look as though you're standing guard."

"Well, I am, in a way," I said, smiling.

"Against what?" His eyes flickered to the closed doors beside me. "You expect someone to try to steal the bronze sheeting?"

"No, I'm waiting for Aunt Luceiia. She's inside." His curiosity was plainly written on his face. "Remembering her husband Publius Varrus."

"Ah, I see." He plainly saw nothing remarkable in that, because he changed the subject immediately. "The Council meeting will be starting soon. You will be coming, won't you?"

"Of course. How much time do I have?"

"An hour or so." He paused. "Have you discussed the Council with your aunt?"

"No. Should I have?"

He nodded, pursing his lips. "I think so, Cay. I didn't want to say anything while Ludmilla was with us, but there are changes occurring within the Council, changes I don't like and I know you won't like them, either."

"What kind of changes?"

"The worst kind, political. Emerging factions, or the threat of them. A threat yet young enough to be stamped out, thank God, now that you are back and well again. Young blood and new faces with an eye to their own position and advancement, rather than to the common good. You'll see, and it won't take you long. But ask Luceiia. She'll tell you more quickly and more accurately than I could. For a very old lady, there's not much that escapes her."

"Tell me more."

"I can't, Cay, I'm late already. Besides, it's better you hear it from your aunt. I should be in the Infirmary now, preparing for the arrival of the main train of wounded from Cornwall. They were sighted this morning entering Vegetius Sulla's old lands, so they should be arriving here any moment now. Talk to your aunt. I'll see you later."

I watched him stride away, suddenly uncomfortable with this unexpected mention of factions within the Council, and all the ominous implications. I have no idea how long I stood there fretting, but presently I heard Aunt Luceiia call my name and went back into the Armoury, where I replaced Excalibur in its case and resealed it beneath the floorboards. She watched me in silence throughout the reinterment of the case, and neither of us spoke until we were once again sitting in front of the brazier in her quarters. I waited, sensing that she had much to say to me, and she did not keep me waiting long.

"Well . . ." she began, pausing immediately. "The mere sight of that sword brought me a new perspective on your talk of dreams." I sat still, feeling slightly uncomfortable, and she snorted, a sound that might have been a smothered laugh or an indication of withering scorn. "The egotist within

me was offended, at first, greatly insulted. That is why I wanted to be alone."
I merely nodded, and she went on. "Why—this was the first, treacherous,
self-pitying thought that occurred to me on seeing it—would Publius keep
the existence of this sword concealed from me? It is plainly the most wonderful creation, and the most precious possession, of his entire life. And if
he had kept this secret, how many others might he have had throughout his
lifetime? What else of Publius Varrus exists beyond my private little world
that I had thought so all-encompassing?" She paused again, but this time
her lips creased in wry, self-disparaging amusement and I immediately felt
better as she continued gently, "I am no less human and insecure than any
other wife, it would seem, even after all this time." She sniffed dryly, accepting the folly of her own words. "Of course, as soon as I began to think
clearly, I realized I was being silly. The mere knowledge, let alone possession,
of a sword like that would endanger anyone. I am quite sure nothing like it
has ever existed. No emperor ever possessed such a weapon. Men would fight
wars to own it."

"Those were your husband's exact words." My interruption was involun-
tary, startled out of me. It won me a smile from her.

"I believe you. So, having made it, Publius could never have unmade it.
And he would wish to see it put to great and noble use. Hence your reference
to his dream and your grandfather's. Did Caius ever see it?"

I nodded, a sudden lump closing my throat. "He was the first to use it,
saving my life. He cut down Seneca with it."

"Ah!" Her voice died away on a long exhalation, then: "Who else has
seen it?"

"You and I. No other eyes alive have looked on it. Father Andros designed
the hilt and cross-guard, Equus worked on the blade and the mould for the
hilt, and Plautus was in the forge when Uncle Varrus cracked it open. And
Grandfather Caius used it to kill Seneca. Only those five had seen it, before
me—except, of course, for Seneca and his animals, none of whom recognised
what they were seeing or survived the sighting."

"Cracked what open?"

"The mould. Uncle Varrus poured the entire hilt and cross-guard as one
solid piece, bonded to the tang. *Excalibur* means 'out of a mould.' "

"I see." She was quiet again, and I saw her lips frame the name before
she said, musingly, "I thought it merely a poetic name, chosen for its beauty
alone, for it has a power to it, a sonority." Her thoughts changed direction
again. "So! Having created such a thing, their need was to conceal it from
men's knowledge until the time had come to make it known, and thus, you
became the Guardian. And now you believe that time will have arrived when
the child Arthur is grown?" I nodded. "Did Uther know of it?"

"No, Auntie, he did not. Uncle Varrus felt Uther was too rash, too headstrong, to be entrusted with the secret."

"Hmm. He was correct, too. That does not surprise me. Publius Varrus
was seldom wrong. Nor did it surprise me, upon reflection, that he had kept
the knowledge of the sword from me. He was protecting me, believing ignorance would keep me safe if things went awry in some unforeseen way."
She fixed me with a gaze that would brook no evasion. "What more can you
tell me of my great-grandson?"

"No more than I have told you already, Aunt Luceiia. He was strong, lusty and in glowing health when I saw him last. He is a big child, and should grow to be a large man."

"Arthur Pendragon . . ." She savoured the sound of it. "Arthur Britannicus Varrus Pendragon." She heaved a great, sharp, gusting sigh. "Well, I shall simply have to find the energy to stay alive until you can bring him back from Hibernia. After that, I shall be prepared for death, knowing that our family will live on."

I returned her smile, but my mind was busy elsewhere now. "Auntie, forgive me, but I have little time and I have to ask you some questions about the Council."

Her face fell instantly into repose. "What questions?"

"About factions, divided loyalties perhaps. I don't know. Lucanus only mentioned to me within the hour, while I was standing outside the Armoury, that I should speak with you on the topic. I'm due at the meeting very soon now."

"Of course you are, how stupid of me. I really am growing old, Cay, forgetting things . . ." She clasped her hands in her lap, stretching and interlacing her fingers. "Very well, I shall speak and you will listen. What I have to tell you is very brief. Armed with it, nevertheless, you will be forewarned and prepared to draw your own conclusions." The next quarter of an hour passed quickly as I sat rapt, caught up in her tidings and assessing her information from two separate, but not dissimilar perspectives. The first of these was concerned with the immediate problems I faced in the resumption of my responsibilities towards Camulod, and the other entailed the effect those problems might have—if not correctly and summarily dealt with—upon the months-old child now being held hostage in Eire. Arthur Britannicus Varrus Pendragon, as my aunt had properly named him, would one day soon return to live here in Camulod, and mine would be the task of rearing him to manhood. Camulod would be his inheritance, and its governance would be his lifelong duty, in obligation to all of his ancestral names. Larger things might befall Arthur in the life that stretched ahead of him, but none of them would be greater than this, his first and foremost charge. Yet what my aunt was telling me—this damnable thing of factions—posed a threat not merely to the child, but to all we had planned for him and for the future. And so I listened closely and thought deeply, engrossed by the subtle layers in Aunt Luceiia's lucid presentation of her tidings.

The Council of Camulod had grown greatly since I had last paid formal attention to it. Where formerly I would have looked to see a single circle of some twenty men, the elders of the Colony appointed for their wisdom, knowledge and tolerance, I now beheld a double ring of chairs, forty-eight in number. Six of these chairs were occupied by women, the senior members of Aunt Luceiia's ancillary Council of Women. The other forty-two were filled by men, and from the information given me by Aunt Luceiia and amplified by my own observations before entering the chamber I could now see quite clearly the factions to which Lucanus had referred.

Four men had greeted me more warmly and solicitously than any others as I made my way through the crowded courtyard outside the Council Hall on my way to the meeting; four men whom I might not easily have recognized without my newly acquired awareness. Two of these were leaders, two followers. Now, in the gathering that swept out and around from where I stood behind the Speaker's Chair, I could still see them clearly. To my left, in a close-knit group fourteen strong, sat the adherents of Lucius Varo, the most notable among them his adviser, Bonno. Lucius was the direct descendant of Quintus Varo, who had been brother-in-law by marriage to my grandfather Caius Britannicus. I knew of Quintus Varo from my readings. He had been a simple, straightforward man of boundless honesty and integrity. From my great-aunt's report, his blood had been sadly diluted to produce this great-grandson, who now saw my eyes resting on him and smiled at me warmly. I allowed my own face to relax into a noncommittal smile and let my eyes continue to rove.

Lucius Varo was young, in his mid-twenties I gauged, some seven or eight years younger than I. He was a politician by nature, using his fresh, open good looks to insinuate his will upon other, weaker men and bend them to his wishes. He had been appointed to the Council two years earlier, while I was suffering from my memory loss, and had established himself as a constant presence ever since. True to his nature, he had done nothing to which anyone might take exception for the first year or so, content merely to bide his time while making himself helpful, amenable and valuable to all. Only in recent months had he begun to emerge clearly as an organizer, using the combined weight and influence of his supporters to influence decisions taken in Council so that they fell to his advantage. Within a close-knit society that had no use for or need of money, he had amassed wealth of another kind: power and influence. His great-grandfather had been one of the Colony's first and finest farmers, whose entire lands had been dedicated from the outset to the provision of edible crops, rather than to the sustenance of livestock. Over the years, that emphasis had produced, unwittingly, an anomaly, an aberration, within Camulod: a concentration of power amounting to a virtual monopoly of a unique kind within the holdings of the family Varo. Much of the finest arable land in the Colony lay in these holdings, and an agglomeration of the Colony's finest agricultural workers had grown up there, owing their allegiance and their welfare to the owner of the Varo estate, originally Quintus Varo and then, upon his death, his only son Quintus Secundus, who had been known to everyone as plain Secundus and had served the Colony and its Council all his life. His son, Quintus Tertius, had continued the tradition until he died tragically while still a young man, killed in a fire. Tertius's son Lucius had then inherited the Varo lands and title, and his father's place on the Council.

With the advent of the fourth generation of Varos, an unhealthy change had arrived in Camulod. People began to grow aware, although but gradually, that the instant and welcome assistance that had been ever available from the Villa Varo, while still available, now bore with it a duty of acknowledgment and obligation that had never before been necessary. Now, in return for favours smoothly granted, each supplicant was expected, rather than simply encouraged as in the past, to align himself with the house of Varo on matters of policy and internal Colony procedures having to do with the acquisition and administration of land holdings. So smoothly had this transition been achieved, however, that it had occurred without resentment and almost invisibly, until several months before, when several people began to remark pointedly upon the proliferation of support for Varo's many new initiatives, and upon the not so simple fact that, in order to achieve anything in the way of change or progress in land ownership or management, ordinary Colonists now had to deal specifically with Lucius Varo.

Although in possession of this information for less than a single hour, I was already convinced that something would have to be done about the affable Lucius Varo and his dangerous ambition. Camulod had no need of men like him, or of the peril his incipient lust for power embodied. There was no room for politicians in our Colony.

A movement at the far end of the room attracted my attention and I saw that my two old friends the Legates, Titus and Flavius, had entered the hall. They did not move forward, but stood attentively against the rear wall, their arms crossed in front of them, both in full armour. I smiled at them, but they were both too far away to see it. Would these two old war-horses ever stop wearing armour, I wondered, even in times of peace? I thanked God that they were here and well, though both far advanced in years. Their presence offered me an anchor. I had not seen either of them since my return but determined to seek them out as soon as I was free of this meeting.

The Speaker's Chair in front of me was still unoccupied, and Mirren, the current president of the Council—the office was another innovation—had not yet entered the hall, although I had seen him outside and exchanged greetings with him. I allowed my eyes to drift now towards my right, to the other faction that I had identified. Peter Ironhair, its prime motivator, was deep in conversation with the man called Rhenus who had accompanied him when he sought me out in the courtyard earlier. Neither man had noticed my gaze turn their way. I took in every detail I could see of Ironhair, whom I would not have known had I not been warned of him. Peter Ironhair was a newcomer to Camulod, but a highly gifted one. He was a metalsmith, a trade honoured in Camulod since the time of Publius Varrus, and he had arrived in the Colony some five years earlier, rising soon thereafter, thanks to his natural skills and despite his extreme youth, to become one of the prime armourers of the Colony. That position had earned him his place in the Council, which he had held, to great acclaim, for almost three years. He, too, I estimated, was seven or eight years younger than I—like Varo, in his mid-twenties. He was a big man, as one might expect of an ironsmith, his hair iron-grey, prematurely whitened in spite of his youth and obvious health. He was gesturing to Rhenus, and from where I sat I could clearly see the massive rippling of the muscles in his arm. He was dressed well, no sign of the working smith in his garments. He glanced up and saw me watching him, but his expression remained unaltered. I knew, however, with complete conviction that he had noticed my gaze and chosen to ignore it. I looked beyond him, casually, at the people seated behind him, several of whom were leaning forward, listening intently to what he was saying. I counted thirteen in his group. Thirteen of his adherents, plus fourteen of Lucius Varo's amounted to twenty-seven men of the total forty-two on Council. Twenty-seven votes, a clear majority should the two groups ever arrive at a common goal, and close enough, singly, for either party to threaten a serious disruption to the business of the Council.

Aunt Luceiia had informed me that the two group leaders detested each other, and that Peter Ironhair's faction had emerged apparently solely in response to the formation of Varo's group. I had no idea at this point of what his power base was built upon. I knew only that, collectively, the two groups were referred to by the Colonists at large as the Farmers and the Artisans. I found it galling that such clear and disparate interests had been permitted to emerge so quickly, and so far I had no idea of how I would disband and nullify them, but I knew that much of my concentration would be given in the near future to that end. Fortunately, I knew also I would not lack assistance. Luceiia Britannicus herself was a fearsome adversary for either group and for any combination of the two, and Lucanus had assured me of the support of Titus and Flavius and many others among the most respected and admired members of the Council.

A bustle at the rear of the hall announced the arrival of Mirren, the delinquent president. A tall, imposing man, another descendant of one of the Colony's founding families, he now raised his arms for attention, speaking above the babble as he strode to the Speaker's Chair.

"Your pardon, all of you, for having kept you waiting. You know I would not normally do so." He arrived at the Chair and nodded to me before turning back to face the Council, holding his arms aloft in a plea for silence. In the hush that followed, he cleared his throat and spoke out strongly.

"I have just returned from the main gates. The train of wounded soldiers for which we have been waiting has just come into sight and I fear it is larger and more awful than we had expected. I have a report of six hundred and more injured men, some of them fit to walk, but more unable. There is work for everyone this day in settling them and arranging for their care, so this meeting must be short and to the point." He turned to glance again at me and nodded.

"First, however, we have a matter of concern to all of us, which must be dealt with now, before anything else." He paused, and every eye in the hall was fixed on him. "Caius Merlyn here returned to Camulod this morning with momentous tidings. I will allow him to pass them on to you himself. Commander?"

I stepped forward and faced the Council. One person shuffled his feet, somewhere in the second row of chairs, and the sound carried clearly.

"Before I deliver my tidings, there is something I would say to all of you, something that is long overdue from me to you." I had their complete attention, because to many of them I was an enigmatic presence nowadays, having been out of my mind, present in body only, for years. Many of them knew me only as Merlyn the reborn, brought back from the verge of death by Luke's medicinal skills. They had not known me before I was wounded. The others had known me in my youth, but the Merlyn they had known for the past few years was another person. I had considered my words carefully, and now I drew a deep breath and spoke them.

"For years now, I have been among you in body only. My mind, my own, real mind, has been elsewhere, smashed into oblivion by a head wound. Know you now, all of you, that it is I, the old and former Caius Merlyn Britannicus of Camulod, now fully restored, who speaks to you today." I waited patiently until the excited exclamations had died down. Before that happened, however, someone began to stamp his feet in applause, and soon the entire hall was filled with the sound of approbation. When it had finally subsided, I continued.

"Thank you, my friends. It is good to be whole again, but you should know I regained my full health, and my memories, intact, slightly more than a month ago. After that, recalling fully who and what I was and am, I set out immediately to find and join my cousin Uther and his armies in the southwest, to help him prosecute the war with Lot. Unfortunately, they had been long gone by that time, and I caught up to them too late." I paused. No one coughed or stirred.

"I bring ill tidings now, I fear, my friends, though some not so ill." I looked around the double circle, seeing each face on its own, separate from its fellows. "The rumours and reports you have heard before today concerning the death of my cousin, Uther the King, Uther Pendragon, Uther of Camulod, are true. Uther was killed deep in the southwest forests of Cornwall after a long, running battle with the enemy—three of Lot of Cornwall's armies. I myself found his corpse and burned it in a pyre where it had fallen. From his finger, I removed his royal seal, the red dragon of his people." I held up the great Pendragon signet for all to see and allowed silence to settle again. "So Uther is gone, and all of us are the poorer for his passing." I paused, looking around the room again, then added, "Lot of Cornwall, too, is dead and he, too, I burned, though in a simple fire. No pyre for him. I found him hanging from a tree, his hands and feet cut off, so that I knew not whether he had choked or bled to death. Suffice that he is dead, and that Camulod need fear his madness no longer." No outbreak greeted this news. The silence held. I continued speaking into it.

"So the Cornish War has ended, even though the last fruits of its madness are still arriving home as I speak. Camulod is at peace again, for the time being unthreatened. It is a time to make repairs, to rest ourselves and prepare for whatever the months to come might hold in store for us. Rest assured, however, that demands will be made upon us in the future, and they might well be greater than all the threats we have stood against to date. The death of Gulrhys Lot is but a breathing space accorded us by God. It is not a final victory and could not be, since our true enemy, the enemy of all we hold in Camulod, does not originate in Cornwall. Our real enemy lives beyond the borders of land and sea that gird this Britain of ours, and wishes only to usurp what we hold dear. The time that lies directly ahead of us must be a time of preparation, of conserving and of husbanding our strengths and rebuilding our forces."

I turned my head towards Mirren. "That is all I have to report, Mirren. Now, if I might add my own urgings to yours, I suggest we adjourn this plenary session to another day, in view of the arrival of our wounded in such large numbers."

Moments later, the meeting had been adjourned until the same day of the following week and I was outside, searching for Titus and Flavius among the throng spilling from the Council Hall, most of whom wished to congratulate me upon my recovery. I located my quarries easily, however, thanks to the visibility of their ornately crested helmets, and soon caught up with them, spiriting them off with me to my aunt's house, where we could speak privately.

By the time we had arrived there, the rituals of meeting after a long parting had been disposed of, and I had informed them of my own activities and what I had learned since my return. They digested my words in silence until we had entered my aunt's house and were seated around the glowing brazier in the family room, each nursing a cup of wine. Both men, initially, were ill at ease in this *sanctum sanctorum* of Luceiia Britannicus, but she herself welcomed them cordially and then sat silent in a corner, listening to what we discussed. I wasted no time in coming to the centre of what concerned me.

"Very well, gentlemen, let's talk about priorities. Something has to be done about these factions, the Farmers and the Artisans as they call themselves, and it looks as though I am going to be the one who has to do it. You agree?"

They both nodded solemnly. "Aye," Titus said. "Your father, had he been alive, would have stamped them out before they had a chance to form themselves, and so would you, had you been in any condition to recognize what was afoot. As it stands today, no one else has had the power, or the guts, to do anything."

"Aye, well, that's in the past. It's the future that concerns me now. Lucius Varo I can understand. He stands to gain strength by denying his assistance to the Colony unless it meets his conditions, and he seeks to bolster his own influence and standing as a leading Colonist and citizen. That, I think, may be easily dealt with. But what about this Ironhair? What does he hope to gain, and how?" Both veterans were gazing at me stolidly, accepting that my question was rhetorical and that I was about to answer it for them. I smiled at them. "I am asking you seriously, my friends, and in good faith, because I had never heard of or seen the man until this morning. I know where he came from and how he won his place in Council, and I have no difficulty with any of that, nor can I see anything reprehensible in his conduct. What I cannot see, however, is how, and to what ends, he built the power base he now so obviously holds. What does he hope to gain in forming such a group?"

Flavius began to say something about Ironhair merely opposing Varo, but I cut him short.

"No, I won't accept that, Flavius. If his concern were merely to thwart Varo he could do that openly in Council, using the full strength of the voting body. That will not suffice as an explanation. The man has formed a group of partisans; thirteen of them, I counted today. If Varo's group consists of fourteen toadies, then Ironhair would need only two of the remaining thirteen councillors to keep him firmly in his place. The corollary is that he could command fifteen votes without forming his own group, these Artisans. Something stinks. So again I ask you, what does he hope to gain? What's his objective?"

The two old soldiers looked at each other and shook their heads in unison, admitting they did not know.

"Fine," I said, accepting that. "We'll find out soon enough, because I intend to bring these matters to a head, and very soon. Now, tell me about the garrison. What's our strength?"

It was Flavius who answered me, and as usual he wasted neither time nor words. "More than eight hundred cavalry, battle-ready, and slightly less than double that number, say fifteen hundred foot-soldiers, fully prepared."

"That few?" This was bad news, indeed. I had been hoping to hear much larger numbers.

"Aye," Flavius sighed. "That few. I may be out on the side of caution, as regards our cavalry, with stragglers still drifting in, but I doubt I'm wrong by much. Lot's greed has cost us dearly."

"Hmm. Are they loyal?"

Both men straightened with shock.

"What d'you mean, loyal?" Flavius asked. "Loyal to whom?"

"To you, to us, to Camulod."

"Of course they are!" Titus sounded outraged.

"Good. We may need that loyalty."

"Caius?" My aunt's voice startled me. I had forgotten she was there.

"Yes, Auntie?"

"I have an idea, a thought. It may be nonsense but it just occurred to me."

All three of us were looking at her now, Titus and Flavius twisting their heads to look over their shoulders. She swept on, now that she had our attention.

"It's about Peter Ironhair, and what he hopes to gain."

"Go on, Auntie, we're listening."

"Well, as I said, this may be nonsense, but I think I have just had an inkling of what may be in his mind. Shall I go on?"

"Of course." I stood up. "But first come over here and sit with us so the noble Legates here will not have to strain their necks." I moved to where she sat and took her arm as she moved forward to sit on the couch beside me, facing the others. When she had settled herself, rearranging the fall of her clothes to mask the speed of her thoughts, she leaned forward.

"Peter Ironhair is married to a great-niece of Victorex, who was the first Master of Horse in Camulod. Her name is Carla." My aunt glanced at each of us in turn and then continued, obviously remembering that we were males and therefore unused to the intricacies of female thinking. "Well, many years ago, my brother Caius acquired the estates that had been bequeathed to a former officer of his, a notorious pederast whom Caius had court-martialled and expelled from the legions for his sins. After Caius's death, the ownership passed on to Publius, my husband."

"Philip Ascanus," I said, recalling the incident clearly from my great-uncle's writings.

"Exactly, Philip Ascanus. A most unpleasant man, from all accounts. Well, after Victorex became too old to work as Master of Horse, Publius endowed him with a portion of those lands that Caius had originally purchased through an agent from Ascanus; a fourth of them, I believe, as his reward for many years of service. It was a valuable bequest, in perpetuity. Those lands passed to his nephew, a man called Gareth, when Victorex died, and Gareth had three daughters, the oldest of whom was Carla." We waited, knowing she would soon make sense. She frowned, remembering.

"Five years ago or so, Peter Ironhair arrived in Camulod. He was an able smith and a hard worker and soon made his mark. He met and wooed Carla, who was not comely, but a solid, sensible young woman. Unfortunately, as these things often go, she yielded to him without talk of marriage, and they lived together for some time. Now," she squinted, thinking hard. "I cannot recall the reasons, though I know there were some, and solid, but Gareth, as an incentive to Ironhair to wed the girl, offered to dower her with a portion of his lands. Ironhair accepted the offer, desirous, as who in his position would not be, of adding to his status that of landowner. Everything was agreed, apparently, until the wedding date, when it appeared there was some impediment to the passage of title to the lands . . . I don't know what was involved, it was years ago and the affair was kept quite quiet, but we can find out if we apply ourselves. Anyway, the upshot was that Peter Ironhair lost his claim to those lands through some prior commitment that his wife's father, Gareth, had made originally to Secundus Varo. Tertius, I seem to remember—Secundus was long dead by then—was loath to press his father's claim, but Lucius, Tertius's own son, was adamant, and refused to settle for less than the family's due. Ironhair protested, and the matter went to Council, but was resolved in favour of the Varo claim."

Aunt Luceiia paused and looked at me. "There, Nephew, I believe, lies the root cause of Ironhair's hatred of Lucius Varo."

I nodded, but my eyebrows were raised in question. "Yes, Auntie, I—"

"Wait, I haven't finished." She paused again, then resumed. "Now, here is a man who detests Lucius Varo; a man who has suffered, personally, from being single and unsupported in a conflict with a well-established, strong and greedy rival. Years later, he sees that rival begin to assemble a strong corps of supporters, who will back the fellow up, it seems, in anything he attempts. But as the years have passed, few though they were, the former friendless victim has amassed some strength of his own, and now perceives an opportunity to challenge, and constrain his enemy. There is the motive behind the formation of the Artisan group."

"That's all very well, Auntie, and it explains his motivation, but what about the ends? What is he aiming for?"

My aunt was ready for me. "What did Lot of Cornwall aim for, Cay? Dominance."

"Dominance?" The surprise in my voice was echoed by the smiles that sprang to the lips of Titus and Flavius. Luceiia Britannicus withered all three of us with a glance.

"Dominance." Her tone was obdurate, her pronunciation precise and clipped. "He seeks personal dominion. No more, no less. His prize is Camulod." She observed all of us and resumed before we could come up with a rebuttal. "Think about it, all of you! Since the death of Picus Britannicus there has been no dominant leader within this Colony. You, Caius, have been bereft of your identity for years, a shadow of your former and true self, a persona that Ironhair never saw. Uther has been totally concerned for those same years with his own mountain kingdom and with the war on Lot. The Colony has been run by you two." She took in both old soldiers with a single glance. "I have no wish to disparage either of you, but your days of being perceived as a potent threat to anyone are as long gone as mine." She allowed that thrust to sink home slowly in the silence that followed it.

"Peter Ironhair is a powerful man," she resumed eventually. "Powerful physically and, of late, in influence. He now controls a solid faction within this Colony's affairs. His followers are all young, all artisans, craftsmen, each with his own apprentices, all physically strong and hence all capable of fighting, if the need for fighting should arise. Against him is ranged the group known as the Farmers, who are farmers indeed, and the remainder of the Council, all of whom are well advanced in years and fundamentally impotent in any trial of strength. No leader has existed to oppose his plans. Do you hear what I am saying, all of you?"

I nodded my head, stunned with the evident truth of her conjecture. "We do. You are saying th—"

"I am saying, Nephew, that saving only your miraculous return to possession of your faculties and memory, the stage has been arranged within this Colony for a revolt, fomented by the bitterness between Lucius Varo, the smooth and unctuous politician, and Peter Ironhair, the hard-muscled and popular champion of the ordinary workers of Camulod, with everything—total control of the Colony, its soldiers and its future—accruing to the victor in the fight that must take place . . ." Her voice died away, leaving us speechless, and then continued. "The truth is there."

None of us sought to argue otherwise.

"So what do you intend to do?" Lucanus had listened wordlessly to all I told him, his face bleak in the dappled afternoon shadows beneath the great tree above us. We had ridden down from the main gates, skirting the edge of the great training campus with its usual activity of wheeling and milling groups of training riders, and sought the comfort of a grassy glade, where we had dismounted and now sat on a fallen tree trunk, sharing a small bag of shelled hazelnuts and sun-dried grapes.

"I don't know yet, but before we even begin on that I want your reaction. Do you believe it? Does it ring true?"

He snorted. "You shouldn't even have to ask me that! Of course it's true. It's as plain as the nose on your face; the only possible explanation of all the things that have been keeping us off balance and wasting our time wondering what Ironhair could possibly be up to. Do you still have doubts?"

I shook my head. "No, Luke. But still, it's hard to credit. I mean here, in Camulod."

"Horse turds! Camulod, Rome, Babylon, Athens or Ur of the Chaldeans, it makes no matter. Men are men, most of them prefer venality, given a choice, and the world is one great latrine. The basest elements survive and float to the surface sooner or later to offend the eyes of others. Whatever you decide, my friend, you have to do it soon. What about Varo?"

"What about him? Ironhair's the danger. Varo is only dangerous as long as he is allowed to persist in this acquisitive lust he has for seizing land. I know exactly how to deal with that and I intend to see to it immediately. Apart from that, young Master Lucius merely provides Ironhair with a focus for the pretence of necessary, righteous outrage."

"Aye, but—Oh damn, I'm being summoned."

His eyes were fixed over my shoulder and I turned to where a messenger approached us from the hillside road, a one-armed veteran mounted on an elderly mule. He saw us notice him and drew rein within earshot.

"Master Lucanus, you are needed in the sick bay."

"Thank you, I will be there directly." The man turned and kicked his mount into its return journey, and as he watched the fellow go I saw Luke's features quicken and then set into a scowl.

"What's wrong?" I asked him.

He shook his head and his scowl changed into a tiny smile. "Passing thoughts," he said quietly. "When did you last wash your hands?"

"What? This morning, why?"

"Because I wash mine all the time, sometimes ten times in the course of a day. I know *why* I do it, too. We surgeons are a cleanly lot. But I had never thought till now of *how* I do it."

I had heard his emphasis clearly, but his meaning had passed me by. I stood up, shaking my head at his non sequitur and sealing the nut bag with its drawstring. "Good for you, Luke. Before the monastic zealots appeared, the Romans used to say that cleanliness is next to Godliness."

He ignored my comment, raising an arm to point to the departing messenger. "A one-armed man can't do it at all, Cay. He must rely on others to do it for him . . . to wash his *hand*."

I froze, suddenly aware of what he meant, as he went on. "Emasculate young Varo, deprive him of his power, and you remove the focus for Ironhair's public motivation. He'll have only one hand to try and wash, and lack the means to do it."

"By God, you're right, Luke, and I know exactly how to achieve that!"

He looked at me and grinned. "I knew you would, as soon as I had pointed it out to you. Now I must go. Coming?"

We barely spoke as we rode back up the road towards the fort. Luke's mind was on the work that lay ahead of him, and so was mine. I had six days to prepare for the adjourned meeting of the Council.

V

THE APPOINTED DAY arrived and I found myself, for the second time in a week, facing the assembled Plenary Council of Camulod, but much had changed in the intervening days. During that time I had convened a lesser council of my own, consisting of my great-aunt; Luke, who was not present at this day's gathering; Titus; Flavius; and a few of the senior councilors, including Mirren, all of whom had expressed concern, one way or another, over the way things had been heading recently. Acting with the concurrence of my small committee, I had busied myself over the preceding week, re-establishing my credentials—essentially my position as Legate Commander of Camulod, a position inherited (and earned, I liked to believe) from my father, Picus Britannicus, who had assumed the mantle from Publius Varrus, who had, in turn, taken over the position and its responsibilities from my grandfather, Caius Britannicus, progenitor of the Colony. Camulod had ever been primarily a military-based society, constructed for self-defense and survival in the face of chaos. Our Colonists were free men, joined together of their own free will, governed necessarily by the rules set forth by our Council and subject to its penalties, the most severe of which was banishment. In all matters of internal administration and civil government the Council's authority held sway. Military matters, however—and these embraced not only the defense, but also the protection of the common welfare of the Colony—assumed priority above all else, and there the Legate Commander held the ultimate authority. Much of my credibility came from being a Camulodian born and trained by the founders of the Colony, and from a long, active and successful career as a soldier of Camulod—a man, in short, who could achieve in very short order whatever had to be achieved.

I had begun by visiting our wounded, freshly returned from Cornwall, and welcoming each man home, and I continued by holding a full General Inspection of the Garrison, the first such event in more than a year. I had then visited every holding in our lands, passing the time not only with the owners and managers of the estates, but with the populace, the ordinary Colonists, visiting many of them in their homes. I had shown my face in every smithy, cooperage and manufactory within our bourne, including the domain of Peter Ironhair, with whom I took care to spend a long time talking of his affairs and concerns.

I had begun anew, this time entrusting the work to personnel carefully selected by my associates, the census of our livestock, abandoned so long before when Lot's Cornishmen first fell upon us, and I had set Titus and Flavius about a similar, exhaustive tally of our fighting strength. Both of these tasks were now complete, and I had the results to present to Council today. I had also ridden long and hard to dine every single night with the most powerful and long-established names among our Colonists, being careful to include among those a pleasant evening in the home of Lucius Varo. In the space of a week, in other words, I had become a politician vying for office.

Now I sat in my proper place in Council, in the front row of the double ring of chairs that circled the hall. I felt more resplendent than I had for years, dressed in full, elaborate Roman parade regalia of polished black bull-hide breastplate, moulded to my torso over a rich, blindingly white tunic bordered with a Greek key design in pure black. Most of the matching accoutrements I wore from head to toe had been my father's and were of that quality which sets the truly ornate apart from the merely ostentatious. My buckles and adornments, from the rosettes of my chin strap to the mountings of my polished leather leggings, were of massive, solid silver. My great-aunt's seamstresses had completely renovated my huge war cloak, transferring the great, embroidered blazon of the rampant silver bear intact onto the back and shoulders of a brand-new black cloak, lined with soft, pure white wool. In the crook of my left elbow I held my finest black leather parade helmet, surmounted with my father's own massive, silver-mounted crest of alternating tufts of black and white horsehair.

A bustle of close-pressed bodies announced the arrival of the Farmers, who moved in a block to the seats left vacant for their use on one side of the circle. Lucius Varo and his closest adviser Bonno—the two were evidently seldom seen apart—sat in the front row, approximately centred among their little group. A short time later, the Artisans entered and made their way to the seats they had marked as theirs. They seated themselves, leaving two central chairs, also in the front rank, ostentatiously empty. Peter Ironhair and Rhenus sauntered in a few moments later and sat down, both of them nodding casually to me in greeting.

I knew that my finery had occasioned much comment among the gathering, but no one, so far, had given me any indication that they considered me too formally dressed. I kept my eyes fixed on middle space and waited for Mirren to call the assembly to order. He did, eventually, and the business of the Council began.

As I had expected, there was nothing of moment to be discussed that day. There had been a long-standing dispute over the borders of parts of Varo's lands, and whether or not they infringed upon the land granted some years earlier to one of Ironhair's adherents. Both clique leaders, however, had visited Mirren privately since my return, requesting that he defer the discussion and judgment scheduled for this day's proceedings. I was quite content to have it thus. The major matter for this assembly to absorb and discuss today lay within no one's agenda but my own, which I had drawn up carefully with Mirren. I paid little attention to the maundering discussions of the few routine matters that remained before the Council, and they were soon dealt with. I was concentrating so intently, in fact, upon the course that lay before me, that I lost track completely of what was happening, so that Mirren's introduction of me took me unawares.

"... the return of Caius Merlyn Britannicus to this Council," he was saying when my mind snapped back to where I was. "Last week, he appeared here in full health for the first time in several years, but appeared before us only as a messenger, bearing the tidings of his cousin's death. Today, however, he is here in a different, a *double* capacity: as one of us, in Council, taking his place among us as an equal, and as Legate Commander of the

Forces of Camulod, the rank accorded him by his own father, the Legate Picus Britannicus, in recognition of his great abilities, and a title, incidentally, that has been assumed by no other since. In both capacities he will address us now, and it is with pleasure I invite you to break the custom of this gathering and welcome him with your applause after so long and regrettable an absence. Caius Merlyn Britannicus." He waved his arm, inviting me to stand and speak, and I arose to a great surge of applause and walked forward to the centre of the circle, where I turned fully around, accepting and acknowledging their plaudits. Varo and Ironhair stamped and clapped as loud as any, but where Varo's smile seemed genuine, Ironhair's face was expressionless. As the noise died down I held up my hand, palm forward.

"Thank you, my friends. I cannot adequately tell you how glad I am to be back here in the hall, in full possession of my faculties once more. I can tell you, however, that I have sworn an oath to develop, based upon my past experiences, a lifelong habit henceforth of keeping my head well clear of swinging iron flails." That brought a round of laughter, even from the Women's Council, and as it died away I spoke again.

"These are warlike times, and we have suffered grievously by that, so I think it is fitting that the Soldier report to you today before the Councilor." I glanced around the circle and then withdrew a folded scroll of papyrus from the bowl of the helmet tucked beneath my left arm. "Let me begin with a summation of our military strengths and weaknesses." I pulled open the scroll and glanced down at it for effect, although I knew the numbers perfectly. "A careful accounting within the past four days has shown that we have a total strength at our command of eighteen hundred and forty trained fighting men fit to do battle today, should the need arise. Some eight hundred and fifty of these are cavalry troopers, the remaining thousand or so are infantry and garrison troops, stationed within the fort itself and in the camps throughout the Colony. A further seven hundred and twenty-eight men are currently recovering from wounds in and around the fort itself, and of that number approximately five hundred, mainly cavalry, should be fit to return to duty within the next two or three months. Some will take longer to regain their strength. Others never will." I looked around me again, and then lowered my head to the scroll once more. No sound marred the stillness of the hall.

"As to livestock: A similar tally tells us that we have fifteen hundred cavalry mounts." Someone hissed in surprise, and a murmur of astonishment rose and quickly fell. I continued speaking. "I have no need to tell you how important those mounts are. Many of them are geldings and infertile or unbred mares, but we have more than eighty stud stallions. We also have a wealth of brood mares, fillies, work horses and pack animals, twelve hundred in all, throughout our lands. In addition, we have a large number of mules, three hundred and eighty of them, and several dozen asses. Of cattle, we have eighteen hundred head in eleven separate herds. Seven hundred of those are milch cows; a full five hundred are heifers, born, thanks only to Fortune, since no one planned it thus, over the past three years and still unbred. The rest are oxen: bullocks kept for food, labour and hides, except for twenty prime bulls. Of other cattle, we have . . . more than six hundred swine, and ducks, geese and hens too numerous to count." I paused, looking up again. "Lest any misunderstand, those numbers leave us richer than any of us had thought to be, because our crops have suffered badly these past few years, and our granaries are poorly stocked. Our prospects, however, for this year at least, are good, even should our crops fail—a disaster that should not occur, all things continuing as they are. We could sustain ourselves on meat alone, eked out by rationed grain, through the severest winter, should the need arise. Again, please God, it will not." There was no stopping the hum of speculation I had stirred up this time. The thought of slaughtering enough animals to feed the entire Colony throughout a whole winter was an amazing one. I waited, and when the time was right I stopped them again.

"I have no doubt that all of you are wondering how we could amass such wealth and not be aware of it. How could it remain hidden? Well, the answer lies in the size and variety of our estates. This Colony we call Camulod embraces no less than fourteen great villa estates today, each of them self-sustaining, in the main. In terms of area, our lands would extend more than twelve miles, perhaps fifteen, in both length and breadth, were they so arranged. Of course, they are not, and few among us have ever visited each estate within the Colony. Has anyone?" No one raised a hand. "I have," I said. "But only in the past week have I set out methodically to do so.

"So, we are wealthy, in terms of livestock at least, almost beyond our dreams, and we have reasonable fighting strength. But before you declare a holiday, my friends, consider this." I made them wait as I turned in a full circle once more, eyeing them all. "Before Lot's pestilence, before his treachery, before the wars he thrust upon us, our cavalry mounts numbered more than five thousand." I allowed that to sink home, before reiterating it with measured emphasis. "Five thousand. More than three thousand of those are gone now, and with many of them went their riders . . . In the past five years, we have lost more than two thousand men, killed in the wars. God knows how many of our allies in Uther's kingdom have gone down to death in addition to those. And Uther's people are not farmers. They will be feeling the pain of lost men far more than we."

These numbers, thus baldly stated, created the effect I had hoped for, and I forged on, seizing the moment. "So our apparent strength, as you may see plainly now if you look, is, in effect, a measure of our weakness. But it is a weakness we can readily remedy, by taking swift, sure steps to stamp it out!"

How? I could see the question written plainly on their faces as they gazed at me, awaiting my guidance, sensing salvation in my confidence.

"We have never lacked prospective Colonists—our biggest problem in the past, in peaceful times, has been in controlling the influx of people seeking safety within our lands; people whose numbers, carelessly controlled, would quickly swamp our ability to provide the very things they seek: safety and security from hunger. That profusion of potential immigrants has provided us in the past with as many willing soldiers as we wished to hire and train. It will do so again today. I seek your formal approval in the dispatching of five teams of recruiters, veteran soldiers all, to raise an intake of at least another thousand replacements for the soldiers we have lost. We have the ability to feed and train such numbers, and the personnel to turn them into Camulodian troopers. More important than either of those, however, is the fact that, thanks to the death of the upstart Cornish king, as he styled himself, we have the time available to train them."

Their approval was instantaneous, a shouted chorus of assent.

"Thank you for that. The recruiting parties are prepared and will go out today." I folded up my scroll and stuffed it back inside the bowl of my helmet, which I then placed carefully on the floor by my feet, giving the three recording clerks against the wall—another innovation since my days of regular attendance here—time to write down the approval I had gained.

"Now," I resumed, changing the subject and arriving at my real agenda for the day. "The topic I will put before you next calls on both of the capacities in which I serve here. I bring it forward both from the viewpoint of our strength, which I am sworn to preserve and foster, and from the perspective of a councilor concerned with husbanding and expanding our resources." A brief pause produced only a silence of anticipation.

"I spoke earlier of the extent and disposition of our lands . . . I have concerns in that regard which I must place before you, and they have to do with balance, with moderation, with the distribution of our resources, and with weaknesses I have perceived within this week. As you all know, I have moved widely among you in recent days, and have had discussions with almost all of you on the conditions under which each one of you must do what Camulod and its people require of you." I looked from face to face, disliking the flattery inherent in the next words I would utter. "You are all people of intellect and probity. That's why you sit in this Council. Each of you knows the practical truth behind the old saying that only a fool carries all of his eggs in one basket, or places all of his precious glassware upon one shelf . . .

"And yet, in my travels about our lands, I have perceived—and I mean *very clearly perceived*—such an imbalance." They were listening closely. "Our livestock is numerous and healthy, but it has been reduced by more than two thousand horses. I have already dealt with that, but the *lands* allocated for those vanished horses have not decreased. We have vast areas of uncultivated grasslands at our disposal . . . going to waste after the years of effort that were spent winning them from the forest. Of all our fourteen villa estates, only one is dedicated completely to the raising of crops. Only one . . . the Villa Varo. It is well run, healthy and prosperous, and we all rely on it completely and quite literally for our daily bread, but God forbid we should ever be taken unawares by an incursion of hostile forces on the Varo lands! Were that to happen, we could, at one stroke, lose all our crops, or the vast part of them. That, my friends, constitutes eggs in one basket on a frightening scale . . ."

This time I made no effort to restrain the tide of comment that swept around the hall, and to avoid the temptation of looking towards Lucius Varo and his group, who huddled tensely, whispering among themselves. I allowed my gaze to drift with apparent aimlessness around the room until it touched on the Ironhair faction. They were agog, straining their necks to watch Varo's people. Only Ironhair himself sat aloof, his face reflecting grave thoughts as he evidently wondered where this was going. Eventually, the tide of comments died down to a murmur, at which point Mirren, with his entitlement as president, rose to his feet. Silence fell again as he spoke.

"Legate Commander Merlyn . . ." Even the phrasing of his address to me at this point had been rehearsed for effect, the emphasis on my titles of Legate and *Commander* clear yet subtle. He performed like a trained actor. "Let me be clear in my understanding of what you have said. You are expressing grave concern about the *weakness* of the Villa Varo?"

"No, not at all." There was no trace of hesitation in my response. "You have misunderstood me if you draw that from what I said. There is nothing weak about the Villa Varo, nothing at all. Forgive me, I thought I had made myself quite clear." I turned my eyes from Mirren to the councilors. "The weakness I perceived, and to which I referred, is a *collective* weakness—a vulnerability within the Colony—brought about by the passage of time and a lack of foresight for which no one can be blamed. My image of eggs in one basket was not intended as a criticism of the Villa Varo in any way. It was a simple reference to a previously undetected weakness in our planning; the planning for survival in the face of chaos that has been the driving force behind this Colony since it began. I set out to speak of balance and the distribution of our resources. I have obviously caused you to lose sight of that, so let me return to it now. I see, fellow councilors, and I feel sure that you will, too, upon very little thought, an imperative need to convert a large part of each of our villa properties immediately to the growing of crops, and to reallocate much of our livestock among the remaining space."

"But *Commander!*" Mirren was on his feet almost before my words were out, forestalling the shocked reaction of the Council, taking the winds of complaint out of their sails before they could begin to blow. I turned to face him as he challenged me.

"Immediately? You said immediately. That is impossible."

I eyed him, letting all see the curiosity upon my face and its slow replacement with a hesitant, but privately much-practised, smile. "How so?" I shrugged my shoulders. "As it appears to me, few things could be simpler."

Mirren's mouth flapped as though he were bereft of words, and I thought again as I waited for him to resume that he would have made a wondrous actor. He turned towards the councilors on his left, as though beseeching them, and then swung back to me, spreading his arms in appeal. "How can you think it simple? With the exception of the Villa Varo, our villas are all run by herdsmen. Their skills are in livestock, as you pointed out, and are amply demonstrated by the welfare of their stock, but their talents rest there. They are not farmers, save of the simplest kind." He stopped, as though realizing the insult in what he had said, then charged on, apparently recovering himself. "I have no wish to disparage anyone, but they're not plough-men, not growers of crops. To expect them to change such things immediately would be folly."

I had allowed my smile to broaden as he spoke, a task made simpler by my admiration for his performance.

"Folly in truth," I agreed when he had done, "had that been what I meant to imply. But I see I have again been less than exact in saying what I meant." I turned again to face my audience, holding up my hands. "Please, my friends, bear with me. I am a soldier, not a man of words. If you will hear me out, however, I will attempt again to clarify my thoughts." I paused, and felt their sympathy flowing around me, tempered by mild distress and perplexity.

"I spoke of reallocation—of lands, and of stock. I see now that I should also have spoken of skills."

Now I looked directly at Lucius Varo for the first time, knowing I had him in my grasp. "We have a rich resource in the Villa Varo. A heavy and potent concentration of the skills Mirren has just described as being lacking in our Colony. The farmers of the Villa Varo are the finest anywhere, even beyond our lands. From that point of view, they are the single greatest strength Camulod owns. Among them, they possess the power to train, to guide and to instruct—as thoroughly and conscientiously as our veterans will train our new recruits—the new farmers of Camulod. By spreading them judiciously among the villas, we can ensure that all the farming skills developed on the Varo lands for the past hundred years and more will spread to all our Colonists, to benefit the future for ourselves and for our children."

I allowed them to digest that thought for a moment, expecting young Varo to protest. He sat silent, however, and I continued. "What I am proposing will require much work, and even some short-term upheavals on the Villa Varo as the task progresses; it will call for much planning by all of us, and a careful reckoning of skills and requirements, but it is far, far from impossible, given the goodwill of all concerned."

Ironhair's face was aglow. He saw the discomfiture and confusion of his enemy, and recognized the end of Varo's bid for power. I knew with complete conviction that he had not seen beyond the moment and had no idea that he was also witnessing the beginnings of his own downfall. A rough, loud voice broke into the stillness, emanating from the back row of chairs.

"By all the ancient gods, Merlyn Britannicus, I think you have it! I stand with you!"

As the man who had shouted rose to his feet, the entire assembly broke up in a storm of support for my proposal. I glanced at Mirren who looked back at me and shrugged his shoulders, his wide-eyed, sheepish gaze a portrait of astonished innocence. I nodded to him, indicating for anyone watching that I was finished, picked up my helmet from the floor and returned to my chair, where I was immediately besieged with heavy-handed congratulations on my clear thinking and vision. I bore the plaudits modestly, watching and waiting. In spite of my concession of the floor, I had not yet completed this day's tasks.

The storm of applause and the confusion that ensued until order was restored within the hall had given Lucius Varo time to collect his thoughts, and he was on his feet immediately the session recommenced, seeking recognition from Mirren in the Speaker's Chair. Mirren recognized him, and a total hush fell upon the assembly. Varo instantly became aware of the intensity of the silence, and I saw the realization bloom within his eyes that he stood alone, his position evident to all. He knew he was trapped and that any overt resentment he betrayed towards my suggestion would be an admission that he sought to preserve his own well-being ahead of the welfare of the community. Nevertheless, to give him his due, he fought courageously and his counter-argument was articulate and reasoned. It would, he said, bring too much hardship to bear on the highly organized Varo estates to make such sweeping changes so suddenly. He and his assistants would require time to plan an orderly conversion—far more time than I had indicated would be available. Adhering to the timetable I had decreed would invite chaos and confusion to flourish, to the detriment of everyone in Camulod.

It was a valiant effort, but fundamentally flawed, for every attentive councilor had marked that I had set no rigid timetable. Yet Varo spoke with authority as though I had, and none interrupted him to point out that I had specifically referred to the requirement for him and his people to be allowed time to plan their changes. No sooner had that thought occurred to me, however, than Peter Ironhair stood up and was given the right to speak. He launched at once into an attack on Varo's argument, recalling and repeating verbatim my own earlier words, throwing them down like a challenge in front of Lucius Varo, daring him to object further. When Ironhair sat down, looking pleased with the impression he had made, no other sought immediate permission to speak, and I stood up again, my eyes on Rhenus, who had been pounding Ironhair's shoulder in approval of his fiery speech.

"Commander Merlyn." Mirren's voice was calm. "Do you have anything to add?"

I affected not to have heard him, keeping my eyes on Rhenus and allowing puzzlement to show clearly upon my face. Mirren coughed.

"Commander Merlyn? You wish to speak?"

"What? Oh, no. Pardon me, I merely had . . ." I moved as though to sit and then straightened again. "Yes, if I may speak again?"

"Of course you may."

"Thank you. I was surprised to see . . ." Frowning now, I stepped to my right to confront Rhenus, who sat back and looked at me in surprise. Every eye in the room was watching me. "Pardon me," I said. "Your name is Rhenus, is it not? You are a newcomer to Camulod since I was injured, if I recall correctly. I met you at last week's meeting?"

"Yes." From the look on his face, he thought I was losing my mind again. I turned back towards the Speaker's Chair, then swung back to Rhenus. "You sat in that same chair then, did you not?"

He frowned. "I did."

"Yes, I remember you came in with Peter here, but I met you outside." I turned back towards Mirren. "I must ask your indulgence, sir, and that of the Council, but I had thought—" I broke off again, as though collecting my thoughts, then said, "Valerius Mirren, may I speak, not of the current debate, but of procedure?"

Mirren nodded, his face dubious.

"Thank you." I continued to look around me as I paused, pretending uncertainty. "It has been several years since I have sat in Council, but there are several things I find confusing here. Changes, it seems, to what I knew in the past."

"What do you mean, Commander Merlyn? Can you cite an example?"

Now I gazed at Mirren directly. "Yes, Valerius Mirren. You."

Someone among the councilors giggled nervously, and several people shifted uncomfortably. Mirren, however, faced me calmly. "I don't know what you mean, Commander."

"You presided at the last meeting, did you not?"

"I did. I am president of the Council. That is my duty."

"Since when, sir? That is an innovation."

He nodded. "It is. An innovation passed by the Plenary Council three years ago, when we were embroiled in war. It was deemed then that the presence of a president would create stability in Council, with so many decisions having to be made each week that passed. The custom of a simple session leader, different each time, became impractical for purposes of continuity under emergency conditions, and so the Council voted to elect a leader to maintain order and to co-ordinate developments in Council with consistency, for one year, until such times as peace returned to Camulod."

"Like a Roman Consul."

He nodded. "That is correct, exactly."

"And you are the third such president?"

"I am."

"I see." I turned to face the councilors, scanning their faces and naming the eldest among them, allowing iron to enter my tone now. "Lars Nepos, Quintus Seco, Agnellus Totius. Were any of you present on the occasion Caius Britannicus stood down as leader of this Council?" All three had been there, and all stood up and said so. They were the eldest of the Elders. I addressed them courteously. "Can any of you tell us what you recall of that occasion?"

They looked at each other and nodded back and forth, and Quintus Seco drew himself erect. "Aye," he said, his voice still strong and hale for all his age. "I can recall it clearly." He looked around to ensure that he had everyone's attention. "On that day, there was chaos in the hall, screaming and arguing. Some of us almost came to blows. Publius Varrus silenced us by blowing on a horn. Britannicus drew his sword and stabbed it upright into the tabletop, prepared to clear the room, which was in his own home, the Villa Britannicus. I had never seen him so angry. He condemned the lot of us as petty, squabbling children fighting among ourselves for prominence and personal aggrandizement, and threatened to withdraw from the Council and never return. He pointed out, for all of us to see, that what he called a spirit of elitism had invaded our proceedings, and he demanded that it had to be stamped out, immediately, if we were to survive. He harangued us for piddling, personal jealousies and political maneuvering to the detriment of all with which we had been entrusted. He made us all ashamed.

"It was on that day that this present Council was born." He swept his arm around the double circle of chairs. "The chairs were rearranged into a circle, so that thereafter all men should be equal in Council, and the rule was made that each man, entering the Council Gathering, should draw a stone at random from a closed bag. He who drew the black would be the leader for that day. Thus, Britannicus said, no man could gain position or influence for any length of time. He himself stepped down that day, and thenceforth sat in Council as an ordinary member—except that he was, of course, Caius Britannicus, extraordinary by any standards." A nervous whisper of amusement greeted his last remark, and he sat down.

"Thank you, Quintus Seco." I turned back to Mirren. "The wars are over, Valerius Mirren."

He drew himself to his full, imposing height and then bowed slightly from the waist. "Thank you, Merlyn Britannicus, I take your point. So is my term of office. The drawstring bag will be by the door at the next meeting of the Council."

I acknowledged that with a deep nod of my head and turned back to Quintus Seco. "Were there other rules made that day, Councilor Seco?"

Agnellus Totius forestalled Seco by the simple expedient of rising ahead of him and speaking without permission. "Aye, there were. The best of them followed the lines of the random selection of a daily leader and made collusion difficult—and it bore directly upon the elitism already mentioned, and upon your question to Rhenus there." His voice hardened and became accusatory. "*No two men were to sit together more often than once in any seven sessions!*"

Now there was uproar, and as it swelled, the rear doors opened and Titus stepped inside followed by two trumpeters bearing great, circular, bronze Roman *cornua*, or war horns. The brazen clamour of them shocked the gathering into silence.

"History repeats itself," I said quietly, into the stunned silence. "The wheel has turned full circle." I turned slowly to Peter Ironhair and pointed my finger at him. He sat frozen, watching me. Deliberately, I raised my other hand, pointing to Lucius Varo, although keeping my eyes fixed on Ironhair. "Let me speak plainly. The Farmers and the Artisans are finished; proscribed, and banned from this Council by my authority as Legate Commander of the Forces of Camulod."

Ironhair leaped to his feet, his face suddenly aflame with fury as he realized how he had been gulled. His entire body stiffened into a crouch, as though he were physically restraining himself from leaping at me. As he glared at me, his lips moving soundlessly, the surge of colour faded from his cheeks, leaving them pallid and gaunt-looking. I glared back at him along the line of my pointing hand so that my finger aimed directly between his eyes.

"Hear me! This is a matter that concerns the safety of the Colony, its unity of purpose and strength in the face of its enemies, and thus it comes within my jurisdiction. By my authority as Legate Commander of the Forces of Camulod," I repeated, "both groups stand proscribed, formally outlawed, by my decree, the written orders sealed with my seal, to take effect upon the closure of this Council session. Be warned. Both groups are noted; the names of all adherents registered. If either group assembles as an organized gathering of more than three from this day forth, it will do so under pain of formal, military displeasure, and will suffer the penalties of martial law according to the laws of Camulod. Banishment, with no recourse. This is not personal, but for the common good of this Colony. No former member of either group shall suffer any consequence, nor be removed from Council, but never again will two such factions function *within* this Council." I waited, counting silently to five. "Do I make myself clear?"

Apparently I had, for no one spoke.

"Very well." I lowered my pointing fingers and addressed the councilors at large. "We have achieved much here today, my friends, but I think our duties are concluded. I would suggest, if I might, that we gather again in one more week, this time in the tradition and according to the customs of the Council of the Colony, to plan our further actions." I turned back to Mirren. "Valerius Mirren, will you move to adjourn?"

Ironhair spoke into the hush before Mirren could respond. I made no effort to turn back to him. His words, low-pitched and choked with anger, were perfectly clear.

"Damn you, Britannicus, this is tyranny. What makes you think you can manipulate this Council to your twisted will? The thought is ludicrous! You come in here, after long years of unconcern, and try to win us with smooth words, masking your sudden, naked greed for power under a guise of caring. Where was your caring last year, and the year before, when Cornishmen were howling at our gates? And now you would use your family's name and your inherited position to decree to us, the *people* of Camulod, its *Governors*, how we must behave? I'll see you damned before I will submit to this. Look at me, damn you! You can't do this! No single person can!"

I stepped to where my helmet sat upon the floor, then bent and picked it up without looking at Ironhair. As I straightened, I glanced to the rear of the hall where Titus stood watching me. I nodded, and he turned and threw open the main doors. A few heads turned at the sound of marching boots as a file of armed men marched in and ranged themselves across the rear of the hall. Most eyes remained on me. I settled my helmet comfortably on my head and only then did I look at my new-made enemy.

"No single person has," I told him, keeping my voice level. "Camulod has done it. The decree is Law and you may disregard it at your peril. Tyranny, lest you think us unaware of what it means, is the bloody and violent rule of one brutal man who cares nothing for the property or the rights of others. My actions here result from the informed concern of others—all Colonists of Camulod—that you, Master Ironhair, might some day seek to set yourself upon the throne of Camulod." I adjusted my chin strap. "Camulod has no throne, Ironhair, merely a double circle of chairs, but it has a spirit—a spirit that may doze from time to time, but will never die—and while that spirit lives and breathes, no tyranny shall ever grow within our Camulod."

The breathless silence continued as I collected my cloak from the back of my chair and swung it hard over my shoulders, feeling the weight of it settle upon me like a cloak of iron ring mail. "Now my duty here is done and my responsibilities as Guardian of this place are many." I looked at him again. "Your duty, as a conscientious councilor from this day forth, yet lies ahead of you and I have not the slightest doubt you can do it brilliantly if you so wish. Valerius Mirren, may we now adjourn?"

As the hall began to empty, Peter Ironhair was left standing alone.

This time there was no throng of people waiting to applaud me as I left the hall. The Council had disbanded quietly, its members making their way to their separate destinations in silence, their minds dealing one way or another with all that had transpired that day.

I stopped by the Infirmary to let Lucanus know how things had gone, but he was not there. Ludmilla sat at Luke's table, writing diligently in a small, clear hand, adding to a long column of numbers that filled the page that lay in front of her. She had not heard me approach, in spite of my nailed boots, so total was her concentration. I stopped beyond the doorway, looking at her, seeing the way the light from an open window brought out the lustre in her hair, making its blackness shimmer. As I stood there, hesitant to interrupt her and aware of an unusual tension in my guts, she looked up and saw me.

"Commander Merlyn, good day. Is there something I can help you with?"

"Good day to you, Lady Ludmilla. I was looking for Lucanus."

She looked surprised. "He went to the Council gathering."

I shook my head. "No, he was not there. I would have seen him. When did he leave?"

"Hours ago."

"Hmm." I nodded my thanks and turned to go, aware of an urge to remain, and yet unknowing whence it came.

"Popilius Cirro is recovering."

Her words brought me around in the doorway. "He is? How well?" Popilius was our senior soldier, *primus pilus*, First Spear of Camulod. I had last seen him far to the south, in Cornwall, where he had lain apart from the field of the last great battle of Uther's army, surviving the slaughter because he had been wounded in an earlier skirmish. He had contracted pneumonia afterwards, on his way back to Camulod with a special escort, and had lain comatose since his arrival.

Ludmilla smiled, a fleeting thing that bared her white teeth for a mere instant. "Extremely well. He awoke this morning, some time before noon, as though he had been asleep merely since last night, rather than since last month. He was hungry, he said."

"Hungry." I cleared my throat. "May I speak with him?"

"I cannot think why not, although he may be asleep again. He is extremely weak." She stood up, and I watched as her long robe settled around her. "I'll take you to him."

Popilius was not asleep, and I saw his eyes light up with pleasure as I walked towards the cot in which he lay. He was an old man now, I saw. When last we met, I had been shocked by his white hair and the white stubble upon his unshaven cheeks. The Popilius Cirro I had known prior to that meeting had been a hardened, veteran centurion, a vision of solid, military ruggedness, clad at all times in crisp, spotless clothes and shining, polished armour. The man who looked up at me now from the narrow cot looked like that other's grandfather. His beard was thick and snowy white, with only a patch of brown beneath his lower lip. Equally white, thick hair lay coiled in tresses on his pillow, and his eyes were sunken deep above hollowed-out old man's cheeks that sagged around deep-graven lines from the edges of his nose to the sides of his thin, lipless mouth.

"Commander," he said, his voice a breathless wheeze. "You came away safe."

I reached out and took his hand, smiling broadly to hide my distress at his condition. "Aye, Popilius, I did. Does that surprise you?"

His eyes narrowed. "What about Uther?"

I shook my head. "I was too late to help him. He is dead. I burned his body."

"Lot?"

"Dead, too, old friend. They are all dead." I felt his fingers go limp. "Now, how much longer are you going to lie here in this useless bed? We have need of you."

He closed his eyes and nodded, his face betraying nothing of his thoughts. "I know you do . . . I am aware of that." His eyes opened again suddenly and he peered at me, almost squinting as he searched for something in my eyes. "Your mind, Commander . . . are you still well?"

I grinned at him. "Aye, Popilius, better than I ever was, and back on duty as I have not been for years."

He squeezed my hand, grunted a sigh, and relaxed again. "Good," he whispered. "That's good."

I waited for more, but gradually realized that he was fast asleep. I disengaged his fingers from my own and left him there. Ludmilla had gone.

I made my way to my aunt's house from there, having no wish to sit

alone in my own quarters, and there in the family room I found Luke and
the others of my minor council assembled and waiting for me, well launched
already upon a celebration of the day's events. Everything had gone exactly
as we had planned it, and Mirren was revelling in the admiration his performance had inspired. I added my own congratulations and accepted a cup of
deep red Gaulish wine from my great-aunt, who merely smiled at me and
squeezed my wrist to show her approval. The mood of that gathering was
one of gaiety and self-congratulation, and I allowed it to wash over me unheeded, attempting to keep my own mind empty of anything resembling
urgency. The week that had passed had been a long and industrious one, and
I felt tired with a bone-deep, aching weariness that was rendered sufferable
by the success of what we had worked for.

It was only long afterwards, after the others had all departed and left me
alone with Aunt Luceiia and Lucanus, that we came to any discussion of the
less pleasant aspects of what we had achieved. Aunt Luceiia had rung the
small brazen gong that sat by the doorway to the servants' quarters and asked
the girl who answered its summons to fetch another jug of the rich wine of
which I had already drunk too much. When the maid servant had gone, my
aunt looked from one to the other of us and smiled again, a gentle, patient
smile. "Well," she observed, "I can see that you two still have much to talk
about, and I may go to bed convinced you will not be talking of me behind
my back." She looked at me. "Caius, you have done well today. Your father
and my husband and my brother would all have been proud of you." Her
gaze widened to include Luke. "I have ordered more wine, in case you feel
the need of it. I know you have no need of my opinion thereupon. Now I
have work to do elsewhere. It is not late enough, but I will wish a good night
to both of you." And she was gone.

Luke drained his goblet. "God, this is good wine!"

"The best," I concurred, "and probably the last of it. Any day now, we'll
be drinking watered *vinum.*"

Luke shook his head with drunken solemnity. "No, you exaggerate, my
friend. Your blessed aunt, endowed with her sagacity, would not permit the
bottom of the barrel to be reached without making alternative arrangements.
She has amphorae hidden elsewhere, have no doubt. I would be prepared to
wager she has made arrangements with the quartermasters to renew the cel-
lars."

"Well, if she has, she has even more of my admiration than before, and
I did not think that could be possible. As for hidden amphorae of this, there
can be very few of them and they must be well cached. We haven't taken a
delivery in years." Lucanus had not heard me. His brow was creased in
thought.

"Ironhair," he said. "What do you intend to do about him?"

I chewed on the inside of my upper lip for long moments as I thought
about his question. Finally I shook my head. "I've done what I intended to
do about him. I've drawn his teeth."

"Before he ever had a chance to bite. You think he'll take it lying down?"

"Lying down, standing up or leaping around, Luke, I couldn't care less.
It's done."

"Aye, but is it finished?"

I sighed and rose to refill his goblet from the jug on the table. "Aye, it is finished, one way or the other." I could tell from the weight of it that the jug was almost empty. I poured slowly, half a cup for each of us, the last drops falling individually into my own cup. "Either he will accept the decree, in which case he may be disgruntled but will constitute no threat, or he will rebel . . . in which case he'll be banished and will also pose no threat."

"You like him, don't you?"

I sat down again, placing the empty jug on the floor by my foot. "I could. I think there might be much in him to like."

Lucanus sniffed. "He'll be a bad enemy, Cay."

"How? What can he do, except dislike me if he stays in Camulod? He won't confront me, and the thought of his displeasure holds no fears for me."

"Hmm. What about Lucius Varo?"

"What about him? Lucius is a politician. He'll create no waves, and he'll survive. What he cannot achieve one way, he'll attempt to gain another way. We're aware of him; we'll watch. What time of day is it?"

Lucanus blinked. "I have no idea." He got to his feet and moved to the doorway, opening it and leaning out into the passageway, where he peered towards the atrium at the far end. He spoke from the doorway. "It's getting dark." He returned to the couch opposite me. "Afternoon drinking, I have remarked in the past, steals more time than procrastination. Popilius came back to us today, by the way, just before noon. He's going to recover, it seems, in spite of all my fears. I stayed with him for several hours. That's why I missed the Council session."

"I know. I saw him before I came here. I went looking for you, but found Ludmilla instead."

As I spoke, the inner door opened and Ludmilla herself entered, carrying a jug of wine. Both of us blinked at her and started to rise. She raised a hand. "Please, stay as you are. I only bring this." She placed the jug on the table against the wall and left as quietly as she had entered. My voice started to stop her from leaving, but my tongue, or some other part of me, would not permit the utterance of the words. I subsided, blinking owlishly at the closed door that shut her from my sight. Luke blew out his breath in an explosive rush. He pushed himself erect from his couch and crossed to the table, where he refilled his goblet before bringing the jug to mine.

"Well, Caius Merlyn, what think you of my student?"

"Ludmilla?" I thought about that for a moment and then smiled. "She strikes me as being a wondrous fine student."

"No, Cay, she is an excellent student, a gifted student, perhaps a divinely inspired student . . . but a mere student, nonetheless. Her wondrousness is of a different order. As you have noticed, she is a wondrous *woman*."

"What d'you mean, 'As I have noticed'?" I felt myself flush, and was embarrassed that I should.

"What do I mean?" He laughed aloud. "Come, Cay, admit it, you are taken with her. A blind man could see that, and why should you not be?"

"Nonsense!" The denial emerged terse and angry-sounding, and the sound of it wiped the laughter from his face. He straightened up, languidly.

"Oh, then I beg your pardon, Caius Merlyn," he drawled, making no attempt to hide the mockery in his tone, and I found myself growing angrier, even though I knew I had no cause and was overreacting beyond logic.

"Fine, then," I snapped. "My pardon is extended—graciously," I added, in a gentler tone, breathing deeply, fighting for composure. "I find Ludmilla admirable, simply because of the terms in which you have spoken of her, but I have no special awareness of her as a woman."

"No special awareness . . . I see. You find her undesirable?"

"Yes!" Far too abrupt, I told myself immediately, and then began again. "No, that is untrue. I find her very . . . attractive, I suppose would be the word, were I attracted to her." Lucanus looked down at his cup, masking his face with his free hand. "Besides," I went on, "I have no allure for her. She is your student, your devotee." I straightened in my own seat now, drawing a deep breath. "What do you plan for her?"

He lowered his hand from his face and raised his goblet in my direction, a slight smile on his lips. "Plan for her? What do you mean? Or should I take that merely as it emerged? I plan, if anything, that she shall become a gifted surgeon, woman though she be. God knows, she has the gifts and the abilities to make me proud of having taught her."

"Taught her? Is that all?"

His smile seemed to grow wider. "All? What more could there be?" His pause was brief, but I sensed a change in the direction of his thoughts. "Caius, when we first met, you did not like me. You told me so in no un-certain words, do you recall?"

I did, and nodded my acknowledgment. He sniffed. "Why did you feel that way, can you remember?"

I shook my head, recalling it clearly. "I was an idiot, young and intran-sigent, arrogant and conceited. I thought I knew everything there was to know of men and life. It struck me that you had no sense of humour; that you were staid and pompous; humourless. Yes, that was it."

He nodded, looking into his cup. "Hmm! Quite natural, I suppose. It was a mutual thing. I found you equally distasteful, although I never told you so. And yet, as time progressed, and circumstances brought us together more and more, our antipathy changed to something vastly different. We became friends."

I grimaced, stretching the skin around my mouth and eyes, trying to shake off the wine haze. "So?" I asked. "What has that to do with Ludmilla?"

"Nothing at all, and everything. How long have we been friends now?"

I thought about that. "Five years? Six, perhaps seven."

Something in his eyes, something enigmatic, alerted me to the import of what he would say next, yet when they came his words caught me unpre-pared. "Seven. And how often have you known me to consort with women?"

I shrugged, puzzled. "Seldom. Never, in fact."

"That is correct." He nodded. "Now tell me, have you ever wondered about that?"

"No," I said, and then paused, frowning. "At least, not until I found you at the campsite with Ludmilla. Then I wondered."

"As well you might, and should have." He shrugged, made a tiny face, sipped his wine and then sat back against the couch. "Caius, my friend, I, as a man, have little use for women."

I felt something sag within me, some bracing, deep within my being, that had been stressed with the anticipation of bearing a different weight from that which it now felt. Luke watched me, that same enigmatic smile playing about his mouth.

"Does that dismay you, Cay?"

I merely shook my head, unable to articulate a response. His smile grew wider.

"You have loved a woman, Cay, and found happiness therein. I never have, but then, I have never sought what you sought and found. It is not in me." He voiced each of those five words separately, leaving their emphasis to fall upon my ear like five clear notes upon a harpist's lyre, then leaned forward quickly, his eyes fastened upon mine as consternation bloomed across my face. "Wait, Cay!" he said, before I could respond. "Before you say a word, or think a thought, consider this: the man from whom you have just heard those words is your close friend Lucanus."

I sat back, leaning away from him, struggling to keep the disgust that roiled inside me from showing upon my face.

"What difference does that make?"

He seemed unruffled, but I detected *something*, a settling, a guardedness descend about his eyes. "Difference, Cay? What difference should it make? None at all. I have not changed in any way since we began to speak of this." He drank again, unhurriedly and naturally. "I have not changed in any way since first we met, or since we became friends. I am myself. Lucanus the physician. Legionary Surgeon. Your friend. I have merely admitted that there is no intimate place for women in my life."

I could no longer sit still and face him. I rose to my feet, feeling the drunkenness falling away from me as though I had been doused with cold water. Stooping, I placed my goblet on the tabletop in front of me and then stepped away from him, my eyes sweeping around the walls of this familiar room as though seeking an anchor, a point of reference from which I could regain my lost perspective.

"How can it *not* make a difference, Luke?" I barely recognized my own voice. "There is a *vast* difference."

"In what?" I heard the challenge in his voice.

"In everything!"

"You mean in your opinion, do you not?"

"Yes, I do, since you push me to admission. It is unnatural, it seems to me, to say what you have just said. How can a man be natural, if he has no place for women in his life?"

"Unnatural? I said no *intimate* place, Cay, not no place."

"Place, space, need, desire, they all boil down to the same thing in terms of men and women, Luke. The need for intimacy exists in all of us. It is an inescapable part of life, one of man's primal urgencies. In normal men, it demands the closeness of a woman."

"And therefore men untouched by such demands must be unnatural. Is that what you are saying?"

"Of course it is!"

"Of course it is. Why then, you are unnatural."

The enormity of that left me speechless for a moment. I was unnatural, when he had just confessed to being homosexual? He pressed on.

"Ludmilla is a beautiful woman, by anyone's criteria. She is young, strong, lovely, healthy, intelligent, articulate and free of encumbrances, and yet you feel no attraction to her. Even worse, it seems to me, you are prepared to fight against the mere suggestion you might find her pleasing. That, my friend, is unnatural."

"Wait, wait. Wait just a moment!" In my haste to interrupt him I was almost shouting. "My feelings, or the lack of them, for Ludmilla have no bearing here."

Now he blinked at me in astonishment, and a brief silence fell between us before he continued. "Are you serious? Then tell me, please, what has?"

I shook my head hard to clear it, thinking I was missing something of importance. "Lucanus," I said. "I am becoming confused, and angry. Let me speak slowly and clearly here. Any feelings I may have for Ludmilla, or for any other woman, are not at issue when we are talking of what is natural and what is unnatural. It is your tastes that are unnatural, your lack of a place for women, which amounts—can only amount—to a love for men. That love, while not uncommon, I've been told, could never be called natural or normal!"

"Oh!" His voice was soft, almost hurt. He rose to his feet again and made his way to the wine jug, where he poured for himself before offering the jug to me. I shook my head. When he had poured, he turned back towards me, resting his buttocks against the table's edge.

"So," he said. "You scorn such relationships?"

"Between man and man? Of course I do."

"Hmm. They are unnatural, of course. Unpalatable, would you say? Unpleasant? Degrading?" I nodded, wordless. "And you could never have a friend who was . . . afflicted by such abnormality." It was not a question. I made no response. "It would repulse you?" I nodded again.

"Yes, Luke, it would. It does."

"How old are you, Caius?"

I frowned. "You know I'm thirty-one. Why?"

He smiled. "You are very old to be so young and innocent."

"Innocent?" I thought he was mocking me. "I am no innocent."

He waggled one hand from side to side. "In some ways, no; in others . . ."

"What is that supposed to mean?"

. He looked me straight in the eye. "It means, my friend, that you are naive in some areas of your thinking. You have gone through life bearing these ridiculous notions within you while practising a selective blindness that is unconscionable."

I was frowning now, beginning to bluster. "What are you talking about? Are you accusing me of wishful ignorance in not suspecting you? You gave me no indications."

"Of what, Caius? Suspecting me of what? Indications of what? A lack of ability, of trustworthiness, of integrity?"

"Of deviance!"

"Ah! Deviance!" He swung away from me, averting his face and holding himself rigid in silence for long moments. Then: "Deviance. A wonderful word, Caius, so rich in meaning, so serpentine in its implications! Tell me, would you call your friend the Legate Titus deviant?"

"Of course not!"

"Quite. What about Flavius?"

"I—What . . . what are you implying?"

He turned again to face me. "Nothing, Caius. Nothing at all, I swear to you. Titus and Flavius are two of the finest men you and I have ever known. They are the best of the best, honourable, trustworthy, dependable, honest and upstanding. They are both old men now and have given their lives, all of their lives, to serving your father and his dreams and hopes and aspirations, and when he died they transferred all their loyalties to you. But have you ever seen either of them with a woman, Cay? For that matter, have you ever seen them apart for more than a few hours at a time?"

"Are you say—"

"I am saying nothing other than that, according to the strictures of your definition, Titus and Flavius are unnatural. Would you not agree?"

"No, I would not." This emerged as a whisper.

"Good. That, at least, is as it should be. Very well. Let us retrace our steps, you and I. This all began by my asking you one particular question— whether you had ever known me to consort with a woman. Now let me ask you another. Other than yourself, have you ever known me to consort with, or have personal, intimate dealings with a man, outside of my work?"

"No."

"Any man at all?"

"No."

"Why do you suppose that is, Cay?"

"I don't know. Because you have no . . . friends . . . apart from me."

He nodded, acquiescing, smiling a little, wintry smile again. "Abnormal, would you say? Unnatural?"

I coughed, feeling awful. "No. Unusual, that's all. You are . . . unique in that."

"Thank you. Now I will tell you something else that might surprise you. Two things, in fact." He raised his cup and emptied it at a gulp, and then looked back to where I sat as though stricken, quivering with shame. "I have had far too much to drink today, which is the reason for this conversation's having taken place, and I have been celibate for thirty years."

"Celibate?" I had heard the word, but I had never considered it, or its true meaning, before now.

"Celibate. Sexually chaste and hence unfettered by my own lusts. Free of involvement. Free of commitment. Free of responsibility to anyone, sexually speaking, except myself. For thirty years. Longer than that, in fact." He picked up the jug again. "And now, if you will drink with me again, I'll tell you why. Are we still friends?"

I nodded, thoroughly chastened now, and held out my cup: He poured, replaced the jug, and then sat down across from me again. When he had settled himself, he grinned at me. "Celibacy," he said. "What does it mean to you?"

I shook my head, admitting my ignorance. "I'm not quite sure, apart from the lack of sexuality involved in it. Doesn't it mean unmarried?"

"It does, but the underlying meaning goes far deeper in certain contexts. In its absolute sense, celibacy entails total, voluntary abstention from any form of sexuality. What I'm going to speak of now is philosophy, Cay; my philosophy, but not of my invention, merely of my adoption. When I was studying to become a surgeon, I had many teachers, all of them brilliant men. One of them, however, was a phenomenon and a genuine magus, in the esoteric sense. You understand what I mean by that?"

"I think so. You mean he was a sorcerer."

He laughed again, delight in his voice. "A sorcerer! Well, I suppose he was, in many ways, but no, that is not what I meant. A magus is a Master, Caius, in the sense of mastery of arcane lore, of knowledge. The Magi who attended the Christ Child were not termed such without reason, but none would call them sorcerers. This magus, my teacher—his name was Philus, by the way—was a living repository of the arts and skills and all the acquired knowledge of the physician's craft down through the ages. He had a phenomenal memory, Cay, and could recall, verbatim, texts he had read in his extreme youth. Nothing Philus read or learned was ever forgotten; nothing he saw went unremembered. And he lived only to teach his knowledge to young, willing minds. He it was who taught me about celibacy, and he had been an adherent all his life. He equated celibacy with power, Cay, with potency. 'Empty your body of the urge to procreate,' he used to say, 'and you release in it the power to think, absorb and grow; the power to know and rule your self; the greatest power available to man.' I had great difficulty with that, at first, for I was young and virile, rudely potent in that other sense. I had never known love, but lust and I were well acquainted." He paused, remembering. "I came to know Philus better, I believe, than anyone else ever had. In time, I became his disciple, and came to believe the truth of what he believed. He died when I had just begun to really learn from him, and soon after that I joined the legions. But I have never wavered from his ways. My life has been my work, and I have been content to have it thus." He grinned again. "And then you came along, with your injured little waif, Cassandra, and we became friends. I had never had a friend before, in the personal sense."

"Tell me more about celibacy and potency." My discomfort of moments earlier had vanished, and for the next hour and more, while the house grew dark and silent around us, Luke talked of his beliefs. The arcane mysteries of all mankind, he explained, were arcane simply because the mass of men were incapable of according them the concentration they demanded in order to be understood. The study, the seclusion and the academic self-absorption necessary for that understanding, he maintained, were incompatible with and mutually exclusive of the pettiness of fleshly things, the merest, yet the most disruptive of which was sexuality. To illustrate that thesis, he cited the misunderstanding we had just gone through, where he had said one thing, and I had heard another altogether and had been outraged, my narrow sensibilities offended. Only my preoccupation with the sensual, he said, could explain that.

I listened, fascinated, accepting the justice of his harsh criticism, and soon we even stopped drinking. I drank only his words thereafter, completely unaware that I was seated at my teacher's knee.

VI

I AWOKE LONG before dawn the following day and made the fundamental error of rolling quickly from my bed as though it was a normal day. Of course, it was not. The day before, and the night that followed it, had been distinctly abnormal, and my body was polluted with poisonous wine residues. I spent much time in the steam room of the baths before the sun came up, attempting to sweat some of the toxins from my quaking frame, and had little stomach for food thereafter. I did, however, force myself to eat, and to drink great draughts of cold water, and by midmorning I was beginning to hope, although with reservations, that I might yet survive.

The day was brisk, with a hint of coldness in the breeze that augured an early winter, and I threw myself into my work, forcing my unwilling body to deal with the necessities of the daily round within the fortress. By noon, I had inspected the Guard and the Garrison, parading the latter formally in the courtyard. I had also visited the invalid troopers in all eleven of our hastily designated, ancillary sick bays, speaking with each of them who was capable of speech. I had looked in, too, upon Popilius in the Infirmary and found him clean-shaven once again, and looking far stronger than he had been the previous day. We spoke for some moments of his return to duty, but did not discuss the form such duty might now take. I had the feeling that he had no more desire than I to deal with the extent of his physical decline at present. I left the Infirmary deep in thought about the advancing age of all our most important personnel, and conscious of a disappointment at not having seen Ludmilla.

That thought led me to a recollection of Luke's passionate defense of celibacy as a path to esoteric power—*whatever that might really mean*, a skeptical voice said clearly in my head—and I shook my head in wonder at the strangeness of his viewpoint, telling myself that we would have to talk again, he and I, in sobriety and at greater length, about his convictions. His pronouncements, as they came back to me now in my distempered state, sat uneasily within me, rendered alien by the harsh light of day and the pounding of a violent headache, but I clearly remembered how impressed I had been at the time by the clarity and logic he had brought to their presentation. But then I had been drunk, and writhing in shame over the unwarranted assumption I had made concerning his sexual propensities.

I had almost reached the stables before I realised where I was going, and the sudden recognition of where I was made me stop in my tracks. I had not set out to go to the stables. I had not set out to go anywhere, in fact. I had merely begun to walk, and my feet had brought me here. Hovering indecisively, I quickly reviewed my list of duties for the day. All that I had set out to do that day, in addition to my normal tasks, had been done. I turned and looked back the way I had come. The scene was peaceful and ordinary. Guards stood at their appointed posts and the people of Camulod went about their daily business, scurrying or dawdling as their natures dictated. I saw the Legate Titus walk by in the distance, accompanied by one of his junior officers whose name escaped me, and then I saw Ludmilla, disappearing around the far corner of my great-aunt's house. I stifled the instantaneous urge to follow her, and turned my eyes elsewhere. A breeze wafted the smell of the stables into my nostrils, and with it came an image of a solitary grave by a placid lake, and a sudden emptiness in my chest. I had not visited the grave of my wife and unborn child since my return from Cornwall, a full week ago and more. Suddenly I knew why I had come to the stables, and I made my way inside and directly to the stall that held Germanicus.

As soon as he was saddled, I sought out Titus and informed him I was leaving the fortress for at least the afternoon, but possibly for longer. I told him I would be within summons, in my secret place—he knew of it, but not of its location—and reminded him of how I could be found in an emergency, by sending out trumpeters to the tops of the three highest neighbouring hills.

A very short time later I approached the main gates of the fortress.

Before I could pass through the portal, however, I had to rein in my horse and swing him aside to allow passage to an enormous wagon pulled by a team of four large horses that had just come up the hill road from the plain. The vehicle was piled high with massive wooden casks, and the driver inched his team forward slowly, cursing the horses fluently and familiarly by their individual names while peering back over his shoulder to where another man stood behind him, on the edge of the first row of casks, craning his neck to make sure that the topmost barrels of the load would clear the lintel of the gateway without mishap. They did, the load passed through and the second man spun nimbly, balancing himself easily with one hand on the teamster's shoulder before he stepped down and sank to the bench beside him. The teamster was unknown to me. The second man was Peter Ironhair, and I recognized him a heartbeat before he saw me.

"Whoa! Hold up there, Tom."

The wagon creaked to a halt and Ironhair faced me, eye to eye, less than three paces separating us.

"Well," he said, his voice pleasant enough. "It's the great Merlyn Britannicus, Legate Commander of the Forces of Camulod."

I nodded to him, keeping my face blank of expression. "Ironhair. Good day to you." He stood up again, looking down at me now, his eyes fixed in an unblinking gaze of cold hostility. Refusing to be challenged to a staring contest, I swung my mount around again to ride on, but the bulk of his wagon, slewed slightly sideways, blocked the gateway. I glanced back at him.

"Your wagon is blocking the gate."

"It's a big wagon." He made no move to signal his driver to proceed. I did it for him.

"Move on, driver."

"Stay where you are, Tom."

I sucked in a deep breath, being careful to show no sign of irritation. I was in an untenable situation, faced with a potentially ugly confrontation I could not avoid other than by backing down completely and riding away. I had no fear of seeming to back down to Ironhair in his own eyes; I would have ample opportunity, even if I had to create it myself, of straightening that matter out in days to come. But already there were people, passersby, forming a crowd around us, awaiting passage, burdened with sacks and laden with bundles, and by that almost magical chemistry found even in the smallest crowd, they were aware already of the tension between us. Besides that, several of the gate guards were watching now. The point was rapidly approaching where a public dispute would be unavoidable. I decided to put as fair a face upon things as I could, and gently guided my horse completely around, taking care to jostle none of the people close to me and urging them to fall back and let the wagon pass.

I rode off for some distance, back into the courtyard, and the crowd followed me. The wagon remained where it was, Ironhair still standing at the driver's bench, his eyes on me.

"Bring your wagon forward."

His answer was flat, unequivocal and provocative. "Not until you and I have talked."

I spurred my mount forward quickly, back to where I had been. The people behind me surged forward. Before they could hear me, I threw a quiet warning to Ironhair. "You are obstructing the thoroughfare. Move it now, or I'll have the guards move it for you and confiscate your load for public mischief."

"Hah!" His shout, and the broad sweep of the arm that accompanied it, were for the benefit of the crowd now within earshot again. "You hear that, people of Camulod? The noble Legate here threatens me with forfeiture of my goods if I do not, this instant, obey his commands. He has, I think, forgotten that his powers apply only to soldiers and not to honest citizens. I have broken no law, that he should bludgeon me with threats. All I have done, am doing, is being slow to move my wagon through this gate."

"Well, hurry it up, damn you, you're keeping me from my tasks!" This issued from the burly throat of the man nearest me, a hulking giant who plainly had no sympathy with Ironhair or his cause.

His interruption took Ironhair completely by surprise. He stopped, and gaped down at the man. "What?" was all he could summon up in reply.

"I said get your damned wagon out of my way. Are you deaf, as well as stupid?"

Ironhair was open-mouthed, and the sight of his surprise took the edge off my anger, so that I found myself having to stifle a grin. Another voice on my left took up the plaint. "Come on, Ironhair, move the shit-filled wagon and let us through the gates. We haven't got all day to stand around here while you preach politics."

"Politics?" I could hear the injury in his tone. "I wasn't preaching politics. This man was threatening me for no reason!"

"Aye," said the big man, "and so what? He had reason enough. You're a fool and a blowhard. Now there's three of us threatening you. Move it!"

"It's a heavy wagon!" There was a note of panic now in his voice.

"Then we'll soon lighten it. Let's have those barrels off, lads!" The crowd surged forward suddenly, and Ironhair had to shout at the top of his lungs to make himself heard above the growls that rose now from all around him.

"All right! All right, stand back! We're moving!" He punched Tom the driver on the shoulder and Tom flicked the reins. The horses leaned into their collars, the wheels began to roll and the wagon lumbered forward. I nudged my horse aside again to give it room, smiling openly now. Ironhair kept his eyes averted as he passed me amid a chorus of jeers and taunts. As soon as the way was cleared the crowd poured through, mingling with others who had waited on the other side of the gates. The two crowds melded into one swirling mass and an unknown voice came clearly to my ears from somewhere in its midst.

"No thanks necessary, Merlyn!"

I shook my head, grinning, and found myself eye to eye and grin to grin with the young decurion commander of the gate guard. He wiped the smile from his face immediately and jerked to attention, snapping me a smart salute. I returned it formally, my own face straight again, then swung my horse around to follow Ironhair's wagon back into the fortress yard, kicking him to canter until I overtook the vehicle.

"Ironhair!"

The wagon creaked to a halt and he swung around to face me, scowling. I gave him no chance to speak.

"Keep your mouth shut and listen, because I will never repeat myself. This once I warn you. In future, I act. The title you threw at me back there was accurate. Bear in mind what it means. You may seek to confront me again, but be aware that no matter what the outcome, you cannot win. By impeding me, or attempting to belittle me publicly, in performance of my duties or otherwise, and by causing confrontations of the type you just attempted, you are endangering the established order and the peace, and therefore the well-being of this Colony. We have problems enough in Camulod, caused from beyond, without internal dissension. That's why I clipped your wings in Council yesterday. You chose to take it as a personal attack, obviously. Perhaps it was, but it came from strength, Ironhair, not from weakness."

I paused, watching him. He glowered but made no attempt to speak. I continued. "Let me add this. You are a big, strong, well-made man and you might think to seek me out and challenge me privately, man to man, some time when I am not on duty." I shrugged my shoulders. "With sufficient provocation you might possibly provoke me into fighting you. Should that happen, I will thrash you, but hear me now, Ironhair, and hear me clearly. If that does happen, no matter what the outcome may be, I swear to you by the blood of the crucified Christ that you will be banished from this Colony for ever, immediately thereafter, upon my preordained decree. My rank, as Legate Commander of Camulod, never goes off duty. Do you understand me?"

He blinked, glowered and turned his back on me again, and the wagon lurched into motion. I watched its progress for several moments longer and then pulled my horse into a rearing turn and aimed him towards the gateway.

I began my downhill ride in anger, my pride offended by the man's audacity, but I quickly recalled the unforeseen support so freely made available to me from the very people he had sought to use against me. *No thanks necessary, Merlyn!* By the time I reached the bottom of the hill road and pointed my horse towards the route to the concealed valley in the hills that held the remains of my wife and child, I had regained my normal humour, aided greatly by the realization that, for the first time that day, my head was clear and my body felt well.

That feeling of well-being lasted for the duration of my trip to Avalon, the name I had given to my secret little vale, but the sight of the lonely grave by the waterside, and the empty hut near by, with its hanging, broken door quickly banished my good humour. The grave was weed-grown, although I had swept it clean only five or six weeks before. I knelt beside it and cleaned it again, digging with my fingers to loosen the roots of the persistent weeds that had re-established themselves so quickly. My task complete, I prayed quietly for a while, remembering the beauty of the silent young woman who lay beneath the dirt, and trying to visualize the child she might have given me which now lay mouldering beside her.

When I eventually rose to my feet again, feeling the coldness of the damp earth drying on my knees, I approached the hut and went inside. It was as I remembered it from years before, except that the coverings on the bed had been removed at some time, exposing the woven hempen rope netting strung across the frame. The rest of the interior, including the few furnishings, lay covered in dirt and old, wind-blown leaves. Even the window, hand-made from pieces of precious, almost transparent glass, was coated with dirt. I looked from the window to the long-dead fireplace, feeling my throat swell with the pain of remembered happiness as I recalled the evenings I had spent sitting there with Cassandra, warm and content in the flickering light of the flames, knowing that the comfort and warmth of the bed behind us was ours alone. As I turned to leave, I noticed the broom in the corner by the window, and remembered making it for Cassandra. I stepped to it and took it in my hands, and looked again around the tiny room, which she had always kept so clean and full of fresh flowers, and I began idly to sweep up some of the dried leaves that lay at my feet. I had no thought of cleaning the place, but what began as a listless, almost aimless recollection of my wife's use of this simple instrument somehow became a determined assault on the years of neglect, so that in a short space of time the room was clean again, no single leaf remaining. I then used the ends of the broom to sweep some of the encrusted dirt from the window glass and ended up polishing each of the glazed sections with a rag from my saddlebag, after which I washed the rag in the lake and used both it and the broom—the latter awkwardly—to scrub and then wash the woodwork of the small table, the two chairs and the plain wooden chest at the bottom of the bed. Only when I had done that did I think to open the chest, and there, wrapped in the skin of a huge black bear, I found all of the sleeping furs we had used, and I plunged my face into them, giving way to my grief at last as I smelled the faint, familiar fragrance of the dried herbs she had used to keep them fresh and purge them of their natural, feral odours.

Much later, emptied at last of tears and self-pitying grief, I rose again and looked around me, then went out to where my horse stood cropping grass and unsaddled him, removing his bridle, too, after I rubbed him down, so that he could roam free. It took but a short time to find kindling and firewood, and as that day drew to an end I sat once more in the leaping firelight, knowing that the broken door must be mended soon if this place were to remain fit for me to live in again. When darkness had fallen completely, I piled the fire high with stout logs and undressed slowly, before climbing naked into the pile of furs that smelled so strongly of her presence and her spirit. I lay awake for hours, it seems, recalling scenes from our happy past, feeling her presence all around me in the flickering shadows thrown by the dancing flames. Somewhere outside, from time to time, a dove cooed, the sound gentle and comforting, soothing the almost pleasant ache within me.

I was awake soon after dawn broke the following morning, and then, having thrown myself naked and bed-warm into the waters of the lake and towelled myself dry by the edge of Cassandra's grave with the lining of my cloak, I decided that I was not yet ready to ride back to Camulod. I was hungry, and I felt wonderful, at peace with myself and my life for the first time since regaining my memory, so I spent an hour fishing and broke my fast on two succulent trout. I spent the remainder of the morning simply lazing around after hauling a fresh supply of firewood from the depths of the woods that occupied most of the valley. Eventually, however, I could procrastinate no longer and I took the road homeward around the middle of the afternoon. Even then, I took a longer route home than was necessary, aware of the needlessness of secrecy now that Cassandra was gone. Yet I had always been jealous of the privacy afforded me by the enchanted and enchanting little place I called Avalon, and aware of a genuine need to keep all signs of my coming and going disguised from others' eyes. My father had known the place many years before I did, and so had Publius Varrus, and although neither of them had been fanciful enough to name the valley, neither had betrayed its location to anyone else other than Aunt Luceiia. Both men had told me long before, when I was a mere boy, that I should keep the knowledge of this spot close to myself, because it would afford me sanctuary at times when I required to be alone, free of the problems of others. Now, besides myself, only five other living souls that I knew of were aware of its existence: Luceiia Britannicus, Daffyd, my Druid friend and his two apprentices Tumac and Mod, and Donuil Mac Athol, my former hostage, now my friend, whose continuing absence had now begun to worry me in spite of the fact that I knew my concern was foolish. He had been gone six weeks, but I had mentally accorded his task three months. Six more weeks, then, might well elapse before I had any real cause for concern about his welfare. On the other hand, the child Arthur could come to harm in the foreign place where he was held, in spite of the fact that it was Donuil's home, long before Donuil returned to Camulod and then travelled with me across the sea to his home in Hibernia, which he called Eire.

I rode in a dream, so lulled by my own unaccustomed peace of mind that I committed errors of carelessness for which I would have had my own troopers harshly disciplined. Almost without noticing, I reached the Cut and swung my horse into it, lost in the beauty of afternoon and the peaceful trilling of the myriad birds in the forest on either side of the path I travelled. It was only the flight of a hare that made me take note of where I was, as it leaped almost from beneath my horse's feet, startling him so that he reared and would have thrown me had I not already been leaning forward, slouched over my saddle horn. The hare went bounding ahead of me, straight as the crow flies, up the narrow incline of the Cut for a good two hundred paces before swerving suddenly to disappear among the heavy growth on my right. Startled by my own heedlessness, I began to pay more attention to my surroundings, but the day was still peaceful and I remained at ease. Soon I began to wonder, as so often before, about the origins of this anomalous stretch of unfinished road that had been called the Cut since time immemorial. It was, or had been, the beginnings of a road; there was not the slightest doubt of that. As a boy, I had dug, with Uther, and found the base layers of the Roman construction. The anomaly lay in the fact that the road had been begun but never completed. The Romans had been meticulous and painstaking in their road-building. Once they began, they always completed their constructions; except, apparently, in this one particular case.

Local legend had it that, in the earliest days of the Roman conquest of Britain launched by the Emperor Claudius but conducted by Aulus Plautius, *Legio II Augusta*, the Second Legion, known as the Augusta, under the command of Vespasian, who would later become Emperor, had begun to build a march route northwestward into the lands of the Durotriges, the original Celts of our region, intending to establish a fortress on the north coast of the Cornish Peninsula. The Durotriges, however, had proved to be as warlike as the Iceni in the northeast and had contested the Roman right of way hotly, harassing the expedition to such effect that the roadworks had been abandoned before they could be completed, the troops involved being required much more urgently further to the southwest. In the aftermath of a hard-won Roman victory, in which the Durotriges, in alliance with the Dumnonii of the far southwest, went down to defeat, the Augusta had settled in Isca, and no purpose had ever emerged for the abandoned road, which had thus been left unfinished. Now, four hundred years later, its path was still clearly discernible, particularly here where it ran arrow-straight for eleven miles before ending abruptly in deep forest. All it had lacked was the finishing layer of paving stones, and the solidity of its construction—it had been incised right down to bedrock along this stretch—had successfully withstood the ravages of the forest for four centuries. An occasional large tree grew out of its foundations, belying its subsurface density, but by and large the Cut retained its essential nature, a long, straight, treeless, man-made incursion into the heart of the thick forests of Britain.

The gradient I had been following was so gentle as to be almost imperceptible, but I knew that anyone approaching me from the opposite direction would be looking down on me and would be aware of me for miles before I became aware of them. I travelled less than two miles along the Cut, however, before veering off to my right and making my way downhill again into more open grassland beyond the heavy forest, about ten miles from Camulod. I could see open land ahead of me, screened by only a fringe of trees, when I found the entrails of a deer which, from the condition of the remains, I knew had been killed the previous day, and probably late in the afternoon or early evening. It took no great degree of woodcraft to tell that there had been four or five in the hunting party; no care had been taken by anyone to conceal the signs of their presence. Cautiously, I followed the signs and found an abandoned encampment less than a mile away, which I estimated had housed upwards of twenty men, several of them with horses. The ashes of the four fires I found were still warm, one of them almost hot enough to contain live embers, so whoever these people were, they had moved on only recently and were still close by. Returning to my horse, I took my helmet from where it hung on my saddle horn and fitted it snugly on my head, fastening the chin strap.

I travelled more quickly now and far more circumspectly, taking the shortest, most direct route to the Colony while seeking the most concealment I could find, intent on raising the alarm. What kind of traveller, I asked myself, leaves an encampment late in the course of a day? I had immediately dismissed any possibility that they might be my own people. This party was made up of horsemen and foot-soldiers. Their signs were clear. Our patrols were never mixed, they were either one or the other, and our foot-soldiers wore hobnailed boots. The footprints I had seen around the fires were smooth-soled, lacking the hard edges common to our footwear. I rode around and down the side of a hill to find myself trapped in an open amphitheatre surrounded by dense trees. I saw movement on my right first, a flash of yellow among the greenery, and then the unmistakable glint of light upon iron. I swung hard left, kicking my horse uphill, but before I could begin to ride that way I saw five men above me, watching me. In my first glance I saw their horned helmets and large, round Saxon shields. Wrenching my mount around I saw, too, that I had been cut off from behind, where another four Saxons, armed with axes and shields, had strung out across my escape route. Germanicus continued to turn, dancing on his hind legs, and I saw the yellow that had first appeared to me, a bright yellow tunic, worn by a huge, bearded man who now stood in the open, surrounded by a group of eight or nine others. All of them had either spears or axes, the Saxons' favourite weapon, and I cursed myself uselessly for having left Camulod without my great bow. I accepted that I was a dead man; it was only the manner of my death that had to be resolved now. And then I saw my escape route: a narrow cleft in a massive stone outcrop on the hillside some fifty paces ahead and to my left, a natural split in the rock, offering me at least the hope of a defense. I dug my spurs into my horse's flanks and charged ahead as my assailants began to run towards me from all sides.

I had never paid any great attention to this spot before, although I had ridden this way several times, so I had no knowledge of what lay ahead of me beyond the entrance to the narrow ravine I entered. Just beyond the entrance, the surface levelled out and the sides began to recede, and I gave my horse his head, beginning to hope, but the floor of the defile curved to the right and beyond the turn the crevice suddenly pinched out, leaving me facing unscalable walls of rock. I pulled up and turned to ride back to face my pursuers, drawing the long sword from where it hung from the side of my saddle, knowing that the best place to meet them was the narrow entrance to the ravine. I stopped, swung my sword, took a long, deep breath, and as I did so, I heard a voice shouting above my head.

"Surrender, Caius Merlyn! You've won me my wager and you're getting too old to be allowed out riding by yourself, anyway!"

Stunned, I raised my head and saw Donuil laughing down at me from where he perched on a ledge of rock at the top of the cliff. Beside and behind him, one hand resting on Donuil's shoulder, my brother Ambrose stood grinning, his long, golden hair shining in the sunlight, and his other arm holding a large, metal helmet adorned with an enormous pair of Saxon horns.

As I sat there, overwhelmed with incredulous relief, I felt the fear and

tension drain from my body like some ethereal form of sweat, while Donuil
came leaping down the face of the cliff like a mountain goat to drag me
bodily from my saddle and sweep me up into a great bear hug. Still too
stunned to react, I was aware of the unyielding bronze of my cuirass, which
saved my ribs from being crushed by his massive arms, and of the sight of
my brother, who had donned his helmet and now followed Donuil's downward route more sedately, a smile of sheer pleasure lighting his handsome
face. I felt my feet leave the ground, and then I felt Donuil lose his balance
so that we fell with a crash and rolled on the sparsely grassed floor of the
narrow gully. Reaction set in then and I began to wrestle back, straining and
wriggling to achieve a headlock on the big Erse prince who was mauling me,
and feeling a brief, short-lived surge of real anger at what they had done to
me. Donuil, however, was bigger and heavier than I was, and so my anger
was quickly dissipated by struggling with the sheer bulk of him and eventually
we both relaxed, by mutual consent, to lie staring and grinning stupidly at
each other like a couple of boys.

As my breathing began to return to normal, I turned my head, still
sprawled backwards on my elbows, to look up to where my half-brother,
Ambrose Ambrosianus Britannicus, my father's son by another woman, stood
grinning down at me. *My father's son by a woman other than his wife, my
mother* . . . The thought caused me no concern, for I knew the amazing, seemingly incredible truth behind it. Picus Britannicus, our father, had known
nothing of what transpired between him and Ambrose's mother. He had been
badly wounded at the time, his throat and neck mangled by an arrow that
had pierced his mouth, and he had spent months under the influence of
strong opiates, bound to his bed much of the time to keep him from thrashing about and further injuring his head, which was muffled in bandages. And
during that time, the young wife of his aged and noble host had used the
faceless, wounded man like a stallion, in the secrecy of night, attempting to
impregnate herself with his seed in order to produce an heir for her feeble
but beloved husband. She had succeeded, but the consequences had been
tragic for her husband and for her. My father had never seen her face or even
known of her existence, and had remained in ignorance of all of this, believing
for a long time that the hazy, episodic fragments he could recall were no
more than erotic dreams brought on by his drugged condition and his own
rude, virile strength. He had told me the tale himself, decades later, but even
then he had been ignorant of having sired a son. Only after my father was
dead had I encountered my half-brother, a mere six months my junior and
my living likeness, in the kingdom of Vortigern, king of Northumbria.

All of these thoughts rushed through my mind in the blinking of an eye
and did nothing to impair the smile that spread across my lips at the sight
of Ambrose grinning down at me. He nodded, silent, and then, removing his
horned helmet again, he combed his fingers through his thick hair and shook
it out around his head before stepping towards me, one hand outstretched
to help me rise. I took it and pulled myself to my feet where I stood watching
him as he stared back into my eyes. I began to raise my arms and he met
me halfway, hugging me in silence.

It was a strange experience, hugging this man, almost a total stranger and
yet blood of my blood, bone of my bone, and resembling me more closely
than my own reflection in the few mirrors into which I had gazed. Therein,

my face was always altered by the colour, texture and sheen of the reflecting metal, be it bronze or silver. The face in front of me now, when I leaned back to arm's length to look at it, holding him by the shoulders, bore no such metallic inconsistencies. The skin was darkened by the sun, as was my own, and the hair above the broad forehead grew thick and yellow, just like mine. If anything was different between us, I thought, it must be simple size. Ambrose, like Donuil, was bigger than I; not greatly bigger, perhaps not even noticeably, but he seemed to me to *bulk* larger than I did, his shoulders more massive, his forearms heavier, his eyes a hair's breadth higher than my own.

"Well met, Brother," I said, and he nodded at me, holding me by the wrists and merely gazing mute and evidently pleased with what he beheld. I looked to where Donuil now stood watching us, his eyes wide with wonder as they moved from my face to Ambrose's and back, the expression on his face one of complete amazement.

"Well?" I asked him. "How great is the resemblance?"

Donuil shook his head. "It would be frightening, had I not seen it before and if I did not know the truth of it. You could be twins. You are identical. The only way to tell you apart is by your clothes."

Ambrose laughed and spoke for the first time. "We may change those tomorrow and confound you." The words seemed to reverberate strangely in my ears and I looked back at him, impulsively voicing the thought that had sprung fully formed into my mind even though I shrouded it in a jest.

"No, Brother, not Donuil, he is too easily confused at the best of times. Something to do with his great height, I think. But it might be interesting to confuse others . . . outsiders." I took the sting out of the first part of my words with a smile, and Donuil grinned again, flushing with pleasure and covering any response to the remainder of my statement with his rejoinder.

"I can see you two will join forces to belittle me because of my superior Erse blood."

"Aye," I agreed. "That, and your outlandish riding skills." Donuil had never mastered the art of riding, which made him noteworthy in Camulod. He had perched precariously on his mounts, rather than seated them, ever since the time of his first arrival, before which he had never approached a horse. Now he drew himself erect and spoke to me down the length of his nose.

"You, Caius Merlyn, have not seen me ride for years."

"Correction, Erseman." I winked at Ambrose. "I, Caius Merlyn, have never seen you ride. Wobble, perhaps; sway, certainly; teeter, frequently, but ride? Never."

A sound behind me distracted me from my baiting and I saw Ambrose look over my shoulder and nod. I turned in time to see the rear view of one of the Saxons disappearing again around the bend in the gully. The sight brought my mind back to my earlier thoughts, before the apparition of my two companions, and my smile disappeared.

"Saxons, Ambrose? Donuil? How could you bring *Saxons* to Camulod?"

Ambrose answered me. "They are no more Saxon than you or I, Brother. They are Lindum men, one and all, my blood guards, merely wearing the Saxon garb."

"Why?" I was not reassured.

He shrugged. "Because we travelled through the Saxon Settlements to come here. Donuil told me your needs were urgent, and that was the shortest route."

His words perplexed me. "What? I don't understand. Are you saying you came along the Saxon Shore?"

"No, at least not all the way. Donuil found me in the far north, up by the Wall. We travelled southward in one of Hengist's longboats, landed on the Saxon Shore north of Colchester, and came straight inland, directly across the country."

"Passing through the Saxon-settled lands."

"Some of them, yes."

"Hmm." I accepted that without further comment, aware of the many layers of significance the words held. "Well!" I looked from one to the other of them. "So what do you intend to do now?"

They glanced at each other, smiling uncertainly, clearly wondering what I was raving about. Again it was Donuil who answered. "What *should* we do? We *intended* to find you as quickly as possible, probably in Camulod, but you came blundering along the pathway back there in a daydream and I recognized you miles away. Now we've found you. What do *you* suggest we do?"

"Hmm." My mind was racing, cataloguing the possibilities and weighing the alternatives as I sought to clear my mind and see my way. "Well, we should return directly to Camulod, of course, and yet . . ." Immediate return to Camulod would create chaos, with all the introductions and explanations that would have to be gone through. I watched them watch me, waiting for me to complete my thought. "And yet," I continued, "it's in my mind, clear as mid-morning light, that taking you directly home, right at this moment, might not be the best idea that has ever occurred to me. We have much to discuss, the three of us, and it could take days, after we enter Camulod and stun everyone with the sight and existence of you, Ambrose, to find the time we need together, free of interruption, without being most discourteous to all our friends there."

"Aye," Ambrose said. "That makes sense. It's more important that we talk together than that we talk to others. What do you suggest?"

I was already looking around me, evaluating the spot in which we stood and rejecting it as a campsite. "Your camp of last night. It's less than two miles from here, and it's secluded; out of the way. Why don't we use it tonight again and ride into Camulod tomorrow morning? That should give us all the time we need."

"Good idea. Let's go."

For the remainder of that day I had the novel experience of observing a score of skin-clad, heavily armoured "Saxon" warriors as they bustled around me, setting up a camp, building cooking fires and attempting to provide privacy and comfort for their Lord and his two companions. There were deer in abundance all around us. Already two small roe had been brought in, dressed and butchered, and several men were busily involved in cooking them. From an oven of stones, prepared by some magic process unknown to and unnoticed by me, came the delicious smell of baking bread. It was still early evening, the sun yet two hours short of setting.

"What are you grinning about, Caius?" Donuil asked me at one point.

I turned to him, still smiling, shaking my head. "All of this. You travel in grand style, with everything considered and allowed for in advance, it seems. But I was thinking it's amazing how much these fellows look like Saxons . . . I'm finding it very difficult to relax with them all around me."

Donuil sniffed. "You'd be even more amazed if you could see how much some of the Saxons look like us—or like your people, at least."

"What d'you mean?"

"Just what I say. The Saxons in the Settlements are little different from your own people. Oh, they talk differently, and they dress differently, I suppose, and all the gods know they fight differently, but they farm the same way and their women don't seem even slightly alien and their children are like children everywhere."

"Farm the same way?" It was the one thing I had heard that struck me as ludicrous. "Come on, Donuil, these people are not farmers—they're marauders, seagoing savages. The only ploughing they do is with the keels of their ships on the belly of the sea. There's nothing of the farmer in their nature."

Ambrose had been standing close by, leaning against a tree as he listened to us, saying nothing. Now Donuil glanced at him, a tiny tic of annoyance between his brows, before his eyes returned to me.

"I see. And how many of these people do you know, Cay? How many have you met, or spoken with? How many have you fought, for that matter?" His voice was almost truculent and I realized, with some surprise, that in all the time I had known him, I had never seen or heard Donuil take serious issue with anything I had ever said. Now he seemed to be challenging me. I felt myself frowning, though more from perplexity than displeasure.

"Is something biting you? I've never known you to sound like this before. I've fought a few of them, as you well know. You were there, and brought me my horse and helmet, the day we rescued Bishop Germanus and his party, near Londinium. How many of them do *you* know?"

"None. But I've met far more of them than you have."

"And?" I noticed that Ambrose had not moved and showed no sign of intervening.

"And it occurs to me you might be wrong."

You are always so correct, Cay . . . Have you any idea how annoying that can be to others? The words came flooding back into my head instantly, remembered from the only confrontation of this kind I'd ever had with Uther. I felt a surge of irritation.

"Wrong about what, in God's name? Wrong about their strangeness? Their foreignness? They are *Outlanders*, Donuil. This is our land, not theirs! They have no place here."

"I'm an Outlander, Cay. Have I no place here?"

That startled me, bringing me up short like a haltered horse. "That is ridiculous! Of course you have a place here. You've earned your place here."

He gazed at me levelly, no sign of anger anywhere about him, his eyes empty of expression. "So did your forefathers, Cay."

"What?" I turned again to Ambrose, seeking his support against such obscure logic, but he was gazing at Donuil, his face unreadable.

Donuil would have said more, was on the point of blurting something out, when a sudden clang of iron upon iron jerked all our heads round in concert towards a clear space beyond the camp, where two men, one of them the giant in the bright yellow tunic I had noticed first earlier that morning, crouched facing each other over the rims of their large, round shields, the bright blades of their swords raised high. Even as I saw them, my view was obscured by the bodies of others who came between us, moving forward to surround the pair.

"Jenner and Marek," Ambrose said. "They're my two best, and worth watching, even in practice. Come."

We moved to watch the two men in their mock combat, our own mild dispute left in abeyance, but even as I watched the skill and speed of the two antagonists, abstractedly admiring their ability, I continued to think about what Donuil had been saying, aware of how closely his sentiments, if not his words, had echoed the unwelcome information I had received not long before from Lars, the owner of the public hostelry I had visited on the road south to Isca.

Now here was Donuil, my own trusted friend, implying in his turn that all was not evil in the people who had usurped our lands. I knew he and I would have to talk more about such outlandish ideas. Ambrose interrupted my thoughts.

"When in Rome, Caius," he said, and I wondered what he meant until I heard his next words. "My men now fight like Saxons, with good reason. One of the first things that impressed me about Hengist's people was the way they fight. I've heard them speak of it as *the weirding way*, or something like that. Whatever it means, it's very strange and very different from the way I was taught. These people have an absolute lack of fear of death. To die in battle offers the greatest state of beatitude they can attain. It seemed to me we would be well advised to learn their methods, since we will surely have need of them some day—not necessarily against Hengist's own, but certainly against their countrymen and former allies."

My attention had focused on the fight the moment he began to speak, and I was already taking note of what was truly happening here in front of me. It became obvious immediately, after the first analytical glance, why the Saxons, or Northmen, as Vortigern's own people called their mercenary warriors, favoured the heavy axe in their warfare. The weapon was awkward and cumbersome, requiring no apparent grace or skilled technique in its employment, both of these sacrificed to pure, brute strength and violence. That strength and violence were demanded, however, by the enemies against whom they fought, or, more accurately, by the shields those enemies carried. These were circular, and because of that, they appeared enormous, although they were no greater in actual extent, from top to bottom, than our rectangular shields, which covered the bearer from knee to chin. Their overall circumference, however, dictated a different style of attack from any would-be assailant, since the extent of the shielded area, laterally, eliminated the normal avenues of penetration that swordsmen, our swordsmen at least, were trained to exploit. There was simply no way to get around these things in a normal attack with a sword, and any effort to do so would expose the sword wielder's body, fatally, to the axe being swung from behind the shield.

Even as I absorbed this, one of the two contestants—it turned out to be Jenner, the giant in the yellow tunic—smashed through his opponent's guard with a mighty, overhand swipe that cut deeply into the edge of Marek's shield, and in moments I received a chilling lesson in our own military shortcomings in the face of such weaponry. The blow landed, the sword's edge bit deep into the rim of the shield, and Marek flung his shield arm up, straight out and away from his body, his own body uncoiling in a surge of strength that locked the edge of Jenner's sword tightly and pulled him forward and off balance, leaving him open and vulnerable so that the only thing he could do was to sweep his own shield across in front of him, thrusting it between himself and his opponent, but unbalancing himself even further, so that all his body weight was pushed to the right. At that point Marek froze my blood by doing something for which I was completely unprepared. He followed the direction of Jenner's crosswise impetus with his own body, turning himself inward into Jenner's imbalance, spinning completely in a wrenching twist until his back was to Jenner, then slamming his left shoulder into the shield that separated them and kicking Jenner's feet from under him with his right heel. Jenner's sword hilt was torn from his grasp and he fell heavily, to what would have been death.

The spectators broke into a chorus of cheers and jeers, but I stood gaping. Ambrose had been watching me and now he spoke again.

"They look heavy, don't they? The shields." I merely nodded, looking at him. "Well they're not," he continued. "But they are very strong. Woven wickerwork wheels, feather light but immensely strong, at least two but sometimes three of them bound together, with an unwoven, handspanwide perimeter of straight canes around the outer edges; the whole covered in a double layer of heavy, hardened hide reinforced and thickened around the rim to catch and snare a sword blade. They're light, immensely strong and virtually impregnable. Arrows, even long arrows, are trapped by the woven layers of cane wickerwork before they can pass through. Same thing happens to spears. And swords, as you have just seen, can't get around them."

"Only an axe," I said.

"Yes, only an axe can give an opponent the chance of smashing one down."

"An axe or a horse."

"True. No man on foot can stand for long against a man on a horse." He signalled one of his men to come forward and asked him to show me his shield, and for the next while we examined the thing, although only I was unfamiliar with the device. I found it completely admirable, and far lighter, much less cumbersome, than I had expected. Somehow, in the course of our discussions, the sun sped across the sky and suddenly it was almost dark, the air around us filled with the smells of newly roasted venison and fresh-baked bread.

When we had eaten and were sitting together by the fire outside our tents, I set out to bring my companions up to date on developments since Donuil and I had parted company, but I quickly found that I had far more to impart to them than I had thought to deal with. Donuil, for example, knew nothing of his sister Ygraine's death, or of her involvement with Uther, and I knew that I would have to approach those topics with a degree of preparation, care and solicitude. Neither man had heard either of the death of Uther or Gulrhys Lot, and Ambrose's first interest was, naturally enough, in the nature of the emergency that had caused me to send Donuil in search of him. In order to explain that, I accepted that I would have to share the secret of Excalibur, and it seemed to me the only way to do that adequately was to tell the entire story of the great Dream of Caius Britannicus and Publius Varrus, and the Colony called Camulod they had founded between them.

I talked for hours, starting from the first meeting between my grandfather and Publius Varrus, and as I spoke, they listened without interrupting and the camp gradually grew still around us until we three were the only ones left awake, and still I talked on. I told them of the foresight of my grandfather Caius, and how Publius Varrus had adopted his vision and helped make it the world we call Camulod, and I spoke of Varrus's own dream of finding a Skystone, and of how he had succeeded, and what he had done with what he found. I talked of the prescient wisdom of these men, combined with that of Ullic Pendragon, and how they had foreseen and set in motion the birthing of an entire new race of Britons, formed of the bonding of native Celts and Romano-British citizens. And I led them along the path towards the culmination of the Dream in the birth of the child Arthur. When I completed my tale with our meeting that day, my two listeners sat silent, each lost in his own world, and I knew better than to expect either to respond immediately. I left them to their thoughts and moved to replenish the fire, which had almost died out.

Donuil was the first to speak, and by the time he did the fire was high again.

"It *has* been five years since I came here. I would not have believed it ... would not have believed I could forget the end of that term." He was speaking to himself and sought no response from me, so I offered none.

"Excalibur." This was Ambrose. "No one else knows of it?"

"No one, except for my aunt. That frightened me when I came to realize the truth of it. I didn't know what to do, then. The best solution I could find seemed to be to explain it in a letter and send for you. Had you arrived and had I not returned within the year, the letter would have been given to you and you would have found the sword."

He looked at me, his face twisted in what was not quite a smile. "What if I had merely kept it for myself?"

"What of it? It would have been yours by then, to do with as you willed."

"So you had no fears of that?"

I smiled, shaking my head. "None, but now the matter is academic. We are both here, and now four of us know."

"What of the boy, Arthur?" Donuil asked. "When will we go for him?"

"As soon as possible. Within the month, if all goes well. It will take several weeks to see Ambrose welcomed and settled into place in Camulod, and then we can leave for your home." I paused, struck by a sudden thought, and looked to Ambrose. "Forgive me, Brother, I am assuming you *can* stay?"

He smiled. "I'm here, am I not? I can stay, at least for a time. Bear in mind, though, I had no idea of what you wanted in summoning me. Donuil's instructions were none too enlightening on that, and now I know why. He had no more knowledge of what you really wanted than had I." His voice faded and his eyes drifted towards the fire, so that when next he spoke, his tone was pensive. "I had expected to remain in Camulod for some time, but I had no expectation of hearing the kind of things you have told us tonight. So many layers within layers of responsibility and duty. I knew none of that, and I did not expect to find filial obligations surrounding me so densely. It makes me feel some guilt towards Vortigern."

"How so?"

"I'm his Captain," he answered, as though I should not have to ask. "He relies on me. Relies on me to help him govern his domains, and to expand them."

In the pause that followed, I decided not to ask of these plans for expansion, knowing that there would be a more fitting time. Ambrose, however, was already launched and spoke what was in his mind.

"Vortigern is ambitious, Caius, but not for himself alone. He is a fine, good man and a strong warrior with a formidable mind. And in a way, his motivation is the same as our grandfather's was. For years he has had to face the question, asked by all who meet him, of what he will do when the Danes he has brought in ask for more land and he has none to give them. Now he is taking steps to solve that problem before it arises."

"What kind of steps?" I was incapable of not asking.

"Expansionist steps; acquisitive steps; territorial steps. Vortigern is extending his boundaries."

"Unchallenged?"

He smiled at me. "Who is to challenge him? His people, thanks to Hengist's Northmen, are the only folk in all the northeast who have not been decimated by the invaders from north beyond the Wall and east beyond the seas. The lands are virtually uninhabited. All Vortigern has to do is hold them. The surviving people welcome him, *with* his Danish Northmen, as a rescuer."

"I see." I had no reason to doubt him. "And when will you return to him?"

He sucked air audibly through his front teeth. "I spoke of a year's absence. I'll go back then, but it might only be for a brief visit, to let him know what I am doing. I have no foolish thought that I am irreplaceable." He smiled. "Vortigern lacks neither champions nor captains, but he has earned of me at least my loyalty and a final, formal leave-taking." He paused, looking me in the eye. "What are you thinking, Brother? That's a pensive, angry-looking frown."

I shook my head, erasing my thoughtful scowl and returning his smile. "I don't really know, but I'm certainly not angry. I'm surprised, I suppose, that you should have made such a momentous decision so quickly, before even arriving in Camulod." My smile widened to a grin. "You may not like it there."

"Oh, I shall like it. Since you began to talk tonight, I have come to realize that it's my home, even though I've never been there. Too many echoes of recognition sounded in my breast while you were speaking, although how I could recognize things totally unknown to me is beyond me. I'm a soldier, not a mystic. It seemed to me, for all of that, listening and hearing much of your tale for the first time—and all of it in sequence for the first time—that this Camulod, founded and governed since its founding by my own immediate ancestors, my father and his father, must have some ties to offer that, having found, I should be loath to lose." I nodded, and he continued. "So, it seems to me there will be work for me, and I am born to do it. You, on the other hand, have other duties. This child in Hibernia, for one."

"Eire," grunted Donuil.

"Eire, pardon me. He is my cousin, and yours, too, and he is Donuil's nephew, as well as titular heir to the Queen of Cornwall and grandson to the High King of Donuil's Scots. That says nothing of the additional truth that he is the son of the Pendragon kings, and great-grandson to Publius Varrus and Luceiia Britannicus of Camulod. A formidable lineage."

"I felt the same when I first saw him," I said.

"It is the simple truth. So!" He clapped his hands and stood up. "To-morrow morning we ride into Camulod and I will finally meet my great-aunt Luceiia and the Colonists who know my antecedents better than I do. A few weeks, you say, to put me in place, providing that I do not prove to be a square peg in a round hole or vice versa, and then you and Donuil can leave for Eire and the boy. Donuil, will you return?"

The question took me by surprise but not Donuil.

"To Camulod?" He yawned and stretched his huge frame. "Aye, can you doubt it? I hardly dare go home, since I am ruined. I've grown used to bathing frequently, and even to horses, and I've learned your heathen tongue and ways. I would be lost in Eire now." His big head swung towards me. "But before we sleep, Caius Britannicus, I have some other questions about the boy. May I ask them?"

"Ask away."

"Did I hear you properly? Connor has no idea the child is his nephew?"

"None. To consider that, he would have had to accept the death of your sister Ygraine. He had plainly decided not to countenance the possibility of that, so I decided to say nothing of the child's parentage, other than that I was his guardian but not his father."

"He accepted that?"

"What else could he do? He had seen with his own eyes that I was prepared to die to save the child."

"Does anyone else besides your aunt know who the child is?"

"No. I saw no point in drawing attention to the child, other than as a guarantor that I would return, bringing you. You yourself told me long ago that not all your brothers and uncles are as mild as Connor. Why place the child needlessly in danger as a potential threat to any of their plans at some future date?"

"Aye. What about Uther's people? Will you tell them?"

"No, not yet." I responded more slowly, thinking about that for the first time. "And probably for the same reason. I have Uther's ring, his signet, in my keeping for the boy. It will serve to announce his right, when the time comes, but before that time it could place him in needless danger."

"Of what, and from whom?"

"Of death, my friend, just as it might in Eire; assassination by any am-bitious malcontent who might construe the child's existence as a threat to his own schemes."

Donuil squirted a stream of saliva between his teeth and into the fire with great deliberation, then wiped his lower lip with the back of his hand. "Good. I'm glad to hear you think that way. I think you're absolutely right. It's not necessary for the child to carry such a load before he needs to; he's already orphaned, and that's burden enough for any mite his age."

Ambrose had been gazing at his drawn dagger, testing its edge with his thumb. "Orphaned, perhaps, Donuil, but he is well uncled and cousined." He looked at me and smiled. "Well connected."

Donuil grunted and laughed as he stood up. "Aye, and well protected. A good night to both of you. I'm for sleep."

VII

"IF VORTIGERN COULD see this, he would die of envy." Ambrose was gazing in awe at the spectacle laid out below us, where we stood on the hillside road to Camulod's main gates, looking down on the great drilling ground that stretched out below them.

"How so?" I asked, knowing what his reply would be, yet wishing to hear it spoken aloud.

"How so? You can ask me that?" He turned to look at me. "Do you not know . . . Are you aware of what you have here?"

I laughed. "Of course I am! I have cavalry, but you've seen it before, in Verulamium when we first met. So why should it amaze you now so greatly?"

He turned back to watch hundreds of our troopers maneuvering their mounts in tightly disciplined formations, rank after rank, squadron upon squadron, responding to the brazen sounds of trumpets and the swirl of brightly coloured signal banners. He remained silent then, lost again in his thoughts, and I expected him to say no more, but he resumed after a spell as though there had been no pause in our colloquy.

"Aye, I saw it then and you are right; I should not be surprised. And yet I am, because I did not really *see* it before . . . I didn't *see* it!" His head moved in a tiny, negative gesture, directed, I was sure, at himself and his own thoughts, and he continued speaking, as if to himself, although I heard his soft words clearly. "We came to Verulamium proud of our strength, secure in our own discipline. And apart from that first meeting, when your men broke off their charge before they reached our ranks, we witnessed, and we shared in, no hostilities."

He was referring to the first time we had met, when, mistaking Vortigern's advancing party in the pre-dawn darkness for the rabble of thieves and mercenaries we had been awaiting, I had almost attacked them. Only at the last moment had I seen their disciplined formations and realized my error in time to halt my attack in mid-charge. He continued speaking.

"At the time, I recall, we thought it was the sight of our defenses that had halted your charge. We were full of confidence, and had just smashed the rabble you mistook us for. The sight of your men approaching us and then breaking off their attack merely confirmed our own self-confidence, I suppose. It certainly prevented me from gauging the true mettle of your force."

"Thank God it did," I said. "Else you and I might not be here today."

"Aye, as you say. But that is beside the point."

"Which is?"

"Voluntary blindness. We became allies, but we never had to fight, so neither took the measure of the other. The confrontation with the thieves in the town that morning was over before it could begin, with no blood spilled . . . We never saw your cavalry fight, Caius, and thus, we could not know your strength; the extent of it." He interrupted himself with another gesture of his head. "I mean, I passed among your people every day. I saw the stirrups they used and I admired the size and beauty of their horses, and none of it seemed significant. I lived among them, but I never truly saw them. I never stood high above them, looking down on them like this where I could see the potential of their mass and the awesome potency of their maneuvres. My God, Caius, look at them! They look invincible from here."

"They are invincible, fighting against the enemy they were designed to fight, boatloads of Saxons."

His eyes swung back downhill. "I can't believe I didn't see it before now, the power of them, the discipline. Do you use any infantry?"

"Some, but not much overall. Most of our men are mounted. But then, horses are expensive in time and effort—slow to breed and to mature—and some tasks are better suited to men on foot. Garrison soldiers, for example, are seldom troopers."

"Why not?" His eyes were fixed on me again.

"It's wasteful, and hard on the men; attendance to normal duties combined with responsibility for their mounts even though they are not using them."

"Do you ever use the two combined?"

"Horses and foot? Not often. Almost never, in fact. If you think about it, you'll see why. Our horses will outstrip our infantry within half a day and our territories are so large that we have need of speed to cover them adequately. We maintain several fixed garrisons, twelve of them nowadays, all small, around our perimeter. Each has a cavalry squadron attached, for local patrol activities and when the need arises, we can reinforce them quickly with additional troopers."

"So you have made no effort to train the two to fight together, in concert?"

"No, no great effort."

"Hmm." He said no more, but together we continued to watch and enjoy the spectacle below us on the plain. This was Ambrose's second day in Camulod and the first opportunity he had enjoyed simply to look around. His first day home—for home is what the place immediately became to him—had been spent mostly with his newly acquired *materfamilias*, his great-aunt Luceiia, although he had met and been introduced to all the notables of our Colony that night at a welcoming dinner held in the great Council Chamber that served as a refectory for grand occasions such as this arrival of an unknown heir to the name Britannicus.

This morning had been spent in introductions, too, beginning with a brief, ceremonial assembly of the Plenary Council to welcome, formally, the second son of Picus Britannicus. After that, I had taken him, accompanied by Titus, Flavius and several other senior officers, on a guided tour of the fortress, including a visit to each of the additional hospitals established for our recuperating wounded from Cornwall, and we had ended up here on the road, arrested on our progress towards the valley below and the Villa Britannicus, which was in the course of being refurbished after the damage it had sustained during Lot's attack several years earlier.

For a day and a half now I had been savouring the general reaction to the first sight of Ambrose, and the novelty had not yet begun to pall, although I was glad I had taken heed of my brother's wishes at the outset. My original impulse, inspired by Donuil's remark on seeing us together again, and fuelled further by Aunt Luceiia's stunned reaction to the sight of Ambrose standing by my side, had been to dress him for this morning's rites in my own best suit of parade armour, to enhance the astounding resemblance between us. Ambrose, however, had demurred at this, and, sensing his discomfort immediately, I had for once in my life been astute enough to diagnose the cause of it accurately and without objection. It was highly important to my new-found brother, I discerned, to present himself as himself and not as a mere duplicate of me. Now I thanked God for enabling me to see the correctness of that. The reaction of our wounded veterans alone had been wondrous to behold. To a man, they had been shocked into awed silence, staring from one to the other of us in stupefaction until one man, in every instance, had muttered some remark that broke the tension and brought forth a roar of laughter and of welcome to the Colony's newest recruit.

Spurred now by a sudden impulse, I turned to address the small group of officers who stood patiently behind us, waiting for us to proceed. "Gentlemen," I said. "I have changed my mind. Tomorrow will be soon enough to show the villa to my brother. It comes to me that he and I might spend the remainder of this day right here with far more profit. Thank you for your time and your company. We will keep you no longer from your duties."

When they had gone, I gripped Ambrose by the shoulder and we walked back together to the fort, saluting the guards at the gate who crashed to attention at our approach.

"You will become my second-in-command as soon as you are ready, Ambrose," I told him as we passed through the main portals.

He looked at me, one eyebrow raised high. "You still intend to move that quickly? Do you think that's wise?"

"I know it is necessary, but not until you are ready."

"And how will you know that?"

I grinned. "I won't. You will, and you'll tell me." I was steering him towards the centre of the main courtyard.

"But I'm not qualified to command cavalry, Caius."

"Nonsense. You are, or have been, one of Vortigern's most trusted captains, and Vortigern's neither fool nor incompetent. How many men have you commanded at one time?"

"Armies," he said. "But armies of infantry."

"How many men, in total?"

He thought for a moment. "Twenty thousand, in our last campaign in the north."

"That's almost four Roman legions. You were in sole command?"

"Overall command, yes."

"Did you win?"

"Of course I did."

"Of course you did, and thus you are qualified to command my men . . . The horses have nothing to say about it, you know. I said you must be my second-in-command. I didn't ask you to share my saddle with me. You'll have to learn to ride with stirrups and a saddle. As you do that, once you begin to grasp the advantages those bring, you'll learn quickly enough what cavalry can do. And here in Camulod, remember, your credentials come built into your appearance, your name and your family. No one will doubt your worth; none will quibble with your authority; and your staff—my staff—will guide your steps until you wish to strike out alone. I have no doubts that will be soon."

We had reached the spot towards which I had been guiding him in more ways than one, and now I reached out my arm and stopped his progress, directing his eyes downward to the ground at his feet. He looked down curiously. The ground on which we stood was hard-packed, but three wide slabs of hand-dressed, dark blue slate were recessed, side by side, directly in front of us.

"What are these, Cay?" I could tell from his tone that he already suspected what they were.

"Your credentials," I said, feeling a roughness in my throat. "Your right to be here in Camulod, and in command in Camulod. In the centre lies your grandfather, Caius Britannicus, founder of this Colony; on his right, your great-uncle by marriage, Publius Varrus; and on his left, the ashes of your father, the Imperial Legate Picus Britannicus. This is the very heart of Camulod, Ambrose, the centre of a dream created by these three. I wanted to show it to you with no one else around."

We stood there for some time and then he sighed, a sudden, gusty sound. "Thank you for this," he said. I did not know if he was thanking me or speaking to the people in the ground.

I cleared my throat. "Come on, there's more to see." I led him now towards the Armoury, that room in the Varrus household that contained Excalibur. He had been there the previous day, late in the afternoon, but he had seen only what all people saw therein: the wealth of weaponry collected empire-wide during the lifetimes of two men, Publius Varrus and his grandfather, to whom Publius had referred as Varrus the Elder. On the occasion of that first visit, there had been too many others around for me to show him the room's hidden treasure. Now we were alone, and having barred the heavy, double doors, I opened the secret hiding-place beneath the floor with the ease of long practise and produced the polished wooden case that held the sword. Impatient now to see his reaction, I remained sitting on the floor with my feet dangling down into the hole beneath as I placed the case on the floor in front of me, springing the hidden lock and handing him the weapon wordlessly, hilt first.

For long moments, neither of us moved or spoke as he stood there staring at what he held in his hand, but then he leaned forward slowly, dipping into a fighting crouch, and began to wield the sword in slow, exaggerated motions, spinning and pivoting, rising and falling on his toes, his movements resembling some solemn, ritual dance of sacrificial awe and reverence. He began by holding the weapon in his right hand, but by the time he had completed his first, tentative series of moves, both of his fists were locked about the long, sharkskin grip and his eyes glittered with the play of light along the edges of the flashing blade that circled his head. Gradually, almost without volition, the tempo of his movements began to increase, until the air hissed audibly with the passage of the lethal, lovely, whirling silver blade.

He stopped, abruptly, his arm muscles tense, holding the sword now motionless, extended at arm's length, and then he grounded the point, reversed his grip, and held the hilt towards me.

"Magical," he whispered, his voice husky. "It should be used, not hidden beneath a dusty floor."

"It will be, Brother, when the time is right." Taking it from him, still sitting with my legs beneath the floor, I yielded to a sudden impulse and struck the blade against the boards, raising the point to the vertical immediately and pressing the cockleshell pommel to the floor to produce the bell-like, resonant effect of which I had read in my uncle's books. In all the years of my guardianship of Excalibur, it was the first time I had done so, and even I was unprepared for the effect it produced. Out of nowhere, springing from the very air of the room, it seemed, an unearthly sound of crystalline, sense-searing beauty sprang into being, transfixing both of us with its power, clarity and shocking strength. Startled myself by its awesome purity and ringing loudness, I jerked my arm upward, breaking the contact between the sword and the solid floor, and the sound faded quickly, to die away completely and suddenly as I touched the blade with a pointing fingertip, feeling a sharp and eerie tingle in my hand at the contact so that I pulled my hand away again.

The silence that followed was profound until Ambrose broke it with a whispered question.

"What was *that?*"

I cleared my throat and smiled again, regaining my self-possession. "Excalibur, singing. I read about it in my uncle's books, but I had never heard it before now." Ambrose was gazing at the sword, an expression on his face of almost superstitious dread, and I knew my own would have mirrored it had I not known what I knew. "Apparently it has something to do with the purity of the metal," I said, for his benefit. "Some kind of vibration. According to Father Andros, the man who first did that the day the sword was made, the ancient smiths could gauge the quality of their weapons by the sounds they produced."

"What ancient smiths? I've never heard of that."

I shrugged. "No more had I, but it is obviously true. The purer the metal, the sweeter the temper, the truer and more powerful the sound produced."

"But there were *sounds*, Caius. That was not one simple sound, not one clear note. I heard several, high and low."

"I know, but don't expect me to explain it. As I said, I've never done that before. It shocked me as much as it did you."

"Do it again."

I did, this time with more confidence, and we listened enthralled as the mighty, ringing clarity of the song of Excalibur made the very air of the room vibrate, setting the dust motes quivering in the beams of light from the roof vents. Then came the sound of running footsteps outside, rushing towards the doors, and I stifled the sound by pressing the blade this time against my leg, feeling again the transient, tingling sting before the blade grew still. Someone thrust against the doors from the outside and I was grateful I had taken the time to bar them. Then fists pounded against the bronze-covered wood and we heard voices raised in anxious questioning. Grimacing at Ambrose, I quickly replaced the sword in its case and dropped it into its hiding-place before replacing the floorboard hurriedly. The pegs that locked the board in place projected still, but I ignored them.

"Open the door, but not too quickly." I crossed the room quickly to a small table, where I picked up one of the devices that lay there, a hollowed-out stone attached to a long, leather cord. I quickly wrapped the small loop in the end of the cord around my right index finger and then nodded to Ambrose, who swung open the doors to admit Trebonius Velus, Centurion of the Guard for that day. As Velus stepped across the threshold, looking uneasily about the room, I saw the press of armoured bodies behind him.

"Trebonius Velus, is there something wrong?"

My question stopped him in mid-step and his face betrayed his confusion as he looked from Ambrose to me and back again, blinking rapidly.

"Wrong, Commander? I don't know, but we heard something strange."

"What do you mean, strange?" I was careful to keep my voice polite and neutral.

He blinked again and shrugged. "I don't know, Commander, but it was very loud. Some kind of whistling sound. Twice, we heard it. The first time, it was brief. I was close by, checking the guards, and we all heard it but could not locate it—it was gone too quickly. But the second time, we heard it coming from here, and we came running." Clearly embarrassed, he went on, "I beg your pardon, Commander. We didn't know you were in here. No one did."

"Think no more of it, Centurion, you behaved correctly." I moved towards him, holding up the hand that held the stone. "This is what you heard, and you were right to respond the way you did. It is a weapon. Have you seen it before?"

Velus shook his head, his eyes fixed on my upraised hand with the looped cord around the first finger joint. I raised it higher, so that the craning guards at his back could see it, too. I was very aware of Ambrose's eyes on me.

"You all know, at least by report, how fond my uncle Publius Varrus was of unusual weapons," I continued, addressing myself to all of them. "Well, this is one of the strangest of them all. We have no name for it, but it was used by the barbarian hordes in the farthest reaches of the Eastern Empire. It was brought back to Britain by our own Vegetius Sulla, many years ago. It is no more than a heavy stone, as you can see, attached to a leather string. It is swung around the head and hurled; a kind of slingshot, but with two differences: first, the stone is attached to the string, and second, the stone is carved, or ground out, so that it generates a whistling sound as it is swung. Observe."

Stepping to the centre of the room where I was unobstructed, I allowed the stone to drop from my hand to dangle at the end of its cord, and then I began to swing it around my head. As it picked up momentum, it began to emit a low, warbling ululation that quickly swelled to a howling shriek that brought at least one guard's hands up to cover his ears. As I began to swing even harder, leaning into my movements to increase both speed and sound, the cord suddenly snapped, cutting the noise instantly and sending the heavy stone shooting up and across the room, fortunately to my rear, where it glanced off a roof beam and smacked violently but harmlessly into a corner pillar before clattering to the floor. No one stirred in the absolute, shocked stillness. I drew the cord through my fingers and examined the frayed end.

"This was an old cord, and therefore dangerous," I said. "But I think you all saw and heard enough."

Velus coughed and nodded. "Aye, Commander. My thanks, and pardon us. We'll leave you alone."

When they had gone, closing the doors behind them, Ambrose turned to me with a grin, one eyebrow raised. "That was quick thinking. I am impressed, but it sounded nothing like the other sound."

"We know that, Brother, but they don't. We were here and knew what we were listening to. They came running to investigate an alien sound that burst upon their ears unexpectedly. I showed them an alien weapon that produced a loud noise. The cord broke before it could achieve its highest volume. They are satisfied and will think no more about it."

He merely shook his head, still smiling admiringly. "As I said, quick thinking. There was more of Merlyn the Celt than Caius the Roman in that spontaneity. I couldn't have come up with that explanation in a hundred years." His gaze settled upon the locking pegs still projecting above the floorboards.

"Shouldn't we conceal those?"

"Absolutely." I pressed each stud with my foot until it sank level with the surface. "Well, Ambrose Britannicus, you have now seen Excalibur, and handled it, and heard it. Any comments?"

He pursed his lips and shook his head. "What could I say? I've never seen its like, but there has never been its like . . ." His hesitation was brief. "But the observation I made earlier comes back to me; it should be used. Who *will* use it? The boy?"

"Arthur? Perhaps. If not he . . ." I glanced around the room, then went and picked up the whistling stone from the corner, replacing it upon the table where I had found it. "I'll make a new cord for that tomorrow. Uncle Varrus was always most particular about the maintenance of even the least of his treasures." Ambrose had not moved and I felt his eyes upon me, deliberating the incompleteness of my answer to his last question. "If not he," I continued, then broke off again, looking around me still. "I'm thirsty. Let's go find a jug of wine and talk some more on this. There are aspects of your question I have never really considered. This could be as good a time as any to confront them."

A short time later, we sat in the day quarters that had been my father's office before it became mine. A small fire burned in the brazier and I had lit lamps and candles to dispel the heavy shadows of late afternoon. Even with the small windows high up on the walls to admit light, summer made little difference to the interior rooms. I had found a jug of wine and released the guard from duty outside my door, which was now firmly closed against interruption. Ambrose had made no attempt to break in upon my thoughts since leaving the Armoury. I took another sip of wine and placed the cup carefully upon the table.

"Excalibur. You said in the Armoury that there has never been anything like it, but that is not strictly true. There is, or there was, a dagger, and a sword—a short-sword—that resembled it. The sword was made by Uncle

Varrus's grandfather for his only son, Publius Varrus's father, but Varrus's father died on campaign with the legions before he ever saw it. It ended up, by some circuitous route, in the hands of the Emperor Theodosius, his most prized weapon. The Sword of Theodosius, men called it. It was the first Varrus blade made from the metal of a skystone."

"From the Skystone? But how could that be? You told me Varrus found the Skystone here, close by."

"That's true, he did. But I did not say *the* Skystone, I said made from *a* skystone. The Sword of Theodosius was made from the first skystone, the one found by the old man, Uncle Varrus's grandfather, about a hundred years ago."

He was frowning. "I see, so there were two stones."

"In fact, there were many of them, all save one of which came down together one night near here, in the Mendip Hills, but that's unimportant." I pushed my high-backed chair back on its legs and put my feet up on the table. "The point I wanted to make is that the sword in question was nothing like Excalibur. I never saw it, but I have read a description of it. It lacked the silver finish, the mirror-bright purity, and it was only a short-sword. But it was made from skystone metal, mixed with ordinary iron, and it would cut other swords in half. And it was stolen from the Varrus forge and ended up being owned by Theodosius. What happened to it in the interim will never be known, but its qualities were such that its ownership succession took it steadily upward from a smith to an emperor."

"What happened to the dagger?"

"Publius Varrus owned that. He buried it with Grandfather Caius, the year you and I were born."

"So you never saw it, either."

"No, but it was flawless, with a blade like polished silver. Peerless. And now there is Excalibur. Can you doubt that men would steal and kill to own it? Uncle Varrus himself told me men would fight wars to possess it. Therefore, brother, it behooved us to make sure, from the outset, that its first owner and user is man enough to hold it and to keep it. It is a king's sword, at least, now that there are no emperors around. We must breed a king worthy of the sword."

"Uther was a king."

"Aye, but a small one. His kingship was small, I mean. There was nothing petty about Uther."

"So his son——"

"His son may be the man, some day. He has the blood of kings—not merely Uther's blood—and he has the breeding. He is Eirish Gael and Cambrian Celt and he is heir to Cornwall's Celts, through his mother. He has the blood of ancient Rome within him, too, patrician Cornelius through our own line, and equestrian Varrus. He could become High King."

"High King of Britain?" I heard amazement in my brother's voice.

"Why not?"

"Why not indeed." Now his tone changed to one of musing. "Vortigern sees himself as High King of Britain some day."

"Does he, by God? By what right?"

His lip flicked upward in a tiny smile. "By default, I suspect, and by right of conquest and possession. What other right is there?"

I had no adequate response to that and so sat quiet for some time, sipping my wine again while my mind raced to follow this new line of thought Ambrose had opened up. If Vortigern's ambitions leaned towards a High King's stature, I reasoned, then we in Camulod might well be able to make use of them to our own, similar ends.

A solid, heavy clunk, accompanied by a flash of movement brought me back from my musings. A small, tanned leather purse, bulky and evidently filled with coins, had landed on the table in front of me.

"What's this?"

"My current wealth, all of it, to purchase access to your gravid thoughts."

I smiled. "We don't use money here."

"I know, no more do we. I keep it as a talisman, a memento of a time long gone. You were thinking of Vortigern, I believe."

"Aye, I was. He will never be High King of Britain."

"Why not? He's already well along the path towards it. He controls the whole of the northeast and works with Hengist to extend his influence southward, into the Settlements."

"That will take him years."

"I agree, but he has years. He's not an old man, Cay. Five, perhaps six years older than you, that's all."

"Very well, he has years. But after those have passed he'll be no more than king of East Britain. Does he have sons?"

"Aye, two. Cuthbert and Areltane."

"Cuthbert? Areltane? What kind of names are those?"

Ambrose shrugged. "Different names; men's names. Saxon names."

"Are they impressive, these sons?"

Again the shrug, this time more pensive. "Who can tell? They are both young, but both king's sons. They have . . . concerns which other men lack . . . I believe, however, that the younger, Areltane, could be his father's heir in more than name. He is a strong young man in every way, approaching his seventeenth year."

"What about the other one, Cuthbert is it? How old is he?"

"Nearing nineteen. He is . . . less of a *presence* than the younger boy. Not less manly, you understand, merely less gifted; less likable, perhaps; certainly less open, less outgoing. I like him well enough, personally, but he is overshadowed by his younger brother in almost everything they do."

"Does he resent that?"

"Again, who can tell what goes on inside another man's mind? He doesn't seem to. The boys get along well together, outwardly at least."

"The other, Areltane; can he fight?"

"Aye, superbly for his age. He's a natural leader."

"Hmm. You admire Vortigern, don't you?"

"Yes, I do, and he has earned that. You admired him, too, when you met him."

"Yes, I admit I did. But High King, eh? Well, perhaps in the Eastern regions, as I said, but never in the West; not in Cambria, or Cornwall, and certainly not in Camulod, even though, as you pointed out, he still has years ahead of him. How many years, would you think, to claim and settle all of Britain to the east?"

Ambrose's face broke into a wide grin as he at last discerned the direction of my thoughts. "Long enough for a boy child to grow up. That's what you're thinking, isn't it?"

"Yes." I squeezed my chin between my palms and nodded my head slowly. "It had occurred to me that Vortigern victorious in the East would keep the pressures of invasion from that direction away from us, leaving us to guard against the South and the West alone."

Ambrose stood up, unable to contain his excitement as the picture in his mind took shape. "Of course! And the boy Arthur is the natural heir—legitimately—to South and West and North!"

"Aye," I added. "Even to Eire, which could reduce the threat from beyond the western seas."

He sat down again as suddenly as he had risen, staring at me.

"You dream wide-reaching dreams, Caius Merlyn."

"Perhaps, but I am bred to it and my dreams are not of my own greatness. We have a land to safeguard here—" I broke off as another thought occurred to me, then voiced it as a question. "Will those dreams cause you problems with your friend Vortigern?"

My question surprised him but he quickly shook his head. "No, not at all. I have already chosen, as you know, to make my life here. I will return to Vortigern and tell him that—another decision long since made. But now I can approach him as a military ally, offering him a guard upon his western flanks; our cavalry. He will be well pleased with that."

"You have no fears that he might seek, some far-off day and then merely to assist his loyal friends, to extend his domain to Camulod and the West?"

"He might," he admitted, after having thought about it for a time. "But by then he'll be too late. I know he has too much ahead of him now even to give thought to the possibility were he aware of it. By the time he does come around to it, if he ever does, his loyal friends will be too strong, too well established in their hilly lands behind their walls of horsemen, for him to consider waging war with them. In the meantime, Vortigern will pacify and unite the East, and Camulod will have those years to grow and prosper, unless something goes radically wrong."

"Aye, and something always will, but at least we have an end in sight— a target to aim for." Now it was I who stood up. "Come on, then. The first step along this path is not a step at all; I want to fork your legs across a saddle and get your feet securely into stirrups, and I want to be aboard a ship to fetch the child before the next moon fills its face."

Within the month, as I had ordained, Donuil and I were ready to set out for Eire. Ambrose was well ensconced and already ranging far and wide throughout the Colony, his feet securely anchored in his stirrups.

Donuil and I would travel light, with only nine men as escort. We would have preferred to ride alone, only the two of us, from my home to his, but everyone around us, from Aunt Luceiia to our visiting Druid friend Daffyd, had warned us of the folly of such a course. The dangers we would face lay on the road, they said, not at the end of our route, and of course they were right. A party of eleven would be small enough to make good speed, and large enough to discourage attack along the way. We picked our people carefully, for their size and fighting skills, and I was content. All nine of them were friends and companions of long standing.

Two days before we were due to leave, awaiting only Ambrose's return from his latest patrol, Lucanus came to visit me while I was in the midst of a meeting with my people, making a final inventory of our travelling needs. I was glad to see him; it had been some time since last we had talked. I apologized for being occupied and asked him if I might seek him out in turn within the hour. In far less time than that I found him in his Infirmary, in consultation with Ludmilla. He grinned at me and waved me to a high-backed chair by his table. "Sorry, my friend, my turn to be engaged, but we are almost done here. Sit, please."

I seated myself and spent the next few moments watching, and trying not to watch, Ludmilla as she leaned over the table beside Luke. She was a well-made woman, long and lithe beneath the voluminous white robe she wore. Black and white, I realized, were the colours I associated with her at all times. And blue, although she wore it too infrequently. Black hair, blue eyes, white clothing. *And red, red lips*, a sudden voice whispered within my ear. I felt my face flush and berated myself for such callow, boyish embarrassment, shifting around in my seat to look elsewhere. The woman flustered me and I could not understand why this should be so. I felt attracted to her, I knew that—the swell of her hips and breasts seldom eluded me for long, despite her loose-hanging clothes—but that was merely lust, and I knew I could cope with that and conquer it. The other confusion that I felt defied definition, but I was aware of it again—an anxiety amounting almost to panic.

The conference ended and Ludmilla moved to gather up the papers they had spread upon the table, and I watched her as she did so. Lucanus was frowning as he scanned a written sheet of papyrus before handing it to her to take with the others. Her load complete, Ludmilla turned and nodded kindly to me with a smile before leaving. Even after the door had safely closed behind her, the knowledge of her nearness kept my heart thudding audibly in my chest. Finally I forced myself to address Lucanus calmly. He was sitting watching me, a slight smile creasing his features.

"Well," I began. "Finally we can talk without distraction. I'm sorry I couldn't leave with you earlier."

His smile grew wider. "You are the Legate Commander. You have duties. When do you leave?"

"Day after tomorrow. Everything's in hand. What's up?"

"Nothing's 'up,' as you put it. A cup of wine?"

"Good idea. Thank you."

He poured for both of us and then resumed his seat, holding his cup at chin level and staring into it for a while before speaking. "I received a letter several days ago. Daffyd brought it."

He had a peculiar expression on his face and I wondered what was coming. Very few men now either read or wrote, since Rome had taken away her clerks along with her armies.

"A letter? That's a great event these days. From whom?"

"From an old acquaintance with whom I had lost touch for many years. It turns out he's close by and learned of my presence here by accident."

"Wonderful, Luke! You must be excited. When is he coming?"

"He is not . . . cannot. Like me, he's a physician and a surgeon, army trained, so he can't simply up and leave his charges. I, however, would like to go to him."

In the previous few weeks our wounded veterans had improved immeasurably and many had already been released to resume their duties. The others, those still confined to bed, now filled less than two of the temporary hospitals set up for them, and none of them now remained in any danger. Those who would die had died already. Lucanus was at liberty to do whatever pleased him. I could have no possible objection to his leaving, nor would I have entertained one, but I wondered why he was telling me this. There was more to come, I felt. Lucanus was not a man to seek another out—even myself, his only close friend—to make mere small talk.

"Then why don't you go immediately? I think that's an excellent idea. You've nothing to detain you here; the work's all done. Your staff can take care of any minor emergencies that might spring up. Are you worried about that? Or is there something else? I have the feeling, for no good reason, that you require something of me. Is that it? For God's sake, Luke, what could you possibly require from me you couldn't simply take as freely granted?"

He made a sound that was both a sniff and a sigh, pulling his shoulders high. "I don't want to go to see him empty-handed, Cay."

"Why should you? Take whatever you want."

"That's rather large. I want to take a wagonload of fresh supplies—food, clothing and medicines."

"A wagonload? Fine, then. See the quartermaster. I'll see him myself and advise him you're coming. But what ails your friend that he should need so much? Not that I begrudge you your gift, you understand—you could have that and ten times more as your due. I'm merely curious. Where is he located?"

"North of here. And thank you, Caius Merlyn."

"Nonsense, not another word. North, you say. By Aquae Sulis?"

"No, more to the west, by Glevum, close to the coast."

"Hmm. We're going that way, to Glevum, to take ship."

"I know you are. That's why I decided to speak. May I ride with you?"

"You have another option that you might prefer?"

He smiled again. "No, not at all."

"Then that's settled. The day after tomorrow. Does that give you enough time?" He nodded, and I went on, my curiosity fully aroused. "May I ask two questions?" He waited, his smile still in place. "What would you have done had I said no to either request?"

"Nothing. I would have stayed here. I could not make the journey on my own, especially with a loaded wagon. What's your second question?"

"Your friend the surgeon. How does it come about that he is in such dire need of basic supplies? Are there none to be had in Glevum?"

Lucanus shook his head slowly. "There may be, my friend, but not for him. His charges are all lepers."

"What?"

"Lepers. I said his charges are all lepers. A large group of them."

"Lepers?" I repeated, still off balance. Lucanus took pity on me.

"Yes, my friend, that's what I said." He watched my face and then said, "Oh dear, there's that look. The look that encompasseth all misunderstandings."

I was listening now, understanding. Luke was going to a leper colony, walking into contagion. I had known there were lepers in Britain, of course, but they were creatures of whispered terrors and nightmares and I had never encountered any. My flesh crawled with horror at the mere thought of them, my mind filled with the grim stories I had heard about them and their disgusting scourge.

Lucanus's sympathetic tone cut through the unreasoning terror of my reaction. "Caius, I beg you, stop looking like that. These sorry people are no threat, and you have no need to fear the very mention of them. Speaking of them won't contaminate us. Their fear of people like us, whole human people, is far greater than our ill-founded terror of them, let me assure you. We see them as the living dead, terrifying in their implications, but they see us, and with far more reason, I fear, as the incarnation of walking death, since we would kill them all out of hand, and with no remorse, merely to rid ourselves of the sight of them." He paused to look at me more closely, and when his voice resumed it was more solemn. "It occurs to me, seeing you react, that I should have given more thought to this. You may find it in your heart, and it lies well within your power, to forbid my visit now, fearing contagion, but I would like your permission to visit them, Commander Merlyn." I stared at him, hearing his formality, until he continued, almost in a whisper, "Theirs is an awful life of suffering and dread, Caius. There might be something I can do to help them. May I go?"

I nodded, suddenly unaccountably unwilling to look him in the eye and unable to speak. I sensed him watching me closely, however, and forced myself to meet his gaze. He was smiling, a small, sad smile. "I promise you, Caius, there is nothing to fear. The foulness and contagion of leprosy are very real, but its reputed speed of contamination is grossly exaggerated. I worked among many lepers during my early years with the legions. My finest teacher, Philus of whom you've heard me speak, was a student of leprosy who had worked for more than three decades among those afflicted with the scourge. He himself had remained uncontaminated and was convinced that the disease is almost incommunicable by ordinary, commonplace means—by casual touch, in other words—although he handled all of them with care for his own safety, and always washed himself thoroughly with astringents afterward. I came to agree with him, eventually, learning from personal experience that he was most probably correct..." His voice died away for a moment, then resumed, "I also learned that lepers are ordinary people, just like us, Caius, but afflicted with a dreadful, bleak, incurable disease that brings death in life and banishment from all human warmth, except among their own kind—but there I have found that human, loving warmth burns brighter than anywhere else in this world."

I watched him as he spoke, then I swallowed hard and nodded again. "The supplies you spoke of—what will you require? Is there anything in particular that you need to take with you?"

He smiled again. "No, almost anything would be welcome. They will have nothing."

"I see. And your friend the physician, what is his name?"

"Mordechai. Mordechai Emancipatus. 'Mordechai the Free,' and he is well named. He is a Roman Jew, educated with me in Alexandria, and then in the legions under Theodosius."

"A Jew. Not a Christian?"

"No, an Aesculapian."

At last I could smile with him. "A brave man, by anyone's accounting. Do you know exactly where to find him?"

"No, but I know where to inquire. Mordechai mentions in his letter that they are located ten miles to the westward of a public hostelry widely known as the Red Dragon, about twenty miles south of Glevum. I'll find him."

"I am sure you will, and I'll make sure you do."

Luke and his forthcoming journey remained in my mind for the rest of that day, prompting me to think about the gifts I should be bearing to Donuil's father, the King of Scots. Luke would go bearing valuable gifts to Mordechai, a friend and colleague. Could mine to King Athol be less substantial? And yet, I asked myself, what did we possess in Camulod that could constitute a kingly gift? The answer was not long in coming. Horses, of course, the like of which were never seen in Eire! I resolved to take a stallion and a brood mare, matched as closely as could be, and I immediately felt better. I set aside the question of equipment, saddles and stirrups for the time being, deciding in my capacity as Legate Commander, as opposed to ambassador, that generosity could be carried too far when it affected safety, strategy and tactics. The gift of breeding stock, I reasoned, was munificence enough; saddlery, including stirrups, provided our cavalry with a military edge it would be irresponsible to relinquish, even to a prospective ally. But then I thought of other weaponry, and resolved to take King Athol one more gift no one could match in magnificence: a matching pair of short-sword and dagger, made by Publius Varrus, with hand-tooled belt and sheaths.

Delighted with my decisions, I summoned Donuil to share my elation, forgetting that we had already arranged to meet earlier that day to select the horses we would take with us on our journey. He listened carefully as I outlined my thoughts on our gifts—I mentioned only the breeding pair of horses, seeing no point in bringing up the potentially sensitive matter of saddlery and stirrups—and when I had done, he nodded his head sagely.

"My father will be most impressed; these are indeed gifts for a king. But they compound a problem I've been thinking about already this afternoon."

"What kind of problem?"

"Transportation, Commander. How are we going to get all these animals across the sea? Now you have added another two. Horses need room. They can't curl up in a corner and go to sleep like a man. We'll never find a ship big enough to take them all."

"Then we'll find several. We'll take enough gold to buy as many as we need."

Donuil was unimpressed. "Buy them where, Merlyn? I know Glevum's a harbour, but it has lain abandoned, or nearly so, since the Romans left. Lot's army went there after Aquae Sulis, remember? They found it just as desolate as Aquae, with nothing left to loot. There may be ships still using it, but I doubt we'll find more than one at any time."

The same thoughts had been running through my mind, but I knew, with an inner certainty I could not explain even to myself, that this was the course we should take. Even if it meant taking a blind chance on having to leave some of our party behind when we took ship, I was convinced deep inside that I was right, and I was confident that all would be well. Donuil listened as I explained all that, and then shrugged, accepting my enthusiasm and optimism.

"So be it," he commented. "You're the Legate, and I'm prepared to trust your judgment in this as in everything else." He paused, looking around him thoughtfully. It was late afternoon by then, darkening rapidly indoors, and we were in my quarters, sitting by a burning brazier and surrounded by leaping shadows.

"What is it, Donuil?"

He shook his head, then decided to proceed with what was in his mind. "Commander, do you remember all the candles you used in Verulamium, lighting up your tent at night like the noonday sun?"

"Yes, I remember them very well." They had been a gift from my friend Germanus, the Bishop of Auxerre in Gaul. "The light of learning," he had called them as a private joke between the two of us. The prelates and clerics who had gathered that year in Verulamium for the Great Debate between the Orthodox Roman bishops under Germanus and the British bishops who had followed the teachings of Pelagius had been superbly well equipped with beeswax candles and tapers of the highest quality. I had acquired half a wagonload of them for my own use when I wrote at night. Now I smiled at the memory. "Why do you ask?"

"I was wondering what happened to them all?"

"They were burned up, Donuil. That tends to happen with candles."

"All of them? You had cases and cases of the things."

"I know I did, but that was years ago. What made you think of that?"

"My father, Commander, and gifts. He's an old man, although you'd never think it to look at him from a distance, and seeing you sitting there in the dark reminded me of how he used to sit the same way, with one of his big wolfhounds' heads resting on his knee. We have no fine, bright candles in Eire, only smoky lamps, dirty old smelly tallow dips and firelight. It came to me that a gift of such things, such bright, clean light, would bedevil and gratify the old man."

"It probably would, Donuil. I would never have thought of such a thing, but it is a marvellous idea. I wonder if we could find some?"

"Nah, you're probably right. They'll all be gone, long since."

Now that he had brought the matter to my mind, however, I began to wonder what *had* happened to those candles. I had not used them all, I now realized, for I had been wounded on the way home and spent the next two years as someone else, without a memory. The last I remembered of them was watching them being loaded onto one of our wagons before we left Verulamium. Lucanus would know.

Another visit to Lucanus elicited the information that he had never seen the things, and that the wagons had been returned, with all their remaining contents intact, to our quartermasters. The following morning, after an hour's questioning and another hour spent searching, we uncovered ten cases of fine candles almost buried in a dingy warehouse against the north wall. I repossessed all of them, since they were mine, and four cases went immediately into our baggage as a tribute to Athol, High King of the Scots of Eire.

VIII

THE MORNING OF the day we were to leave turned out to be a momentous one for several reasons, and as a result we were obliged to postpone our departure for ten days. It began innocuously enough, when I awoke at dawn filled with a sense of well-being after a dream I could recall with perfect clarity.

Some people, I have learned, never dream of flying, of soaring above the earth like a bird. I have always had the power to fly, in my dreams, and always as an eagle. My pinions had borne me high in this grand dream, and the pleasure of it woke me with a smile upon my face. Nothing foreboding or prophetic marred my enjoyment. I had been gliding, I recalled, high above the training ground at the bottom of Camulod's hill, with the towering stone walls of the fortress on my left, and beneath me all the forces of the Colony had been marching and riding in parade, their ranks and formations bright with ceremonial colours and the metals of their harness burnished to inspection quality. A flash of light had attracted my eyes to a rostrum erected on the hill, and there stood Ludmilla, garlands of flowers in her long, black hair, her eyes and face aglow with happiness as she received and accepted the salutes and plaudits of the passing troops.

Folding my wings and curling my great pinions, I swooped down to where she stood, and as she heard the sounds of my swift passage she raised her smiling face to greet me. I threw wide my wings then, feeling the air arrest me so that I hung there, spilling the wind around me, almost stationary, and as I did she raised one hand to me, holding out my Aunt Luceiia's silver mirror. I saw myself reflected there, but as a man, not a bird, and yet as I reached to touch it, she laughed at the clatter of my talons against its surface. Startled, and panicking, I felt myself begin to fall, and the swift-beating feathers of my wing tips touched the ground before the air lifted me up again, allowing me to beat my way aloft to where I could become myself once more. And finally, feeling the thrill of freedom in my breast, I tilted myself and planed above the army, hearing their cheers as I passed overhead.

It was at that point I awoke, a smile upon my face, and for a while I lay there, breaking my lifelong custom of leaping from my bed the moment my eyes opened. I had spent much of my life avoiding my dreams, most of which were dark and frightening and, I had come to believe, prophetic. This one, I felt sure, had been very different, benevolent, and I believed I could interpret it.

I had been making myself miserable ever since my return from the southwest, I now realised, attempting to avoid my own attraction to Ludmilla, and, having made that admission freely to myself, I now examined it more closely. I was almost thirty-two years old and had lain with no woman since my wife, and my wife had been dead for more than four years! And now, unexpectedly, my mind, my thoughts, my days were filled with visions of Ludmilla. She was more than merely lovely; she was enchanting, beautiful, graceful and lithe. And she was clever; clever enough for Luke to value training her in his own arcane profession. She was accomplished in every other way, too, a valued and highly regarded member of Aunt Luceiia's household. And then I had another thought, quite startling in its novelty, yet strangely lacking any power to surprise me: she suggested, and exactly resembled, the portrait Publius Varrus had set down in words of the woman who had bewitched him when he was my age, Luceiia Britannicus herself.

"So be it," I thought then. "Today I will seek her out and talk to her and spend some time in courting her and then, when I return from Eire, we shall see what comes of it."

That decision made, I leapt out of bed, pulled on a tunic and my heavy, sandalled boots, and went for a long run, down the hill to the plain and across its dusty surface to the edge of the forest more than a mile away, where I turned right and ran around the perimeter of the training ground until I could run no more. Then, as I caught my breath before tackling the hill again, I heard a warning trumpet from the guard post at the gate above and turned to see Ambrose's patrol column approaching from the forest.

I waited for him and ran up the hill with him at the head of his troopers, my hand on his stirrup leather. The patrol had been an uneventful one, he told me, with nothing to report. We parted at the gate and I made my way directly to the bath house.

Something over an hour later, bathed, refreshed and fed, I made my way to the Infirmary, hoping Ludmilla might be there already. She was not, but Lucanus was, checking some final details with his staff before leaving them to their own devices while he was away. He dismissed them just as I arrived and turned to me with a head-to-toe look of wry appraisal.

"Well, good morning. You're looking full of vim and vigour. What's on your mind?"

"Nothing at all," I lied. "Other than our journey, of course. Are you all prepared?"

"As much as I'll ever be. When do you want to leave?"

"Before noon, although we're in no hurry other than to get away. I feel like a boy turned loose from his tutors for the summer. Is Ludmilla here?"

He was looking down at his desk, his thoughts elsewhere. "Hmm? She was a moment ago, didn't you see her?" He corrected himself immediately, his attention fixed on something on his desk. "Oh no, she's in the wards; she left before you came . . . Damnation, I told Cato to take this with him." He picked up the item, a small wooden box, then paused, his eyes widening with surprise as he looked beyond my shoulder. "Ambrose," he said. "Welcome. What brings you here for the first time? You're obviously not sick."

I had turned as soon as he began to speak, to see Ambrose looming in the doorway at my back. He looked enormous, and again I found myself thinking he must be much bigger than I, although I knew that was not so.

"Forgive me, Luke," he said, smiling. "But they told me Cay was here and I need to talk to him before he leaves." His eyes swivelled to me. "It's important, Cay, or I wouldn't trouble you, but I forgot to mention it when

I first thought of it, before I went out on patrol, and I've only just remembered it again, so I thought I had better do something about it before it slips away again. May I have a moment?"

"Of course," I said. "What's—"

I was interrupted by the sound of running feet and Ludmilla dashed into the room through the rear door that led to the interior sick rooms.

"Lucanus, come quickly! It's Popilius Cirro. He can't breathe!"

"Stay here, all of you!" Lucanus was gone in a swirl of robes, leaving the three of us alone.

I spoke to Ludmilla, noting even as I digested her words the way in which she seemed to sag against the door frame, her full breasts emphasised by the way her robe was caught between her and the wall.

"What d'you mean, he can't breathe?"

"I don't know what's wrong, Commander. He simply cannot catch his breath." She had not looked at me at all in speaking. Her eyes were fixed on a spot somewhere behind me and her face was flushed a deep red; from fright, I supposed, and the effort of running.

"Who is Popilius Cirro?" I heard Ambrose ask, and I realized then how truly new he was to Camulod.

"Our Senior Centurion," I answered, my eyes still on Ludmilla. "A good friend, and *primus pilus* to our father for many years in the legions, under Stilicho. He is an old man now, but he was active until he took a wound in the last campaign against Lot, and then he became ill. But he's recovering, and almost fit enough for duty again; at least I thought he was." Even as I was speaking the words I had the strangest sensation that something was wrong here; something that did not concern Popilius. My stomach grew tense and I glanced over my left shoulder to see if anyone else had entered the room behind me. No one had, and I looked back at Ludmilla.

"Don't you think you should go to Lucanus, Ludmilla? He might need some assistance. I think it was us he told to remain here, not you."

She looked at me for the first time since entering the room, a hesitant smile flickering on her face. "Yes. Yes, of course, I probably should." She straightened up, preparing to leave, and then her eyes moved away from me again, back towards the point at which she had been staring all along, and finally the realisation came to me that she was staring at the point behind my right shoulder from which Ambrose's voice had come. I turned my head quickly and saw her gaze mirrored in his eyes as he stared back at her, his face entranced. Still not comprehending fully what was going on, I looked again from one to the other. They were completely unaware of my presence, let alone my scrutiny; each was aware only of the other.

"Ludmilla?" The sound of my voice broke the spell, actually startling her.

"Oh, Popilius Cirro! Excuse me." She turned and was gone, the door swinging shut behind her. I turned back to my brother to find him gazing at me, his entire face radiating awe.

"Cay," he said, his voice quiet and filled with wonder. "Who is she?"

"Her name is Ludmilla," I answered, waiting for the anger I knew must be inside me to come boiling to the surface.

"I know that, I heard you call her that, but who is she? Does she have a husband?"

Suddenly, inexplicably, instead of feeling anger or jealousy, I found myself on the point of laughing, and a part of me wondered how I could possibly find any humour here. "Not yet," was all I said.

"Ludmilla . . ." He was looking at me, but his thoughts were elsewhere.

"Aye," I said, "Ludmilla. What was it you wanted to discuss with me?" His eyes widened in surprise. "You said there was something you wanted to talk to me about."

"Oh, yes. It was a thought I had about Uther's people and their bows. Do you think we could arrange to have some of them stationed here permanently?"

"Permanently? You mean living here in Camulod? I doubt it. Why?"

"Because I would like to start training them to fight with our men, tactically. It would be easier if some of them were based here. Why do you doubt it? Wouldn't you want them here?"

"No, it's not that, not at all. I simply doubt they'd come down out of their hills, particularly now that Uther's dead. I don't even know who will rule in his place now, but it's quite possible that whoever does might wish to have no more to do with Camulod."

He frowned. "You think that's likely?"

"No, but again, I don't know. It is possible. Uther rode to war for Camulod, rather than for Cambria, although Lot moved against Cambria, too. More to the point, unfeeling though it may seem, the fact is that most of those men lost their bows along with their lives, and Uther's people have never had enough bows to be able to afford to lose any of them. It is against their law for any man to own a bow."

"What do you mean? I don't understand."

"I know you don't, but it's quite simple. The Pendragon bow, as they call it, is a new weapon. It is made from a specific wood, a wood that has never been in abundant supply, and each individual bow takes years to make. For every bow made, there are a score of men waiting to use it, so each man takes custody of one bow for a year and has the responsibility of caring for it, but he must share it with others. The Druids are growing yew saplings everywhere throughout the Pendragon lands today, but that is a new development and the trees grow but slowly. There must have been hundreds of bows lost in Uther's campaign against Lot. They will be difficult to replace, and impossible to replace quickly."

Now my brother looked quite crestfallen and I reached out to clasp his shoulder. "Look, I may be wrong. They may have more resources than I thought. In the meantime, however, they have to replace a king and recover from a war, as we do. When Donuil and I return from Eire, we will journey to Uther's land and talk to whoever rules there. The alliance of Pendragon and Camulod is advantageous to both parties. We will work at it and build upon it."

As I spoke, the rear door opened again and Lucanus came back into the room. I swung to him immediately. "How is he, Luke?"

He stepped to his table and sat down, reaching out to pick up the small box he had been so concerned about earlier. He gazed at it, as though wondering what it was, and then replaced it on the tabletop.

"Popilius Cirro is dead. Respiratory failure." His voice was flat and emotionless, but then he turned to look at me, although even as he spoke his gaze drifted away over my shoulder. "I am sorry, Commander, there was nothing I could do for him. He was in paralysis when I arrived, and I was powerless to help him. He died almost immediately, while I was trying to clear his windpipe."

"Clear his windpipe?" My voice sounded strange to me. "You mean he *choked* to death?"

"No," he said, shaking his head distractedly. His eyes were fixed on some infinity within his mind, and for several moments he said nothing more, then resumed in a normal tone. "No, he did not. His trachea was unobstructed. He died of some kind of internal convulsion, probably related to the pulmonary condition—the pneumonia he had been suffering from." Lucanus paused and pinched the bridge of his nose between finger and thumb. "Anyway, he's gone . . . What will you do now?"

"Do? What d'you mean?"

"About leaving today. I imagine this changes things."

"Oh." I had not even thought that far ahead. "Yes, yes of course it does. I couldn't even think of leaving now. We will stay here a few more days and honour Popilius Cirro with the funeral he deserves." It was too sudden, too final, too brutal to be true. How could death come, so swift and unexpected and so final, lacking war or violent strife? And yet Popilius was dead. I could see Lucanus was as shaken as I was. "May I see him before I go?"

He rose to his feet again immediately, his face expressionless, set in lines of distant coldness that I knew to be the detachment of his professional persona. "Certainly, come with me."

The *primus pilus* still lay in the cot where I had seen him last, but he looked very different now. The shape beneath the coverings was still the one I remembered, but the once-familiar face was now hideously lifeless, the skin chalk white except around the blue-lipped, sunken mouth and cheeks.

"Why is his mouth blue?" I found myself whispering.

"It's a condition caused by the way he died, the respiratory failure. We call it cyanosis, because of the blue coloration it produces. Much the same result is seen in death caused by cyanide poisoning."

I glanced at him sharply. "He was *poisoned?*"

Lucanus shook his head, a tiny, weary smile twisting his lips. "No, not at all; I merely said the effect was the same."

Popilius's right arm lay on top of the covers and I reached out and took his hand in my own, finding it still warm as I had known it would be although already I fancied I could feel the chill of death beneath the skin. It was a large, old hand, calloused, hard and heavy. Anguish swelled in my throat, hurting so that I could not swallow.

"Old friend," I said to the recumbent form, "I will undertake your last commission." I had to stop, waiting for the end of a surge of grief that robbed me of my voice. When it had passed, I spoke again. "You built an armed camp at the bottom of our hill and held it for us in the face of Cornwall's thousands. Later, you tore it down again, but not until all danger was long past. Tomorrow, on the spot where you built the praesidium in the centre of that camp, you will be buried, alone with the glory you have earned, as befits a *primus pilus*, yet in a place of honour among the others who fell in that battle. Farewell, Popilius Cirro."

I turned on my heel, with a nod to Lucanus, and went to begin the arrangements for the funeral. Outside the sick ward, in Lucanus's office,

Ambrose was still waiting, presumably for me but more hopefully, I guessed, for Ludmilla's return. I reached out and grasped his shoulder in passing, pulling him into step with me. "We have a funeral to arrange," I told him. "Your first, but not your last in Camulod. As well you accompany me now and find out how we do it, because sooner or later you're going to have to arrange one on your own."

As we emerged from the Infirmary and swung towards the administration block that housed my office and those of Titus and Flavius, we came face to face with Peter Ironhair. He stopped, stock-still, several paces in front of us, his face setting into a scowl as he saw me and then betraying shocked amazement as his eyes went from my face to my brother's. Unsure of what to say or how to react to the evidently unexpected sight of two of me, he drew himself to his full height. I gave him no chance to recover from his shock.

"Ironhair," I said, acknowledging him. "You've been away, obviously. You have not yet met my brother, Ambrose Britannicus. Ambrose, this is Peter Ironhair, one of our smiths and a member of our Council."

Ironhair nodded to Ambrose, a cautious, hostile gesture. For me he had nothing. No trace of a smile or sign of any courtesy marked his features. Ambrose, sensing the man's dislike, merely nodded in return, his own face blank. This unforeseen exchange dispensed with, Ironhair walked on, swerving slightly to go around us. We proceeded in silence for several paces before Ambrose spoke.

"Who was that?"

I glanced at him. "I told you, Peter Ironhair, a smith and a councilor."

"I know that, but who is he? Why does he dislike us so intensely?"

I smiled half-heartedly, thinking of Popilius. "Not us, Brother, me. He thinks I did him a disservice, when all I really did was save his life."

"From whom, or what?"

"From me. He is an ambitious fool and a newcomer who cares nothing for the way things are done here. He had pretensions of a future role for himself here in the Colony that bore no resemblance to the role designed for any man in this place." I told him the story of the Farmers and the Artisans, and about the confrontation Ironhair and I had had by the main gate the following day, and he listened without interrupting until I had finished. We were at the entrance to the administration building before I reached that point and I held him there until my tale was done.

"Hmm," he said, when I had finished. "Sounds like a danger well identified. Certainly looked the part. It's a good thing you returned home when you did, in time to neutralize him. Had I arrived before that, or even later, I would not have noticed anything amiss. I have a lot to learn, Cay, before I'll be fit to deputize for you. D'you think he'll cause any more trouble?"

I thought about that for a moment and then shook my head. "No," I said. "I doubt it. He knows I'll kick him out of Camulod if he misbehaves from now on; and as you will be responsible in my place whenever I'm away, the same threat will hold good for you. Does that cause you any concern?"

He shook his head with finality. "Not in the least . . . as long as I know what I should be looking for."

I laughed. "You'll know, Brother. You'll know."

*   *   *

The arrangements for the funeral were well in hand by late afternoon, and Ambrose followed them all with interest. It was an unfortunate sign of the times that such rites had been sufficiently numerous in the recent past to entail no great logistical or procedural difficulties. Popilius, however, had been highly ranked and highly regarded, so the formalities of the occasion were more elaborate than most and it was decided that an honour guard of senior centurions should attend his bier and I myself should deliver his eulogy. No priests were involved. Despite his official Christian status, Popilius had been an old soldier, bred in the old ways, and was a disciple of the ancient military cult of Mithras. We had no Mithraic priests or representatives in Camulod, so we honoured his convictions by interring him as a soldier of his soldier's god, dressed in his finest armour and weapons. The ceremony took place the following afternoon and, in spite of the relentless rain, it was attended by almost every adult in the Colony, including my aunt and her women, the only people there afforded shelter beneath a leather awning.

In the middle of my oration, while I was speaking of the Popilius I remembered from my boyhood, a face leaped out at me from among the rain-swept crowd. Peter Ironhair again, the cowled hood of his cloak thrown back from his forehead, looking at me in scorn from the faceless, huddled ranks, a bitter sneer twisting his face into a mask of resentment. The sight of that sneer, the anger and rage it bespoke, almost succeeded in making me forget what I was saying, but I closed my mind to it, forcing myself to feel instead the trickling rainwater inside my harness, and brought my mind to bear again upon Popilius Cirro and what he had meant to Camulod. My own anger, however, once kindled, did not fade; it merely moved aside and waited. I knew that some day, come it soon or late, Ironhair and I were destined to meet sword to sword.

After the funeral, as soon as I had stripped out of my armour and passed it into the care of my orderly, I made my way to the bath house to find it, as I had expected, jammed with people who, like me, had stood for hours beneath the chilling rain. I had never known the place so crowded in all the years since it had first been built, and my immediate reaction was to leave again and make my way down to the Villa Britannicus, where the baths were vastly superior. But that would have meant another journey through the icy rain, and it was too far and I was too lazy, so I accepted the jostling of the close-packed mass of bodies and resigned myself to merely absorbing the heat and thawing out my bones.

I made my way in the accepted fashion through the formalized pools of graded temperatures, dawdling little in any of them and elbowing my way almost surreptitiously and with many apologies through the throng, determined to arrive at the steam room ahead of the main crush. There was no rank in the bath house; first there, first served was the rule. The man directly ahead of me in the line for the *calidarium*, the hottest pool before the steam room, eventually gave up in disgust and quit the line. I glanced at him as he passed me and did not recognise him, and that surprised me. I had thought I knew everyone in Camulod by this time, having worked hard at the task since regaining my memory. Puzzled, and curious, I turned around to look at him again, only to find him close behind me; too close behind me, and moving towards me inimically, pale grey eyes wide with violent intent.

Reacting instinctively, I turned my side to him and sucked in my belly, rising to my toes, throwing up my arms and bowing my middle backwards. The knife in his hand sliced a straight line across the muscles of my stomach as my right hand slashed down to close over his wrist and I pulled him forward, smashing my left elbow into his nose. Before the man on my other side could even react—his back had been pierced by the point of the assassin's knife when I jerked it forward—I had spun again, to face my attacker, driving my right knee up into his naked groin. He bent forward, clutching at himself, and as his head came down I brought my other elbow crashing against the back of his neck, the full weight of my frame behind it. He fell to his knees and remained there, restrained from falling farther by the press of bodies around us. Now the man who had been stabbed, his wound a mere scratch, was turned towards us, his eyes staring and his mouth wide with terror as he tried to reach behind his back to staunch the blood that flowed from him. My own belly was covered with fast-flowing blood. Somebody shouted an alarm, and the first flush of panic began to spread, although the danger was over. While I had never seen the baths so crowded, neither had I seen them empty so quickly. I sagged at the knees then, staring at the open edges of the cut across my abdomen.

"Damnation, I won't accept any argument on this, Titus, it was Ironhair." I was almost hissing through teeth clenched against the pain. "It had to be him; there is no other conceivable explanation. He had just returned to Camulod after an absence of days—Ambrose and I met him just inside the gate yesterday—and I heard someone say later in the day that he had brought some strangers with him. Now he and the strangers have vanished, judging by the time Ambrose has been gone; all except the one we have. Have they found out who he is yet?"

Titus was looking at me in dismay, and behind him, against the wall of the sick bay in the Infirmary, Flavius stood close by as always, his brows knit in a furrow of concern. An attempted assassination within Camulod was unheard of, and that the intended victim should be me appalled them both.

"Answer me, damn it!"

Titus shook his head. "I don't know, Caius. As far as I know, he's still unconscious. Lucanus is with him now." He set his jaw in determination and faced me squarely. "Nevertheless, at the risk of incurring your anger, I repeat that I must doubt the involvement of Ironhair in this." He held up his hand, palm towards me, to cut me off before I could respond. "I am not saying I believe the man incapable of such a thing, not at all. But I am saying that it defies credence that he could have planned the event when no one, including yourself, knew that you would go directly to the bath house after the funeral."

"But I didn't go directly to the bath house. I went back to my quarters and changed out of my armour. Had I remained there, he would have made the attempt there. As it was, he followed me to the baths. The only planning necessary was the decision to kill me today, while my mind was occupied with the funeral. The assassin is a stranger, unknown to me, but here in the safety of Camulod I would expect no threat, and even his strangeness ought not to have alerted me. I see many little-known faces around me nowadays. What saved my life, in fact the only thing that saved my life, was that I am aware of such lacunae in my knowledge of the folk here, and so turned around to try to place his face more firmly in my recollection. That's when I saw him lunge at me."

Flavius broke in here. "That's another thing I've found impossible to understand! How could anyone have got in there with a knife?"

I looked at him. "The bath house? He carried it in a towel. Do you examine all your friends while bathing to make sure they are unarmed? No one saw him armed because no one, including me, would ever have thought to look for such a thing there. Even after I had been stabbed, Flavius, no one noticed the blood until the other man screamed."

Neither man had any response to that.

I had tried to walk out of the bath house on my own, but it had been beyond me. Ambrose and Donuil had found me sprawled by the shallow tepid pool as I watched my own blood discolour the water. They had come at the run, bellowing for assistance, and soon the echoing chambers of the bath house were full of the clatter of running boots. I had pulled Ambrose down to me and whispered in his ear, sending both of them running to arrest the man called Ironhair, because I knew he had been behind this. I'd watched them go and felt my head fill with roaring emptiness, and then I lost all awareness.

Others had carried me here to the Infirmary, covered with blankets, and Luke had lost no time in coming to my assistance. Banishing everyone from the Infirmary save Ludmilla, Titus and Flavius, he had washed my wound with a painfully astringent solution that he told me would prevent sepsis of the cut. Then, when he was satisfied that the cut was clean, he had sewn it up—this almost painlessly, I was glad to discover—with seventeen small, carefully fashioned stitches, which he told me would have to remain in place for at least seven days. Only then had he gone to attend to my assailant, held under guard in a separate room. My wound had not been as serious as I had initially feared, and Lucanus's demeanour alone had reassured me as he worked. The incision was long but shallow, little more than skin deep in fact, so the muscles had not been damaged. The instinctual desperation with which I had sucked in my gut and arched my back had saved my life.

Now the door opened and Luke came into the room, looking directly at me.

"What did you hit him with, Cay?"

"My elbow, it was the hardest thing I had available. But I hit him clean and well, right at the top of the spine."

"You certainly did. You killed him. Now we'll never know who he was."

I tried to sit up straighter and regretted it immediately. "But he can't be dead! He was alive earlier."

"So was Popilius. I wonder who'll be next? They say death comes in threes."

I winced at the pain in my belly. "That whoreson Peter Ironhair is number three, when I get my hands on him. What in blazes is taking Ambrose so long?"

As though in answer to my question, Donuil strode through the door.

"Donuil! Did you find him?"

He shook his head and gave a short, sharp sigh. "No, we missed him. You were right, obviously. He wasted no time. Must have had someone posted either in or just outside the bath house. As soon as he knew the attempt had failed, he was gone. The guards saw him leave by the main gate with three other men, moving quickly. That was before the news of what had happened even reached the gates. We arrived there much later. I had wasted time checking his known haunts first, the places you told us to search. Stupid of me. I should have sealed the gates immediately."

I waved that aside. "Don't blame yourself for that, my friend. By your own mouth you've just confirmed that he was gone before you could have caught him. At least you found out when he left. Did you send after him?"

"Aye. Ambrose took a full squadron of troopers, and two of his own trackers. His men are bloodhounds. They'll find them."

"Good man, I know they will." I lay back then, seeking respite from the band of fire that seared across my belly, and Luke was at my side immediately, a cup of some foul-tasting brew in his hand. I drank it unwillingly and fell into a deep sleep shortly thereafter.

Luke's soporific had been potent, because by the time I awoke night had fallen and the room in which I lay was lit by several lamps that threw a dim, yellow, comfortably warm light. I made a small movement, an attempt to change position slightly, and was rewarded with a searing blast of pain across my stomach, so that I lay still from then on and dwelt only on my thoughts. My eyes closed after a while, and I lay there dozing, not asleep but merely drifting in and out of awareness, and eventually I heard Ludmilla approach my cot, recognizing her by her quick, light footsteps. For some reason, and whence the impulse came I know not, I kept my eyes closed and feigned sleep. I felt her hand cool on my forehead, and then she moved away from the bed but remained in the room. I heard her sit down, and then the silence stretched, broken only by my own breathing. I opened my eyes after a time and looked at her without moving, but she remained unaware, staring into the light of one of the lamps, her thoughts evidently far away. She was always beautiful, as I had cause to know, but here in the lamplight she was ravishing and I allowed my thoughts to drift as I drank in the pleasure of watching her.

I realized with surprise that I felt neither rancour nor jealousy over the situation that had sprung into being between her and Ambrose. How could I have, I asked myself. What could be more natural than that this beautiful woman and my beloved brother should be attracted each to the other? But what of your dream? a small voice asked within my mind, and I smiled as the answer to that question came to me immediately, filling my chest with gladness and relief.

In the dream, Ludmilla had held up to me Aunt Luceiia's silver mirror, and I had seen myself reflected therein. But what I had seen was my mirror image—my alter ego—Ambrose my brother. I myself had been an eagle at the time, as witnessed by my talons striking the silver surface when I reached for it. Ludmilla had not shown me myself as reason for her happiness, but a semblance of me that she could love with ease, and I recalled the thrill of freedom as my beating wings bore me aloft again from the place where I had almost fallen to the ground in trying to touch her.

Now other footsteps approached the sick room and as they came, Ludmilla rose to her feet. I closed my eyes again before she could notice that I was awake, but kept them open the merest slit, so that I could see who came.

It was Ambrose, and he froze in the entrance as soon as his eyes lit upon her. They stood mute, staring at each other, each afraid to speak. Then Ambrose nodded, his face flushed with pleasure and constraint, and spoke in a low voice.

"Lady. How is he?"

Ludmilla, too, spoke softly, her voice barely more than a whisper. "He is well. Asleep. Lucanus gave him a sleeping draught against the pain."

"Is his wound bad?"

"No, merely superficial. He was fortunate. Lucanus stitched him up and he should mend completely within the week. My name is Ludmilla."

I saw him nod. "Ludmilla . . . what?"

"Sir?"

"Ludmilla what? Have you no other name?"

"Oh, I see." I could tell she was smiling. "No Roman name in the style you would recognize. I am of the house of Pendragon, cousin to Uther. Ludmilla Pendragon, then, would be my Roman appellation."

"Ludmilla Pendragon . . . I am Ambrose Britannicus, half-brother to Caius Merlyn."

"No! Had I not heard you say so I should never have guessed." I heard pure raillery in her whispered tone, and so did Ambrose, but he mistook it for scorn. I opened my eyes fully and saw him flush even deeper.

"Forgive me, Lady," he said, appalled. "Have I offended you?"

Ludmilla was instantly contrite and moved towards him quickly, hand outstretched. "No, that was cruel of me. I did not mean to tease you, but did you honestly think I could be in any doubt of who you are? The resemblance between the two of you has been the major topic of conversation in Camulod since the first moment you were seen. Shall I wake Commander Merlyn? Do you wish to speak to him?"

"No! Not yet." He smiled, now, gaining confidence. "I would much rather speak to you first, before anyone else appears. How is it that I could be here for weeks and not have seen you?"

No raillery now. Ludmilla had evidently been asking herself the same question and her voice betrayed that. "I don't know," she whispered.

"Would you not at least have come, through curiosity, to see this marvel of comparison?"

"There is no comparison, but no, I would not."

"I do not understand. No comparison?"

"Please, Commander Ambrose, be seated." Her voice was gentle and Ambrose sat down obediently, his eyes never leaving her for an instant as she moved to stand closer to him. "I have many duties," she went on, "and in these last weeks they seemed to swarm upon me. I heard all about the marvel of your resemblance to Commander Merlyn, but I know Commander Merlyn well, by sight, and I find him amiable and admirable."

"But?" Ambrose leaned forward, an elbow on one knee. "You did not speak the word, but my ears heard a 'but' in there, somewhere."

Ludmilla giggled gently, something I could not remember having heard her do before.

"Your ears are keen . . . Let me see, then. How shall I put this? I cannot, without sounding improper and immodest, but I will in spite of that . . . Commander Merlyn is a wondrous man and everything a woman looks for in a man is there in him. For me, however, there is a blindness involved. I find him amiable and admirable; as I have said, but he holds no *wonder* for me. Do you understand that? I feel towards him as I would towards a brother. And therefore, when the talk was all of you and how much you two were alike, I found it no great sacrifice to dedicate what time I had to my duties. They were pressing and necessary, whereas the simple meeting of another amiable brother seemed to have no urgency. Does that make sense? I simply did not know . . ."

A pause of heartbeats, during which I decided it was time I sprang awake, but before I could do anything, Ambrose asked his next question. "Did not know what, Lady?"

"How different two identicals could be."

I coughed and spoke, "Ambrose," and in an instant they were both beside me, Ludmilla taking my right hand to feel my pulse, and Ambrose seizing the other to wring it heartily. Several moments of activity went by before I could ask the question that superseded all others in my mind.

"Did you catch Ironhair?"

"No, Brother. We caught his companions, three of them, but he was not with them."

"What do you mean? Where was he, then?"

He shook his head. "We don't know. The other three swore he left them as soon as they reached the bottom of the road down from the gates. He swung off to the north, they said, leaving them to make their own way south and east to Isca and thence to the coast and Gaul."

"Where are they now, these three? Did you bring them back with you?"

"No, they are on their way to their destination."

"What?" I attempted to sit up and merely managed to drive the breath from myself in a whoosh of pain.

Ambrose waited until I had recaptured my breathing, then resumed. "They told me they did not know him well, that they had met him only days earlier, him and one other, on the way to Camulod. They themselves had come to deliver a cargo of wine, ordered by our quartermasters this time last year. Ironhair rejoined them as they were preparing to leave, during the funeral or shortly after it, and rode with them from the fort. I believed their story, and did not interfere with them any further."

"What do you mean you believed them? Why should you believe them? And why permit them to go on?"

He looked at me wide-eyed, his eyebrows high on his forehead. "I mean I believed them, Caius, nothing more than that. They had made no attempt to flee from us, or hide. When we approached them, they were prepared to fight, as anyone would be on meeting a force of strangers on the road, but once they saw who we were, they offered us no contest and were courteous and open with us. I believed them implicitly. They spoke the truth. I have met liars before, you know."

There was nothing I could say to that without sounding completely boorish. I let go my breath with a sigh. "Aye, you're right. I had no right to snap at you. I am angry Ironhair escaped, that is all."

"He will turn up again, sooner or later, Cay, and if he does, you'll have him. And even if he should never appear again, you will benefit by that; all of us will."

"Aye. What hour of night is it?"

He grinned at me. "Late. We returned some hours ago, but I met Luke and he told me you were a prisoner of Morpheus and would remain that way for hours, so I bathed and had some food."

"Good. I hope your bath was uninterrupted?"

"No one attacked me."

"Excellent." I sighed again, uncomfortable with my injuries. "Ludmilla, did Lucanus leave any more of that foul brew he fed me? I'll never get back to sleep without it."

She had moved away while Ambrose and I were speaking, but now she reappeared, holding a cup. "Yes, Commander, I have it here." She held it for me while I gagged it down, and then she and Ambrose returned to their fascination with each other. Neither of them was any more aware than I was of when I fell asleep again.

IX

WE HAD RECEIVED no further news of Peter Ironhair by the time we eventually left Camulod nine days later. He had disappeared completely, swallowed up by the forests that stretched unbroken in every direction beyond our fields, and I was forced to come to terms with the fact that there was nothing I could do to remedy that, other than to keep searchers in the field in the increasingly forlorn hope they might stumble upon his hiding-place. I called them off after a wasted week. In the interim, however, I had mended quickly enough, although I bitterly resented the enforced idleness. Luke had estimated the healing time to the day.

I had put the time, which otherwise would have been lost, to good use, nevertheless, even though it was to be years before I saw the benefits of my days of convalescence. I had begun with impatience, thinking fretfully about the child now held in Eire, and what he would mean to my great-aunt and to all of us in Camulod in the years to come. From that point, I began to think more analytically about what the future might hold for him, and that led me to a train of thought that was completely new to me: the problems any and all children must face, growing to maturity in the bubbling broth of the Britain that was forming now and changing from day to day, sinking towards anarchy and chaos. Those problems would be particularly enhanced when the child in question was blessed, or encumbered, with the blood that flowed in young Arthur's veins. By the time my thoughts had clarified along those lines, I was in a fever of impatience to discuss the matters in my mind with someone, any one of my closest friends. But Ambrose was patrolling again, Donuil had his own duties and Lucanus was Lucanus, constantly immersed in his surgical responsibilities. I spent most of that frustrating week alone.

Lucanus came bustling into my room, finally, on the afternoon of the eighth day and removed the stitches that had bound me. It was the day before we were again scheduled to leave, and he examined my wound closely, peering at it from a handsbreadth away and poking and stretching the newly formed scar tissue with his fingers before professing himself well enough satisfied with the healing process, but warning me of the dangers of violent movement for a few weeks. Riding did not qualify as violent movement, he assured me. Fighting most certainly did.

I glanced at Donuil, who had also come to visit me and was standing by my bedside when Luke said that, but he smiled and shook his head, holding up his hands, palms towards me. "No danger of violence around me, Commander," he said, his native lilt strongly pronounced. "It's Eire we're going to, a sweet and pleasant land. Of course, we still have to get there from here, so I'll make no promises about that stretch of the journey."

"How will you dress?" Luke's question surprised me.

"What do you mean?"

"I mean will you ride armoured? You'll be but a small party, in a strange land. Armour might attract unwelcome attention."

"That's a risk we'll have to take." I looked at Donuil. "What d'you think, Donuil?"

"Of course we'll ride armoured." He sounded indignant. "We can be sure of our welcome at my father's hearth, but any attention we attract before we reach his lands could be unwelcome. Better armoured against it than not."

I spoke again to Luke. "Why would you ask that?"

He sniffed. "Because, my friend, you are still an invalid, that's why. Look at yourself. Your belly's still bare and the holes made by the stitches are still open. They'll itch, probably, as they heal. You'll have a frustrating job trying to scratch them beneath your breastplate, but that suits me well, because the worst thing you can do is scratch them."

"So be it," I said, affecting a sniff of disgust. "I shall ride armed and itching, and I shall heal without complaint."

The following morning, having taken leave of everyone including my great-aunt, who was already impatient for my return with her great-grandson, I met with my travelling companions in front of the stables. We were a small party, but a strong one. Nine trusted men, including the centurion Rufio, who had become Donuil's shadow, and two trainees to care for our extra horses, would accompany Donuil and me on our journey, and we would act as escort to our surgeon Lucanus as he rode, with his wagonload of supplies and gifts, to visit his friend and colleague Mordechai Emancipatus. Luke and I had decided that we would say nothing of his destination, other than that he rode to visit an old friend. Leprosy was an illness that no one spoke of lightly. The very mention of it brought terror leaping into the throats of ordinary folk, as I had discovered for myself.

I was surprised to find Ambrose waiting with the group, mounted on the massive chestnut gelding he had chosen for himself, and watching me with a smile as I approached. I greeted everyone and hauled myself up into my saddle, turning immediately to Lucanus who sat on the wagon bench, the reins gathered loosely in his hands. He winked at me gravely and I smiled, turning back to Ambrose.

"Good morning, Brother. I didn't expect to see you again so soon after our farewells."

He grinned. "I decided to ride with you for a few miles. It's a beautiful morning, and my horse here has not had a stretch in three days. I'll ride with you as far as the main road and then give him his head on the way back."

"Good," I said. "Let's go." I gave the signal to move out and the small crowd of onlookers who had gathered to see us off parted to let us pass. Lucanus went first with the wagon, and we fell in behind him, and I was aware of a deep feeling of well-being, released as I now was from all Camulodian responsibilities for the duration of our journey.

It seemed I was not the only one to feel that way. I chose to savour the drifting of my own thoughts, and I found that no one in our party showed any inclination to do otherwise. We rode in companionable silence for more than a mile, until the hill of Camulod behind us had been screened from us by the trees of the forest that now stretched unbroken ahead of us to the main north road. I had glanced at my brother from time to time, expecting him to be the one who broke our silence, since he was unaffected by any feelings of departure, but he rode as wrapped up in his own thoughts as the rest of us and appeared completely unaware that no one had spoken. Finally he straightened in his saddle and looked up wonderingly at the massive trees beneath which we were riding. I happened to be looking at him as he did so, and my curiosity had the better of me.

"What are you thinking, Brother?" I asked him, nudging my horse closer to his.

He looked at me and smiled, shaking his head. "Merely how peaceful it is here. We could be miles and miles from the nearest signs of habitation, and yet I know there are fields and farmsteads all around us, hidden by this wall of trees on either side."

I glanced at the forest lining the road. "Hardly a wall," I demurred, "but they stretch a good hundred paces to right and left, most of the way from here to the main road. There are spots where they run far deeper."

"Why is that, Cay? Why have these trees never been cut and the ground cleared? The fields on either side are fertile and rich and the land would have more value, surely, if it were given to crops?"

"Several reasons," I answered. "All of them attributable to the earliest of the Britannicus family to settle this land. I suppose the main reason originally was to provide a screen between the agricultural lands and the main road, and then later to maintain one between visiting dignitaries and the sight of honest labour on either side, but there's also the matter of the trees themselves. Look at them. They are all prime: elm, beech, chestnut and oak; not only decorative, but good building materials, and hence too valuable to destroy merely to clear land. When the Villa Britannicus was new, no one ever perceived that there might be a need for more farming land. This was hunting territory. That's why there's no heavy underbrush; it's all burned out regularly to leave the grazing free for deer and other animals."

"Are you serious?"

"Of course I am. Why should that surprise you? Don't you do that where you come from?"

He shook his head, a rueful grin twisting his face. "Burn out the underbrush? No, that would take forethought, and the luxury of time to hunt anything other than raiders. I suppose it might have been done, long ago, but if it was there's no memory of it. We have forests aplenty, but they grow on their own, without help from us, other than an accidental burning or two." He broke off and looked at me. "Of course, you've never been to Lindum, have you?"

"No, Verulamium marked the northern limit of my progress through Britain."

"Hmm. Well, it's very different from this area. Not nearly so ... what's the word I'm looking for? Settled is not accurate; Lindum has been there forever. I suppose established would be a better way to put it. This area was wealthy and established long before it became Camulod. The villas and estates around here are old and magnificent. We have villas around Lindum, of course, and several of them are quite large, but nothing there, no aspect of the wealth they display, comes even close to matching the luxuries you take for granted here."

I laughed aloud. "Well, you're fortunate to live here in that case, as are the rest of us."

"I'm aware of that . . ." His voice faded, as though his thinking had changed direction, and then he resumed in an entirely new, much quieter tone. "Caius . . . I have something to ask that I would not care for others to hear. Will you ride ahead with me?"

"Of course." I kicked my horse to a canter and guided it around Luke's wagon, then kicked it again to a full gallop, closely followed by Ambrose, so that we soon outstripped our companions. For more than a mile we galloped, giving our mounts their heads until the first flush of pleasurable exercise began to pall on them and we reined in, slowing them down again to a walk.

"Well," I said, grinning. "You want to ask me about Ludmilla, so ask away, although I don't know what you expect me to say in response."

The fall of his jaw was ludicrous, and my own pleasure at his discomfort was heightened by the elation caused by my awareness that I had not, since the first moment of divination in Luke's Infirmary, experienced a single pang of envy or jealousy concerning him and Ludmilla. "You *knew* what I was going to ask you? How could you *know*? I had no idea myself I was going to ask you until the moment arrived."

"Come, Brother," I laughed. "Haven't you heard the tales about Merlyn? They say I have magical powers, and divination is the least of them." I was not at all inclined to tell him I had witnessed their first meeting, and thereafter listened shamelessly to their whisperings while I supposedly slept.

"Aye, I have heard them, but I had thought them idle talk based on your friendship with Druids."

His answer brought my head around to face him sharply. There was a tone in his voice I had not expected. "What does that mean? You sound as though you half believe them."

He looked straight back at me. "I think I do. I mean, you have just told me something that you could not possibly know. How could you, when I did not know myself? And besides that," he added, after a long pause, "I remember the way you explained my mother's actions to me, and the truth in your voice that convinced me you were right. It was impossible for you to have known the truth of that, when the actions you described took place almost before you were born." He was half frowning, half smiling. "You said yourself, at the time, you didn't know whence your explanation came."

It was true. When first we met, I had reconstructed his mother's reasons for abandoning him in childhood, using nothing more than intuition to connect the few facts I knew to be true with the description I had gleaned of Ambrose's mother and her circumstances at the time when she had met and availed herself of our temporarily incapacitated father, in her great desire to provide her husband with a son. Neither Ambrose nor I would ever prove the accuracy of my reconstruction, but it had *felt* correct.

"Oh, for God's sake, Ambrose!" I snapped now. "I was guessing, that's all, guessing predicated upon some self-evident truths. And the same thing happened here! You are my brother, and a new brother, at that. I watch you closely all the time, now that you've come back into my life. It took no sorcery to see that you were smitten with Ludmilla and she with you from the first moment the two of you met. You have had eyes only for each other ever since, but do you think the rest of us have lost ours?" He was still staring at me, unconvinced, as I rushed on. "You had that solemn look about you, all at once, and wanted no one else to overhear your secret. What other secret could you have in the space of these short weeks? Ludmilla and I are almost related, through Uther, and she is one of Aunt Luceiia's treasures. Of course you would wish to ask me about her and about what you should do. That is only natural. No magic and no sorcery in guessing that. That should be apparent in what I say hereafter. For I have no idea what to tell you, or what you should do, other than to follow your instincts. Ask Ludmilla what to do! She probably knows far better than any of us, anyway. Marry the woman, but wait until Donuil and Luke and I are back in Camulod. You can do that, I hope?"

He was staring at me, only half hearing what I had said, I was sure. "Others know?" he asked, after a short silence, his voice filled with wonder.

"Only those who are not blind and care to look. Don't worry about it, man. Why should you care what anyone thinks, save you and your love? Such things happen, and it is natural."

His face broke into a smile and it was like the sun shining through a break in heavy clouds. "She may not have me," he said in a voice begging to be contradicted.

"She will have you, Brother. Of that I have not the slightest doubt. And if you label *that* prediction sorcery, I will lose respect for you."

"How can you be so sure?"

I had to smile at his innocence. "Because I have seen her look at you, stonehead! We are not discussing unrequited love here. This is no tragic tale! The woman is as besotted with you as you are with her."

"She is? God! I thank you for that news! I will ask her tonight—today, as soon as I return." His face fell. "Aunt Luceiia will be furious."

"Ambrose, why would you even think such a thing? Luceiia will be delighted. She has not known you for more than a month, but already she thinks as much of you as she does of me. She will be delighted at the thought of such a marriage, binding the families of Pendragon and Britannicus even closer. Don't forget, her own daughter was the first of our family to marry into Pendragon blood." I cleared my throat. "Now, having done all in my power to make you feel better about the fate that awaits you, may I ask you to speak about something else before we rejoin the others?"

He looked at me, eyebrows raised. "Certainly. What?"

"This nonsense of my being magical, a sorcerer. What exactly have you heard?"

"Oh, that." He flushed, slightly embarrassed, as was I. "Well, nothing, *exactly*. I overheard one of the soldiers saying something about you one day, and I asked Donuil about it afterward. Donuil would tell me nothing, but when I pressed him he advised me to speak to some of the old-timers, so I approached the Legates Titus and Flavius."

"And? What did they tell you?"

"Nothing concrete. Certainly nothing to indicate that any of the whispered stories might be true. Titus told me that they had all arisen from an incident concerning the woman who became your wife, Cassandra. Something about her disappearance from a guarded room."

"I see. Did he tell you how it happened?"

"No, only that something mysterious had happened and had grown into a kind of soldiers' legend. He assured me that the magical mutterings were nonsense, but understandable in the face of soldiers' boredom and their tendency to gossip among themselves, fostered and fed by the mysterious, unsolved nature of the event."

"Hmm," I said, arriving at a momentous decision. "Tell me, Ambrose, do you ever dream?"

He grinned at me. "All the time. Nowadays I dream of Ludmilla."

"Those are daydreams. I meant, do you dream at night?"

"Of course. I understood you and I meant what I said. I dream frequently, almost every night."

I looked at him in surprise. "Do you, by God? Do your dreams frighten you?"

Now it was his turn to laugh. "Frighten me? Of course not. I usually can't remember them by the time I wake up, but they certainly don't frighten me."

"Then they don't come true?"

He reined his horse to a standstill. "What?" My horse continued walking and eventually he had to kick his to catch up with me, talking to the back of my head. "Caius, you are serious, aren't you? No, my dreams don't come true, except in the case of Ludmilla, and I'm not even sure of that. Do yours come true?"

"On occasion. That's why dreams frighten me." I did not look at him as I spoke the words and he fell into silence, riding beside me. Finally I turned to him again. "Look, Brother, I have never told anyone what I am about to tell you now, so listen quietly, please, without interrupting. It is not an easy tale to tell.

"The tale of Cassandra's disappearance is simply explained. Cassandra was never in that guarded room. It was a trick to protect her life, since I did not know whom I could trust, other than a few close friends who helped me smuggle her away from danger and conceal her. It suited my sense of humour at the time to be mysterious, but that single incident has now grown, as you say, into soldiers' legend. On other occasions, I have enjoyed good fortune, mainly in war, that might seem to be beyond the normal fortunes man is heir to. Fuel was added to the tales each time. Add that to the facts that I can read and write and have a gift for languages, and that I trained in boyhood with the Druid Celts, and I am set beyond the understanding of many who had none of these advantages. Now they whisper, and there are some who believe, that I have magical powers. It is all nonsense. And yet, I have a power that terrifies me and sets me truly apart from ordinary men and women; a cursed power of which I have never spoken to anyone. For years I fought the knowledge of it in myself, trying to make believe it was not so. But then, one day, I could no longer deny the truth of it, and now I have to live with it and with the terror of it. I have dreams, Ambrose, and all too frequently they do come true and they are seldom pleasant. I have had them all my life, despite the fact that I abhor and would happily abjure them."

I pulled my horse to a stop and so did he, and we sat staring at each other for long moments. "Well," I asked him eventually, "what have you to say to that?"

"Tell me about these dreams."

For the next hour, until we reached the Roman road and stopped to wait for the others to catch up, I told him everything I could recall of every prophetic dream that had ever harrowed me, including the deaths of Equus, Picus our father and Uther, and the apparition of Ygraine before I ever saw her. When I had finished speaking he sat silent for a long time, and then he asked me a surprising question.

"The child, Arthur. Did you dream of him?"

I thought about that for a moment. "Of him? No. But I dreamed something with him, when we lay asleep in the birney, off the Cornish coast. At least, I think I did. Not a dream, perhaps, but a fragment."

"What was it?"

"A sword, standing in a stone. That's all I can remember."

"A sword? Standing *in* a stone, not on one?"

"No. In it. Point down. I don't remember it well, but I do recall that."

"Was it Excalibur?"

"It may have been, but I don't really know. I think I would have recognised Excalibur. Why do you ask that?"

"Because Excalibur came from a stone. The Skystone."

"Hmm. That had not occurred to me. Now that you mention it, of course, it becomes obvious. That's probably the explanation for what I dreamed. As I said, it was strange, and only a fragmentary thing, but it was not frightening, like all the others."

He sat gazing at me with narrowed eyes, his mind obviously elsewhere, but before I could ask him what he was thinking I heard the jingle of harness back along the path and the first of our companions came into view, riding now ahead of Luke and his wagon. Ambrose flicked a glance back towards them and leaned closer to me.

"We must talk more about these dreams, Brother, but I doubt if you should fear them. I believe they occur, and I believe they are prophetic, but I cannot think of them as being omens of evil, not in you. They come to you for a purpose, and there is power in them. You must learn to use that power."

Our companions were upon us by that time and I could do no more than nod my agreement before they joined us, loud and brash and gay now with their new-won freedom. Ambrose left us there, by the side of the great road, after wishing us well on our journey and we watched him until he had disappeared, waving back over his head as he put his spurs to his big horse.

"Well, my friends, we won't get to Eire by sitting here." We swung north and left Camulod behind us.

Donuil's remark about attracting unwelcome attention became reality far sooner than any of us expected. It occurred some time in the course of our second day of travel, although we remained unaware of the fact until after we had made camp and eaten a hot meal. We had built our encampment in the southwest corner of a long-abandoned Roman route camp, in the shelter of two corner walls that looked as strong as the day they were built, centuries earlier, and we had posted two sentries. Mine was to have been the third watch, and I was on my way to sleep when Rufio, Donuil's centurion mentor, approached me casually and threw an arm around my shoulders. I knew immediately that something was wrong, because none of my men, particularly Rufio, who held me in some awe, would have dared actually to touch me in the normal way of things. There was no rule against their touching me; it was simply the way things were. Forewarned by his direct approach, I

betrayed no surprise and as we walked together towards my tent he told me
that we were being watched. He had seen movement in the bushes around
the walls, but had no idea of how many men were out there.

Careful now to do nothing that would signal our awareness of being observed, I turned back and moved to where Donuil had already stood up from
the fire. He, too, had noticed the way Rufio approached me. I briefed him
quickly and then quietly, moving unconcernedly, we alerted the others and
unobtrusively doubled the guard before retiring as we would have normally.
Few of us had any sleep that night, lying awake and waiting for the alarm,
but nothing happened.

When daylight came, we broke camp routinely and moved out, having
seen no sign of anything unusual. Rufio, however, found the fresh tracks of
six men in the area where he had seen the shadowed movements the previous
night. We rode on, wary and alert, our weapons close to hand. All day we
rode steadily, though not in haste, stopping only to relieve ourselves, and as
evening approached we made camp again, this time some distance from the
road, on a grassy knoll protected on three sides by a fair-sized, swift-flowing
river. We ate a cold supper from our saddlebags that night, since hunting
was out of the question. It would have been folly for any man to ride off
alone to hunt for meat. Again, we were watched but unmolested and again
Rufio found the same signs of six men come morning. This time he called
me over to look at how two particular pairs of footprints identified the group,
whoever they were. The first belonged either to a giant or to a man whose
feet would appear grotesquely large; the second to either a child or a dwarf.
Lucanus had been watching me and he called to me as I went to mount my
horse after examining the tracks in the soft earth no more than twenty paces
from where we had lain.

"Cay, come, ride with me for a spell."

When I had tethered my horse to the back of his wagon, I pulled my
bow stave and quiver from their wrappings and clambered up onto the bench
beside him. He clucked at his horses and slapped the reins, and we moved
forward with a lurch.

"Same people as before?" I grunted an affirmative, my mind still upon
the disparity in size between the two pairs of unusual footprints. "Well," he
urged me. "What do you think? Will they attack us?"

I grunted a negative this time and busied myself with stringing my bow
before answering him properly, bracing the end of the stave against the
wagon's wood frame and bending the bow with my foot. Strung, the weapon
was formidable. I pulled it, feeling my shoulder muscles flex and harden
against the tension of the compound arc. "I doubt it," I answered him then.
"We are fourteen, eleven of us armoured soldiers, and they are six. So long
as we stay together we'll be safe enough. They're probably hoping we'll split
up, so they can take us piecemeal." I propped the bow beside me, leaning it
against the bench, within easy reach.

Lucanus was looking at me quizzically. "You don't think they know we
know they're there?" His voice held mild disbelief.

"No, I don't." I selected an arrow from the quiver on the seat beside me
and held it up to my eye, squinting along it. It was straight and true. "Think
about it, Luke. If they suspected we were aware of them, then they would

know we'd stay together, safe in our numbers. Knowing that, they wouldn't be here now. They'd have gone looking for easier prey."

"Hmm. So what d'you intend to do about them?"

"Nothing, except hope they'll give up and go away. I certainly don't intend to fight them if I don't have to. But I'm worried about you. How far are we from your friend's settlement?"

"I don't really know, but we'll know when we come to the inn called the Red Dragon. I expect we should be there by tomorrow afternoon."

"Good, but after that you have ten miles or so to ride west alone, while we keep going north. Let's hope our friends out there become impatient before then and disappear. Otherwise we'll have to escort you all the way to where you're going. Can't let you ride off alone with a wagon full of goods and six thieves waiting for you to do exactly that, can I?"

Instead of answering, he surprised me by changing the subject. "How d'you feel about Ludmilla nowadays, Caius?"

I absorbed the non sequitur and merely grinned, knowing what was coming. "Better than I have in a long time," I answered him. "Now that she is completely besotted with Ambrose, and he with her, I seldom think about her, other than as a future sister."

He blinked, hiding his surprise almost completely, and then he smiled. "I didn't think you knew."

"Come on, Luke! I'd have to be blind and a fool not to be aware of what happened the first time they saw each other. I was there, if you recall."

"Oh I recall, very well. I simply was not sure that you had seen it . . . or recognised it might be more accurate. I must say you seem to have taken it in stride." He was still smiling, a gentle, wistful little smile.

"I took it in gratitude, my friend, with profound, almost abject relief. The moment I saw what my eyes beheld between the two of them, I recognised the nature of my own discomfort over the young woman. My attraction was lust, pure and simple, alloyed with a modicum of fear and doomed by feelings of guilt."

"Hmm." He busied himself with his reins, giving himself time to think, and I used the interval to glance around us, noting our line of march and scanning the terrain on both sides of the road for signs of our unwanted escort. The countryside through which we were passing offered open, natural stretches of rolling meadow with scattered copses of tall trees. High up on our left I saw a solitary stag, his magnificent antlers sweeping along his back as he stood motionless, gazing down at us, and I stifled the immediate urge to go after him, taking comfort instead from the implicit assurance that no other humans ranged the woods between him and us. I turned to look at the other side of the road, but nothing moved there, either, that I could see. In front of me, Donuil and Rufio rode with two others, all four of them alert and watchful, their heads moving constantly. I checked over my shoulder and saw the two boys riding placidly behind us with the extra horses, and behind them our other five outriders.

"I understand the lust and, to a lesser extent, the guilt, which I believe is nonsense, but the reason for fear eludes me."

I had almost forgotten that Luke had been absorbing my last comment. Now I looked at him, grinning ruefully. "Age, Luke," I said. "I'm growing old."

"Horse turds! You're what? Thirty-two?"

"Almost. I was barely twenty-nine when we rode off to meet Germanus at Verulamium. That was three years and more ago, and I lost more than two of those years."

"Good God! It doesn't seem that long ago. Anyway, your fear of growing old is ludicrous."

"Was ludicrous," I corrected him. "It no longer applies."

"How so?"

"I mean that my fear, if fear it was, came from the threat I perceived at the time of being unable to attract a woman, because of my age. It was irrational, I can see that clearly now, but not before the scales fell from my eyes. And with that realisation came the thought that I must speak with you more carefully, and at much greater length, about the celibacy you espouse. Since then, there hasn't been enough time to mention it to you. Now there is."

"I see. And why is it so urgent, suddenly, that you and I should speak of celibacy?"

"Because I'm curious. I want to learn more about it."

"In what sense? There's nothing obscure or arcane about it ... all you have to do is remain sexually continent. Sexual continence constitutes celibacy. It's quite straightforward."

I felt myself bridling at his tone, reacting to the faint hostility I sensed, and I had to make an effort to keep my own voice dispassionate. "I know that, Luke," I responded, willing my face to form a rueful little smile. "But when we talked of it last time, you spoke about it as a tool to self-mastery."

"I had been drinking far too much on that occasion, as had you."

"I know that, too, but I also know the old saw about truth emerging from wine. You meant what you were saying that night and it fascinated me."

"*After* you had decided you could not have Ludmilla ..."

"No! ... well, yes, I suppose that's true ... but there was more to it than that, Luke. You planted a seed in my mind that night, and I've been aware of it ever since. The episode with Ludmilla, a one-sided thing, I know, was ..." I searched my mind for the correct word and settled upon a compromise. "It was a sign, I suppose, of something that has been bothering me, a feeling of ... I think dissatisfaction's the closest I could come to describing it." I could hear my own frustration.

" 'Symptom' is the word you were looking for. Your feelings for Ludmilla were a symptom of an ailment." His face flickered in a grin and his voice became softer. "What kind of ailment is this, Merlyn? A fear of becoming impotent? That happens to all men, I'm told, with time."

"No, it's not that, Luke, that doesn't bother me at all, one way or the other, although I'm potent enough ... My body's fit enough, and the urge is still there often enough to keep me aware of it. No, it's not that at all. It's my mind, my feelings, my sense of who I *am* that's troubling me."

"Hmm." He looked away from me, back to his plodding horses. "That sounds troublesome enough. Don't you know who you are, Caius Merlyn Britannicus?"

I had to laugh. "Yes, my friend, I know who I am, as well as you do, and I can see that I am not explaining myself very well, so let me try again. Bear with me for a moment."

I gathered my thoughts and tried to focus them. Finally I began again. "I still might not get this right," I said, "but it's important to me. Ludmilla, as you acknowledge, was a symptom of something. My difficulty is defining what that 'something' entails, but I know it has to do with my memories of Cassandra and the feelings I still have for her in spite of the fact that she has been dead for years. I lost the main part of those years, so to me, the loss of her is still something new and painful. Does that make sense?"

He nodded, not looking at me. "Completely."

"Good, I'm glad to hear you say that. But don't you see wherein lie my feelings of guilt?"

His concurrence emerged more slowly this time. "I do, from your perspective."

"Thank you, but since there is no one else who can influence what and how I feel inside, there can be no other relevant perspective, can there?" He did not even attempt to respond to that, so I continued. "So Cassandra—I can never really think of her as Deirdre—and my memories of her, fresh as they are, are a dominant force in how I think and behave . . . Tell me when you think I start to make no sense . . . My body has been without her for years, longer than might normally be required to forget her, I suspect, but my mind is struggling as though with a recent bereavement. And the conclusion I have reached is that I wish to remain faithful to the memory I hold of her. In my lusting for Ludmilla, I was aware of a betrayal of Cassandra." I hurried on, before he could be tempted to interrupt me. "I *know*, at least, a part of me knows, that is nonsensical, Luke, but it's true, nevertheless. And the fact remains that, as I am today, and with the way I feel inside, I have no desire, not the slightest, to come to know another woman. My body does, from time to time, but that is ephemeral and purely physical, and therein lies the reason for my interest, not in mere celibacy, but in the manner— the confident and assured manner—in which you spoke of celibacy as a powerful means to a particular end. You said it was an aid to concentration, to knowledge, to self-mastery and self-awareness, and to power over one's baser instincts. You were describing a power, Luke; a permanent and enduring power over one's self, leading inevitably to betterment and fulfillment. That intrigued me at the time, and since then, after long hours of thought, it has become more and more alluring. This is a knowledge I want to possess." I paused, then finished almost in a whisper. "But I suspect it's not to be achieved by simple abstinence."

He cleared his throat explosively and spat, something I had rarely seen him do, following the result over the wheel of the wagon with his eyes. Then he sighed deeply. I waited, feeling no impatience, knowing he was concentrating.

"So," he resumed after a spell. "You're right. Abstinence alone is not enough. There is also a requirement for discipline and training, as there is in all things worth while. But the training requires a lifetime of commitment and concentration from a very early age." He left that hanging in the air between us.

"How old were you when you began this training?"

"Eighteen, nineteen, when I first became aware of the phenomenon, twenty-something when I began to apply myself to learning it. Twenty-four, I believe."

"So I've lost eight years. That's all that means."

He glanced sideways at me. "That is almost a decade, Merlyn. Most healthy men have only five or six of those, and by your own admission yours are more than halfway gone." He stopped and then hitched himself sideways, to look directly at me. "Without evasion of any kind, without reservations, give me a quick and honest answer to this question: Why should this . . . this *condition* . . . suddenly become important to you?"

The question was a test, I knew, and I also knew that I had no time to think about my answer. "Philosophy," I said. I watched his right eyebrow arch.

"Philosophy?" His lips stretched slowly into a smile containing more than a little incredulity. "You will pardon me, I hope, my friend, for smiling at the thought, but I have never seen you as a philosopher."

"Nor could you have. I have never been one, and perhaps even now that is the wrong word. Philosophically speaking, I have come to believe that I am here on earth for one sole purpose, and thus it behoved me to exert all my energies towards the achievement of that purpose with devotion and single-mindedness. Sexual abstinence might help me to achieve my purpose, but would entail distractions . . . Celibacy, on the other hand, as I have understood you, is something that may be learned and practised to a higher end than mere self-denial."

He was still looking at me, one knee hitched up now between us on the wagon bench. "You have my complete attention, Caius. What is this single purpose you have defined?"

"The child, Arthur."

He blinked at me, saying nothing, and then, when he saw that I had said all I was going to say, he coughed, clearing his throat gently. "Forgive me, my friend, for seeming so obtuse. The child Arthur . . . ? What about him?"

"He is my purpose for being here, alive." I could see that Luke was completely mystified. "He is my responsibility," I went on. "He holds the essence of the Dream dreamed by my grandfather and Publius Varrus. Surely you see that?"

"No . . . But I can see that *you* see it. You forget I am not as familiar as you are with this dream of which you speak. I've heard you speak of it before, but never at any great length, and never in detail. Enlighten me, please."

"I will. I've been thinking about little else these past eight days." I began immediately, and he listened in absorbed silence as I told him about the vision of my ancestors, how they dreamed of resurrecting the greatness that had once been Rome, the great Republic, here upon this island of Britain, and how they had established Camulod as the first bastion of survival in the face of the chaos that would follow hard on the heels of Rome's desertion of Britain. When I had finished, he looked at me astutely.

"Uther was a king," he said. "His son, the child Arthur, may follow him into kingship one day. Is that your wish?" I nodded, and he smiled. "Kingship, my friend, the regal state, sits ill with the spirit of republicanism. The two are immiscible."

"No, Luke, not so." I had been through this matter in my own mind already. "On the surface, I will grant, the two seem at odds, and they are incompatible by definition. But what I am talking about now is not the essence of a republic, or of kingship, other than in the purely nominal sense. What I am propounding to you here is the difference between darkness and light, between civilization and barbarism, between chaos and order, between anarchy and . . ."

"Monarchy," he supplied the word I had been seeking.

"Monarchy. Yes." I felt deflated.

"Kingship."

I shook my head, impatient now with what I saw as sophistry. "Not merely kingship, Luke. I see it as leadership—the offer of enlightened leadership by one man: order and decency and literacy and justice and civility and all the things that make life worth living."

"Ah, I see. Enlightened despotism!" All of his sophisticated, Roman-bred distrust of the mere notion of kings was there in his voice.

"Damnation! How can I make you see what I mean?" He waited, saying nothing. "For four hundred years, this country was at peace, wealthy and prosperous under the *Pax Romana*. It was Britain, one Province, divided into several parts for administrative purposes, but those parts no more than sections of a complete entity. It had one set of laws and one system of government. It was united and its citizens were prosperous and content, and it was peaceful until shortly before the end of Rome's presence. That era ended the year that I was born. What have we now, in Britain? Within my lifetime we have seen the growth of Camulod, an enclave of sanity, and we have Vortigern, king in Northumbria and civilized enough, save that he has had to import aliens to help him hold his lands. We also had Lot, king in Cornwall, and Derek, king in Ravenglass, and Uther Pendragon, king in Cambria. How many other kings are in this land today? Only God knows. I, certainly, have no idea, but I suspect there may be dozens, and perhaps even scores or hundreds. All kings, Luke, and all supreme in their own petty realms, ruling by force and whim and whatever other methods take their fancy. Derek of Ravenglass is no arbiter of enlightenment; nor, God knows, was Gulrhys Lot, nor even Uther, rest his soul. These men are not kings, Luke, they are warlords, but they have assumed the power of kings. And then there are the 'kings'—again, God only knows how many—who now rule in the eastern lands along the Saxon Shore. Britain, in less than forty years, has fallen into utter anarchy."

"And you think this child may change all that?"

I looked him in the eye. "I do."

"How, in the name of all the ancient gods?"

"By uniting the people again, but even more strongly than they were before, when they were unified by Roman Law and Roman rule. This time, the people will be Britons, all of them, unified by the rule of a King of Britain, with an enlightened system of common laws."

Lucanus shook his head, gently and with sympathy. "My friend, I accept the dream has passed to you, down from your forebears, but it is a dream, I fear, and hardly likely to be realized."

I gave a self-deprecating laugh. "Aye, Luke, you're right, and more so than you know. It is a dream. But dreams are bread and meat to me, and they do come true, from time to time. This will come to pass. I know it will. It's why I'm here. It's why I am Merlyn Britannicus. My duty, my life's purpose, is to train the boy, to teach him all I have learned from all the sources to which I have been exposed, to make him High King of all this land. And that, my friend, will demand all of my attention, for all my life."

He was looking at me now in amazement. "You believe that! With conviction . . ."

"Completely, Luke. Never doubt that again. And I intend to become celibate from this day forward."

"But surely, if you intend to raise the boy, you'll need a woman's help."

"Aye, but there are many women, and I shall use as many as I need. But no wife. I have had a wife, whom I loved dearly, and she was to have borne me a child. She and the child were lost, and I will never know who took them from me, but I have come to believe, deep in my being, that they were taken to leave me free to assume the charge of this boy Arthur. I am convinced of it."

He shook his head again, and his voice was subdued. "Very well, I am convinced that you are convinced, and I will do what I can to help you, although I may never understand whence this . . . this sudden passion . . . this *conviction* arose. You will teach the boy well, I have no doubt of that. You will teach him your knowledge as thoroughly as my own tutor taught me his. But I'm afraid I may not be the teacher *you* require."

"I have no fear on those grounds, Luke. I want to learn, and am prepared to spend the time required."

"I told you, it will take years, Cay."

"I have years."

"Hmm. Tell me . . ." He paused, blowing out his breath noisily, and then began again. "How can you be so *certain* of all this, and so suddenly?"

"It's not sudden, Luke. I have been bred towards seeing that truth, and to recognise it for what it became. I saw it but recently, that is all."

"What? What did you see?"

"A dream." I grinned at him, feeling the euphoria of conviction sweep over me. "I had a dream, and recognised it. I've had them all my life and spent my life running away from them. Now I know them for what they are. I'll tell you about them some time, I promise you. But not today. I've astounded you sufficiently for one day."

"Aye," he agreed. "You have that."

"So, when can we start my lessons?"

"I knew you were going to ask me that." He sounded both resigned and regretful. "Cay, I have no idea. At this moment, my mind is completely blank on the matter of a simple starting point. In fact, I don't believe there is any such thing as a simple starting point. You have caught me completely unprepared." He thought for a moment. "Look, it's going to take some time for you to reach Donuil's home and then return. How long do you estimate you'll be away?"

I shrugged. "As long as is necessary. It may take a month, but I doubt I could be so fortunate as to find everything progresses as smoothly as I would wish it to. It could take half a year."

"Hmm. Well, will you grant me that time to consider how we can approach this matter of your training?"

"Absolutely, but my program of celibacy is already under way." I picked up my bow and dropped the single arrow back into my quiver. "We have talked for long enough. I think it's time I checked on our companions." I glanced over my shoulder into the body of the wagon and noticed a large iron pot, filled with cloth-wrapped bundles, among the profusion of crates and packages that filled most of the wagon bed. "What's that for?" I asked. "The cooking pot."

"For cooking in." He was grinning. "It's not as frivolous as you might think. Remember, I told you that these people have nothing. I meant that quite literally. Cooking pots rust and wear out. It occurred to me, while I was preparing this load, that an extra one might be appreciated."

I had been on the point of leaping down from the wagon, but now I sat down again, struck by what he had said, and before I had completed the movement, my mind was made up. "You know, I never would have thought of that?" I turned my head, scanning the woods on either side of the road. They encroached closely, all evidence of open grassland long since fallen behind us. "Look," I said, "we still have seen no signs, other than footprints, of whoever it is that's been following us, and they may have given up long since. But whether they have or not, the fact remains that you and your cargo here are too valuable to allow me to put you at risk by leaving you alone before you reach your friend Emancipatus. Half a mile can be too far from help if you run into trouble. Ten miles is out of the question, and yet it's but a couple of hours' journey. We'll stay with you until we've seen you safely arrived. No buts, Luke—my mind's made up." I had seen the protest forming in his eyes, and now he smiled and nodded, acquiescing.

"So be it," he murmured. "Thank you."

"No need. I'll be back." I swung myself down, collected my horse from the tail of the wagon and rode to join Donuil and Rufio at the head of our column.

We camped that night beneath the trees, and split the watch into two-hour, four-man shifts, so that none of us had more than four consecutive hours of sleep, but there were no alarms and we found no footprints around our camp the following morning other than our own. Our escort had vanished as silently as it had come. We made good time again throughout a morning that brought showers and a blustery wind, and came to the inn of the Red Dragon before noon, stopping there to eat. After our meal, I had gone to relieve myself among the bushes by the road—repelled by the stench in the public latrine attached to the hostelry—and I was reentering the courtyard when I noticed Donuil standing in a corner, by the door to one of the outhouses, staring down at his feet. Curious, I walked over to see what he was looking at, and there, clearly outlined in the moist dirt of the yard, was the signature that had been absent from our campsite: the giant feet and the tiny.

"Damnation! Have you seen any sign of these people?" Donuil shook his head. "They could be anywhere now, hiding in one of these buildings or far gone on the road to wherever they came from." I was looking around me as I spoke, angry at myself for not having checked the place thoroughly on our arrival, but it was too late now to do anything useful. "Well, that's wonderful," I said acerbically. "From now on we'll ride with scouts out, although not too far away to be cut off. I hope we come upon these people. I'm just in the frame of mind to deal with them now. Roust out the others and let's be on our way."

Donuil was looking at me in puzzlement. "What are you talking about, Merlyn? Have you seen these footprints before?"

"Of course I have! You have too. They belong to the people who have been following us. They were all around our campsite the night before last, and the night before that, too. Don't tell me you didn't see them."

He shook his head. "No, I didn't. I knew you had found tracks. Rufio mentioned that, but I didn't see any need to go and look at them."

"Then why are you looking at them now, if they have no significance to you?"

"Oh, they have a significance." He was staring down at the marks again. He looked up at me again, the beginnings of a smile dawning in his eyes. "If these belong to the people I think they do, then you can forget about being attacked, unless you decide to do harm to me." He saw my mystification and grinned. "I believe, although I could be wrong, that these footprints were made by two of my father's most trusted men, a giant called Logan and a midget called Feargus. If I'm right, then they're watching over me, which means that Connor came safely home, with the child, and has told my father of meeting you." He nodded his head. "Aye, that would be the way of it. My father would have sent them off to find Camulod and you, and to discover what had become of me."

"You know these people!"

"They are my friends."

"Then why would they not come forward and say so?"

He grinned again and shook his head. "Come, Caius Merlyn, are you serious? They are Outlanders, remember? Would you have them trust your open honesty and goodwill without ever having met you? What would you have done if they had confronted you when I was not around? You would have cut them down."

There was no disputing his reasoning. I shrugged my shoulders. "Aye," I said, "I would have. But not now. Call them in now."

Donuil was still smiling. "I can't, Commander. They are not here. They would have faded away once they discovered where we were headed. We might pick them up again on the road. I'll be watching out from now on, now that I know who I'm looking for. But still, as I said, I could be wrong, so I'll do as you said and roust out the others. There might well be another two sets of feet like those in Britain, but until we know one way or the other, we'll do well to be ready for anything."

Some three hours later, Rufio came riding back towards me over the crest of a hill, and even from afar I could tell by the way he moved that he had ill news to report. I had been riding slightly ahead of our little party, swathed in my war cloak against the chilling rain, and had just returned to ride alongside Luke's wagon.

"Rufio looks upset," Luke said from above me.

"Aye, something's wrong."

When he reached us he reined his horse in a tight circle before speaking, so that none of the men behind us might overhear his words.

"Lepers, Commander, up ahead. A large group of them."

"How many?" This was Lucanus.

"About fifteen, I think. We came on them unexpectedly and they ran.

There's a house of some kind, built of logs, half buried in the ground. No way of telling how many there are inside. Not without going in." His tone made it clear that was beyond consideration.

"Stop looking like that, man, you have no need to fear anything," Luke snapped. "They won't contaminate you. These are the people I have come to see. Stay here with the others, if your fear is that great. I'll ride on alone. Who else was with you when you found the colony?"

Rufio was gazing at Luke as though the physician had lost his mind. "Prince Donuil," he answered. "He's still there, watching the place."

"Why?" Luke's scorn was withering. "Does he expect them to attack him? Sick people?" He turned to look at me. "Would you like to accompany me, Commander Merlyn?" He paused, awaiting my response, and I swallowed hard before nodding, unwilling to trust my tongue. He smiled and turned again to Rufio. "Where are they?"

An hour later we approached the lepers' place by a narrow but well-trodden path that struck away from the main road for half a mile, so that the dwelling place of Mordechai Emancipatus and his charges was well hidden from the eyes of passers-by. Donuil and Rufio had found it simply because they were scouting, on the lookout for anything unusual. Lucanus steered the wagon carefully as we made our way forward and Donuil, pale and tense, now rode beside me.

The path led us into a tiny, bowl-shaped depression too small to be called a valley, floored with fine, white sand that gleamed like snow through the grass that fronted the log structure housing the lepers. The building, of the type known as a byre or longhouse, was built, as Rufio had said, into the side of a low hill. Flanked by two rough outhouses of the same construction, it looked both large and ancient, its walls—those portions of them that projected far enough to be seen—thickly crusted with lichen and mosses. Its roof sagged dangerously in the middle, weighted down with the accretion of years of moss and weeds, so that it would have been invisible from any angle but the one from which we approached. A large cooking fire was smouldering into ashes in front of it, but apart from that sign of life the place appeared to be abandoned. The sight of our scouts, Lucanus assured me, would have driven the lepers inside, to the illusory safety of the building. He drew rein less than twenty paces from the only doorway and climbed down from his seat, slinging his big leather physician's satchel over his shoulder as he did so, and told us to remain where we were for the time being. I was appalled by the place, but it was Donuil who spoke out.

"You're not going in there?"

Lucanus looked up at him and smiled. "I am indeed. Are you suggesting I should come all this way for this sole purpose and not enter? Of course I'm going in, and I'm coming out again. Then you can help me unload the wagon." He lowered his heavy satchel to the ground and crossed to where I sat watching. "Can you reach inside the wagon and hand me down that big pot, Merlyn?" Transferring my weight to one stirrup, I stepped from my saddle onto the wagon platform and leaned inside, up-ending the pot gently to allow its contents to fall out undamaged, before handing the vessel down to him. He carried it to Donuil, grinning widely. "Here, fill this with clean water and set it on the fire there. I'll need it later."

As Donuil slowly dismounted, his face darkened by a troubled scowl,

Lucanus picked up his bag again and slung it back over his shoulder. He approached the building and knocked heavily on the door, and I heard a surprisingly deep and normal male voice shout to him to go away, that they were unclean. Luke's only response was to step forward and push against the door. It swung open slowly, and he disappeared inside.

I leaned closer, trying to pierce the darkness beyond the doorway, but could see nothing. I turned then to Donuil and we looked at each other in dismay, but neither of us voiced his thoughts, and Donuil went off on his quest for water.

How long I sat there before Lucanus came out again I do not know, but it seemed like hours. Finally, however, he emerged and approached us, stopping first by the fire where he tested the heat of the water in the pot with his fingertip. When he reached my side he looked up first at me, then at Donuil, and then at me again.

"Merlyn," he said at length, "I am going to invite you to come with me on a journey into Hades, and you will see the true value of the gifts you have given these poor people."

I heard his words without surprise, for I had long since ceased to be surprised by the depths of this man's humanity and compassion. My sole wonder about Lucanus nowadays was due to my own remembrance of the time when I had thought that he was humourless, inhumanly cold and efficient, and that he and I could never be friends.

"Will you come?" He was still gazing at me.

I nodded. "Of course I will."

"Merlyn—" Donuil again, his voice sounding agonized. I cut him short.

"You stay here, Donuil. Don't let that fire go out."

On the threshold, my heart thudding loudly in my ears, I paused and drew a huge, deep breath of clean air. Then, holding it in my lungs as though it were the last I should ever know, I followed Lucanus into the darkness.

I did not know then, nor can I now imagine, what I really expected to find inside that place. A charnel house, perhaps; a hell pit of some description. What I found was Stygian blackness after the bright light of outdoors. I stopped inside the threshold, still holding my breath, and gazed around me, seeing nothing, hearing nothing. The stillness inside those walls was absolute. No one moved, and no one spoke. My head began to swim from the effort of holding my breath, and as my eyes began to adjust to the darkness, I exhaled noisily, explosively, then fought down a surge of panic as my lungs sucked in more air . . . contaminated air. I began to discern the shape of Lucanus, standing just ahead of me, and long lines of military-looking cots extending along both walls, right and left, the way they did in Lucanus's own sick bay in Camulod.

Lucanus spoke into the silence.

"You may light the lamps, Mordechai. This is Caius Merlyn Britannicus, my Commander. You have nothing to fear from him."

When he had finished speaking, the silence returned, and then the sharp sound of a flint striking metal made me jump, so close was it beside me. Recoiling instinctively, I turned quickly to my right and saw sparks falling, and then a tiny glimmer of light that grew into a small, bright flame. A thin wax taper dipped into the flame and caught, and then its unseen bearer

moved away from me, cupping the flame in one protective hand and receding
in silhouette against its flickering brightness, lighting a series of lamps down
the length of the room, which emerged gradually into view. As the brightness
grew and my eyes adjusted, I stared in amazement. The place, for all its
Spartan bareness, was meticulously clean and neat. The floor of hard-packed
earth was swept bare of dust and dirt, and strewn down the central aisle with
fresh, carefully aligned, new-dried rushes. The beds along each wall were
uniform; plain, unvarnished, hand-planed wood frames furnished with thin
mattresses, and on each mattress sat or lay a human form, most of them
swathed in long, voluminous drapery that covered their limbs and faces as
well as their bodies. The air I breathed smelled clean. There was a smell, to
be sure, and it hinted of sickness, but there was nothing about it of rot or
filth, of carrion or contagion.

I became aware of Lucanus watching me. When I looked at him, he
motioned me forward, towards the bed by which he stood. As I approached,
the occupant of the bed stood up and looked at me. He was a big man, clean
shaven and massive of chest and shoulder and wrapped in a single robe that
hung, toga-like, to his ankles. His hair was thick and flaxen fair, hanging in
ringlets to his shoulders, and his hands were thrust into the folds of his
garment.

"Merlyn, this is my friend Mordechai Emancipatus," Luke said. "Mordechai, I present to you Caius Merlyn Britannicus."

I nodded to the big man, who returned my nod in silence.

"Mordechai, as I have told you, is supreme commander here, much as
you are in Camulod," Luke went on. "He is a physician, as you already know,
trained with me in Alexandria. He is also the breadwinner here because he
is the strongest and, to this time, the least afflicted."

Afflicted! There had been no mention of affliction when Luke and I had
talked of this before. I gazed at the man Mordechai in consternation. I could
see no sign of sickness about him. I found my tongue at last.

"You are a leper?" I asked him, realizing the futility and stupidity of my
question as it left my lips. He nodded solemnly.

"Show him your hand," said Luke.

Mordechai withdrew his left hand from the folds of his robe and stretched
it towards me. I could see nothing wrong with it. Lucanus reached out and
picked up the nearest lamp, bringing it to where its light showed the hand
clearly. In the brightness of the lamp, the skin looked . . . *scaly* was the only
word that occurred to me. Luke moved the light closer and I saw the discoloration of dry, painful-looking lesions, red in the centre fading to a dead
whiteness at the edges, between the knuckles and on the joints of the fingers.
The light moved again, throwing its brightness now on Mordechai's face.
Again, the skin looked, upon close observation, somehow dry and flaky, although no flakes were apparent. The man's face reminded me somehow, and
I shied away from the thought, of some kind of animal, familiar and yet
strange.

"Note the leonine swelling of the features." Lucanus was speaking in his
dry, professional voice and his words jarred me. The animal I had been
visualizing was a lion. "A classic symptom of this illness. The whiteness and
swelling of the skin around the brows and forehead, and the thickening of

the nasal bridge and nostrils characterize and emphasize this leonine appearance. Note also that his eyebrows are quite white, not yellow like his hair. How long have you been afflicted, Mordechai?"

Mordechai shrugged his massive shoulders. "Eight years now."

"And before that? How long had you been tending lepers?"

"Since finishing my last tour with the legions, in Gaul. More than twenty years."

"You are now what? Fifty?"

"Forty-eight, I believe."

"Hmm, that's right, you were several years younger than I, the youngest student of us all, in fact. You look good, my friend, in spite of everything."

A smile flickered briefly on the big man's face. "Not many lepers are told that."

"Undo your robe."

The hair on Mordechai's chest was thick and darker than the hair on his head, but it was patterned with white patches, some small, some large, all roughly circular in appearance. Lucanus pointed these out to me, continuing to speak in his clipped, didactic physician's voice. "The whiteness of the hair over the emerging lesions is another unmistakable symptom, but the disease is notorious for not being uniform in its emergence to view. Sometimes the lesions themselves are white, and frequently scabrous, but they may just as easily be red and pus-filled, easily mistaken for common boils in the early stages of the sickness. As you have heard, Mordechai has had this scourge for eight years but shows remarkably few serious blemishes and is hardly debilitated at all, thank God. I have seen others, and I know you have too, Mordechai, who have degenerated to the point of digital decomposition in far less time than that." He broke off and glanced at me. "You understand digital decomposition? The finger joints and toe joints atrophy and fall away."

I nodded, fascinated, unable to tear my eyes away from Mordechai's piebald chest hair, but from the corner of my eye I saw Lucanus straighten up and look around the huge room.

"Eighteen of you," he murmured. "How many in extremis?"

"Seven," came Mordechai's response.

"How are you treating them? What medicines do you have?"

"Medicines?" Mordechai's bitterness was all the more apparent because he expressed it in a laugh. "I have water, Luke, and home-made soap, cloth bandages and gentleness. What more could I have? Whence would it come?"

Lucanus flicked a glance at me and I cleared my throat nervously. "What about light?" I asked, thinking of the cases of fine wax candles I was transporting to Donuil's father. "Is it always this dark in here?"

Mordechai looked at me kindly, his mouth twisting into a smile. "Most of the time," he answered. "With this sickness, the absence of revealing light is frequently a benison. I am the only one of our community you have seen. Some are not as comely as I am. I am still almost whole, look." He now extended his right hand, and it was sound and pink, unblemished. I coughed again, feeling painfully awkward.

"It was simply . . ." I ran out of words, then began again. "I asked only because I have a box—a large box—of fine wax candles among my possessions. They are a luxury to me, but it occurred to me they might be a blessing to your people here. I would be glad to leave them with you if they could be of use to you."

He inclined his head with great dignity. "Thank you, Master Merlyn. They would be more than useful."

"Good. They are with the rest of your supplies in the wagon. We will unload them directly."

"Wagon?" Mordechai glanced from me to Luke and back to me again. "You bring supplies for us?"

I felt my face grow red. "Lucanus brings them. They are his gift to you, apart from the candles. I merely brought Lucanus." As the two began speaking, the one offering and the other declining gratitude, I looked around the long room again. Its occupants were silent still, most of them gazing at the three of us standing in the middle of the floor, but they were no longer isolated shapes. They sat in small groups of three and four, close to each other, touching and sharing warmth and comfort and strength. I glanced at Luke again and found him watching me.

"Luke, a word with you please, outside."

He excused himself to Mordechai, as did I, and we went out again into the grey daylight, feeling the fresh, cool air snap into our lungs with our first breath. I saw Donuil straighten up in relief as we emerged, but my thoughts were with Lucanus.

"The candles are not in the wagon, Luke. They're on one of the packhorses, back at the camp. It had occurred to me that Donuil and I might unload the wagon, but that's a task that might better wait until tomorrow, when Mordechai will have had time to think about where to store everything. In the meantime, I'll leave Donuil here with you to help you with anything you might need, while I fetch the candles."

It was almost sunset by the time I returned with the box of candles, and I found Donuil sitting his horse exactly where I had left him hours earlier. There was no sign, however, of the wagon and its team of horses. Donuil told me he had stabled the horses and the wagon in a shed at the side of the longhouse. He also told me how Mordechai's eyes had filled with tears when he saw the profusion of what we had brought for his people. The two physicians had been working ever since I left, he added, cleansing the sick and changing dressings, and as we spoke they emerged from the longhouse, stripped themselves to the waist and began washing vigorously in hot water that was white and pungent from the astringent chemicals Lucanus had added to the pot. Surprisingly, I found an air almost of gaiety pervading the small community now, fostered by the sudden wealth that had come their way.

Long after darkfall, Donuil and I made our way back to our encampment, having bidden farewell to Lucanus and his friend Mordechai. I had achieved, I felt with some pride, a modicum of understanding of the fate of these people smitten by the most dreaded illness in the world. I had spoken with most of them in the course of the evening, and had found them to be very much like other people. But neither Donuil nor I had been able to bring ourselves to share their meal as Lucanus had, and some time in the middle of the night I sprang into wakefulness, shuddering in horror at the sight of my own leprous, fleshless face in some dream mirror.

X

DONUIL WAS ASTIR before any of us the following morning, up and out hunting. He brought back a brace of hares and a handful of wild garlic for that night's pot. I had gone to relieve myself and then to wash in a nearby brook as I did every morning on awakening, and he returned to camp at the same time I did, the hares hanging casually from his left hand and the garlic clutched in his right. I noticed them and nodded to him in passing before the significance of what I had seen struck home to me, but then I spun on my heel and called to him.

"You've been hunting, out of camp." He nodded, smiling faintly, and I continued, hardening my voice. "You know better than that! That was fool-hardy. You know the rules."

"Aye, Commander." He was still smiling slightly, his response accompanied by a nod. "But I knew what I was about and I was careful. There's no one out there; neither friend nor foe."

I breathed deeply to keep my flaring anger under restraint. "Don't do anything like that again in hostile territory, ever, without my specific permission," I snapped. "I know you think these people who have been following us might be your friends, but you yourself admitted you don't know if it's them or not. You could be lying out there now, gutted like one of those animals you're holding."

His smiled widened, infuriating me. "I hardly think so, Commander."

"Oh, really, you hardly think so? Trooper, I don't give a damn what you think! It's what *I* think that's important here. It's not your place to think under these circumstances." Only now did his eyes widen with the realisation of the depth of my anger. "As far as your father's people are concerned you are still a hostage to my goodwill, and they have no cause to trust me. You are already late in returning home. Had there been enemies out there, you might have been killed, slaughtered like the fool you appear to be, perhaps after a heroic fight in which you satisfied your stupid Celtic honour, but where would that have left me? I'll tell you where! It would have left me looking like a liar in your father's and your brother Connor's eyes, a self-serving, lying coward with no hope of rescuing the child they are holding against your safe return. Your corpse, and all my tears, would have been useless in gaining his release."

He looked stunned, crestfallen, recognising and accepting the truth of that. His big head dipped in a chastened bow. "You're right, Commander. I didn't think about that."

"Of course you didn't think, you idiot! That's why I'm angry. I said it's not your place to think, but it is, Donuil. It is! I cannot afford to have you or anyone else, but most particularly *you*, operating thoughtlessly now. There is too much at stake here to permit such foolishness."

Donuil nodded contritely. "It was irresponsible of me, I can see that. It won't happen again."

"Good. Please make sure it doesn't." He nodded again and turned away, showing no evidence of being upset by my displeasure, then turned back.

"May I say something, Commander?"

"Of course you may. What is it?"

He pursed his lips, then inhaled deeply through his nostrils. "We're getting very close to Glevum. Have you thought any more about what you're going to do if there are no ships there? We have thirty beasts for transport: a spare for each fighting man, the matched pair for my father, and six packhorses."

He was right. It would be virtually impossible to find a vessel, any vessel, large enough to transport our men, let alone all, or even half of our livestock. My own father, more than thirty years earlier, had been forced to leave behind more than six hundred head of prime stock in Britain—stock that now formed the breeding herds of Camulod—because of the overpowering and insuperable logistical difficulty of transporting livestock by sea upon short notice.

His words, unexpected as they were, made me realize that, until this moment, I had been drifting along, blithely convinced, utterly without reason other than some inner prompting, that everything would work out and we would cross to Eire without difficulty. The enormity of my hubris, and this sudden reminder of it, brought me to my senses. I expelled a gusty, deepchested breath. "Well, we may have to make adjustments. We were aware of that before leaving Camulod. If everything goes against us and there are no boats big enough to take us all, the others will have to return to Camulod with the horses. If necessary, you and I will cross the sea alone."

"We should take Rufio with us. He's a good man in a tight corner."

"Aye, perhaps. Very well, the three of us."

"And our horses."

"What?"

He spread his hands, palms upward. "We have to cross by boat, and we had intended to find one big enough to carry thirteen of us, counting the boys, and thirty horses. We might still be able to find one that big, something from beyond Britain, unloading cargo."

"Consigned to whom?" The irony on my face made him shrug, conceding my point.

"You're right, it's probably impossible. But we should be able to find one, even a fishing boat from along the coast, that can transport three men, instead of thirteen and perhaps three horses where the other eleven men would have been."

"We'll see. Call the men together."

When they were all assembled, looking at me in curiosity, I cleared my throat and reminded them that, on the face of it, it was highly improbable we would find a vessel capable of transporting all our horses. If that were the case, I said, only three of us, Donuil, Rufio and I, would embark for Eire with, or without, our personal mounts. Thereafter, the remainder of the party would return to Camulod.

These men had all been personally chosen by me. They were not only excellent soldiers, but comrades-in-arms of long standing, and that gave them a certain freedom in responding to what I had said. Two of them, Quintus and Dedalus, were veterans who had ridden with me on the earliest patrols I shared with Uther in our boyhood. Now Dedalus looked at me through a frown.

"You'd really go without us? I don't like that, Merlyn. It's too damn dangerous for only three of you, heading into a land filled with Outlanders. Donuil there's one of them, and we all trust him, but even he makes no secret of the fact he can't speak on behalf of any other than his own people, and not all of them, either. Why can't we all go with you, and leave the horses here with the boys? We can fight as well on foot as from horseback."

I smiled at him. "None of us can go at all if we can't find a boat, Ded. I'm wagering on finding one. If I do, as many of us will go as is feasible. The others will remain behind. I merely wanted you all to know my mind."

There was a deal of muttering and mumbling, but no one could alter the truth of what faced us. Everything depended upon what we would find in Glevum.

The former port town of Glevum, which we reached early the following morning, was an abandoned ruin, devastated by war and time. I had expected that. I knew it had been ravaged by Lot's second army several years earlier, the army, originally bound southward for Camulod via Aquae Sulis, that had caused me to ride into the fight that cost me my memory. On that occasion the army had changed direction and, leaderless, had ravaged both Aquae and Glevum before disbanding. I had also seen the effects of time and the lack of civic government and maintenance on other towns, such as Noviomagus and Londinium itself. Glevum, I decided, had been at far greater risk than all of these during the past two decades since, as an open river estuary port, it had no protection from sea-borne raiders. I had spent the intervening day railing at myself for my own idiocy in even presuming to find sea transportation of any kind available, and my men were all aware of my frame of mind. With all of this taken into consideration, we approached the place very cautiously, yet prepared, by the time we arrived, to find it completely deserted.

I was surprised and excited, therefore, to discover that not only was there a ship at the wharf, but that it was enormous, a massive bireme with a towering mast and huge spars that would support a vast expanse of sail. We saw it first from a distance above the town, on a low hill, and at first I saw only the mass of the huge vessel itself, and the two vertical banks of long sweeps that stood along its side against the wharflike palisades. There appeared to be hundreds of men involved in the feverish activity that was going on about it, with people scurrying everywhere like angry insects whose colony had been disturbed. Then I noticed that much of the activity seemed to be concentrated either at the rear of the vessel or on the section of the wharf directly beyond it and hidden by the bulk of the ship. I swallowed my impatience and forced myself to analyze as much as I could see before committing myself or any of my people to going closer.

As far as I could estimate from our vantage point, the Roman-built craft—what other type could it be, I asked myself—had more than thirty oars in each of its double banks, which amounted to one hundred and thirty or forty sweeps. From the length of the sweeps themselves, it was obvious that at least two men, and possibly three, would be required to manipulate each blade, indicating a crew of four hundred or so oarsmen. In addition to those, I knew there would be warriors responsible for attack or defense when the ship was moving, for Roman biremes were mainly ships of war, constructed for battle and intended as moving fortresses, so that they carried a military force as well as a naval force.

Who could these people be, I wondered, and what was their purpose? It was evident at first glance that they had an urgent purpose; the energetic nature of their activity bespoke it. But even as I watched, the activity died down and altered. Now there was a definite and unmistakable movement of people towards the ship, and they began pouring up the two steep gangways in a living tide.

"They're making ready to leave." The voice belonged to Rufio, who was standing closest to me.

"You think so?" I asked.

"They're leaving. Whatever they were loading, the job's complete. They'll be gone within the hour."

I accepted his judgment completely. "Then we must stop them and negotiate passage."

"Hah!" His laugh was more of a bark, harsh and derisive. "I doubt you'd want to bargain with those people, Commander."

I threw him an ill-tempered look. "Why not?"

"They're carrion eaters. Pirates. They'd gobble us up and not bother spitting out our bones. We're twelve against five hundred."

"We're not against them, Rufio. We are a source of potential revenue to their captain."

"Aye," he grunted a laugh. "We are that." But then he caught himself and looked at me as if he thought me mad. "Commander," he exclaimed, his tone outraged. "They're pirates, they'll take our *revenues* and all else we have and kill us all, can't you see that?"

"I can see the possibility, but it's a risk we're going to have to assume. You could be right. On the other hand, this is too good an opportunity to pass up. We'll approach them cautiously, but approach them we must, my friend, and we don't have much time. Tell the herd boys to stay here with the extra mounts until we wave them down. Let's go!" This last was a shout to the others, and I waved my arm high to urge them on as I dug my spurs deep and aimed my horse downhill at a run on the shortest route to the outskirts of the town, leaving Rufio to make sure that the boys remained behind.

It was a hard gallop, but in less than a quarter of an hour our horses were clattering through the paved streets of the deserted town, veering abruptly this way and that to avoid the haphazard piles of debris with which the thoroughfares were littered. At one point the entire street was blocked with great piles of masonry and rubble, so that we had to swing right, along another, and ride for several blocks before we could turn back again towards the waterfront. Now we rode among warehouses, most of them wooden and in a state of collapse, but eventually we broke out of the buildings and emerged on the broad, cobbled roadway that ran the length of the long stone wharf. In the time that had elapsed since we left the hilltop, the ship had moved away from the wharf and was now manoeuvring in the deep water of the river channel about thirty paces from where we emerged, its oarsmen swinging it completely about, almost around its centre point, so skillful was their work, to point downstream towards the sea. Dedalus, who rode close to me, had a brazen horn, and now he blew it wildly to attract the attention of the crew aboard the craft.

Our appearance brought consternation on board the bireme and among the group of forty or so men who had remained behind on the wharf to watch the vessel pull out. As we left these behind and galloped along the wharf, keeping abreast of the vessel and waving to attract attention, I saw intense activity on the raised stern platform, where a cluster of men seemed to be arranging themselves in some form of disciplined order. Then, as my disbelieving eyes adjusted to what they were seeing, a blizzard of arrows came winging towards us. I heard a horse scream and a man shout in alarm, and then a hideous clatter told me that one of my men, at least, was down. No sooner had I heard the sounds than a mighty bang exploded against my helmet and I felt myself wrenched sideways and falling, seeing the cobbled street rushing up to meet me from between my horse's hooves. Somehow, instinctively, I managed to check myself, my right hand clutching the horn of my saddle by some reflex and my bent left leg, its foot jammed in the stirrup, absorbing the weight of my falling body. Germanicus veered left, dragged by my weight, and came to a halt, and I managed to haul myself partially upright before falling to the ground. There was confusion all around me now, pierced by the wicked whistle and crack of hard-shot arrows striking stone, a sound I had not heard in years. Someone came running and grasped me beneath the arms, then dragged me into a doorway before lowering me to the floor and running out again. I lay there for some time, shaking my head to clear it and regain my senses, and then I rose to my feet and ran outside, only to find myself alone on the wharf.

"Merlyn! Get back inside!" someone yelled, and I threw myself back into safety again as two arrows smacked into the wall behind me, one of them shattering with the force of its impact. The next time I approached the doorway, I did so on my belly. The big bireme was stationary in mid-stream, its decks lined with bowmen. In the water behind it, two small boats, each sculled by two men, were feeding ropes up to the stern of the larger vessel. As I watched, the ropes were pulled aboard, dragging the ends of two much thicker cables behind them. I heard the clacking of winches, and then the bowmen lining the sides disappeared, followed shortly afterwards by a groaning sound as the great oars were lowered into the water again. A drum struck up a steady cadence, and the bireme began to move downstream. Behind it, attached to the two massive ropes that were now almost taut, drifted two barges, low-sided, flat-bottomed, ugly craft of shallow draft; no more than floating platforms for the hauling of heavy cargo. As the bireme pulled away I stood up again and stepped back onto the wharf. Immediately, an arrow sought me out, falling short and almost spent. They were moving rapidly beyond bowshot and I began to look around me, calling to the others. A dead horse lay to my right, about thirty paces from where I stood.

Quintus was the first to emerge, from a doorway only a little farther down the wharf from where I had lain. He was staunching the blood flowing from a cut on his nose with the edge of his short cloak. As he appeared, others began to come out from the various places they had sought safety. I began counting them quickly.

"Was anyone hurt?" I asked Quintus.

He shook his head, wiping his nose again and sniffing to clear his nostrils of blood. "No. Metellus went down just before you, but it was his horse took the arrow, not him. He's unconscious, but not injured apart from that. Then you went down and—" He looked at me and stopped speaking abruptly, gazing at me with his head slightly tilted, his eyes on the space above my head, then he stepped towards me, grinning through the mask of blood on his face. "Well, I'll be . . . Let me look at that. Take off your helmet."

I undid my chin strap and pulled off my helmet, which he took from me, holding it up for everyone to see. "Hey, fellows, look at this!" When I saw what he was holding, my whole body chilled. An arrow had pierced the metal framework of the crest on my helmet, and was now lodged there exactly by its centre, the flighted and the barbed ends projecting equidistantly on either side. The matched tufts of alternating black and white horsehair of the crest itself seemed undisturbed. And then I witnessed one of those phenomena that can occur only in moments like that. Completely oblivious to the fact that they had all been in mortal peril only moments before, my men all crowded around to marvel at the sight of the arrow in my helmet as though it were the greatest wonder in the world. I watched them in amazement for long moments before my good sense reasserted itself.

"That's enough of that! Give me that helmet. Where are the horses?"

"In there," Dedalus answered, nodding towards the large doorway of the nearest warehouse. "They're all safe—save for Metellus's."

"Good, then bring them out, please, and let's remember where we are." I snapped the shaft of the arrow and pulled the longer part out through the hole in my silver crest-mounting, leaving an eye-shaped aperture. "Those people tried to kill us, and there was a large group of them still standing on the wharf to our right when we swung left to follow the ship. They're not going to be any more friendly than their fellows were. How is Metellus?"

Donuil came out of the warehouse as I asked the question. He was carrying his helmet under his arm and rubbing his eyes. "Metellus is fine, Commander. He's just come to his senses. He can't stand up yet and his head hurts, but he doesn't appear to have broken anything and he won't die on us."

I noticed that Quintus had stepped away from the others and was standing alone by the edge of the wharf, staring downriver to where the bireme and its trailing barges were now mere dots. He was still mopping at the blood on his face. I stepped to his side.

"How is it, your nose?"

He sniffed again, hawked, and spat bloody sputum into the water. "Ach, I'll live, Commander. Self-inflicted wound. I banged it against the hilt of my sword when I dismounted in a manner I'd flay my recruits for even thinking of. It'll clot in a while. I'm a bad bleeder, the medics tell me. Once I start, it takes some time to stop."

I turned and gazed back to where the remaining group of men had been, at the far end of the wharf. There was no sign of them. "Well, as soon as you are mobile again, mount up and follow us. I'm going to see what happened to those people left behind, and to see if I can discover what kind of cargo they were towing in those barges." I called to Dedalus and Donuil, telling them to assemble the others and have them at full readiness, then I went to find my own horse in the darkened warehouse. Germanicus seemed none the worse for his escapade, and as I pulled myself up into the saddle I saw Quintus preparing to mount his own horse. I stopped him and ordered him to stay behind with Metellus, whom I could see sitting in the shadows against the wall, shaking his head and resting his elbows on his upraised knees, obviously still disoriented. Quintus looked for a moment as though he might object, but then thought better of it and moved to lower himself down beside Metellus.

When the others were all mounted, I assembled them in a defensive formation, Donuil, Dedalus and I riding in front, with the water on our left and the other six strung out behind us to the right, each man half a length behind the man on his left and carrying his shield on his right arm in anticipation of attack from the buildings in that direction. Nothing moved in front of us as we proceeded cautiously to the far end of the dock, where we had last seen the men. There was still no sign of them. The cobbled roadway ran directly to the gabled end of a stone building and vanished beyond a massive pair of wooden doors the full width of the street. The interior was dark and windowless, the only light a sharply lined wedge spilling inward from the doorway. I held up my hand and drew my horse to a halt, wishing I had thought to bring my bow with me, and we sat there gazing into the huge shed. On my left, Dedalus hawked and spat.

"Are you thinking about going in there, Commander?"

I did not look at him. I was almost sniffing the air, searching for threat, attempting to define the danger my instincts told me was there. "I think we have no choice, Ded."

"Hmm. Well, at least you have a choice of who goes through that whoreson door first, and it won't be you."

Now I glanced at him. "Why not? It's my place, and who's to prevent me?"

"I am. The first man through that door will draw whatever fire is in there. He'll be stone blind, silhouetted against the light and ridiculously outnumbered. There must have been thirty, forty men in that group we saw."

"At least." I could not contain the smile his threat of insubordination had stirred in me. "So what do you suggest we do?"

"Oh, we have to go in; no argument about that, but there must be at least one other doorway . . . an entrance. This is an exit."

He was right. The doorway we were facing had but one function: to allow the goods held inside to be brought out for shipping, or to allow access for unloaded cargo. There was no other way on or off the wharf at this point. The entrance to the first side street lay some thirty paces behind us.

"So we should find the other entrance."

"Aye, or entrances. Then we can hit all of them at once. Let's turn about and ride back the way we came in. Once we're out of sight, we can stop and send half the men to ride around to the other side of the building. If there are only two entrances, we'll go five and five. If there are more, we'll divide ourselves up to fit, and by that time we'll know at least the size of the building, 'cause there's no telling from here."

"You're right. You agree, Donuil?"

Donuil, however, was not listening. As I spoke to him he kneed his horse forward and rode to the edge of the wharf, looking down into the water, about the height of a tall man below the edge. I followed his gaze and saw an empty barge of the type that had been towed behind the bireme. It was long, wide, ugly, flat-bottomed and empty, of no interest or use to us.

"Donuil?"

"I agree with him completely," he said over his shoulder. "I wonder what they ship in these things?"

"Anything they can load and tow. Come on, let's fall back."

We withdrew in order, alert for any signs of movement in the buildings we were passing and as we went I was greatly relieved to see Quintus and Metellus riding to join us from the warehouse where we had left them. They were double mounted, Metellus riding behind Quintus with his arms around his waist. His face was ashen and he looked exhausted, but he seemed firmly seated. When they joined us, I could see that Metellus was far from well. His face was vacant, his eyes staring, and he did not seem to be aware of any of us.

Quintus shook his head at me. "He's badly shaken. I think he must have landed on his head when he hit the cobbles, but he'll be fine once he can lie down and rest for a while."

I said nothing, returning my attention to the business at hand. We reached the junction with the side street and I stopped and again explained our plan. We would proceed up this street to the first cross-junction, I told them, then four of us would remain there while the other six turned left again and rode to the rear of the waterfront warehouses to look for the other entrance or entrances to the farthest one. If the exploratory group were attacked, they would turn at once and head back to rejoin us. If they were cut off from us somehow, both groups would converge on the point of attack. It was the best we could do, since it was inconceivable that we should simply turn around and ride away, leaving the field uncontested before this aspect of it had even shown any signs of dispute.

Those signs of dispute, however, materialized immediately upon our arrival at the junction of the cross-streets, just as we turned left but before our group had any opportunity to split: a hail of arrows poured down on us from attackers concealed on the rooftops of the surrounding buildings. Fortunately for all of us, our assailants were so jumpy, and so intent on remaining safely hidden, that none of those first missiles found a target. Before they could launch another volley, we had swung our mounts around again and were spurring them back out of the junction, swinging left once more, headed now directly away from the waterfront and the dangers it contained. I cursed the narrowness of the streets, because for several moments there was utter confusion as ten horses tried to enter a space that would permit no more than three abreast. From my position at the rear, time seemed to slow down as I waited for the first arrows to strike among the massed bodies struggling to pass through the small entrance. But suddenly they were through and I was the only one remaining in the open junction. I put my spurs to Germanicus and followed them.

Donuil and Dedalus were directly ahead of me, both of them reining in to wait for me. I waved them on and crouched down in my saddle, feeling my horse's stride lengthen as he settled into a flat run, and I quickly caught up to them. As I approached, angling my mount into the space between them, I could see that they had fallen about twenty lengths behind the others. The air thundered with the clatter of iron shoes on cobblestones. And then suddenly, with absolutely no warning, a man leapt out into the road from a doorway ahead of us, swinging some kind of enormous axe. It took Donuil's horse from beneath, in the outstretched neck, and killed it instantly. I had almost drawn level with them, my horse's head between the rumps of theirs, and the attack had occurred and was over before I could react. I had a blurred image of Donuil's horse crashing to the ground in a spray of blood, of Donuil himself flying over its head, and of the killer whirling nimbly away, back into the safety of the doorway from which he had sprung.

I swung my own mount around, hard, whirling my sword backhanded and uselessly at the killer, and then I was falling, too, my horse rearing and screaming as his hooves trampled his downed companion, kicking wildly in its death throes beneath him. I kicked my feet free of the stirrups and landed on my hands and knees beside the chaos of their thrashing bodies, smashing the fingers of my right hand between the cobblestones and the hilt of my sword. Above me, the killer sprang out again, his blood-covered axe upraised to cleave me. I let go of my shield and threw myself sideways to my left, scrambling with the speed of desperation to remain clear of the horses, and landed against the opposite side of the doorway that had hidden my attacker, just as his axe struck sparks from the stones of the road beside me. Then, scarcely aware of what I was doing, I braced my left arm against the frame of the doorway and launched myself at him, my body fully extended, stabbing my long-bladed sword like a spear into the softness beneath his rib cage. I felt no impact as my blade took him, but saw his eyes widen in surprise, then he released his axe handle and clutched at my blade with both hands. I jerked it free, slicing through his hands as I rose to my knees, and saw another man rushing at me from the passageway behind him. Before the newcomer could reach me, I was on my feet again, waiting for him. I brushed aside the short spear he thrust at me and killed him with a single, two-handed chop to the join of his neck and shoulder. Neither man had worn armour.

And now I became aware of Dedalus shouting my name, his voice shrill with urgency, and telling me to mount up, mount up, for the love of Christ! I spun towards the sound of his voice, my body still tingling with the fever of combat. Germanicus stood close by, his eyes rolling, and beyond him I saw Ded, leaning from his saddle, supporting Donuil, who was shaking his head groggily, blinking furiously to clear his vision. To my left, the way we had come, the street was filled with running men, still distant, but coming rapidly. There were far too many to fight. I snatched up my shield again and ran to my horse, jamming my foot into a stirrup and swinging myself up into the saddle.

"Come on!" Ded was shouting. "Grab his other arm and we'll carry him!" My hands were full. I jammed my left arm completely through the larger sling at the back of my shield, forcing the thing up my arm towards my shoulder until it would go no farther and hung there, anchored and offering some unforeseen protection to the back of Donuil's head. Then, my hand free, I leaned down and grasped Donuil by the upper arm, grateful for his height, if not for the weight of him, holding both the reins and my sword in my right hand.

"I have him! Let's go." We spurred our mounts and began to move, supporting Donuil's dead weight between us. As our horses began to gather speed, however, he regained awareness and began to run between us, unsteadily at first, but strengthening rapidly, so that by the time our speed had increased to a gallop, he had taken hold of each of our saddle cinches and was leaping along between us, bearing his own weight and pushing himself off the ground with one foot at a time in huge, distance-burning strides. One arrow hissed at us, clanging off Ded's metal-covered shoulder, and then we were safe, our pursuers left far behind us. On the outskirts of the warehouse area, where the thoroughfares broadened out, we met the others starting back, somewhat belatedly, to rescue us.

The aftereffects took hold of me a short time later, covering me in icy gooseflesh and rattling me with shivers as we rode quietly and sedately through the outlying area of the town, in the direction of the hilltop where we had left the boys and our extra horses. There had been little talk of who and what we had encountered. Time enough for that later, when each man had had time to absorb the fact that he was safe and whole. Now we rode each in his separate silence, reliving those few, terror-filled moments. We had been defeated and repelled by a force we had not even identified; driven off almost casually. I told myself that we had been heavily outnumbered and that there was little else I could have done. Then I remembered Rufio's warning with perfect and humiliating clarity, and there was nothing I could invoke to excuse myself for my arrogance in ignoring it. Since mine was the biggest horse among our group, and Donuil's the largest body, he rode now behind me, his arms loosely encircling my waist. Like me, he had not spoken since we met the others. Now I felt him stir and his voice spoke into my ear.

"Stone," he said.

"What? Stone?"

"Aye, marble. Isn't that what you call that smooth, shiny stuff? That's what they were taking on those cargo boats. Marble stone. I saw some broken pieces in the empty one, but I only now realized what it was. They were small, all broken, but one surface of almost every piece was smooth and shiny, polished. Some green, some white, and one reddish piece. Why would they take stone?"

His words suddenly came together in my mind, and I remembered something I had noticed earlier, on our way into Glevum; something that had been anomalous, yet insignificant at the time.

I looked around me, knowing what I was looking for now, and called to the others to halt. On a slight rise, just a little to the right of where we now sat, were the ruins of what had once been a temple. Its pillars gleamed softly in the afternoon light. I told the others to wait for me and kicked my horse forward. Donuil remained silent until I reined in and dismounted, freeing my feet and swinging my right leg forward over the horn of my saddle before slipping to the ground without disturbing him. I heard him dismount behind me as I walked forward to the temple steps. We climbed them together and stood staring in silence at the scene before us. The floor of the temple seemed artificially smooth and bare in places, gouged and rough in others, and scattered here and there with the broken remains of several of the square, black and white marble tiles that had covered it. The walls were bare, too, and it was equally evident that they, too, had once been covered with marble; entire sheets of polished, pale green marble; once again, the broken evidence remained. The facade, too, had been stripped of decorative panels in several places and the portico formerly supported by the marble Doric pillars was gone without a trace. Two pillars only remained, and they looked structurally sound in their smooth, unblemished whiteness, almost new. Four had disappeared.

"Well," I said, "there's your answer, my friend. They, whoever they are, are systematically stripping the buildings and transporting them."

"But why? What's to be gained from that? And where would they take them to?"

"There's wealth to be gained, Donuil, great wealth, I would think. Marble is the most valuable building material in the world. Now the Romans are long departed, and entire towns like this are lying abandoned, so someone has had the bright idea of dismantling them, the public and sacred buildings, at least, and shipping them to where they can be put to use by people rich enough to want to build that kind of thing elsewhere, probably in Gaul, across the water."

Donuil was gazing at me in wonder. "You're serious, aren't you?"

"Of course I am, although I can see why it would make no sense to you or me or any of our people. These, however," and I nodded to the signs of pillage all around us, "are not our people. These are scavengers. Do you know what locusts are?" He shook his head and I smiled. "Well, I've only read about them, but they are a kind of grasshopper in Africa, and they fly in swarms so dense they can black out the sun at noon. They consume everything in their path and leave nothing behind them but destruction. That's what you're looking at here. The work of human locusts. They'll strip this land of ours until nothing remains but the hills and the trees."

He sighed and shook his head. "I don't doubt the truth of it, but I'll never understand it. It seems insane."

"Oh, it's sanity, of a kind. Do you remember the Carpe Diem, in Verulamium?"

"The tavern? Aye, what about it?"

"We called it the Carpe Diem because of what it signified, and the shortness of its life. It was open for less than a month, you know, but its owner earned a lot of money during that time."

"Aye, but he provided a good service."

"Of course he did, I'm not denying that. But *carpe diem* means 'seize the day' . . . grasp the opportunity now, while it's available. Do you see what I mean?" He shook his head again, his eyes still troubled. "Donuil, thousands of people descended on that deserted town within a matter of weeks to attend the great debate. The Carpe's owner—I think his name was Paulus or something like that—saw and grasped the opportunity to profit by it. He opened a hostelry and enjoyed a thriving business while it lasted."

"Aye? So did a dozen others."

"That is exactly my point, Donuil: there will always be a breed of men who can take any circumstance and turn it into profit. And that's why these . . . these people, are here, dismantling Glevum. They're taking fortune where they find it. They'll probably spread their activities outward, eventually, to the abandoned villas all around, and unless someone does something to discourage them, sooner or later they'll come swarming towards Camulod like dung flies."

Donuil thought about that. "I understand," he said at length. "But what

I don't understand is why they would attack us like that, over a pile of stones? Why would they think we might want to steal their silly stones?"

"Because they perceive those stones as having monetary value, Donuil; great value, too, probably greater than you and I could imagine, judging from the number of people involved. They must have purchasers lined up somewhere, awaiting delivery. And even though their stolen cargo might be worthless in our eyes, they would kill us out of hand to protect it. Come on, we had best rejoin the others."

Two hundred paces farther on, just as the track we were following began to ascend the hillside, we found ourselves surrounded yet again, before we had any intimation of danger. A circle of men, many of them holding pulled bows, stood up out of the long grass all around us. Perhaps because of what we had just survived and our reaction to it, all of us were caught completely unprepared. My heart pounding in consternation, I cursed and stood up in my stirrups, pulling at my sword to unsheath it, then felt Donuil's arms pinion mine as he roared in my ear, for everyone to hear.

"Stand fast, men of Camulod! These are my people!"

My men all froze, staring around them in stupefaction, and I made an instant evaluation, then sagged backwards into Donuil's embrace, fighting for composure, forcing myself to sound unconcerned in spite of the fact that my heart seemed lodged somewhere in the region of my throat.

"Well then," I said, hearing and marvelling at the lack of even a tremor in my voice, "for the love of our God and theirs, tell them to point those arrows somewhere else before someone gets hurt."

Over the course of the hours that followed, we became acquainted with our new companions, whose leaders were the giant and the midget whose footprints had caused us so much concern on the journey from Camulod. Their names were Logan and Feargus, Logan being the giant. It had taken but moments for Donuil to convince them that we were friends and that he was in no way being constrained by us. As he told them the truth of his "captivity" and of how he had become a soldier of Camulod, they watched him in silence, making no attempt to interrupt him. When he had finished his tale, the tiny man, Feargus, made his way to me, followed by big Logan. He stopped directly in front of me, his head tilted far back to look up into my eyes.

"Merlyn Britannicus," he said, in a surprisingly deep and normal voice, the lilting Erse syllables pouring from his tongue like honey. "I extend to you the thanks of my Chief, Athol, King of Scots, son of Iain, son of Fergus and of all his people, for the honour you have shown his son."

Uncomfortably aware that I lacked a suitably formal response to his words and impressed by the simple dignity with which he had delivered them, I could only bow my head in acknowledgment. Donuil, however, felt no such reservations. His delight at seeing these people was complete and heartwarming. He ran forward to embrace the two leaders, then demanded to know, immediately, why they had taken so long to come forward, since they had been following us for days.

It was the giant, Logan, who responded, avoiding the question by pointing out that we were all still mounted, and that their story could wait until we had made camp and eaten. We moved forward then, still in our two separate groups, until we had rejoined our herd boys and their charges. Fires were lit shortly after that, though it was still only early afternoon, food appeared from a variety of sources, and a guard was posted on the hillside to make sure that none of our former assailants from the town came creeping up to finish what they had started. And as we ate, the two companies finally melded into smaller, mixed groups around the fires, communing somehow, in spite of the fact that neither group spoke the other's tongue. Logan and Feargus, between them, told Donuil and me their tale.

Connor had returned home safely, bearing the child hostage, but having failed to find his sister Ygraine. Donuil and I exchanged glances at that. King Athol had listened closely to Connor's story, gazing all the time at the tiny boy who had been brought into his kingdom as a hostage. He had questioned Connor closely on whether he had believed my tale of Donuil's safety and, at the end of it all, neither of them had known what to believe. They knew, however, of Camulod, from other sources, most notably the words of Lot, the Cornish king to whom Athol had wed his daughter. And Donuil's uncle, whom I had released at the time of Donuil's capture, had recognised me from Connor's description, and upon the strength of our one brief meeting had been inclined to believe what Connor reported. I made a mental note to seek him out and thank him when we came to Eire.

Logan and Feargus, two of Athol's most trusted friends and retainers, had been dispatched with two galleys to find Camulod and discover whether Donuil was alive or dead. They had landed to the west of where we sat now, and had seen us on the first day out of Camulod, recognising Donuil immediately, but finding themselves unable to approach us openly since they were too few in numbers to deal with us if we proved hostile. The last thing they wished was to endanger their prince. They had followed us closely for two days and nights, until we approached the place where they had left their galleys, at which point the two leaders stayed close to us, but not close enough to alert us to their presence, while the others were sent to bring more men; enough to confront us successfully, irrespective of our attitude to Donuil. They had suspected, Feargus told us, that we had known about them on the second night they came close to our camp.

Donuil had been listening intently, frowning a little, and now he interrupted Feargus.

"Why did you move across the country with only six men, Feargus? You have two galleys full."

Feargus sniffed and looked at Logan. "Aye, true enough," the big man said. "But your father the king was most exact in his instructions." He glanced at me, then back to Donuil before continuing. "Remember, you stood as safeguard of the word of your father that there would be no war with your captors so long as you were safe. Five summers was the term. We had no proof that you were dead, and none that you were alive. And so the word of King Athol was that we were to find a place to lie with our galleys, safe hid, until the word of your life or death was known beyond dispute. If you were now a free man, according to the agreement, then there would be no need to show a warlike force. If you were prisoner still, we were to march and deliver you. If you were dead, we were to exact vengeance. But until we knew, one way or the other, we were to do nothing to endanger the peace to which your father had committed all of us. And so we had to make towards Camulod, few enough in number to occasion no alarm, but strong enough in number to protect each other. So we were six, and but lightly armed." He paused and grinned. "We arrived back today with enough of us to make you safe, one way or the other—until we heard that you had ventured into that town, among the snakes. Gave us a bad time there, you did." He swung his head to include me in his next question. "Are you mad, to ride in, twelve against half a thousand?"

I dipped my head in acknowledgment. "I must have been, for a short time. Rufio over there warned me against it, but I would not listen. I was too intent on shipping our horses aboard their vessel."

"Horses? Aboard a ship?" Feargus was blinking at me in amazement. "And where were you thinking of going?"

"Home, Feargus," Donuil answered. "We were going home to Eire."

Feargus blinked again. "All of you? With horses?"

I grinned, feeling distinctly foolish. "That was my fault, Feargus. I had not thought the matter through. Or perhaps I had set greater store by my instincts than by sound planning."

Logan was as perplexed as Feargus appeared to be. "Why would you even want to take horses to sea?"

The question rocked me for a moment. "To transport them, to take them with us," I explained, as though speaking to a child. I could see that he still could not understand why anyone would wish to pursue such folly. "We are cavalry, Logan. We operate on horseback, and our horses are essential to our . . ." Strategy and tactics had been the words I intended to say, but no equivalents for them existed in the Erse tongue as far as I knew. I looked to Donuil for assistance, saying the words in Latin. He smiled and took over from me without pause, directing his words to both men.

"Caius Merlyn was about to say 'essential to the way we fight,' but he found himself in the same situation as you were when you landed your galleys down the coast from here. He had no intention of fighting in my father's land, but his presence there might be unwelcome to some. His purpose was to bring me to my home, greet my father and Connor in courtesy, collect the child, his godson, and then return to his own home in Camulod. To do that, nevertheless, he knew he might have to pass through strange and perhaps hostile territories, particularly when returning. He was thinking in terms of self-defense, and self-defense to the people of Camulod entails horses."

Both listeners appeared satisfied with that explanation, and the tension faded visibly from their bodies.

"I still don't see how you could have done it," insisted Logan. "There's no room on a galley for animals, other than a few trussed sheep or pigs for slaughter on a long journey. The very thought is madness."

I agreed with him. "We would not have been looking for a galley like yours, a longboat. We would have required something much larger, with a wooden deck and some means of shelter for the beasts. Something like the bireme that left this morning."

"Hmm." Feargus interrupted, waving Logan to silence. "How essential are these horses to you?"

I shrugged. "They are not, now that the choice has narrowed to remaining here with them or going without them. We'll leave them behind. Do you have a favoured weapon, Feargus?"

"Aye," he answered, dropping his right hand to the shaft of a short, heavy-headed axe with a wide blade that hung from his belt. "This. I rely on it because of my size. I find it gives me an advantage over bigger men that's more than enough."

I nodded. "I think the same way of our horses. Mounted, each of us can master six or seven on foot."

He turned to Donuil. "And you, Prince Donuil, do you feel the same?"

"I do." Donuil paused. "I do now. It took me a long time, though, to learn the truth of that."

"Hmm." Feargus stood up, his face furrowed in thought, and walked around to the other side of the fire, his head bowed, his tiny hands clasped at the small of his back. Watching him, I found nothing ridiculous in the size of him. He paced for a while, then turned and beckoned for Logan to join him, after which the two of them walked off to a distance, muttering together. I looked at Donuil.

"What d'you think that's all about?"

"Your guess is as good as mine," he said, his eyes on the ill-matched pair across the fire.

Their colloquy, whatever its content, was brief, and they returned directly to where we waited. Feargus, whom I had long since identified as the senior of the two, dropped to the ground, his back against a log and his elbow crooked over it, and spoke his mind without preamble.

"I think King Athol would enjoy seeing his son atop a horse as big as those you ride, accompanied by good friends. You know that empty vessel in the town, tied up by the dock . . . the thing like a big coracle . . ."

"It's a barge. What about it?" I felt a flutter of excitement.

"A barge. Would it transport your horses?"

"Aye, and all of us, but we can't reach it, and even if we could, we could not move it, since it has to be towed."

"Behind a bireme?" He was smiling slightly now, and my excitement increased.

"Aye, or even a longboat, were it big enough."

"What about two fair-sized galleys?"

I was sitting erect now. "How would we reach the barge, guarded as it is?" I asked, knowing the answer from the grin that now split his elfin features.

"We go in from the water and take it. No one will expect anything like that. An empty barge is worthless. We send swimmers in before dawn to cut it loose, and then attack when the sun comes up. One galley to pull it off empty and the other to discourage interference."

And so it came about that the banners, the men and the horses of Camulod travelled to Eire in an open barge, pulled slowly behind Erse warriors and at the utter mercy of the winds, which graciously held their breath.

BOOK TWO

EIRE

XI

Eire appeared to us as a mystical dreamscape, emerging silently and almost imperceptibly through the thick fog of an eerie dawn when nothing moved, not even the waters beneath our keel, and the only sounds to be heard were those we made ourselves. Ahead of us, attached by the long, heavy tow rope that sagged now beneath the motionless waters between us, Logan's galley drifted, looming dimly like a spectre in the fog, its big sail furled and its oars raised clear of the sea, so that the water dripping from the blades could be clearly heard by all of us. We lined the sides of our floating platform in silence, the moisture condensing on our armour and rolling down leather and metal like rain, each of us gazing intently to where, ahead and to our right, the fog bank seemed to thicken into solidness. Beside me, Dedalus leaned forward, his hands braced on the rail, the heavy wool of his cloak beaded with drops of water. Quintus stood next to him, and in the dim light I saw vapour coming from his mouth and nostrils as he breathed, and water dripping steadily down the back of his cuirass from the neck guard of his helmet. Someone behind me cleared his throat nervously and the stillness settled again, pressed down beneath the weight of the fog, absolute and impenetrable. A horse moved restlessly, stamping a hoof once on the solid planking of the deck, the sound damp and muffled and echoless, and still the silence persisted as we drifted. No one had warned us to be quiet. We had assumed our mantle of stillness in response to the sudden absence of sound from the galley. If those fierce Ersemen chose to proceed in stealth, we on our ungainly barge were glad to follow their example without prompting.

Then came a muffled order from the galley and the oars dipped again to the water, pulling strongly in a maneuver that won my admiration even as I marvelled at its strangeness. Five times the oars dug deep before the rope that joined us to the galley became taut and pulled us into motion, and then four times more, so that we surged forward in its wake. Then some of the oars rose vertically again, while the remainder on one side pulled forward and on the other backed water. The huge galley swung on its own centre, all oars shipped now, and came to rest facing back towards us, parallel to our course, between us and the invisible land mass as the momentum of our continued forward motion brought us alongside. Men stood ready to fend us off with long poles, but the judgment of the maneuver had been so exact that they were unnecessary. We glided perfectly to rest beside the larger vessel and Logan himself leapt effortlessly down to our deck. Until he opened his mouth to speak to me, no one had uttered a sound.

"Well," he said, holding his voice low, "we're here. Welcome to Eire. You can't see it yet, but the shore is less than half a bowshot from us now. The tidal drift will take us in closer, but I want to take us out again until we know exactly where we are. I merely wanted to warn your people to keep all noise down. Don't let those horses make a sound."

"Why not, if we've arrived?"

He raised one eyebrow at me and glanced at Donuil. "Because we don't know where we are exactly. The fog has seen to that. If we are more than three leagues south of where we should be, we could attract attention we don't need. We have no friends to the south of us. Feargus went farther north during the night, to find our anchorage, the spot we should have reached if not for this damned fog. He should be back soon, and then we'll know."

I had looked over his shoulder as he spoke, and now I saw the top of a massive tree emerging through the tendrils of fog that wreathed its branches. "We may be closer to the shore than you think," I said, nodding towards it.

He turned to look, uttered an oath and ran, using the low side of our barge as a step and launching himself upward to his own vessel, where waiting hands pulled him aboard. Thereafter all became confusion. The oars on the side nearest us levelled towards us from above like spears and pushed us away, forcing us sideways in a sluggish, wallowing, ungainly dance, moving their own galley as much as our heavy barge, so that its high mast rolled drunkenly. As soon as we had drifted apart far enough to give them room, the oars dipped again into the sea and began to pull, but not soon enough. Their gathering impetus was immediately aborted, the sweeps stilled in the water amid chaos as the central oars on the right of the galley dug into a rapidly shelving bottom, lodging there and throwing their rowers off balance. We did not discover what had happened until much later, but we clearly heard the violent cracking splinter of at least one oar and a chorus of shouts and screams mingled with the sound of falling bodies as the prow of the galley, propelled by the partial, yet powerful, thrust from the unfouled oars on the landward side, began to swing back violently towards us, its high, pointed nose towering over us until the heavy, reinforced beam crashed slowly, but with amazing power, into our side, splintering our heavy vessel's timbers as though they were made of eggshell. I saw the barge's side bend inwards like a colossal bow and shatter with a noise that almost deafened me, and at the same instant the planking of the deck closest to the side and running from prow to stern heaved upward, splitting into fragments, some of which flew whirring viciously through the air, spinning like wind-blown leaves. Beneath the planks, within a fraction of a heartbeat, I saw the lateral struts to which they had been nailed give way, sprung apart like the sides of a log beneath the axe that was the galley's thrusting prow.

The violence of the collision threw all of us, including the horses, to the deck, where the animals immediately began screaming and whinnying in panic, scrabbling and flailing vainly to regain their footing. I landed hard on my buttocks, my shoulders slamming against the side of the deck farthest from the point of impact, and Dedalus immediately fell sprawling on top of me, his elbow ramming sickeningly into my crotch and blinding me momentarily with pain and nausea. By the time I could drag myself to my knees again, reeling and gasping for breath, everything around me had degenerated into chaos. Dedalus was gone, but Quintus lay squirming close by me, his face ashen, bleeding copiously from the nose again and clutching his right thigh in both hands. That much I saw in the first glance, but then I saw him flinch again, struck by one of the wildly flailing hooves of my own big black, Germanicus, and I knew what had happened. I reached him in a lurch, still on my knees, and grasped him by the armholes in his cuirass, hauling him clear of the horse's reach. "Broken!" he hissed in my ear, and then I was on my feet again and looking all around me. The deck beneath me was tilted steeply towards the point of impact, where the prow of the galley still thrust through our shattered side as though locked in a vise. Where the two vessels joined, sea water lay deeply pooled, its level creeping upward even as I looked. And then I saw a pair of legs sprawled on the deck, its owner's head and torso lost beneath the water. I threw myself forward and down, barely avoiding being kicked by a horse myself, and grasped the ankles, dragging the drowned or drowning man out and up the sloping deck. It was Metellus, who had not fully regained his senses since falling from his horse on the wharf in Glevum. I had no time to check him for signs of life. The silence of only moments before had been obliterated by a Hadean chaos of noise, with men and horses adding their voices to the tortured shrieks and groans of splintered, twisting timbers, and suddenly I found myself looking up at Logan, perched on the very point of his galley's prow and shouting down at me. As I stood there, trying to decipher what he was telling me, Donuil appeared at my side.

"Can't hear you!" he yelled, his hands cupped around his mouth.

Logan heard him, and did the same with his own hands, funnelling his voice towards us. "We can't backwater to free ourselves! Too close to shore. Stern's aground. We'll have to push you like this. Donuil, come aboard!"

"I'm staying here! Do what you must. Push us out if you can, then turn us."

Logan hesitated for a moment, high above us, and then turned and disappeared. Donuil grasped me by the arm and leaned closer, shouting into my ear. "Did you understand what he said?"

"Aye, he's fast aground. I heard that. But how will he push us out, if his men can't row?"

"They'll push, until they have enough water beneath the keel. It shouldn't take long. Only the stern's aground. Once they're clear, they can throw their full weight on the oars and push us around. They hit us aft of centre, so we'll swing fairly easily. The motion should break our hold on them and allow them to break free of us."

"Aye, and what then?"

"We'll sink, once they've pulled free. The barge is broken well beneath the waterline. We'll have to swim ashore." As he spoke, the motion of the barge changed suddenly, and with the change came an agonized groaning of wood from the junction of the two craft. I glared around me at my men, my mind in a turmoil.

"Damnation, Donuil, we're all wearing armour. We'll sink like stones and drown!"

He had anticipated me. "We'll swim with the horses. They'll carry us, but we have to get them on their feet. Come on!"

I ran immediately towards my horse Germanicus, feeling the barge's deck lurch again beneath my feet as Logan's men thrust their long oars against the sea bottom, poling both vessels away from the land. "Up!" I yelled to everyone. "On your feet and get the horses up! Quickly, or we all drown."

We had haltered the animals to four stout ropes slung from side to side across the deck and fastened by heavy iron spikes hammered through their knotted braids, which meant that the horses themselves stood facing either front or rear. The sidelong impact had sent them all tumbling, and only a very few had regained their footing. I reached Germanicus and knelt in front of his head, grasping his bridle in both hands, and talking to him, seeing the rolling of his eye that bespoke utter terror. "Come on, big boy," I told him, fighting to maintain the familiar level tones he knew from me. "Come on, let's get you on your feet again. Come on, up!" I raised myself, pulling the straps of his headstall, raising his head clear of the deck, then straightening and heaving as I almost dragged him to his feet. Slowly, hesitantly, but gathering confidence from my persistence, the great animal shrugged himself around until his front hooves were flat against the deck, after which he pushed himself up, as a man will on his arms, until his legs were straight. Once there, the rest was fairly simple. He tried once, then again, and on the third attempt gathered his haunches and lurched to his feet, where he stood spread-legged and unsteady, bracing himself delicately on the tilting deck, his nostrils flaring, ears laid flat along his head and his eyes still rolling wildly.

Now, all around me, I saw my men doing as I had done, pulling the animals upright. Only one still screamed, and I looked towards the awful sound and saw a beautiful roan with a mangled right foreleg, the skin broken and pierced by a long shard of bloodied bone. As I looked, absorbing the animal's wound, one of my men smote the animal between the eyes with a hand axe, killing it instantly. The sudden cessation of its agonized screaming made the remaining tumult seem like silence. I used that instant to capture everyone's attention with a shout.

They listened attentively as I explained what was about to happen, shocked, but plainly aware of the need to waste no time in making preparations. As soon as I had finished speaking, they fell to work, saddling their own mounts and stowing their weapons before loading the packhorses. I had told them not to worry greatly about cinching the saddles perfectly. It would be difficult on the sloping deck, and all that was really required was that the saddles should stay in place. They would not be riding ashore, but swimming alongside their mounts, hanging on and kicking, trusting their animals to keep them from drowning. As I turned back from fastening my own cinch, tightening it as firmly as I could, I saw Donuil back at the broken side, talking to someone up on the prow of the galley. And then, amazingly, I saw a figure dive from the side of the galley, straight down into the sea. He surfaced almost immediately and came swimming to where Donuil crouched, ready to pull him out. The diver emerged, dripping, and then Donuil helped him climb back up to the craft above again before turning and making his way to me.

"I asked for someone to dive down and see how deep the bottom is," Donuil explained. "He touched bottom on his dive, so it can't be much more than the height of a tall man."

"So? That's deep enough to drown in."

Donuil actually grinned at me. "Aye, but it's also shallow enough to dive in. The sun will be up soon enough, and that means the fog will disperse, so we'll be able to recover anything that we lose in swimming ashore. Shields, for example, and heavy weapons. All we have to do now is hope that we are either in friendly territory, or that there's no one around to ask awkward questions before we can reorganize ourselves. We—" His voice was suddenly lost in an upsurge of the grinding, wrenching noises from the join of the two ships. As we had worked to prepare ourselves, Logan and his crew had been labouring mightily, heaving on their oars in a series of complicated maneuvers and pushing us first outwards and then around, so that our own prow now pointed towards the land, which was clearly discernible, although still mist-shrouded, in the early morning light.

My attention was immediately all for the horses. The sides of the barge were not high, but they were certainly high enough to deter a balking animal that had no wish to leap overboard.

"Tell Logan to stop, quickly!"

Donuil turned and yelled an order to the man on the galley prow. The great oars stopped churning almost instantly.

"Now," I told him, speaking loudly for the benefit of my men, "it is imperative the horses go over facing in the right direction, otherwise they're likely to swim out into deep water. Tell Logan that, and explain it. He knows nothing of horses and how stupid they can be at times. His ship is parallel to the shore now. If he reverses the thrust of his oars, he should be able to pull free, and the same motion should pull our stern around again, towards the beach. As soon as he breaks free, this thing will start to sink, tilting shoreward, if we have any luck at all. That should make it more than simple to put the horses in facing the proper way. Tell him to do it now." As Donuil sprang back towards the galley, I raised my voice to the others. "Cut the halters and hold fast to them. Those of you who can handle two, do it. When the deck starts to really tilt, lead the horses down and try to keep them calm. They'll want to panic, so don't allow them to. Go with them, and hang on. They'll get you safe ashore. You heard what Donuil said. We can come back later for any weapons you lose, so don't weigh yourselves down any more than you have to, but don't leave yourselves defenseless, either. Now, wait for my word." I glanced around me. "Where's Metellus?"

It was Dedalus who answered me. "He's dead. Kicked in the head, I think, by one of the horses."

"What about Quintus?"

"Quintus is here. He should be fine."

I turned to see Rufio standing behind me, holding two halters. Quintus was draped face upward and tied firmly to the bare back of one horse, the only white one we had, a huge gelding that dwarfed even my own mount.

"Where is his saddle?"

Rufio nodded. "Over there, on the king's stallion."

"Good. Look after him."

I saw a wave of movement as the banked oars of the galley came down into the water again and thrust backward in unison. The barge shuddered and lurched and an evil, highpitched rending sound was ripped from the mouth of the barge's open wound. For long moments nothing happened; the oars cleared the water and dipped again, accompanied by a heaving, grunting, concerted roar of effort from the galley's rowers. And then came a sudden screech and the deck beneath our feet shuddered as the galley sprang free, tossing its prow in the air, the scars on its bow planking showing new and bright against the darkness of the timbered hull, although the damage appeared superficial. The old barge, however, was mortally wounded and heaved upward, threatening to topple all of us again and sending the pool of sea water swirling around our feet before the vessel's returning, downward roll brought the holed side down beneath the level of the surface and the sea came pouring in. There could be no recovery. Within moments, what little liveliness the ungainly craft had ever had was gone, and it began to settle quickly, as the space beneath the shallow deck was inundated.

I had misread what might happen. The barge sank downward on an even keel, steadily and appallingly swiftly, so that we had no need to coax the horses over the side. The sea, instead, came up to meet them, gurgling between the planking of the deck, and before they knew it they were swimming strongly for the shore, carrying their normal passengers, although in a most abnormal fashion.

For the second time in two months I found myself immersed in the sea, out of my depth and weighed down by heavy armour that threatened to drag me to the bottom. I hung tightly to the horn of my saddle, trusting my horse's strength and attempting to kick my legs to relieve him as much as possible of my dead weight. I might as well have tried to fly! My leather-lined chain-mail coat and leggings, almost weightless in the saddle although uncomfortably bulky when walking, were lethally dangerous in water. Each futile thrust of my overburdened legs threatened to tear them from their sockets. I gave up and clutched with my hands and arms, my eyes tight shut, wrapping my right elbow tightly about the saddle horn and praying I had cinched the saddle securely enough to prevent it slipping sideways and drowning me. And then I felt Germanicus falter, then push himself erect, his feet solidly planted on the sandy bottom. Almost without pausing to adjust his balance, he began to push forward strongly, walking now, and I felt the pressure of the water against me change. A moment longer I clung to my saddle's safety, and then I let go with my elbow, feeling for the bottom with my own feet, but retaining a firm hand grip on the horn. I touched bottom immediately, my toes dragging through sand so that I had to brace myself to get my legs beneath me properly. Then, first slowly, but with increasing ease and speed, I walked towards the beach until the sand beneath my feet was dry. Only then did I fall to my knees.

As I knelt there, catching my breath, I became aware again, for the first time since it had happened, of the heavy ache in my balls caused by the blow from Dedalus's elbow, and then a gust of wind set me shivering with cold. I forced myself to my feet and looked about, seeing my men and horses all around me, most of the men already loosening the cinches and removing the heavy, waterlogged saddles from the beasts' backs. I saw our two herd-boys, too, one of them clutching the bridles of the matched chestnut roans that were my gift to Athol. The stallion wore Quintus's saddle on its back, but the mare was unencumbered. The other boy was running among the men and animals, gathering up and herding the extra horses, many of which were laden with bundles of our baggage and supplies, and I wondered briefly how much had been spoiled by sea water.

We were on a small, sheltered, steeply sloping, crescent-shaped beach with tree-covered arms sweeping out to sea on either side. The upper edge of the beach was less than the height of a man below the level of the surrounding ground. Beyond that rim, the land seemed to stretch level for a distance before sweeping sharply upward, covered completely with trees as far as the eye could reach before the low clouds obscured the view. I turned towards the sea behind me, and there was Logan's galley, riding calmly less than fifty paces distant, held in place by an occasional backward or forward sweep of a few oars on either side. I could see Logan himself up on the forward platform, gazing towards us; I waved to him and received an answering wave. I heard someone approaching me and turned to see Donuil walking head down, tugging at his clothing. He had already divested himself of his cuirass, leggings and helmet.

"Well," he said, peering down at a knot he was attempting to undo, "we're all safe ashore."

Behind him, I saw Dedalus and a couple of others lifting Quintus down from the back of the big white that had ferried him safely.

"How's Quintus, do you know?"

"Aye, he's as well as he can be, I suppose, but I wish Lucanus were with us. His leg is badly mangled. Bone right through the flesh. We'll have to set it and splint it, although I don't know where we'll find decent splints. There!" The knot at which he had been tugging came loose, and he stripped off his tunic, leaving himself naked except for a breech cloth. His huge chest was covered with goose bumps and his skin had a bluish tinge to it. "Now we have to light a fire."

"With what? You'd have to go up off the beach to find kindling and no one is strolling off alone until we're sure there's no enemy up there watching us and waiting for us to be stupid. That means you stay here until we are organized and that, my friend, is a direct command. Anyway, it would be futile—everything will be soaked from the fog." I glanced up towards the sky, surprised to see bright blue up there. The fog had vanished and the sun hung low in the sky above the horizon to the east. "It may take some time for the sun to develop enough heat to dry things out, so we will simply have to settle for being cold for a spell."

Now Donuil looked directly into my eyes, smiling. "Ach, Commander, you are in the hands of an Erseman now, in his homeland. We can always find dry moss, even in a downpour. Besides, I wouldn't go alone. Let me take Ded and Rufio with me, and I'll have a fire going before you have time to grow another goose bump." He broke off and looked at the impenetrable trees surrounding the beach. "I wonder where we are exactly? Best we make no smoke until we know for certain. I'll fetch my fire-making tools and a knife, and then I'll get started. Can I go?"

I glowered at him, stifling the urge to laugh at his audacity, yet thinking that if there were enemies up there among the trees, we would be better off knowing now.

"Take four men, all of you armed, and be careful."

He grinned at me and nodded, then turned and loped away, heading back towards the pile of gear and armour he had cast off on landing. I was shivering with cold and knew that movement was what I needed. I turned and climbed the sloping beach, feeling the sand cling heavily to my sodden footwear as I trudged towards the overhang of a little cliff that rimmed the inlet. Once there, I leaned an elbow on the hard, grass-stubbled ground and peered towards the trees.

Behind me, I heard the sounds of someone approaching and I assumed it to be Donuil, but it was Rufio. Donuil followed behind him, leading Philip, Benedict, Paulus and Cyrus, all of them except Donuil still fully armoured. Almost naked, but carrying a sword and an axe, Donuil paused at the top of the bank, looking at me. "I would suggest you too strip off, Commander, before you freeze or rust solid. Then move around. The sun will warm you, and the quicker you get warm, the sooner you'll be prepared for any company that might come by." He disappeared into the fringe of trees, followed by the others in his party, and Rufio and I watched them go, then waited for any sound of conflict that might follow. None did, and I eventually decided we were alone. I hauled myself up onto the level ground and turned back to Rufio, pulling him up beside me.

"Donuil's right. Wet clothes and wet armour over cold bodies will cripple us. Better to warm ourselves first and then put on damp clothes again over the warmth if we have to." Quickly, with a minimum of effort, we helped each other remove our armour, each undoing the other's wet and slippery buckled straps, and then we undressed completely. The others on the beach, seeing where we were and what we were doing, began to move up to join us until only Dedalus was left, kneeling over the shape of Quintus. The horses, too, remained on the beach, most of them rolling in the sand, drying the sea water from their coats. They would have no way of climbing up to where we were until we created a causeway of some kind for them.

Donuil had returned without my noticing, and now I smelled the tang of smoke. I looked behind me and saw him crouched on his knees, blowing gently and lovingly on a tiny tendril of smoke. As I looked, he knelt up straighter and began to lay twigs carefully across the crackling grass and moss and bits of bark he had ignited, and the flames began to leap higher. The mere sight of it, and the promise it contained, put heart in all of us, and my sense of purpose found its feet again.

Less than an hour later, three large, roaring fires were ablaze, surrounded by steaming clothes and armour, all stretched out upon an amazing array of dead branches and sticks. Logan's galley had anchored alongside one of the protecting arms of the small bay, so that his warriors could land and form a perimeter about our small encampment, standing guard against unwelcome visitors until our clothes and armour were dry and we were fit to take care of ourselves.

Benedict and I had set and splinted Quintus's broken leg between two narrow lengths of heavy planking, split and trimmed to size with a hand axe. I had been assisted by four of our biggest men, who had had trouble holding Quintus down until he passed out from the pain of the procedure. Now the worst was over, and his wounded leg was clean, washed out and scoured by the salt water. I had hopes that he would recover, and Logan, who had provided clean, dry cloth to bind the leg, had agreed to transport him on his galley to our destination. Logan's ship had also provided us with food, a porridge made of ground, salted oats, and pots in which to cook it, and we were all feeling much better and stronger. A team of ten men, some of them ours, most of them Logan's, all strong swimmers, had dived down to the sunken barge and prised loose a number of whole deck planks, bringing them ashore and lashing them together, after which they had returned and salvaged almost everything that we had lost. Before beginning that operation, however, two of them had retrieved the corpse of poor Metellus, towing him between them to the beach, and I set two more of my men to digging a grave for him, up on the solid land far from the water. While that was happening, another group of men had laboured to break down the lip of the bank at its weakest spot, creating a ramp for the horses to climb up from below. Most of the horses' grain supply was ruined, but there was enough grazing nearby to sustain them, and they themselves had been thoroughly dried and groomed. Within another hour, I estimated, we would be self-sufficient again: rested, well fed, dried out, re-armoured—although a little stiffly and uncomfortably—and remounted.

A single glance around having shown me that everything was happening as it should, I crossed to where I had left Publius Varrus's great bow leaning against a tree bole in the sunlight. It had been among my first concerns, after the welfare of my men. At the earliest opportunity, I had dried it carefully and coated it with a fresh covering of the light oil I always carried in a tiny bottle in my scrip, working the lubricant thoroughly into the surfaces with a soft, dry cloth. It was the same oil that Publius Varrus had always used in the bow's upkeep. I had been concerned about the effect of sea water on the old weapon's triple-layered composition—the smooth, deeply polished wood of its outer curve was backed by a layer of carefully grafted animal horn, which, in turn, was reinforced by a third layer of densely woven animal sinew, painstakingly plaited into a resilient strip, then stretched, glued into place and carefully dried and shrunk by a master craftsman now dead for more than a hundred years. I had been grateful to see no signs of deterioration in any part of the huge bow, although the rational part of me knew that its highly glossed finish was proof against a mere soaking, that the glue that bonded its layers together had endured for more than ten decades and showed no signs of deterioration, and that in any event, the weapon had not been immersed for long enough to have sustained damage. Satisfied that it was unharmed, I hefted it and turned it in my hand, checking the condition of the half-dozen bowstrings of woven gut I had wrapped tightly around the shaft, spiralling from one end to the other, to allow them to dry out, too. They were drying evenly; still too damp to use, since they would stretch when moist, but showing signs of hardening again.

A leather satchel inverted over a nearby bush had been filled with my supply of arrows, each of which Donuil had dried individually, to avoid rust on the heads, and laid out flat while I took care of the bow. I could see traces of salt riming the feathers of the flights, but that would easily be dislodged between a finger and thumb. As I stood there, looking down at them, I heard a voice shout, "There they are!" and then a chorus of cheers told me that Feargus's galley had returned. As I looked, it came surging around the headland to the north, under full oars and sail, its prow slicing through the waves that had risen with the slight wind. Their lookout had seen us before we saw them, for the long, sleek vessel was turning sharply, cutting towards us, headed directly towards Logan's moored craft. It came impressively, swooping like a hawk and then slowing dramatically as the rowers backed water in unison and then allowed it to find its own way until it glided to a halt alongside Logan's vessel and was made fast. I saw Donuil striding along the beach towards the newcomers and I followed him, restraining myself against a ridiculous urge to run and catch up.

Feargus crossed into Logan's galley immediately, ignoring Donuil and me when we climbed aboard and greeted him. Only by a warning gesture of his upraised palm did he indicate his knowledge of our presence, but the peremptory gesture contained enough authority to inform both of us unmistakably that, irrespective of our rank elsewhere, our presence was unwanted until he had discussed the situation with his own subordinate. Donuil and I exchanged a glance and waited by the mast in the middle of the ship, out of earshot of the discussion taking place on the rear deck, until the little man snorted violently, pulled himself up to his full height, and walked to the edge of the deck. There he stared out towards the dark shape of the sunken barge for long moments, his hands clasped together at the small of his back.

I cleared my throat and straightened my shoulders, thinking to myself that this might be the proper time to assert my own authority, but Donuil's voice murmured gently in my ear.

"Give him time, Merlyn. He takes his responsibilities very seriously, our Feargus, and there's no point in upsetting him more than he is already. In his mind we are in his charge, for the time being, in spite of what we ourselves might think, and we'll remain so until he has delivered us safely to my father's Hall, fulfilling his obligation. He will be seeing our misfortune as his own fault, for all that he was nowhere near when it occurred. As he will see it, his is the command, so his must be the fault. Of course, he's an Erse Outlander, and they're all strange, don't you agree?"

I spun to look at him and saw him smiling. Recognizing his wry allusion to my own attitude to command, I resigned myself to waiting until Feargus was ready to speak. Moments later he turned from his musing and made his way down the central spine of the ship towards us, beckoning Logan to come with him. He stopped just short of us, looking up at Donuil first and then at me.

"This is dangerous. We are in hostile territory, almost ten leagues south of where we ought to be, and by now we should be overrun and dead."

"At whose hands?" He did not even dignify my question with an acknowledgment, let alone an answer. His attention had now focused upon Donuil.

"Yourself will have to remain here, aboard my vessel. The others will have to take their chances on the land, unless they care to come on board and leave the animals here for the Wild Ones."

I straightened up at that. "The Wild Ones" was not what my ears heard but what my mind supplied as a rough translation. Years with Donuil had enabled me by this time to speak his tongue fluently, so close was it to the tongue of Uther's Celts, but now that we were among his own people again, he was conversing naturally with them at great speed and using words and phrases and entire constructions that were alien to me. The phrase I had translated as "The Wild Ones" was one of those. The disdain with which the words were uttered—forming an epithet rather than a name—carried overtones of implacable savagery and inhumanity.

"The Wild Ones?" I looked at Donuil for help, but he was already shaking his head at Feargus.

"No, Feargus, I will not leave my friends here, and they will not leave their horses."

"Don't talk like a fool, Mac Athol! Your father charged me with the guardianship of you, and you will obey me in this as you would himself. I will send half my men to escort your friends overland, out of this place, but your welfare is more important than all of them together."

Donuil turned to me. "What do you say? Will you leave the horses here and come by boat?"

"No." I did not even have to think about it. "How far are we from the nearest road?"

My question startled him. He looked at me and laughed. "From the nearest road?" He waved his hand out to sea. "The nearest road is back there in Britain, Merlyn, beyond the sea! We have no roads in Eire, not in the sense you mean. We have tracks and paths, beaten by passage over the years, but there are no Roman roads linking towns and regions. This is a different land. It has never been conquered or colonized."

I blinked at him and then turned to Feargus, trying to hide my dismay. I had never envisioned an entire country without roads. "Who are these Wild Ones you mentioned, Feargus?" I used my own words, unable to recall the exact phrase that he had used.

He looked at me in disgust. " 'Wild Ones?' That's a pretty name for such as those. They are the creatures of the dark who infest this place. Savages is too weak a word for them. They are mindless and pitiless. They have no system: no king, no chiefs worthy of the name, no government of any kind, no clan structure."

"You mean they are outcasts? Alien?"

"Outcasts?" His bark of savage laughter was derisive. "Cast out of what? They have never belonged to anything except their own madnesses. Alien? That's a strange word I've never heard before, but if it means different then yes, they are alien, as different from ordinary people as the wolf is to a boy's pup. Different indeed. They are all blood mad and all they do is fight. They spend their lives looking for folk to kill, and when they cannot find them they kill each other. It is our law that any of them we find, we kill on sight."

I frowned. "Invariably? I find that hard to accept."

"That is your right." He stopped abruptly, and then his voice changed, becoming more pensive, less outraged. "Look you, Merlyn Britannicus, I know not how it is in your land, this Camulod, but my mind tells me, from the very look and presence of you, that it must be similar to here. Here in Eire we have always known that people cannot live together without laws. The laws of each clan may differ in substance, but each *has* laws, and rulers, kings and chiefs and family heads to make and defend those laws, and you would be surprised to know how little most of them differ, even among clans and groups set far apart. The people you so innocently called the Wild Ones have no laws. None at all. They know no loyalties, even among themselves. They live in savagery and they are completely merciless. Woe betide any man, woman or child unfortunate enough to encounter them alone."

"Come now, they must have families!"

He cut me with a glance. "They have mates, and broods. No more." He looked around at the heavily treed land beyond the beach. "We are in their lands now. Deep within them. It is not a good place to be. I blame myself. We should have remained together."

"Don't," I told him, accepting the almost supernatural fear I sensed in him. "That would have changed nothing. You did what you thought was for the best, and it was. It was the fog that brought us to grief, not your leadership. Now, here's what I want to do. I agree with you about Donuil. He

should go with you, and you must take our wounded fellow, Quintus, too."
I cut Donuil's protest short with an upraised hand and continued speaking
to Feargus. "As for an escort of your men, we won't need them; they would
only slow us down. Fortune has been with us so far. Now all we require is a
short time to allow us to dry our gear completely and make a fresh start.
After that, we'll head north, following the coast as closely as we can, and try
to keep in touch with you. Are there any settlements along the coast between
us and where we are going?"

"Nah." His headshake was emphatic. "If there had been, we would not
be here like this, undisturbed."

I looked back to Donuil. "How far is a league? In Roman miles? He said
we are almost ten leagues too far south."

"About three miles to a league, I think, but that's only a guess. I'm staying
with you."

"No, Donuil, you are not. You will travel with Feargus." Again I stopped
his protest before it could be uttered. "Remember why I came with you,
man! If we should meet any of these Wild Ones and fail to make it through,
then at least the child will have a chance to return home to Camulod in
your care. I know I can rely on you for that."

He looked at me long and hard, then sucked his lower lip between his
teeth. I stared back at him, waiting. Finally he sighed and jerked his head in
a nod. "Very well, Caius Merlyn. So be it. I do not like it, but I will do as
you say. Just see that you come safe through."

I grinned at him, feeling much better. "I will, Donuil. I have no intention
of dying at the hand of anyone as degenerate as the people Feargus describes.
In fact, I have no intention of dying at all, ever." I turned back to Feargus.
"Do any of your men use spears?"

"Spears? Aye, many of them do. Why?"

"Because I would like to borrow some. We have our shields, but only
three of us carry spears and it seems to me now that we might all have need
of more. We will be riding fast and hard, and if we have to fight these demons
you describe, I would choose to fight from horseback, at a run, and with a
strong spear in my hand."

He grunted. "I wish all requests were that easy to grant." He swung on
his heel and shouted to one of his men, sending him running back towards
the platform at the rear of the galley. He returned moments later, accompanied by three others, each of them bearing an armload of assorted spears.
The weapons all looked heavy and serviceable and were of varying lengths.

"Excellent," I said, nodding my approval. "We won't need anywhere near
that many, but there are enough to let each of my men pick one that suits
him. My thanks. We can be prepared to move out from here within the hour.
That should give us five, perhaps six hours of travel time before nightfall;
close to your ten leagues, if fortune smiles on us and we're lucky enough to
avoid your savages."

Feargus looked impressed. He turned his head to look towards our horses.
Donuil, however, shook his head, looking doubtful.

"I think not, Merlyn. You won't be able to move that quickly. No roads,
remember? The entire route along the coast is heavily forested. You'll be
riding through trees and underbrush the whole way. It could cut your normal
speed by half."

*   *   *

From the outset, it seemed as though Donuil had the right of it. We said our farewells within the hour, some time shortly after noon, and rode into the forest, leaving him staring after us from the deck of Feargus's galley. By the time we had progressed the distance of a bowshot, our speed had been reduced to a slow, torturous walk, and I knew that none of us had ever encountered a wilderness such as this. My vision of a steady, cantering passage had already been proved ludicrous by the difficulty our mounts had found in even placing their hooves to walk. Every step offered a potential hazard, threatening a broken leg or ankle, for this ground, beneath a canopy of mighty, soaring trees, had never been cleared. The forest was beautiful, but utterly alien and apparently unpenetrated by man; every leaf and twig and tiny branch, every limb and tree trunk that had ever grown here, down through the ages, had fallen in the course of time in random chaos and lain undisturbed thereafter. There was a verdant, lush stillness everywhere that choked all sound and made the rich greenery of Britain's great forests seem anaemic and tawdry by comparison. Moss clung to the tree trunks here as it did over there, but the moss of Eire was thicker, *fatter*, and it grew everywhere; on the ground, on the rocks, on the countless fallen trees, some of them enormous, that littered the ground in every stage of decay, and on the upper portions of the trees themselves, hanging in green garlands from the branches. The earth under our hooves was of rich, reddish loam beneath the carpet of dead leaves that coated it, and crusted with fungi of all shapes and sizes, many more of which also clung to the boles and branches of the trees. A few of those, I knew, might be edible, but many more would be deadly, and I had no way of knowing which was which in this new and threatening land through which we rode.

To our left, inland as we made our plodding way northward over the forest bed, the terrain rose vertically in a series of ancient, green-scummed cliffs from which giant slabs and boulders of granite had been wrenched in ages past and now leaned drunkenly in every conceivable posture, as green and lichen-scabbed as the cliffs that had mothered them. Huge trees grew up there, too, upon the cliffs and slabs and boulders, clinging impossibly to the living rock by vast networks of roots that stretched across, between, along and around the fissures in the stone, and everywhere grew clumps and thickets of brilliant, ancient-looking ferns, many of them taller than a mounted man. Little light penetrated the roof of leaves high above, but wherever a ray of sunlight did succeed, it shimmered gold-green in the silent, surrounding darkness. I was aware of rich, reddish-brown fecundity everywhere I looked, but the pervading impression was of total greenness.

I was in the lead, and now I hitched myself around in my saddle, looking back to Dedalus, who was following me closely. He saw me turn and shook his head, and the disgust in his face was echoed in his tone as he called to me. "You thought to make thirty miles before nightfall? We'll be lucky to make one at this rate." His eyes shifted from my face to the wilderness ahead of us. "Mind you," he added, "the ground's rising. We might ride out of this soon, if we're not just climbing a hill with a down slope on the other side."

I glanced forward again and he was right. There was a definite upward slope to the land ahead. I pulled my horse aside and waved him past me, telling him I would catch up later. Then I sat and watched my pitiful little parade as it trooped by me, offering a word or two to each rider in turn. There were eight of us left—ten, counting the herd boys—of the original group of fourteen. Lucanus had been the first to depart, as planned. Metellus was dead. Quintus with his broken leg and Prince Donuil had gone with Feargus and Logan. But we still had all the horses except the three that had been killed. Eight men, two stripling boys and twenty-seven horses. I cursed myself for my folly in bringing all of them across the sea. They were behaving placidly, nonetheless, and for the time being I had no great concern over them. When the last of my men had passed me, nodding wordlessly to my greeting, I fell in behind him, immediately aware of the beneficial effect twenty-six sets of hooves in single file had had on the ground underfoot, and there faced a dilemma: were I to pull aside now and attempt to overtake the entire train to regain the point, I should be risking my horse irresponsibly on the uneven ground. I decided to remain where I was for a time. And then, within a matter of moments, the man directly ahead of me changed his gait, kicking his horse to a trot, and as I followed him I saw the file ahead of him extending to my left. Dedalus, at the point, had evidently found and was now following a game trail that led along the bottom of the towering cliffs on our left.

Our pace picked up steadily as soon as we were all on the beaten path of the narrow track, and after a mile or so it quickened again as the main path widened after converging with yet another, that joined it from our right. I saw the junction as I drew level with it, and followed it idly backward for several paces with my eyes before suddenly reining in my horse and returning to look more closely. It was a deer track, but I had never seen deer tracks like those I gazed at now. Each hoofprint, clearly visible in the soft loam of the beaten pathway, looked as large as my horse's own, and yet the signs were undeniably those of a cloven-hoofed deer. The track itself, now that I looked at it more closely, was far broader than a mere game track should have been. Unable to doubt what I was looking at, I shook my head in wonder and then rode to catch up with the others, grappling with the outlandish idea of a deer as large and heavy as a cavalry horse. I had lagged behind about a hundred paces, and as I cantered to catch up I took note of the way the path had widened. I called to the last man ahead of me to warn him I wished to pass and was able to do so quite easily, so that my progress from the rear to the head of the column was swifter than I would have thought possible mere moments earlier. As I drew abreast of Dedalus, he glanced at me, his eyes crinkled.

"No roads in Eire, huh? This is almost as good as one of ours. Not as straight, and narrower, but serviceable enough."

"Aye, Ded, but have you thought to ask yourself what made it?"

I caught his glance from the corner of my eye. "What d'you mean? Deer made it."

"I know, but if the wolves and bears in this place are as big as the deer I hope we don't meet any."

He frowned at me, and then raised himself in his stirrups, peering forward at the ground between his horse's ears.

"By the Christus," he muttered, in a voice filled with awe. "I hadn't noticed! You're right. What kind of deer are these?"

"Very large deer, Ded. We can only hope they have deer-like natures and no horns."

The game path was clearly ancient. Saplings had grown up along its edges in many spots, sprung from seeds scattered in the dung of its users, and their leafy branches brushed against us on both sides as we rode in silence for a spell, travelling two abreast easily now at a steady lope on the gently rising gradient that showed no signs of coming to a crest. At one point, where a giant tree had fallen across the track long years before, the route switched sharply, following the enormous trunk for many paces before bending tightly again to pass beneath the bole that continued angling sharply upward to its torn-up base, where ancient roots more than four times the height of a mounted man reared far above us. Whatever its cause, the great tree's downfall had created a clearance, sweeping lesser trees to ruin in its wake, so that now the space around it was filled with light and lesser growth. Ded was looking back at the place where we had passed beneath the tree. We had had to duck our heads to do so, but only very slightly, which indicated to me that the animals who used the path required almost the same clearance as we did. Dedalus was evidently thinking the same thing, for I heard him mutter "Big deer!" again, beneath his breath. Now he looked up towards the blue sky visible above us.

"You know, Merlyn, it occurs to me that we might be enjoying unusual weather in this land of Donuil's."

"How so?"

Before answering, he leaned sideways from his saddle and grasped a trailing garland of moss, tugging it free of the branch from which it hung and holding it towards me. "This stuff. It requires moisture. Haven't you noticed how green everything is? And all the fungi? It must rain here all day, every day, seems to me . . . And if that's the case, it's going to be a whoreson to live here without rusting up solid, our weapons and armour and all."

He was right and I was on the point of agreeing with him when he jerked up his arm, holding it high and cutting me short. "Wait!" His eyes stared fixedly into the middle distance over my shoulder. "What was that?" The men behind us stopped, too, some of them having seen his upraised arm, but the noise of their movement masked whatever it might have been that had alerted Dedalus. I swung around to look where he was looking, my ears straining to hear anything beyond the sounds we made ourselves.

We waited, motionless, our senses on edge, even our horses seemingly spellbound. Nothing stirred. After long moments, Dedalus relaxed, blowing out his breath and settling back in his saddle. "There's nothing there, but I could have sworn I heard something."

I dismounted without speaking and he watched me as I pulled my bow stave from its fastenings beneath my saddle skirts.

"What are you doing?"

"Feeling vulnerable." I fished a bowstring out of my scrip and strung the bow, bracing it with my knee, then hung a quiver of arrows from my saddle horn before remounting.

Dedalus was smiling. "Not used to seeing you jumpy."

I raised an eyebrow at him. "It happens. Keeps me alive sometimes. If we have to leave this path for any reason, we'll have to do it slowly." I nodded towards the tangle of broken trees all around. "My arrows give me speed. It's being unprepared that's dangerous. Let's go."

He pulled on his reins and raised himself up in the stirrups. "All right," he announced. "False alarm, but keep your eyes and ears—"

His voice was drowned by a bellow of rage from very close by. Something came charging towards us from our left, against the base of the cliff. I saw the wild, surging movement of it, and had the immediate impression of low-slung, solid bulk and sorrel brownness before the creature came clearly into view, causing panic among our close-packed horses. It was a boar, massive and fuelled by rage, and it attacked in a terrible, weaving, impossibly swift charge, right into the middle of our column. The untended horses scattered, screaming in terror, from the rank, feral stink of the beast. Before I could even swing my mount around, the nightmare creature had caused death, scything wildly with the strength of its brutal neck and shoulders, its wicked, spiralled tusks slashing to right and left, ripping upwards into the soft bellies of two of the animals within moments of reaching them.

"Spears!" Dedalus was yelling from behind me. "Get down there! Use your spears!"

The pathway between me and the slaughter, comfortably wide a moment earlier, was now all too narrow and completely impassable, choked with men and rearing, fear-crazed horses. Forcing my own panic down, I looked around me, searching for some way to ride back to where the chaos was spreading, but it was hopeless, and I was forced to watch the utter disintegration of my force under the attack of a brute beast. The noise of the conflict escalated madly, the shouts of men mingling with the screams of the animals. No sense of order remained anywhere in our cavalcade, every man trying uselessly to control his demented horse. Impatiently, curbing Germanicus grimly and using his bulk as a battering ram, I forced my way back through the press until I could see some of what was happening. Five men surrounded the enraged boar, I could see now, two on horseback, three on foot, and as I saw them one of the men afoot, Rufio, leapt in and stabbed the beast deeply, thrusting the spear with his whole body, the shaft clutched in both hands and tucked beneath his arm. The creature reared and spun, showing another, broken spear in its right flank, and in its awesome rage flicked Rufio into the air and out of my sight. And then suddenly, with a final, deafening squeal of pain and rage, it broke off its attack and fled into the trees. Long after it had gone, the horses continued to plunge and scream in terror and the men waited tensely, glaring about them, anticipating its return.

It took us a full hour and more to regroup. The panicked horses had scattered widely, in spite of the impossible terrain, and we had the devil's own trouble catching some of them. By the final accounting, we were five horses poorer, three of them disembowelled by the beast, one with a broken leg, and one with a haunch so lacerated by a slashing tusk that it had no hope of surviving the remainder of the journey through such hostile land. Rufio, for whose life I had feared, was merely stunned and hideously bruised. He had landed in a tree, like a javelin shot from a catapult, and fallen heavily to the ground. The others were merciless in their treatment of him, calling him "the Bird Man," a name he was to carry for the rest of his life, although it was eventually shortened, as all such names are. Rufio, from that day forth, became The Bird.

When order was finally restored, I authorized an hour's rest. It was unlikely the boar would return now, and it seemed pointless to me to push on any farther without giving everyone a chance to recover. A good rest, followed by an early camp and a solid night's sleep, it seemed to me, would do all of us good.

Some time later, Dedalus's voice close by my ear snapped me out of a doze. I roused myself and looked at him questioningly. He looked at Rufio, who lay sleeping beside me, and then he raised his eyes towards the sky. "I was saying it's very obvious, to me at least, that there are no Outlanders around here. That commotion would have been audible for miles in every direction. No one's come to see who caused it, so I think it's safe to say that no one will." He stopped, waiting for my response.

"So? What are you telling me?"

He shrugged his shoulders and ducked his head, managing to appear sheepish and conciliatory at the same time. "Nothing, but that boar was badly wounded and bleeding heavily, arterial blood or I'm a blind man; two spears lodged in him when he broke away, both deep and well-placed, one of them intact so it would hamper him in running far through that." He nodded towards the surrounding undergrowth. "So, he's probably lying close by here, at the end of a plain blood trail. If I'm right, and I'm prepared to wager against anything you might wish to part with, we could have, for the price of a short walk, fresh-killed pig tonight. We have a clear sky, fresh water close by, an injured companion, and we're all tired. It has been an eventful day. We've been shipwrecked, half drowned, abandoned, lost in an alien forest and savaged by a ravening beast that cost us five prime horses. And yet there's more grazing here, of a kind, for the remaining stock than any other place we've seen since setting out this morning, and we have a master with us"—he bowed his head and clenched his fist over his heart in mock modesty—"of the art of dressing and roasting fresh-killed pig with garlic, onions and truffles."

"Truffles?"

He nodded sagely. "The greatest of all fungi. Our swinish visitor was rooting for them when we came along. I found where he was digging, and I found his prize."

"So you think we should stay here tonight and eat like pigs."

He sighed. "Caius Merlyn, I swear you have the gift of reading minds."

I nodded, pretending surliness. "Very well, you have an hour to find the beast. If you don't find it within that time, come back here and we'll eat horse meat. If you do find it, your truffles had better be superb."

XII

It took us until noon on the second day after our encounter with the boar to make contact again with Donuil and his father's galleys, but the weather held fine, with only scattered clouds and one heavy shower, and our progress was uninterrupted. We saw no sign of Feargus's Wild Ones, nor, although we saw ample evidence of the giant deer that had created the route we followed, did we see a single animal.

Our long night's rest and solid food had performed miracles for our well-being, and Rufio, our "flying man," had almost fully recovered from his misadventure, with only an aching in his ribs as a reminder. Ded's truffles had been epicurean, and the wild pig had provided a meal that each of us would remember with fond nostalgia in the years that lay ahead. While waiting for his men to finish scalding the bristles from the haunch that he had butchered, Dedalus had vanished back along the path, returning some time later with a helmet full of tiny, wrinkled, almost dry red apples. What he did to them I do not know, but when he served them with the succulent wild pig in the form of a thick, heavy sauce, they set every man's taste buds reeling with delight. We slept well that night, bloated with wondrous food and cushioned on thick, soft beds of springy moss.

An early start in the dim glow of dawn, begun tentatively with an eye to new and unlooked-for dangers, gave way gradually to a leisurely, carefree trot along our meandering route, following the path of least resistance with only occasional halts to negotiate natural hazards where trees or rocks, and once an entire cliff face, had fallen recently enough to block the way. Only the fallen cliff face caused us grief, forcing us to leave the smooth game trail completely and climb down a slippery, steeply sloping bank to bypass the tumbled obstruction at a crawl, carefully testing each tentative step along the base of the bank before committing to it, then clawing our way back upward to the pathway with much impatient, ill-tempered cursing. The experience reminded us forcibly of the impassability of this primeval forest and the debt we owed to our guiding spirits, the giant, unseen deer. It took us an hour to negotiate the downward slope, far enough away from the debris of the fallen cliff to be safe from loose, rolling boulders, and then as long again to make our way across the short space at the bottom of the sprawling pile that loomed above us. It took us more than twice as long again, however, to regain the pathway from the bottom on the other side, worming our way up sideways with the horses, whose hooves scrabbled and slithered and fell back on the soft, greasy loam.

And then, slightly before midday on the third day of our journey, we emerged without warning at the top of a high cliff and saw the two galleys of Feargus and Logan below us, drawn up onto a stone-grey, sheltered beach. Behind them, an arm of the sea swept inland and out of sight, masked by the high cliffs on which we sat. The cliff that had towered on our left throughout our journey pinched out here, on this high plateau. I waved to the tiny figures on the beach below, and shouted, but received no response. Finally, I nocked an arrow and launched it gently, watching it fall to earth beside one of the fires that burned brightly on the strand. That captured their attention, and they ran outward, staring up at us and waving, gesturing wildly towards our left. Sure enough, there was a downward route where they indicated, but it was terrifying in its steepness. Dedalus, beside me as usual, spoke the words that were in my mind.

"I hope that's not a river estuary behind them, or we're stuck here. Don't think it is. Water's too clear; no silty outflow. Must be a sea arm, what the Celts call a lough. Anyway, that's north, Donuil's country, over there, and we have to get there." He paused and spat over the edge, watching the flying spittle fall away. "You agree?"

I nodded. "So far. What else is in your mind?"

"Well, since you ask, it seems to me that taking the horses down there entails one certainty: we'll have to bring the whoresons up again."

"Why? We might be able to ride right along the beach, as far as the inlet extends."

"Aye, and it might extend for miles and then pinch out, leaving us to ride all the way back and still climb this cliff again . . . I say leave the horses here, hobbled, where they can graze along the fringes of the trees. We can carry our saddlebags and go down on foot. That's not a roadway, and horses have no hands. A man can climb down backwards, if he has to. If there is a way along the beach, and if it's possible to lead them down, we'll come back up and get them. If not, we'll have to come back, either way."

"Done," I said, and wheeled to make the arrangements.

After our perilous descent and the welcome we received from Donuil's Scots, they sat in silence around us while we ate, and listened intently as we told them the story of our meeting with the boar. One of our number, a normally taciturn man called Falvo, grew lyrical in his description of the monster, and his account of the battle fitted strangely with my own recollection of the debacle I had witnessed.

When Falvo had finished his tale, translated in the telling by Donuil and its verity endorsed by the approving murmurs of the rest of my men, Feargus looked at Dedalus, who had found the boar's body afterwards, then turned to me. "How big was this beast, truly?"

As I shrugged my shoulders, Dedalus reached for a blanket-wrapped bundle I had noticed hanging from his saddle earlier. "Big enough." I answered, watching him idly. "He cost us five horses and almost killed Rufio there."

Something large and yellow flew through the air from Dedalus to Feargus, who caught it in an outstretched hand and held it there for everyone to see. It was one of the beast's huge, spiralled tusks and the sight of it brought a concerted hiss of surprise from the assembled Scots. I turned to Dedalus.

"I didn't know you'd taken that."

"I took them both." He tossed the second one to me. "They'll be impressively barbaric once they've been cleaned up and polished."

I hesitated, struck by a thought. "How did you know what Feargus asked me?"

Ded grinned. "I didn't. I guessed from the tone of his voice. It's what anyone would have asked, isn't it?"

Fascinated to see the thing up close, I examined it carefully, aware of the glances of the others moving between me and Feargus who still held its mate. It was heavy, solid ivory, yellow with age and dirt, save where it was worn white towards the tip, and it was thicker than the base of my thumb at the blood- and bone-encrusted end where Ded had chopped it free of the jaw in which it had been set. From there, it swept outward in almost three complete, tapering curls, perfectly round in section save for the last part of the third curl, the width of my hand in length, which was edged with wickedly sharp, blade-like ridges capable, as I knew, of shearing and destroying anything they struck. From end to pointed end, the thing extended almost the full length of my arm from wrist to elbow.

"Dermott, come forward." The voice belonged to Feargus and an old man stepped forward at his bidding. "Show them."

The man, whom I could not remember having seen before, extended his right arm, and I looked with wonder at the bracelet wrapped around it, embracing the entire lower part. It was a tusk like the one I held, but it had been worked into a thing of beauty, polished to a creamy, glowing whiteness and carved, its ends capped with hand-crafted gold.

"Dermott is our bard," Feargus said, his voice solemn and filled with respect. "But in his youth he was a fearsome fighter and the greatest hunter of our clan. His wife, Moira, wears the other tusk, the twin to that. The arms of each of them have shrunk with age, but these symbols of their prowess that they wear with pride do not age. They killed the boar between them, with two spears, before any of you were born. A man-eater it was, ancient and evil and cursed for years. The biggest boar ever seen or known in our lands. Look!"

He held up the new tusk until it was level with Dermott's, and the polished whiteness of the old man's bracelet was dwarfed beside the dirt-smeared mass of the new-killed monster. A murmur of awe rose and fell into silence. Long moments Feargus held the tusk there wordlessly before passing it to me. I felt the solid weight of it matching that of its fellow in my other hand. I handed both tusks back to Dedalus, who rewrapped them in his blanket, and then I led the conversation towards the things I needed most to know.

Dedalus had guessed correctly. The water beside us was a sea lough, stretching inward for two leagues, or six of our Roman miles, and there was no open way along the beach. Half a mile inland, the precipice fell straight into the lough, its bottom lost in the depths. The only route for us to follow was atop the cliffs, where our horses already awaited us, but we were pleased to learn that our journey was more than half complete and we could travel from this point onward without fear of the Wild Ones, whose territories now lay behind us. Not that we should ride carelessly, Feargus added, since the Wild Ones knew no boundaries. When we reached the inner rim of the lough, Logan told us, taking over from Feargus, we should strike out to the north and west where, after another eight leagues, we would come to a river estuary with a road along its bank on our side. To the left, that road would lead us straight into King Athol's stronghold, the heartland of the Celtic Scots. If the galleys arrived there first, as they ought to, he said, they would row upstream to their point of anchorage close to home, and await us there, sending runners on ahead to prepare our welcome.

Having seen the surprise on my face that this "heartland" should lie so close to the domain of the Wild Ones, Donuil interrupted Logan to explain that his father had built his stronghold in the south of his domain because of the richness of the soil and the openness of the country. Fully four fifths of all the land the Scots claimed as their own was either heavy forest or rugged, barren uplands.

I asked next about the giant deer whose prints were everywhere, but of which we had seen no other sign. Elk was their name, a Norse word, Feargus told me, and he went on to explain that the legends told that they had been imported, two hundred years earlier and more, by a Norse king who had settled in Eire but pined for the giant deer of his homeland. He had sent his longships home to bring back breeding pairs of the huge beasts, and they had thrived in Eire's forests, where no predator but man was large enough to stalk them. They lived in the deep forest and preferred marshy land and boggy streams, since that was where they fed. Seldom were they seen beyond the deepest woods, and when they did venture that far they were easily killed. They were gentle creatures, he said, like all deer, but large enough to be dangerous, even lethal, when threatened, for their massive horns were like the horns of no other deer, being heavy, broad and spatulate, sculpted like great, flat spoons and as wide across as a big man's arms, with only tiny, blunted tines around the outer rims to mark them as deer horn. When the rutting males fought for dominance every year at the time of mating, he said, the clatter of their head-butting could be heard echoing through the forest for many leagues.

Dedalus broke the mood, tired of listening to interminable tales in a tongue he could not understand. "Merlyn," he growled, "it's mid-afternoon. Do we stay here tonight and climb that whoreson cliff in the morning, leaving the horses alone up there all night?"

"No, Ded. We'll sleep up there tonight and get an early start."

"Well, we'd better get going soon. I'd hate to attempt that climb without sunlight to guide me."

I sighed, and rose to my feet, and we took our leave again of Donuil and his Scots.

As soon as I set eyes on Athol, High King of the Scots of Eire, standing among his advisers on a raised dais, awaiting our approach, I saw the false presumption in the term *Outlander*, an expression I had used throughout my life. An Outlander was foreign, alien, someone from another land and therefore barbarian. Athol the King, however, despite his advanced years, would have been unmistakably a king in any land, regal in every aspect, including the stillness with which he watched us come. He seemed to embody his entire race, his upright bearing stamped with that unmistakable air of authority and magisterial presence the Romans had called *dignitas*. I was immediately thankful that I had called a halt and insisted on my men taking the time to clean themselves up before riding in, for though I knew nothing of this man, I saw at once that he was king in more than name, and while I could have no indication of the thoughts that must be swarming in his mind as he watched our approach I knew they would be far from trivial. He was forming his first impressions of the men and power of Camulod as we advanced. We were the victors who had made a hostage of his son. Now we were escorting that son home, but he must be wondering to what ultimate purpose. I felt sure, somehow, that he must be reassessing the potential worth of the child he held as surety for this return.

We had encountered no difficulties on the route from the shore where we had left Donuil and his party, and we found the road along the side of the river estuary exactly when we had expected to. The wide, shallow river had been deserted, and I had assumed that the two galleys had already passed and were awaiting us somewhere upriver to the east. I was right; we met them about five miles upstream, and they had been awaiting us for no more than a few hours, ready to escort us into the realm of their king.

Now, as we rode slowly towards the king himself, across the flatness of a central court ringed by silent watchers, I sucked in my belly and made an attempt to sit straighter in my saddle, even though I was already straight as a spear, encased in my unyielding parade armour. Donuil rode on my right, half a pace ahead of me as was his right in this, his father's place, and Dedalus was right behind me, in charge of the king's gifts: the pair of horses, their coats burnished to a blaze, and the decorative case that held the Varrus weapons. Athol looked only at Donuil, assessing the difference that five years had wrought, and schooling his features to give no hint of what he was feeling. The rostrum on which he and his advisers stood was set at about the height of a man's chest, on a scaffold of some kind, its entire front shielded by the king's guard, who stood shoulder to shoulder on the ground, facing us, their weapons cutting us off completely from any close approach to their leader. They were impressive, even though there was no hint of uniformity in either their dress or their appearance. Only in the wary watchfulness of their eyes and in their stance was there unity.

When we had approached to within a few paces of the guards, Donuil drew rein and the rest of us, who had been waiting for his signal, followed his lead, stepping down from our saddles and holding our mounts close-reined, their muzzles by our right shoulders. Donuil dropped his reins to the ground and stepped forward; the guards parted silently to give him access to a flight of steps their bodies had concealed. He mounted the steps in silence and went directly to kneel in front of his father, bowing his head and clasping the old king's outstretched hand. I watched only them, taking great care not to allow my eyes to look around. Behind me, my men did the same, I knew, because they had strict orders to do so. Donuil had explained to all of us that idle curiosity would be ill regarded, prior to his father's formal acceptance of our presence.

The old man gazed down at his son's head without speaking or moving for long moments, and then I saw his arm tense as he pulled Donuil upright and stepped forward to embrace him. The younger man, whom I would have expected to tower over his father, was not much taller than he. They spoke together in quiet tones and at the edge of my vision I was aware of several of the men behind the king leaning forward, trying to catch what was said. Eventually Athol nodded and Donuil turned towards me, beckoning me forward. I dropped my own reins and mounted the steps to the rostrum, aware of the king's eyes studying me. I gazed back at him, studying him with equal frankness.

He was slim and erect and, for all his advanced age—I guessed him to be well beyond sixty summers—his arms and neck were hard and tightly muscled, clearly showing the physical strength these Celts demanded in their kings. His long hair was shining clean, not white but paler than silver, parted in the middle and cut so that it fell bluntly to his shoulders. His eyebrows, however, were thick and snowy white on his sun-browned face above large grey eyes that held the fire of a man half his age. It may have been the greyness of his eyes with the pale grey of his hair, but at first sight from across the courtyard I had defined him as a man of silver, and that impression was heightened and confirmed with nearness. He wore a heavy overgarment, much like a cloak, of rich, hand-worked pale grey wool above a long, equally heavy tunic of darker grey, flecked with white, that was belted at the waist and kilted to his knees. His belt was buckled in silver, and the long sword it supported was hilted in silver, too, housed in a silver-worked scabbard. From the knees down, his legs were sheathed in supple sheepskin, worn fleece inward and bound with silver-decorated thongs, and silver straps gleamed, too, on his sandalled feet. Decorative bosses of the metal covered his breast, and the cloak was held in place at his left shoulder by a massive silver disc pierced with a pin and housing a great purple stone that looked like glass. Only the single filet of metal binding his brows was different. It was of bright gold, fashioned to look like a knotted cord with acorns on each end. Athol the King had dressed for a grand occasion.

He regarded me with solemn grey eyes as I stopped directly before him, then he reached out his arm in the Roman fashion, his hand spread to grasp my forearm in the grip of friendship.

"Welcome, Merlyn Britannicus," he said softly, his voice a deep, growling purr. "My son tells me you speak our tongue."

I was caught off guard by the directness of his greeting me, for I had not known what to expect or how to behave. My knowledge of regal protocols was severely limited. Uther Pendragon, Vortigern of Northumbria and Derek of Ravenglass were the only kings I had ever met. Each of them had been signally different from the others and none of them had cared for ceremony. I had been afraid of committing some unseemly indiscretion, cursing myself for not having thought to ask Donuil how a stranger was supposed to greet his father. Now I found myself gazing into this man's eyes and gauging the strength of his arm while my mind floundered, seeking an adequate response.

"My thanks for your welcome, King Athol," I said, and then I found it easy to smile. "If you will permit me, I should like to ask you first, and before all else, about the welfare of the child you hold in trust for me. Is he well?"

The king nodded gravely. "Aye, and not merely well. He grows like a young shoat. You have returned my son to me in better health than I have ever known him to enjoy, and I will do no less for you, although the child in this case is not your son. Is that not so?"

I nodded. "True, Sir King, but he could be no more dear to me were he indeed my son."

"Good. You will see him soon, I promise you. He lives in the house of Connor, with my son's own brood, and takes no ill from anyone." He paused, smiling now, but eyeing me shrewdly nonetheless. "You speak our tongue remarkably well, Master Merlyn, for an Outlander."

I returned his smile, aware of his pointed use of the term I myself had used to describe his son years before, and feeling immeasurably better by the moment.

"You are kind, my lord. I speak it poorly and inadequately, but I was unaware of that before I came into your lands. Your son is a fine teacher, but lenient."

He glanced now towards Donuil, still holding my arm. "Lenient? How so?"

"In permitting me to stumble, without seeking to improve my hesitancy. I speak, as you can hear, at less than half the normal speed."

He smiled again, returning his gaze to me and releasing my hand. "That is mere usage, soon cured by time and custom." He looked beyond my shoulder, to where my men stood at attention. "Your men look fine, Caius Merlyn; a credit to you. But where are the rest of your horses?"

"Outside your gates, my lord. I thought it wise to leave them there until we, or you, should decide where best to keep them. But of those you see here, two are for you in person, a matched breeding pair selected by your son with the guidance of our Master of Horse."

"Hmm. I noticed them as you approached. You honour us. Before we look at them, however, there is a ritual we must share." He raised one hand and a man stepped forward from behind him, bearing a small platter on which lay a flat loaf of bread and a tiny dish of salt. Athol broke the bread, tearing off a small piece and handing the remainder to me. As I, too, broke off a piece, he sprinkled his with a small pinch of salt and then salted mine, too. We ate together. Then, the ritual completed, the king stepped forward and raised his arms in a gesture requiring silence, although the stillness all around was profound.

"It is done," he said, raising his voice by a mere shade, knowing that everyone present, including the advisers ranked behind him, hung on his every word. "My son is returned to us in health. Caius Merlyn Britannicus, Commander of the Forces of Camulod in Britain, has shared our food. He and his men and all his goods are under my protection; treat them as you would me and mine. For now they will rest and recover from their journey. Tonight we will celebrate their coming."

There was no acclamation, no markedly visible or audible reaction, and yet a sense of wellness filled the air as the throng around the courtyard immediately surged into motion and dispersed about their tasks. Athol turned, placing himself between Donuil and me, and taking each of us by one elbow, led us back to where his advisers stood waiting to greet us. Behind us, my own men relaxed and clustered together, awaiting disposition.

There are times when one experiences instinctive revulsion towards a person whom one is meeting for the first time. It doesn't happen often, but I learned long ago to trust the feeling, despite the apparent lack of logic that frequently attends its occurrence. Of course, in most of these cases, the aversion is easy to explain and understand, inspired by the physical appearance of the stranger. It is far easier to like, at first sight, a man or a woman who conforms to one's own notions of attractiveness than it is to feel drawn towards one who is unwashed, ill formed or burdened with some grotesque, dehumanizing affliction. When an unexpected introduction to a total stranger sets my internal alarms jangling discordantly without rhyme or reason, experience has taught me that this gut-level reaction is infallible. During my brief introduction to Athol's counselors, I experienced three such episodes, each of them different from the others.

The first man fell into the category of the easily understandable. His physique, his appearance, the very way he stood and moved repelled me. His name was Mungo, and the sound of it, completely alien to my ears, conjured an image of a large, ugly fish stirring heavily in the bottom mud of deep, murky waters. To my eyes, however, he presented no sign of fishiness. Mungo Rohan was a squat, rock-like presence, massive of chest and shoulder, with enormous hands and wrists that were coated with thick, wiry black hair. A great bush of black and grey beard hid the lower half of his face and obscured what little neck he had. His head, however, was bald as an egg and his eyes were small and porcine, squeezed too tightly together for my taste on either side of a misshapen nose that had been smashed beyond repair in the distant past, and almost hidden beneath the thick bar of eyebrows that sprouted wildly above them. I marked him immediately as one I would neither like nor trust. He glowered at me for long moments before stepping forward to greet me, nodding affably enough once he decided he had made the impression he wished to make, and extending his hand in a fair semblance of courtesy and friendship. I clasped his hand, inclining my own head slightly in return, aware of the deadness of the glaze that hung between his eyes and mine and was evidently intended to mask his true feelings. Adviser to the king he might be, I thought, and senior by age and rank, but any advice this man dispensed would be well weighted to incline any outcome towards the benefit of Mungo Rohan.

As I clasped his hand, aware of the weight and strength of it, I allowed my gaze to drift beyond him to where Connor stood watching me from the far end of the line, his face creased in a smile of . . . what was it? Anticipation? Or was it mere contempt? Mungo released my hand and stepped back, and the king moved me along to the next man in line, who made no more lasting impression upon me than a stranger passing in a crowded street.

Next to him, however, was a face I recognized immediately, and it was smiling in welcome. Fergus, son of Iain, son of Fergus, brother to King Athol, grasped my wrists in both of his and thanked me for safeguarding his nephew as I had promised. We had met only once, on the day I took Donuil hostage and allowed this man and his surviving warriors to depart from the battlefield with their weapons, and therefore their honour. I was as glad to see the big man as he evidently was to see me.

The fourth man was very different, and the sight of him brought my heart bounding into my throat. I knew we two had never met before, and yet I knew this man! I recognized the size of him; the colour of his yellow hair so like my own; and the way his face would twist awry when he laughed in the teeth of a strong wind, showing his own teeth, white and strong but flawed by a missing canine; but I failed completely when I sought a reason for this sudden presentiment. I must have frozen in shock, for the smile on his lips faltered and his eyes clouded momentarily with concern. I had to make a strong effort to collect myself and behave casually.

"Well met," I said, before he could speak.

His smile, which had been on the point of failing, came back admirably. "Your name and fame are well known here, Merlyn Britannicus. Welcome home, Brother." This last to Donuil, who stepped forward to embrace him. When they stepped apart, the yellow-haired brother addressed me again. "I am Caerlyle, brother to Donuil here, whom you have returned to us, and to Connor, whom you have met elsewhere. They call me Kerry. Welcome to Eire."

I nodded, my thoughts still awhirl at the feelings his appearance had brought out in me. "My thanks . . . Kerry? Should I call you that? Not Caerlyle?"

"No, Kerry suits me well. I sometimes fail to answer to Caerlyle, it's been so long since any but my mother called me that." This man was charming, full of self-confidence and strength, his face open and bereft of guile. Why then, I asked myself, were all my internal warning systems vibrating? And whence came this unsettling familiarity I felt with him? I held his hand, gazing directly into his eyes.

"We've never met before, have we?"

His eyes flared with surprise. "No," he said, laughing at the strangeness of the question. "How could we? I have never been away from here and this is your first visit to Eire. Where could we have met?"

I shook my head. "You look amazingly familiar. It must be that you remind me of someone else, someone from long ago." I smiled. "I find that as I grow older I see more and more resemblances with people I have met long since. It disconcerts me sometimes."

King Athol spoke from beside me, his hand on my elbow steering me gently towards the next man in line. "You will find, my friend, that the phenomenon you describe grows even stronger as you approach my age. People tend to fall into types. Meet my good-brother, Liam. I was once wed to his mother's sister."

Liam was a hunchback, small and wiry-looking, with large eyes and a liquid, lilting voice of surprising resonance and beauty. "Twistback, they call me," he said, grinning. "No imagination, some of these people." I grinned back at him, liking him instantly, and turned to the next man in line.

The basilisk stare of utter dislike from this one's eyes caused me to blink at him in astonishment before I could stop myself. Even King Athol, who was on the point of introducing us, hesitated visibly, evidently as nonplussed as I.

"Fingael?" I distinctly heard the note of uncertainty and surprise in the old man's voice. "Fingael, what ails you?"

"Nothing. I'm fine, Father." The man's eyes never left my own as he spoke the words from one corner of his mouth in a whispery voice that was sibilant and ominous. Apart from that response, he made no move either to recognize my presence or greet me in any way. His father cleared his throat, in embarrassment, I thought, and spoke again, this time with iron in his tone.

"Then perhaps you will greet our guest as befits his rank and status, rather than leaving him to suspect that we have lax rules of hospitality in this, my kingdom!"

"His rank and status?" The words came out like a challenge to combat, their insulting tone clear for anyone and everyone to hear. "He is Brother Donuil's friend and jailer. There are those of us who don't make friends that easily or that dishonourably."

I saw Athol stiffen on one side of me and sensed Donuil gathering his strength to move forward angrily in his own defense. I forestalled both of them with raised hands, pressing the back of my right hand against Donuil's breast, restraining him gently. He subsided, although I could feel his unwillingness, and I addressed myself to his uncivil brother.

"You must excuse my uncertainty, but do you and I have some unsettled difference between us of which I'm unaware?"

He sneered at me. "No. We have nothing between us. I don't like you, and that's all there is to it."

"Damn you, Finn, you pig-headed dolt!" Donuil moved forward again, and again I stopped him, this time facing him and stilling him with my eyes and tone.

"Donuil, my friend, this is my concern." I turned back to Fingael. "I can see that you dislike me. Everyone can." I kept my voice level and forced myself to pause, having no wish to add to the damage this lout was attempting to do. "Dislike might even be too mild a word." I paused, looking him straight in the eye and allowing my silence to stretch until I saw him start to say something more. Before he could, I spoke again. "Well, doubtless you have your reasons, sufficient for your own mind at least. But your dislike has the air of long usage, and until we came face to face I had no awareness of your existence. You form your judgments quickly, it would appear."

"Quickly enough." He had ignored Donuil completely and the sneer was still pasted to his face. I resisted the urge to wipe it away. He was a big man, but not as big as I, and younger, and beneath his present scowl he would be, I saw, pleasant-faced, clean-shaven, with bright red hair and green eyes that blazed from a stark white face that was sunburned on nose and brows. His bearing radiated challenge and I knew I could not yet walk away; this man would assume from that a victory of some kind.

"How old are you, Fingael, son of Athol?" I asked him, seeing his eyes widen in surprise at my level tone.

"Old enough to know my mind."

"Aye, but not to trust it, eh?"

"What?" The sneer vanished. He had no idea of my meaning. Neither had I, but I had retained the initiative.

"I would guess you to be two years, perhaps three, older than Donuil. Twenty-six or -seven. I'm thirty-two. Do you understand my point?"

He frowned ferociously, indicating that he did not. I continued speaking. "I had lived for more than half a decade before you were born, young Finn. To this point, I have lived throughout your entire lifetime without seeing you or hearing of you until this, our first meeting. I would happily forgo a second meeting for the remainder of it in equal ignorance."

Someone caught his breath in surprise and then there came a shout of laughter in which everyone joined save me, Fingael, Donuil and their father King Athol. While it was ringing, I turning casually away from him, dismissing him as I moved towards the next man in line. Athol the King stalked beside me, rigid with fury at the insult offered me, yet saying nothing that might add to an incendiary situation. I know I greeted the man but have no memory of it. My mind was awash with other, far more serious matters: anger at Fingael's insults and confusion over my strange, unshared recognition of Caerlyle. And so I progressed until I faced the last of Athol's counselors, his son Connor. Here, at least, I found interest and pleasure in his welcome and in the open frankness with which he hugged his brother Donuil.

"You impressed my brother Finn, Yellow Head," he said to me eventually, when he and Donuil had finished belabouring each other's back and shoulders. "He has not met many who can best him either in words or a fight. I must warn you, he makes a bad enemy and cares not for losing."

"Hmm. He's lucky never to have met my cousin Uther."

He smiled at me. "Two of a kind, are they?"

"Aye, you might say they're similar, in much the same way that certain lambs are similar to bears—both may be born black." I turned to look back towards Fingael, but he was nowhere to be seen. "Where did he go?"

"My father marched him off as soon as you had moved away. I imagine the king is speaking to him now of hospitality and the rules of Eirish courtesy."

"Is he always as pleasant with strangers?"

He looked at me, one eyebrow raised. "Who, my father? Or Finn?"

"Fingael."

"He's a boar, with a boar's manners," Donuil muttered.

Connor's gaze, still amused, went to Donuil and then back to me. "In truth, he is not. Neither a boar nor generally unpleasant without reason. I've never seen him quite that way before today. But Finn is . . . difficult at times. He has his own ways. My father, who is no more patient than most kings, has yet great patience in some little things. For twenty years now he has been trying to teach Finn to school himself, but without much success." He threw an arm around my shoulders and I caught a whiff of the remembered smell of him, leather and light, clean sweat and a tang of some wild perfume in his hair. "Come, let's drink some ale before I die of thirst. I have a vat long cooled beneath the ground. And I have a babby in my house you might wish to see. And if we are to speak of boars, I'd rather hear the tale of the one you killed in the south than of the one you bested here today." He led the way down from the rostrum and directly to his hut, walking with the familiar, rolling gait I recalled so clearly. The cordon of guards that had lined the rostrum had long since disbanded and my own men had disappeared, back to the camp we had established beyond the walls. Only a few of Athol's people paid us any attention as we crossed the now-empty central space.

I spent more than an hour of the time that followed with my young cousin Arthur who was, as the king had said, growing like a young pig. The child was now at least six months old, and possibly seven, by my best reckoning, and was already a large child, although distinctly lacking in regal attributes. He was, indeed, closer to a young shoat than a young king, for his home was the dirt floor of Connor's house, and he sprawled naked and dirty before a banked-up, guarded fire with a large number of other mites, some of them little older than himself. Connor had to search for him amid the tangle of small, bare bodies before hauling him out and handing him to me, and as I waited for him to identify and extract the future Commander of Camulod from the squalling company of his current peers, I found myself smiling in disbelief. In truth, I picked the boy out before Connor did, recognizing him by his startlingly coloured eyes, and feeling gratification at the evident, sturdy strength of the child. But he was filthy, and there was no denying that, stripped of all the rich swaddling that would have covered him in Camulod, and liberally daubed with a moist compound of dirt from the floor and fresh urine from one of his small companions, his regal heritage was far less evident than was his common humanity. I was already reaching for him by the time Connor hauled him out of the press, and I felt ridiculously pleased when the child grinned at me immediately upon being passed to me. I exulted in the solid weight of him at the end of my outstretched arms, and pulled him to me quickly, smiling into his eyes and then opening my mouth in laughing protest as his chubby fingers immediately reached out for me and closed on my face, his tiny nails sinking into the sensitive skin at the end of my nose. Connor did not notice. He was staring down in mild bemusement at the pile of children about his feet.

"These are not all mine, you understand," he said, unfazed by the din and activity all around. "We just seem to attract them, somehow. My wife enjoys the sounds and smells of children, and all the gods know they can produce enough of both for anyone, so mothers who don't share her pleasure are happy to cater to it by lending her their own to care for while they do other things. Come and meet her. Bring the babby." He led Donuil and me out and into another hut standing apart from the one shared by "the brood," as he referred to the children, and there I met his wife Margaret, a jolly, laughing young woman of generous build who hugged Donuil and then welcomed me shyly, disguising her nervousness by fussing with the baby Arthur, whom I clutched firmly in the crook of my right arm. I thanked her warmly for the care she had evidently lavished on the child, and her confusion and embarrassment increased, so that I had, for pity's sake, to suspend my praises. She did assure me, however, and I had no doubt of it, that she would continue to look after young Arthur for the duration of our stay here among them, and that I need have no worries over his welfare. Some short time later, still flustered and red-faced, she made excuses and left the hut to see to the other children, leaving Connor, Donuil and me alone with the child and the jug of ale Connor had promised. I placed my squirming young charge on the ground at my feet, and the three of us sat and talked of trivial things before the brothers left me alone with the child for a spell. When they had gone, I sat gazing at the boy who lay quietly for the moment, looking up at me wide-eyed, and again I found myself marvelling at the beauty of his strangely golden eyes. I knew from my reading that my grandfather, Caius Britannicus, had had similar eyes, so I accepted that they must be a Britannicus family trait, although one that was seldom seen. But it occurred to me now that they must pass downward through the maternal side of the family, for Caius Britannicus had been this child's great-uncle. It was my aunt Luceiia who gave Arthur his Britannican blood, and therefore his yellow-gold eyes. Eagle's eyes, Publius Varrus had called them, and that memory led me to thinking again about who this child was and what he represented. I shook my head in wonderment at the making of him. So much mingling of noble bloodlines and so much family strength and character had fused together, so beautifully, in this one small boy child: Roman blood of two great families, and all the inborn strength and fortitude and dignity of the leading families of the great Celtic clans of Cambrian Pendragons and Eirish Scots. Surely, I thought, if Destiny awaited him, as I believed it did, the spirits of his ancestors would combine with sufficient potency to make him master of whatever lay ahead of him.

I realized that I was straining, leaning forward in my armour so that breathing was becoming difficult, and the boy lay staring up at me, kicking occasionally with bare, plump feet. I leaned forward further, with some difficulty occasioned by the unyielding metal length of my cuirass, and poked him in his swollen little belly, making those inane, speech-like noises that all grown people seem to make when looking at infants. Then, embarrassed by the noises I was making, and by the way the child regarded me, as though to ridicule my efforts at addressing him, I stooped further, grunting with the effort, and picked him up, holding him above me at arms' length while I sat back, thankful to be stretching, and frowned up at him in perplexity. He continued to stare back at me, solemn faced.

"What are you going to be, young Arthur Pendragon?" I growled. "Who are you going to be? Will you be a warrior? And if you are, what kind of fighter will you be? What will your enemies have to say of you?" Without warning, a stream of water leaped from his tiny spout and the sound of it spattering against my parade breastplate was ample commentary on how he cared about what his enemies might think. I sprang to my feet with a curse, laughing despite my shock and holding him still at the extension of my arms, turning him so the jet of his urine arced away from me. He gurgled, laughing with me, no doubt because of the sudden, swooping movements of my startled reaction, and a warmth swelled up in my throat, making me want to hold him close and press him to my breast. But he was very small and fragile, and my breast was encased in armour, so I merely set him down again while I dried my dripping harness, and then I carried him very cautiously back into the room with the other children. It seems strange to me now that I had no fear of handling him on that occasion, for his smallness awed me at other, later times. Perhaps it was his sturdy nakedness that day that made me realize he would not break from handling. Later in his babyhood, in Britain, where he was always clothed, he seemed far more delicate and vulnerable.

Fingael, son of Athol, was conspicuously absent from the festivities that began before nightfall, by which time the odour of spit-roasted venison had permeated the entire community and brought a throng of people back into the central communal space before the rostrum in the expectation of feasting and music. Within an anteroom of the great long hall that took up one side of this gathering place, while the crowd outside was becoming more noisy and festive with every passing moment, my friends and I were welcomed yet again, less formally this time, at a reception attended by the king and all his most trusted followers. At the urging of Donuil and Connor I had laid aside my armour for the first time in weeks and had ordered my men to do likewise, so that we paraded ourselves in our finest clothes, without weaponry of any kind, in a clear gesture of trust and confidence in our host and his people. In contrast to our unarmed trust, however, all of Athol's people save himself and his sons came armed to the teeth, as the saying goes, and decked in their most savage finery, most of which set my Roman-instructed teeth on edge.

I had been raised in the old Imperial tradition, to Roman tastes and sensibilities, in spite of the fact that my entire family on my father's side prided themselves upon being "British" and not Roman. By comparison with these Eirish Scots, however, even my mother's Cambrian Celts were restrained in their tastes and use of colour. I had noticed from the outset that Donuil's people had no fear of mixing colours, but this gathering in the Hall made all the bright raiment I had seen up to this point seem muted and drab, as the daily wear of most people is by comparison with their festive finery. With an evening of festivity stretched ahead of them, they had arrayed themselves in their finest and I had never seen so many bright and vibrant, violently opposed colours used in such profusion: yellows and greens and reds and blues intermixed haphazardly enough to challenge the eyes. And yet, as I grew inured to the welter, I began to perceive certain unities in the chromatic chaos. All of the clothing was patterned, I could see, and all of the patterns were based upon a simple check design common in the monochromatic work of all weavers. In the case of these Scots, however, the colours of the yarn the weavers worked were wildly mixed, dyed in a multitude of hues. Thus it might be seen that all the members of one family group might wear the same pattern of green and red, with cross-lines of hazy blue or white or even yellow offsetting the dominant checks, but the reds and the greens might vary from person to person in shades that ran from the palest, near-white green of sun-blocked grass to the deep green of forest conifers, and from anemic orange to the crimson of clotting blood. And sometimes, I could see, these colour variations would appear in one large garment, such as the great, toga-like robes in which several of the older men were swathed. The younger men, no less garishly caparisoned, wore armour with their brightly coloured clothes: breastplates and arm guards and sometimes even greaves or leggings of iron, bronze, brass or layered, toughened oxhide. All of them carried sheathed daggers of one kind or another at their waists, although there were no swords or axes to be seen.

I mentioned the weapons to Connor, who sat beside me at one point, partly reclined upon a long, low couch that would once have graced some Roman household and that I guessed had been placed here for his special use, since the other furnishings in the anteroom were few and far more primitive. He looked at me with a half smile.

"You find that strange, that men should go armed at all times?"

I shrugged my shoulders. "Aye, in the King's Hall, among friends, on a festive occasion."

He grunted, in what I assumed to be a stifled laugh. "They're not really armed, my friend. They left their swords and axes and their spears outside."

"But not their daggers."

"No, not their daggers. Their daggers are not thought of as weapons—more as a badge of free manhood."

"Those badges all look lethal."

"Aye, and they would be, were they ever drawn. But to the bearer, most of all. It is death to bare a blade in the King's Hall."

I blinked at him, surprised. "Then why wear them at all? A man in drink might be provoked to draw."

"True, but it's custom. No true man should ever be weak enough to permit himself to be provoked into suicide, therefore the custom has become a test of a man's true worth."

"Speaking of that," I smiled, thinking it a good time to change the subject, "what has happened to your brother Finn? He's not here."

"No, he has gone hunting." He looked away to where his father sat talking to Donuil and the hirsute Mungo. "My father decided he has a taste for goat."

"Goat? And Finn had to go hunting for a goat? The paddocks I have seen are full of them."

"Mountain goat," Connor continued, his face carefully schooled into emptiness.

"Mountain goat. I see. And how close are the nearest mountains?"

"Oh, very close, but they are not high enough to harbour mountain goats."

"Are any?"

"Aye, but the closest of them is a good three days' journey from here."

"Three days. And three days back. How long to catch a goat?"

"Long enough, my astute friend, to enable you to settle down here in peace for a while."

"Aye, until Finn comes home. Does your father think an enforced exile will make him see me in a more friendly light?"

Now Connor turned and looked at me directly. "My father is no man's fool, Caius Merlyn. His enduring kingship bears that out. By the time Finn comes home, my father will have formed his own opinion of your worth, from his own observation, uninfluenced by any other's perception. You will have earned your own place among us by then, your own identity. Thereafter, anything that transpires between you and Finn will be your own affair and will not reflect upon my father or his hospitality. As I said before, Finn has his own ways, but my father the king has his, too."

I nodded, then asked what he had meant in referring to his father's enduring kingship. His answer surprised me, adding once more to my knowledge of these strange people.

"You don't know our ways? Hasn't my brother told you of our rules of kingship?" I shook my head. "Well, we are different here in Eire from you, and from any other people I have met, including our neighbours. I know you call us Celts, and I suppose we are, since every other people in these lands is Celtic, save for those born, like you, from Roman stock, but we call ourselves Gaels." He pronounced the word almost as "Gauls," and I immediately took it to mean that his people came from Gaul and questioned him on that, but he shook his head. "No, I think not, although there might be something to it, back in the long ago. To my knowledge, though, we have no connection with those other Gauls. We are of this land, and have always been."

"Whence comes the name then?" I saw from his face that he could not answer, and waved him on. "No matter, it's not important now. You were about to tell me of your custom of kingship."

"Aye. The law of our people states that our king be of the people . . . king of the people."

I stared at him. "I don't understand. Surely that is self-evident?"

"Oh no, not so. How many kings do you know?"

I shrugged. "Very few, a mere handful: my cousin Uther, who was always more of a brother to me than he was any kind of king. King he was, of course, after his father's death, king of the Pendragon strongholds in the Cambrian west. But Uther never ruled, in the kingly sense. He was a warrior chief, paramount, but king only in name. Then there was Lot, who called himself King of Cornwall, although the title was self-assumed; Vortigern, King of Northumbria; and Derek, King of Ravenglass, although again I assume that to be a false kingship, more vaunt than verity since Ravenglass is but a town, and a Roman one, at that. And now your father, the High King of Eire."

"No!" His denial was so abrupt as to be near violent. "My father makes no claim to being High King of Eire. There can never be such a High King so long as there is one other king who disputes that claim. All of them would. Any High King of Eire would have to fight to gain and hold that rank. None has, to this day."

"I see. But I have heard Donuil speak of your father as *Ard Righ*, I am sure. Is that not what the title means?"

"Aye, in some sense, although in ours it simply means high chief, and therefore king. But Athol Mac Iain, my father, is King of the Gael—you would say King of Scots—and therein lies the distinction."

"What distinction?" I felt foolish having to ask, for Connor looked at me as though I were feebleminded, and in truth I was beginning to wonder myself about my powers of perception, for there was something here that was eluding me.

"Think about it, man," he exhorted me. "You said the words yourself: 'Lot, King of Cornwall; Derek, was it? King of wherever, which you said was only a Roman town; and Vortigern, of whom I have heard, King of Northumbria. Then Uther, your cousin, king of the Pendragon strongholds. You have defined the norm in your own words. Even the emperors of Rome conform to the common way: they are all kings or emperors of some *place*. They rule their people's holdings. They hold the *land*. Our kings are kings of the people and the *people* hold the land. We are unique in that, and so my father is the King of Scots and rules his people in trust—not their land, for it is theirs."

I shook my head ruefully. "Now I see what you mean. It is indeed a distinction, and as you say, unique. I would never have seen it, had you not pointed it out to me."

He grinned now, suddenly more relaxed. "Oh, you would have seen it, eventually. You would have noted that the kingship my father holds has its own encumbrances. As king of the people, he remains one of the people and is therefore under constant scrutiny. As a king without land of his own, he relies upon the goodwill of his people in time of war and in time of need to supply him with what he otherwise lacks, the resources of the land."

"Wait a moment, Connor, this is too much too quickly for me. There is a contradiction here, involving the very idea of kingship. How can any man be a king and hold no land? Land, as you yourself have only now pointed out to me, is the very essence of kingship."

He sat up straight and reached for the cup that sat on the ground by my feet, emptying it at a toss. "No, you are wrong, my friend. Think about it. Kingship, in its purest sense, untrammelled by language, involves rule: the governance and guidance of the people. It involves things spiritual and moral. It involves those elements of life and rules of living that dictate the difference between sane living and mere mindless savagery. The land itself is really unimportant . . . it is no more than the space a people occupies, and from time to time it may become unhealthy or untenable. The king of a land has nowhere else to go. The king of a people, on the other hand, may take his people anywhere they wish, or need, to go."

I had lost all awareness of where we were, oblivious to the noise and movement all around us. Here, in the midst of a strange, unchristian people, in conversation with a man I would have dubbed a barbarian short months before, I was hearing talk of morals and philosophy the like of which I had seldom heard in Britain. Connor was still speaking.

"That ability, that capacity, is what I meant when I spoke of my father's enduring kingship. Great burdens lie upon the man unfortunate enough to bear the title 'King' among our folk. He must have, and show at all times, great physical strength, and a soundness of mind to match it. When he becomes too old, too weak or too untrustworthy to serve as king—leader, guardian, champion and . . . what's your Roman word? Mentor? . . . That's it, mentor—in all respects in his people's eyes, he must step down or be deposed, allowing a better or a younger, but certainly a more able man—more able at that time, I mean—to assume the kingship. My father Athol is old to be a king, but he is hale and strong and his word is law to all. His justice and his wisdom are renowned and, to this date at least, his fighting skills are unimpaired. I tell you honestly, Merlyn, I'm almost twenty years younger than he is, but I would not care to cross him."

I turned to where Athol stood talking with another group, looming over all of them except Donuil, who still stood by his father's side. "Aye," I said, smiling. "He looks formidable, for all his years." As I spoke, a man approached the king and whispered to him, and Athol turned to look at me as though he had been warned that I was watching him. Then, excusing himself from the group around him, he made his way directly to where I sat with Connor, Donuil following him closely.

"Master Merlyn," the king said as he approached, speaking in the accents I now knew to be the courtly, formal style of the Erse tongue. "I have been aware of spending little time with you, but I'm reassured by the sight of you two together. At least I know you have not been bored or ignored." He nodded to Connor, who merely smiled and held his peace. The old king's eyes flicked up and away towards the great doors of the Hall, which were being pulled open as he spoke. "The festive part of your welcome is about to begin. The people are gathered and the food prepared. Our bards and minstrels are assembled and awaiting our arrival." He smiled again. "You may find much that is strange to you in this evening's fare, but I think you will enjoy it. More than your men may, I fear, since I understand most of them do not have the tongue of our people."

I had risen to my feet at his approach, offering my hand to Connor who, in spite of his wooden leg, pulled himself up by it without the slightest sign of discomfort. "King Athol," I said now, feeling completely at my ease, "my men will have no difficulty enjoying themselves. The food I smell would assure me of that even had I not tasted your drink. Besides, there is nothing like the warmth of welcome to assuage the weariness of a tired, far-travelled man. Words have a strange but welcome way of falling into unimportance beside shared peace and openness of mind." Beyond his shoulder, I saw Donuil's face soften as he recognized my reference to the love I had had for his mute sister.

"Good," said the king. "Let's away, then." He stepped to the side to make room for me on his right, and together we walked from the Great Hall, followed by Donuil, Connor and the others, out into the open space where huge fires blazed, their leaping flames banishing the evening shadows and adding their own noise to the voices of the crowd and the sounds of wild and alien music. He raised his arm, and at the signal someone blew repeatedly on a great horn until the sounds of revelry had died away and all eyes were on the king. Athol raised his voice and invited everyone to the feast and the doors of the Great Hall behind us swung fully open.

The feasting continued for many hours, accompanied by music, dancing and the enthralling songs and tales of the king's bards, of whom there were five, ranging in age from a very young boy who was a gifted harpist and whose voice was pure and clear as mountain stream water, through a trio of fine singers of varying ages, to old Dermott, who wore the boar's tusk about his forearm and whose prodigious memory for intricate details made insignificant the fact that his voice wavered with years. Vast quantities of food were paraded in style and then consumed, and two different kinds of beer, one dark brown and one almost clear amber, were served in huge jugs drawn from enormous wooden casks. There was no wine, and only the king's table held jugs of potent, fiery, honeyed mead of a kind I had never tasted. King Athol drank little, and was equally abstemious in his eating. His self-appointed function there, I gathered, watching him closely, was to preside over his people's pleasure, to ensure that all were looked after and none was left untended. On his right, Donuil, too, drank little, although he ate hugely. I sat directly to the king's left and guided myself by his example, and Connor sat on my left.

And then there came a time when the songs died down and gave way to a brief lull that was quickly drowned by a rising babble of noise as the drinkers, free now of the constraints of listening politely to the performers, began to vent their euphoria. Athol turned to me.

"We may leave now, Master Merlyn, or stay, as you wish. The remaining part of the festivities will look after themselves." He was smiling slightly, his eyes on mine, prepared to accede to whatever I might wish.

I shrugged and shook my head, smiling back at him. "I remember my father's dictum for such occasions, sir. He maintained that the presence of senior officers became more than unnecessary beyond a certain point at all such gatherings."

The old king smiled. "Unnecessary and unwelcome. Your father was a wise man. Shall we go?" He rose to his feet as he spoke, and the evening's festivities had progressed to the stage where very few of the revellers were even aware of the movement on the high table platform. Moving without haste, Athol led the way from the Great Hall, patting a shoulder here and there and exchanging pleasantries with many of the older people present. As we moved behind him, Donuil drew abreast with me and grasped me gently by the arm.

"What will you do now?"

I looked at him. "What do you mean, what will I do now? I'll do what any sane man should do. I'll sleep. What else should I do?"

"Have you had any thought of speaking to my father about Deirdre?" I looked quickly over my shoulder. "Don't be concerned, no one else heard me. But don't you think you should say something soon? She was his daughter."

"Aye, and your sister." I was still looking around me, uneasy at the thought of being overheard, but no one appeared to be paying any attention to us. Connor had moved ahead to walk beside his father and everyone else who had been at the head table had stopped along the way to talk to others. Now I looked back at Donuil. "I am aware of my responsibilities in this, Donuil. But it's a story that will be long in the telling, so I had decided to wait until tomorrow, when your father would be rested and there would be less pressure surrounding all of us."

He nodded, but any agreement he might have offered was forestalled by his father, who had stopped to wait for us to draw level with him at the exit from the Hall.

"Master Merlyn, the night is not yet too old, and I would like to speak with you in less . . . public circumstances. Will you come to my quarters?"

"Of course, sir, with pleasure."

"Good." He glanced at Donuil, then towards Connor. "We will be three, then, with your—what was the word—your *adjutant*? Will you object if Connor here makes four of us?"

"Not in the least."

"Then please, come with us."

XIII

IT TOOK US only moments to cross the space between the Hall and what I took to be the king's own hut—it could hardly have been called a house, even though it was the most commodious building I had yet seen in the enclosure apart from the Great Hall itself—and once inside, I was immediately struck by the shadowy darkness of the place and forcibly reminded of the gift of candles we had carried all the way from Camulod. I turned to Donuil at once, but he was smiling already. "I'll bring them," he said, and left at once. His father watched Donuil leave, raising only one eyebrow to indicate his curiosity before waving me to one of the four backless Roman-style chairs that were grouped around an open hearth pit in the middle of the floor.

"There is no ceremony in this place," Athol said. "Here, we serve ourselves." He moved away and began to pour ale from a large, earthen pitcher into four mugs of kiln-fired clay. Connor moved to assist him and I looked around me in curiosity. This was a one-room dwelling, with only a single, fur-covered cot against a side wall. The wall with the doorway was blank and undecorated, with two small window embrasures covered on the outside by wooden shutters. The remaining three walls were hung with a strange variety of skins, none of which seemed to be decorative, and with a variety of swords, shields and other weaponry, including a pair of large, unmatched axes and a smaller, lethal-looking hatchet with a heavy head and a widely flared cutting edge. It was, I decided, a distinctively unregal dwelling. When Athol spoke again, the humour in his tone embarrassed me greatly, for my amazement had evidently registered upon my features.

"I do not live here, Master Merlyn. I merely sleep here from time to time. My living quarters are behind the Hall, where we dined tonight, but there are times when I find it convenient to escape, and my people are considerate enough to leave me to my own devices when I come here."

"Forgive me—" He cut short my apologies with a laugh and a wave of his hand.

"For what? For looking about you? That is natural, and you are a stranger here. Now, where did Donuil disappear to?" He stepped towards me, holding out a drinking mug for me to take, and then seated himself beside me, leaning comfortably into the side arm of his chair with the ease of long usage.

"He has gone to fetch a gift we brought for you," I told him, sniffing the aroma of the cool ale before tasting it. "We had both forgotten about it in the excitement of arrival."

"Another gift? Those you have given me already are magnificent enough to beggar any I have ever received. And the return of my son himself is gift enough to gladden all of us." The delight in the king's voice was unmistakable. Connor was grinning as he, too, came to sit close by the fire, which was leaping brightly in its pit. "Well, by all the gods," the old man continued, "we'll drink to your new gift now, Master Merlyn, before it comes, since it is not possible that it could disappoint us."

He sipped his ale tentatively and waited for me to try mine. It was cold and delicious, and I nodded in appreciation. Seeing my approval, Athol nodded, too, and took a longer drink before setting his mug down and fixing me with a straightforward gaze. "You have done well by my son, Merlyn Britannicus, and I am grateful. He speaks very highly of you, and in the short time since we two have met, I can perceive why that should be so." His face broke into a smile again. "And he is fiercely proud of the fact that he is now a horseman . . . what is the word you use, a cav—?" He stumbled over the alien sound.

"A cavalryman, sir. Organized, disciplined horse troops are called cavalry."

"Cavalryman, aye, that's the word. He's fearsome proud of that." He had fallen out of the courtly language of his formal bearing and spoke now in the liquid, rolling Erse of the common folk.

"And so he should be. You have no cavalry here in Eire at all?"

"We have no horses. Och, we have ponies, wild creatures and strong enough to carry a man, but small they are, scarcely bigger than asses. They look little like those massy creatures you have. There's nothing in all Eire to compare with those beasts of yours for size."

I smiled. "Except your giant deer. There's nothing in Britain to compare with those."

"The elk? But they're not Eirish! They came from beyond the seas, in the old days, brought by an Outland king. You don't have their like in Britain? I thought you must have. Anyway, they liked it here, I suppose, for now there are hundreds of them. But they're stupid things. There's no sport in hunting them, although they carry much meat. They are too big and slow. The most difficult part of the hunt is finding them, because they live in the deepest woods, among the swamps. Give me a small deer any day. Hunting one of those is a challenge." He paused, then: "But I was talking of your horses. Would you . . . ?" He broke off and cleared his throat before continuing. "My people are fascinated by your horses, and by this whole idea of cavalry. Tomorrow promises to be a fine day. Would you consider showing us what your cavalry can do that makes them such a powerful force?"

"You mean an exhibition? A *cavalry* demonstration? But there are only eight of us, nine counting Donuil. One of my men was killed on the way here, and another broke his leg."

"Nine cavalry may be an awesome force to people who have none."

My eyes went from him to Connor who was watching me closely, and I realized that I was being tested in some way I could not define. "Of course," I said. "There won't be much I can show you, but there are enough of us to give you some idea of what's involved in our maneuvers. Where could we arrange such a thing?"

It was Connor who answered me. "That's easy. Right outside our main gates there's a clear space of common grazing. You crossed it this morning on your way in. It's bounded by the river on one side and by the forest on the other two. We could do it there."

"Then we shall. At what hour?" I had noticed the place, but had been too preoccupied with our imminent reception and the appearance of Athol's stronghold to pay much attention.

Now Connor looked at his father. "What do you think, Father? Early or late?"

The king hawked and spat into the fire. "The place will be full of thick heads in the morning. Better wait until they've had to eat and drink again and recaptured their senses. Some time after midday." He glanced at me. "Would that suit you? After midday?"

"Of course, whenever you think best. There's no great need for preparation, since my men and their mounts are ready at all times for whatever I call upon them to do."

The door opened as I spoke and Donuil entered again, lugging one of the boxes of candles we had brought from Britain for his father. He crossed directly to stand in front of the king's couch and then dropped to one knee, lowering the heavy case carefully to the ground, where he prised off the lid, using the flat of his knife to spring the nails that secured it. Athol and Connor watched in silence as the lid was removed and set aside, after which Donuil removed a thin covering of straw and pulled out a single long candle of translucent, golden-looking wax, offering it to the king. Athol took it from him, holding it delicately between his fingertips, evidently in complete ignorance of its purpose.

"It's very fine," he said eventually. "And wondrous pure in its smoothness . . ." A lengthy pause produced no reaction from either Donuil or me, and Connor's blank expression warned his father that no help could be expected from him, either, so that the king was finally forced to ask the question he would dearly have loved to avoid. "What is it, Donuil?"

Donuil grinned now and took back the candle from his father's hand. "It is a gift of light, Father. Light more pure than any save that of the sun itself. Watch this." He rose to his feet and placed the candle on the floor by the case before crossing to where two tallow lamps flickered on a table against the wall. Wetting his finger and thumb with saliva, he snuffed the wicks on both of them, plunging that area of the room into shadow and filling the air with the heavy stink of smouldering. Three more lamps burned at various places in the room, and he dealt with each of those the same way, leaving the fire in the hearth as the only source of light in the large chamber. "Now," he said, moving swiftly to the hearth. "Behold the light of the Christian priests." He knelt in front of the fire, scooping up one of the dried rushes that covered the floor and folding it into a narrow spill, which he lit from the fire. Shielding the small flame carefully in one cupped hand, he brought it back to where we sat and held it out towards his father and brother.

"See," he said. "It's yellow."

I could see from the looks of them that they were hard put not to scoff openly, since it took no great feat of observation to perceive that the flame of a dried-out rush would be yellow. Now, however, Donuil reached down and scooped up the candle from the floor, lighting it and immediately shaking out the flame of the spill. In the comparative darkness, the tiny bead of light at the tip of the new-lit candle burned white and pure, strengthening and growing steadily as the melting wax began to saturate the wick, until the brightness of it far outshone all five of the tallow lamps that had burned earlier. As his father and brother sat rapt, Donuil silently drew more candles from the case on the floor, lighting one after another until twelve of them surrounded him in a semicircle, each stuck to the floor in a congealed pool of its own wax. No one spoke, no sound marred the stillness in the room, and I experienced a feeling almost of awe at seeing the effect such a simple thing as a wax candle could have on people who had never seen its like.

It was Athol the King who finally broke the silence.

"This room has never been so bright after the set of sun, and has seldom seen such brightness even at full noon. What are these things? You called them the light of the Christian priests?"

Donuil looked now at me, for the first time since he had re-entered the room. "Aye, Father, but they are called candles, and Caius Merlyn here thought to bring them to you. He once used them to write by, late at night, as do the Christian clerics. He obtained these long years ago, from a Christian priest, before a battle in which he was wounded, and he had forgotten them since then. I recalled them some time ago, when we were talking one night and, thinking them long since lost, mentioned that you could have made great use of them here. Caius found them and decided to bring them to you, as a gift. We brought three cases. There are two others, just like this one, in our tents."

The king rose up and extended his hand to me in thanks. I shook with him, feeling slightly embarrassed by what I saw as an inappropriate reaction to what was, in essence, a paltry gift. He left me in no doubt that I erred, however.

"Caius Merlyn," he said, his voice deep and low, his delivery slow enough that I could hear, in the two words of my own name, all of the sonorous, lilting cadences of his native tongue. "There can be few gifts more valuable, or more welcome, than the gift of light in darkness. This land of ours is bright and green, rich and full of colour in the summer when the flowers are in bloom . . . but the summer is too short, and all too soon the nights stretch out again towards winter and the gathering darkness starts to make its terror felt again. We are a simple people, but we are hagridden by our fear of darkness. Our Druids and the night-tales of our folk are all concerned—far too concerned—with terror and the threatenings of the dark; with that great portion of our lives when folk can see no trace of the world around them and therefore dreadful things are free to move about them, unsuspected and unseen. The darkness of the unlit night means blindness and deprivation and the fear of madness. The only thing that keeps men sane is light—firelight, torchlight, tallow light and lamplight. Children dread the night, the darkness, and if the truth be told, every grown man and woman dreads it, too, in the rooted depths of their being. One of these candles, burning as it does, could keep an ailing child, or man, in comfort through the longest, blackest night and see him safely into day again. I will keep two of these cases aside, in your name, for just that purpose. They will be night lights for the sick, and I will set my people to providing the same quality for future use. It can be done, and the existence of these you have brought proves that. Men made these things in Britain. Our men will make the like of them here in Eire. Of what are they made? It's not tallow."

"No, Sir King," I responded. "It is wax. Pure beeswax, but I know not what the wick is made from."

"Wax? The wax of bees? Is that so?" Athol looked to Donuil, as if for confirmation, but Donuil merely shrugged to show his ignorance. "And how do you acquire bees' wax without being stung to death?"

It was Connor who suggested an answer to that. "Probably the same way you acquire their honey for your mead, Father. By smoking them into a stupor, then taking what you want."

"Aye." The king's voice was musing. "And we've been doing that for a hundred years and more, yet no one ever thought to burn the wax as fuel."

"Why would they, Sir King?" My question earned me a high-browed look almost of pity.

"Why? Because the possibility was there for the recognition and the taking. Christian clerics thought of it, and Romans before them, I would wager, but none of my people did, though they are no more stupid than any other." He stopped and cleared his throat with a great noise. "Well, at least we can begin to use it now. Again, my thanks, Lord Merlyn. I hope we will find something of equal merit with which to send you on your way when your visit here is ended. Two of my sons have befriended you, and I see much that moves me to commend their judgment."

His words, and their unexpected warmth, filled me instantly and unexpectedly with writhing guilt and made nonsense of my earlier resolve to remain silent, for this night at least, on the other matters, completely unsuspected by him, that lay between us. I took a deep breath and glanced at Donuil, who was watching me closely, and then at Connor, who sat easily on my right, smiling slightly. Suddenly, for no good reason, I felt afraid for the outcome of my venture here in this alien land.

"Suspend your judgment until you know me better, King Athol," I heard myself say in a tone suddenly distant and formal. "We are far more closely bound than you suspect."

The king frowned slightly now, puzzled, the small smile still upon his lips. Then, in wary recognition of my sudden formality, he rose slowly to face me, settling himself firmly in an attitude of wariness, his weight distributed evenly on spread feet, his body seeming to lean slightly forward as though to resist the pressure of anything I might throw at him. All of us watched him as he did so, awaiting a further reaction, although for a spell he did not respond beyond rising, merely scanning my face, particularly my eyes, with his own gaze. I sensed then, rather than saw, Connor's body stiffen on my right, but a hand flick from his father, caught from the corner of my eye, albeit tiny and backhanded as though he waved irritably at a buzzing pest, forestalled any reaction or interruption Connor might have been tempted to make. The silence stretched, and the king's eyes left my face and sought Donuil's. Evidently having found nothing there to alarm him, Athol eventually spoke, in slow, even tones.

"More closely bound than I suspect? How so?"

I knew that my next words would be among the most important I should ever utter. A misplaced inflection or mannerism might bar Arthur, and me, from Camulod forever, confining him, or both of us, to this foreign place as prisoners. I stood up slowly and moved towards the hearth, placing myself so that its fire burned brightly at my back.

"I know more of your family, Sir King, than you do. But before I tell you what I know, I must speak of two things . . . things I must say in advance of anything else, since failure to speak of them now might—no, they would—give Connor, if not you yourself, apparent cause to doubt my truthfulness hereafter."

Even though my heart was galloping like a horse with anticipation of the unknown outcome of my course, I admired the old king's self-possession in the face of what he must have perceived as extraordinary and mystifying behaviour on my part. He merely nodded, maintaining his silence and indicating courteous patience. Connor sat leaning forward, his peg leg straight out before him, his left hand gripping his good knee, his right hand holding his ale pot as though to throw it. Donuil was rubbing his long nose with a forefinger, looking downward.

"The first of these two things is this: I came here, into your kingdom and into your presence, fully resolved to speak my mind and tell you all that I will tell you now. Until moments ago, however, I had intended to speak to you of them some time tomorrow. Donuil and I were discussing that when you invited me here after the feast, and I had just finished telling him I have had no suitable opportunity to speak with you in private since we arrived, and these matters demand privacy, I believe. Now that has changed. We are here, in private, and I cannot, in conscience, hold back longer." I paused and tipped my head towards Donuil. "The major part of what I have to tell you will be attested to by Donuil, who has experienced the truth of it at first hand. The remainder, that which Donuil cannot personally verify, you must judge for yourself, based upon your own assessment of the matters I shall disclose."

Athol nodded once again, concealing any signs of impatience with my hedging, and retaining his outward mien of good-humoured courtesy. He glanced briefly at Donuil, who nodded his head wordlessly. "I accept that," Athol murmured. "Though it sounds mysterious, even ominous. What is the second thing?"

"I will deal with that now," I said, hating the stilted quality I could hear in my own words, yet utterly incapable of changing them. "It concerns the propensity that exists in all of us to cleave to that which we wish to believe, rather than to that which our senses indicate to be the unpalatable truth." I turned my gaze now upon Connor. "Connor, when we first met, when you hauled me out of the sea, I told you the truth. I recognized you, do you recall?"

He nodded, plainly not knowing what was coming next.

"We spoke then of Donuil, and the friendship between him and me. You chose to doubt my truthfulness—a reasonable choice under the circumstances—and decided to keep the child, Arthur, as hostage against the safe return of your brother to your father's Hall; a shrewd ploy, since you well knew the child to be worth more to me than my own life, although you knew not why."

"Aye." Connor's voice was low-pitched. "I was wrong to doubt you, I know now. But I had no way of knowing it then."

"I agree, and I harbour no ill feelings. You freed me thereafter to seek Donuil, and you yourself remained behind to await your sister, Ygraine, disbelieving what I said of that, too."

Now his face flushed red and he moved to struggle to his feet. Again, however, he was restrained by a gesture from his father, whose own voice now betrayed a hint of anger. "What of Ygraine? I have heard nothing of this."

Connor was glaring at me now and answered his father without removing his eyes from mine. "There was nothing to hear, Father. Mere rumours and foolishness."

"Not so!" I turned towards the king, facing him squarely. "Connor refused to accept my word of Ygraine's death, but your daughter died in my own arms, King Athol, on the beach that day that Connor found me. She had fled her husband, Lot of Cornwall, days before, and she and all her women and her guards were slain in a fight I witnessed from afar. I was in pursuit of them, or of the man I thought to be pursuing them, but I arrived too late to be of any help. They were all dead or dying by the time I reached them. Very few of their assailants, a mere handful, had survived the fight. I slew them with my bow." I saw no benefit in adding that I had allowed the last of them, their leader, to depart unmolested.

The king's face had whitened to a pallor resembling the beeswax candles that had so delighted him mere moments earlier, and he clasped his hands out of sight behind his back, closing his eyes with such concentrated effort that the skin tightened upon his face, the wrinkles on his brow smoothing out to show clearly against the paleness of his high forehead. I spoke on gently, attempting to lessen the pain for both men, father and brother.

"I told Connor of this later that day, but he argued that the woman who died in my arms that afternoon could not have been his sister. And, by his lights, I will admit, he had strong room for doubt. I had told him myself that I had never previously met his sister, or even seen her in the flesh. Nor did we find her corpse when we returned to seek it. She, and all the others, had been washed out to sea by the returning tide before we could win back. We found one naked female, floating in the waves, a stranger, unknown to Connor or any of his men. So he reasoned that this woman I had cradled in death was another slain by coincidence upon the strand where he had sought to find his sister. It could not possibly have been Ygraine, he chose to believe, because her bodyguard of your own Scots was strong enough to safeguard her against any danger, as was their blood duty. His reasoning was sound enough, but flawed. His knowledge was incomplete. He had—he could have had—no notion of the carnage that had been wrought for weeks in the blighted Cornish lands through which I had been riding, too late at all times to achieve anything worthwhile in any matter."

Silence, then in a quiet, calm voice: "Yet, knowing that, you made no effort to convince him of his error."

It was a statement, not a question, and I lowered my voice in responding. "No, I did not. I accepted his need to believe what he believed, and saw no profit in angering him. Besides, I had concerns of my own, which would have been endangered had I sought to convince him otherwise."

"The child."

"Yes, the child."

Athol sucked air audibly through his front teeth. "What is the import of this child, Caius Merlyn? He has great influence, it seems, for a mere babe in arms. Who is he?"

"He is my ward. Who he is, exactly, will become clear as my story unfolds, but I have no wish to name him now."

He sucked at his teeth again, in a quirk I suddenly recognized as one he shared with his son Connor. "Something you said . . . you told Connor you had never seen or met his sister. How, then, could you assume this woman was my daughter? And how did you know that her name was Ygraine?"

I suddenly wanted this to be over. "I knew she was Ygraine, wife to Lot of Cornwall, because I recognized her."

Now the king's frown became a deep-graven scowl. I counted to fourteen before his voice grated, "There is a lie here, somewhere amidst all this. How could you recognize her, never having seen her?"

This was proving to be as painful for me as for my listeners. I swallowed hard, to dislodge the lump that had swelled suddenly in my throat, and when I spoke again my voice emerged as a whisper. "Because, save for the colour of her hair, she might have been the twin of my dead wife, her sister . . . your other daughter, Deirdre."

The stillness that struck the room was total. Athol stiffened, his eyes fixed upon mine and I watched his pupils widen. Connor froze in mid-movement, so that he hung awkwardly in his seat, appearing to be off balance and yet poised, almost comically, on one buttock, his right arm braced to drag the weight of his false leg to a new position. Only Donuil appeared unaffected, slouched against the right arm of his backless chair, chin down, his eyes upon his hands cupped between his thighs. As the stillness stretched, he looked up slowly, taking in the tableau presented by the three of us, then heaved a deep, audible breath and spoke for the first time.

"That is the truth, Father. Deirdre, whom we all thought long dead, was Merlyn's wife. I met her and knew her again, spoke with her often in our own sign language, lived in Camulod with her, and tended her grave there after she was killed." He raised one hand gently, palm outward, in a sign to forestall his father's questions, speaking calmly and with great dignity into the shocked silence. "We assumed her dead, Father, when she disappeared the second time, after her second fever. She never returned and was never seen again. She was dead to us. But the fact is, she lived, and travelled far . . ." He broke off and sighed, looking to me for aid. I stared back at him, expressionless. This part of the tale was his alone. He sighed again and carried on.

"I had been in Camulod for many months before I saw her, because she had been assaulted, grievously—she was still mute and deaf—and Merlyn had hidden her to protect her from her attackers until she could identify them for him. The two of them fell in love while she was in his care, and one day, when he believed it safe, he brought her home to Camulod. That is when I saw her."

Donuil's father interrupted him at this point. "You are sure it was her, your sister?"

Donuil's surprise at the question was so great that he laughed aloud, biting the sound off immediately it issued from his lips. "Am I sure? Father, she was Deirdre, my loving little sister, and she flew to me the moment she set eyes on me. I told you, we talked long in our own private language of signs. Of course it was her." His father nodded acceptance and Donuil continued his tale.

"I asked her, of course, what had happened to her, why she had left us, but she had no more idea than we have. She remembered only awakening one day and being frightened by her own reflection, which was that of a woman, where she had expected to see a child. The years between what she expected to see and what she saw were lost. She was with people who treated her kindly enough, and who knew her well, but she did not know who they were or how long she had been with them."

"Madness." This was a whisper from Connor, and Donuil answered it immediately.

"No, Brother, not madness. There is a term for her illness, which I learned from my friend Lucanus, the surgeon of Camulod. It is amnesia. Deirdre had lost her memory, the result, he guessed, of the high fevers I told him had consumed the child. She was no more mad than you or I, or Father here. She had simply lost her memory of all that had happened to her . . . Anyway, there she was, alive and well and happy to see me again. Merlyn and I thought to bring her home here, to visit you after they were wed, but war broke out, and we were absent for a time from Camulod, and when we returned, she was dead, murdered by someone, with the babe she carried, while she was out of the shelter of Camulod. Merlyn knew nothing of it. He himself had lost all memory, his mind driven from him by the smashing of a swinging iron ball that should have killed him and would have, save for the skills of the same Lucanus I spoke of."

I watched the king struggle to control himself as he listened, attempting to come to terms with what was being thrust upon him. He had loved both his daughters, I knew this from Donuil, but Deirdre had been his favourite and he had grieved long and hard twice in the past, believing her dead. Now, as he learned that she had lived through all his grief, only to die again, by mindless violence in a far land, conflicting passions betrayed themselves, sweeping across his face, each in its turn to be dismissed and condemned and disallowed. I saw sorrow, compassion, anger, disbelief, suspicion, resentment and dismay each register upon his face and in his eyes, but after they had passed in a fleeting thought, his face grew calm again and he mastered himself. His eyes moved back to hold my own as Donuil continued speaking.

"Two years and more went by, and Merlyn knew nothing of his former life. But then his memories came back, and he believed that Uther, his cousin, had been the killer of his wife. He had suspected long before, though he could not prove his suspicions, that Uther had committed the first violence on her, the attack that led Merlyn to hide her far from Camulod. Now he believed in Uther's guilt and set out to find and kill him. Uther was at war, in the southwest, against Lot. By the time Merlyn caught up with him, Uther had been killed and his armour stripped from him. Merlyn knew nothing of his death, or of the theft of his armour, and so pursued the killer who appeared as Uther from afar. The chase led him to the beach where he found Ygraine, and with her the child Arthur, drifting off in the birney. He climbed aboard the boat but could not return to shore. Connor found them drifting that same day."

When Donuil finished speaking the king sat down, staring off into the middle distance for a long, long time before he eventually straightened his back, rose to his feet again and spoke to me in slow, deep tones.

"We will speak more of this later, Caius Merlyn . . . You are, in truth, my son by marriage?"

I nodded. "I am."

"And this child, this Arthur. He is yours? Yours and Deirdre's?"

"No, Sir King, he is not."

"I see." I heard first the regret, then the bafflement, plain in the old man's voice. "Then who is he? I had thought . . . almost hoped, for a moment there, listening to Donuil, that he might be my grandson."

I opened my mouth to speak, but the words congealed on my lips, and the words of my great-uncle Publius Varrus, unthought of for years, flashed clearly before my eyes; words he had written recalling the occasion when he stood beside my own grandfather Caius Britannicus and heard that noble man deny what he had always claimed to be his birthright, abjuring his Romanness and claiming British identity. As it had for Grandfather Caius on that long-past day, as it must at some time for all men, my own moment of truth had arrived. I overcame the surge of cowardice that had stricken me mute and forged ahead, unmindful of the threat to all my plans and those of all my kin, knowing all at once the rightness of my course.

"He is."

A pause, the length of several heartbeats, while the king looked at me, grappling with the meaning of my words.

"What did you say?"

"He is your grandson, born of Ygraine, your daughter, to my cousin Uther. Uther Pendragon."

The king sat down again, subsiding suddenly back into his seat as though the strength had left his legs. Once seated, he turned immediately to Donuil, seeking verification, but Donuil merely shrugged and cocked his head, indicating ignorance. Connor, however, had shrugged off all restraint and now leaned fiercely towards me, clutching at the arm of his chair in preparation to rise and face me beard to beard.

"Damn you, Merlyn," he rasped. "You told me none of this!"

"Damn me if you will," I responded. "What other course lay open to me? You refused to believe me when I spoke of Ygraine. What would your reaction have been had I told you the child was her bastard, bred between her and her light of love, my cousin, whom I had been pursuing? And if you had believed me, what then? Would you have permitted me to keep the child, as I am sworn to do? I doubt that! More likely you would have fed me to the fishes then and there and brought the infant home with you. Am I not right?"

He hung there, angry words trembling upon his lips, threatening to spill, and then he recovered himself and subsided, sniffing loudly and breaking eye contact with me. "Aye," he muttered. "Mayhap I would, at that." His father, however, had seized upon what I had said last, and now questioned me.

"To what are you sworn, Caius Merlyn? What is the boy to you? Why would you claim any right to him and why would you even wish to, were he the son of the man who killed your wife and your own child unborn? Were I you, I should have killed the child out of hand, purely for vengeance, blood upon blood. Is that your intent, even now?"

"Father!"

"Quiet!" Donuil's protest was cut short by a peremptory slash of his father's hand. "I am speaking to Master Merlyn here."

I turned my back to them, gazing into the fire, hearing the sound of

Athol's angry breathing behind me as I sought the proper words. Finally I turned back and spoke.

"The child is very special, Sir King," I began. "He is unique; bred to a purpose, and of the blood of many kings and champions. He is your grandson, and the blood of your people runs in his veins. But he is also the grandson of Ullic Pendragon, King of the Cambrian Celts, and by his mother's marriage, at least, he can lay claim to Cornwall, once he is of age. He also claims the heritage of Camulod, its builders and its kings, though they sought not to be kings in name: Caius Britannicus and Publius Varrus—noble names of ancient lineage, springing direct from earliest Roman times. His destiny is greatness, for he will be king of all Britain, *Ard Righ*, High King of all the land, uniting its peoples to withstand the growing influx of the Germanic Saxon hordes." I had spoken forcefully, willing my tongue to articulate without the slightest pause, unwilling to permit the expostulation I thought must cut me short in mid-delivery, but the king had shown no sign of wishing to interrupt. Now I stopped, curious, and waited for a reaction.

Athol stooped from the waist and picked up his clay cup from where it had lain untouched for a long time. He sipped at the contents pensively before moving to stand beside me in front of the fire, gazing down into the glowing coals. Donuil and Connor looked at each other, but neither spoke. I turned again, shoulder to shoulder now with the king, and stared with him into the fire.

"An impressive destiny," he said, eventually. "High King of Britain. A name like that brings its own dangers and breeds enemies from stones."

"I am aware of that, Sir King."

"Aye." He drank again, then spoke over his shoulder. "Donuil, you have been there, in this place Camulod. I ask you as my son, a Prince of the Gaels of Eire. Is this claim true, and could it come to pass as Master Merlyn says?"

"Aye, Father, I believe it. It will come to pass."

"Will? Not could, or might? You are that sure?"

Now I heard Donuil rise for the first time, and as I glanced his way I saw him extend a hand to help his brother to his feet, after which the two moved closer to us. As they approached, Donuil said, "Sure enough to have decided that my own destiny lies with Merlyn and the child. I will return with them to Britain when they go, to play my part in whatever the fates hold stored for them."

The king glanced over his shoulder, one eyebrow raised sardonically. "*If* they go," he said. "If I permit them to leave. I am king here, remember, and the child is my grandson, all that I have remaining of his mother, whom I loved."

I was watching closely, hearing the threat and its implications, but I was surprised to see Donuil smile easily, undismayed by his father's words.

"And why would you forbid it, Father? Had the child been born legitimately, it would have been Lot's heir, bearing his blood, and I have heard your opinions regarding Lot and his true worth. Nevertheless, the child would have been king of Cornwall and you'd have been well pleased. Now he has no taint of Lot about him, he has a claim to the Cornish kingdom, and he has, besides, the promise of all Britain, certainly of Camulod and Cambria . . . High King of Alban, Father! The blood of our clan will flourish with his prosperity."

"Aye, or suffer with his death. You are foolhardy, it appears to me, my son, in this decision. It will bar you from all chance of inheritance here in your own right."

Donuil's smile grew even wider. "What chance is that, Father? I am your youngest son and the pole of claims above mine reaches high. I'll never be king here after you are gone, and you will admit that, if you are pressed. Besides, it might even be less perilous fighting in Britain than it would be here in Eire. Arthur, the child, has a chance of gaining the *Ard Righ*'s chair there. No man will ever have that chance in Eire, by your own admission."

The king pursed his lips, his eyes expressionless. "And my familial blessing? You would forfeit that?"

The smile disappeared from Donuil's face immediately. "No, Father, I would not in truth, if it could be avoided. I would hope to leave with your goodwill."

"Hmm." Athol turned his gaze on Connor. "And you, Lord Connor, what think you of this?"

Connor had been listening, his eyes on me most of the time. Now he coughed slightly. "I do not know what I should think, Father. I have heard more here than I ever thought to know."

"Your brother here trusts Master Merlyn more than some of his own kin. Have you anything to say to that?"

Connor grimaced and glanced at Donuil. "His good sense surprises me. He has hidden it well, in the past." He looked back to me, his gaze now openly speculative. "I agree with him, too, which also surprises me. I believe Master Merlyn, in spite of all my wishes to deny him. Ygraine is dead, I now accept, as I accept the fact that I have mourned her without knowing. So is our sister Deirdre. But if he won Deirdre as he has won Donuil and almost my unwilling self, there may be more to him even than meets the eye, and that's impressive enough."

I said nothing, sensing that it was not yet time for me to speak. Now the initiative passed again to Athol. He swung away and sought my cup, then handed it to me, and when he spoke again he had lapsed back into the courtly language he used as king.

"So be it. You said you thought this discussion should be private, Master Merlyn, and you were correct. Let it remain so. None but we four shall know of its occurrence, for now. Are we agreed?" Connor, Donuil and I all muttered our agreement. "Good, then here is what has formed in my mind while we have talked. You spoke of the boy's destiny, Master Merlyn. Destiny, I think, is a wondrous but perilous thing for those selected to attain it. Most men live and die without ever hearing or thinking of it, for Destiny is not the truck of ordinary mortals. Destiny attains the stature of godhead, of immortality. It gives rise to legend. It reeks of the whims of gods, goddesses and priests. Those who speak of such things, and there are many of them, mostly priests, would have us believe it will come, to those touched by it, without effort. I adopt a more hard-headed view of it, when I think of it at all. I find I prefer to believe it should take hard work to achieve. A child of Destiny, a High King, must be taught, it seems to me, how to be first a man that other men will respect and admire, then a chief whom they will follow, then a king who can command them in peace as well as in war, and only then a High King, who can impose his vision on a people. Do you agree?"

"Completely."

"I thought you would. You have thought, then, on this training?"

"Deeply."

"And what have you decided? How will you see to it the child is trained?"

"At my own hand, Sir King. I have made up my mind, long since, to give my life to the training of him, but I believe it must be in Britain, where he is to rule."

"You see no hope for him in Eire, then."

"No." I shook my head. "Not in this matter. He must be taught, from earliest boyhood, to perceive the land he rules: the people in it, its problems and its requirements. Afterwards, armed with a clear understanding of those things, and a sense of his place at the head of them, he might have some chance of succeeding in the task ahead of him, which is to combine those peoples, and the solutions to the problems that confront them, and to weld them into a common folk."

"You see him as a lawgiver?"

"Aye, among other things, but first as a soldier. A leader, as you have said, and a champion."

"Hmm. Well, you can train him in that, at least, but what of the other things?"

I shrugged, finding it easy now to smile. "The rudiments are all in place. He will learn the structure of a civilized society in Camulod, taught by its finest minds, and he will learn his place within that structure, responsibility and leadership. There, too, he will learn of weapons and of warfare, of cavalry, and of tactics and strategy. He will also study the basic elements of education, literacy, logic and polemics. He will study metallurgy and engineering, and his teachers will be the finest we can provide."

"And who will supervise these teachers?"

"I will."

"Hmm." Athol looked away again, staring into the fire, and then he spoke, announcing the decision he had reached. "So be it. My trust in you shall be no less than my sons'. You shall return to Britain, Caius Merlyn, with my grandson, at winter's end—as soon as the weather on the seas has moderated to allow you safe passage. Donuil will accompany you as my appointed guardian to the child. Connor, whose galleys dominate the seas between our two shores, will act as liaison between you and us, carrying information and, should the need arise, assistance from one to the other. We will discuss more details in the time ahead. For now . . ." He turned to face his sons. "You two will please me greatly if you leave us. I wish to speak to my goodson Merlyn of his wife, my daughter Deirdre, and your presence may hinder him from speaking with the depth I seek." The term he used to speak of me was not "good son" but rather "goodson," a single word, carrying connotations of family attachments. I had heard it used before, during the day that had passed, but never beyond the land of the Scots. Donuil and Connor excused themselves and took their leave, and I was left alone with Athol, who moved directly to refresh our cups while I threw fresh wood on the fire at his request.

We talked far into the night, the king and I, by the brightness of his new candles and the leaping flames of the fire. I talked to him of his daughter and of my love for her, omitting nothing that I could recall. I spoke to him of her athletic abilities, of how they had amazed me at the outset when I realized that I had never known a woman or a girl so strong and supple, or so fleet and self-assured in matters of sport and physical prowess. I spoke, too, of my own frustration in never having learned how she came by such skills, and in never having learned to "speak" with her, using my hands the way she and her brother did. I told him of my youthful, arrogant belief that I could leave her for a while and then return to find her and the child she would bear me and to take up at the leaving point and spend my life thereafter pleasing her. And I told him of the times I spent with her and of the love I bore her, how it grew from nothingness into the fire that blazed to become the core of my existence, then was extinguished, utterly and devastatingly, for years, to spring back blazing, phoenix-like, into full life with all the agonies of true love lost and long unmourned. I talked of the home we shared in my tiny hidden vale and spoke to him of how she had felt, nestled in my grasp and how she tasted on my lips; of how I held her sheltered in my arms; of how she succoured me when I was weary and in pain; and of how she glowed with health and life and fullness when I last beheld her, advanced in pregnancy. And last, I spoke to him of how I found myself, beside her grave, close by the darkened waters of the little mere in Avalon, and of the agonies I suffered by that grave, tasting for the first time a lifetime of guilt and grief and loss.

Through all of this, King Athol sat and listened, speaking no word, allowing me to pour out my heart and soul into his ears and understanding. He was the perfect listener for my tale, because I knew that he, too, had mourned for my lost love, not once, but time and again, and was doing so now afresh. He listened minutely, absorbing every word, every flicker of expression that crossed my face, bearing the pain I suffered during this, my first complete mourning for my beloved love and for the nameless, faceless child she had prepared for me.

Only long after I had fallen silent, emptied of everything, did he speak, and then he asked of Uther. Did I still believe that Uther had violated and finally killed my love?

Exhausted as I was from purging myself, I thought long before answering, and when I did I spoke with a new confidence, finding a certainty inside my soul that told me of Uther's innocence in all I had condemned him for so ruthlessly. No, I told Athol, I did not believe that Uther was at blame. His guilt had been in my mind alone. That led me to speak of my own father, Picus Britannicus, and his unwavering sense of truth and justice; of his staunch belief in according the benefit of doubt in the absence of absolute proof of guilt. Of his belief, in other words, of the essential good in man, and of the enormity of those dark passions that could lie in all of us, capable of overwhelming anyone, but not without great struggle. I explained how he had brought me to doubt Uther's guilt, and of how that had sufficed until I fell in battle, to awaken to myself years later and find that, once again, my love had been struck down by an unknown assailant.

From there, I went on to describe my pursuit of Uther through the battlefields of Cornwall, revealing to the king, for the first time, the story I had heard from Popilius Cirro, our veteran *primus pilus*, concerning the capture of Ygraine by Uther and the liaison that had flourished between the two, resulting in the birth of the child Arthur. Athol listened in silence to all of this, making no judgment either of his daughter or my cousin, although at one point he uttered a single, scathing remark consigning his erstwhile ally and goodson Gulrhys Lot to eternal perdition. I ended my tale with the culmination of my hunt, when I found myself face to face, not with Uther Pendragon, but with another who wore Uther's clothes and armour. The circle was complete, and we sat silent together until the fire died down one last, long time. Finally, the king stood up.

"It is late, Goodson," he said, "and I have learned much of you this night. Thank you for telling me the things you have, and know that I consider my poor daughter Deirdre fortunate to have known you, and you fortunate to have found the happiness you had, fleeting though it may have been. Few men are blessed with love such as you have depicted here to me tonight. Get you to sleep now. Tomorrow you must show your cavalry to all my folk. This night, however, you have shown your self to me, and I shall regard it highly the remainder of my life." He dropped his hand onto my shoulder. "Sleep well. And sleep sound, for you deserve kind sleep."

XIV

THE FOLLOWING MORNING, soon after sunrise, Athol sought me out again, and once more we sequestered ourselves in his "sometime" house, free from interruptions and the daily commerce of the settlement. He had thought further, he told me, on what we had talked of the night before, and had lain awake almost until the sky had begun to pale with the new day. His bearing gave no hint of sleeplessness, for all that, reminding me of Luke's observation that the aging process differs in each of us. It evidently affected Athol only superficially if, at his age, he could so easily forego a night of sleep.

He began by questioning me on Britain, particularly on the lands that lay between Camulod and Glevum, where we had met with his envoys, Feargus and Logan. He asked about the nature of the countryside; whether it was densely wooded like his own territory, or more open to the sun. He wished to know about the people: Was the territory populated? If so, by whom? Did they farm the land? Who claimed the land? He knew it was not Camulodian ground, but to whom, then, did it belong?

I tried to answer all his questions, although I wondered why he would ask such things and asked several questions of my own, inquiring whether he had plans for colonizing Britain. No, he assured me, smiling, all he sought was local knowledge. If his grandson were ever to be living in that place, he felt it fitting to know as much about the region as he could learn. I accepted that and told him that all of the territory around Glevum lay in the Pendragon lands, to which Arthur himself was the true heir, and it was clear the information pleased him greatly, because he changed the subject and we moved on to talk of other things.

Soon after the noonday meal I begged leave of him to ready my men and made my way out through the gates of the Scots' stronghold to where my cavalry, such as it was, had already assembled to wait for me. Only Donuil was missing. I had left him behind with his father and the other counselors, charged with the responsibility of explaining the few brief maneuvers we would be presenting for their amusement. The delegation was an act both of self-preservation and consideration; Donuil's horsemanship was still far from the equivalent of the others', and his participation might have endangered the brief exhibition we were to mount. Besides, I saw no point in making his shortcomings as a cavalryman obvious to his own people. As it was, I felt acutely embarrassed at the paucity of the resources at our disposal in this exercise, and had I been able to conceive of any means of avoiding what lay ahead I would gladly have grasped it. Always a believer in the strength of initial impressions, I felt strongly that there could be no advantage to Camulod or its reputation in presenting a vague shadow of its potency. If the thing could not be done right, I saw no benefit to anyone in doing it at all. The thought of eight men attempting to portray the power of Camulod's thousands seemed ludicrous to me. The king, however, had requested a demonstration, and I felt honour bound to indulge him.

My men looked their best, dressed in the finery I had insisted they bring along for formal occasions, and their equipment and armour gleamed in the watery afternoon sunlight. It had rained heavily through most of the morning and I had begun to hope that the day might be too inclement to permit a public gathering, but these hopes were dashed in the late forenoon, when the sun broke through the cloud cover and encouraged great wedges of blue sky to follow it. I saw Dedalus sitting his horse slightly apart from the others, holding the reins of my black, and made my way towards him. There was no formalized order of rank among my companions; all of them were capable of command and each of them had known his fellows too long for such niceties to be necessary. On this occasion, however, Ded seemed to have assumed the lead. I went straight to where he sat, thanking him with a nod as I took my reins and pulled myself up into Germanicus's saddle. He nodded back, indicating the crowd of Scots who had already assembled on the gently sloping meadow outside the walls.

"They're out in force, expecting a spectacle. I hope they won't be disappointed. Eight men won't amount to much of a cavalry charge."

I grinned at him, refusing to allow my face to show how much I shared his misgivings. "Rely on it, old friend, they will be impressed. Bear in mind they have never seen anything like us before. The mere size of our horses is enough to awe them, and their armour, even the best of it, is paltry beside ours. When they see a line of us, leg to leg in formation, charging them at the gallop, they won't even think to count and see that we are only eight. They'll see only force and power, weight and threat, and terror is the only thing they'll feel." I looked him over carefully, from the freshly unpacked and carefully brushed centurion's crest of horsehair bristles on his helmet to the polished silver mountings on his spurred boots. Dedalus wore the crest of a senior centurion, a *primus pilus* of the Second Augusta Legion, which had served faithfully in Britain for almost four centuries, based in the legionary fortress of Isca Dumnoniorum, now reduced to the sad, dilapidated huddle known merely as Isca. He had never served in the Second Augusta, gone since before his birth, but his great-grandfather had, and the crest had been passed down from him to Dedalus, who wore it with as much pride as had his ancestor. It was dyed to a startling, chalky white and the horsehair bristles projected a full handspan above the crest's silver mounting, which sat across the helmet's crown from side to side, rather than from front to back like a staff officer's. The effect was striking.

"You look magnificent," I told him. "So do the others, but that centurion's crest is finer even than Rufio's."

He grunted. "It is. It's Second Augusta. Rufio's is a mere imitation: Twentieth Valeria."

"Careful, Centurion," I grunted. This was an oft-repeated piece of raillery. "My own grandfather commanded the Twentieth, as Legate. Given the opportunity, he would probably have kept your grandfather hopping. In his day, the Twentieth took second place to none."

Dedalus sniffed. "Aye," he said disdainfully. "So I've heard. Second place to none. That's why the Second Augusta lads were proud to call themselves

'None.' " He looked around at the others, most of whom were watching us, waiting for my signal. "But you're right, we look good. And so we should. When you sent word to me last night about this nonsense, the men were all too far gone in drink for me to make any arrangements, so I let them sleep. But they were all up at dawn, cursing you and me, and I've had them hard at work preparing for this ever since."

Dedalus was the only man among us who would drink neither wine nor ale nor mead. The only things I had ever seen him drink were water and the juice of fresh-crushed fruit: apples, pears and plums. All of us had long since grown used to this strangeness in him, and I knew from many past experiences that it made him utterly reliable at times when, were it not for him and his sobriety, no man could have done service.

"Look at the size of that thing," he muttered, gesturing with his head to some point behind my shoulder. "Surely in the name of all the ancient gods he doesn't throw it?" I turned to see what he meant and saw Rufio talking down from his horse to a stocky, massively muscled Scot who clutched an enormous spear, bigger than any I had seen before. As I looked, Rufio reached out and grasped the shaft of the thing, trying to lift it. It was as thick as his forearm at the base, and scarcely tapered towards the head, which consisted of a heavy, wickedly barbed, spade-shaped blade that reared up far above the head of the mounted centurion. Curious, both about the Scot and his weapon, I kicked my horse into motion and walked across to where they were. He saw me coming and eyed me calmly and I nodded a greeting as I approached. Rufio turned to me, alerted by his companion's look.

"Good morning, Commander," he said in Erse. "I was admiring this. Cullum here tells me it's a boar spear. We could have used a few of these when we met the one that attacked us."

"Aye," I replied, in the same tongue. "But you'd have to be the size of Cullum to carry it, and then you'd be too heavy to ride a horse. Good day to you, Cullum, I am Merlyn Britannicus. How do you use this thing?"

The man called Cullum grinned at me. "You only take it on the hunt. You drag it behind you. When you find a pig, you attract his attention. Then you dig the butt of this into the ground, crouch down beside it, and make certain that the pig runs onto the end of it. If it misses, the thing is of no more use. Neither are you."

I returned his grin. "Aye, I can well believe that. I can see you have never missed."

"Oh, that I have, Commander, twice. Both times, though, I was lucky. They were small pigs; small enough to kill otherwise."

I assumed that if he judged bulk according to his own, then even the fiercest boar might seem insignificant. He was enormous in chest and shoulders, with arms that seemed as thick as an ordinary man's thigh and huge hands that easily circled the thick shaft of his massive spear. He was also flat bellied, although his overall dimensions made it difficult to appreciate that. I could detect no sign of fat on him. Cullum was a formidable figure. I nodded to him again and spoke to Rufio.

"Are you clear on what we will do here? The order of maneuvers?" He nodded his head. "Good, then we had best line up with the others." I spoke again to Cullum. "I hope you'll find this spectacle to your taste." He smiled and bowed his head very slightly, saying nothing more. Behind him the meadow was rapidly filling now with people of all ages. It seemed the entire populace had come to watch us ride.

When I rejoined Dedalus his face was closed and guarded, a sight sufficiently unusual to prompt me to ask him what was wrong. His response was short and terse. "I'm upset, and I'm nervous."

I laughed aloud, hoping to put him more at ease. "Of what? This? It's only a demonstration, Ded!"

He was unimpressed. "Aye, so you say. But it's a test. These Outlanders, fine people though they seem to be, will judge us by our performance here today. I'm telling you, Merlyn, I haven't felt this vulnerable since the first time I stood on defaulters' parade waiting for your old man to come down on me from his godly height."

"You? On defaulters'? God, Dedalus, that must be thirty years ago!"

He threw me a scathing look. "No, young man, it was twenty-three years ago and I remember it well. I was a lowly trooper and I'd been in a drunken brawl and belted a young tribune by mistake. A killing crime. I thought I was for a flogging, at least. The General had that look in his eye. But he knew what was what, and I found out long afterwards that he would have enjoyed the seeing of it. The tribune was not well liked. But I'll never forget that morning. Turned my bowels to water."

I laughed at the look on his face. Dedalus was of old, pure Roman blood. He had a beak like an eagle and a thin slash of a mouth, and he had always been something of a dandy among his peers, dressing more flamboyantly than anyone else, and getting away with it because he was capable of disembowelling anyone with his bare hands.

"Don't tell me you were afraid of him, Ded?"

He looked at me through narrowed eyes. "Afraid? Of your father when he was on the rampage? Only a fool wouldn't have been. Picus Britannicus was implacable, once he decided that punishment was called for. Should have thought you'd know that. He must have had the hide off you a few times."

The thought surprised me. In all my years of childhood, my father had never raised a hand against either me or Uther: his voice, yes, and loudly, but never his hand. I had never thought about it before, but I thought about it now and saw that it was surprising, for he was a strict and fearsome martinet. I knew his men had walked in dread of him most of the time although, paradoxically, they loved and admired him, too. I had seen men flogged and even executed at his command, for his discipline was absolute. Dereliction of duty carried a death sentence, whether it was for sleeping on sentry duty, cowardice in the field, absence without leave, or theft from a comrade. Rape meant execution, as did murder. All of these offenses were tried by military tribunal and clemency was extended only under the most extenuating circumstances. I knew of only one instance, a case of suspected but unproved theft, in which the accused was given the benefit of the doubt and freed. One instance in all the years since I had started paying attention to such things, but it had been at my father's insistence that the man was given his life.

Abruptly, all thought was driven from my mind by the explosion of a bellowing roar of rage from the woods that bordered the meadow to the right of the main gates of the stronghold, and a giant bear burst into the open, in pursuit of a fleeing, terrified man who died as we all watched, smashed to extinction by the sweep of a massive paw. The beast was less than sixty paces from where we sat. It had come bounding into the sunlight, killed its tormentor and now reared up on its hind legs in triumph, a nightmare thing whose heavy, matted, blackish brown coat seemed to draw daylight physically into its enormous bulk. Again it bellowed, its weak eyes now attracted by the press of people on the slope above, and the volume of the sound stirred the short hairs on my neck. Someone behind me, a woman, screamed, and I sensed, rather than saw, a ripple of terror-stricken movement along the front line of Athol's people at my back.

"Stand fast!" Dedalus's bellow was almost as startling as the bear's, and such was the power of his roar that even the people of the settlement stilled their panicked rush for safety, freezing where they stood. Dedalus pulled his horse up into a rearing turn and faced the rest of our men, defying any of them to show fear.

I saw all of this from the corner of my eye, for from the moment of first hearing that awful sound, I had felt myself swept up into something beyond my control and my eyes were fastened on the bear to the virtual exclusion of everything else. It stood there, erect and huge, emanating menace and destructive power, and then the prancing movement of Ded's horse caught its attention so that the beast swung its massive head towards us, dropped to all fours and broke immediately into a lumbering charge. Dedalus had his back to it at the time and the skittish agitation of his horse had placed him between the bear and me. I saw, without being able to believe, the speed at which the monstrous animal was coming, and I knew that it would be upon Ded before he could regain control and kick his horse to any speed, but I was horrified to find myself kicking my own horse and going straight towards the abominable thing.

It saw me coming and reared up to a halt, flinging itself erect again to wait for me. I hauled on the reins, leaning far out to my right, and brought my horse heeling hard over, almost within grasp of the dreadful animal's great claws, galloping past it and on down towards the line of brush that had concealed the beast. Standing erect, the monster towered above my head, even mounted as I was. I glanced back over my shoulder and saw that it was chasing me now. I kicked again, letting my reins fall slack, and gave Germanicus his head. There was one isolated clump of bushes straight ahead of me; one single, fair-sized thicket. I guided my mount as close to it as I could, knowing the beast was gaining on me, and then twisted his head into a savage turn, risking a fatal fall. Thorns and branches ripped at my clothes, but I kept the big black's head pulled down, far to the right, making almost a complete circle around the clump. Then I kicked him flat out, back towards the line of my mounted men. I heard a cheer and knew that my ruse had worked. The bear had gone charging ahead and I had gained some distance. I was almost back to the line by the time I heard another bellow of rage over the thudding of my horse's hooves and glanced backwards in time to see the bear drop back to all fours and come after me again. But suddenly there was Dedalus, cutting across diagonally between us at full gallop. The bear, confused, stood up and roared again as I brought my horse to a sliding stop almost upon the line of Athol's spearmen who were advancing, grim-faced and shoulder to shoulder, towards certain death. Cullum's wicked boar spear reared up among them, closest to me.

"Give me that!"

Cullum blinked at me in surprise, then stepped forward and handed me his weapon. It was bigger and thicker than I had thought, wickedly heavy. *Sarissa . . . Alexander . . .*

The words rang in my head in the tones of Uncle Varrus, and I remembered him telling me that the Great King Alexander's Companions had ridden into battle with a spear six arm's-lengths long, the sarissa, balanced on their shoulders and angled forward and down. The spear I now held was less than two-thirds that length, thick in the shaft and grossly heavy, and no thought had been given in its design to serving a man on horseback. I knew as soon as I took hold of it that I could not hope to balance it on my shoulder, but the bear was there, bellowing, and my own reflexes were in control of me. I tucked one end of the gross shaft beneath my arm and kicked Germanicus back into a run, the butt of the ungainly weapon held close to my hip, against the back of my saddle. It was too heavy, far too cumbersome, so I jerked it up, allowing the point to fall forward and catching the butt directly beneath my armpit, struggling with gritted teeth to keep the point up and free of the ground as I flew towards what I knew to be certain death. The muscles of my arm and shoulder were already screaming with pain and I knew I was going to drop the spear. I *had* to drop it, to save my life. But I dropped the reins, instead, and used my left hand to pull the spearhead upwards. I was leaning backwards in my saddle, my legs braced solidly in the stirrups, when Germanicus felt the freedom in the reins and swerved violently. I saw a mighty paw swinging from above and screwed my eyes closed, and then came a jolt the like of which I had never felt, and I was plucked bodily from the saddle and sent flying. I heard my horse scream as the ground came flying up to meet me, and I fell into darkness.

When I came to my senses again, I was strapped to a cloak of some kind stretched between two spears, being carried through Athol's gates by four men, two of my own and two of the king's. Donuil's face loomed above me, creased with concern. I tried to speak, but a dizzying blackness fell on me again.

Later, of course, I discovered that I had killed the bear. The swerve of my horse and the pull of my left arm had brought the point of the heavy spear up to a perfect entry point in the creature's throat, and the angle of penetration, combined with the speed of my approach, had driven the great head of the weapon with sufficient force to sever the animal's spine. The bear had gone over backwards, the mighty spear's shaft had snapped, and I had been catapulted into the air while my poor horse had fallen heavily, frightened almost to death by the feral smell of the giant beast that sprawled beside it.

My early protests of an accidental victory fell on deaf ears. Everyone had watched me take a spear and charge a maddened bear, killing it on the spot, alone and without help of any kind except for that one diversionary pass by Dedalus that had given me time to arm myself. I gave up arguing and enjoyed being a hero.

Hearing that I had regained consciousness, Donuil and his father both reached me at the same time, the latter frowning and the former now grinning widely.

"Merlyn, how do you feel?" Athol asked. "Can you stand? It shames me to think that you might have been killed defending my people while a hundred and more of my own warriors stood idly by."

I stilled his anxious protestations with an upraised hand. "Peace, King Athol. The responsibility is mine alone. The bear was already attacking, and none of your warriors was at fault. There was no time to do anything else."

He shook his head. "No, not so. My spearmen should have made short work of it. You should have left it to them."

Donuil interrupted. "You saw the size of that thing, Father. It's enormous! It would have killed a dozen men, perhaps more, before they killed it. Caius Merlyn was born for deeds like that. We should simply thank the gods that he was there." Donuil hunkered down beside me, grinning again. "By your Christian Christ, Cay, you must be mad! I've heard men tell that you're a wild man when you're roused, but I wouldn't have approached that thing with fifty of my father's spearmen!"

I grinned, feeling foolish again. "I didn't intend to, Donuil, it just happened. There was no time to think, only to do something, anything, it didn't matter what."

"Aye!" He laughed. "The thing really is enormous, at least three times the size of the boar your people killed last week."

Donuil's father cut his banter short with a wave of his hand, then stood gazing down at me on my cot. From my position, looking back up at him, the old king seemed even larger than I remembered. He stood silent for long moments, his lips sucked inward, then nodded as if to confirm what he had been thinking.

"My son is garrulous, Caius Merlyn, but he may have much the truth of things. I heard about the boar you killed in the south; the size and weight of it and the splendour of its tusks. And now this, with the bear. Measured erect, I am told, it was almost twice the height of our tallest man, the largest creature of its kind any of our people have seen. But it was folly to do what you did, no matter what the provocation. One man alone against a creature of that size should have been killed immediately. There should have been no contest. How did you do it?" Before I could frame an answer he held up his hand to forestall me as he had his son. "No matter. I do not think I wish to hear your answer to that. I am content that you succeeded and in the process saved the lives of several of my people. For that, atop all else, you have my gratitude." He smiled then, a smile of genuine amusement. "I told the people they would see a demonstration of the power of cavalry. What we saw, all of us, filled us with awe. We have no need now to watch more. One man alone has convinced us."

"Well, sir, not one alone. I had some help from Dedalus."

"Aye, a diversion. That was bravely done. But Dedalus did not front the beast by himself and kill it. We will speak further later, when you have regained yourself." He lowered his head, almost in a bow, and left Donuil and me to watch him go.

"So," Donuil said, perching himself on the edge of my cot and wasting no time with niceties. "Tell me what happened. I was late in arriving, after my father, and I saw only the closing dash. I missed all of what had gone before, and since then I've heard four different versions. Tell me your version of the foolishness."

"There's not a lot to tell," I said, swallowing against a soreness in my throat. "It didn't seem foolish at the time. It was as though the entire thing was predestined, and I could not really believe it was happening even as it occurred. There was simply nothing different I could have done. Had I not moved when I did, the bear would have killed Dedalus. I simply knew I had to divert the thing's attention. Once it began, I had no other course."

"Hmm!" His voice sounded reflective. "I asked Dedalus about it. He told me that you behaved with brilliance. That's his word, not mine. He said you hauled your horse around a clump of bushes in a move he has never seen any rider equal."

I grinned. "That was desperation. It was a matter of making that turn or being caught by the bear."

"How did you get the spear?"

"I took it from Cullum—is that his name? The thickset fellow with the enormous muscles." Donuil nodded. "Aye," I continued. "Anyway, Dedalus saved my life by his charge and gave me time to get Cullum's spear, so we are equal there. I saw the spear with its huge blade thrusting up into the air and remembered what Uncle Varrus said about sarissas, the great, long spears Alexander's men used to carry. It seemed to me that even a boar spear would be a better weapon against that beast than a sword, so I seized it and charged and the rest was pure, blind chance. I killed it, but should not have. It was fortune, good fortune, thank God. My horse swerved, I managed to haul the point up into the air at last, and it hit the bear in the neck. No judgment, no skill involved, mere blind chance. A couple of finger breadths to either side and I would have missed it completely and be dead now."

Donuil grunted. "Hmm! That's what my father meant by folly. You could have been killed and that would have been a tragedy, especially in such a useless, unpremeditated way as that."

"Unpremeditated, perhaps, Donuil, but far from useless. It led me to Cullum's spear."

"What d'you mean?"

"I succeeded by accident, but I did succeed."

"So?" He unslung a wineskin from his shoulder where it had hung unnoticed by me and swallowed a mouthful of its contents. "You were fortunate Cullum was there. On the spot, by your own admission."

"I know, but that's not what I mean. The spear was wrong, but it felt right, too. I killed the bear by chance, but I could easily have killed it the same way on purpose."

He glanced sideways at me, and his response was heavy with irony. "Forgive me, Commander Merlyn, but what you are saying sounds like nonsense to me. What, exactly, are you trying to say?"

"No, it's not nonsense. Give me some of that." He passed me the wineskin and I gulped at it heartily before asking, "Where did you get this?"

"Camulod. I brought it with me."

"Damnation," I said, regretting that I had not thought to do the same. "Anyway, I don't think what I'm saying is nonsense. Before Uncle Varrus died, the last thing he said to me was that we still had much to learn from the weapons, the old ones, in his Armoury, and he mentioned Alexander and the sarissa specifically. Alexander's chosen bodyguard, the Companions they were called, rode into battle carrying an enormous spear over their shoulders.

They charged and left the spear in the first man they struck. Created havoc among their enemies. But that's what made me think of seizing that spear from Cullum." I stopped, and took another mouthful of wine. I was thinking carefully about my words now, wanting to clarify my thoughts to Donuil and to make him see the potential of the half-formed idea that was exciting me.

"I don't know the feel of a sarissa, but I know that boar spear was too heavy—too much weight in the head, and the shaft's too thick. And yet the sarissa was five, perhaps six arm's-lengths long and Cullum's spear no more than four. When I hit that bear at full gallop, it was like riding headlong into a wall. It stopped me solidly. But the ridge of the saddle against my back added to the impact. I flew off and almost broke my back, because I had both hands on the spear. I wasn't holding the reins. If the saddle hadn't stopped me, I would have been pushed from the back of the horse at the first impact. Do you follow me?"

"No, quite honestly, I don't, but go on."

"Donuil, I think it was that extra punch from the saddle back that drove the spearhead all the way through the bear's neck. You remember the tale of the first time I smashed the vase in Uncle Varrus's Armoury?" He nodded, his eyes betraying his interest. "Well, that's the kind of leverage I'm talking about. I think, I'm not certain, but I *think* that if I had been holding a lighter spear, still strong, but with a smaller head—or even a longer one like the sarissa—and *if* I had been holding it under my armpit, and *if* I had been leaning forwards when I hit the bear, instead of backwards, and *if* I'd had the reins tight in my left hand and my legs braced properly, controlling my horse . . ." My voice trailed away.

"A profusion of 'ifs,' Merlyn."

"I know, I know, but bear with me, Donuil. What I'm trying to put into words here is important. I believe that if I had done all of those things, I could have driven that spear clean through that bear, even through its chest, *without being unhorsed.*"

He looked me straight in the eye, all trace of levity gone. "Without being unhorsed. You really believe that?"

I nodded. "Yes. Completely. Anyway, I want to try it. Alexander's Companions always lost their spears on their first charge, because they had no way of holding on to them, they could not brace themselves against shock. We can. Our stirrups give us the option of using spears, hitting hard with them and retaining them to use again."

Donuil was frowning now, deep in thought. "You could be right, Caius, but not with a spear as long as the one you seem to be describing. That's far too long, it seems to me. I know I'm no cavalryman, not yet, but it seems to me that what you should be talking about is a spear that's long enough to take a man in front of you chest high, whether he be mounted or on foot, knock him down, and be short enough to pivot under you and be pulled out by the force of your momentum as your horse goes on past him."

"Exactly, Donuil! That is exactly what I mean. So perhaps it might be half the length of a sarissa. Three arm's-lengths."

"Aye, that's more like it. Three arm's-lengths, at the most. A light, strong spear, heavier than a javelin, stronger than a pilum, with a long, unbarbed head that will pull out clean. Should I have our smith attempt to make one? I can have him start on it tomorrow morning. It shouldn't be difficult to make, merely a variation on the spears he makes already." His enthusiasm was total, and infectious. I grinned at him.

"Why not? I'll come with you when you talk to him. The sooner he tries, the sooner we'll see whether or not I'm right. Now pull me up, I'm beginning to feel like a tired old man, and that illicit wine of yours has made me hungry. Is it still raining?"

Donuil returned my grin. "It's always raining, that's why the land is so green. Our gods want to ensure that we never become ungrateful for the sunlight, so they dole it out to us in tiny rations; each day of sunshine reminds us of the beauty of our land, but they're few and far enough between to make sure that we never become overused to it. Come then, let's get you up and moving, and if you feel up to it, we can eat with Connor. His wife killed a young pig three days ago and she's roasting some of it tonight."

It was still raining heavily the following morning when we went looking for the local smith, trudging almost ankle-deep through muddy water that seemed to have nowhere to drain to, although in fact it all drained into the nearby river. The smith to Athol's people was a man called Maddan, and no one setting eyes upon him for the first time could have thought him anything but a smith, even discounting the ingrained soot and charcoal that polished his visible skin to a glossy black in places. He was short and stocky, broad of shoulder and thick of forearm, wearing only a rough tunic beneath the thick, heavy leather apron that protected him from flying sparks. I smiled on seeing him, for he was, as I had expected, clean-shaven and therefore something of an oddity among the hirsute, bearded and mustached Scots. I had never known a bearded smith except my Uncle Publius, and even he had kept his beard close-cropped and neat in the Roman fashion, not, as he had once explained to me, because he thought that highly of Roman styles, but simply because a beard was a hazard for a smith, liable to ignite at any time while he worked at his forge.

Maddan knew his craft and understood very quickly what we were seeking. He had, of course, been present in the meadow the previous day and had seen my struggles with the bear and the boar spear. When I began to explain how my thoughts had developed after that encounter, he nodded his head immediately and thereafter listened in carefully attentive silence as I outlined my idea. As soon as I had finished speaking he grunted and disappeared into the farthest recesses of the gloomy cavern that was his smithy, emerging shortly afterward with a spearhead that was almost as large as the one on Cullum's weapon.

"This might do, to start out with," he suggested, dropping it on a countertop with a metallic clang. "It's rusted, but that's easily mended. Forge'll take care of that. I made it last month, but I was in too much haste and I made it too big and too heavy. It's too big for what you want, but not by much. I can lengthen it and narrow the head, and by the time you decide on the kind of shaft you want, it should at least give us a working model we can make adjustments from. What d'you think?"

I thought it might be close, and told him so, looking to Donuil for his concurrence, but he was looking elsewhere, his eyes wide and filled with pleasure and something else that I defined instantly and without reason as awe. Curious, I turned my head to follow his gaze and saw a figure crossing the open space outside the forge, head down against the pouring rain, its shape tilted to one side from the weight of the burden it bore. I saw no more than that; a shapeless, indeterminate figure, obscured by the rain and by a long, heavy cloak. Intrigued, I glanced back to Donuil, seeing him still rapt, and then returned my gaze to the newcomer. As I did so, the figure lost its footing in the mud and slipped, almost falling, dropping its burden. It was no more than a momentary loss of balance, but it provoked a surge of energetic resentment from the cloaked figure, who seized a fresh, firm grip on the heavy bundle and swung it mightily, releasing it to fly through the air and land with a sodden thump mere paces from the open front of the smithy. Even before the bundle had landed, the thrower was moving towards it again, grasping it afresh with surprisingly small hands and propelling it, with a heave of shoulders and a guiding knee, into the open doorway.

"Shelagh," Donuil said, his voice almost a whisper. The figure stopped in surprise, then straightened, peering into the darkness of the smithy and raising one arm to pull back the hood from its head. Beyond surprise for some reason, I saw that it was a young woman, whose long, dark hair hung down in rain-plastered ringlets over a featureless face.

"Donuil? Is it you then?" She stepped forward into the shelter of the doorway, combing her wet hair off her face with the fingers of one hand, and stood there for a moment, staring hard at Donuil, her expression unreadable. None of us moved. Finally, her lips formed what might have been the beginnings of a smile and she nodded, a tiny movement of her head, and then her eyes moved to where I stood watching. She ignored Maddan completely. She regarded me from head to foot and back again, and spoke again to Donuil.

"I heard you were back. I met Finn on the path to the mountains yesterday. I would have been here to greet you, but none of us knew if you were yet alive, let alone coming home." Her gaze returned to me, looking me straight in the eye. "You must be the Merlyn fellow. You're almost as big as Donuil. I've seen you before, but not clearly, and even so, you're better-looking than I expected from what Finn told me of you, but it was obvious even then that you and he had not made friends the moment you met. I'm Shelagh. Donuil and I were friends once, long ago, before he went off to be your prisoner." I was confused, and becoming more so by the moment. What had she meant by saying she had seen me before? She could not have, unless she had been in Britain recently, and had I met her I felt sure I would have remembered.

I bent my head in a courteous nod, but before I could respond she had turned her attentions once more on Donuil. "Well, I can see they didn't starve you over there. Have you been to my father's house yet?"

"No." I could tell from the slow, deliberate way Donuil shook his head in emphasis that he was far from being at his ease in this meeting.

"Well, that's something, at least. Why not?" She answered her own question. "Och, never mind. I know why not. My father was probably waiting for me to come home, to look after him as well as you. There's little comfort in a house that has no woman in it."

"No," Donuil finally rallied some words. "We haven't had time."

"Time?" She threw him a look of wide-eyed astonishment. "Then what have you been doing since you came back? Never mind. Will you have time

tonight?" Donuil nodded, wordless again. "Good. Then we'll expect you."
Her eyes flicked back to me. "You, too." Now she turned to Maddan, indicating the sodden bundle on the threshold with a wave of her hand.

"There are eight wolf pelts there, Maddan, a bearskin, a badger and four
of them lovely tree fellers with the big, flat tails." I did not recognize the
name she used, but it was plain that the animals were the dam-building
creatures the Romans called *castora*. "They're all salted down," she continued, "but they need to be stretched and dried out. Will you be a love and
make some frames for me? You can have the bearskin, if you will." Maddan
merely nodded, smiling patiently and saying not a word. I could see that
these two had worked together before. Shelagh smiled at him now, in a flash
of white, even teeth. "And I'm carrying half the soil of Eire on my body and
in my hair with this rain and the mud. Would you heat me some water for
a bath?" Again, a silent nod from Maddan. "Thank you, sweet man. I'll see
you two tonight." And suddenly she was gone, leaving Donuil and me staring
at each other.

He smiled at me, suddenly shy and awkward. "That was Shelagh."

"Aye, I gathered that," I answered, making a determined effort to keep
any trace of irony out of my tone. "But who is she, and who is her father?"

"Liam, Liam Twistback's her father."

"Liam?" I was too surprised to dissemble. "Is she . . . ?" I broke off, belatedly, not wanting to ask the question. The long cloak could have hidden
any deformity.

"Is she what? Oh, you mean is she a hunchback?" He laughed, and I
heard Maddan behind me laugh with him. "No, Cay, she's no hunchback,
not Shelagh. She was always the pretty one in the old days . . ." His voice
faded, and then resumed with wonder. "But I'd no idea she'd grow to be
so . . ." He coughed and turned his attention immediately to the long-
forgotten spearhead on the bench beside us, picking it up and hefting it in
his hand before stooping to peer at it closely, angling it towards the light.
"There's a lot of rust on this thing, Maddan."

I covered my smile and respected his reticence for the time being, and
we returned to the topic that had brought us to the smithy, picking up our
discussion almost as smoothly as if we had not been interrupted. We agreed
that the existing spearhead, with minor modifications, would be as good a
starting place as any, and Maddan thrust it immediately into the fire of his
forge and began to work his bellows, making it clear to Donuil and me,
without the insult of words, that our continued presence in his smithy was
likely to be a distraction thereafter. We pulled on our heavy, waxed wool
cloaks and walked out into the downpour.

"What now?" I asked Donuil, raising my voice above the hissing roar of
the rain.

He glanced up at the leaden clouds and sniffed. "Doesn't make much
difference, seems to me," he shouted back. "Whatever we do, we'll be wet."

"Hmm. I think I'll go over to the camp and visit the others. Will you
come?" Aware of the pitch of both our voices against the noise of the weather,
he merely nodded now, and we made our way towards the main gate and
out towards where "the horse camp," as the townspeople were already calling
it, had been set up. Donuil hitched his cloak more comfortably around his
shoulders and spoke again, loud-voiced against the elements, but without

looking at me this time, his eyes fixed on the waterlogged ground where we walked.

"Well, Caius Merlyn, you have been here two nights now. Different from Camulod, isn't it?"

"Aye, it is," I called back. "Very different. But I expected that. It's a different land altogether."

"Aye. Primitive, would you say?"

I stopped walking immediately, forcing him in turn to stop and look at me. "What do you mean?" I asked, lowering my voice and moving close to him so that he could hear my words clearly enough. His face was flushed, as though angry, but I knew I had given him no reason for anger, so I sought another cause for his evident discomfort and could only come up with defensiveness. I knew immediately I was correct, although his reasons and the timing for such feelings escaped me.

"This is your home, Donuil, and I have been made welcome as a guest in it. Do you suspect me of comparing it to Camulod and finding it less agreeable?" He made no move to respond and so I prodded him. "Well, do you?"

He shook his head, obviously ill at ease, then mumbled, "No, no, I merely pointed out that it is primitive. It is, compared with what you are used to."

"Horse turds," I snapped. "I'm a soldier, Donuil, and you know that as well as I do. I'm more accustomed to sleeping in a leather tent in pouring rain than I will ever be to sleeping in soft beds with fine coverings. Your father's home is not primitive. It is civilized and well governed and its people are safe and happy. Its houses are soundly built and functionally strong, as strong as any in Uther's land." He was looking at me in surprise and I continued speaking, unwilling to allow him any time for interruption.

"Don't forget that while Camulod may be unique in some ways, it is frequently as cold, wet and uncomfortable as any place on earth. Its uniqueness lies in the fact that many of its buildings were erected by Romanized people, using Roman techniques: Roman architects and Roman skills and Roman building materials. But you've already seen how useful Roman building materials are when the Romans leave. That's what those pirates were carting out of Glevum on their barges—Romanism—so I don't wish to hear any more of that sort of rubbish. I have seen no reason, anywhere, since I arrived here, for you or anyone else to feel shame over where or how you live. The ordinary folk of Britain, outside of Camulod, live in settlements and small towns very like your own here—many in far worse case—and if you have not been aware of that in your travels, then you must be either blind or stupid. You have also seen the once-great Roman towns of Britain ruined and abandoned: Isca Dumnoniorum, once the headquarters of the Second Augusta Legion, now an empty wasteland. Verulamium, Londinium, Colchester, Lindum: all of them lying empty, save for a few last citizens either too stubborn or too afraid to leave the false safety of their walls. Don't talk to me of fine houses, Donuil, as though they housed only fine people and vice versa. A fine marble villa built by a Roman nobleman's fortune is no more than a large, empty space to catch the howling wind when its owner is gone. It's far too big for one small family unconcerned by affairs of state and government. A family needs warmth and comfort. My family in Camulod has warmth and comfort, thanks only to fortune. That they are where they are is almost accidental; they are blessed and highly unusual." I paused. "Your family has warmth and comfort, too, man, and happiness, as much as any large family can have that gift. I count myself fortunate to be here. Am I clear?"

He nodded, chastened, yet visibly relieved. I began walking again and he fell immediately into step beside me.

"Good," I said, and then remained silent for another twenty paces or so. "Now tell me about this young woman Shelagh. She means much to you, I could see that."

Now he coughed and cleared his throat and made a useless but determined effort to wipe the streaming rain from his face. I said nothing, simply walking, my head hunched down against the teeming rain, and waiting. We had progressed a further ten or twelve muddy paces before he attempted to respond. As he began to do so, however, drawing a deep breath and turning slightly towards me, we were hailed by a figure that loomed out of the murk just ahead of us. It was Rufio. Donuil shook his head, sharp and hard, as though to warn me from saying more. "We'll talk about it later" was all he had time to say before Rufio joined us.

"God's balls, Donuil," he spat. "Is it always like this in this godforsaken place? Don't you ever have a single day without rain?"

Donuil was grinning again, his earlier discomfort vanished. "Aye," he said. "Sometimes, but not often at this time of the year. Why do you ask?"

Rufio rounded on him, then realized that Donuil was laughing at him. I cut both of them short before he could form a retort. "Were you looking for us, Rufio?"

"Aye, I was," he answered, ignoring Donuil thereafter. "Dedalus and Quintus and I were talking about how long we're going to be staying here, and we realized that none of us knows, and that led us to the awareness that we haven't seen you since yesterday, when we left you to go back to camp. We expected you to come over this morning, but when you didn't come and we had heard nothing, we began to wonder if you were as well as you ought to be, and so Ded asked me to find you and check on your health."

"I am at full strength. How is Quintus? Is his leg mending?"

"It must be, he has done nothing but complain for the past three days, and he wouldn't give out as much as a grunt if he were really in pain, so I suppose that means he's mending. Anyway, he's sitting up in his cot, being waited on hand and foot by everyone else around, including an entire covey of young Eirish girls. I've been giving some thought myself to slipping and falling heavily."

I grinned and slapped him on his armoured shoulder. "Is Ded warm and dry?"

"Aye, and as lazy as ever, and just as cunning. Why d'you think it's me out here looking for you in the pouring rain, and not him? He's safe by the fire, keeping it fed for your advent."

I looked at him in surprised disbelief. "Dedalus *ordered* you to come and find me?"

He had the grace to shrug and deny it. "Well, no. Not exactly. We tossed for it."

"You tossed for it. Against Dedalus. Rufio, there are times when I wonder about your wit. When did you last know anyone to win the toss against

Dedalus?" Dedalus had a reputation of long-standing for never having lost on a spin of the coin. His luck was legendary in Camulod.

He shrugged. "Never. I know that, but the coin was mine, out of my own scrip, and I spun it. There must be a first time."

"You really believe that, Centurion?"

"Yes." He was completely serious. "I really believe that, Commander."

"Well, when it happens, I want you to let me know, and if you are the one to beat him, I will personally pay you twenty times the value of the spin, or of the coin you spin, whichever is greater. Do you believe me?"

"Aye."

"Good. And do you believe I believe I'll ever have to pay?"

"No."

"Even better. Now, do you believe it's possible to drown, simply standing out in the rain?"

"No."

"No more do I, but I have no desire to find out whether or not I'm right. Let's get inside." We lumbered into a run, clanking and splashing, all three of us, to the warmth and smoky comfort of the wooden hut Rufio shared with Dedalus and Quintus. Once there, and drying quickly in the heat of the roaring fire in the open hearth, we were soon at our ease and the talk turned to soldiers' matters, so that the remainder of the day passed quickly and the rain lost all importance.

XV

I DID NOT know what to expect in the home of Liam Twistback that night, so I dressed with some care. I decided to wear neither armour nor weapons, acting upon the assumption that our hostess this night might be seeking an opportunity to redress any false impressions Donuil and I might have drawn from her soaked and bedraggled condition earlier in the day, when she had just returned from a long journey. I guessed that this night, in consequence, would be a time for easy conversation and social intercourse, an occasion where the emphasis would be more likely placed upon the feminine arts than on the masculine. That assumption, let me admit, was bolstered greatly by my having heard the young woman arrange for Maddan to prepare a hot bath for her that afternoon, and by my anticipation, based upon my own observation and intuition, that her interest in Donuil might be at least as keen as his evident interest in her. It was an assumption almost completely undermined, however, by the uncomfortable awareness that I had no real idea of how the women of this society were accustomed to behave in social situations within their own homes. I was entirely unaware of the local customs or of standards of protocol in such circumstances. The only guide to whom I might have turned for enlightenment in such matters was, of course, Donuil himself, and, for one reason or another I had had no opportunity to question him on any of these things.

Donuil had steadfastly refused to speak of Shelagh at all throughout the day, and I had eventually decided not to pursue the matter, aware that his discomfort stemmed more from doubts over his own feelings about the young woman than from any natural reluctance to discuss her with me in front of strangers, even though those strangers had become his friends. Given the opportunity, I guessed, allied with a modicum of genuine encouragement from me, he would have talked me to death on the subject.

The rain had abated but still fell steadily as I made my way through the darkness to the house of Liam Twistback, which was, next to that of the king himself, the largest building in Athol's stronghold. I had learned, at least, that Liam was the wealthiest of all Athol's people, a situation, strangely, that had resulted from Liam's physical condition. Born unfit by his deformity to be a warrior among a people who prized physical abilities above all else, Liam had used the brilliance of his mind and the power of his personality to become the most successful landholder among his peers. He had expended years of singleminded effort in the husbanding of arable land and the gathering and breeding of cattle, goats and oxen, and had established himself as the prime commercial source—indeed, the only reliable, consistent source—of provender to his people. All this, Donuil had told me, Liam had managed to achieve without provoking either jealousy or envy among his fellow Scots who, over the long years during which Liam had amassed his wealth, had simply come to accept that in the little hunchback's industrious but eccentric nature, they had been gifted with a unique asset that was worthy of protection and pride. Liam was wealthier than his king, and wealthier by far than any of his tribe, but he bore his riches casually and self-effacingly, giving offense to none. The only things upon which he lavished his wealth were his house, and his daughter Shelagh.

As a young man, he had wed a cousin of the king, an unmarriageable young woman born, like himself, with a physical deformity. In her case—her name, Donuil had told me, was also Shelagh—the disfigurement had been twofold, consisting of a withered right leg, malformed at birth, and an unsightly, dark red blemish that stained her neck and lower jaw on one side. That both she and Liam had been permitted to survive their birthing had been akin to miraculous, apparently, but each had been born to prominent, elderly and otherwise childless couples. Liam, the elder of the pair by a decade and more, had watched the little girl grow up, an outcast like himself, and had befriended her. By the time Shelagh began to approach marriageable age, Liam had long been successful in impressing his people with the powers of his mind and intellect, and his industry and single-minded application to whatever tasks he set himself had attracted the friendship and admiration of the young king, Athol, to whom Liam had become, at the youngest age in living memory, a personal adviser. Athol it was who, at the risk of scandalizing his entire people, had given his regal and personal blessing to the union of the two most unsightly people in his lands.

That two such people, each set far outside conventional comeliness, had combined to generate a child of such exquisite, glowing beauty as their daughter Shelagh had been a wonder still unforgotten among Athol's Scots. Liam's wife, however, had died in presenting him with their child, and for years Liam had been inconsolable. As the child grew lovelier and stronger, however, the hunchback had transferred all of the love he had harboured for her mother to her. He would never have a son: but he had more: his daughter Shelagh was living proof that his flawed exterior was capable of generating more beauty than any of his sound-bodied contemporaries. He had built her a house to live in, rather than a hut, and had filled it with everything he could devise to make her happy.

As I approached that house for the first time, curious to see inside it, it seemed I was the only person astir in the entire settlement, and yet I could smell the smoke of many cooking fires in the moist air, a blend of woodsmoke and some other, unrecognizable but distinctive-smelling fuel. As I raised my hand to knock on the door, the top half of it swung inward and Donuil himself looked out at me and then sprang backward in fright, as surprised as I at the unexpected confrontation. He had been about to come looking for me, he told me moments later, but had not expected to find my face within a handsbreadth of his when he opened the door. And so I entered Liam's home amid lighthearted laughter that was to be sustained throughout the major part of an extremely pleasant evening.

Liam's house was justly famed among the Scots. Large and spacious, thick-walled and rectangular like the Great Hall, it was high-roofed and quite untypical of the other dwellings in the settlement, which were, in the main, squat, circular, solidly built huts of a material Donuil called wattle—clay strengthened and bound with a strong, interwoven framework of willow sticks.

The interior of the house into which I stepped directly from the door-yard was partitioned into at least two large, separate areas by high screens of plaited reeds, painted and varnished in bright colours. The entrance door, the only one of which I had been aware, was situated far on the left of the longer wall of the rectangular structure, which stretched laterally from there to my right, to where my view was blocked by the painted screens that stretched inward from front and rear walls, overlapping approximately in the centre of the room to create a passageway to the other half of the building. The large main area in which I now stood was brightly lit, and my admiration for our young hostess grew as I recognized the source of the brightness as a large number of the fine candles I had presented to King Athol. I accepted her enterprise in this immediately, for it did not cross my mind for a moment that Liam himself might ask for such bounty from his king. The candles were clustered in four main concentrations of candelabra: one cluster, by far the largest, on the massive, black wooden table that stretched the length of the shorter wall of the house to the left of the door, another on a smaller, circular table in the centre of the room, and one more on either side of the great stone fireplace that filled up much of the long wall opposite to where I stood. My eyes were filled with impressions of bright colours, flickering light and hospitable warmth. Donuil stood beside me, one hand on my arm, and another man sat opposite me, by the side of the great fire that roared in the hearth, holding a small harp in the crook of his arm. As I saw this man, recognizing him as one of the minstrels who had performed the previous evening and whom I had met twice now although his name escaped me, Liam Twistback himself came into the room through the gap in the over-lapping screens to my right.

"Caius Merlyn! Welcome to our home." He moved quickly towards me, his hands outstretched to enfold my own, and I had time to admire the way the long, rich-looking robe he wore was cut and draped to minimize his deformity. When he took my hands, his large, intelligent brown eyes looked smilingly into my own, and he hitched his left shoulder, the humped one, and glanced down at it quickly, smiling a wry smile. "If you'll recall, they call me Twistback for good reason, but the twist is no more than physical. My mind has no unwelcome kinks, at least none I'm aware of, and I am looking forward to listening to your words this night. Be welcome, and sit down over here, close by the fire. It has been a foul day, but my daughter assures me that the evening will be very different. Have you met Cardoc, our minstrel?"

Cardoc. That was the name I had forgotten. I nodded towards him, smil-ing, and he returned my gesture, smiling easily. Liam, meanwhile, was ush-ering me towards a solid, wooden chair with a deep, curved back, one of a grouping of five that had been placed in an arc in front of the open fire. As I sat down, Donuil dropping into the chair on my left, another figure emerged from behind the screen, this one a woman, carrying a heavy tray on which stood a jug and a number of cups. She placed it on the circular table and withdrew without speaking. As I watched her leave, Liam sat down on my right, then rose again immediately and went to the newly stocked table where he busied himself pouring what I took to be some kind of mead into four cups.

"Donuil, come help me. Take one for yourself and one for Cardoc there." He brought the other two back to where I sat, handing one of them to me,

then sat down again and sipped deeply. I tasted mine. It was delicious, and
I said so.

"Aye," he said. "It is, is it not? Shelagh makes it, and holds the secret of
its preparation to herself as if it were her child, which, in a way, I suppose
it is. Anyway, she'll tell no one what it is she adds to give it that peculiar
tang of heat it carries. Others have tried to copy it, but none has come close
so far."

I drank again, this time more deeply, and nodded appreciatively. The
drink, whatever it was, was excellent, fiery and potent, yet sweet and smooth
on the palate.

"It's some kind of mead, but I could not begin to guess at that flavour."
I looked around me. "Will your daughter join us?"

"Join us?" He laughed. "Aye, she will that, and will not quit us until she
has decided it is time for you three to go home. But for now she is seeing
to the cooking of our meal. She insists none but she can oversee these things
in the proper manner." He nodded, staring into his cup. "She's quite right,
too. None can."

Donuil was saying nothing and looking at no one. He sat staring into the
flames of the fire. Cardoc was tuning his instrument, his head cocked sideways in total concentration upon the pitch of each string. "Your house is
very fine," I said, glancing up into the darkness beneath the roof tree. "Donuil
was telling me it is the largest and finest in all King Athol's land."

"It may be so." He nodded modestly. "Except for the King's Hall. It is
unusual, I know that, but we like it thus, Shelagh and I."

"Do you have a large household?"

He blinked at me. "What do you mean, household?"

I blinked back at him, surprised in turn. "You know, servitors."

"Servitors? I don't know this word."

"Forgive me, servants. You know, a housekeeper, a majordomo . . ." Even
as I spoke I was recalling where I was. He was watching me closely and now
his face crinkled in amusement.

"Servants, is it? You will forgive my bluntness, I hope, Caius Merlyn, but
you are a long way from your home in Britain, when you are here in our little
kingdom. There are no servants here, not even in the king's house. There's
little of the formal in the way we live our lives, but no man of ours, or woman
for that matter, would ever consider accepting the indignity of actually working for another, in that other's *house*, as a *servant*, for recompense." He
paused, his eyes fixed on mine, and his next words were aimed at putting
me at my ease. "I am not offended by your suggestion, Master Merlyn, understand that clearly, please. I know such things are common in your land,
where wealthy people have servants and entire retinues of followers and retainers. We have retainers here in Eire, too, but only in the role of warriors,
sworn to defend and to assist their king in waging war whenever and wherever
war may occur. But we have no *servants*."

I glanced at Donuil, who was perched sideways in his chair, watching me
with a tiny smile hovering about his lips. I nodded, taking no offense where
no rebuke had been tendered, but then I asked the question that had been
in my mind since Liam started speaking of this.

"Then who, if you will forgive my asking, was the woman who brought
in the mead?"

Liam's face split into an enormous grin. "My neighbour, the wife of Maddan the smith. And I must now concede your point. We do have people who work, from time to time, assisting others in the preparation of major events and festivals, but their contribution is always voluntary and they expect the right to share in those events as equals, once the work is done." He hesitated, still smiling. "And, I will admit to you here, as my guest, they do, from time to time, receive other . . . considerations in return for the willing provision of their help."

I nodded, schooling my features to permit no trace of irony to show. "I see," I murmured, nodding.

"Aye. I can see you do." Liam made no attempt to disguise his irony. He turned then to Cardoc, who had finished tuning his instrument. "Cardoc, a song, if you please. Something short and tuneful, until herself joins us." Cardoc inclined his head and began to sing, stroking the strings occasionally to enhance the mood his song evoked, and for a spell all three of us sat entranced, enjoying the smooth, mellow tones of his deep voice and liquid words.

When Cardoc's song eventually died away to silence, no one spoke for a long time, until Liam turned to me again and said softly, "Master Merlyn, I have been sitting here thinking, as I listened to Cardoc, that there must be many things in this land of ours that are strange to you, perhaps confusing. I know how ill it is to be a stranger in an unfamiliar land, unused to the customs of the folk around you, and fearful of committing some offense through simple ignorance, so I wish you to understand you run but little risk of offending anyone here by such an accidental slip. Ask me anything you wish about anything you do not understand. I will answer you as plainly as I can, without evasion." He nodded to where Donuil sat beside me, listening. "Young Donuil here I have known since the day of his birth, and he is an able, worthy young man, but not sophisticated in the ways of such as you and your people. There is much that will simply never have occurred to him as being needful of explanation." He stopped, and then grinned at me, the expression taking years away from the age in his face. "Listen to me, the world traveller. In truth, I can be little better than Donuil, but I am older, and I have travelled farther and more freely than he has, having travelled to your land in my youth."

"You have been to Britain, Master Liam?"

He nodded, his eyes on Cardoc. "Aye, several times. And on one occasion, when I was a mere boy, I remained there for more than a year, living among the Romans, in Londinium."

"You surprise me," I admitted. "What took you there?"

He smiled again and sniffed, turning his gaze back to me and hitching his humped shoulder as he had done before, when I first arrived. "This did. I was an acrobat. That should surprise you even more greatly, I suspect." It did indeed, but he gave me no chance to say so, continuing with that self-deprecating smile I was coming to recognize as one of his key attributes. "Contrary to what most people believe, Master Merlyn, a young hunchback is not necessarily at a loss for normal, bodily movement—within certain clearly defined limits, of course. As a lad, I was agile and physically gifted. What I lacked in dexterity because of my twisted spine was more than compensated for by the greater than normal ease of movement I had in my arms

and legs. An ability to contort them, allied with my small size and weight
and the naturally amusing quality of my . . . differentness, made me a popular
figure at entertainments, and I did well for myself for several years, travelling
the lands with a troupe of showmen. We were particularly popular in Britain,
where we travelled widely among the various garrisons and military bases,
amusing the troops. I have always had a good head on my shoulders, thanks
only to good fortune, and I managed to acquire enough in silver, and even
a little gold, to start me off in my life here when I grew too old to perform."

"How old were you then?" His recitation had fascinated me.

He drew his brows together, reckoning. "I began to stiffen up in my
thirteenth year . . . Once it began, however, it progressed quickly. I began to
suffer, as did my performances. Within the year came three consecutive occasions when, where a short time earlier I would merely have fallen and
bounced easily to my feet, I broke bones instead; once in my arm, twice in
my right leg. By the third time, my tumbling days were finished. I was home
less than seven months later, having used my small store of hoarded coin to
purchase six healthy, breeding pairs of well-matched goats from the hill country in the north of Britain and then to ship them back here to Eire with me.
Iain, Athol's father, who was our king in those days, gave me back the right
to farm my father's land—my parents had been dead, and thus my claim
forfeit, since shortly after I left home, although I had been unaware of it—
and I began to build my own herds and mind only my own affairs from that
day forth. By the time King Iain was killed, a half score years later, and Athol
elected king in his place, I had established a fine herd of goats and another
of cattle, and a few sheep, too." He shrugged, a tiny, self-deprecating gesture.
"I suppose I had earned myself a reputation, too, for being both fortunate
and singleminded. At any rate, the new king, Athol, sought me out more and
more often in the first few years after his election, always to ask for my advice,
it seemed to me, on things about which I knew very little, if anything at all."
He sniffed again. "I thought at first he came to me merely to placate his first
wife, Rhea, who was sister to my mother, but he always seemed to listen to
what I had to say, to follow my advice and to value my judgment . . ." He
shook his head and sat silent, staring into the fire, obviously overtaken by
thoughts that were far removed from where we sat. Neither Donuil nor I
sought to interrupt them. I, however, raised my cup to sip again and discovered, to my great surprise, that it was empty. Liam sensed my plight immediately and returned from his wool-gathering.

"Och, you are dry! Donuil, have you no eyes at all for seeing to our guest?
Here, Master Merlyn, let me bring you another." He took my cup and looked
at Donuil, one eyebrow raised high. "I suppose yours is empty, too? Cardoc,
another?" Cardoc shook his head in polite refusal, but Donuil proffered his
cup sheepishly and Liam snatched it from him in mock surliness, smiling as
he moved away to refill both. While he was doing so, his daughter Shelagh
swept into the room, moving quickly and with confidence, her hand outstretched to greet me and the hem of her long garment brushing the floor,
concealing any movement of her legs and giving the distinct impression that
she glided rather than strode with long, sure steps.

"Master Merlyn, welcome to our house." She looked me straight in the
eyes and made no attempt to apologize for not having been here to greet me
when I arrived, and as I took her hand in greeting, her eyes were already

scanning the rest of the room, taking a brief, keen inventory. Apparently
satisfied, she looked back at me. "Has Cardoc been singing for you?"

"He has, and very well."

"Aye, he is our finest bard, in my opinion, although I keep that private,
for the good of all." She flashed a smile at Cardoc and then her gaze moved
on to Donuil, who was gazing into the fire again, but her next words were
still for me. "I can see Prince Donuil is as talkative as he has been since he
arrived. Father? Will you pour a cup for me? I'm parched from the heat of
the kitchens. Be seated, Master Merlyn, and I will, too." She sat down immediately, in the seat her father had occupied, and he returned silently,
holding a cup for her and one for me, after which he returned to collect his
own and Donuil's before settling into the next chair on his daughter's right.
I, too, sat down again, holding my cup aloft and smiling with admiration at
this mercurial young woman.

There was no sign in her of the harassed and road-weary traveller I had
met earlier in the day. The creature who sat easily beside me now, taking a
deep draught of the brimming cup her father had poured for her, was wondrous to behold, with long, carefully tousled, burnished hair of a deep, rich
brown, interspersed with lighter textures that caught the light in streaks and
reflected the glimmer of flames from fire and candle. Artless in their abundant artifice, her tresses were luxuriant, waved, rather than curled, and held
casually in place by several jewelled pins and one finger-wide band of polished
amber that circled her high forehead a fingersbreadth above her eyebrows.
Her eyebrows were remarkable: straight and full, they rose slightly upward at
the sides, creating a dark band the entire width of her face, broken only by
the space, again a single finger's width, between them. Beneath those startling
brows, her eyes tugged at my consciousness, suggesting something I could
not at first define, and therefore demanding my closer attention. They were
the colour of hazel, neither brown nor green and yet a blend of both with
overtones of grey, but it was the shape of them that had caught my attention,
I decided moments later. They were straight, almost as though ruled across
the bottom, making them starkly different from the eyes of others. Most
young people's eyes are rounded, top and bottom. Only the advance of age
mars their perfection, tugging and twisting inexorably downward with the
years, until the eyes of older people become as individually different and
wrinkled as their owners. Shelagh's eyes were straight across the lower lids,
and only slightly curved upward across the top, yet they were huge, large and
lambent and beautiful. She was speaking now to her father, turning her head
slightly towards him and away from me, allowing me to look more closely at
her, seeing her almost in profile, and only now did I recognize another artifice
to match the skill with which she had arranged her hair: she had highlighted
the shadow of her upper lids with some kind of cosmetic, very faint and only
slightly darker than her natural skin colour. That hint, the merest suggestion
of additional depth, lent her eyes the appearance of slanting slightly upward
as they swept out from the narrow bridge of her nose, and lent emphasis also
to her cheekbones, which were already full and high, smoothing the skin that
covered them to polished planes. Her nose, narrow, clean-edged and perfectly
proportioned to her face, was very slightly hooked; not aquiline in the sense
of the great Roman beak of my own forebears, but a gentler, less aggressive
yet unmistakably avian curve. A *hawk*, I thought, seeing that. *This woman is*

a hawk! She is a kestrel, soft to the touch and beautiful, once trained, and a pleasurable, exciting companion, but intrinsically savage and untamable unless she herself has chosen to accept a master, after which her loyalty will be unswerving until death.

Surprised and slightly uncomfortable with these thoughts, I glanced away again, towards Donuil, only to find him gazing at the woman as raptly as I had been. There was an open vulnerability in his expression that I found even less comforting than my own thoughts, and so I returned my eyes to Shelagh, aware that I had absorbed no word of the conversation taking place between her and her father.

Now I heard her say, "They should be ready now. I'll go and start them moving so we can eat." She tossed back the remainder of her mead, tilting her head backward and gulping it like a man, then stood up, smiling widely at Donuil and me. "We will eat within the quarter hour, I promise you, but now I'm back to the kitchens." I watched her lips, wide and bright red and full, forming the words, and admired the perfectly shaped brightness of her strong teeth. Belatedly, remembering my manners, I began to rise to my feet but she was already gone, and I watched her move quickly and surely across the floor and disappear behind the screens that masked the far end of the house, where I could now hear the sounds of other people talking and moving.

Liam himself had twisted around in his seat to watch his daughter leave, and now he turned back to me, a small smile of bemusement on his lips.

"She's the wild one, and I love her more than is good for either of us, I fear, but there are times when I cannot help wondering what she is, and times when I wonder if she knows, herself." He saw my look of mystification and his smile grew a little broader. "Daughter or son, I mean. Oh, she's all female; the gods know, a blind man could see that, but she has some fearful male attributes about her from time to time. She refuses to be . . . what's the word I want? . . . constrained's as good as any, I suppose. She refuses to be constrained by her womanhood." He paused, his head cocked to one side, regarding me. "D'you understand what I mean by that, Master Merlyn?" I shook my head, not trusting myself to words. "Well, I'm not complaining, you understand, not really. She could not be a better daughter, and she lacks none of the affection or the warmth an old man looks for in his daughter. She looks after me as though I were an egg, too fragile to be entrusted to any but the gentlest care. And she's beloved, I truly believe, of all the other women in this place, helping them with their troubles and their children, and as you can see, she keeps a house for me that is unlike any other in this land, in terms of comfort and cleanliness." He finished off the contents of his cup before continuing. "But there's the other side of her. She prides herself on being a hunter and a warrior and, truth be told, she is one of the best and strongest fighters in the place. No other woman can match her with sword or spear or club, and precious few men would care to face her in earnest, either. And with a knife, she is almost a demon. She can throw a knife—any knife—and pierce a target, clean and centre, nine times out of ten . . ." This time his pause was long. "No other that I know—no one anyone else knows, either—can do that. But she's my *daughter* . . ." I heard a note of agonizing plaint in his voice, but before I could respond, another voice broke in.

"She could always do that." I turned in surprise. This was almost Donuil's first contribution to our talk since I had arrived.

"What? With the knives?"

"Aye," he nodded. "When she was no more than ten years old, she could hit and kill a running rabbit with a knife; with the point of it, I mean, not just the weight of it."

"A running rabbit?" I could hear the doubt in my own voice. "Not regularly, surely? I mean, she might have hit the odd one. I can believe that. But not consistently, Donuil. That's not possible."

He shook his head, smiling and pursing his lips. "I can't blame you for doubting, Merlyn, but it's not only possible, it is true. I saw her do it often, and she missed no more than occasionally. Mind you, the rabbit had to be quite close, and not yet settled into its run, but she could do it. We used to spend hours, creeping about, knives in hand, stalking the things. I never killed a single one, but we seldom came home empty-handed."

I shook my head again, believing him this time in spite of myself, and then we were disturbed by the beginnings of a period of activity radiating from the kitchens, during which the main table by the side wall was laden with food brought in by a half-dozen people, each of whom made a number of return journeys to the kitchens, where the proceedings were evidently being supervised by Shelagh. At length the hubbub died down, Shelagh rejoined us, and we each pulled our own chairs over to the table, which groaned now beneath the riches piled upon it. Before we began to eat, I gazed at the bounty provided from Liam's kitchens.

"Are we to dine alone, the five of us? There's enough here for fifty."

He smiled at me again. "Aye, so we must try to leave some for our friends who worked so hard preparing this. Normally we would all eat together, but tonight is a special night. My daughter has returned from a lengthy journey, as has Prince Donuil, and you yourself are an honoured guest, so our friends have graciously decided we may eat alone, to talk of things we wouldn't think to discuss were they all with us. Where would you like to start?"

I ate far more than was my habit, succumbing to the excellence and variety of the food laid before us. And as we ate, we talked and drank, although I sipped but sparingly at the fiery, potent mead, and then we talked further, barely pausing as the table was cleared and the fire replenished and we dragged our chairs back into the crescent they had formed before we ate. Liam was the perfect host, in the grand, Roman style—although he might have been appalled to hear the thought—attentive to his guests and assiduous in making sure each had enough to eat and drink, and topics enough on which to speak. Donuil had found his tongue again as the meal began, and Cardoc had proved himself to be a gifted thinker and a quick-minded debater. Shelagh was a complete delight, quick-tongued, as I already knew, and possessed of a devastating wit that she used mercilessly and without compunction on each and all of us, including her father. As the night wore on, I grew increasingly pleased with the open and wholesome attraction that she and Donuil were rediscovering for each other, each of them, I thought, losing the reticence born of long separation and intervening maturity, and returning almost seamlessly to the friendly intimacy they had shared throughout their childhood. *Lucky man, Donuil Mac Athol,* I thought on more than one occasion, for it was plainly evident, to me at least and surely to the others, that the friendship of old between these two had been transmuted into an attraction deeper and more adult than they had known before.

It was late in the evening by the time we were interrupted by the arrival of a rain-soaked young man looking for Cardoc, who took him aside and listened carefully to what he had to say. The bard then asked him several low-voiced questions before returning to where we sat watching, curious about this new development. Rud, his sister's husband, he informed us, had failed to return home from checking his traps that afternoon in the neighbouring forest. His sister, Cardoc explained to me, was heavily pregnant and frantic with worry, and he begged Liam to allow him to leave and go to her.

Liam had risen instantly to his feet when Cardoc began to speak, all concern and offering immediately to accompany Cardoc to his sister's house, and to assist in forming a search party if need be, but Cardoc would not hear of such a thing. He knew where Rud had his trapping territory, he insisted, and he and his own two brothers, aided by Rud's two brothers and his oldest son, would be more than enough to find the missing man, who had probably injured himself and fallen along the path.

In spite of Cardoc's embarrassed protestations, nevertheless, Donuil and Liam insisted upon accompanying him to his sister's house to see what might be required if the need arose for a larger search. I was ready to go with them but was overruled and persuaded to remain with Shelagh, by the fire, since Donuil and Liam would not be gone long and would return to take up our evening again, doubtless wet and cold and in need of more mead and a welcoming blaze.

XVI

LIAM'S HOUSE WAS very quiet after the door closed behind the three men. No sounds came now from the kitchens as Shelagh and I stood side by side, facing the closed door, our backs to the fire. I cleared my throat and waved a hand towards the screens at the far end of the room. "Has everyone gone, back there?"

She nodded, moving away to stand in front of the great fire. "Some time ago. They all went home to share their supper with their families." She was holding her hands out to the blaze and speaking to me over her shoulder. "That is one of the benefits my father enjoys from his wealth. He can't do it often, for fear of offending the fierce pride in some people, but from time to time, when we have an occasion important enough, like this visit of yours and Donuil's return, he takes the opportunity of preparing a private feast much too large for our own needs, and insists that the remains be divided equally among the folk who worked preparing it. They then take the food home and their families eat better, while the leavings last, than they would normally." She turned back to face me and smiled. "The most difficult task, apart from making the events look natural, is deciding in advance which families we will ask to help us with the preparation each time."

Now she moved away from the fire again, walking to the table that held the mead flasks, where she lifted a cup, holding it towards me with one eyebrow raised in question. I nodded, not having drunk anything for some time. I had been nursing a small drink, sipping it only occasionally, since early in the meal. Now she took two cups and moved back to the chairs by the fire, where I joined her.

"Of course," she continued as I sat down, "I could be cynical about the entire thing and regard it as an elaborate game, allowing myself to believe that everyone knows exactly what's happening, but that no one wants to break the conspiracy of silence and run the risk of having the 'special occasions' stop."

I turned to face her, sitting almost sidewise in my chair. "A conspiracy of silence? That does sound cynical, and you are too young and fresh for cynicism. Do you really believe that?"

She laughed, shaking her head, and we sat in silence for some time, staring into the flames, and then she asked me about the life young women lived in Camulod. She could hardly have asked me anything to tax me more, but I did my best to answer, basing my remarks upon my imprecise recollections of the daily lives of the nubile young women who had shared my aunt Luceiia's household over the years. I found it ironic that I could have spoken with far more authority in the area of their night lives, but that would have been insulting to this vivacious young woman. My halting recital seemed to satisfy her, however, for she began telling me of her own life here in Eire,

pointing out the differences between the Eirish customs and those I had so
inadequately described.

The most significant point she made addressed the question of feminin-
ity—an area utterly alien to me. She was amazed that our young women
received no military training, and pursued no athletic activities, like running
and climbing. I listened happily, agreeing from time to time with what she
said and remembering with nostalgia my early days with Deirdre, when she
and I had run and walked and wrestled strenuously among the hills surrounding Avalon.

It was only when the fire collapsed upon itself, belching a cloud of sparks,
that I realized I had lost track of time and that an hour must have passed
since her father and Donuil's departure to search for the man Rud.

"What about the missing man? Will he be found, d'you think?"

"Oh aye, he'll be found, but whether whole or injured, dead or alive, I
cannot tell. I suspect some accident has happened to him. But they will find
him. Rud is a steady man, solid and trustworthy, and unliking of things new.
Of all the people in the place who might be expected to lose themselves,
Rud would be the least likely, for he seldom travels far in trapping his animals, and he never wanders from the track he has beaten over the years
through the woods behind his house."

"Hmm." I sat back in my chair, feeling totally at ease with this impressive
young woman. "You think your father will be gone for long?"

"Mmm-mmm." The sound, accompanied by a brief headshake, was a firm
negative. She put down her cup, leaning over to place it on the floor, and
then sat back, twisting her body sideways to rest her back against the arm of
her chair so that she could look directly into my eyes. "So, Master Merlyn,
what think you of my man, really?"

Her question caught me unawares, and I realized that I had been looking
at her breasts, aware of them for the first time that evening only because of
the way in which she had twisted to face me, throwing the right one, small
but perfectly formed, into sharp relief beneath the heavy covering of her robe.
Now I flicked my eyes hastily upward to her face, seeing again, as though
afresh, the startling, hawklike beauty of the eyes that gazed back at me with
no sign of discomfort, from beneath her brows. She smiled at me, displaying
her fine teeth again, supremely confident of who and what she was.

"Your man? Oh, your father."

She cut me short with a shake of her head, her smile growing wider. "No,
my man. Donuil Mac Athol."

"Oh . . . I see." I cleared my throat. "Well . . . what do you mean, what
do I think of him? I respect and admire him greatly. He is my friend, and I
am honoured by his friendship."

"He is young, though, to have you as a friend, would you not think so?"

"Young?" That observation disconcerted me slightly, and I had to think
about my answer, attempting to ignore her question's implications about my
own years. "Aye," I said, finally. "I suppose nine years might be seen by some
as a large gap in age, particularly between close friends . . ." I hesitated only
briefly. "But Donuil is unique, and he and I have come to know each other
well over the past five years. I have found nothing in him to dislike or to
mistrust. Absolutely nothing . . . But tell me," I went on, unable to resist the

urge to ask. "Is he aware of your conviction? Does he know you regard him as 'your man'?"

Now she laughed, her voice as clear and ringing as the tone I had struck from Excalibur in the Armoury at Camulod. "Of course not, no! He has no idea!" The mere thought of such a thing clearly struck her as ludicrous and her laughter grew even stronger. "Oh, poor Donuil! He doesn't even know *himself* that he is!" She held up a hand, begging me to sit still while she mastered herself, and then, when her laughter had died down she coughed slightly and said demurely, although smiling still, "As I have said, Donuil is young, and in some ways very young, but he will learn."

"I see," I said again, and this time I did, and clearly. "I think he will, too. But have you always known that he was yours?"

Now her smile grew gentler, more subdued. "Almost, Master Merlyn, almost. I have certainly known since I was very young. Donuil and I were destined each for the other."

"Hmm, Destiny." I almost added "again," but caught myself in time. "And how can you know that with such certainty?" I was smiling now, too, not doubting her sincerity for a moment.

"Because I know. He and I will be wed and I will bear him two sons, called Gwin and Ghilleadh." She raised one eyebrow, looking at me serenely. "I simply know these things, Master Merlyn, but were I to tell you how I know, you would disbelieve me and think me foolish."

"Call me plain Merlyn, without the 'Master,' or Caius, if you prefer. I doubt that I could think you foolish." She bowed her head in gracious acceptance of both compliments and I stopped speaking, staring into her eyes. She waited, knowing that I had more to add. Finally, when I had straightened out the thought that had returned to me, I continued. "You said something to me this morning, when we first met, something strange. You said you had seen me before, but not clearly." She blinked, a long, slow, birdlike closing of her wide, exotically slanted eyes that was deliberate, I felt; an attempt to guard herself against my gaze. When her eyes opened again, looking into mine, I pressed on. "I know your father has been in Britain, but I did not think he had been there recently. Has he? And did you accompany him? Because unless you did, you could not possibly have seen me before today, clearly or otherwise."

Shelagh's smile had disappeared as I spoke, and now she reached upward to her mouth, smoothing the softness of her lower lip with the tip of the smallest finger on her right hand. I watched the gentle pressure push the pillow of her full lip slightly askew and then she curled her fingers, cupping her chin delicately.

"It was a slip of the tongue. Is your full name Caius Merlyn or Merlyn Britannicus? Which is correct?"

"Both. My name is Caius Merlyn Britannicus."

"It's a good name, strong and solid."

"My thanks. And what is yours?"

"My full name?" Her smile had returned. "Shelagh. Shelagh, daughter of Liam, known as Twistback. But I am not Shelagh Twistback, simply Shelagh."

"Then, 'Simply Shelagh,' I will congratulate you on your attempt to divert my attention, unsuccessful though it has been. A slip of the tongue, you said.

I hope you will forgive me if I doubt you. You were looking at me as you said the words this morning and I believed you recognized me. You had seen me before. So how could that be?" My heart was suddenly beating hard in my chest as I waited for her reaction, because I had begun to feel, all at once and without logic, that she and I might have far more in common than either of us could ever have suspected. She stared back at me, her face now in repose.

"I meant what I said, Merlyn. It was a slip of the tongue."

"No." I shook my head, dismissing her response. "Pardon me, but a slip of the tongue is an inadvertent yet revealing lapse. An error of statement that contains a truth."

"Really?" Her eyes glinted with amusement and a hint, I thought, of stirring anger. "And what does that mean?"

I decided to gamble, but began by prevaricating. "Nothing, really," I said, pretending resignation. "It was mere curiosity that prompted me to say it."

"Curiosity about what?"

Now I smiled at her. "About you, about who you are and how you think. I found myself wondering if you had dreamed of your future with Donuil, and of the names you would give your sons."

"Well, of course I have." She smiled at me now with all the guile of womankind. "All young women dream of such things. Surely you knew that?"

I shrugged my shoulders. "To an extent, I did. But I had not known they dreamed quite so minutely. Most of my own dreams are formless pictures, difficult to recall on wakening. I had presumed everyone's were the same."

"No, not so. I dream quite clearly, most of the time."

"Aye, I believe you, and you dreamed of meeting me before you saw me."

Her face underwent a sudden, startling change, her eyes narrowing and her colour receding rapidly. I held up a hand quickly to forestall her flaring, evidently frightened anger, feeling a surge of excitement in my breast. "Wait, Shelagh! Before you fly at me, know this: I am not *accusing* you of anything. I, too, have dreams that come to pass, dreams that come true."

She froze, her eyes wide, staring into mine. Silence settled and lay between us, solid and tactile as a heavy veil of drifting smoke. In the stillness, I could feel my heartbeat rally and slow down, and still she sat motionless, tense and poised as though for flight. Then, when I had begun to feel concern that she might never speak to me or move again, her voice came in a whisper, each word hissed separately.

"What . . . what are you saying?"

Unable to define the tone in her whispered words, I allowed myself to relax and raised my cup to my lips again, drinking slowly before responding.

"I am saying that I dream strange dreams," I answered finally, speaking slowly and without heat. "Prophetic dreams, and frightening. And I have done so all my life. Never, at any time, have I met another person with the same ability."

She was gazing at me fixedly, but the colour had returned gradually to her cheeks. Another silence grew and lengthened between us.

"Why would you tell me such a thing?" she asked eventually. "What attraction could such perilous knowledge hold for me? And why would you even think to entrust it to me?"

"Perilous?" I was confused, caught unprepared by the unexpected answer.

"Why would you say that?" I asked her. "There is no peril involved for me in your knowledge, how could there be? Nor is any need for trust involved. It is simply a thing, an ability—I know not whether gift or curse—that has troubled me throughout my life, although I became convinced of its potency only recently. It's a personal burden, a secret of my own, of which I have spoken to but very few, because it has frightened me for years, but only for my mind, not for my bodily health. There is no danger involved in it, no peril."

Now it was she who looked confused. Her eyebrows drew closer together and her eyes scanned my face, looking for I knew not what, before she pursed her lips and spoke again.

"The power you speak of is sorcery. The Sight, it is called. The known possession of it means banishment from the world of ordinary folk."

"What? Banishment? By whom?"

"By everyone. It is the law."

"But, Shelagh, that is ridiculous!"

"Ridiculous?" Her anger flared again. "Laughable? How dare you mock me, Caius Merlyn! I speak the simple truth. Foreknowledge—the ability to see the future, godlike—is unhuman. No man or woman can possess such powers without being touched by the gods, and therefore without the taint of immortality. The law decrees banishment from the homes of men."

"I see. It is akin to leprosy. Its possessors are unclean." She had begun to frown again and I pressed on. "To where, then, would I be banished?"

"To anywhere you wish to go, so long as you remove yourself from all human contact."

"And if I should refuse?"

"You would be killed."

"In the name of God, that is barbarism!" Even as I said the words, I saw, belatedly, the reason for her earlier hostility. The thought of banishment, of a life of eternal solitude, cut off from her father and her folk for her entire life, must terrify her. I nodded my head in understanding, letting the sympathy I felt soften my voice. "So that's why my questions frightened you so much." She made no move, but I saw gratitude in her eyes. "But tell me, if you will," I continued, keeping my eyes fixed on hers. "Tell me why you would speak of dreams to me at all, even light-heartedly, if you had any fear of being thought to have . . . what was it you called it? The Sight?"

She nodded, a tiny gesture, acknowledging the legitimacy of my question. "You are a stranger, with no knowledge of our ways. I thought I might toy with you, in the safety of your ignorance." Her voice was soft now, reflecting her changing mood.

"You had no thought that I might share your gift?"

"None." She shook her head and then realized what she had admitted, and her alarm flared up anew, her eyes widening in panic. Again I raised a hand, palm outwards, to soothe her.

"Hush, Shelagh, be at peace. You risk nothing with me. It is a gift we share, remember?"

She nodded again, nervously, appearing suddenly and sadly cowed, her hands clasped tightly on her lap, her eyes darting around the room as if in terror of being overheard, so that my throat swelled up with compassion for her.

"Come, girl," I whispered, gentling her as I would a frightened horse. "There is nothing to fear. We are alone. But take heart from the knowledge— and I will swear the truth of this on any oath you care to name—that such laws do not exist in Britain, nor anywhere else save here that I know of. There's nothing wicked in the ability you have, Shelagh; nothing willful either, for that matter. It is something born within you, as it was in me, something over which we have no control." I broke off, thinking of what I had just said. "Can you summon your ability at will?" She shook her head emphatically. "Well, then, in that we are alike, the two of us. But you can recall your dreams clearly, is that not so?"

"Sometimes," she whispered, more strongly this time.

"And do they frighten you, these dreams?"

"No," she looked at me, wide-eyed. "Do yours?"

"Aye, they have, on almost every occasion, although I have no clear memories of them on waking. You can recall the events in your dreams?"

"Yes, clearly." Her voice was growing stronger with every word, her confidence increasing as her fears abated. "But I cannot always understand what I have dreamed. There are times when I can recall a dream clearly and see the pictures in my mind in detailed colours, and yet have no idea of what any part of it means. That happens often."

"Often? How often do you dream such things?"

She shrugged. "Oh, I don't know. It varies. Sometimes I may have several in the course of a single year, but I have known whole years to pass without one." She leaned down again and collected her cup from the floor, then drained it at one gulp, after which she sat back and breathed deeply. I sat still, saying nothing, my thoughts racing. I had found someone who shared my gift, someone who knew the strangeness of the alien power exercised in me! The sound of her voice brought me back from my reverie.

"I saw your face in one of those . . . the kind I never understand, I mean."

I sat up straighter. "How so? What did you see?"

She gazed intently into my eyes for several moments and then turned to stare into the fire. The logs had burned away almost completely, and now she rose and crossed to where a fresh supply lay in a stout, wooden frame. I made no move that might interrupt her thoughts as she selected several sawn lengths and threw them on the fire, finally pushing and prodding them into position with a long, heavy iron poker.

"There was a bear," she said, her voice almost lost in the snapping and flaring of the fuel so that I had to lean forward to hear her. "It devoured a boar, and then it killed and ate a dragon that was black, with green scales, and breathed fire. Then, later—I think it was later, but it may have been directly afterwards—it rode on a bull's back to where it met another bear, and all three creatures fought each other in a ring of wolves, among waterfalls of blood, and when the fight was done, the bear, the first one, was sorely wounded and prepared to die among the wolves, but a darkness fell, and out of the darkness, on a broadening beam of light, came a great eagle to attack the wolves and scatter them . . ." Her voice died away completely and she remained there, head down by the fire, staring into its depths.

"And?" I prompted her. "What happened then?" She gave no sign of having heard, and I stood up and went to her, standing beside her. She paid me no heed. "Shelagh? What happened then, after the eagle came?" She turned to look up at me, frowning and shaking her head as though unable to remember, but I persisted. "You said an eagle came, upon a broadening beam of light. What then?"

"It killed the dominant wolf, a giant, and then stripped the coat from its back with its great talons . . . and underneath its coat, the wolf had green dragon scales, and it roared its breath of fire at the eagle, burning its feathers, burning it to death, and as it fell dying, the eagle, too, became a dragon-shape, crimson with its own blood. And the light faded, and I saw you, standing among the shadows, masked in almost darkness, and all else disappeared but you, with the crimson dragon bleeding on your shoulder and the great eagle itself, fully restored, perched upon your wrist."

As I stood there listening, my heart pounding, I realized that she had no more to tell me. I swallowed hard and stepped back from her, looking around me for my cup of mead. It sat on the floor by my chair, where I had no recollection of having placed it. I stepped to it and picked it up. It was empty. Breathing a great sigh, I crossed to the small table and poured a fresh supply for both of us, after which I returned to my chair and sat down.

"Shelagh," I said. "Come, join me."

She moved back to sit beside me again, taking the cup I offered her. We sat for a spell in silence, and then I asked her the question in my mind.

"You have no idea of what it means?"

"No." Her voice was still subdued with the memory of her dream. She looked at me. "Have you?"

I gusted a sigh. "No, I have not, although there are some elements of it that might make sense, in a demented way."

"Oh?" Her tone was livelier now, responding to my reference to dementia. "And what are those?"

"The animals, some of them at least. I myself might be the bear. It is my symbol. But I am only one bear; you saw two and I know of no other. Uther, my cousin, who is dead now, wore the symbol of the dragon, but his was red, not green. Lot, King of Cornwall, whom I believe Uther slew, had for his sign the boar. But there it ends. Of bulls and wolves and eagles I have no knowledge." I sighed again. "It is nonsense. I have the same problem with the dreams I dream, and they are less succinct than yours. Most often, it is only after seeing the things I dreamed about that I become aware of having dreamed at all. You are the only other person I have ever known to share the curse, and I had begun to hope for a moment there, having found you, that your dreams might be more intelligible than mine. Obviously I was wrong." As I spoke, we heard loud voices outside in the rain, and both sat up straighter, almost guiltily. "Here comes your father, so we will speak no more of this tonight," I said. "But if we have the chance, let's talk again when we can do it safely." Shelagh nodded and then rose and left the room hurriedly, exiting through the screens that masked the other end of the dwelling. I crossed idly to the fire again, where I stood gazing into the heart of the blaze, puzzling over Shelagh's dream and awaiting the entry of Liam and Donuil.

When they stomped in, muffled in close-wrapped cloaks and dripping wet, I eyed them closely, seeing the failure of their mission in their bearing and the air of weary frustration that hung about them.

"Oh, you're still here?" Liam began to unwind the cloak from about his shoulders as Donuil barred the heavy door behind them.

"Aye, are you surprised? You asked me to wait and you have not been gone that long. You didn't find him?"

Donuil's loud sniff was eloquent, and he crossed in front of me to spit violently into the fire before responding otherwise. "No," he growled then. "No sign of him. We might have passed him in the dark, lying dead or unconscious somewhere, but I doubt it. There were six of us and we searched thoroughly, though we were damnably hampered by the rain and mud. I think he's gone."

"Gone? Gone where? Shelagh says he is a creature of habit, never known to change his settled ways."

"And Shelagh's right, he is," Liam put in. "But even cattle can change their habits." He dropped the last of his sodden outer garments and crossed directly to the table where the mead sat in its jug, then poured out two fresh cups, looking at me with a raised brow to see if I would have some. I shook my head and he busied himself in bringing a cup to Donuil, who still stared into the fire. "The problem is," Liam went on, "that once a bullock or a cow changes its pattern, a mere man has little chance of understanding the change, or predicting its outcome." He sipped his drink loudly, then gasped in appreciation of the silken warmth of the mead.

"So? Are you saying he has absconded?"

Liam looked at me with a small, bitter smile. "Absconded? To where? No, Master Merlyn, I am saying merely that we were unable to find him. He might have wandered farther from his path than is his habit. If he did, and if he is to be found at all, it will have to wait until daylight. We will sleep now for a few hours, and search again at daybreak."

"I'll come with you."

His eyes travelled the length of me, from head to toe, and he smiled. "Not in those clothes, you won't."

I had forgotten how I was dressed, and now I returned his smile. "Of course not," I agreed. "I'll return before you leave."

"I don't think you should, Cay," Donuil muttered, almost inaudibly.

I looked at him in surprise. "Why not? Another pair of eyes will aid your search."

"We have no shortage of pairs of eyes. I'd rather you stayed here. There's something wrong, something beyond the loss of Rud."

I looked quickly to Liam and saw his gaze sharpen, his brow furrow as he seemed to lean towards Donuil. "What do you mean?" I asked, though my eyes remained fixed on Liam.

Donuil turned now to face me. "I don't know what I mean. But something is amiss, I feel it in my belly. Rud's vanishing is one thing, perhaps easily explained. We will know quickly, come morning. But in the meantime, something else is nagging at me, annoying me, something I ought to know, yet have missed seeing in the passing."

I heard a sound behind me as Shelagh came back into the room, and when she spoke I knew she had overheard what Donuil said. "You think there are enemies out there?"

Donuil looked at her and shrugged. "There could be. Have you ever felt yourself being watched, Cay?"

Shelagh answered for me. "By whom?"

"By someone, or some animal, that remains hidden."

I immediately recalled the feeling I had had the first time I discovered my brother Ambrose watching me, in Verulamium before we met face to face.

"I know that feeling," I replied. "It is unmistakable."

"Aye, well I had it tonight, while we were searching in the forest."

"Pshaw!" Liam's voice sounded relieved somehow, as though some kind of tension had been removed from it. "That was mere night nerves! I felt something of the like myself, but it was only because, even with our torches, the place was black as the pit. 'Twas nerves, nothing more."

"No, Liam, it was not. I know the difference. The lad who left here five years ago has grown up now, and can distinguish between fear and fancy. I felt we were being watched."

"By whom, then, lad? Who would be watching us, rooting about there in the dark? Rud himself, unwilling to be found?"

Donuil shrugged helplessly, looking to me for aid, but I had not been there. I could only shake my head. "I don't know, Donuil, but say you were right, and you were being watched, who could it have been, apart from Rud? An enemy? A single enemy? What could he hope to achieve, other than being caught? Did you look about you?"

"Of course I did! But it was pitch black. I could see nothing."

"Even with a torch?"

He frowned. "What d'you mean?"

Now it was my turn to shake my head. "Foolishness. I was about to ask how anyone could have seen any more than you, lacking a torch, but of course he could have watched you by your light and you would have been flame blind, peering into the darkness . . . which means, I suppose, there could have been someone there."

"Who, in the name of all the swarming gods?" Liam's exasperation was growing and it was his daughter who answered him, her tone cutting through his impatience.

"It doesn't matter who, Father. If there was someone out there, and the possibility cannot be overlooked, then he was no friend of ours. If no friend, there remains only an enemy, there in the forest close to us in darkness, waiting for light. If that's the case, we have until dawn to prepare ourselves."

"Aye, but—"

"No buts, Father. There's either someone out there or there isn't. If there is, it could be a whole host, a raid in force. If no one's there, we will all have an early start in our search for Rud. Either way we'll be prepared for whatever comes with the day."

"Damn me, Daughter, think what you say. The only people who could be out there are the Wild Ones from the south, and they lack the skills and even the discipline to do what you suggest they're doing. They never could—"

"Och, hold your tongue, Father!" Shelagh's voice cracked like a whip. "You're wasting time when we have none to waste. If I am wrong you'll have all day to tell me so tomorrow; for now, I'm thinking Donuil could be right." She spoke now to Donuil. "Go to your father. Tell him what is in your mind. Have him make ready, but be sure to warn him of the need for stealth. If there are enemies out there preparing a surprise for us, foolish we'd be to warn them we suspect it." She swung to me. "Merlyn, we could have need of you and your horses. Will you stand with us?"

I smiled at her, seeing clearly her father's sometime dilemma as to whether he had sired son or daughter. "Your peril is ours, Lady. Of course we stand with you. I'll go right now and prepare my men."

"Go then, but wait a while before you have them prepare. We still have several hours of darkness and nothing will occur before daylight. No one can fight well in the dark. Whoever is out there will be terrified when you and your beasts appear. They could not have seen you before now. Any approach before nightfall would have been detected by our people, so if they are there indeed, they must have approached after dark, in the secrecy of night. Early they might have been, which would explain their finding Rud, but that would have yet been distant from our walls. Now go, both of you. I must arm myself. Father, the king will need you, too, for your counsel."

We three men left together, taking our separate ways immediately, Donuil and Liam to the King's Hall and I towards my own camp outside the gates. The rain had stopped finally, but the ground was wet and slippery underfoot and I had to place my feet with care. The settlement lay dark and quiet around me, no lights discernible in any of the huddled, night-still dwellings. I made my way to the main gates without seeing another sign of life, and as I passed through, I heard the deep, even sounds of snoring against the wall to my left. A sleeping guard? I had not been aware of seeing any gate guards since we arrived, and I had assumed, I realized only now, that outposts ranged the forest. From what I had learned tonight, however, I knew now that that was not the case. On impulse, I sought the source of the snores and found one man huddled at the foot of the wall, dead to the world. As I leaned over him, I caught the smell of ale and vomit. No guard, this. I left him where he lay and passed out through the open gateway.

"Hold!" The challenge, peremptory yet not too loud, came as I approached the huddle of seven empty huts outside the walls, used for some summer purpose I had not defined, that had become our camp. I recognized the voice of Philip, the youngest of our band apart from Donuil. For as long as I had known him, more than fifteen years, he had been called Philip Broken Nose for reasons none could miss. A blow from a wooden practice sword had flattened his eagle beak forever when he was a mere lad.

"Philip, it's me, Merlyn. Is everyone abed?"

He emerged from the shadows beneath the eaves of one of the huts. "Merlyn. You're late afoot. We've been turned in for hours, since darkness fell. Too miserable a night even for drinking. Mine is the second watch, relieving Rufio. Is something wrong?"

"Perhaps, perhaps not, but I'm glad everyone has had some sleep. Has your watch been quiet?"

"Aye, yours was the first movement I have seen or heard since coming out here. What's up?"

"I don't really know, but Donuil should be coming in a while. We may or may not be receiving visitors come dawn. Either way, we should be prepared. Stay alert." I left him to his watch and went directly to Dedalus, who awoke as I approached his cot. I told him briefly of Rud's disappearance, and of Donuil's misgivings, and he swung up out of bed, rubbing the last remnants of sleep from his face and eyes.

"Are we beset, then? How long do we have?"

"Until dawn. If there's to be an attack it won't come until then. There's no moon tonight, and heavy clouds. Too dark to see, too dark to fight."

"Hmm. What hour is it, anyway? Who's on watch out there? Philip? Good, his is the second watch. That means there's four and more hours of darkness left. Have you been to bed?" I shook my head. He yawned and stretched, grunting with pleasure. "Well, you had better try to sleep, then, if you can. I'll let the others lie for another hour, then get them ready. I'll wake you in good time." He paused, frowning. "If Donuil's right, Merlyn, and there's an enemy out there, waiting to come in with the first light, where will we deploy ourselves? We can't go charging off into the forest; we would all be unhorsed before we saw anything. The only space open enough for us to fight in is right here, outside the gates."

"True," I said. "So our task will be to wait until the attackers swarm around the gates, then hit them from behind. I'll sleep two hours, if I can, but no more. Wake me then."

I left him moving around in the darkness of the hut and made my way to my own cot, convinced that sleep would be impossible to achieve.

I was wrong. Two hours later, Rufio had to shake me hard to bring me back to awareness, though I collected myself quickly enough, once stirred.

"Everything's prepared," he told me. "Dedalus and the others are fully armed and the horses ready and safely out of sight in the empty huts."

I was sitting up by that time, looking around the interior of the hut in the light of two lamps. The shutters were closed tight over the windows, so I knew no light would spill outside. "Whose idea was that, to hide the horses? That was good thinking."

Rufio grinned at me. "Mine. I was talking to Ded, and we guessed that whoever is out there might not have seen us or our horses, if they sneaked in here after darkness fell. Remember when we arrived? We were the first horsemen these people had ever seen."

"I know. Old Liam's daughter Shelagh pointed out the same thing to me last night, when first we heard of this alarum. Did Donuil arrive?"

"Aye, not long after you had gone to sleep. Said to tell you that his father's people are prepared, but will give no signs of life until the attack begins. The gates lie open, too, he said, though forces are in place to close them quickly once the attack begins. In the meantime, they are an invitation to tempt invasion."

"Good; Athol's thinking matches my own. What's that?" I had noticed a leather washbag steaming at the foot of my bed, where it hung from a wooden tripod, and could not take my eyes away from it. "Hot water? Is that for me?"

Rufio was grinning still. "Aye, to wash in. Ded again. He said if you had less than two hours' sleep you wouldn't be fit to walk unless you had the chance to wash the sleep out of your weary face. Personally, I think he spoils you." He walked to the door. "Take your time. We have about an hour, perhaps more, before first light. But remember, we may have to fight, so tighten all your buckles properly . . ." He left, still grinning at his own wit, and I moved to the steaming water.

A short time later, feeling alive again and fully refreshed, I fastened the final buckles on my armour, took up my long, sheathed sword and carried it in my hand as I went to join the others in the largest hut, which had been selected as our gathering place when we arrived. They were all there, waiting for me, and I greeted each man personally. When I had done, Dedalus waved me towards an empty stool beside a table that held a partial loaf of bread, a bowl of roasted grain, a morsel of hard cheese, four withered apples and a cup of water, weakly flavoured with vinum, the harsh, red wine for which we had inherited a taste from Rome's legions. "That's the last of the vinum," he said, as I picked the cup up and sniffed it. "From now on, it's water or Eirish ale."

As I broke fast, we discussed strategies for dealing with whatever might befall. Fundamentally, as Ded had pointed out three hours before, our choices were limited by geography. We could not fight among dense under-growth, nor would our horses be of any tactical advantage within the settle-ment. We were confined, therefore, to the open space before the gates. If we had to fight, Quintus would be sequestered in the farthest hut, guarded by the two herdboys while we were gone. That settled, we spent the in-tervening time before dawn as soldiers do, talking among ourselves and pre-paring ourselves, each in his own way, for the death that might lie in wait for us.

At length the door opened and Paulus, Philip's relief, came inside to join us in concealment, warning us that the sky was showing signs of lightening. We rose and made our way to our horses, moving in silence broken only by the muffled squeaks, chinks and clinks of harness and weaponry. We did not mount, but remained there in the darkened huts, each man holding his own horse's bridle, waiting for a signal, a summons of some kind in the stillness of the dawn. When one came, it was not at all what we expected. There came a stealthy movement outside the door of the hut in which we stood, and then a fumbling at the latch. Everyone froze. A breathless, anticipatory pause, and then the door swung inward, revealing a hulking shape in the doorway against gathering light outside. Someone, I knew not who, moved swiftly forward, grasping the shape and jerking it into the room, then swing-ing, pushed it against the wall inside the door. These movements were ac-companied by a grunt, the metallic scraping of a dagger being unsheathed and then the sound of a blade being hammered home into a torso.

"Commander, take this!" As the whispered words hissed in my ear I felt a set of reins being pressed against my hand and seized it as a second shape loomed in the open doorway, peering in. Then I saw Rufio, whose voice it had been, lunge forward, dagger-wielding arm above his head, to bear this fellow backward and to death. The doorway was now filled with figures, ham-pering each other at first as they sought to leave. I heard the clang of blade against blade in the air outside, and then a chorus of shouts and the sounds of hand-to-hand fighting.

"Out! Bring out the horses!" someone yelled, and I moved forward, Ru-fio's bridle in my left fist, my own in my right. I released Rufio's horse to follow me and led my own horse out. There were figures struggling every-where, evidently more of them than us, and I decided I would do more good above than I might on foot. I seized my saddle horn and hopped on my right foot, finding the stirrup with my left on my first attempt and hauling myself up above the ruck. My long blade cleared its sheath as my right foot housed itself in the other stirrup and I pulled my horse up into a rearing turn, seeking a target. They were there in plenty. One tall, lanky fellow stood agape close on my right, his sword arm arrested as he stared up at me in stupefaction, and I clove his skull with my first swing, even before my mount touched all four feet to earth again. Rufio, his horse directly behind him to my left, was unable to mount, facing three men, and I kneed my way towards him, riding them down, then guarding him until he could swing up to his own saddle. Ded, too, was having trouble reaching his seat, using his horse as a barrier between himself and four feral assailants, one of whom began to dodge around the horse only to meet death at the end of Rufio's blade. I pulled my horse into a rear again and he kicked out, as he was trained to do, braining another. Rufio's horse breasted the other two aside, and Ded was mounted, shouting his thanks. Philip was up, too, as were two others, leaving only two, one of whom was Donuil, still afoot.

At a shout from me, we five who were mounted rallied, forming on our two beset companions, winning them time to mount. Then we were unassailable, wheeling and moving as one entity, and our opponents fled, some of them throwing down their weapons.

"Let them go!" I roared, reining my horse tightly. "Now listen! What's afoot there, over by the gate? Listen!"

Over the dwindling sounds of retreat from our erstwhile opponents we could clearly hear the sounds of battle coming from our left, still hidden by the pearly morning mist, yet swelling by the moment. Our horses snorted, their nostrils blowing plumes of vapour into the coldness of the morning air. Idly, my ears attuned to the noises in the distance, I glanced around at the corpses scattered on the ground. Ten I counted, before Rufio broke in on my thoughts.

"Well, Commander? Are we to sit here all day while they have all the glory?"

I glanced at him wryly, knowing he was being ironic. No man here among us retained the smallest illusion on matters of "glory" in battle. We were all too experienced for that, having lost too many friends in too many ungodly places.

"We are no more than eight, Rufe," I said. "And all we have on our side may be surprise. After our first appearance, that will be gone. So we will wait a little longer, to ensure that our appearance is appreciated. We'll hit them line abreast the first time, hard and fast, right in the centre of their press, for my guess is they'll have no line of battle. Then we'll swing away and form an arrowhead on the gallop, circling completely to the left, and hit their centre, right before the gate, cutting through them and veering left again, along the line of the wall. As soon as we've won free of them the second time, we'll turn, form staggered lines, four to a front, a sword swing apart from side to side, and hit them again. Remember, the surprise will be gone after our first charge. After that, they'll fight for their lives, so we'll be relying on our weight and speed. Let's hope the horses frighten them to death before they think of striking at the mounts, rather than the riders." I listened again. The noises to our left seemed to have reached a crescendo. "Very well, let's ride, and God grant we may all feast well when this is over."

I kneed Germanicus to a walk, pointing his nose towards the distant gates.

By this time the light had brightened enough to be almost worthy of the name of day, but a heavy ground mist hemmed us in and swirled about us as we rode forward. Dedalus remarked on it, observing that it would help our efforts by keeping us concealed until we charged through it, and I knew he was right. The noise grew more appalling as we travelled and soon I brought my horse to a trot, then to a canter, straining my ears and eyes to find the optimal spot at which to kick us to the gallop and full charge. And then a breath of wind scattered a patch of mist and showed me running figures, travelling from our left across our front towards the walls of Athol's stronghold.

"Come together! Dress your lines. On me!" I had been leaning forward as I rode, one hand downstretched to grasp the handle of my iron flail, where it hung from my saddle bow. Now I unhooked it, feeling the dangling weight of the heavy ball on its iron chain. I sank my spurs deep and swung the thing aloft and around, feeling the pull of it in my arm and shoulder muscles as my horse lengthened his stride, gaining full momentum.

And then we were among them, falling upon their crowded press like a crushing mass of stone, our mighty horses trampling and battering their way forward and through them as our weapons rose and fell, swung from above and dealing death and crippling wounds to all who barred their passage. On the instant, it seemed the air was filled with noise of a different kind. Exultant battle cries gave way immediately to piercing screams of terror, and I saw faces raised to us in direst awe, screaming mouths widened in panic and superstitious disbelief. Mere moments we were among them, then we were through and swinging our horses wide and to the left, regrouping to narrow arrowhead formation as we rode, me at the point, tightening the circle, charging back again into their midst, scattering them like wind-blown leaves before us. I struck far fewer blows the second time, for there were none who sought to withstand me or argue passage. The gates loomed before me and I swung my mount hard left again, galloping flat out, then left again, where we regrouped to a double line of four, the rear filling the gaps left in the front, and back to the slaughter, save that slaughter fled us, in a rout, streaming to both sides of our charge, leaving the field scattered with abandoned weapons and the corpses from our first and second passes. I raised my arm and slackened my reins, allowing my horse to slow, and the gates swung wide and Athol's Scots emerged, howling with glee, to pursue their shattered foes.

I looked about me. All present. "Is anyone hurt?" I shouted, ignoring the rabble of vengeful Scots pursuers who streamed by us. Miraculously, it seemed, no one had taken so much as a scratch. I turned my horse around, placing my back towards the open gates, and watched the slaughter being performed on the edges of the forest where some of Athol's blood-hungry warriors had caught up with the straggling remnants of the fleeing enemy. Dedalus moved into my line of vision, bringing his horse up to stand alongside mine so that only I would hear what he had to say.

"Well, that's about as heavy a draw on Fortune's bounties as any of us can hope to effect for a long time. They thought we were devils, straight from Hades. I don't think I saw one thrust aimed at any of us. They folded and ran at the mere sight of us."

"Aye. Total surprise, allied with terror. We'll never have a success like that again, for next time, no matter when it comes, they'll be expecting us and they'll fight us." I turned in my saddle to address the others, who were sitting patiently, awaiting my word. "My thanks to all of you, my friends. It has been short work, but effective. I doubt if they'll stop running before their legs give out. But I find myself wondering who they were. As you all know, there would be little point in taking to the forest in pursuit; they're being pursued thoroughly enough, and once we rode off the traffic-beaten paths, we would be at their mercy. I don't know how you feel about that, but I think I prefer matters the way they are." That won me a smattering of grins and chuckles, and I held up my hand for silence, aware that a number of Athol's people were standing around us, gazing up at us where we towered above them. "I doubt we'll see more trouble today, but it would be folly to assume all danger past, so we will remain mounted and ready, here, where we are. I go now to find the king, to discover his intentions. I'll not be long. Donuil, come with me."

I swung Germanicus around and rode through the gateway, only to find Athol, Liam, Connor and several others on their way to find us, their jubilation evident even from afar in their bearing and their gait.

"By all the spirits," Athol said to me, gripping my stirrup leather and gazing up into my face. "I have never seen, nor will I see again, the like of that attack of yours."

"You saw it?" My surprise made me forget the formalities of addressing a king.

"Saw it? Aye, I saw it. I was up yonder, on the tower to the east."

I glanced in the direction he indicated and saw the square-framed tower, built of logs, the top of which was jammed with waving, cheering Scots. "A good vantage point!" I shouted.

"Aye, for watching, though, not for being involved. Come you, to the Hall. Your men will not have eaten, and there's bread, and ale, and meat left over from last night. Bring all of them and join us there."

"But sir! King Athol, is it wise to leave the gates unguarded?"

He laughed aloud, a deep-bellied shout of a laugh. "Unguarded? When more than nine tenths of my own men have not yet wet their blades? Come, bring your people."

XVII

THAT EARLY-MORNING MEAL turned into a day-long celebration that escalated every time another contingent of warriors returned in jubilant triumph from the chase through the forest. It had become clear, almost from the first moments of the attack, that the invaders were the people I had come to think of as the Wild Ones, the anarchistic renegades in whose territories we had first been blown ashore. It was equally clear, however, that their attack could not have been occasioned by our trespass on their lands, for had they known of us, they would have been aware of, and prepared for, our horses.

Whatever the reasons for their presence in Athol's territories, they had been destroyed by the sudden apparition of our cavalry, utterly demoralized by our swift and savage onslaught, and their lack of any form of discipline had doomed them. Once broken in their initial attack and frightened into flight, they had continued running, leaderless and without plan of any kind, ruthlessly hounded to the death by their intended victims.

Estimates of their original strength varied from one hundred and fifty to three hundred men. My own guess was that there had been two hundred or so before the gates when we arrived, but I had been too preoccupied in closing with them to assess their numbers consciously. Some people, most of them observers from the walls, argued that as many as two hundred others had remained in the fringes of the forest, holding back from the attack on the gates, awaiting its success before committing themselves. I found that hard to credit, simply because it suggested a discipline that had otherwise been proved lacking. I felt confident that my own reckoning was close enough to the truth. Reports of the slaughter in the forest, however, became confusing. If the stories we heard were all to be believed, close to five hundred raiders had been hunted down and killed among the rocks and trees. It seemed to me there was much exaggeration in the celebrations taking place. No matter, I thought. The victory was real.

The celebrations were truncated, late in the afternoon, by the arrival of two unexpected guests, Rud, whose disappearance had triggered the entire affair, and Fingael, the most truculent of Athol's sons, who returned without the mountain goat he had been sent to kill. They arrived slightly more than two hours apart.

Rud's unexpected reappearance added, initially, to the celebrations, which had become almost riotous by the time he arrived. He had been found in the deep woods, tied and stifled, abandoned there to be collected later and hauled into slavery, and subsequently forgotten in the flight of his captors. He would have died there, hidden away from the main paths, save for the call of nature that fortuitously took one of his neighbours in search of privacy right where Rud lay.

Pleased enough about being freed and delivered, Rud's blunt-hewn features were yet grim enough to intrigue me, so that I mentioned his apparent unhappiness to the king—who stood beside me at the time—asking him if Rud were always so dour at such celebrations. Athol, who had not noticed anything amiss until I pointed it out, called Rud to him and asked him what was wrong and why deliverance should cast such a shroud of gloom about his face. The answer he received quickly cast a pall on all within hearing distance.

Rud had become captured just before dusk, he told us, when he had finished checking his traps and was preparing to head homeward. He had taken a prime marten in his last trap and was busy skinning it, bent upon his task, when he himself had been taken, all unawares, by someone who crept up on him from behind and clubbed him over the head.

On regaining consciousness, he had found himself tightly bound, hand and foot, with a gag filling his mouth, making him want to vomit. There had been a small fire close by, masked behind a screen held up by sticks, and he had heard voices discussing him, briefly, and then the attack they would launch come daylight. One of them sought to kill him out of hand, not wanting the encumbrance of a prisoner. After tomorrow, this one said, they would have slaves aplenty, so he could see no need for keeping this one alive. Another, however, the one who had taken Rud, was adamant that Rud would be his slave. He had need, the fellow said, of Rud's size and muscles. Rud had felt a chill of despair on hearing that, knowing his life was over, no matter which way the discussion was resolved.

Another voice diverted the first two from their argument, however, and Rud's fate was forgotten. This one, clearly a minor leader of some capacity, was unhappy that they should be here, in these woods, at this time, rather than awaiting the arrival of their allies, as they had promised. His opinion was unpopular and stirred up an altercation that attracted others to the unseen group around the fire, where the argument became loud and bitter. Most of the men, clearly, were in favour of the planned dawn attack on Athol's stronghold, and bitterly scornful of any dubious advantage that might be gained by waiting for outsiders to join them. They were strong enough by themselves, they said, to deal with Athol's folk, and their dawn attack would be sudden and lethal. Victory would bring them the treasures of Athol's people: weapons and tools, stored grain and livestock, strong men and ripe women. They had no need of help and no desire to share the plunder with foreigners. No one suspected their presence, and the gates of the stronghold had not even been closed, according to the information brought back by one of their own scouts. Gladud—Rud had assumed they spoke of the objector— was mad and deluded if he thought to put faith in the MacNyalls and the Children of Garn as allies. Creatures of night these were, and fit only for lies, greed and betrayal.

Gladud had responded angrily to the slur on his integrity and had come to blows with at least one of his fellows. Unable to see what was happening, Rud had listened to the sounds of strife, terminated by a sudden, gargling cough, after which Gladud's voice had become permanently silent. In the relative quiet that ensued, no one had said anything to indicate the outcome of the sudden fight, and the gathering had soon broken up as men sought shelter and a few hours of sleep before the attack.

I watched King Athol closely as he listened to Rud's tale, noting the unease that brought wrinkles to his brow when Rud named names. The names meant nothing to me, but they were plainly of concern to Athol. He restrained himself with difficulty, I could see, from interrupting Rud at their mention, and allowed the man to finish his story in his own way before congratulating him again on his deliverance. Rud nodded his thanks and stood there, obviously waiting to be questioned.

"MacNyall," the king said, his voice low-pitched. "And the Children of Garn. You are sure those were the names you heard?"

"Aye." Rud took no offense at the king's question.

"Hmm. Did you hear talk of other names?"

"No."

"Nothing of the Sons of Condran?"

Rud frowned, thinking hard, searching his memory. "No. But I heard the name Brian. Nothing more than that, only the name, and it might have been one of them."

"Aye, it might. Thank you, my friend. Get you home now to your wife." The king watched Rud walk away and then spoke to Connor. "Summon my Council now. Cullum!"

At the king's shouted summons, the giant whose boar spear I had used to kill the bear two days before stepped forward. Athol spoke crisply, issuing his orders.

"Close off the ale. I want no more drinking this night. We may have need of clear heads again, come morning. See to it." As Cullum nodded and resolutely moved away, the king turned to me. "Merlyn, come with us." He swept away, followed by Connor, Donuil and their brother Kerry, Liam, me and several others of the king's counselors. I saw Dedalus standing off to my right, talking with Benedict and Paulus as I approached the doorway. I beckoned him to me and told him not to wait for my return, but to get the men back to our quarters and hold them ready. I did not have to tell him to mount a guard.

Donuil had waited for me as I spoke with Dedalus, and now he led me to the skin-hung room where Athol had taken me the night I told him of my wife. By the time we arrived, the others were already seated, seemingly in no particular order, crowding the chamber, which had seemed spacious to me on my first visit. I sensed their Council meeting was about to begin without ceremony. Donuil found us two stools, and we seated ourselves at the rear, where we could see and hear clearly. Athol watched me until I had arranged myself, and then spoke, his first words bringing silence.

"Master Merlyn and my son Donuil are here at my request, and neither of them knows of the matters for discussion. I intend, therefore, to speak of what has passed to this point mainly for their benefit, but also because the retelling may refresh all our recollections and hence bring some new insight into our current problem." There was a muttered chorus of assent and some nodding of heads among his listeners, two of whom, the corpulent man called Mungo and Donuil's other brother, Kerry, turned to look over their shoulders to where we sat. Mungo glowered, his face strained and red from the effort of twisting his great frame around, but Kerry grinned and winked at me, and I nodded back to him, permitting myself a slight smile of acknowledgment and wondering again at the familiarity I found in him.

Athol sucked in a great breath, drawing himself erect and marshalling his thoughts, and then began to speak.

"Let me begin by thanking you, Caius Merlyn, as king of my people, for your assistance this day. You and your . . . cavalry"—he pronounced the alien word with scrupulous care—"saved perhaps hundreds of my own, for this attack would have cost us dearly had you not been here." He paused, and as he did so I felt a liquid stirring in my bowels and a sudden cramp, not strong or long-lasting enough to cause me great discomfort, but sufficiently assertive to let me know that my intestines were about to demand my attention. As I tensed my stomach muscles against it, the king spoke on. "We are a strong people, and prolific, and our values, the love of family and clan, mark us as very different from our neighbours, some of whom you faced today. But at this moment we are weak in numbers, and hence open to attack." The cramp subsided and he had all of my attention now as I wondered whence this numerical weakness, which I had not suspected, had come. He did not leave me wondering.

"For some years now, five at the least, no, even more, for Donuil had not yet left when we began, we have been removing ourselves—our entire people—from these territories, from this land. It is too much enclosed, as you have seen, and is not fit for grazing on the scale we need to raise our beasts and feed our folk. We can cut down the trees, and the soil is rich enough to bear crops, but the lack of sunlight is a hazard to the harvest every year. So, as I said, we decided to move—Have I said something amusing?" His voice was chilled, suddenly, as he glared at Connor, who had smiled at me. Connor was immediately contrite, his smile vanishing as he turned to face his father's abrupt displeasure.

"No, Father. Forgive me, but your words brought to mind a discussion Caius Merlyn and I had only nights ago on the nature of kingship."

"And? To what end was this discussion of *kingship?*" Athol was far from placated, and Connor shrugged his shoulders.

"I remarked that the king of a land was tied to that land, but that the king of a people could take his people wherever they wished to go."

"I see. An astute and learned observation." His voice dripped with sarcasm. "May I continue now?"

"Of course. I beg your pardon." Connor's face was expressionless, but I fancied I saw humour glinting in his widened eyes.

"My thanks to you, Lord Connor." Still somewhat stiffly, the king returned his attention to me.

"What my ill-mannered son said is true. This land, which we have held since time out of mind, is no longer sufficient for us. We have outgrown it and the time has come to move beyond." His eyes moved away from me to sweep over the faces of his councilors, as though his words were meant to reinforce their memories. When he had scanned each face, he returned his gaze to me. "Such a move, Master Merlyn, as I am sure you have already decided, may not be lightly undertaken. It requires much planning and great organization . . . More than anything else, however, it requires great resources to be expended on exploration, for it is futile to think of moving if there is no place where you may go. And to go blindly, without searching for that place ahead of time, would be suicidal." I nodded slowly, keeping my eyes on his.

"To that end, therefore, we have searched hard and long. We have found, not surprisingly, that all the living spaces that surround us are inhabited. We could take them by conquest, but that would solve nothing, since the land we won would have the same disadvantages as that we quit. So we sought farther afield. And finally we found a land that suits our needs. It has no name, but it is suited to our purposes, even though inhabited."

Beside me, Donuil raised his hand tentatively, seeking recognition. His father glanced at him. "You wish to speak?"

"Yes, Father, but not to interrupt. This was afoot long before I left home, though I was too young then to enter Council. Do you still speak of the same place? The islands and the land to the northeast?"

"Aye, I do. You have something to add?"

"A name for it. The Romans, and now the people of Britain to the south of it, gave it the name of Caledonia."

I felt gooseflesh stirring on my arms and back as he said the name, and its utterance crystallized the thoughts that had been stirring vaguely in my mind as I listened to the king's words. These Gaelic Scots were speaking of annexing Caledonia in exactly the same way that the other Outlanders we called Saxons were sailing onto Britain!

"But what of the Picts?" I blurted.

The king looked back at me, smiling now, a glint of humour. "The Picts? You mean the painted people? What of them? They will make room for us, one way or another. They hold only the mainland, anyway. Most of our outposts are among the islands off the coast—we have established only three small settlements on the mainland, in three of the mountainous glens that descend to the coast. And besides, these Picts, as you call them, are hunters only. They grow no crops and tend no beasts or cattle. They live off the things that live off the land itself, eating their flesh and fruits. They are not a people as we think of a people. They are too primitive to hold such wealth." He cleared his throat, collected his thoughts and returned to the main topic. "Let it be understood, this matter is afoot and well in progress. My firstborn son Cornath has been given the task of organizing our new settlements; Brander, his brother, is our admiral, in charge of the fleet responsible for moving our people to their new home. That task goes on, even in winter, save for the darkest months when the danger of sea crossings is too great. Each year, before that time, Brander returns home to make ready the next fleet of travellers. We expect him daily, and with him he will bring three hundred men, manning his fleet of galleys, roughly twenty to each craft. The normal complement of men per galley is twice that many, but those places will be filled come spring, when the fleet sails again, taking women and children with them . . . to Caledonia." He glanced towards Donuil as he added the name and then continued, speaking more briskly.

"In the meantime, until Brander arrives, we are undermanned. Half of our remaining men are scattered throughout our holdings, organizing the withdrawals, putting things in order. We would be badly at a loss, had we to fight a war at this time."

He stopped speaking, evidently waiting for me to say something. I could only shrug my shoulders. "The punishment we inflicted today should keep you safe enough for a time, at least until Brander arrives."

He nodded, agreeing with me, though I could see that he had more to say.

"Aye, Caius Merlyn, that is so, but there is more at risk here than you know." Again his eyes flicked to the men of his Council and again I had the feeling he was prodding them, somehow. "It seems that we are not the only clan thinking of moving north and east, beyond the sea. Word came to us several months ago of a fierce sea fight waged there between our galleys and those of a king who holds vast territories to the north of us. His name is Condran, and his fame as a warrior is widespread, extending far beyond the bounds of his own lands. He is aging now, but his people hold him in high regard and call themselves the Sons of Condran. You heard me speak the name to Rud, earlier."

"Aye," I nodded. "But he said he had heard no mention of these Sons of Condran."

"He did so. But Condran is aging, as I said. He is still hale enough, but his eldest son now acts as commander of Condran's forces on land, while his younger son, named Liam, like our old friend here, controls his ships. These people, unlike the Wild Ones who attacked today, know discipline. That eldest son is called Brian. And Brian's name was heard by Rud."

"But inconclusively, I believe, Sir King," I ventured.

"Aye, inconclusively, as you correctly say, but ominously, when you know all of it. The sea fight I spoke of occurred long months ago, early in the summer, and Brander's galleys were victorious, taking many captives and sinking many of Liam's vessels while capturing many others. More than a few fled to safety, nonetheless, and took word back to Condran that our folk were there in the northeastern seas. Then, mere weeks ago, word came to us from the north, sent by a friend in my employ who dwells amid Condran's folk, that Condran and Brian have been spending time with other tribes, long enemies of them and theirs: folk of the Clan MacNyall, and others of a verminous horde who dwell in the west and call themselves the Children of Garn. Alliances were forming, the message said, and a gathering of armies to stamp out the Gaels. Those whisperings seemed strangely echoed in Rud's tale, would you not agree? We are the Gaels, Caius Merlyn, we whom I know your people call the Scots. And now you know the reason for this Council gathering. You are welcome, should you care to remain, and any thoughts or ideas you might have in listening to our talk will be listened to and heeded by all here."

I nodded courteously, indicating my willingness to stay and listen, and the meeting came properly to order as Donuil and I exchanged glances and grimaces.

For the next hour or so, the Council talked and I listened, but I heard nothing that stirred my mind to life or motion, and I found myself drifting into my own thoughts more and more, digesting the implications of what was happening here and attempting to ignore the steadily increasing upheaval in my gut. I had no idea how many of Athol's people had been moved to Caledonia thus far, or how many remained here in Eire, but I knew he had dispatched three thousand men against Camulod a mere six years before. Two thousand of those, however, had perished at our hands, and such losses must have been wellnigh insupportable. I leaned forward to whisper to Donuil, asking him how many people his father ruled. He gazed at me blankly, eyebrows raised, and shrugged his big shoulders in ignorance. I sniffed, and returned to my own thoughts. If Brander were returning with three hundred men, twenty to a galley, he would bring fifteen vessels with him. Fifteen galleys seemed like a paltry fleet to move an entire people, for I had not missed the king's reference to other settlements throughout his holdings. The more I thought about that, the more it concerned me, and I leaned towards Donuil again, feeling slightly guilty, like an inattentive student, and fully expecting to be chided by the king. Donuil leaned to meet me, his ear cocked to hear what I had to say.

"Twenty men to a galley? Is that what your father said?"

"Aye," he nodded, whispering back. "Skeleton crew."

"And three hundred men? That's only fifteen galleys, nowhere near enough!"

He flashed me a grin and shook his head, holding up three fingers. "Fifty, at least," he hissed. "Each manned boat tows at least two more, empty. The larger ones tow three or four, stretched out in line astern of them. It's easy, if the weather holds."

"That's more like it. But what if they're attacked?"

"That's only half the fleet. The other fifty, fully manned, come with them halfway, to see them safely past the Condran shores, then they return. From there, Brander is safe, unless they meet an unexpected storm."

"How do you know all this?"

"My father was wrong. It started seven years ago, not five. The first two seasons, the return of the fleet was the biggest event of the year. I remember it well, because I wanted to ship with Brander that first year, but my father said I was too young. By the following year, I was preparing to go to meet you." Now one of the councilors did turn to glare back at us, and we fell silent again.

So, I thought, fifty loaded galleys at a time began to resemble a migration on a tribal scale, especially if the feat were repeated annually over seven years. That would amount to three hundred and fifty galleys, laden with folk and goods, cattle and possessions, each galley capable of shipping at least forty oarsmen and a tight-packed cargo of bodies uncaring of comfort.

As I was mulling over those numbers, the door of the chamber swung wide and Fingael strode in, his face tight with urgency. At his entry, all sound in the room was stilled, save for the clump of his shod feet. Athol rose to meet him.

"Fingael. What are you doing here?"

The young man continued to advance until he faced his father. "My regrets, Father, and I must beg your pardon. I was unable to procure your mountain goat."

"Oh? And why was that?"

"My way to the mountains was barred by a host bigger than any ever seen in these parts, I believe."

"Whose host?" Athol's voice was grim, his acceptance of his son's tidings unconditional.

Finn shook his head. "The one we heard of, I assumed. I know not who leads them, but I saw MacNyalls among them by the hundred. No mistaking those colours of theirs. And others, many others, marched under massy banners of some kind, green and yellow, with black bars descending from one side to the other."

"The Children of Garn. How far away?"

"Two days' march, perhaps longer, for their numbers restrict their speed and movement. But they weren't coming here. They cut across my path, headed to the south. That was yesterday, some time after noon. I watched them for more than an hour, but they were still crossing to my left when I crept away. I came straight back, stopping only the once to sleep for a few hours when it grew too dark to see."

"Hmm. You did well. Your news confirms what we have been discussing here. You must be tired. Go, eat and sleep and then come back to me. We have much to do."

Fingael bowed to his father and left the room without even having been aware of my presence, and from that point onwards the Council took on a palpable air of urgency. Runners should be sent out, the king decreed, to summon all his people to the stronghold, and every able-bodied man would be put to work strengthening the defenses. I watched the king handle the crisis and saw the real reason behind what Connor had called "his enduring kingship." Athol reminded me of my own father at his best, a consummate general, handling his people surely and with ease, the fullness of his confidence and competence riding his shoulders like a mantle. And as we sat listening I became sure, after a while, that no calls would be made upon my advice. Athol the King commanded now, and had no need of assistance. As the thought occurred to me, my guts twisted violently, jerking me erect, and I felt a painful surge that threatened not to be withheld. I gritted my teeth and fought the pain down until it was bearable, then I nudged Donuil and motioned with my head for him to come with me, and we quietly left the room. Athol, however, stopped us in the doorway, bidding me wait on him after the Council. I replied that I would, and left, but as I closed the door behind me another cramp clawed at my bowels and I had to fall back, my shoulders against the door as I battled to restrain my sphincter from giving way.

Shelagh was the first person Donuil and I saw as we left the Council room, and despite my immediate concern, or perhaps because of it, I saw her in great detail. She waited against the wall of the building opposite, leaning at her ease, clothed in full armour of mail shirt and leggings over strong, thick-soled boots. Her shoulders were encased in a broad iron collar, studded with decorative bosses, and deep enough in front to cover and protect her breasts. Above this collar, slung from right to left, she wore a broad leather belt from which hung a heavy sword and an array of identically hilted knives. Greater in bulk than I had ever seen her, she seemed yet smaller, somehow diminished by her warrior's garb. As she saw us, she straightened up and moved towards us. Only then did Donuil turn and discern my condition.

"Caius! What ails you?" His voice was filled with sudden tension but I was grateful for his presence of mind in sweeping up his hand to stop Shelagh's advance. She stopped at once, several paces distant, her face showing concern and puzzlement.

Whatever ailed me, it had struck with ungovernable ferocity, unmanning me completely. I felt as helpless as a young boy. "Nothing serious." I grated the words between clenched teeth, seeing his near panic. "Nothing fatal, anyway. Stomach cramps. Need a latrine, right now."

His shoulders sagged visibly in relief. "Christus! For a moment there I thought you were going to die on me. Can you walk?"

"Aye, but not far." My teeth were still tightly clenched with the effort of controlling my bowels. "I'm in dire shape, Donuil, and I'd hate to lose my dignity while your lady's watching."

By this time he was right beside me, holding my arm to brace me. "Lean on me. The king's own privy is close by, no more than twenty paces. Can you manage that?"

He helped me to Athol's private latrine, quite an elaborate affair with rails on which to perch above the hole beneath, and left me to do what I had to. I hung there for what seemed like hours, my guts twisting like snakes, prolonging my torment long after everything within me had been expelled. By the time the spasms eventually died away enough to give me confidence that I might be able to leave the noxious place, my brows and hair were wet with sweat and I knew beyond doubt that I was too ill to wait on Athol as he had requested. At length, after another age-long period of resting, preparing myself, I stood up and began to rearrange my clothes, but as I stooped over in the process, my stomach heaved and I vomited, retching in agony as my throat and abdominal muscles rebelled at this new atrocity. Dimly, as if from somewhere far off, I heard Donuil calling to me, and then his arm was about me, holding me up as I sagged against him.

"*Dia!*" I heard him say, then, "Shelagh! Cay is sick, and too heavy for me. Fetch someone strong to help me. Anyone!" I felt motion then, and blackness claimed me, until I opened my eyes again and found myself being carried into the hut I shared with Quintus, Rufio and Dedalus, whose face now loomed above me, brows creased in concern. They lowered me onto my cot, then stripped me rapidly, turning me this way and that as though I were a baby, finally wrapping me in blankets. Ded approached me shortly after that, carrying a stiff, leather bucket which he placed on the floor beside my head.

"Here," he growled. "If you have to puke again, use this. Use it to shit in, too, if you get the runs again. Benedict's building a wooden frame for it, for you to sit on. When did this start? Have you not got the sense of a boy, enough to keep you indoors when you don't feel well?"

I managed to smile at him, but I was very weak. Somehow, the thought of what he had said was amusing. I had not been sick in years, and neither had any of my fellows, apart from the infrequent unpleasantness of over-indulgence in wine. Our bodily functions, matters of simple human routine, were acts we took for granted and seldom had occasion to consider, other than in the casual performance of them. Now I could see the unsettling effect my condition had on my companions. I had to lick my lips before I could speak, and when the words emerged, they were a whisper.

"I must have eaten some bad meat. Is anyone else affected?"

Ded was frowning. "No, not like you. Cyrus threw up an hour or more ago, but he's fine now. No one else has been behaving any differently than usual." He paused. "Course, I haven't checked Athol's people."

"Cyrus," I said. "The bird. We shared a cold fowl earlier, before noon, a partridge I think, but he only ate a leg. I ate more of it, but I noticed a strange taste and threw the rest away."

His brow cleared immediately. "That's it then, you're poisoned, but at least it was self-administered. I was beginning to think one of these Outlanders had slipped something into your cup." He paused, squinting at me in speculation. "It might get worse, but I don't think you'll die. You're too damn strong and far too stubborn to go that way. Besides," he grinned for the first time since I had been brought back, "from what I heard about the way you puked and shat, the poison must be out of you by now."

I closed my eyes. "I hope so, Ded. I hope so."

During the remainder of that day and night I awoke frequently to drag myself—and there were times when the intense pains racking me made me think I would never succeed—to the bucket beneath the wooden frame Benedict had built for me to use for either of my two urgencies, and on each occasion, I remember, the room was lamplit and the bucket was empty and clean. The last time, somewhere in the deepest part of the night, Cyrus thrust his head through the doorway as I was crawling back into my cot.

"How are you, Cay? It's my watch. Can I help?" I shook my head, unable to trust my voice, and he stepped forward to collect the stinking bucket. "By the Christus, I'm glad I wasn't as hungry as you were when we started on that bird. Sleep, man, and forget all else. Things are well in hand and there's nothing for you to do or to fret about. I'll clean this and bring it back."

When I opened my eyes again it was full day, and Athol himself was standing by my cot. Somewhere outside a bird was singing, and I realized I had been listening to it for some time. Athol saw I was awake and leaned forward, pressing his hand against my forehead.

"The fever's broken," he said. "How do you feel?"

"Better." I had to work my mouth to gain enough saliva to wet my lips with my tongue, for they felt as though they had been stuck together. "I hear a bird singing."

His eyes crinkled. "Aye, you do, and it sings for you. It's a blackbird."

"A blackbird?"

"Aye, with a wondrous power of song. We call it a merlen."

I drew a deep breath, filling my lungs cautiously, aware that I was no longer in pain, yet expecting my outraged stomach muscles to cramp again immediately. "What time of day is it?" I asked him.

"Late afternoon, nigh on evening. The sun has been shining all day long."

I was shocked. "You mean I've slept the day away?"

The king's smile grew broader. "This day, and yesterday, and the day before that. You have had some kind of fever, from the poison in your system. But it's past now, and you look stronger already. You'll be up and moving again by tomorrow, I'm sure."

Alarmed by his words, I moved to sit up, but the weight of the blankets that covered me kept me pinned to the bed. I was completely without strength.

"You're weak now," Athol said, as though he had read my mind. "But that will pass quickly, as soon as you have some solid food in your body.

Welcome back, Caius Merlyn. Your friends will be happy, and they are loyal, honest friends. Not a man among them but is genuine in his love and admiration for you. Not a bad word, or a shallow affection for their Commander in any one of them. I will send Dedalus in as I leave, and I shall come back tomorrow early. You and I have much to discuss." He turned to leave and I sought to stop him.

"Wait! Sir King—"

He turned back to me, smiling. "No more 'Sir King,' Merlyn. My name is Athol. Only those I govern treat me as a king, and then only when I am being King. To my friends, I am but a man like them. I have learned much of you from your own people these past few days, while you lay sweating, muttering to yourself. And I have spent long hours with my errant son Donuil, while he, too, told me of his love for you, the love of a warrior for a Champion and Leader. I have been much impressed and will be honoured if, from this time forth, you think of me as a friend." He left then, before I could summon a response.

Moments later Dedalus strode into the room, sweeping aside the screen around my bed. Until he moved it, I had been unaware of the thing. Now I gazed at it, noting its construction of woven wicker and the bright colours that adorned it.

"Where did that come from? That screen."

Dedalus glanced at me and continued folding the device, leaning it eventually against the wall by an open, unshuttered window. Finally he clapped his hands together as though dusting them and turned to face me. "From the Lady Shelagh. She came to see you the first day, before dark, shortly after Donuil and the big fellow, Cullum, brought you back. The next morning she came again, bringing this and an army of women. Erected the screen to give you privacy, she said, and cleaned out this hovel from roof to floor, then opened all the shutters. Made me promise to leave them open, too, even at night, no matter what the weather; claimed the clean air would do you good, as long as you were well wrapped up against the chill. Perhaps it worked, perhaps not. I only know that Paulus and I almost froze our arses for the past two nights. You hungry?"

Was I? With the question, I was suddenly ravenous, the mere thought of food triggering a flood of saliva. "Aye," I said.

"Good. I'll be back." He started to leave, then stopped. "You need to piss or anything?" At my headshake he nodded and then quickly left.

I lay there in the sun-bright room, looking at the long, afternoon shadows from the window and listening to the bird outside, the merlen. Three days I had been sick! The thought spurred me, and I made another effort to raise myself, this one less feeble, but no more successful than the first. Subsiding, I lay still for a time, gathering my strength, then loosened the tight-wrapped blankets that swathed me and tried again. This time, by gripping the edge of my mattress and using it for leverage, I managed to sit upright, swinging my legs free of the side of the bed. I was naked, I discovered, as my feet fell to the floor as though my legs were made of wood and I sat there, swaying and clutching at the edge of the mattress. A wave of giddiness almost overcame me, but I fought it off and forced myself to breathe deeply, willing the room to stop gyrating. It did, after a short time, and I sat motionless, gathering my strength again before I attempted to stand up. Then, when I felt I had my mind and body under my control once more, I stood, and swayed, and fell, twisting my body at the moment when I knew I must fail, and managing to sprawl facedown on my right side across the bed, rather than crashing to the floor.

"Sweet Jesus, there's no leaving you alone, is there? You're not fit to be trusted on your own at all. Here, wait a moment." I felt Ded haul me bodily until I lay where he wanted me, properly positioned on the cot. He then covered me up, tucking in the blankets before gripping me beneath the armpits and hauling me up into a sitting position, after which he wrapped a soft, warm woollen shawl about my bare shoulders. I protested at being treated like an old man, and he growled.

"No one's treating you like an old man, but you're a sick man and you might have killed yourself, eating that rubbish the way you did. Bad meat! By the Christus, Merlyn, even a child knows enough not to eat tainted meat, especially fowl!"

"It didn't all taste bad, Ded. The leg Cyrus ate didn't taste bad to him. Am I to live without eating meat? What's in that bowl?"

"Meat, but good meat, and there's little of it. Mainly it's broth, with onions, garlic, mushrooms, some cheese, some green things and a generous taste of salt. And bread, floating on the top. Get it into you. Here, I'll hold the spoon, otherwise you'll spill more than you sup."

"Cheese?" I said, as he began to spoon the broth.

He paused and grinned at me. "That's what I thought, too," he said. "Until I tasted it. It's some kind of hard goat's cheese, and they grate it into powder, then mix it into foods of one kind or another. It's wondrous stuff, you'll love it."

I did, and as I ate and the flavours of salt and garlic and that Eirish cheese mingled on my palate I felt the strength flow back into my body. When the bowl was empty, I lay back, savouring the flavours that lingered in my mouth.

"You're right, Ded. That cheese is wondrous stuff. Now I need to piss."

"Well, your throne's still there. Here, I'll help you." He crossed to replace the bowl on the table and then came back and helped me to rise. It was much easier this time, and I barely had to lean on him as I took the two paces to the bucket and relieved myself, leaning on the frame and smelling the strong, ammoniac stink of my own urine. I even smell sick, I thought. Then, as I was finishing, I asked him if the bucket and its frame had been moved closer to the bed.

"Moved from where?"

"From where it was. It was much farther from the bed than it is now, that first night I was here."

He shook his head. It had not been moved, he told me, since the moment he had brought it into the room on that first occasion. Benedict had built the frame and placed it over the bucket. Besides, he pointed out, there was no room for the thing to have been placed anywhere else. I could see the truth of that for myself even as he said it, and was left shaking my head over the memories of the struggle I had had on several occasions to reach the spot from where I had lain. He helped me turn and supported me again for the two steps back to the bed. I was glad to arrive. As he tucked me in again, flat on my back, Paulus, Philip and Benedict crowded in at the doorway to

see me. I waved to them and smiled and they seemed delighted at my talent.
Ded chased them away. I noticed that the sunlight had vanished and that
the sky beyond the window had turned a deep, dark bluish grey. Ded crossed
to the door and stopped to look back at me.

"It's getting dark. I'll bring some lamps."

I was asleep when and if he did.

By the time Athol arrived to visit me again the following morning, I was up
and fully dressed, wearing a quilted tunic. The sunshine of the previous day
had given way to overcast skies, although there seemed to be no rain clouds
threatening for the time being. I felt ten times stronger than I had the day
before, and had broken my fast on another bowl of the delicious broth,
brought to me this time by Donuil and Shelagh.

I had watched them as I ate, feeding myself, so much was I improved,
and it was plain to see that matters between them had progressed apace.
They touched each other frequently, each going to great lengths to do so,
and to make the contact appear casual or accidental. They were concerned
for me, I could see, and glad to see me so much improved, but a blind man
could have seen that they had eyes, in truth, only for each other. Love had
visited Athol's kingdom, it appeared, while I lay sick. They talked brightly to
me, promising to return again, and soon left, and I watched them from my
window, walking hand in hand now that they thought themselves unobserved.
A short time after they had gone, the king arrived, and we sat together at
the table beside the open window, where, after the pleasantries concerning
my improved condition, Athol came straight to what lay on his mind.

"The army that Finn saw lies quartered in the south. I believe their intent
was to join with the Wild Ones, but those animals could not wait, or would
not, and hoped to wipe us out before their allies arrived."

"Then why are the newcomers waiting now?"

"I don't know, but I suspect they are waiting for others to join them."

"Others? From where? Have you had further news from your spy among
the Sons of Condran?"

He shook his head. "No, but I sent men to mingle with the people already
there in the south. None of them saw any sign of Brian or his forces. The
warning I received was that Brian and his tribe were to ally themselves with
the MacNyalls and the vermin of Garn. That has not happened, yet the other
two are here and have not moved against us. That makes me suspect that
Brian has been delayed for some reason, but has sent word of it. Otherwise
there would be no question of their waiting."

"And what could that reason be? You suspect he has waited to engage
Brander and his fleet?"

Athol's headshake was emphatic. "No," he growled. "Brian is a land warrior, not a seaman. Besides, his brother Liam does not lack for men to fill
his galleys, especially now, when he has so few galleys to fill. No, that's not
the reason. Even had they the will, Condran's brats no longer have the
strength to tackle Brander. I fear something else, something different . . ."

"Like what? Have you any suspicions?"

Again Athol shook his head. "None that I can define, but the uncertainty
has made up my mind on one thing." He paused, tugging at the beard beneath his lower lip, and I waited. At length he straightened his shoulders and

spoke again, looking me straight in the eye. "You talked, the other night, of your plans for the child, to make him High King of Britain." I said nothing, waiting still. "A great part of his task—the greatest part, as I understood it, listening to you talk—will be to unite his people against the invader, the Saxons who are chewing at your shores, is this not so?" I nodded. "Aye. It could not have escaped your attention, I suppose, that what I plan for my people in the land you call Caledonia is exactly what the Saxons are attempting to achieve in Britain?"

"No, it had not passed me by."

"And how do you feel about that?"

I shrugged. "Were I a Caledonian Pict, it would move me to defy you. But I am not. I am a Briton, from the land beneath the great Wall built by Hadrian to keep the Picts locked out of Britain. The Wall is useless now, ruined and overrun, but the Picts are still a threat to us. Should you succeed in occupying Caledonia, coming to terms in whatever way you must with these same Picts, we would have a friend and ally thereafter beyond the Wall. How could I be aught but pleased? I have thought about it, Athol, this colonization and conquest you propose, and it would be to my advantage, solving a great part of our problem at no cost to me. But it has also made me consider something that could never have occurred to me before this time . . ." Now it was he who sat silent, waiting for me to gather my thoughts.

"Seeing your dilemma through your eyes has taught me that my judgments are too often based on too little knowledge, an old fault of mine I thought I had outgrown. My cousin Uther once accused me of being overly judgmental, and the accusation caused me grief, but I came to see he was right. I saw that I had been a prig, and I set out to change that. I will never know if I have been successful, though I live to be a toothless old man. But I feel I know your people now, thanks mainly to your son, and will never again think of them as Outlanders, as I did before. You and yours are now, and will remain forever, people like my own, with lives to lead, and dreams, ideals and families you love. Your planned invasion has the appeal of logic, when listened to in the terms you used to me. I think, now, that for the sake of the boy and of the king he will become, I have to find some accommodation in Britain, among the Saxons. Not all the Saxons—I am not completely mad. Like your own Eirish folk they come from many tribes and clans, some good, some bad. But some of them have been in Britain for many years, even generations. So I ask myself, have they the right to be there, to hold the land they have farmed for years? I confess, I have no answer for my own question, but I am highly aware, at last, of the question's importance."

He looked at me long and hard before responding, then nodded and took up an earlier point. "We have no strategy for occupying all of this Caledonia. But when we gain a foothold there, my grandson will profit by it. I want you to take him home with you to Britain as soon as you are well enough to travel."

I blinked at him, astonished, as he continued. "Winter has not yet come, and Brander not yet arrived, so there is still time, and opportunity, for you to make a safe passage home, rather than sit here until spring and find yourself trapped. I said that I had no idea what might have delayed Brian, but sitting here listening to you talk of invasions and Saxons, I have become convinced there is a possibility that he is on his way directly from the north.

I told you his father Condran's lands are enormous. So are the numbers that he rules. It came to me, listening to you, that there are many lesser tribes in the coastal territories between his land and ours. Condran, and Brian, control no harbours at this time, south of their own strongholds. If they have decided to move against us, sending their allies down from the northwest, southward through the interior, it would provide a perfect opportunity for Brian to conquer all those lesser tribes between him and us while free of any threat from his own western allies. That would delay him, but it would also strengthen him greatly, providing harbours for his brother Liam all the way down to our river entrance.

"If I'm right, and that is what he's about, then we are plunged into war for a long time to come. We are in any case, with the MacNyalls and Garn about our ears, but this of the coastal harbours could make all the difference between victory and defeat. By now, Brander will be far south of Condran's coast, and he should arrive within the week. His escort will have turned back towards Caledonia, having seen him safely past all threat of interference. I need those galleys here, however, not in the northern isles, so I have ordered six of my swiftest galleys here to bring them home, where there is work for them. If those six ships leave now, within the next few days, before Brander arrives, Brian will not know they have gone, and we'll retain a chance of setting him on his rump in the months to come with a surprise attack of our own." He paused, assessing my reaction. "Six galleys will go out; three pairs in tandem, in the hope that one pair, at least, might escape attack by Liam's remaining vessels—for you may be sure Liam will be following Brander, in support of his brother, as soon as his way is cleared by the removal of the remainder of our fleet. One pair of my messengers will escort you, with the child and your men and horses. They will leave you safe on your own coast, then make their way northward. You have something to say. What is it?"

My frustration almost made me stammer. "We can't . . . It's not . . . How can we go? We lost the craft we used to bring our horses over. We would have to build another to replace it."

He dismissed that with a wave of his hand. "Already foreseen and resolved. We have such a craft, or Liam does: a small galley, a toy ship he has been building for his daughter Shelagh. Not a fighting ship; more of a pleasure vessel, if you can believe such a thing. It is broad in its middle, much more so than our war galleys, and draws little water, gaining balance from its extra breadth and from a weighted keel. For your purposes, however, it will suit perfectly, since it is unfinished; undecked, I mean. It will accommodate your horses and your people. Donuil has told me how you shipped the last time. This craft will be easier to tow, and more seaworthy. Our builders are fitting temporary decking now, and that should take no more than a day. You could sail as early as tomorrow or the following day."

"And what does Liam have to say about that? It is his galley, after all; his gift for his own daughter."

Athol sat straighter, squaring his shoulders.

"That is what I wanted to discuss with you, the night of our Council gathering, when you fell sick. Because of the lack of time, I have proceeded in the hope that you will take no ill of my suggestions and the arrangements I have made without your knowledge." He smiled briefly, a swift, wintry lightening of his sombre face. "Much has occurred while you lay ill."

"Hmm. I had noticed some of it," I murmured, thinking of Donuil and his evident, newfound love. "Tell me."

"Liam will go with you to Britain. No, let me finish!" I swallowed the retort that sprang to my mouth. "So, too, will Donuil and Shelagh. Those two will be wed. Liam and I had decided on that long since, when Donuil first went away, but now the pair of them have arrived at that decision on their own."

"I guessed at that," I told him. "But this of Liam going to Britain sounds foolish. Why, and to what end? What would he do in Britain?"

"He would live, safe under your protection, as will my grandson. I have no confidence that I could say the same were he to stay behind, here in my lands, with enemies the like of which we face swarming all over. Liam Twistback is no warrior, but beyond doubt he is the most valuable of all my counselors, his wealth aside. He has abilities and skills no other of my people can provide: the breeding—the *selective*, skillful breeding—of livestock; the organizing of regular, useful traffic between our outposts in the northern isles ... We think, the mass of us, in terms of warfare and of conquest as a means to ensure our safety to raise our families and live our lives as simply as we can. Liam thinks in terms of trade and the means of *improving* life. I can't afford to lose those strengths of his, not when we are on the very brink of needing them more than ever before, in our new home."

"I understand that, Athol, but why send him to Britain? Why not directly to your new holdings in the north?"

He inhaled, then smiled again, without mirth. "Because they are so new. Some of our people are already living there, as you know; some, but nowhere near enough. And their life is harsh, far harsher than here, where at least we know the land and its problems. There in the northeast, everything is different. The islands are mountainous, bare on the high slopes, the valley choked with forests. The earth is fertile, though, in places, but such places have to be first cleared, then broken to the plough by hand, and shelter from the weather has to be built by hand, of stone and sod. Such work does not yet come easily to our men."

"What about creatures? Game, and the like?"

"Deer, on most islands, wolves, bears; goats and some mountain sheep on the heights. Very few cattle, and those only on the largest of the isles. And you have placed your finger on the need for Liam's skills. Donuil steered my thinking, when he told me of your troubles with your horses, the difficulty of sending them by sea. We face the same problems. We have shipped very few beasts with our people. Now, with this war threatening us, our cattle here are at grave risk and we'll lose most of them no matter what the outcome. That is why I have decided to do what I must, if you will grant your aid. Liam's breeding stock, his prime animals, goats, sheep and cattle, are too valuable to risk losing. If we are to save them, we must ship them out, soon. To do that, we'll have to build vessels to carry them, and now that can be done, using Liam's small galley as a model. But no matter how quickly we build, the winter storms will be upon us before they can set out, and the journey to the northeast through winter seas would be impossible. Far safer, I thought, though still hazardous, to ship the beasts across the narrower sea to your lands—to some part of your holdings close by the sea, where no one lives, and where Liam Twistback can perform his wonders breeding new stock. His closeness to the sea will mean my galleys can remain in touch with him and you. Then, when the weather changes, not next year but the following one, my galleys can remove the young stock in safety, shipping them north to where our people are. Do you follow me?"

I nodded. "Aye, and it makes good sense." I drew a deep breath. "Would Liam join you in the north eventually?"

"Of course. As soon as we are settled and the wars are done. I'll need his counsel then far more than I need it even now, providing I'm still alive. And even if I'm dead by then, my folk will need him."

"And what of Donuil and Shelagh? What plans have you in mind for them?"

Athol grinned this time. "Think what you ask, man! What plans does any man, king or father, dare make for a newly lovestruck pair? Donuil is your man above all. What was the word? *Adjutant?* He speaks of being your adjutant some day. I asked him what that meant and what he told me mystified me, and yet, for all my lack of understanding, I found myself approving of the notion. He will learn much that is unknown to us in Éire, and his ward, my grandson, will learn thereby from him." He paused, and then his tone became almost musing. "Apart from that," he said, "young people being what they are, Donuil and Shelagh will have sons. It would be good for our young High King to have cousins to grow up with, don't you think?"

I nodded, pleased by the thought, and then considered all else he had said.

"Athol," I said, eventually, "I can see no objections to your scheme, providing we can have the agreement of Uther's people. It's their land you'll be on, not mine. Camulod lies too far in from the sea to suit your needs."

"Will that be possible, to gain such agreement?"

I thought about that. "It ought to be simply done. None of their people live there, south of Glevum, and the town itself lies ruined. Their relationship with Camulod has always been as allies. I knew most of the elders, when Uther's father was alive, though I have not set foot in the Pendragon lands since Uther became king. I'll visit them again when I return, and seek their agreement, based upon your own promise and mine that Liam's presence will be but a short one—two or three years."

He nodded and stood up. "No more than that. And now I have to meet with Finn and Connor. My thanks, Caius Merlyn. You'll have no cause for regrets in years to come."

"I don't doubt that, King Athol. I, too, should be abroad now. I've been too much out of touch these past few days. I need to inform my men of what's afoot and ready them for the journey home. You have not told them anything, I presume?"

"Nothing at all. No one has. I forbade mention of it until I should have the time to speak with you. You might have refused me, after all . . ."

"What about Donuil and the others?"

"Oh, they all know, and are already making their preparations to depart. The woman Turga, whom you brought to Connor that first day, is still the baby's nurse, ferociously attached to the child. She is a changed woman from the half-witted creature that was led ashore from Connor's galley. She is comely now, and at peace in her mind, still young enough to bear more children of her own. Food and rest, some kindness from our own, and great love for the child she suckles have made a new being out of her. She will go with you, too. It seems to me the morning tide the day after tomorrow might not be too soon."

"It is very soon, Athol."

"Aye, but our enemies could well be about our ears before then. As it is, every day free from attack surprises me. Still, most of our people are here now, safe behind our walls, their villages abandoned. The swine of Garn and MacNyall will be hard put to stamp us out."

"You think they might succeed?"

Athol smiled and grasped my arm. "That, my friend, lies in the dominion of the gods. But I intend to remind those same gods where their loyalties should lie. We shall meet again some day, you and I, when this is over."

I walked with him to the door and watched him walk away, escorted on either side by Fingael and big Cullum, who had been outside together, awaiting him. As he went, I wondered what the future might hold and whether he and I would ever meet again, and then my thoughts focused on Finn, who had not acknowledged my presence as I emerged from the hut with his father. That young man was no friend of me or mine, no matter how his father felt. They disappeared from view around the corner of another hut, and I re-entered mine, flexing my right arm against the pressure of my left fist and thinking I would have little time for exercise or training in the days that lay ahead. I called through the open window to Dedalus, who was practising formation maneuvers with the rest of our companions in the grassy space behind our camp. While he made his way towards me, I thought briefly about the woman Turga, young Arthur's nurse, whose name I had not known. I had forgotten her completely, assuming that she had served her purpose and been released somehow, though where, and to what end, I could not imagine when I brought my mind to it. Now I realized that I would not have known her had I seen her, which led me to assume that I must have, at some time during my stay here. I resolved to visit her and take her measure, since she was as important to the child Arthur as he was to me. And then Ded entered and our preparations for departure from Eire began.

I told him briefly about the tenor of what Athol and I had decided, and was only mildly surprised that he listened solemnly and merely nodded when I had finished, accepting all I had said without demur. Our discussion thereafter was equally brief, the subject matter being simple and soon dealt with; having decided to return to Britain, there was little for us to do in preparation. Athol's people were the ones who would have to make the necessary arrangements. It merely remained to us to advise our own men and those few others who would travel with us, to pack our possessions, and to present ourselves on the wharf at the appointed time on the chosen day.

As soon as Dedalus left, I draped myself in my heavy cloak and went looking for the woman Turga, determined to set my neglect of her aright and to thank her for her assistance in saving the baby Arthur. Even as I phrased that thought, however, I recognized its towering inadequacy. She alone it was who had saved the baby's life, nourishing him from her teats. All of us who cared for the child were forever in her debt, for the strongest man among us would have been powerless to save young Arthur's life, lacking her contribution. And I had ignored her completely since my arrival here in Eire.

I walked cautiously at first upon leaving my hut, recalling my weakness

of the previous day, but I was soon striding confidently, exulting in the growing awareness that my incapacity seemed to have disappeared completely
overnight. I saw Connor's wife, Margaret, standing by the open door of her
house, talking with another woman, and I made my way directly to her. She
blushed deep red and smiled at me nervously as I approached and stopped,
and remembering how agonizingly shy she was when faced with strangers, I
smiled and nodded amiably as I greeted her, inquiring slowly and with great
courtesy if she knew where I might find the woman Turga. Her eyes immediately flew wide in confusion and she darted a glance towards her companion, but before she could say anything, the other turned to me, meeting my
gaze boldly, almost defiantly, as though challenging me.

"I am Turga. What do you wish of me?"

The words were strange-sounding, but intelligible, a rough blend of the
local Celtic tongue of Cornwall and the liquid, rippling Erse of Athol's people, and I realized that Turga, in her few months here among strangers, had
adapted to their ways and to their language more aptly than my own Latin-
speaking soldiers could have. But that awareness was swept aside even as it
occurred to me, in the face of the new realisation that swept me immediately
afterwards. My shock was so great that for several moments I stood gaping
like a fish, bereft of words or any kind of sane reaction. I had known I could
not remember what she looked like, but I would never have recognised this
woman who faced me now as the half-mad wretch I had found keening by
her murdered child in front of her ruined house. This woman was a virago,
tall and strong, with a commanding presence and a haughty, truculent air
about her. She carried her head high and her breasts were proud and thrusting—full of milk, I realized belatedly, as I felt my eyes drawn to them and
found myself unable to resist the impulse to stare at them. She stood gazing
at me directly, making no move to avert her eyes or her body, or to assist
me in my confusion. Finally I found my tongue and looked her straight in
the eye.

"Forgive me," I said, speaking in her own tongue, almost stammering in
my discomfort, cursing myself for not even knowing how to address her. "I
did not know . . . I came to thank you . . . for the boy."

A tiny frown ticked between her brows and her pale blue eyes narrowed.
"What do you mean, thank me? What did I do?"

"You saved his life."

"Oh, that." Her tone said that was insignificant. "Why now?"

"Why—?" The astonishment on my face must have been eloquent, for
she took pity on me, although her voice remained heavy with hostility.

"That was months ago, and you came here days ago. Why do you seek
me now?"

Poor Margaret was hovering in an agony of apprehension, her eyes flickering from one to the other of us as if afraid we might quarrel and come to
blows there on her doorstep. I took a half step backwards and came to attention, bringing my clenched right fist to my left breast in a crisp, military
salute.

"I was at fault in that, Domina," I said, speaking easily now that I had
begun. "I should have come first to you, to give you my thanks, and those
of my people, for your services to the child who is my heir. Without you, he
would have died where we found him, starving among helpless men whose

food was useless to him. We could not have saved his life, for all our so-called strength and power. You alone did that, and for that service I, and all my people, will be eternally grateful. That should have been my message to you, directly and in person, on the day we first arrived. That it was not so is something I shall always regret, since it reflects an ingratitude that was not really there. I know not what I was thinking of, to be so inconsiderate and uncivil . . . so ill-mannered . . . but I have no excuse. I can only ask your forgiveness and forbearance, and I stand here now to do precisely that."

As I spoke, I had watched the expression on her face change from haughtiness to puzzlement, then to a stirring anger as she began to think I was mocking her, and then finally to one of . . . what? It was not disdain, nor was it scorn, rather it was a combination of skepticism and barely disguised impatience with such foolishness. And still the small frown creased the center of her brows. Margaret, in the meantime, merely gazed at me wide-eyed with amazement at my sudden fluency.

"Hmm!" My mind scrambled to assign a description to Turga's grunt, but before I could define it, she spoke on. "You'll want to see him, I suppose, since he's your heir?" There was only the slightest emphasis on the last word, and once again, she left me wondering what her tone entailed. I nodded, suddenly afraid to say any more.

"If I may," I managed to say.

She turned away to Margaret. "I'll come back later, and I'll bring the salve." She glanced back at me, over her shoulder. "Come, then."

I followed her wordlessly to a hut three buildings down from where Margaret stood, still watching us, and she bustled inside and disappeared, leaving the door open behind her for me to follow. I stopped just beyond the threshold, blinking my eyes against the sudden darkness, and then, as my eyes adjusted, I saw the child's crib, a plain wooden affair on rockers, close by the fire that smoldered in the hearth. The woman was bent over in front of the fire, stirring the fuel to angry life, and a shower of sparks whirled upwards into the rough stone flue.

"He's asleep," she said, over her shoulder. "You can look at him, but don't wake him. He's not due for feeding for another hour."

I hitched my cloak back over my shoulders and crossed to the crib, where I bent forward, peering down at the baby who slept there. He was naked, except for a breechclout, and the unmistakable smell rising from it told me it needed to be changed. Turga's sigh startled me because it was so near. She had approached behind me and stood gazing down with me.

"He's a smelly little beast," she said. "A typical boy, all shit and shouting. Here, sit."

She held a three-legged stool in one hand, and now she placed it beside me. I mumbled a word of thanks and lowered myself to the seat, and she moved away again, back to the fireplace, where she piled several blocks of some kind of fuel on the fire.

"What is that stuff?" I asked. She twisted to look around at me, then grunted.

"Peat, they call it. They burn it all the time, here. They dig it up from the ground and dry it, then burn it. When I first came here, I couldn't stand the smell of it. Now I barely notice it. If he smells too rank, you can come and sit over here." She had a strange voice, for a woman, deep and gruff, and yet I sensed a tenderness there that her gruffness denied.

"No," I said, "I'm fine here. Do you . . . do you know who I am?"

The look she threw me was utterly sardonic. "Merlyn," she said. "Merlyn of Camulod, no? Like Uther of Camulod. Is he kin of yours?"

"He was," I replied. "He's dead. But he was never Uther of Camulod. He was Uther of Cambria, Uther Pendragon. He seldom came to Camulod."

She stood staring at me now, her face cold, her voice flint-hard. "Seldom came to Cornwall, either, the black whoreson, but he killed my man and my children, and Uther of Camulod was the only name I ever heard him called. I hope he died badly."

"He did," I said, chastened by her hatred of my cousin. "He died the day I first met you."

Now she frowned, clearly perplexed. "What are you saying? I never saw you before you came here."

"You did, Turga, but you don't remember it. I found you kneeling on the ground outside your house in Cornwall, mourning your family. Your baby was newborn. That's why I thought of you when we found Arthur starving. His mother was dead, and I knew your baby was dead. He needed milk and you needed to give suck. That's why we came back for you. You have no memory at all of that?"

She shook her head, her frown deepening. "No . . . or only very vaguely. The first memory I have is of feeding the child—this child, Arthur—by a fire on a beach. I didn't know where or who I was. Later, when we had crossed the sea, I remembered my own family, my man and my little daughter—" Her eyes filled with sudden tears and she wiped them away with the back of her hand, but her face remained expressionless. She drew a great, deep, sudden breath. "So, this boy . . ." She waved her hand towards the crib. "He is your *heir*, you say. Is that the word? What does it mean? Is he your son?"

"No, he is my nephew, and my cousin. His mother was my wife's sister and his father's mother was the daughter of my grandfather's sister. That sounds complex, but it is the simple truth. He is bound to me by family ties in two ways." I thought it might be unwise to name his father at that time. Turga blinked at me.

"And what do you intend to do with him?"

"I'll take him home, to Camulod."

"And me? What will you do with me?"

"Do with you? I'll do nothing with you. You are free to do whatever you wish."

"What if I wish to stay with the boy?"

"Then you shall. I was hoping that you would, and I suppose I had assumed you would. He's nursing still, is he not?"

Her face had relaxed, and now her voice sounded slightly less hostile. "Aye, he is, and will be for another year before he's weaned, although he's bigger and stronger than most." She crossed back to where I sat and stood close to me, looking down at the sleeping infant, and when next she spoke her voice was softer yet again, as though she were speaking to herself alone. "I saved his life, you said. But he saved mine, too. We are close bound, this child and I, and I would kill to keep him safe and by my side." She turned to look at me. "*Will* kill . . . so if you have thoughts of taking him away from me, best kill me now."

I shook my head. "Turga, I have no slightest thought of separating you from him. The boy is orphaned. You are the only mother that he has, and he needs you. Therefore, I need you, too, to care for him and keep him safe from harm. There is a place for you with him in Camulod, and you will be happy there, at peace. What? What is it?"

She was looking at me strangely. "You tell me the answer to that question, Merlyn of Camulod, because there's more to this than I can see. A babe's a babe, and there are countless others to be found where it came from. But here we have a baby causing great concern among grown men and soldiers, warriors and kings."

I shrugged, accepting and acknowledging her insight. "He will be a king in Britain, in his own right, and he is grandson to Athol Mac Iain. He is a very special boy."

"And you? You must be a very special man, to be his guardian."

"No," I sighed, shaking my head. "I'm merely his cousin and his uncle both, but I am sworn to see to the raising of him, in memory of his . . . mother." That was not strictly true, but better, I thought, than stirring up questions on his paternity. She might have asked me about that then, but that was when the boy awoke and voiced his own displeasure at his smell and his condition.

"*Dia!*" she said, and bustled away to where a wooden bucket filled with water sat in a corner by the door. She picked it up effortlessly, swaying with it slightly so that the slopping contents barely spilled as she carried it to the fireplace, where she poured the contents into a deep, blackened metal pot with a semicircular, iron bucket handle. Then, carefully and deliberately, she settled the heavy pot among the coals of the fire, twisting it and testing its balance until she was satisfied that it would not tip over. "Here," she said. "Watch this and don't let it spill over."

I moved my stool over to the low fire, where I could now see that the pot sat supported on an arrangement of flat stones that had been buried and hidden by the coals, and as Turga picked up the howling infant, I kept one eye on the iron pot while watching her openly and admiringly as she tended to the child.

The soiled breechclout was disposed of quickly, loosened and removed and thrown into another wooden bucket before I had had time to see how it was fastened. That done, she seized the child by his ankles, holding them easily in one hand while she lifted and twisted him gently, cleaning his caked and soiled nether regions with another cloth before throwing that, too, into the bucket. She showed no repugnance as she performed the unpleasant task, and watching her, it occurred to me for the first time that this was a commonplace thing in a woman's life, that all mothers and nurses must do daily for their helpless charges. The realization, new as it was, surprised me and filled me with a novel admiration. I had performed the same task, when I had first found the child abandoned in the birney that had borne us out to sea, but I had done so merely because I had seen no alternative, and the entire exercise had sickened me, with its stench and foul stickiness. Now I watched it done with dispatch and the confidence of long practise and found it fascinating. In moments, it seemed, the child was clean again and had stopped wailing. Turga half turned in my direction, glancing at the pot on the fire, then brought the boy to me.

"Here, hold him while I get his bath ready." I took him in my arms, holding him against my quilted tunic, but ready to turn him away the moment he showed any sign of pissing on my tunic as he had on my armour. He blinked up at me, then his features twisted into a tiny scowl and he began to wail again.

"He's hungry, the brat," Turga said, not even glancing at us. She had wrapped a rag around the metal handle and lifted the pot from the fire, holding it away from her as she carried it to the only table in the small room where she tipped it, using another rag to hold the fire-heated bottom as she poured water into a large, shallow basin that had been hollowed from a wide section of log. She tested the warmth of the water with her elbow—something I had never seen anyone do before—and then she set down the water pot beside the fire again and took the child from me. He stopped howling as soon as she lowered him into the tepid water and I moved to stand beside her as she bathed him, holding her left hand behind his head as she washed him with a soft cloth held in the other. His eyes seemed enormous, and I watched in amazement as he kicked and splashed, his tiny limbs jerking reflexively in the freedom of the warm water.

"He's swimming," I said, hearing the amazement in my own voice. "He was swimming in the sea, when I went after him the day they threw him overboard. I didn't see it until now."

"That's silly, babies can't swim." Turga did not even glance at me. "He's splashing, that's all. He likes the warm water. Don't you, you little ruffian?" She released the washing cloth and tickled the baby's ribs, and he smiled up at her and gurgled, kicking harder. She scooped water over him gently for several more moments, then took up the cloth again and wiped his face and head, and I laughed at the way he screwed his eyes shut but made no signs of protest. Finally she picked him from the water in both hands and dangled him above the surface, shaking him gently to dislodge the water that still clung to him, and nodded towards a thick roll of cloth on the tabletop.

"Hand me that towel."

She wrapped him warmly, drying the top of his head with soft, gentle movements, and then removed a small, circular box from a pocket in her robe. She twisted it open to reveal some kind of unguent, pale lilac in colour and smelling strangely familiar, then undid the wrappings of the towel and hoisted him again by his ankles, smearing a thin covering of the fragrant stuff over his buttocks and into the deep creases between them and around his groin.

"Lavender," she said, filling my mind instantly with recognition of the scent. "Replaces the stink for a while, and stops him from getting sores and rashes." Another, fresh, breechclout appeared in her hands as though by magic, and within moments the child was covered and securely wrapped again and I was holding him, moving to sit again on the three-legged stool by the fire. Gazing into the child's face, I was aware that Turga stood close by, gazing down at me. I looked up at her.

"What are you thinking?" she asked. I shrugged, smiling.

"That I've been foolish. I have learned more about infants in the past half hour than I have learned in all my life till now . . . And I was wondering how anything so small and helpless as this babe might ever grow to be a man, a warrior, and a king."

Turga said nothing at first, merely gazing at me with a speculative look that I could not define, and knowing she would speak when she was ready, I looked closely at her for the first time since meeting her earlier. She was a handsome woman, I decided, though large and somewhat coarse-featured, and I estimated her age as somewhere in the middle twenties. Large-breasted, as a wet nurse ought to be, and full-hipped, she had broad shoulders to support those breasts, and I knew her legs, beneath the long, plain homespun robe she wore, would be firm and muscular, heavy and strong. Her hair was dark brown but otherwise indeterminate in colour, and her eyes, evenly spaced and very slightly protuberant, were a pale, startling blue in the swarthiness of her weathered face. The pores on her nose were clearly visible from where I sat. As I examined her, trying not to stare too obviously, she pursed her lips and raised her hand to one breast. I saw the dark, wet discoloration of discharged milk beneath her finger.

"I need my stool. It's time for him to feed."

Flustered, I rose and she took the boy from me as she sat down. I did not know what to do then, whether to stay or to remain. She made the decision for me without embarrassment, adjusting the front of her gown and easing a swollen nipple out to where the boy could reach it. He needed no guide, and began to guzzle noisily. She leaned her head back slightly and closed her eyes and the skin of her face seemed to smooth itself as she drew a deep breath and then released it.

"When will we leave for Britain?"

"Soon now, before winter sets in." I was gazing at the suckling boy. "Athol will tell us when."

She opened her eyes again and looked up at me, cupping one hand protectively over the child's head. "The boy would do well here, with Athol's folk. Children are welcome here, and loved. Will he fare equally in this place you come from, this Camulod?"

I nodded, feeling a smile tugging at me. "Aye, he will, and better . . . So will you, Turga."

She nodded, her face expressionless. "So be it, then. We'll go. But bear one thing in mind, always. He may be yours, and may inherit all you have, but he is mine, as well, as I am his, and harm will come to him only after I am dead, for I'll kill, or die trying to kill, any who threaten him."

"Then I'll lie dead beside you, Turga, for I have sworn the same oath."

She looked at me, and for the first time, her lips twitched in what might have been the beginnings of a smile. "Good," she said. "That's good. You do your part for him, and I will do mine, and he'll be well protected. And perhaps he will live to become the king you wish him to be."

I stooped and took her free hand, raising it to my lips, and she watched me quizzically, making no move to withdraw it. "I promise you, Turga, no matter what may transpire in the future, no matter where young Arthur's road may lead, you will go with him, under my protection, for as long as he and you may wish." She stared at me a moment longer, then nodded her head very slightly, accepting my promise, and returned her attention to the child at her breast. I turned and left quietly.

XVIII

I HAVE A vision stamped into my mind, a memory that fills me even now with anxious helplessness, in which I see myself standing on the foredeck of what I came to know as Shelagh's Galley, my hands clutching the rail tightly as I look back to watch the distant shores of Athol's kingdom shrink into a narrow line of grey, like clouds edging the horizon. Behind me, I know without looking, Shelagh herself stands beside Donuil, sheltered in the bend of his arm beneath his cloak, while the others of my party stand, sit or lie here and there wherever they have found space. To my right, in the wide, middle part of the vessel, our horses are secured, tethered by headstalls to stout wooden rails that cross the deck from side to side. But in the thinking of these things, in the act of recalling them, they are eclipsed from my mind by the looming vision of the hawklike eyes of Shelagh, filling up my mind.

The wind had been fair and steady that day. Above my head, a great square sail bellied from the central mast, and at prow and stern on either side, four teams of Eirish oarsmen swept their oars, their efforts carefully timed to marry with the mighty, sweeping strokes of the vessel that towed us, Feargus's great galley. Astern of us, riding easily in our wake, Logan's galley breasted the waves, making easy progress, awaiting the moment when it would take up the strain of towing us, relieving Feargus and his crew. We seemed to fly over the water, which was calm beneath blue skies dotted with scattered clouds.

I kept my eyes fixed on the distant hills of Eire, grasping the handrail even more tightly as a shapeless dread that filled my chest sought to overwhelm me.

Angered at my own senseless feelings of foreboding, I jerked my gaze away and looked around to where Feargus's galley pointed its nose to sea. Feargus, I knew, had more valid cause for deep concern than I had; my fears were obscure and formless, his sharp and crisply limned. Feargus misliked to head straight out into the unknown sea, for once beyond sight of land he would have no way of knowing where he was, or whither he was moving. His galley was overmanned, as was its consort, crowded with half again as many rowers as either craft would need in the normal scheme of things, and depriving Athol's forces of much-needed strength at home.

Feargus was gambling heavily on speed and strength, and fortune, hoping to exploit to maximum advantage the unusually mild break we were enjoying from the normal weather patterns at this time of year. If the wind held and the seas stayed calm, and if his crews, aided by the extra men aboard, could maintain the astounding pace he would set both day and night, he hoped to

bring us safely across the narrowest part of the open sea between his land
and mine in two days and nights, despite the terrors of losing sight of land
by which to steer.

Beyond Feargus's sail, lighting it brightly from behind so that the shapes
of sail and mast were thrown into silhouette, the morning sun climbed steadily into the sky. The last of the gulls that had followed us from the river's
mouth broke away, swooping low over the waves and turning towards the
distant land, rapidly diminishing until it vanished. The sail above me shifted
with a loud crack as the wind veered slightly and once more the eyes of
Shelagh filled my mind.

A large crowd had assembled on the pier along the bank of the river
estuary immediately before our departure. Athol was there, and Connor and
another ten or so in the king's own party gathered to bid us farewell and a
safe journey. The horses were aboard and secured, and our possessions stowed
away beneath the temporary decking installed to hold our horses. My men
had said their good-byes and filed aboard, four of them handling Quintus
with great care, keeping his stretcher level as they transferred it aboard, lest
he reinjure his fast-healing leg. The tide was high, and about to turn. I had
bidden my last farewell to Athol and to Connor, and then climbed aboard,
leaving Donuil and Shelagh and her father to make their parting with the
king in their own way.

Once aboard, I made a swift inspection of our status and found it satis-
factory. A pair of massive, solid-wooden thwarts had been mounted on the
foredeck, hard by the pointed prow. Solidly braced and bolted at their base
to the structural beams inside the ship, down near the waterline, they were
well buttressed by two flanking beams braced against the prow. There was
but one purpose for these new thwarts, added by Athol's shipbuilders in
recent days: to hold the end of the cable tow that would join our vessel to
our larger, faster escorts.

A sudden swell of noise attracted me to the side and I saw people running
towards the king and his party from the shipyards that lined the edges of the
riverbank. A crowd of people, all of them men. Curious, I scanned what I
could see of the shipyards, searching for a reason for the exodus, but there
was nothing to see. The shipyards, which we had not seen until the time
arrived for us to leave, seemed peaceful, dotted along the water's edge with
galleys in all stages of construction, most of them new-looking, of bright,
unpainted wood. On our arrival from the south, we had emerged from the
forest upstream from these yards, turning away from them to Athol's stronghold without ever suspecting their existence. I watched as the first runners
swarmed onto the pier, thronging around the king. Something was wrong, I
knew, but I felt no desire to leave the deck to find out what it was. And now
the king and Donuil were arguing, the one peremptory, the other expostu-
lating fiercely; their voices, raised, came to me muffled by distance and by
other noises so that I could make out no words. Shelagh pulled Donuil's arm,
tugging at him, willing him to go with her, and the king waved his arms in
turn at Liam, bidding him depart quickly. The three turned and made their
way towards the plank that led up to the deck, Donuil unwilling and with
many a backward glance. The king hurried away, his retinue in train, and
abruptly the wharf lay empty save for two hurrying figures who cast off the

ropes that bound our galley to the land. Distant movement atop the walls of dirt and logs that surrounded the shipyards drew my eyes. There was great activity there now, and the smoke of fires being lit.

I heard shouting from behind, and from on board, and the deck beneath my feet heeled slightly as the tow rope tightened, water squirting from its straightening length, and our craft began to move out from the wharf, dragged by the nose so that it turned almost within its own short length. As soon as we had left the land, our Eirish oarsmen lowered their sweeps and there was a rush of feet and the creak of more ropes as the spar that supported the sail was hoisted to the masthead and secured. In the space of mere heartbeats, it appeared, we were progressing at great speed, the river mouth already far distant behind us. I saw a seaman leap up to the rail and gesture northward and as I looked where he was pointing, I was unsurprised to note the other sails that dotted the skyline. Brander had come home.

Donuil, Shelagh and Liam had remained apart from the rest of us after boarding, talking urgently among themselves, and only now did Donuil step away from them and come to stand close by my side.

"What was that about?" I asked. "You looked for a time there as though you would remain behind."

"Aye, and I still think that was my place, in spite of what my father and the others say."

"What has happened?" I knew, before he answered, what his words would be.

"We were attacked, in heavy force, at dawn. From the south, as we expected. Finn was in place, and met them before they could build up momentum. He was hard-set, but holding them before the stronghold. He will not retreat inside the walls as long as he has strength to keep them back from the gates." Donuil gestured now to where his brother's fleet grew closer in the north. "Now that Brander is here, his men should make the difference and may enable Finn to turn the marauders back."

"And what of Brian? Any news of him?"

"No, nothing yet. But Kerry's dead."

The day went dark about me and the shapeless fear leapt, sudden, newborn, to my throat.

"Kerry? How?" But deep within my entrails I knew how.

Donuil was shaking his head. "No one knows, but he was killed before the attack began, slain after he left the post where he and Finn had spent the night."

My guts were roiling and black shadows danced across my vision, for all at once I knew why Kerry's face had seemed familiar. My stomach heaved and I lurched to the side to vomit. Below my hanging head I watched the water surge along the planks that kept the ship dry and afloat. Donuil was close beside me, but I asked him to leave, and he rejoined Shelagh, behind me.

That remembrance, as I have said, fills me again with sharp anxiety and fear each time I think of it, to this day, despite the fact that I have long since come to terms with what it was that ailed me. It was another of my accursed dreams, of course, but it was the first to which I had opened myself com-

pletely, prepared to accept the strangeness of it all and to attempt some form
of understanding of the experience.

That I could not initially accept it, however, that I constrained it uselessly
and searingly within my soul for such a length of time before I faced it, was
due to the shock of having seen Lord Caerlyle, the smiling Kerry, face to face
without recalling anything at all, save an annoying sense of having met the
man before. There had been no sign, no suspicion that I might have dreamed
of him. The thought had occurred to me on one occasion, but I had searched
my mind and dismissed the possibility. My memory had been blank.

I turned my back to the sea and watched Donuil and Shelagh murmuring
together, and, my mind open now, the memory of my dream returned to me.
For the first time in my life, I recalled a dream in detail, even though long
months had passed since I had dreamed it. I felt the prickles of superstition
as the flesh on my upper arms rose into gooseflesh. Determined, I stepped
towards them, noting that Liam had moved to where Dedalus and Rufio
lounged against the opposite rail. Donuil looked up as I approached.

"It didn't thunder last night, did it? There was no storm?"

He shook his head, his eyes widening in surprise that I should ask. He
and I had spent much of the night together, preparing for departure.

I looked at Shelagh, who was watching me, half smiling. "Shelagh, I must
talk with you. It is important." I glanced at Donuil. "Would you permit us
to speak alone for a moment?"

Mystified, he shrugged his huge shoulders and moved away to join Liam
and the others. I took Shelagh by the elbow, leading her to a space close by
the prow, beside the tow rope, where we might speak without being overheard. Without demur or question she seated herself on a coil of rope, beneath the shelter of the vessel's side. I crouched beside her.

"Have you said anything to Donuil of what you and I discussed the night
I came to your father's house?"

"You mean about the dreams? No, I have not. There has been no time
even to think of that since then."

"You mean you would have, had you had the time?"

She brought her brows together, puzzled, but not frowning. "I might have,
I think. He has the right to know the kind of woman he will wed. Why do
you ask that now? You said this was important. Does it have to do with this
curse?"

"Aye, Shelagh, it's important. I have had another dream. This time a
dream of Kerry's death, and I believe I know the truth of it. But you are the
only one who might believe me."

"Tell me," she said at once, her eyes level with mine. "Last night? You
dreamed of this last night?"

"No, months ago. Do you recall my telling you how I often fail to recognise my dreams until they have come to pass?" She nodded. "Well, I saw
Kerry killed in a dream I had long months ago, before I ever met or heard
of him. I only recalled it this morning, moments ago."

"Dia! But you have met him since then! Why did you not speak before?"

"Because I didn't know him! Didn't recognise him. I had forgotten the
dream, if I ever recalled it at all. I knew only that he looked familiar, but I
could not think why and so I passed it off, thinking he resembled someone

else from long ago . . . Until Donuil told me of his death, and then I knew at once."

"*Dia!*" She said the word again, an incantation to some Eirish god. "Tell me about your dream. Why did you ask Donuil if it stormed last night? Did it storm in your dream?"

"Aye, thunder and flaring lightning of the kind to terrify, and a great wind, but no rain. I was in a forest, among great trees, and it was pitch dark, save when the lightning flared, as it did almost without respite. I stood in a glade, beneath a tree, and a man approached me, outlined moment to moment by the flickering glare so that he seemed to leap to where I waited. He smiled at me and I knew him . . . and I hated him. As he approached, his smile grew wider and he came right to my side, as though to greet me, and then the dagger in my hand knocked him backwards as it stabbed up, beneath his ribs. He fell against a tree root, striking his head against the huge bole, and his mouth was filled with blood, black in the lightning's glare as I bent over him to wipe my blade clean on his cloak. He tried to speak to me, but died as I stood up again . . ."

She hissed at me, impatient with my lengthy pause. "What are you saying? *You* killed him? *You* killed Lord Kerry?"

"No, Shelagh, I dreamed it! This was my dream, no more. Last night I worked with Donuil far into the night, and then we slept together, side by side on the same cot, among the others. I do not even know where Kerry was last night, or when he died."

She pulled her head back as though she had been slapped. "Then . . . what is this, this dream? It makes no sense!"

"They never do, I told you that . . ." I drew a short, deep breath. "But this one did, or does. This one was different . . . I have not told you everything." I paused, thinking, then continued. "As I stood there, above the body, the lightning flared again, throwing my shadow on the tree where he lay dead." I stopped, then spoke again before she could interrupt. "It was not my shadow."

"Not . . . How could you know that? A shadow is a shadow."

"I don't know how I knew, but I knew—and still know—that shadow was not mine!"

Her eyes grew wide, because she had guessed at the sequel. "Whose . . . whose was it, then?"

"I swear it was Mungo Rohan!" I jerked myself erect, straightening my knees convulsively as I heard her gasp, and leaned my back against the right side of the ship's high prow, spreading my hands and feet for balance. She remained seated, her head directly beneath the tow cable, gaping up at me as I continued speaking, my eyes staring seaward. "Shelagh, I *know* there is no sane, logical explanation for such knowledge. And even more than that, I am aware of the gravity of all I have said. I know that by my simple repetition of these words to more impulsive ears than yours, Mungo Rohan's life would end abruptly. I know all that." I looked back into her eyes. "But, Shelagh, I know it is pure truth. Somewhere, somehow, at the depths of my being, I am convinced. I recognised that shadow beyond doubt. It was not distorted, nor altered by the flickering of the heavenly fires. It was—*I* was, there in that grove—Mungo Rohan, as surely as I breathe."

As suddenly as I had arisen, I dropped back down, bracing myself with one hand as I perched beside her, so that her head as she sat now was above me. "Nor is that all I know, Shelagh, although the God I revere must be shaking His head about how such knowledge came into my ken. The thing was planned. I knew, in my dream, that Kerry would come by there. I waited for him, and I knew that he would be alone. The thought was in my mind as I dreamed. Kerry would come this way, alone, and he would die, and we would have our way. We, Shelagh, for I was not alone in having plotted this death. We would have our way!"

I could see from her eyes that she believed, and was afraid to ask, and so I told her.

"Finn was the remainder of that We. Finn and I would prevail. The enemy would fail and be repelled, but in the achievement, Athol would fall— one way or another—and the Gaels would seek another king among his clan. Cornath, the firstborn son, is safe in Caledonia; Connor is crippled, hence unfit; his next-born brother, Brander, is at sea, involved in the new colonies; and Fingael, next in line after Caerlyle, would claim the King's Corona with its golden acorn points. Donuil did not even enter my mind. Fingael would rule, but I, Mungo, would be supreme."

In the silence that followed, Shelagh's face was deathly pale, her eyes filled with pain and deep, though unwilling, belief. She rose to her feet, pulling herself erect with a firm, one-handed grip upon the rail in front of her, after which she remained standing, leaning her shoulders against the taut cable, gazing out to where Feargus's galley laboured ahead of us, dragging us through the waters. She had thrown back the hood of her large travelling cloak and the wind, spilling and gusting all around her as it swirled about the prow, caught at her hair and blew it every way, so that much of the time it obscured her face and I could not observe her expression. I held myself in patience, awaiting her decision. She had immersed herself completely in what I had told her, and I had utter faith that she would know what I should do next—a knowledge completely without reason or logic, but both of those had disappeared completely with the news of Kerry's death.

My own thoughts were chaotic and, I fear, far less concerned with Athol and his grief and danger than with myself and my own reputation. No matter what I did now, I was thinking, I would be ill-regarded once the word was spread that I had dreamed this thing and then put credence in my own imaginings, perhaps enough to cause the death of high-placed enemies. I had no doubts that I was not the only one who had noticed Fingael's plain distaste for me—or Mungo's, for that matter. Added to that, the rumours that had caused my brother Ambrose deep concern back at home in Britain would be strengthened immeasurably by this development, and I could see no way of avoiding that. The word would spread. Tales of scandalous doings and supernatural deeds knew no borders or boundaries. Sorcerer, men would call me, and they would retell the tales of Merlyn's strangeness, whispered since his youth. Worse than that, however, was the concern caused by my new knowledge of the penalties for such abilities among Athol's own people. Possession of the Sight earned banishment. It mattered nothing that the curse I bore was born in me without my wishing it, or that I would be happy to abjure it. I was accursed. The mere suspicion of such abilities as mine would place me beyond the bourne of ordinary men.

I must have made some sound of distress, because Shelagh swung to face me. "What?" she asked. I shook my head and shrugged my shoulders, unwilling to be a cause of distraction to her. She looked away immediately, her eyes moving speculatively to where Donuil stood with his companions by the rail, farther along the deck.

"Donuil will know what to do," she murmured, almost to herself. "We must tell him, immediately."

"Tell him what, Shelagh? That I've had a bad dream? He wouldn't believe it. I wouldn't either, were I he."

"He will believe it, after I have talked to him." We were both looking at Donuil now and he glanced in our direction, as though aware of it. Shelagh beckoned to him. "Leave me alone with him for a while, Caius. I need to make him listen."

Donuil and I passed each other with a nod and I took up his place with Dedalus, Liam and Rufio, where the talk was of the death of Kerry, the morning's attack and the timely arrival of Brander from the north. Much of these speculations passed by me unheeded, since my mind was fastened on Donuil, Shelagh and the truth revealed to me.

After an interval that seemed like hours, I heard Shelagh call my name and I made my way back to where they stood by the prow. Donuil watched me approach, his open face troubled. Shelagh wasted no time, but it was to Donuil that she spoke first.

"Tell me, my love, would this man, Caius Merlyn Britannicus, ever lie to you, do you think?" The question clearly took Donuil unawares, because his eyes went wide and he blinked, but there was no hesitation in his denial.

"No! How can you even ask that, knowing what I have told you?"

"Because I want that knowledge freshly stated in your mind before you listen to what he will tell you next." Her eyes met mine. "I have told Donuil all about myself—my dreams, I mean—and he believes me, although the idea upsets him. I also told him of our talk the night he and my father went to search for Rud."

"You have such dreams, Cay?"

I nodded. "Aye, infrequently, but I do."

"And you believe their . . . power?" The word came to him with difficulty.

"Not fully, and not willingly, until today."

He frowned, and Shelagh interposed herself between us, pressing against him, snuggling under his arm beneath his cloak, pulling him with her into the narrow angle formed by the rigid bar of the tow cable and the right half of the prow itself, artfully distracting him before he could say whatever had occurred to him.

"I have told him nothing of today, Caius," she said, once they were settled there. "That's your task. Tell him now."

I glanced over my shoulder to make sure no one was paying us attention, and then leaned towards both of them, resting one hand on the rail and the other on the cable, so that the three of us were curtained from the rest of the ship by the spread of my cloak. There is no privacy aboard a galley. Then, keeping my voice low, I repeated my tale to Donuil.

His face drained of colour as he listened, and his mouth changed into a tight-clamped, lipless line. When I had finished he did not even question me, but stared off, over my shoulder, fury smouldering in his eyes.

"The question is, what do we do now?" I added, seeing that he was not about to speak. "I could tell you about this, with Shelagh's help, but we can't tell the others, not about a dream, with nothing to back up my fears. They'd think me mad, or worse, a sorcerer or demon of some kind."

He glanced at me, his eyes empty. "I don't care what they think, we have to turn around; go back."

"How, Donuil? Think, man! Feargus is your father's man and won't heed you. He knows you didn't want to leave, and that Athol ordered you away. Feargus will not turn back. He has his duties clearly in his mind. If he turns back, he risks losing the weather and perhaps the chance to sail again. His task is to drop us in Britain and then make all speed up the coast to bring your father's galleys back, for he cannot afford to assume the other ships will win through Liam's forces safely. And anyway, what would you tell him? That your Outlander friend has had a dream in which your own brother, the Lord Finn—who might even now be a hero, dead or victorious in this morning's fight—has played ignobly, plotting to murder his own brother, and his father next? Feargus would throw me overboard before he would permit me thus to sow the seeds of rebellion! He could never believe such things from a stranger's dream. We must do something, I know that, but we cannot turn about."

Angry at my words, unwilling to listen, but unable to deny the truth in them, Donuil had turned away, freeing his arm from Shelagh's shoulders and showing me the breadth of his back as I spoke. Now, suddenly, I saw him straighten, his whole body tense and alert as he gazed towards Feargus's galley surging ahead of us. He turned again, his gaze, keen now, going over my shoulder to the line of land still edging the horizon to the west. Then he broke free, pulling my right hand free of the rail and rushing back partway towards the stern, where he leaned outward, peering down. Satisfied of something, he spun and came back to us, ignoring the curious stares of the others. When he reached us again, his eyes were glowing, alight with decision.

"The boat," he said, smiling ferociously at Shelagh. "It has a sail, and oars. We're still in sight of land. I can be back home by tonight, even alone, and I'll land in darkness, unseen."

"I'll come with you."

"That you will not!" he said. "I'll have my hands full, and I need my wits about me. I won't be able to do what I might have to do if I'm concerned about your safety." He raised a hand, stopping her angry retort before it could emerge. "My love, I'm not saying you could not help me . . . I am saying that if I have only myself to worry about, I'll be better off and more able to react however I must." He turned to me. "Take her to Camulod, Caius. I'll join you there come spring, or even sooner. The galleys they are building to carry Liam's animals will cross before then. If I'm successful, I'll come with them."

"And what if you fail?" The question, asked by Shelagh in a cold, dead voice, quelled even my chaotic thoughts.

Donuil stopped and looked at her, then smiled and reached with a cupped hand to caress her cheek. "I won't fail, my love. I can't. I have two sons to father, don't you remember?"

She stared at him, still angry, then smiled, slowly, a tremulous, trusting smile, and the moment hung there between them. I coughed, to break the spell.

"What will you do, once there?" I asked him. "You have no way of proving anything."

He reached beneath his cloak, loosening the blade of his long cavalry sword in its sheath. "I'll do whatever seems right at the time," he answered. "I'll confront Mungo first, though, to his face, alone, just him and me."

"That might not be wise. I think you had better tell your father first what you suspect."

"Hmm . . . Perhaps . . ." He hesitated. "Tell me, you said my brother's mouth was filled with blood in your dream, and you wiped your blade clean on his cloak. Did any splash on you?"

"Blood?" I stared at him, trying to remember. "I don't know, but then I didn't look down at myself. My eyes were all for the man I had killed."

"Then it might have? Blood might have stained your clothes?"

"Aye. There was blood in plenty. Some might have splashed on me. But . . ."

"But what?"

"I saw it only in the lightning, Donuil, and there was no storm last night."

"No, Cay, there was no storm, but there was murder done, and if my brother had red blood in him, it would have spilled, storm or calm, regardless. The whoreson Rohan might be stained, or might have taken off his blood-stained clothes. He might have hidden them, if he did, but he'll have had no time to burn them yet, not with MacNyalls attacking." His eyes moved from me to Shelagh and back. "If blood is there, I'll find it, and then I'll carve his fat carcass and feed it to my grasping brother Fingael." He looked around him again. "I have to leave. Each oar stroke sets more distance to reclaim." Exuding a confidence that I had never seen in him, he stooped and kissed Shelagh, a long, lingering embrace, and then he gripped my arm as though I were now the neophyte and he the commander. "Take care of her. I'll see you soon."

He spun and left us, adjusting his sword and armour as he strode to the stern, where he set two seamen to hauling in the rope securing the small, sail-equipped rowing boat the sailors used for everything too petty for the larger galley to achieve. As soon as the tiny vessel was alongside, he climbed over the side and leapt down into it, then cut the rope that tethered it to us. Free of its line, the boat responded instantly to the pull of the water, falling away behind us at a startling pace as Donuil fought, leaning into the tiller, to bring its nose around to meet the waves that threatened to engulf it. Everyone had watched his passage the length of the galley, but until he swung his leg over and dropped from sight into the boat, their interest had been mere curiosity. Now Dedalus and his group surrounded me and Shelagh.

"What's going on?" Dedalus asked for all of them. "Where's Donuil off to?"

I held up my hand, bidding him wait as we watched Logan's galley ship oars, the banks of sweeps rising to the vertical, the vessel ceasing all forward motion as Donuil's boat approached it. As he came close alongside, someone threw a line, and he secured it to his boat, so that the small vessel swung in under the larger's side. I could see Logan leaning over, shouting, but could not hear his words. Presently, I saw movement behind Logan, and four armed men swung themselves down, one after the other, to join Donuil. As soon as they were safe, he cast off again and the tide swept him behind the galley,

out of our sight. Moments later, Logan's oars dipped again and his crew
began to pull. By the time it had moved far enough to reveal Donuil's craft
again, the little boat had hoisted sail and was scudding away towards the
distant land. I turned then to the others.

"Donuil had to leave," I told them. "There was something he had to do,
some business neglected in the heat of leaving." They stared at me as though
I were twitting them.

"We had guessed he had to leave," Ded said.

"Well then," I smiled. "What more can I say?"

He shook his head, and his eyes flickered briefly towards Shelagh. "Well,"
he sighed, "it must be a matter of great import for Donuil. If such a matter
had been mine to deal with, no matter who else thought it important, I
would have set the world on end to save the doing of it for a better day. I'd
have to be an older man than he before I'd tend to anything if it meant
leaving my love on a ship bound for another land."

I relented slightly, for the sake of Shelagh, nodding my head in acquiescence. "Some information came into his possession, something I knew and
he did not . . . something I told him with no anticipation of how he might
react. He chose to leave and rejoin his father." That was as close to the truth
as I could come without admitting to my dream and opening a full Pandora's
box of troubles. I looked from face to face, seeing the friendship there and
feeling guilty for my reticence.

"My friends, when I have decided how I should proceed henceforth, and
when I have learned something of the outcome of Donuil's sudden departure,
I will tell you what has occurred here today. But accept this: Donuil had no
other recourse open to him, once he had heard what I told him. It would
not be possible to turn the galleys back without losing time that might be
vital to the survival of our friends in Athol's kingdom."

Ded had one more comment. He eyed me shrewdly. "Do you believe he
took the proper course?"

I looked him in the eye. Did I, in fact, believe it? I nodded. "Yes, Ded.
I do."

"So be it, then. I've not known you lacking in judgment in the past, so I
won't look for it now." He looked now at Shelagh, and then back at me. Will
you translate my words for the lady?" I nodded, and he turned again to
Shelagh. "Lady, until your man returns, we—all of us—will be at your command, so call on any one of us without delay should there be anything you
require . . . among us, we can handle anything. Your man may be a heathen
and a giant, but he has earned our friendship and our trust." A growled chorus
of assent from the others confirmed what he had said.

Shelagh had been staring at him, her head cocked to one side as she
listened, and now as I translated what Dedalus had said, she blushed, a dark
flood of red stealing over her face. She nodded graciously and whispered, "I
thank you."

On that, the men turned as one and left us to ourselves, Shelagh, Liam
and me.

The remainder of the voyage passed quickly and uneventfully, apart from
a short visit from Feargus, who boarded us nimbly from the little boat that
brought him from his galley as soon as Logan had taken the tow from him.
He was much less angry than I had expected, listening to my explanation—

the same one I had given to my own men—in silence. His reaction afterwards
was much akin to Ded's, too, save that Feargus accorded the good judgment
in the affair to Donuil, who was, when all was said and done, he pointed
out, the son of Athol Mac Iain and much like his father in his thinking. He
spent some time with Liam and Shelagh after he had done speaking with
me, and then returned to his own galley.

Thereafter, the weather and the wind both held, and the moon rode in
a clear sky overhead throughout the night, so that we kept both our consorts
in sight at all times. At dawn on the third day, dark clouds came rolling
towards us from the west. The new day had already revealed the broken
skyline of land directly in our path, however, and Feargus now had no fears
of foundering. Logan was towing us again and heavy rain squalls were breaking around us by the time we drew near enough to the coast to begin looking
for landmarks. Never having seen the coast of Britain from the sea before,
except in leaving it, my men and I were useless to the lookouts, but Feargus
and Logan both knew where we were, and soon we changed direction, speeding diagonally under full sail and oars to the south until we gained, and
passed, a point of land that stretched out farther than any other. The massive
inlet we found beyond it, we were told by those on board who knew, was
really an outlet, the mouth of the estuary to the south of Cambria, which
now lay directly on our left. The ruins of Glevum lay ahead of us, farther in,
on the south bank.

We felt the change in motion as soon as we entered the estuary, and
soon we noted the changed colours of the water beneath our vessel. None of
us had been sick at sea, to the great surprise of our Eirish oarsmen who, I
sensed, felt cheated because of that. Before the sun had risen halfway up the
sky, we were sweeping along between the banks of a broad but rapidly narrowing river mouth, with sand flats and shoals on either side of the deep
channel we followed. As we progressed, a low ground fog clung to the land
on either side like smoke, obscuring our view, but the water ahead of us was
clear of it. The wind died suddenly, blocked by the land around us, and four
men hauled down the sail, so that, in the absence of wind and waves, the
galley's hull hissed audibly through the water between strokes of the oars.
And as we progressed, the fog receded, until the banks lay clear and open
and the huddled buildings of a town emerged from the distance. Glevum.

A short time later, there came a shout from Logan's galley, and a series
of hurried maneuvers, and the heavy tow cable went slack and was thrown
overboard by four more men. The loud clacking of a wooden winch came
clearly afterwards, as Logan's crew hauled the bulky cable aboard.

We were in mid-stream, but now our oarsmen went to work again and
brought us slowly towards the town that lined the bank, and we saw the very
wharf from which we had stolen the barge, mere weeks before. All three ships
came to rest a safe distance from attack, but none of us saw any signs of life.
The desolate ruins seemed empty. Uneasy nonetheless, I had my bow strung
and an arrow nocked as soon as we were within bowshot—my bowshot, which
none other could match.

Feargus was first on the wharf, surrounded by his men, a number of whom
he sent to scour the seemingly empty buildings. He stood there without
moving, his arm extended to hold us away until the word came back that it
was safe. As soon as he received it, he waved us in and set his men to finding

ways to bridge the space between deck and dock for our horses.

It took close to two hours before we were unloaded and the little man turned to me with a sniff and a smile. "Well, Master Merlyn, you are home again, and so's Lord Donuil, safe in his own land."

"Aye, Feargus." I glanced to where Liam, Shelagh and some others stood with the woman Turga and the babe she held close to her. Young Arthur had reached the age at which he grew restive quickly in confining arms, and he was wriggling mightily. But Turga held him easily. I turned back to Feargus.

"Do you have time to walk with me awhile?" I saw him start to frown and pressed on. "I wish to speak to you of Donuil, and his departure, but it is for your ears alone. I could not speak of it aboard the galley, with so many about."

He nodded. "Aye, then. Let us walk."

"Good. I will not waste your time."

During the next quarter hour I told him my strange tale, holding back nothing in spite of my fear of his reaction. I had determined that since he was King Athol's most trusted associate, he had every right to know the reason for the strange defection of his chief's son. And so I told him of my dream, and of Donuil's reaction to hearing of it. Feargus listened closely, walking head downward, his hands clasped behind his back, and I could not see his face. When I had finished, he stopped and looked up at me, chewing a ragged end of his long moustache.

"One of your men told me the Druids had the raising of you?"

"Aye." This was half word, half laugh; he had surprised me. "Some of it, at least. My grandsire's people in the hills had Druids among them. Some of them were my teachers."

"Did you tell them aught of your Sight?"

"No. In those days I had not been aware of it."

"Aye, well, treat it with respect. It is a gift, and a curse, given to few men. Do not abuse it."

"Don't abuse it?" I was astonished. "Then you don't think I should be banished from the haunts of men?"

The look he flashed me was of pure scorn. "Old women's fancy, that! Punishment born of terror and the fear of the unknown; sorcery and the like. No man with a mind of his own can doubt the existence of the nether world. We talk of gods, which means we give credence to things other than natural. Your gift is not unnatural, Master Merlyn, merely unusual. Your visions come to you in sleep, do they not? Nothing is more natural or more needed than sleep." He grinned, sudden and wicked. "In the meantime, I'll be in Caledonia the day after tomorrow, and back home in Eire within the week following that. The Lord Donuil will not lack swords to do his bidding after that. When this is over, and the vermin plaguing us are sent back home licking their wounds, I'll bring Lord Donuil back to his Lady myself. You have my word on that."

As we stood on the wharf, watching them depart with Shelagh's empty galley in tow again, it did not cross my mind to doubt him. We watched them until they had shrunk to dots in the distance, and then I turned to Rufio and Dedalus with the word that we ourselves should prepare to leave—to discover that they, along with me, Liam, Quintus on his litter, the women

and the child, were all who remained on the wharf. Farther along, on the
stony road fronting the warehouses, our two trainees were working with the
horses.

"Where are the others?"

"Searching the buildings for a pair of wheels. Quintus still cannot walk
or ride, you know." Dedalus spoke without expression, but Rufio grinned at
me and jibed, "That sounded insubordinate to me, Commander, now that
we are back in Britain. Am I not right?"

"Yes, it was insolent, Centurion Rufio. But then, it was Dedalus who
spoke, was it not? We have to consider the source from which the matter
springs." I turned away smiling and moved to Quintus, who lay watching me,
his back propped against a bundle of saddle blankets.

"How are you feeling, Quint?"

He smiled and touched his hand to the thigh beneath his covers. "I'll
mend, Commander. I doubt if even Lucanus could have bettered the work
done on this leg by the boys. It's clean, it's sound, it's all sewn up, and healing
rapidly. I don't know who it was that choked me and half-killed me, but I'm
glad he did, whoever it was. I'd hate to have been conscious when this bone
was set. I saw it when they hauled me from the sea."

"Aye—" I was interrupted by a shout from along the wharf, and watched
Benedict and Cyrus approach, pulling a two-wheeled cart. Even from a distance it looked agued, rocking from side to side alarmingly. As they drew
closer, the reason became clear. The thing was ancient, with high, ungainly
and badly warped wheels lacking a large number of spokes. The others began
to appear, drawn by the noise, all of them empty-handed, and the chorus of
cheers and jeers grew louder as the crowd around the sad old cart grew.

Quintus had been gazing at all this in alarm and as the small procession
reached us he called out to Cyrus. "Hey, I can't ride in that! The thing will
fall apart and I'll be thrown out and break my leg again."

"Well, walk then, ingrate! In all this town there's only one conveyance,
and we are worn out finding it for you, and you would turn up your nose at
it?" Cyrus was delighted with his find and his infectious gaiety encouraged
the spontaneous good feelings of returning home. I called them to order and
we began inspecting the cart. Benedict, who was something of a carpenter,
offered some quick, monosyllabic suggestions of how to improve and
strengthen the frame and sides, but there was nothing to be done about the
wheels, he said emphatically in the crude way common to soldiers everywhere. I told him to do the best he could, and he began issuing orders, so
that by mid-afternoon the cart had been much improved, even its shaky
wheels strengthened by struts of planking from a dismantled door, placed
hexagonally around the decrepit rims and fastened into place with horseshoe
nails, then reinforced with cross-braces. We piled Quintus, Liam, the women
and the child into the body of the cart with as much extra baggage as the
contraption would hold, hitched our most placid horse between the shafts,
and made our way from Glevum to the southeast, towards the leper colony
of Mordechai Emancipatus.

BOOK THREE

THE
SAXON
SHORE

XIX

IT WAS THE taciturn Benedict who put into words the happiness we all felt at coming home. Ded and I had been riding at the head of our small column and, on being relieved by Philip and Paulus, had fallen back to check that all was well behind. We found Falvo riding where he should be at the rear, but peering back over his shoulder, where there was no sign of Benedict, who had fallen behind, presumably to relieve himself. Falvo was about to go back to check on him, but we bade him ride on, and Ded and I kicked our horses to a canter in search of our missing companion. We were not alarmed, merely being cautious.

We came upon him almost immediately, standing by the side of the road, concealed by a thicket of evergreens that overhung the roadway, his reins in one hand and his head bent, staring down at something green he held in the other. As we approached him, he looked up and waved what he was holding. It was a large, broad-leafed weed of some kind. When we reached him, I saw the mark between the cobbles at his feet where he had uprooted it.

"What have you there? Looks like a weed."

"Aye. Growing in the road."

I looked at Dedalus and he raised one eyebrow in return, saying nothing. One seldom knew what went on in Benedict's head. Now, however, he had chosen to show more eloquence than Ded or I had ever suspected him to possess.

"I saw a lot of Empire when I was a boy, long before I came here, but until now I never thought to note how dangerous growth is." Slowly and with great deliberation, Dedalus crossed one arm over his chest and leaned the other on it, masking his mouth behind cupped fingers and schooling his face to show no expression. I, too, fought hard not to smile, but Benedict did not notice. "Today it's a weed, growing between the stones," he continued, gazing down at the uprooted plant he held. "In ten years, it'll be a tree . . . In a hundred years, this road will be destroyed." He looked up at us. "Until we went to Eire, I never thought about roads. It never even crossed my mind that some lands might have no roads. Gaul has roads. Even the Saxon lands have roads. The whole Empire has roads."

"Rome never conquered Eire," I said, no longer feeling the urge to smile.

"I know, but I've only come to see that now," Benedict said, turning his gaze to me. "No Roman conquest means no roads. So Rome *means* roads . . . And *roads* mean towns at each end and along them . . . So without Rome, we'd have no place to go and no way of arriving. And here I am, forty and more years old and never knew that till now! I've spent much of my life being glad the Romans left Britain, but I'll spend the rest of it being glad they came . . ." He threw the weed aside and climbed onto his horse, then rode off back towards the column without another word to either of us. Dedalus

looked at me wide-eyed, his face still extravagantly empty of expression. I
shrugged and kneed my horse into a turn.

"I think he means he's glad to be back home."

"Aye," Ded agreed. "A veritable Benedictish benediction. Amazing."

We had ridden fifteen miles after that incident, counting the milestones,
when Rufio, who had been ranging a mile and more ahead of us, came spurring back, waving his arms as soon as he came into view. A large body of
armed men was approaching, he reported. He had managed to remain unseen
only by good fortune, having picked up the signs of their movements as they
crested a hill ahead of him, about three miles from where we were now. He
had left the road immediately and made his way back along the verge, hidden
by foliage, until he no longer risked being seen, and then had galloped the
rest of the way. He had been too far away to recognize anything about them,
he reported; they might be friend or foe, but they outnumbered our small
party, as far as he could estimate, by no less than three to one.

We had to assume, as Rufio had, that all strangers were enemies, so my
first concern was for the cart holding Quintus and the women. I ordered
Liam Twistback, who held the reins, to get the vehicle off the road and out
of sight among the trees as quickly as he could. Then, while Liam was looking
around for a place to leave the road safely, I turned my attention to our extra
horses, setting Cyrus, Paulus and Philip to assist our two trainees in leading
the animals from the road, too, spreading their exit points as widely apart as
possible in a short time to obscure the evidence of their exit. That done, I
turned back to hiding the cart. It was a slow and awkward process, hampered
by the poor condition of the cart itself and its high, narrow wheels, which
sank alarmingly into the soft ground, leaving deep tracks. I assigned three
men to that task, too: Benedict to lead the horse forward by its halter, steady-
ing it and eliminating the need for a driver, and Falvo and Paulus to walk
alongside, one by each wheel, to help maneuvre it among the bushes and
obstructions that littered the ground. I followed behind it with Dedalus, both
of us working to conceal the signs of its passage.

As we laboured, Ded talked. He was convinced, he told me, that the men
approaching were the same who had attacked us in the town the day the
great bireme had sailed away. They had been left behind for some purpose,
he observed, reminding me that I myself had feared they would range farther
afield in their search for booty, once the town had been stripped bare of
marble. Already there was not much left to plunder and they had gone scouting for a new supply, perhaps even as far as Aquae Sulis. Now they would be
returning.

As soon as the cart was safely out of sight of the road, I shrugged out of
my heavy, black cloak, with its conspicuous white lining, and left it on the
cart. Then I strung my bow and hung a quiver of arrows from my shoulder
and Ded and I returned alone to find a spot from which we might watch
whoever passed without being seen ourselves. As we drew close to the road
Ded stopped and looked up, pointing to the tree that soared above us, an
ancient, massive oak hung with dense clumps of mistletoe. He jabbed upward
with his thumb, raising an eyebrow in silent query. The sight of the mistletoe,
and the idea of climbing up there, immediately took me back across a gulf
of thirty years to the day I had fled for my life, aged six, from a Saxon pursuer
and found salvation in the person of Flavius, my father's friend and Junior

Legate. By the time I had recalled the incident, Ded was already far above me, climbing strongly, apparently unaware that he was wearing heavy, bronze armour. I slung my bow across my shoulders and followed him, pulling myself up surprisingly easily to where we each found a sturdy crotch among the upper limbs and settled down to wait, with an unobstructed view of a clear stretch of road no less than thirty paces long.

For a long time after our ascent nothing happened and the forest settled into utter stillness around us, broken only occasionally by the sounds of birds. Then, gradually, noise began to swell in the distance, first the sound of raised voices, laughing and shouting, and then the creak of laden wagons and the clop of hooves. I glanced at Ded, who seemed to have better hearing than I.

"What language is that?"

He shrugged, making a face. "Nothing I've heard before. Might be Saxon."

"Saxons? Here in the west?" I shook my head, still listening to the alien sounds. "They're a long way from home, if they're Saxons . . ."

"Well, we'll see them any moment now." Almost as he murmured the words, the men leading the party came into view, four of them, all heavily armed and armoured, arguing hotly. They trudged by our vantage point without looking left or right, two of them looking down at their own feet and the other two glaring at each other as they exchanged angry-sounding words, although there seemed to be no acrimony in their posture.

I had heard Ded's hissed intake of breath at his first sight of the strangers, but his surprise had been no less than my own. These men were like no others I had ever seen, but I had recognized the bows they carried instantly as being related to the one I bore. Despite their smaller size, about half the length of my own great weapon, I knew from their elaborate, double-curved form that they were made of laminated layers of different materials, and that marked their bearers in my mind as Africans, since it was out of Africa that the bow I held now had come, brought to Publius Varrus's grandfather by some returning legionary a hundred years ago or more. They were swarthy of skin, these men, dark brown, with coal-black beards, and their dress and armour were exotic. Their necks and shoulders were protected from behind by thick, armoured leather flaps suspended from the bottoms of the shining metal helmets they all wore—helmets uniform in shape and design, more conical than domed and each crowned with a high, sharp spike. They wore heavy cuirasses, front and rear, of the same shining silvery metal fastened over mid-thigh-length tunics of ringed mail. Their legs, seemingly unarmoured, were covered by long, loose black trousers, and from each man's waist, slung low and almost dragging on the ground, hung a long, heavy sword with a curved blade. I had never seen metal curved in such a fashion and the sight of them told me that these people, whoever they were, were master smiths, far more skilled in ironwork than any in our land.

Before the first four had passed from our sight the main body of the group began to appear from the screen of leaves that had masked them from us. We counted thirty-eight men, twelve of them pulling an enormous, four-wheeled cart filled with a chaos of goods, among which I saw a heavy wooden table and two high-backed Roman chairs.

We watched them pass, holding our breath when one fellow left the road to defecate almost beneath us, within two paces of the rutted tracks of Liam's cart, which, from our elevation, stood out like fresh-burned brands upon the ground. Fortunately, the fellow squatted with his back to them and concentrated solely on his task, wasting no time afterwards, but running to catch up with his companions who had passed from sight. We waited again, still silent, until the sounds of their withdrawal had faded, then Ded hawked and spat.

"I almost emptied my bowels before that whoreson did, when I saw where he was headed."

"They're Africans," I said. He glanced at me, surprised enough to stop himself in the act of swinging his legs up onto the bough on which he had been sitting.

"Aye," he said, musingly, after a pause. "Perhaps . . . North Africa could have spawned them, but I'm more inclined to think them Barbarians."

I grinned at him, feeling light-headed with the relief of danger safely past. "Of course they're barbarians, Ded. They're not civilized like us."

"No, that's not what I meant. I mean they're Barbarians, the Berbers, from the far end of the Middle Sea, across from Africa. I've been there, seen them in action, ran from them once, when several of their accursed galleys almost caught us alone, close by the Pillars of Hercules. You think Athol's Eirish galleys are fearsome? You'd never think so again if you once saw some of those Berber galleys come slashing towards you on a bright blue sea. There's a sight to loosen your bowels! They're fast, and sleek, and built exactly to their purpose, crammed with savage, fighting predators, and all their rowers are slaves, chained to the oars. The sight of them has emptied the bladders of bigger and braver men than you and me . . ." He stopped abruptly, peering down between his knees to the ground far below. "Come on, we'd best get down and on the road again."

As we climbed down, I questioned him further. "I didn't know you had been that far away from Britain, Ded, to the Middle Sea. My father never served in that area, did he?"

"Nah," he grunted, hanging from one thick branch while seeking another with his feet. "I was only a tad at the time, travelling with my father. He took me with him when he went to Constantinople." He found his footing, the last difficulty between us and the ground, and from that point on our descent was swift and he talked non-stop, his eyes moving constantly as he sought his next hand- or foothold. "I didn't join your father until years after that and even then, I was still but a lad. Hadn't even begun to grow a beard. Your father was my first Imperial Commander, and my last. I was serving as a runner to him when he was betrayed. I brought him the word of danger just ahead of the killing squad Honorius had sent to arrest him. Consequently, I was one of the ten he took with him when he escaped. The rest of our contingent stayed behind to give him breathing space. God knows what happened to them, but if they weren't killed fighting whoever had been sent, they'd have been executed out of hand for simply being Picus's men."

We reached the ground, he slightly ahead of me, and paused to sweep the dirt and bark from our dress. "Anyway," Ded concluded, "Berbers makes sense. They came on that big bireme, which they probably captured in some naval fight. Their own galleys, fearsome as they are, are too light and small to survive out of the Middle Sea, and far too small to pull the kind of cargo they're dealing in now."

We joined the others, then made shift to haul the cart back out onto the road. We were eight miles and more from our destination and the sun had begun to sink already, lengthening our shadows on the road. Rufio rode out ahead of us again and I sent Philip rearward to make sure the strangers had not reversed their course for any reason. We made good progress after that, but it was deep twilight when we finally approached the small valley that provided refuge to the lepers.

Lucanus was astonished and delighted to see us returned so soon. He had thought us gone for at least six months. That our absence would last less than six weeks had not occurred to any of us as a realistic probability. While our men set up our tents at some distance from the leper longhouse in the barely adequate light of two large fires, Luke and I sat by the larger fire, and I began to tell him of our journey. He had examined Quint's leg as soon as we arrived and the greetings were over, and pronounced it healing splendidly. Quintus would have some deep-trenched scars, he pronounced, but should have full use of the limb once the bone was fully set. More men than Quintus had sighed with relief on hearing that, and one of them was Benedict, who had set the bone and splinted it.

Now, as we sat and talked, his eyes sought Shelagh, who was preparing food with Paulus, the best cook among us, and Turga. The baby slept safely, wrapped in a bundle of blankets close by Turga's side.

"The woman, Shelagh. Who is she?"

"Liam's daughter, I told you when you met her."

"I know that, Cay, but who is she? Why is she here?" His eyes had not left the young woman, whose long, tousled hair disclosed and obscured her face and eyes alluringly in the leaping of the flames. I had to take my own eyes from her deliberately.

"She is to be Donuil's wife."

His head swivelled slowly towards me. "Then where is Donuil?"

"At home in Eire." Before he could question me any further, I launched into the tale of what had happened in the past week, omitting nothing, and as I talked the tent-raising around us was completed and the men began to gather close around the fires, although they took care to leave us room to continue speaking in private. I ended my tale with my agreement with Athol to acquire a concession from Pendragon that would permit Liam to raise his animals on their lands for at least a year.

"You think you can obtain such a concession?" he asked, when I had finished. I could only shrug and observe that it seemed reasonable. There was no ill-will between Uther's people and my own of which I was aware. To my concealed dismay, however, Lucanus named the single concern that had been gnawing unacknowledged at the edges of my mind since I had spoken of this to Athol. I myself had not visited the Pendragon lands since the accession of Uther to his father's throne, and Uther's support of Camulod in the recent wars had cost Pendragon dearly, not in men alone, but in losses of the precious longbows that were so hard to replace, since each one took so long to make. Those losses, allied with the apparent lack of gratitude and concern expressed by me, or any in Camulod, either privately or publicly, might well have eroded the goodwill that had existed between our peoples since the days of King Ullic, Uther's grandfather. In the eyes of the Pendragon, he said, I might well have earned the reputation of an ingrate. Untrue as that might be, it was not an unlikely perception.

Chastened considerably, I admitted that I had given insufficient thought to this possibility, and we agreed that this was a matter that demanded an immediate journey by me into the Cambrian mountains, to express that gratitude, belatedly, and to explain to whoever now held power among the Pendragon the many reasons for the lapse of time since I had burned Uther's corpse and returned home to Camulod. From there, we moved on to talk of other things, and he told me how they had lost five of their number, several days before, struck down by arrows from an unseen enemy. I stared at him, but he had nothing more to say.

"What do you mean, an unseen enemy? You were attacked, yet saw no one?"

"That's what I said. Whoever it was shot at us from the woods, there. From the summit of the hill behind us."

"And killed five people, without attacking further after you had run and hidden? Did you show them you were prepared to fight?"

"To fight? Fight with what, Cay? These people are lepers, not soldiers . . . And no one ran to hide. The five who died were all outside, walking, most of them with the aid of staves and crutches. They were too weak to run. Whoever killed them knew well what they were, and did their slaughter from afar, running no risk of contagion. It was butchery, callous and inhuman."

"The Berbers," I said, and told him of the armed band we had seen returning from this region. As he listened, his face grew troubled.

"Then they will return, is that what you are telling me? They'll pass this way again and come looking for further sport, and Mordechai has no way of deterring them."

"Mordechai may not, but Camulod does," I told him, feeling a monstrous anger boiling in my gut. I looked to where Dedalus sat talking with Benedict and Cyrus and called them to us, bidding them summon the others. Briefly then, once all of them were listening, I repeated what Luke had told me of the arm's-length slaughter of helpless invalids, and I spoke of the inherent threat of further outrages by the alien Berbers, and I saw the same anger stirring in their eyes.

"Now," I said. "We return to Camulod tomorrow and should arrive within the next three days. As soon as we have won back and I have settled several matters within the Colony, I must leave again for Cambria, to visit the Pendragon lands and find out who rules there today. You, Ded, will accompany me and so will you, Rufio. The rest of you, however, all five of you, will return here under the command of Cyrus and Benedict, bringing with you a full cohort of our troopers, and you will cleanse Glevum of this barbarian filth that has polluted it. Do you hear me?"

"Aye!" All five spoke as one.

"Good. So be it! Now eat and then get some rest, all of you. We will be up and away, come dawn. I'll need Lucanus's wagon harnessed ere the sun comes up, and the women and the baby safely installed in it. Eat well, and then sleep well, and deeply."

As soon as they had gone, clustered around the cooking pots and the delicious aromas they emitted, Lucanus and I sought out Mordechai, so that I could bid him farewell and inform him of what would happen upon our return to Camulod. Mordechai listened and then thanked me, although his eyes told me he had a question. I prompted him, curious, and he shook his head, the hint of a smile on his lips.

"I was merely thinking how strange the ways of people are," he murmured. "These Berbers you speak of stand far back and kill us from concealment, because they are afraid to come too close to us, risking contagion. Now you tell me your own men, who are equally afraid of us, will return in strength for our protection. It is a non sequitur, my friend."

"Not really, Mordechai. There is ample logic there. Granted, my men fear your people and avoid their presence, as I do myself. But it is leprosy they fear, rather than lepers, and the avoidance of contagion is mere prudence. These are simple soldiers, ordinary men with ordinary terrors. They dread the sickness far more than the sick . . . But they are decent men, and casual slaughter of the kind that happened here outrages them. As for these Berbers, if that is what they are, they represent a threat to us, and to our Colony, so we will wipe them out and guard against their return. The service we will provide for you is incidental, an entailment to your benefit. However, my men will not come anywhere near your encampment on their return. I see no need to feed the idle curiosity of our troopers by telling them of your presence here. The aliens must be cleaned out of Glevum; that is sufficient reason for our punitive expedition, and all that will be given."

He nodded, accepting my words, and thanked me again with great dignity. When we left him, assuring him he would be quit of us come dawn, Lucanus walked with me back to my tent. I paused there, before entering, and looked him up and down, as friend to friend, the exigencies of the day all dealt with.

"Well," I asked him. "Are you well? Convinced you have contracted no disease?"

"Leprosy?" he responded, smiling. "No, Cay, I am convinced there is nothing of the leprous in me now that was not here ere we arrived."

"I'm glad of that, my friend," I told him then, only half jocular. "As I told Mordechai, I am not at ease in proximity to such potent threat as is concealed beneath the clothes of even such a friend as he." He stared me directly in the eye and I nodded. "So be it. Are you hungry, or have you already eaten?"

He pursed his lips and shook his head. "No, to both your questions. But I am tired. I have not slept properly since the night of the attack, waiting for a return visit."

"Well, you can sleep now. No one will bother us tonight and we leave for Camulod at dawn. Sleep well, Luke. It will be good to reach home again, even for a few days."

We passed by Aquae Sulis late the following day without looking for signs of life, making twelve additional miles before we camped for the night, and as I made the rounds of our small camp before seeking my own bed I was aware of the feeling of anticipation that filled everyone. Even the women seemed to be looking forward to tomorrow, although neither of them had ever seen our Colony. We would be up and on the road before first light, travelling at campaign speed, and we hoped to sight the towers of Camulod before noon. I wrapped myself in my cloak and an additional blanket beside the fire and then discovered, to my great surprise, that I could not sleep. I

lay awake for a long time, tossing and turning, feeling the earth grow harder
beneath me, before I accepted my insomnia and crawled out from my blankets to throw more wood on the sinking fire. As I did so, I heard the sound
of the baby whimpering somewhere close by, and then the sound of Turga's
voice crooning and whispering to him, soothing him to silence again.

Returning to my blankets, I lay still for a while with my back to the fire,
watching the shadows form beyond me as the new fuel ignited, and listening
for more sounds from the baby, but he was silent again. Something had struck
me as different in the sound of his crying, however, and I found myself
wondering if his voice was deepening, then smiling in the darkness at the
silliness of the thought. And yet, he was growing like a weed—even my un-
sophisticated masculine eye could see the change in him since we had first
landed in Eire. The child had grown visibly, not so much in height—length,
I amended—but in overall bulk. He had *thickened*, that's what it was.

That notion, the thickening and strengthening of his small body, reminded me of Benedict's comments that morning, concerning the weeds
growing in the roads of Britain. In a hundred years, he had opined, the roads
would be destroyed, fractured and torn apart and ultimately replaced by the
inexorable growth of millions of plants, beginning with green, healthy weeds
that would root between the cobblestones, as had the one he noticed, and,
over time, would widen and then split the surface cracks before giving way
to shrubs, bushes, saplings and eventually mighty trees whose roots would
sunder and obliterate all that the legionaries had achieved. The idea grew in
fascination as I considered it; the notion that a simple, everyday broad-leafed
plant—a weed—could have the capacity to precipitate such mass destruction
of man's greatest achievements.

From that point, somehow, and by some logic that escaped me then, the
weed in my analogy transfigured itself into the child, Arthur. He, too, I realized, possessed the potential of that thickening, ever-thriving weed. Seeded
almost by chance between the enduring, close-knit edges of Britain's contig-
uous clan territories, with their differing, but equally rigid and unyielding
systems of survival and their lack of anything resembling a centralized core
of laws, young Arthur Pendragon could become a wedge that would break
apart the cobblestones of Britain and reshape them into a bonded surface
that would cover all the land. Nurtured by the Roman-bred, republican ideals
of his immediate ancestors, the boy might bring about a revolutionary change
in the ancient ways, if he were properly instructed and guided. The raw
potential was there in his makeup. But then I saw his laughing, innocent
face clearly in my mind, for a moment, and tried to imagine it in manhood,
frowning and solemn with righteousness. The attempt was ludicrous, and I
turned onto my other side, emptying my mind of such nonsense and staring
wide-eyed into the leaping flames.

The darkness beyond the firelight was absolute, and the stillness of the
night was disturbed only by the crackling of the new wood on the fire, and
I soon found myself thinking about my brother Ambrose for the first time
in days and wondering how he had progressed with Ludmilla. Those thoughts
led me to Donuil and his love for Shelagh, a love that seemed almost to have
sprung into being magically, although in truth I knew the seeds of it had
been planted years ago and had merely lain dormant until the two set eyes
upon each other once again. From there, my thoughts passed on to Luke

and the matter of his celibacy, and my own. He had promised to think about
how he might counsel me in that matter during my absence, but I had been
gone far less long than either of us had thought possible, and I knew he had
had much to occupy him during that brief time. I resolved to ask him about
it on the journey to Camulod, but the idea lacked urgency somehow, and I
realized, after some time and with great reluctance, that I was being distracted from my task by Shelagh's face, mainly her eyes, which interposed
themselves between my own and Luke's image in my mind.

Surprised at myself, and feeling more than slightly guilty, I took myself
to task, questioning the source of such thoughts. And of course, as is normal
in such matters, the answer I found was even more disconcerting than the
question I had asked: I had not willed myself to think of Shelagh. She was
simply there, in my mind, but now I realized that she was seldom absent
from my thoughts, even when I was unaware of them. With that awareness
came an increase in the guilt I felt. Shelagh was to be Donuil's wife, and
Donuil was my friend above all else, entitled to my unswerving loyalty. And
damnably, with that conviction came the insidious thought that the two
must now wait months to lie together, to consummate their bond . . . and I
visualized that consummation, save that it was I, not Donuil, who reared
above Shelagh's exultant body, supported on my outstretched arms and
watching the ripples of pleasure distort her lovely face. Frightened now in
my soul by the intensity of what had sprung unbidden to my mind, I rose
up from the fire and blundered off out of the firelight, blind from the flames,
seeking I knew not what. I was fleeing from myself, I knew, terror-stricken
by my own sudden arousal; fiercely, demandingly engorged and seething with
surging lust and guilt. The mere existence of such unsought, urgent wanting
in my body seemed to me a betrayal of Donuil's friendship and a violation
of his trust.

I crashed headlong into a tree trunk and knocked myself off my feet,
seeing flashing lights all around me in the darkness and knowing they were
only in my head. Stunned and confused, I raised myself to a sitting posture
and remained there for a while, asprawl on the damp ground, until the coldness penetrated to my buttocks, after which I pulled myself to my feet. My
eyes had now adjusted to the dark and the riot in my blood had abated
considerably. As I turned to return to the tents, however, I heard a sound
that froze me in mid-step. I strained to recognize it, then smiled at myself.
It was only the splashing of water from the brook that curled around our
campsite. Somewhere upstream, beyond where we had camped, there must
be a small waterfall, and the sound of it had caught at my ears. I walked in
the direction of the noise and found a pool, some fifty paces removed from
where we slept, where the water swirled over some large boulders and fell
into a small basin. Above my head, the moon shone through a gap in the
clouds, lighting the place with silver, and I remembered the advice of the
Legate Titus to young men on long patrols: "When your lusts bother you,
and if you have the opportunity, seek out a pool of cold water and steep
yourself. It will clear your head and your veins." I stepped forward and knelt
by the little pool, then leaned forward, supporting myself on my hands, and
plunged my head slowly beneath the water. Sure enough, my fires were
doused, for the present, at least. I towelled myself dry with the lining of my
cloak as I returned to the fire and took my seat again, thinking once more

of Shelagh, but this time with awareness and circumspection.

"Have you been dreaming again?"

Shelagh's voice startled me, making me jump. I had not heard her approach, but now she stood beside me. I turned towards her, standing up as I did so and willing myself in the moment not to look too closely at her.

"No," I managed to say, attempting to smile. "I couldn't sleep. Excited at returning home, I suppose. What are you doing awake at this hour?"

She nodded downward, indicating the bundle she held, and only then did I become aware of the sleeping infant she held in her arms. "He is fretful, upset by something, so I took him. Turga has had no sleep these past two nights." She peered more closely at the child. "Look, he's sleeping now. Isn't he beautiful?" She pulled the covering from the boy's face and I leaned closer to look at him, acutely aware of her proximity. He slept peacefully, his tiny eyes gently closed, showing the dark lines of his long, thick lashes against the softness of his baby skin.

"Look at his lashes," Shelagh said quietly, as though she had read my mind. "Have you ever seen such lashes on a baby?"

I was gazing at the child in wonder, my discomfort at being so close to her miraculously abated. "I don't think I have ever seen another baby," I answered. "Not like this, I mean, not up close. I've never really looked at one before."

She glanced up at me, smiling broadly. "Then look more closely at this one. Here, hold him. He's heavy. Come on, take him! He won't break. But take him gently, don't wake him."

Before I quite realized what was happening, I was holding the future King of Britain in my arms, my muscles locked in panic lest they flex too suddenly and crush him. And Shelagh was laughing at my evident discomfort.

I willed myself to stand still and simply relax, allowing my arms to adjust to the minuscule size and weight of their burden and to hold it easily and without awkwardness. The child slept on, long lashes feathered against the incredible smoothness of his cheeks. He represented total innocence, unmarred by any vice or weakness, and an unformed thought teased me with hints of the sadness of all he must learn in future to equip him for the tasks we, his future trainers, had in mind for him.

"He doesn't look much like a High King, does he?" I murmured.

"Not now, of course not. But he will, Caius. As he grows, those yellow eyes of his will note and change the entire world. I have never seen a baby with golden eyes; nor an adult, for that matter. Have you?"

I shook my head. "No, but I've read of one. His great-grandmother's brother, my own grandfather; the same Caius Britannicus after whom I'm named. He had golden eyes. Eagle's eyes, Publius Varrus called them."

She glanced at me sidelong, a tic of puzzlement appearing on her brow. "Who's Publius Varrus?"

The question took me unawares, reminding me forcefully that she really was alien to our ways. I smiled at her. "He was this young man's great-grandfather, husband to my own great-aunt Luceiia Britannicus. I'll tell you all about him one of these days."

"And this great-grandmother, what did you call her, Luceiia? She is still alive?"

"Aye, very much alive, in Camulod, which was founded by her husband

and her brother. She's waiting patiently to see this young man."

"She must be very old."

"Extremely old, and tiny now, shrunken with age. But very strong, too, for all that. In her youth she was a great beauty."

Shelagh was looking down at the baby again, and now she reached out and laid one fingertip against the tiny fist with its dimples on each knuckle. "Yes," she said. "This one will be High King, right enough. He'll be big. He has the size already, and the strength, of an older child." As she spoke, the child opened his small fingers and grasped her fingertip. She smiled. "And the strength of him! What this one owns, he will hold. Someday those fingers will grasp a king's corona."

"Aye," I thought. "And a king's sword." I had received an instantaneous vision of the child, aged about twelve, holding Excalibur. He stirred and wriggled in my arms, uncomfortable, no doubt, against the hardness of my metal cuirass.

"Here, give him to me. I had better sleep for a while. Dawn will come too soon."

I watched her leave, with the baby, and then I, too, sought my blankets again, and this time I slept.

We arrived within sight of Camulod in the middle of the afternoon of the next day, having ridden the entire way from our previous night's camp without encountering a living soul. The countryside had become more familiar all around me as I rode, and when Philip came spurring back to tell me we were there, I made sure to ride beside the wagon holding Liam, Shelagh and Turga as we breasted the last rise, so that I saw them see Camulod for the first time. It was an impressive sight, even from an eminence as low as that on which we stood.

The valley that embraced the main holdings of the Colony lay spread in front of us, angling sharply westward in a carpet of greenery, among which the rectangular shapes of cultivated fields stood clearly etched. In the distance, dominating everything at its feet, the hill of Camulod stood out proudly upon the landscape, the silver grey of the stone walls that crowned it clearly visible. We were too far away to make out signs of human activity, but the shapes and angles of the castellated walls and towers spoke of strength and durability even at this distance. I heard the catch of Shelagh's breath as she registered what she was looking at. Liam was more serene. This was not his first time in Britain, and he had seen Roman-style fortifications before, as opposed to Roman ruins like the abandoned towns of Glevum and Aquae Sulis. His eyes narrowed as he took in our fortress, and then swept down into the valley, towards the fields.

"Much land under the plough, Caius Merlyn."

"Aye," I responded. "But the fields you can see are only the largest, about one quarter of the total on this side of the fort. The smaller fields are shrouded from this height and distance by the trees surrounding them. We have a large number of Colonists, and all of them have to eat. Most of us are farmers."

He looked across from the driver's bench of the cart, smiling slightly. "I thought most of you were soldiers?"

"Not most, many," I responded, returning his smile. "You dealt with the

Romans in your boyhood, I recall, so you are probably aware that the Roman citizen soldiers who built the Republic, before the Empire, prior to the time of Gaius Marius and Caesar, were all farmers and landowners; free men who wore their swords while they walked behind their ploughs. We are much the same, in many ways. Our soldiers exist primarily for the protection of our farmers. It may sound strange to you, but that is the truth. The horsemen provide the farmers with peace and protection while they grow the crops that feed them and the soldiers. Come, we have another ten miles to ride, but the good road lies some two miles to our right, and once there, the way is straight and easily travelled." I kneed my horse forward and heard Liam cluck to the horse between the shafts of his cart.

An hour later, we came to the first guard post on this approach to Camulod. It was a small, fortified farmhouse, built of stone and elongated to accommodate its permanent garrison, its outhouses long since altered to provide stabling for the horses of the troopers who shared the posting with the infantry. The young centurion in charge greeted us with delight, slightly awed to have so many veteran superiors descend on him at once, and Dedalus, being Dedalus, set out immediately to inspect the installation. While he was doing so, I bade the others alight and rest while I spoke with the young commander, whose name was Decius.

"How many men have you here, Decius?"

"Fifty, Commander. One multiple squad of thirty-four afoot; two squads of cavalry."

"Since when, and why? The normal complement here is half of that, is it not?"

"Aye, Commander, it was, until a few weeks ago. Commander Ambrose changed the duty roster for all outposts."

"I see. Thank you, Decius. You may return to your duties. We pause here only for water and a rest, and then we strike on to the fort. Is Commander Ambrose in Camulod?"

He shook his head. "I have no idea, Commander. We have been here for ten days; four more to go."

"Very well, Centurion Decius, you may go." He saluted me, bringing his clenched fist to his left breast, and spun away.

We had lost no time on the road, but the news of our arrival far outran us, and an entire cavalcade, headed by Ambrose himself and his entire staff, came riding out to meet us as we approached the outer edge of the great campus, or drilling ground, that stretched out at the foot of the hill of Camulod itself. It was a joyous reunion, and as soon as Liam, Shelagh, Turga and her charge had been introduced, they were made as welcome as the rest of us. We would feast that evening, Ambrose told us; the stewards and the commissariat had already received their instructions and the quartermasters had been ordered to open their precious stores of luxury goods to welcome home the escort to the great-grandson of Publius Varrus. The Legates Titus and Flavius were stirring their aged stumps supervising the arrangements and the following day had been declared a holiday. Even though the guest of honour himself was much too young to recognize the honour done him on his first visit, his great-grandmother would welcome all comers to the feast in his name.

His great-grandmother was my primary concern, now that we were safely home, and she was the object of my first question once the civilities were done and I could ride alone with Ambrose on the way up to the fort. He told me that she had been ill, failing visibly ever since I left, but the news of our return, outrunning us magically hours before, as such news always seems to travel, had brought her from her rooms for the first time in weeks and the change in her, according to my brother, had been truly remarkable. That she intended to preside over the evening's festivities had completely astounded him. I looked at him when he said that.

"Is she capable of doing so?"

He grinned at me. "You know, Cay, I find it hard to credit that I have known her only for a few months, but if I have had time to learn anything about Luceiia Britannicus Varrus, it is that neither she nor I has ever found anything she is incapable of doing. She will be there, and she will play the hostess to all of us. Her pride in her great-grandson will bear her up. She may not last the entire course, but she'll be there for most of it."

"With all her women. Which reminds me. How is the Lady Ludmilla?"

He grinned at me, all eyes and flashing teeth. "Magnificent! I am in love . . . we are in love."

"Do you tell me so?" Returning his grin, I made no effort to hide my irony, but I sobered quickly. "I am glad of it, Ambrose. Will you be wed?"

"Aye, we will, come spring."

"Good. I look forward to your nuptials. For the moment, however, there are other matters that must concern us. The question, for example, of why you have doubled the strength of all the guard posts. Are you expecting trouble?"

His grin changed, becoming more rueful. "No, Cay, no trouble." He turned in his saddle, glancing around at the group that followed us closely, almost surrounding us, giving himself, I thought, time to phrase a response.

"It is an experiment," he said finally. "Ever since arriving here, I've been aware that we have a need to combine our tactics, allowing us to gain the best advantage from both our forces, infantry and cavalry." He paused, looking a question at me. "Were you—Are you aware we have a serious rivalry between the two, Cay?"

I shrugged. "We have always had rivalry, ever since the day Britannicus and Varrus decided to mount our men on horses. Rivalry is good; it keeps people mettlesome."

"Aye, but it can be damaging, too. I said we had a serious rivalry, not mere competition."

"How so? What d'you mean?"

"I mean it's bad, Brother. I began watching closely as soon as you had left for Eire, and I did not like what I saw. Your cavalry are elite troops; none better anywhere that I have seen, but that undoubted excellence has bred a sullenness among the other troops. Remember, I am an infantry commander by training. I know what I am talking about. Anyway, I began asking questions, and I would not accept any expedient or placatory answers. I spoke to the senior officers in both divisions, and to the rank and file as well, and what I found convinced me that we must make some effort, expeditiously, to heal the rift that has sprung into being over the past few years since Lot first marched against Camulod. And so I have been working closely with our infantry commanders, developing strategies that will enable us to draw full measure of the potential of our infantry in fighting with our cavalry in future. The doubling of strength in the guard posts is the first step towards that. Not because I want more strength there. I want more *men* there, living together in harmony, getting to know each other, and working together on developing the plans I've put in place."

"Hmm. And is it working?"

"Too soon to tell, but it seems to be."

"Tell me about this rivalry. You say it's only recent, since the start of the war against Lot? If that's so, then I would not have been aware of it. I've spent too much time being someone else since then."

Ambrose began his account, but we were too close by then to Camulod's gates and the waiting throng of welcomers that choked them. We agreed to talk again, later that night, and he abandoned me to the well-wishers. It took me more than an hour to win free of them and then to remove my armour, wash quickly and change into fresh clothing before going to collect the child from Turga. That done, I made my way directly to Aunt Luceiia's rooms, for I knew she was waiting there, curbing her impatience, to welcome me and her great-grandson. And as though he knew that this was a momentous occasion, the six-month-old child who was Arthur Pendragon rode easily in the bend of my elbow, wide-eyed, alert and staring at his new home with great, golden eyes.

I had been preparing myself for some time, ever since hearing from Ambrose that my great-aunt had been confined to bed by illness, to be appalled by the changes in her. She was a very old woman, having long outlived all of her own contemporaries, and genuinely merited the word "ancient" in the eyes of everyone else around her, and her advanced age had brought her to that stage of life where the smallest irregularity of health could wreak startling changes on her appearance. She stood up quickly as I entered the room bearing my small ward and moved immediately towards us, her eyes fixed upon my burden to the exclusion of all else so that I was able to scrutinize her as she approached. I could see no sign of illness. Her skin, as pale and delicate as fine papyrus, seemed to shine with health, although it may have been the simple radiance of her anticipation, and her great blue eyes, faded but still remarkable, sparkled in the late afternoon light from the unshuttered window she had ordered added only recently to the long rear wall in the family room, admitting welcome light from the small atrium beyond. She had a brief smile of welcome for me, open and heartfelt but nonetheless distracted in the urgency of greeting her great-grandson.

"Careful, Auntie, he's heavy," I said as she reached for him. She ignored me and plucked the boy from my arms as though he were a feather, carrying him directly into the light from her new window, where she held him aloft, peering into his tiny face. The child returned her scrutiny with complete equanimity, his eyes wide and calm, so that she gave a surprisingly girlish little crow of delight and pressed him quickly and lovingly to her bosom before holding him away from her again to continue her examination.

"Hello, young man," she said to him, for all the world as though only she and he existed. "Aren't you the wonder I never hoped nor thought to see? Arthur Britannicus Varrus, bearing the likeness of your ancestors as though to show the entire world who you are and whence you sprang." Now she turned her head and spoke to me, inviting me to join their tiny circle. "The eyes are pure Caius Britannicus—I never saw Cay's equal in eye colour until now—and the golden hair is a family heritage my brother used to blame on a too-loved northern slave of former days. You and your father have made it commonplace within the family nowadays, but it was once rare. But look at this fellow! Look at the strength of him, the shoulders and the depth of chest! How old is he? Six months? He has the body of Publius already, and could be the strongest smith in Britain. You could, couldn't you, were you not destined for other, greater things?" Responding to her tone, the infant smiled at her and she hugged him again, kissing his baby cheek.

I was beginning to feel stirrings of concern for her, because all of this time she had been standing, holding the child away from her easily, despite the fact that what I had said was true: the child was heavy, a solid lump of bone and sturdy muscle that could remind even my arms of what they bore. Now, however, she moved to a couch and sat down, holding the child seated on her lap, and the eyes she turned to me glowed with happiness.

"Thank you, Cay, for bringing this wonder home to me before I die. He is the future—the future of this Colony of ours and of this land. Look at him! That certitude is stamped into the essence of him. He is my entire life story, the history of all my loves made into one small boy." She fell silent again for a while, gentling the child at first when he began to squirm impatiently, and finally bending to allow him to slip down to the floor by her feet, where he lay kicking and waving his sturdy little arms, his eyes roving all around this strange, large room, registering the play of light and sparkle upon furnishing and ornament and ignoring the two people who watched him.

When she spoke again, her words had a musing, self-absorbed intimacy. "I can see all of them there, when he moves in certain ways: Publius Varrus in the very way he breathes and clenches his fists; my brother Cay in his eyes; even Ullic Pendragon and his own father Uther in his bearing, though how a child can have a 'bearing' kicking on his back is beyond me . . . it's there, nevertheless." She paused, then glanced at me. "His hair has a red tinge to it I have never seen before. Even as babes, your own hair and your father's were more yellow, more fair than this."

"His mother had red hair," I told her.

"Ah! Then that would explain it. It may change as he grows, to red or to pure gold like yours, or it may not. Only time will tell. Was he born with red hair, or did the change come afterwards?"

I shook my head. "I don't know, Auntie. It was that colour when I found him, but by then he was three months old. Is that long enough for a child's hair colouring to change?"

"Sometimes, but it is unimportant. Did you know the mother? What was her name? Ygert?"

"Ygraine. No. When I found her she was already dying. Lot's wife. And young Donuil's sister. And my wife's too."

Aunt Luceiia shook her head, smiling gently. "It's strange, stranger than anything I have ever known through all the years I've lived, the influence that this unknown, alien clan from another land has brought to bear on you, Nephew. Does it not amaze you?"

I had to nod in agreement, for the same thought had often occurred to me and been the subject of long mental deliberation in my quiet times. I disliked and distrusted coincidence, and had been taught by my own father that coincidence *per se* did not exist. The relationship between Donuil, Ygraine, Connor and myself was explainable, involving the politics of kingship and territorial alliances more than anything else. Having captured Donuil legitimately in a war waged by his family, and having befriended him thereafter, it did not seem strange to me in any way that I should later meet the members of his family who were involved in all the varying activities of warfare and alliances. The one coincidence that defeated me, that I could not explain, was meeting Donuil's sister, my dead wife, long months before I went to war and captured Donuil. The probabilities against two such unrelated encounters assuming the significance they had, defied credence. And yet it had occurred, and my life had been utterly changed beyond redress. My aunt was sitting still, watching me closely.

"Aye," I admitted, finally. "It does seem strange."

"God's will always seems strange to simple people."

"God's will?" I smiled as I looked at her. "Come, Auntie," I twitted her, seeking to ease my own sudden pain. "You think God's will extends to making sure that I would meet my wife and go through the joy and suffering I did before—and after—I lost her?"

I was well aware of my Aunt Luceiia's lifelong dedication of herself and all she did to the Christian God and His Church here in Britain. I considered myself a Christian, I believed in the existence of God, but my religious conviction was a private thing, and I seldom thought of God or of His Son, the Christ, as contemporary personalities. More Roman in such things than anything else, I felt, deep within myself, that God—as in "the gods"—had more important things to do than worry over individual people and the details of their abject little lives. Aunt Luceiia, however, refused to be teased. Ignoring the child at her feet for the time being, she composed herself, hands folded in her lap, and looked me straight in the eye.

"You are being flippant, Nephew, and I will not dignify your levity with discussion. But think of this: Had something not guided your feet to where you found her, on that patrol with Uther, none of the things that happened after would have come to pass the way they did. All of them might have happened, certainly, but they would not have been interconnected so intimately. Donuil would have remained a trusted hostage, perhaps even a friend. And you would not have pursued Uther so angrily nor so jealously—" She interrupted herself, responding to the sudden expression of shock I felt registering itself upon my face at her knowledge of what I had thought to be a secret known only to myself. "Oh, yes, I know the truth of all of that and what you thought and did. And while I am aware of the kindness with which you sought to shield me from your conviction of 'the truth,' I am neither blind nor feeble-minded . . . Most of all, however, I find myself accepting that had you not believed you had cause to suspect Uther in the death of your beloved wife, you would not have pursued him into Cornwall and my great-grandson would have perished. Instead, here he is, kicking at my feet. Your suspicion of Uther thus prevented the destruction of the great Dream you described to me but recently, the Dream of my brother and my husband Publius, personified in this child and his apparent Destiny. Without your doubts and beliefs, all of it would have gone unrealized. Will you make fun of that?"

By the time Aunt Luceiia had finished speaking I had mastered myself. I had also lost any urge to treat her observation with levity. Chastened, I realized that what she had said was the simple truth and that my own convictions regarding coincidence involved a contradiction in terms. Belief in Christianity, or any acknowledgment of a supernatural order of existence, entailed a willingness to accept that coincidence, or any series of synchronous yet apparently illogical events arranged in rational sequence, somehow related to the supernatural will. I drew a deep breath.

"No, Auntie, and you make me feel ashamed. I will never commit that error again, I promise."

She smiled and relented, waving her hand to dismiss the topic. "No need to feel shame, Nephew. You must merely keep an open mind in future. Remember your uncle Varrus. All of his learning told him no stone could fall from an open sky without first being hurled up into it from earth. Had he chosen to accept that, he would never have found the Skystone that he sought, and that wondrous sword Excalibur would never have existed." She paused, allowing her words to sink home in me. "Keep your mind ever open, Cay. Accept no other's dictum as the final word on anything you think to question. Now, get you off and bathe and steam and shave, and leave me with my grandson here. Who is his nurse, by the way?"

I told her about Turga, and then spent a full half hour telling her of the baby's other family in Eire, and of his other grandfather, Athol, King of Scots. Finally I told her of Liam Twistback and his daughter Shelagh and the absence of Donuil. She listened to most of this in silence, asking only a few questions, and then suggested that both Shelagh and Turga should move into her own household as guests, the one to await the return of her husband-to-be, the other to guarantee her hostess constant access to the child. I smiled again and again as I listened, and then kissed her fondly before leaving to find Ambrose, with whom I had much to discuss.

XX

I DISCOVERED THAT Ambrose was out on the hilltop lands behind the fortress walls, conducting target practice with some of our younger foot-soldiers whom he had decided to train as bowmen. Intrigued, I started to make my way directly to the spot, but then I recalled my aunt's instructions and paused, considering them. I had washed and changed out of my travel clothes before going to her, ridding myself of the uppermost layer of human and horse sweat, but I was still far from being either clean or refreshed. I knew that a visit to the bath house would revivify me. A quick glance at the sky showed me some hours of daylight yet remained, and so I beckoned to a passing soldier and sent him to Ambrose with a message that I was bathing and would join him, bringing my own bow, within the hour. That done, I headed for the sanctuary of the baths as quickly as I could, and regaled myself in the luxury of the hot pools leading to the *sudarium*, or steam room, where I surrendered myself willingly to the ministrations of the two masseurs then on duty.

Later, refreshed and feeling new born, and clutching Uncle Varrus's great bow and a quiver of arrows, I made my way to where Ambrose had set up his new target range at the rear of the fort, beyond the postern gate that had given access to my father's assassins years earlier. In those days, the rock-strewn, grassy hilltop had lain empty, but I knew that the space was now put to full use, with buildings, horse pens and roofed stables filling most of the area. Ambrose, apparently, had commandeered the last clear, level stretch of terrain for his current use, and I heard the laughing shouts and jeers of the participants as I approached. I had no idea what to expect when I arrived, but what I found amazed me.

There must have been close to thirty men there, all of them clustered at the end of the range opposite a row of four clearly marked, black-and-white ringed targets, each one spread over what I later discovered to be bound bales of densely packed straw. Ambrose stood to one side, watching the proceedings with his back to me as I approached, and most of the milling throng over which he presided I identified immediately as young recruits and trainee soldiers. Several other faces among these, however, distinguished by the untrimmed beards and hair that framed them, leapt out at me; older faces these, well known but unexpected in this place and at this time. As I walked towards them, still unnoticed, two more young men stepped forward to the rough line gouged in the earth that marked the aiming point, their heads bent and all their attention concentrated upon the long, tapered Pendragon bows each of them held with the awkwardness of learners. The sight of the bows shocked me even more than had my recognition of the several faces I had last seen in Uther's company, and checked my advance. This sudden stop attracted the attention of one thick-set, bearded Celt, who turned his head towards me and then earned my gratitude by breaking into a smiling roar of recognition, so that suddenly I became the centre of attraction, surrounded by the enthusiasm of old, back-slapping companions whose existence I had all but forgotten.

There was Huw Strongarm, direct descendant of Publius Varrus's old friend Cymric, the Pendragon bowyer who had made the first long yew bow stave, and with him was his son, another Cymric, whom I had last seen as a stripling lad. Behind Huw loomed the enormous bulk of Powys, the largest and strongest man I had ever met, who could lift a struggling heifer in his arms unaided. Other names flashed back to me, unthought of in years, as their owners greeted me: Owain of the Caves; the trio Menester, Gwern and Guidog who, I had learned long since, had been born within four days of each other and had done everything together since childhood. Cador the Fisherman was there, as was Medrod, who had been one of Uther's most trusted retainers, and Elfred Egghead, who had lost all his hair, including lashes and brows, almost before attaining manhood. These nine I knew immediately. Five others stood with them whose names I did not know, although I recognized them all by sight. By the time their boisterous greetings had died down and I was able to look beyond the circle of them, I saw Ambrose standing watching me, a slight smile on his lips, and grouped beside him were his trainees, almost a score of them, some clutching Celtic bows, and all of them staring at me with expressions varying from slack-jawed awe to something approaching reverent admiration. Several heads swung back and forth from me to my brother, remarking and cataloguing our amazing resemblance to each other. None of these young men was known to me, and that realization made me more aware than anything else until that time of how far I had drifted, all unawares and for a multiplicity of reasons, from the daily life, activities and people of the Colony that was supposed to be my home.

I raised my clenched fist to my breast, saluting Ambrose, and he returned the greeting gravely, though his eyes were dancing, but when I would have moved to meet him I found myself confronted by Huw Strongarm with a challenge to test my Varrus bow—that was what he called it—against his homegrown pride. Though his tone was one of friendly raillery, I knew at once that this was not a challenge I could easily refuse, for the growl of approbation that sprang from the throats of his fellows was unanimous, and so I shrugged and accepted. Two men ran immediately to spread new targets over the existing ones, which were already pierced and tattered, although I noticed, even from this distance, that the central rings of all four targets were almost unmarred. They were plain enough targets, made from raw cloth stretched over square frames of woven reeds like the circular Saxon shields carried by Ambrose's men on their arrival. Black rings, concentric circles, had been drawn on the plain cloth, each circle growing smaller by a handspan until the smallest, itself a handspan wide. They were set up a hundred measured paces from the firing line, which Huw and I approached together.

Each of us glanced sidelong at the other, eyeing the other's weapon. Because of its double curve and triple compound layers of construction, my bow looked bigger and somehow more formidable than Huw's, and my arrows were perhaps a palm's width longer, but I took no satisfaction in that appearance of superiority. Huw's bow, bent and strung, looked graceful and slender, and much shorter than mine, although I knew that was illusion.

Unstrung, his bow was equal to his own height and was painstakingly carved
from a single sapling, the result of years of care and conscientious labour,
carefully dried and straightened, worked with heavy linseed oil, then planed
and shaved by hand to taper perfectly from its central thickness, which filled
up a grown man's palm, to its notched extremities, each the size of a fingertip. My bowstrings were of dried animal gut, stretched wet, then plaited into
single strands of great strength. His were of spun-hair twine, braided and
waxed. Only our arrows bore comparison, made from straight ash shoots—
mine the longer—and fletched with goose feathers, slightly curved, to make
the missiles they adorned spin smoothly.

The sun was behind us on our right, more than halfway down the sky, so
that it threw our shadows, long and slanting to the left ahead of us. Huw
sniffed and grinned at me. "Ready?"

"Aye," I murmured. "But yon centre's a massy ring, and close."

"That's true enough, but none of your boys have hit one yet."

"Then perhaps what they lack is inspiration?"

He cocked an eyebrow. "Something smaller, then?"

"Much smaller," I said with a smile.

He thought for a moment, then grinned and reached up to his breast,
where he unpinned the kind of brooch I had remarked King Athol wearing,
although Huw's was much smaller. It was a simple circle of silver, held by a
straight pin. The rim was half the width of my small fingernail, its central
space as wide as the distance from the tip of my thumb to the first joint.
Turning, Huw threw it to the closest bystander, big Powys.

"Powys," he said. "D'you think your fingers delicate enough to place this
thing in the centre of the target there? But mind you don't close the pin!
Stick it straight into the target. We'll be putting arrows through the ring and
I don't want my fine brooch broken." Few of our young men understood
what had been said, but as the giant Powys strode forward and affixed the
silver circle to the centre of the first target, a murmur of awe arose around
us. When Powys was clear of the line of flight, I turned to Huw with a small
nod.

"Your brooch, your shot."

He nodded back and raised his bow immediately, hardly seeming to
bother taking aim. The bowstring smacked against the heavy leather arm
guard that protected his left arm and as it did so the sound of his arrow
smacking home echoed it immediately. There was a shout of acclamation,
and I saw the feathered end of his shaft slanted across the distant silver circle.
The point was buried in, or close to, the ring itself.

"Fine shot," I said. "Did you hit the brooch?"

"I hope not, for if I did, there's ruined it is. I missed the target, anyway.
I think you could insert a thumb between the arrow and the mark. Make
sure you do the same, either in or out. Don't hit the brooch, for 'twas a
recent gift from one who'd have the hide off me if she knew how I was using
it."

I smiled and drew the string back to my ear, aware of lack of wind or
distraction. As the tip of my arrow crossed the line of my eye, I loosed and
watched the shaft speed straight and true, hearing another roar of admiration.

"That missed, too," I told Huw. "But I think it's closer than yours."

"Well then, we'll check it. One shaft at a time is all we can try here, for more than that will block the view and endanger the brooch. A clean shattering from a single, well-aimed shot I could live with, but to do so carelessly simply because either one of us could not see clearly would be unforgivable." He raised his voice to Powys, who had remained at the far end of the range. "Powys! Which one was closer?"

The big man crossed to the target and leaned close to it, measuring carefully, it seemed, before straightening up and pulling out both arrows.

"Merlyn's," he called back. "But not by much. His to the right and centre, yours to the left and high. I had to use one finger to my thumb's end to mark the difference."

"Stand away then. The next one's mine." As Powys walked away, Huw nocked another arrow and then froze in the half stoop used by all men who pulled these mighty bows, his eyes fixed on the distant target, his bow arm hanging almost loosely by his side, his right arm bent across his middle, holding the bowstring gently. Long moments he stood there, his concentration absolute, and then he straightened, stepping into his shot, bringing the full strength of his upper body into play as his weapon swung up and he pulled and loosed, again without having seemed to aim. I watched the arrow's flight, marvelling at the big man's coordination and speed of delivery. I knew how good I was, and knew that few men were my equal in this arena. Huw Strongarm, however, was one of those few, and I knew that I could never match his speed and ease. This time I was almost unaware of the cheers coming from the watchers. Huw's shot was closer than his first had been. It might even have pierced the centre. We were too far away to know beyond doubt.

Drawing a deep breath once, twice and then a third time, blowing the air from my chest so hard that my cheeks puffed out, I nocked, then willed myself to relax and gather my strength as my eye sought and followed the flight of the arrow I would send towards the target. Then, when I knew my eye was true and my mind satisfied, I released the series of rippling moves that would unleash my thunderbolt, leaning into my pull so that I actually pushed the bow stave forward as I brought the taut string back towards my ear. The shot sped clean once more, and I knew Powys's thumbnail would be employed again. This time, however, it was my arrow that lay farther from the mark.

"One more to decide?"

I grinned and nodded. "But no more than one. I think you have been practising more than I have."

"Practising? I don't practise, man. This is what I do!"

This time, as I watched my opponent prepare for his shot, I listened to the silence around us. Thirty and more grown men all held their breath and watched as I did, enthralled by the rapt attention Huw gave to his task. Again I marvelled at the taut stillness of him, and then at the explosive force as he snapped into motion, seeming to expand simultaneously in all directions as he released the pent-up energy that had sustained his trance. This time big Powys whooped and went capering across to the target, where he peered downward and then spun around, leaping in the air and crying that Huw's shaft was in the ring. I felt the tension drain from me like water.

"Well done, Huw," I said, meaning it sincerely. "That was a master's shot."

He looked at me in surprise. "What, you mean you're giving up?"

"Giving up?" I laughed aloud. "God, man, you pierced the ring! I can't beat that."

"No, but you could equal it. There's room in there for two."

"Not if you hit dead centre, and I'd guess you did."

"No, I hit to the left of centre, almost against the side."

"How can you know that?"

"I saw it! I'm not blind, man."

"By God, then I am, and that's enough for me. You can see so clearly that far away?"

"Aye. You can't?"

"No, and I would wager not one other man can, either, except you." I turned back to Powys, who was still standing by the target. "Powys," I shouted. "Where was the hit?"

"Left of centre. Against the rim," came the reply. I turned again to Huw, my face, I knew, betraying my amazement. But Huw was already shouting to Powys.

"Is there room in the circle for another shaft?"

"Aye!"

Huw looked at me. "Well? Will you shoot, or are you prepared to give up the legend that the Varrus bow is superior to the Pendragon?"

His tone was jocular, but I knew he spoke in earnest, and the gravity of what he said came home to me. For decades now, the great African bow brought to this country by Publius Varrus had remained a thing of legend. This was the bow that had inspired Cymric the bowyer to build the first Pendragon bow, which Ullic the King himself had been the only man with the strength to pull. From that first bow of yew the rest had sprung, so that over a period of short decades the Pendragon had become the most effective fighting force outside Camulod, the fame of their dread weapons spreading far and wide throughout the South and West. Now, in this confrontation that had begun between two old friends, I saw the challenge clearly. If the Varrus bow were found wanting, then the name of Varrus himself would suffer neglect hereafter. I sighed, a gusty sound of anger and sudden frustration.

"No, I don't think so, Huw," I answered him, hearing my own voice grating on the words. "Not yet, and not without a fight." I pulled another arrow from the quiver at my shoulder and stepped back to the line, putting my thoughts in order. That was, I found immediately, more easily attempted than achieved. I found myself in the grip of an unreasoning anger, and I knew it would obscure my judgment if I allowed it to persist. Aware of the deep silence that had fallen all around me again, I forced myself to stand motionless and concentrate upon the task at hand. As calmness began to assert itself and my anger faded, I turned away from the mark, glancing at Huw, searching his face for any sign of mockery or scorn. I saw none. He stood motionless, his bow grounded, watching me calmly and without any expression other than the respect due from one opponent to another in a contest of skills.

I nodded to him and turned again towards the mark, exhaling completely and then breathing deeply in the pattern I had taught myself over the years. And the world around me vanished, to be replaced by a long tunnel that stretched away ahead of me to where a silver circle shone, large and clean-lined, against a field of dun, untreated cloth. As I loosed my shot I knew it was my best ever. I had turned away to Huw before it even hit the mark, aware that the watching crowd yet held its breath, waiting for Powys's verdict. But I knew, and Huw knew, judging by his grin, that my shaft had lodged with his, inside the ring. As we shook hands, the air around us shattered under the noise of the watchers' cheers.

"So it was meant to be. The Varrus bow has lost nothing with the years, including its master's skills." Huw's admiration was genuine and ungrudging.

"Had you not said what you did, your victory would have gone uncontested, my friend."

"I knew that, Merlyn, but I knew, too, that you had not seen it, did I not?"

"Aye, you're right. It needed to be said. My thanks to you. But why are you here, Huw? Why in Camulod, and since when?"

He made a wry face. "Since life in our own place became unbearable," he answered, as the throng bore down on us, led by Powys, who brandished Huw's brooch above his head. "We'll talk about it later."

Once again I found myself surrounded by well-wishers, and it occurred to me that here was a day for interrupted conversations.

After the sun went down, destroying any hope of further shooting, the recruits were dismissed and dispersed, and Huw and his fellow Celts accompanied Ambrose and me to the refectory, where I prevailed upon one of the presiding cooks to pack up a quantity of foods, both hot and cold, to feed sixteen of us. Ludo, my effeminate old friend from boyhood days, had died some time before, but he had disciplined his staff over the years to accede to any demand that I might make at any time. Then, armed with good food and ale, we sought a firepit by the road outside the walls by the main gate. We found one, manned by some of the recruits who had been with us earlier, and sent them searching elsewhere for a fire, while we sat down to eat and talk. There was a chill nip to the evening air, but most of the men wore cloaks and the day had been pleasant, with more pale, wintry sunshine than showers.

Conversation was desultory while the food lasted, but Huw was quick to show me his brooch, returned to him by Powys, which had now become a trophy. It bore two small, parallel identical scars where the inside upper rim had been nicked by our arrows, and Huw was immensely proud of it.

"Look you, Merlyn," he pointed out to me, kneeling beside me and balancing the meat he had crammed inside a wedge of bread precariously on one bent knee while he held the brooch out for my inspection. "If you were to draw crossed lines, splitting the circle in four parts, each arrow's point would pierce above the level cross line, you see?—but exactly the same distance on either side from the vertical, so that the upper edges of the arrowheads have nicked the rim! It looks as though the marks were made a-purpose, doesn't it?" I agreed that it did, gaining great pleasure from his simple excitement, and he went off to share his explanation with the others.

"He'll get drunk on that brooch for years," Ambrose murmured from where he sat beside me.

"Well, why not?" I responded, watching Huw's progress. "He's entitled to. That was probably one of the best shots he ever made in his life; I know it was mine. That the two should occur together like that almost goes beyond belief, but fortunately for Huw, he has witnesses aplenty. Now, to business." I turned and faced my brother as squarely as I could when we were seated side by side on the same log. "Where did he and the others come from, and when and why?"

Ambrose threw his remaining, well-gnawed bone into the fire and wiped his grease-covered fingers on the hem of his tunic before answering, finishing his toilet by scrubbing at his lips with the back of one hand. "Arrived on the day you left," he said. "All fourteen of them together. Frightened the marrow out of the sentinel. He neither saw nor heard them until they spoke to him, right in his ear. They had crawled up on him from behind . . ." He paused, reflecting. "I almost had the fellow charged with dereliction, until I thought the matter through. Obviously such a thing could not have happened had Huw's men not been so thoroughly familiar with our ways and territory, and of course that does nothing to relieve the guard of any fault, but it served to point out one of the many weaknesses in our current system. Had Huw's people been hostile for any reason, possessing the same knowledge, they would have been among us before we knew they were near. So instead of punishing the guard, I embarrassed him by making him explain the whole affair to his companions: how and why he was at fault; what might have happened had these not been friends; where he had been careless; how, *exactly* how, he would take steps to be more vigilant in times to come. I was merciless on him, but I think the lesson worked. All our guards are more alert now, everywhere. Anyway—" He broke off what he was saying to pick up his ale mug. "Huw says there is much trouble in our dead cousin's Cambrian hills, Brother. Minor, perhaps major wars are being waged over the vacant kingship. Uther had no natural successor, being the last of his direct line, but I gather there is no dearth of secondary claimants; uncles on his mother's side, cousins and a whole host of far-flung relatives."

"Hmm. I thought that might be the case, although I must admit I am surprised to hear you speak of warfare. That kind of war pits brother against brother."

"Aye, and mother against son, in some instances."

"So why did Huw's people leave?"

"Ask him. He thought I was you, when he first saw me, and came right to me. He was much nonplussed to find I did not recognize him." His face broke into a smile. "But he was really stunned when he found I was not you. I made him at ease, for all that, and there were many others around to welcome him and his men. Titus and Flavius both made much of them, and they helped me tremendously in gaining their acceptance. Later, when Huw had come to know me slightly better, he spoke of his reasons for leaving the hills and coming here. Fundamentally, he and his men had been away too long to enable them to form sudden, clear-cut loyalties to any of the contenders in the struggle that they found when they reached home. Uther had been their lord, and they his men. So after spending an entire war against Lot, surviving as a unit, they maintained their unity at home, without committing to one faction or another. And that failure to commit, as I am sure you will already have surmised, bred hatred from all sides. Originally twenty-four, their party was depleted one by one, by stealth and treachery over the course of less than four months, to the point where only fifteen remained alive. Huw decided to come here to save the others, their loyalty transferred from Uther to you as Uther's natural successor."

"Uther's successor? I have no claim on Uther's kingship!"

"They said nothing of kingship, Cay. Their talk was all of loyalty and commitment."

"Ah! Do they know aught of the child Arthur?"

Ambrose shook his head. "Nothing. I reasoned it was not my place to tell them."

"Good. I may tell them later, for we will have need of them and their loyalty. Tell me about your school of bowmanship."

He stretched his legs and rose to his feet, massaging his buttocks, then sat down again, straddling the log so that he faced me directly. "Huw offered to teach some of our men to shoot, and I seized on it. It fitted in perfectly with my design to meld the elements of Camulod's forces into a single entity. I told you about the rift I have discovered between our horsemen and foot-soldiers. At the most fundamental level, a schism—which may be groundless but is nonetheless extremely real—has been created between the two." Again he stopped himself, and I could almost see his mind working as he scanned the words he would use next. "Understand me, Brother, I see little of this stemming from you yourself, but from all I have gathered you have been, albeit unknowingly, part of the problem. When you lay injured, and even afterward, when you were up and about, the guiding hand, the strength and wisdom you had formerly lent to all in Camulod, were sadly lacking. During that time, too, Camulod was at war, and principally under the command of Uther and his staff of officers. Most of those were cavalry, for the simple reason that Uther, when he required the men of Camulod to supplement or complement his Celtic Pendragon, required them urgently, insisting they be capable of moving quickly to prosecute his aims. He took large bodies of our infantry as well, but those served as foot-soldiers always do, slogging through mud and mire and sleeping on the ground in filth and squalor: no wondrous feats recorded of them; no deeds of brilliant daring; no glowing victories . . . no privileges, and no new equipment, whereas the vaunted cavalry received, it appeared, the best of everything.

"And so, over a span of years of brutal war, a division was created, born of the simple envies and resentment bred in men who see themselves as put upon and not appreciated while others more fortunate than themselves are lauded for performing similar but more ostentatious and less meritorious deeds at far less cost and under far fewer hardships. Schism . . ." He paused, then added, "An unpleasant word, Cay, and a far less pleasant fact."

"Aye," I said. "I can see it now, listening to you, but I had no idea. Thank God you came to Camulod, Brother. What's to do now? You have already started, I'm aware, by doubling the presence in every outpost, mixing the men. But if the schism is as deep and angry as you say it is, how will that help? The mix, at such close quarters, might be incendiary."

"It could be, but I think I have forestalled the danger, at least in part. Now that you've returned, the matter should proceed more quickly with your support." A couple of the men around us had moved closer to where we sat, seeking the fire's heat. They were paying us no attention, but once Ambrose had become aware of them, their presence inhibited the flow of his speech. He glanced at them again and then stood up. "Walk with me a little. I'll explain as we go."

No one paid us any attention as we strolled out of the firelight into the darkness, which was now almost complete, and we made our way automatically to the paved road that wound down the hill from the fortress gates, seeking the soundness of its surface beneath our feet. As we went, Ambrose told me of his plans to unify our Camulodians, as he referred to them, more tightly than ever before. He knew that they had always been a single force until the present difficulties had begun, and he was confident they would soon be again. He would arrange the military affairs of the Colony, provided he had my support and assistance, so as to ensure that neither arm of our forces would ever act entirely independently of the other again. Patrols would be organized in such a way that each of the outlying guard posts would be in constant contact with the others on either side of it. There were twelve such outposts placed around the perimeter of Camulod's territories at the present time, and Ambrose had allocated each an identifying number, from one through twelve. Six double squadrons of cavalry would soon begin to ride the bounds, each double unit beginning its tour from one of the even-numbered camps, progressing at a pre-set pace and continuing from camp to camp until they had completed the entire circuit, a course that would take a month; twenty-four days for travel, six more in which to deal with unforeseen developments. Infantry support from each camp would accompany each group of riders to the half-way point between camps, at which an infantry detachment from the next post would be waiting. Each outgoing infantry patrol would then return to its own camp to await the arrival of the next mounted group, while the mounted troopers rode on to the next camp, escorted by the infantry who had awaited them. This activity, Ambrose believed, would keep all the men active and on the move at all times, neutralizing the danger of boredom or dissatisfaction.

I was impressed by his vision of how his innovations would work, but I had not yet heard the really ambitious part. Each soldier, he told me, horse and foot, would henceforth do a month of patrol duty at one stretch, and then would have two months in Camulod itself. We had the resources to arrange that, I knew. But during his two months in Camulod, as rapidly and intensively as possible, each soldier would learn the other force's skills. All mounted troopers would train as infantry; all foot-soldiers as horsemen. That way, Ambrose maintained, each would learn the benefits and the drawbacks of their fellows. It might be chaotic at first, and he was prepared for that, but he believed the chaos would be short-lived. Some troops would wish to change, he said, and there might be apparent imbalances for a time because of that, but his belief was that eventually the balance would settle again to resemble the current status quo. The best of both groups, however, on a voluntary basis, would be given the opportunity to join a new branch of Camulodians: to become bowmen, armed with the long Celtic bows.

By the time his recital was done we had reached the bottom of the hill, turned and made our way up again almost to the point from which we had set out. I saw big Powys above us, clearly outlined by the flames from the firepit.

When I was sure Ambrose had no more to add, I grinned at him and shook my head in admiration. "You have wasted no time since my departure, have you, Brother? To say that I am impressed would not do justice either to what I feel or to what you've achieved, in planning, at least. How long will all this take? I'm assuming you have plotted all of it?"

"A year or so; certainly no longer than that. As I said, it will be slow at first, then all will follow like a landslide for some hectic months, and then there will be a period of months for slowing down and refining. Less than a year, when all's been said and done."

"And after that the schism will be gone."

"After that? God, Cay, it should vanish within the month, as soon as we can see we've truly begun."

"And when will that be?"

"Tomorrow, if you're in accord with me. The basic elements are all in place."

"What will you require of me, apart from my personal involvement?"

"Total, visible and vocal support and commitment." He had been waiting for me to ask that specific question.

"You have all of it. How do I express it?"

He grinned. "First, in Council; next, to the assembled officers of Camulod, high and low; then to the troops themselves, in formal parade. Time we had one of those. The last formal parade we had here was the one you called to signal my arrival."

"Agreed in full, and here's my hand on it. Let it be done." As we clasped hands to forearms, I added my single condition. "I hope you can begin without me, for at least the first week or two."

"I can," he said with a nod. "What have you planned?"

"An expedition of a hundred troopers to Glevum, without me, the reason for which I'll explain in a moment, and for me, a journey to Cambria, although I see that might be difficult and dangerous, from what you have told me."

"Potentially fatal, I would say. Take my advice and speak with Huw on that. He will have things to say that will make more sense than anything I've told you. What's this about Glevum?"

I told him briefly about the Berbers we had seen, and their attack on the leper colony, and he listened, tight-lipped, then nodded. "You're right. Something has to be done about those people. Otherwise, they'll grow like a nest of wasps. Best to get rid of them before they can settle in to a nesting spot. There's a formal Council meeting the day after tomorrow. Can this wait that long for Council's approval?"

"Yes. It will take that long to make ready. The expedition can leave the morning after the meeting."

He pursed his lips. "Tell me, has the Council ever withheld approval of a venture like this?"

"You mean a punitive expedition? No, how could it? The mere idea is ludicrous. Things like that are only undertaken for the good and protection of the Colony itself and the Council is the legislative body of the Colony."

"What would you do if the circumstance ever arose? For the sake of argument, let's say that, for some reason inconceivable to either of us now, Council should some day decide to withhold its approval of an expedition like the one you now propose. What would you do, hypothetically?"

I grimaced and shook my head slowly. "Hypothetically? Well, I suppose hypothetically I'd do the same as I would practically. I'd override them and imprison any councilor who sought to stay me."

Ambrose grinned. "That, Caius Merlyn, is the response of an autocrat."

I grinned back at him. "Is it really? Well, I might quibble with you over that, Brother. I'd say it's the response of a professional soldier to a question that is, by definition, hypothetical—a soldier, bear in mind, whose title is Commander of the Military Forces of Camulod and whose responsibility is to the safety of the Colony . . . In my opinion, Ambrose, and perhaps it would apply within this context alone, a councilor is but an adviser with a grander title. The function of the Council in such purely military matters, in my 'official' eyes, is to counsel and support, by providing a consensus—a concurrence and a commitment—of the senior minds within our Colony. It may strongly advise against a particular course, but it is never to forbid."

"Hmm," he murmured, still smiling as his eyes focused on something behind me. "Here's Huw now. Ask him about the journey you intend to make."

"What journey?" Huw was one of the few among Uther's Celts who spoke our Latin tongue with anything approaching fluency. I swung around to face him as he joined us.

"To Cambria, Huw. I have to travel to your country, to speak with whoever is in command there now."

His face twisted into a scowl of disgust, and to express it he lapsed back into his own tongue. "In command? No one is in *command* there. The place is a morass—a bog of shit and waste and treachery. That's why we are here, myself and the others. The pride we've borne all our lives in being Pendragon has been blasted like a tree in a thunderstorm and all that's left of it is a smoking stump riven into shattered pieces, each leaning like a drunkard in its own direction." His eyes had been fixed on mine throughout this and I was struck by the image his words brought into my mind, but he had not yet finished. "I'm serious, Merlyn. Nothing you have to do is important enough to warrant a journey into that nest of rats."

His vehemence, and the words he chose to express it, gave me more cause for concern than I had yet considered. "Nest of rats? Huw, that is your own home you are speaking of."

"I know that!" He snapped the words at me, their utterance a rebuke for my ignorance. "But the rats I refer to are no relatives or clansmen of mine. Rats thrive among people, Merlyn; they always have. They feed on the waste people discard. That doesn't make rats of the people who supply their food, nor does it make rats' nests of their homes, but as surely as you'll find green shit in the guts of a cow, you'll find rats' nests among human dwellings. All I meant was that there's a plague of two-legged rats running around my homeland nowadays in all directions; a plague; a sickness—an insanity."

"Hmm!" I thought about that, and sighed gustily. "Still," I said. "There's no help for it. I have to go there."

"Why, in the name of all the Druids and their gods?" His exasperation made him sound angered at me.

"Because I have given a promise, Huw, perhaps foolishly, to achieve something. It may be unachievable, but that is something I will have to prove for myself, and to the satisfaction of those concerned."

"And who are they, these concerned people?" Huw's voice had regained a tone of normality. "Do you want to tell me?"

"Aye, willingly, if you'll sit down and stop barking at me like an angry dog." He sat down by the fire, close to Ambrose, and I told him of Liam Twistback and his breeding cattle, and of my promise to King Athol to arrange a temporary sanctuary for the man and his animals in the little-used grazing lands to the south and west of Glevum.

"That's all it is?"

"Aye, but I would not choose to dismiss it as scornfully as that. I made a promise. I must honour it."

"And what does this King Athol offer in return for this . . . what did you call it? Sanctity?"

"Sanctuary. A Roman word, meaning a safe haven, a place free of danger, conflict and penalty."

Huw barked a loud, hard laugh. "Sanctuary! A strange term to be applying to Pendragon country nowadays."

"I can see that now," I agreed. "But it did not seem so silly when I made the promise. I knew nothing of what's going on up there."

"Aye, much can happen to alter the world in a short time. Anyway, I asked what this king offers in return."

I shrugged my shoulders. "Nothing, in effect, because we did not discuss the matter in those terms. I would suspect, nevertheless, his people would be willing to make some form of payment, perhaps in kind, for the use of the land. I see no risk of conflict there. The risk is involved in finding whoever it may be who can confer such rights on Liam and his people."

"How many people?"

I felt myself frowning, perplexed at his pursuit of such detail. "Ten . . . Perhaps a dozen . . . The people who would tend the beasts. No more than that."

"Done, and settled, providing your Outlanders are dreaming no surprises. Bring me to this Liam Twistback." He grinned, fierce and sudden, at the look of surprise on my face. "Those lands are mine, Merlyn, south and west of Glevum—mine and my clan's, which means mine and my son's, since all the rest of us are dead."

"Yours? They're yours?" I found myself almost blustering.

He gazed at me, an expression akin to compassion complementing the smile in his eyes. "Aye, that's what I said. Those lands are mine and have been in the care and keeping of my people since before the Romans came. They thought to conquer us and called us Belgae and Silures because they didn't know the names of our clans, but we are of Pendragon, and our land was ours and well ordered long before the Caesars came and called our country Britain. The Romans are long gone, but our land remains ours as it remained ours throughout their occupation. We were never conquered, Caius Merlyn; we merely stopped fighting."

"Then I have no need to enter Cambria."

"That is what I am saying. No need to go. I can extend the right to your friend Twistback to live on the land . . . What I cannot do is guarantee his safety, any more than I could ensure my own, were I to attempt what he will. To breed his cattle, he will have to stay in one place and defend it against all who come his way. I have no envy for him there, because all of

Cambria is in chaos and he may find himself in the way of many unwelcome
visitors."

"Well, that may be looked after in due time, by one means or another.
God! Is there any of that ale left, Ambrose?"

"No." My brother leaned forward and groped for a flask by his side. "But
I have some good mead."

Later that night, in the comfort of the family room after Aunt Luceiia had
retired, I discussed the entire day's happenings in flickering firelight with
Lucanus and Ambrose. We talked at length of the expedition to cleanse
Glevum of the Berbers' occupation, and of the need to provide some means
of protection for Liam Twistback and his people in their temporary home
south of Glevum. Those territories lay outside the bounds of Camulod—far
outside, in fact—but the unrest reported farther north in Cambria might
spill southward, and it seemed sensible to all of us to establish some form
of defensive outpost in Huw's territory. It was Ambrose, my far-sighted
brother, who pointed out that it might also be politically astute to arrange
for a constant presence in the coastal waters, to be provided by Connor's
fleet in protection of their own interests. I determined to find some means
of making such arrangements with Connor, and from there the conversation
drifted aimlessly for a while as we discussed a range of matters distinguished
only by their lack of urgency.

It was Ambrose, too, who led the discussion on to its next stage. He had
been sitting silent for a time, staring into the fire, but suddenly he stirred
and turned towards me. "You know," he said, "it has just occurred to me
that you are free to lead the raid on Glevum if you wish to, now that you
won't be going to Cambria."

"The thought had passed through my mind," I answered, "but I decided
against it. If you and I are to work together as closely as you suggest, and if
the task ahead of us is as complex as you believe, then I think my time would
be better spent here with you, getting on with it. My lads have no need of
me to do that job. They know what's necessary and they have the motivation
and the spirit. They'll make short work of it and be back here within ten
days. Your task and mine, which is much more important, would not be
begun too soon were we to tackle it tomorrow. Don't you agree?"

"Aye . . ." A slight hesitation turned his positive response to a negative.

"What's wrong? You foresee a problem with so quick a start? Do you still
have preparations to make?"

He sighed and sat up straighter. "No, Cay, not at all, but my mind was
on other things. I was lulled by the fire, dreaming about Vortigern. You know
I still have to return and tell him I intend to stay here in Camulod."

"Aye, but you said you felt no time constraints in that. You spoke of
returning after a year, and you have been here less than three months. Has
something changed your mind? Have you news from Vortigern?"

"No, nothing like that. I have been thinking about him recently, that's
all, and I thought for a moment I might achieve that task while you were off
in Glevum. But it would not be possible. The timing is wrong in all aspects.
I had been thinking your expedition might take longer than you clearly expect
it to. Ten days would hardly be long enough for me to reach Vortigern's
territories, let alone find him and return."

"No, a month would not be long enough, especially at this time of the year. There will be snow on the mountains by this time, and you might have difficulty in the high passes. Better to wait for spring. How long do you anticipate this melding of our troops would take were we both devoted to the task?"

"If we can throw ourselves into this thing together, side by side, without permitting anything to distract us from our intent, it should be achievable in a matter of two or three months. All we have to do is supply the outline and define the pattern we wish to follow, and convince our men that it is sane, desirable and good for all of us."

Lucanus leaned forward and stirred the coals. "So, you believe it could be done by spring?"

"Aye, easily."

When Luke responded, his words were to Ambrose, but he looked at me. "Then your task and your time lines are clearly defined, and you can journey together to meet Vortigern come spring, if you so wish."

"Together? I have no reason to travel across Britain simply to visit Vortigern."

"You think not? I can give you at least two, here and now, with no further consideration."

"Then do so, please. I'm curious."

He stood up and wrestled a big, fresh log onto the fire before he responded. "Very well then," he said finally, dusting his hands and returning to his seat. "The first of them is self-evident. You two have much yet to discuss and share. A ride across the country would give you the time and the leisure to deal with much of it and to enjoy each other, free of duty for a spell."

Ambrose smiled and nodded at me and I grunted. "Aye, agreed, if duty will spare us. What is your second reason?"

"Your own curiosity about the parts of this land you have not seen, and the people who inhabit them. Those Saxons who live along the Saxon Shore, and Vortigern's mercenaries. I know you are concerned about some of them, at least; those of them who have lived here now for several generations. You spoke of them when you returned from the south, after Lot's War . . . of how the people there feared the Saxons far less than Lot's Cornish mercenaries and Uther's bowmen. Am I not correct?"

"Aye, you are. What of it?"

"And again, you spoke of it when Ambrose here arrived with his men all dressed as Saxons, having travelled through the Saxon-occupied territories to reach us . . . It seems to me that a journey to Vortigern's kingdom might provide you with a wondrous opportunity to look more closely at some of these people . . . to meet them and assess them. Ambrose speaks their tongue—"

"One of their tongues," Ambrose interjected.

"One of their tongues, so be it. And he and his men have the clothing and the weaponry to pass unremarked among them."

"With good fortune," Ambrose interrupted again.

"As you say, with Fortune on your side. But—" He broke off and looked from me to my brother, leaving his thought unfinished. Ambrose nodded.

"Luke's right, Cay. Know thine enemy. It's an opportunity to meet some of these people face to face and pass among them. It would be valuable."

"Of course it would be valuable, but it would also be highly perilous."

Ambrose grinned at me again. "Life is highly perilous, Brother, had you not noticed that before now?"

I found myself suddenly impatient with the tone of this entire conversation. "Damnation, Ambrose, be serious! It would be folly to undertake such a journey, and you know that. We could both be killed, and where would that leave us?"

"Dead in a forest or a meadow somewhere, removed from all further concerns. Unbend, Cay. We were but making idle conversation. There's no need to grow angry over it. And yet I agree with Luke. It would be worthwhile to scout the land, and enjoyable to do it in concert with you. What would be lost by it, given that we return alive?"

"Discipline, for one thing." I moderated my tone, but I was far from mollified. "With both of us gone, at the outset of a program as ambitious and portentous as the one you've been describing, things could fall into chaos again within days of our departure. Who would you leave in charge? In the three months since you arrived, have you found anyone you might trust to such an extent?"

His eyebrows went high on his forehead. "Aye, several. If there is one thing Camulod does not lack it is ambitious, bright young leaders, in both arms of our force."

"Name some."

"Young Brian Melitas, and his two companions, Cornelius Nimmo and Jacob Cato; Jacob's own father, Achmed Cato, although he is not young; your own companions on your journey to Eire, every one of them; Silas Agorine, one of the most brilliant young infantry commanders I've ever seen; Johan Sitrabo, another of the same calibre. There is no lack of deputies in Camulod, Cay."

I sat staring at him for long moments, aware of Luke's eyes on me. Then I cleared my throat. "Apart from Achmed Cato, his son Jacob and my own companions, I know none of those men. That is unconscionable." Neither of my friends said anything to that, and I continued, speaking now almost to myself. "Only today, watching your young bowmen at practice, I realized that I have been away too long, both physically and mentally. I no longer know my own people. Even worse, I don't know our best and brightest young commanders. You have been here mere months, and you know them all far better than I do. I have a task ahead of me."

Ambrose laughed gently and leaned forward to the fire, reaching for the great iron poker that lay in the hearth to stir the logs. "Don't berate yourself, Brother. Your neglect could hardly be described as willful." He busied himself with his task. "Besides, by the time you and I have immersed ourselves in our new program for a few days, you will know all of them. Such things come quickly, you and I know."

Thereafter we sat silent, staring into the fire, each thinking his own thoughts, and the time went by until the logs began to settle, more than half consumed. The entire household was still, we three its only waking occupants. Lucanus was the first to move, standing up and yawning, ready for sleep. His action stirred a like response in us, and the last thing that was said that night was mine. I told them that I would consider riding to the east with Ambrose in the spring, to see for myself how matters were progressing elsewhere, but that my self-appointed task throughout the coming winter would be to come to know the Camulodian Colonists again—all of them, farmers, artisans and troopers—which prompted me to wonder what had become of Peter Ironhair since his departure. No one had seen him. No word had come of his whereabouts since the day he fled.

We doused the candles and the lamps and left the family room in darkness that glowed with the embers of the dying fire, and I made my way directly to my quarters. I lay awake for a long time, thinking about all that had happened in the past few months, and was happy to be aware that Shelagh demanded little of those thoughts. Most of them, in truth, concerned the boy, Arthur, and the growing influence I suspected he was going to have upon my life from that time forth, and they had been precipitated by the short discussion of Peter Ironhair and his whereabouts and doings. No one had heard of him, but I had no reason to believe him dead, or indifferent to our affairs. He had simply faded from our immediate awareness, and that, I suspected without any real reason, might bode ill for us along some future way. Ironhair was alive and well, somewhere, I was convinced. But now, for some reason, I could not put the man out of mind. I tried to tell myself that he had consigned all of us to perdition and decided to live out his life elsewhere, far removed from sight and sound and memory of Camulod, but there was something within me that prevented me from being so sanguine. I tried eventually to banish him by thinking on the baby Arthur, and discovered to my mild astonishment that the mere contemplation of the child's existence was a source of delight to me, something I would not have believed possible mere months earlier, and I fell asleep some time after that, filled with the warmth of the memory of his tiny, sleeping face with its long, thick, almost feminine eyelashes.

XXI

FIVE DAYS AFTER that evening in the family room, seething with frustration and a debilitating fear, I decided—or to be more accurate and truthful, my friends decided after long and sometimes impassioned debate—that for the sake of my own sanity and the welfare of the men under my command, particularly the younger officers, it would be best to remove myself from all human contact for a while, and so I sought the stillness of the forest, armed with my bow and a quiver filled to capacity with arrows. There, for an entire week, and never less than five miles from the fortress, I hunted singlemindedly, cleaning my frequent kills and leaving them for collection at predetermined points by soldiers sent by Ambrose, with whom I had made the appropriate arrangements. None of the collectors ever saw me, although on each occasion I watched from concealment to ensure that they arrived and the meat was not spoiled. Each time, once assured that my orders had been carried out, I moved on to my next selected location and began my hunt anew, and all the time I struggled with my thoughts, my plans, my desires and my various dilemmas, one of which was what I should do about Shelagh, who had become, through my own carelessness, the second woman ever to set eyes upon Excalibur.

The incident had occurred the day after my arrival home, before I became involved in the matter of Ambrose's schism. I had been up and about early that morning, full of good cheer and enthusiasm for the days ahead despite the fact that the rain was falling steadily outside, and I was on my way to Uncle Varrus's Armoury to search out a reference to Alexander's cavalry I had remembered from one of his books. On my way I had met Shelagh, quite accidentally, rounding the corner of a passage. She was carrying the infant Arthur, straddled across her right hip and supported in the bend of her arm, and had been pleased to see me, laughing and talking to the child about me. He, for his part, had seemed singularly unimpressed by his "Uncle Merlyn," as Shelagh had called me. His large golden eyes had observed me without expression and then moved on to gaze at other, more interesting vistas down the passageway.

On discovering that I was merely headed for the Armoury to read something, and in no particular hurry, Shelagh had asked me to mind the child for a few moments while she attended to something that she had forgotten to do. I took the child from her and watched her walk away, enjoying the sight of her firm buttocks moving tautly beneath her robe. When she had gone, and the child and I were alone, an impulsive idea occurred to me and I took the babe into the Armoury, mere steps away. I laid him on the floor while I pulled up the floorboard and retrieved the case from its concealment. Quickly, kneeling beside the infant, I wiped the dust from the polished wooden case with a cloth and then brought out the wondrous sword itself, waving it slowly now above the supine infant's form, and his eyes fastened immediately upon the shifting patterns of light along its shining blade.

"There, Sir King," I breathed. "What think you of that? Pretty, is it not? This is your own sword, Excalibur. Would you like to hold it?" As quickly as the thought came to me, I held the weapon, pommel down, towards him. "See," I whispered. "It is yours. Take hold of it." He did, immediately, with both hands, and I felt the hairs stir along my nape. It was probably the polished gold of the pommel that attracted his eyes, carved as it was in perfect replication of a large cockle shell, but his tiny fists clamped just above it, at the junction of pommel and hilt, below my own hand; first the right hand, then the left, and both with authority.

Long moments we remained immobile, and then I smiled and moved to break his hold, pulling the weapon gently back towards me. The child, however, would not let go. His golden eyes stared straight upward, fixed on the length of the great blade that reared above him, and his chubby fists hung on. Intrigued, and still smiling slightly, I increased my pull gently, seeking to break his tiny grip, but he clung staunchly, refusing to quit even when my greater strength began to lift his shoulders clear of the floor. Astonished now, I continued pulling and watched him continue to rise without effort, so that he was almost sitting up completely. A sudden vision of his grip breaking and his tiny skull striking the wooden floor made me stoop immediately to cup my free hand behind his head, but still he maintained his grasp on Excalibur. Finally, shaking my head in wondering admiration, I relented and lowered him gently and carefully back to the boards, removing my guarding hand only when he was supine again and using it to pry his tiny fingers loose from the hold he seemed determined to maintain. When I had done so, his eyes gazed now at me and I grinned at him and shook my head.

"Not yet, Sir King," I told him, whispering still. "Not yet, but one day, surely, when your own size is greater than your sword's. Then you will grasp it firmly, and relinquish it to no man." The mighty sword still reared between us, but now the child seemed to have eyes only for me, as though he heard and understood my words. "Do not forget this day," I admonished him. "Nor this. Its name is Excalibur. Excalibur . . . Remember it."

Done then, I began to rise to my feet again, only to be confounded by the sound of Shelagh's voice behind me, by the door she had opened noiselessly.

"Merlyn, what are you doing?"

I must have appeared either ludicrous or dangerous, or possibly both, scrambling to my feet and whirling towards her while attempting uselessly to conceal Excalibur behind my back. Her eyes were wide with alarm as she took a step further into the room, one hand reaching out towards the baby on the floor.

"Stop!"

She froze in mid-step, beginning to frown.

"You're not supposed to come in here," I spluttered, hearing the futility in my own voice.

Her brows came together now and her eyes flashed. "And why not? No one told me anything of that. It seemed a room like any other—" She stopped speaking abruptly and glanced quickly around the walls, noting the array of weapons that hung there, and the large books that lay on tables here and there. From there, her eyes went quickly to the child still lying placidly by my feet, then to the sword I held so ineffectually behind my back, its long, silver blade quite evident where it reached beyond my body, and thence to the open case with its leather-lined, sculpted cradle for Excalibur. I knew then, all at once and with despair, that I had forfeited all chance of diverting her from the sword. Had I possessed the presence of mind merely to hold it casually when she appeared, I might have smoothed things over, brazening it out. But my own horror in discovery had betrayed me.

For long moments, neither of us moved nor spoke. Then, apparently satisfied that the child, at least, was safe, Shelagh drew a deep breath and stretched to her full height, turning her back to me and moving away resolutely towards the door. Once there, however, she increased my consternation by closing the half that lay ajar and turning back towards me, laying her shoulders flat against the join of the bronze-covered panels.

"So be it, Merlyn Britannicus," she said, speaking in level, courteous tones. "I should not have come in here. Unfortunately I did, seeking you and the child and knowing no better . . . And now I have seen that weapon you are trying so uselessly to hide behind your back and the case in which it is kept, which evidently causes you great concern and makes you both afraid and angry, although I know not why. What is done is done. I have seen what evidently should not have been seen. So what am I to do? We may regret such things, once done, but we are powerless to change them."

I gusted a great sigh then, I recall, and shook my head, shamefaced, then lowered my eyes to the floor, unable to meet her gaze and allowing Excalibur to come to rest with its point on the floor by my right foot. She waited for me to say something and when I did not, she moved swiftly to stand beside me, placing her hand upon my wrist, above the sword's hilt. When she spoke again, her voice was gentle, filled with sympathy.

"The sword is wondrous, Merlyn, and plainly worth more than anything I have ever seen. Is that it? Is that your concern, that having seen it I might talk of it with others? Should I be unaware of its great value?"

"Of its existence," I said, looking at her and watching her eyes narrow in surprise and incomprehension.

"What did you say?"

I sighed again. "I said you should not be aware of its existence. Almost no one else is."

Distractedly, to give herself time for thought, she knelt and picked up the child, straightening immediately and settling him anew across her hip, where he leaned forward and began to nuzzle hungrily at her breast. She pushed his mouth away gently with the back of her fingers and hitched him higher. "There's nothing there for you, young man," was all she said, before squinting up at me.

"What is it that is so remarkable about this thing's existence?"

"It is the only one of its kind in the world."

She pursed her lips, dropping narrowed eyes to where the huge cross-hilt gleamed in front of my fist, and then she reached out with one extended fingertip and placed the ball of her finger gently against the silver of the blade.

"I can see that the guard there is different. That may be unique, as far as I can tell, and the colour of the blade is vastly different. But the blade itself is of a length with your own sword, so there's nothing special there. How then is this so magically rare that it's unmatched in all the world?" She glanced back at me. "Can you tell me? Will you? Wait! Before you answer, let me ask this: Has Donuil seen this sword?"

I shook my head. "No, he has never seen it, but he knows of its existence. That he has never seen it is due merely to circumstance. The opportunity to show it to him has never arisen. Donuil is one of a very special group of living souls who know of it. The others are myself, my brother Ambrose, my great-aunt Luceiia, and now you. There are no more."

Her eyes were wide with wonder. "But why?" she asked. "Why keep it secret? It is no more than a sword!"

I found, quite suddenly, that I could smile again. "Ah, Shelagh, there you are wrong; in grievous error. This is far more than a sword. This is Excalibur, the High King's sword, and that young person in your arms is the High King himself. And now, if you will bear his regal hunger to be satisfied, I shall wait here for your return and tell you the entire tale of Camulod, Excalibur, and the Dream of the Roman Eagles who created both."

She hesitated, tugged by the wish to leave and then return, and by the fear that I might leave while she was gone. "You will wait here?"

I laughed then, feeling immensely better. "Aye, you need have no fear. A modicum of knowledge is greatly dangerous and now, to disarm that danger, I must tell you all there is to know. Only then will you be able to comprehend the secret you must hold from this day forward. Go now, and send someone to light a fire in here against the cold, then come back quickly."

By the time she returned, Excalibur had been safely cached once more, the fire had been kindled and was burning brightly. She had taken time to change her dress and comb out her hair, and I thrilled with guilty pleasure as she crossed the room to sit beside me, close to the leaping flames. We talked then, or rather I spoke and she listened, for a space of hours, and in spite of my familiarity with the tale I told, its power consumed me yet again, so that I soon lost all awareness of her as a woman and spoke only for her ears and mind. So wrought up in my tale were we that we forgot eventually to tend the fire, and by the time I had finished, it had been reduced to glowing embers. As I replenished it, knowing the drying warmth to be beneficial to my uncle's books, Shelagh began to ask me questions, and we talked further, and the time passed quickly. But now that my self-absorbing tale was told, I found myself aware of her again, watching her body's supple sinuosity; seeing and sometimes sensing the motion of breast, belly, buttock and thigh; the flashing, laughing, flaring, breathtaking eyes; the casually tousled curls that hung and swung in such profusion, inviting contact, apparently wishing to be touched, caressed and smoothed. The physical disturbance caused by all of these things was almost overwhelming, and utterly deceptive. I knew implicitly that Shelagh felt no such desire for me. The invitations that my mind supplied were of my mind alone. Finally, almost in desperation, I stood up abruptly, interrupting something she was saying.

"Shelagh," I could hear the tension in my own voice. "I have lost track of time. Forgive me, but I promised Ambrose I would spend the afternoon with him, talking to people on a matter of great urgency, and it is long past noon. The time has flown. Will you permit me to . . . leave now?" The hesitation had been very slight, but I had almost used the word "escape." I wondered fleetingly if she had noticed, but her response showed she had not. In a moment she was on her feet, taking my hand in a tight, two-handed grasp.

"Of course, Caius," she said. "Go now, but before you do, tell me this. Do you believe, completely without reservation, that I will guard your trust in this?"

I raised her hands to my lips and kissed her fingers, feeling the fiery contact searing into my memory and being branded there with the scent of her skin. "Completely, and without reservation. Now pardon me, I must go." I spun on my heel and walked from the room, humiliatingly aware of my own arousal and cursing myself for my perfidy.

Recalling that as I lay in my cot that first night in my solitary hunting camp, I felt myself stirring again and turned my thoughts to another topic: the matter that had taken me to meet with Ambrose that same afternoon.

I had originally accepted Ambrose's opinion on the schism within our forces without argument, simply because I had been convinced with that curious, half-blind arrogance that seems to lie within all of us, that the opinion he expressed was merely that—a personal perspective on a minor problem. I had not questioned his belief in the troublesome division he reported, nor did I doubt the existence of the dichotomy itself. The unfortunate corollary was that I had equally little doubt that the phenomenon must be no more than a minor, distracting irritant—a barrack-room philosopher's complaint, born of some misunderstanding, then broadcast and blown out of all proportion. I had, at root, no doubt of my own power to correct it merely by directing my attentions towards healing the rift. In consequence, I began my remedial efforts on the afternoon following our discussion, blithely confident that the problem, once defined and isolated, and once I had shown that I was concerned about it, would dry up and disappear in a spontaneous explosion of Colony-wide goodwill and military solidarity.

By the end of the second day, however, it had become obvious, even through an intransigence as vast as mine was then, that matters were far from well within Camulod's once close-knit little army. Dismayed by what I had already discovered, I had taken leave of Council that morning to absent myself from the regularly scheduled session, for even by then it had become undeniable that Ambrose was right, and that the rivalries between the men who formed our two main forces were much less than amicable. Underlying, deep hostilities had surfaced rapidly in the recent past and now I could see they were but thinly masked, and that impending violence between our cavalry and infantry lay buried by no more than a single, shallow layer of ill-borne discipline.

The recognition of another pair of competing factions destroyed my complacency. Aware that the consternation caused by the affair of the Farmers and the Artisans had not yet had time to fade from the minds of the Colonists at large, I was appalled to find myself facing a similar, frighteningly comparable situation, this time within my own command. And in this instance there appeared to be no obvious progenitors—no identifiable group who were recognizably at fault. My initial, instinctive reactions to what I found beneath my nose were fear and dismay, quickly followed by a violent urge to roar and rend—to vent my anger and outrage on my disgruntled troops—which, of course, I could not do without the risk of provoking them to outright rebellion. The officer cadre, however, was another matter, and for a short time I came close to yielding to the temptation to create havoc within those ranks. I gave thanks to God many times thereafter for the presence of my brother and his placid, unruffled perception and wisdom. He cajoled me and calmed me, diverted my anger, and made me see and finally accept that my own complicity, through simple ignorance, was as great as any other's. I slept poorly that night, nevertheless, and then for no more than an hour or so.

On the morning of the third day, we held the meeting we had planned, assembling all the officers in garrison at the time—Staff, Field and Warrant ranks, Cavalry and Infantry. Dedalus and his six comrades from our Eirish travels were in attendance, their expedition to Glevum summarily postponed for the time being pending the outcome of this plenary officers' conference, the first formal Tribunal ever held in Camulod for the resolution of a purely military domestic emergency. It was convened, for the sake of privacy and security, in the old, now-empty but still well-maintained Villa Britannicus on the plain beneath the hill of Camulod. No guards were assigned to duty there that day, and no servants permitted within the Villa confines. We fed ourselves between sessions from cooking fires lit outside the gates. The word had been passed among the attendees the previous day and everyone arrived at the Villa at the pre-ordained time, within half an hour after the break of dawn. The Colonists must have speculated wildly at the sight of the entire complement of the garrison's officers blearily making their way, singly and in small groups, down the road from the main gates in the pre-dawn darkness, but their speculation would go unresolved for many days, since everyone who attended that extraordinary session was sworn to secrecy.

The order of the proceedings was straightforward, and the first directive was that the two disciplines, horse and foot, should mingle in equality, no two of either discipline sitting together. There were almost two hundred officers present, and Ambrose and I shared the office of Convenor. I began by outlining the situation succinctly and forcefully, apportioning no blame and voicing no criticism. I defined the Schism, as I had come to think of it, as a military fact requiring an immediate solution, and then threw the topic open for debate.

By the end of the day, as the sun was going down, we had made progress, but the process had been noisy and at times almost unruly. Voices had been raised in angry disagreement at various times, and acrimonious insults had flown freely, but I believed that no new enmities had been forged and no lasting ill will fomented. A consensus had been reached: the problem that faced us was dangerous, inimical to the well-being of the Colony. It behoved all of us, therefore, to act together, according to the dictates of a carefully defined agenda, to pour soothing balm on the hurts, real and imaginary, suffered by each side in this dispute at the hands of the other. The primary difficulty, of course, would lie in the identification and definition of a solution, and in the development of a means of putting it into effect.

As I might have expected, it was Dedalus who came up with the most practical observation, after having sat for some time, bent forward, in a huddled conversation with Philip, Quintus and Rufio, all of whom were grouped close by him, interspersed among infantry officers.

"Commander!" He held up his hand, demanding my attention, and when

I recognized him he rose slowly, looking around at his assembled colleagues while addressing me. "I've been talking with some of the people around us, from both sides—" He broke off, apparently realizing too late what he had said, and then grinned his rogue's grin. "Your pardon . . . from both *viewpoints* might be a better way of phrasing that." Everyone laughed and I immediately felt more sanguine about the outcome of this affair.

"Aye. It might, Captain Dedalus," I answered him, allowing my face to crease into a slow smile and provoking more, but restrained laughter. "But guard your mouth from now on. No more seditious talk. We are one force, you know."

"I know that well enough, Commander. But so do you and Commander Ambrose." He lapsed into silence. I blinked at him.

"Forgive me, Dedalus, but I fail to see your point."

"You two are my point, Commander, with respect." He nodded from one to the other of us. "Peas in a pod," he grunted. "Flowers on a bush. Identical. Both of Camulod. Both Commanders. To look at you, you're indistinguishable one from the other, and yet one of you's an infantryman and the other's a horseman. Why don't you assemble all the troops—as you've assembled us—and let them see that? I mean, they know it, but they haven't *seen* it, if you know what I mean." He sat down again, looking at his hands and allowing his words to hang there over the assembly.

I sat there for several moments, going over the implications of what he had said. The same comment had been made, although in different words and in another context, by Ambrose several nights earlier when he had suggested a formal parade. The silence in the room, which had been sustained, was suddenly broken from somewhere at the rear of the large room, where someone began to applaud, slowly, and the sound spread quickly until I had to stand up and spread my arms for silence.

Dedalus's recommendation was adopted immediately and unanimously. Such a gathering would take place, but it would have to be, by definition, extraordinary. For the space of at least two days, it was agreed, we must assume the risk of leaving our outlying lands unguarded. We had no alternative, since it would be an admission of defeat before we began were we to preclude anyone, of any rank or for any cause, from attending on this occasion. That decision made, we began to discuss the best timing for such an unprecedented convocation, and decided that it would be held on the eleventh and twelfth days after our meeting, coinciding with the recently adopted monthly changing of the guard patrols. This time, and this one time only, the old guard would come in, but the new guard would remain at home for two extra days before departing. Our most distant frontiers would be unguarded for the better part of three full days—one day for the departing guard to return to Camulod, one more for the convocation, and a third, or some portion of the third, for the new guard to return. That vulnerable time would be greatly reduced in the case of those outposts closest to Camulod, where the guards would remain in place longer before leaving and could return more quickly. Before that happened, however, and as close to the appointed time as possible, we would conduct an intensive, high-speed reconnaissance of the lands beyond our lands' perimeter, to assure ourselves as far as we were able, that no impending attack was building prior to our deliberate suspension of vigilance.

Thereafter, slightly reassured of our eventual success but greatly apprehensive of our initial method of achieving it, I spent two more days and much of both nights fretting over what we would say to the troops, until Ambrose and several of my friends virtually threw me out of Camulod with my bow, bidding me gather viands for the festivities, which would be held the day following my return.

In the grey dawn of the last day of my hunt, I experienced a phenomenon that I have never known repeated. I spent a full hour in a hunter's paradise, in a place I had discovered the day before, where a large number of deer trails, many showing the hoofprints of large animals, converged amid low, sparse bushes at the base of a jumbled pile of whitish rock. I had identified the spot as being a natural salt lick and had made my camp close by, wakening early to creep stealthily into concealment in full darkness, and confirming that the direction of the breeze had not changed overnight before placing myself well downwind of the lick, at the base of the large tree I had marked out with a dagger the day before. From here, I had estimated, I would have an unobstructed shot at whatever creatures passed the convergence of the trails that morning.

As the sky began to pale, however, the breeze strengthened to a brisk wind and then grew even stronger, blasting in hard, violent gusts, whipping the bushes wildly, rattling the bare branches of the winter trees and frequently even snatching the air from my lips as I sought to breathe. I cursed my ill fortune but remained in place, huddled against my tree bole, hoping that the sudden change would abate with the same speed that had brought it, and that no rain would follow it. Daylight grew almost imperceptibly, a long and weary struggle with the dominance of darkness, but at length I found I was able to distinguish the dense, roiling masses of clouds in the leaden sky, and all the time the wind kept rising until it was a howling gale.

I lost all judgment of the length of time I had spent huddled there, and eventually rose to my knees to leave, abandoning my hunt, only to find myself looking into the largest herd of deer I had ever seen in these parts. There must have been fifty animals in my immediate view, most of them grazing, heads down in the low brush, apparently unconcerned by the violent wind. On a low knoll less than forty paces ahead of me and to my left, the patriarch stood poised, head up, his magnificent spread of antlers almost flat along his back, his nose pointed directly into the storm. Even from where I crouched I could see his eyes were closed, and I reached for an arrow. Before I moved again, however, I looked once more at the herd and counted twelve strapping young males, all less than two years old, and thirty-nine females. I had no doubt that there were others, hidden from me by the woods and rocks.

Regretfully, I returned my attention to the herd leader, the largest animal there. I knew that the moment I killed him the others would vanish, despite their swarming numbers, swallowed up by the forest and the greyness of the day. I took aim carefully, knowing that the fury of the wind would have no effect on such a short-range flight, and then I stepped into my shot and fired, sending my arrow straight into the spot I had selected. The stag went down immediately, his brain transfixed by the missile that had entered behind his ear. I stood frozen, awaiting the bounding panic that would greet his fall, but nothing happened. The herd continued grazing, the death of their leader unnoticed, and I realized that the fury of the wind and the chaos it created had dulled their senses somehow, robbing them of their legendary acuity. Scarcely daring to breathe, and expecting to be discovered at any moment, I moved cautiously around and selected another target, this one directly on my right, close by the edge of the forest proper and even closer to me than the first had been. Directly ahead of me, between the two of us, a shoulder-high bush lashed from side to side. I took note of it, allowed for its movement, and thereafter ignored it. Again I sighted and fired, and again the animal fell to its knees, out of my sight and into death without disturbing any of its neighbours.

Aware now of a visceral excitement, I cast my eyes around in search of another available target and saw a young doe close by, almost completely hidden from me by another flailing bush. She was farther away than the others had been, however, and I could not obtain a clear view for a killing shot, so I set out with the utmost care to close the distance between us, crouching low and fully cognisant of the sea of movement all around that cloaked me. I drew as near as I dared go, for fear of being seen by the doe I was stalking or by another animal, and risked what I knew to be a hazardous shot. I loosed, and watched a vicious gust of wind snatch at the speeding shaft and send it high, so that it almost grazed the feeding creature's back. And once more, miraculously, the animal paid no heed. Emboldened now, I sighted and shot again, and this time my aim was true and she went down.

In the half hour that followed, buffeted and shaken by the wind until my clothes seemed useless and I was chilled to the bone, I wrought havoc among that herd, nocking my arrows with cold, nerveless fingers, keeping myself downwind at all times, so that the buffeting of the gale hit me directly in the face, and moving laterally in a narrow arc, hither and yon, remorselessly killing the beasts on the outside of the dwindling herd. A score of them fell to my deadly attack before the twenty-first, a massive-muscled young stag, leapt about and fled, bugling a note of panic. Watching him go, I wondered what had frightened him, for I knew by that time that it would not have been my presence. Perhaps, I thought, he had caught the scent of fresh-spilled blood, borne on an errant eddy of gusting wind. Whatever the cause of his fright, however, they were gone.

Slowly then, I walked around the scene of my slaughter, counting my kill. Twenty fresh deer, of a kind unknown to me, far bigger than the common red deer to which I was accustomed in these parts. Twenty large deer! I had not the slightest hope of being able to clean and dress them alone, but I had to do something with them.

Four hours later, shaking with exhaustion, I gutted the last of them and dragged it, with the help of my horse, to lie beside its fellows. After that I returned to my campsite and finally broke my fast before breaking camp and heading towards the spot where I had left my three-carcass kill the previous day, safely cleaned and, unlike the other twenty, hung high from the branches of an oak. The wind had died down a little, but the day was still unfit for man or beast. I arrived at the spot before any of the collectors had arrived, so I found a depression out of the wind beneath a fallen log, wrapped myself in my cloak and sat down to rest. The twenty deer might be discovered by a predator, but that was something over which I now had no control, and so

I dismissed them from my mind for the present, concentrating, with a sense of well-being, on other, more pleasant things.

I must have fallen asleep, because the voices startled me into a panic-stricken crouch, my dagger in my hand and my knees protesting at the sudden movement. There were four men in the party, and I knew all of them. Even better, I had the pleasure of surprising them as much as they had me, for they had not seen me lying asleep beneath my log. Now I winged an arrow into a tree trunk beside them and laughed as they scattered, cursing and clawing for weapons. I stepped forward immediately and they shuffled together uneasily, crestfallen at the apparent magic with which I had "crept up on them" across an open glade. I said nothing to disillusion them, but set them quickly to lowering the three carcasses from the oak tree, and then I led them to the clearing where I had left my twenty new prizes. These had remained untouched, Fortune continuing to favour me throughout the day.

I still recall with pleasure the effect that cache had on those soldiers, for I had been through a sufficiently long period of self-doubt the previous week to enable me to revel in their wonder. Their eyes grew wide and their mouths gaped, for never had such bounty been seen as the result of one man's solitary hunting in a single day. Again, I offered no explanation of how I had achieved such a harvest, and such was their awe, they would not have considered asking me. I apologized, however, for the unskinned condition of the catch, pointing out that I had neither had the time nor the tools to skin all twenty beasts. I left them to their task then and they set to work immediately, muttering in wonder among themselves and casting superstitious glances my way whenever they thought they were unobserved.

Directly the men were finished loading the meat onto the wagon they had brought, I returned with them to Camulod and made my way straight to the bath house, where I spent little time in the intermediate pools before lodging myself for an hour and more in the steam room. Thereafter, although November's early darkness had not yet begun to fall, I sought my cot and slept like a baby.

They wakened me hours later, in the dead of night, with a hurried summons to present myself in the Praetorium, nominally my own working quarters but in fact the headquarters of the Officer of the Watch at any time of day or night. Alarmed by the appearance of the white-faced, stammering young soldier who had been sent to roust me from my bed, I threw cold water on my face, pulled on a heavy winter tunic, wrapped myself in my cloak and made my way directly to the Praetorium, where I found Ambrose, as tousled as I was, huddled with a group of senior officers including Dedalus, Rufio and Achmed Cato, who, as I perceived immediately from his immaculate uniform, was Officer of the Watch. They broke off their colloquy as I hurried in, each of them scanning me from head to foot as I approached. I saw and accepted that without a thought. I felt fresh and well rested, and I gauged I had already been abed for six hours or more.

"What's happened?" I asked as I strode up to the table. Ambrose reacted first, picking up one of the objects that lay on the table and tossing it to me as I drew near. The silence held as I pulled the flying object from the air and looked at it: part of an arrow, much like my own, save that the shaft had been cut through, leaving no way to tell how long the missile had originally been. Six more exactly like it remained on the table. I sucked in air as I glared at the thing in my hand. Its barbed head and the first handspan of its length were coated with dried and clotted blood, and the cut shaft had been deliberately severed with a sharp blade. I scraped the barbed iron head with my thumbnail, noting the way it had been made and the size and weight of it.

"This is Pendragon." I rapped out the words, an indictment in themselves, looking around at each of them. "Who has killed whom?"

Achmed Cato cleared his throat. "Are you sure of that, Commander? That it is Pendragon?"

"Don't be dense, Achmed. I'm as sure as you are. This was made for a Pendragon longbow. The arrowhead betrays that. It's far too large and heavy for a short bow." I turned to Ambrose. "No one has answered my question. Tell me."

Ambrose shrugged his shoulders and scratched beneath his armpit. " 'Whom' is some of us," he answered in his clear, ever reasonable tones. " 'Who' is unknown. One of our outposts has been wiped out: Calibri, the one farthest to the northwest, closest to the Pendragon lands. Fifty men, all dead, and all the horses stolen. Twenty-four animals—mounts for two squads, one with remounts. The raid occurred less than a week ago. The patrol from the next camp, Horse Farm, waited for them this morning, since they had been scheduled to join the Horse Farm group. When they had not arrived by mid-morning, Saul Maripo, the officer in charge at Horse Farm, led a contingent of his men to see what the problem was. He arrived at Calibri before noon and found everyone dead. A head count showed no one was unaccounted for. There were no enemy corpses."

"Shit and corruption! When did this occur?"

Ambrose shook his head, but it was Achmed Cato who answered me. "Maripo had been there five days earlier and all was well when he left then, just before nightfall. Whatever happened must have taken place the next day or the day after that. From the condition of the bodies, he estimates they had been dead at least three days."

"Damnation!" I curbed my angry reaction and looked around at each of them. All of them met my eyes, and I burst out again. "The *raid*, you say? Fifty garrison troopers dead and you think this was a mere raid? Are you all mad?" I paused then, looking about me again. There was something in the bearing of all of them that struck me as strange. "What is going on here?" I snarled at Cato. "You are the Officer of the Watch. Have you sounded the Assembly? I heard no horns."

"No, Caius, we have not."

His words astounded me, but I was aware of the general attitude here and realised that I had not heard all there was to hear. I drew a deep breath, stifling the urge to rant further.

"Very well," I said when I had mastered my breathing again, hearing the ominous quiet in my own voice. "Would someone care to tell me why?"

"Saul Maripo will tell you himself," Cato said, his own voice calm and dignified. "I regret he was not here when you arrived, but he arrived himself only a half hour ago, having spent the entire day in the saddle, riding hard, and I gave him leave to go to the latrine while we awaited you. He should be back at any moment."

Even as Cato spoke, I heard the ringing of metal-studded boots on marble and turned to see young Maripo stride into the room and skid to a halt as he saw me. He snapped immediately to attention and smashed his fist against his cuirass in a salute, flushing scarlet. He was stained and dirty and travel-worn, dark rings of exhaustion clearly visible beneath his eyes from where I stood across the room. I waved him down and put him at his ease.

"Saul," I greeted him, nodding. "I hear you have had an eventful day."

"Aye, Commander." He was still at attention, swaying on his feet.

"Sit down, lad, before you fall down. And relax. No one is going to dis-embowel you." I moved to the chest that stood behind my desk, stooping to raise the lid and withdrawing the flask of mead and one of the cups I kept there for occasions like this. Around me, I could almost feel the tension drain from the other officers. I poured the cup to the rim with the honeyed, fiery drink and carried it to where young Maripo had subsided into a high-backed chair brought forward by one of the others. He accepted the cup from my hand, nodding gratefully, and drank deeply, then caught his breath and coughed against the fire in his throat. No one laughed. When the young man had regained his composure, I nodded to him again. "Take another one, more slowly this time." He did, and then sat back, relaxing visibly, his eyes on mine.

I moved back to the table and leaned against it, placing the mead flask by my side. I took my time now, knowing the floor was mine and no one would interrupt me. Perhaps to compensate for my earlier volubility, I waited longer than I might have and then spoke slowly and clearly.

"The others have told me part of your story . . . the distressing part. All that remains now, it would appear, is for you to explain why no one is raising our army to repel a possible invasion of our territories. Can you enlighten me?"

The young officer nodded. "Yes, Commander. There is no threat—no immediate threat, I mean."

I sighed, loudly. "I see. And how have you arrived at that conviction?"

He flushed again, hearing the irony in my tone. "I looked, Commander. And I looked with great care, and at great length, and with as much speed as I could."

I dipped my head slightly, accepting his word. "Explain, if you please. From the beginning."

Now it was his turn to heave a quick, sharp sigh, and I watched him search for the words to tell his tale. When they came to him, they emerged in the clipped tones of a formal report to a superior.

"I assembled my entire command at dawn, Commander, and set them to breaking camp completely, knowing that this was an unusual day, in that the post would be abandoned overnight, today and tomorrow. It seemed an ideal opportunity to clean up and prepare the post for a new start by the returning guard, who might appreciate a clean and wholesome billet at the outset of their stay. I also knew I needed to keep the men occupied until the arrival of the force from Calibri—there was a festive spirit in evidence that morning, because of the occasion, and I thought it might be mildly prejudicial to good discipline to allow the men to indulge it. I expected the Calibri contingent to arrive before mid-morning." He paused, evidently remembering, then resumed. "When they had not materialized by the expected time, I became concerned, but decided to allow them half an hour of leeway, thinking they might have decided to clean up their own camp before leaving. Eventually, however, my discomfort drove me to investigate their absence. We ourselves had experienced nothing out of the ordinary prior to that time, and so I took the entire mounted force under my command and made my way towards Calibri at all speed. Before I left, however, anticipating that there might be something amiss, I also sent a rider on our fastest horse to summon the cavalry troops from the next camp to the southeast, bidding the commander there, Decius, to take note of my concern and send his men as backup for my own."

I interrupted him. "Pardon me, Decurion, I have no wish to interrupt your report, and so far I am impressed, but how many horsemen did you have?"

"Sixteen, sir. Two squads; half a squadron. And thirty-four infantry, whom I left in camp, standing to arms."

"I see. Go on."

He cleared his throat, collecting his thoughts after my interruption. "We made good speed to Calibri, and when I was sure that no one was coming to meet us, I sent four scouts ahead on our flanks. The camp was silent when we reached it. It had been burned and there were dead men everywhere."

"I see. All ours; no enemy dead?"

"No, sir." He blinked and I watched his eyes focus on a point somewhere between himself and me. "As soon as I had confirmed the death toll, I began to fear that the enemy, whoever they were, might have outflanked us along the way, hiding until we had passed by, and then riding to attack my own camp at Horse Farm. I knew I had to ascertain, immediately, their numbers and the direction they had taken when they left Calibri. I deployed my men in line abreast to sweep around the perimeter, using the camp itself as a pivot. Fortunately, we found the sign immediately, beginning at the paddock where the horses had been kept, and heading away directly towards the northwest. I examined the signs myself and gauged the raiding party to have been less than a hundred strong . . ." He broke off and his eyes became troubled, then fixed directly on my own. "Those bows, Commander. We've known what they can do for a long time, but they have worked for *us* until now, suiting our purposes. Used *against* us, they represent an entirely new form of attack against which we're utterly ill-equipped for self-defense. All our dead were killed by arrows. I know that because I examined each body individually. Not one man bore a sword cut or an axe wound. Every single one had been shot to death by arrows, and most of the arrows had been ripped out of the bodies afterwards. I had one of my men cut some of the few remaining from the bodies of our dead, and brought them with me in the belief that they might be important to the identification of the raiders."

"Aye," I nodded. "They are. The arrows were reclaimed to be used again. They are difficult to make, and much too valuable to be abandoned when they might be salvaged. The few that were left were probably too deeply lodged to be freed quickly, so they were cut through in order to deny their usefulness to others." *Or to disguise their source,* my mind added, tacitly. "Carry on."

"Sir. One of my men, called Kenith, is a Celt, highly skilled in tracking, and he confirmed my estimate of their numbers. He also divined, and later confirmed from his own observations of the tracks, that the attackers were Celts. He is a scout and a tracker, as I have said, and he pointed out to me that the trail was old, by several days at least. All marks other than the deepest gouges and footprints had been wiped out; the grass straightened by time. And yet their trail was plain, beaten by the hooves of the horses. No rain had fallen in the interim, Kenith indicated, and we might follow them with ease. I so decided, and left a pair of men behind; one to await the arrival of the riders from the other camp, who would be following behind us, and bring them in pursuit of us; the other to return to Horse Farm at all speed, with orders to Sextus Sulla, the infantry commander there, to march his men to Calibri and bury our dead in a common grave." He broke off again, clearly feeling a need to explain. "There was no time, Commander, to do other than that. We could not bring fifty three-day corpses home for burial, nor could we bury them in single graves."

I nodded in agreement, saying nothing, and he continued, apparently relieved by my concurrence.

"That done, I set out directly with my remaining fourteen troopers to follow the raiders' tracks. At all times, Commander, I deployed half of my force as scouts, ranging far out on both sides of our route. I also kept all my men on full alert, so there could be no possibility of missing any sign of a body of men departing from the principal trail. We followed it for four hours, riding hard even through the deep woods—although those we pursued had avoided the worst of the forest and kept to clear game trails—before I called a rest stop in a large clearing where the evidence of their passing was un-mistakable. The raiders had stopped there themselves, and had built fires and rested, evidently a clear day ahead of us, since the ashes of the fires were damp and we had had clear skies throughout that day. The horses had grazed on one side of the clearing where the grass was rich, and the men had slept apart from them. We found the days-old guts of a deer just inside the woods, and I knew then that what Kenith had said was true: these men had not anticipated any swift pursuit." Again he stopped, his face reflecting puzzle-ment. "The raiders had remained on foot, Commander, throughout the en-tire withdrawal. They made no effort to ride the horses, and they left the saddles and bridles in the stables."

"Probably didn't know what they were," I said. "These are mountain men, Decurion. They've never ridden anything other than their own small moun-tain ponies. The sheer size of our horses might have inhibited them from trying to master them while still so deep in hostile territory. Carry on with your report; you're doing well."

"Thank you." He cleared his throat again, frowning in concentration. "We cleared the forest, eventually, and came out into rolling grassland. I began to grow convinced our quarry was in full flight, headed for the mountains we could see in the distance north and west of us each time we topped a hill. When I became sure of it, I increased our speed—the open country made that easier—and we covered more than twenty miles, until we came to the crest of a long rise, where the ground fell away beneath us, exposing a vista that was flat and bare as far as the eye could see—probably another twenty miles, since the sun was shining then and the light was clear. There was nothing moving anywhere out there, though all of us scanned the entire valley carefully for signs." He paused and sniffed, then drew another deep, long breath.

"We did see *something* there, however, Commander. A broad swathe of tracks, disappearing out of sight in a large arc to either side of us, cutting directly across the tracks we were following." He looked around at the assembled group. "We moved down to investigate these signs and saw they had been made by a large party of shod horses, riding from west to east. Again, it was Kenith who observed that they were cavalry, most likely our own, since we know of no other. He pointed out that they had ridden in files, four abreast, and once that had been mentioned the tracks became plain to see. We moved on to the point where these tracks met with our quarry's and found that the cavalry tracks had crossed the other, older tracks. They had stopped there, then followed the old tracks for a while, but the marks of their return were clearly evident. At that point, assuming that this earlier pursuit had proved fruitless, I decided there was nothing to be gained by my proceeding further with such a puny force. I knew the entire garrison of Camulod would be meeting here tomorrow, and I had determined to my own satisfaction that no army on foot could cover the distance from beyond our sight to Camulod in sufficient time to take us by surprise, once I had made my report. I also knew that I had made no move to ascertain, at that point, whether the next camp on the other side, to the west of our perimeter, had been molested. I judged from the regularity of the cavalry arc we had found that those riders, whoever they had been, had ridden well clear of our borders on their way around from the west. So I turned back and met shortly thereafter with Decurion Decius, who was leading his cavalry to join us. I dispatched him, with his own men and mine, to check the next camp west, at Acorn Lake. I then made my way directly here at top speed, stopping only briefly at Calibri to set my own infantry back on the road to Camulod via Horse Farm, and then at my own camp again to change to a fresh horse. Decurion Decius, had he found anything amiss at Acorn Lake, would have sent his fastest rider to confirm my report and add his own. No such messenger has yet arrived, although one may arrive within the hour. If no one comes, we should be able to assume that all was well at Acorn Lake when Decius arrived and he is now on his way with the Acorn Lake garrison as scheduled. I arrived back about an hour ago, and made my initial report to Tribune Cato. That is all I have to report, Commander."

"Hmm. You have acquitted yourself well, Decurion Maripo. Your report, and your presence of mind, are both laudable. Your assumption about the identity of the cavalry whose tracks you found was on the mark. They were our own, sent out in four separate groups to sweep around our entire perimeter, each to a quadrant twenty miles outside our bounds, to check for signs of alien activity that might affect our standing down today and tomorrow. They returned this morning, early. The only sign found by any of the four groups was the one you followed. The sweepers found those tracks a day ahead of you, so your judgment on the timing was accurate, too. You have our gratitude. We will take over from here, so get yourself off to sleep. You have earned your rest."

The young man stood up, snapped to attention, saluted me crisply and left. All of us watched him go.

"Well, gentlemen, I now concur with your decision not to sound a General Muster at this time. The question we must answer now is what do we do next? I am open to suggestions. Ambrose? Cato? Anyone?"

Dedalus responded with a question. "Are we at war, then, Commander, with the Pendragon?"

"Certainly not!" My retort, stung from me by the suddenness of the question, from him of all people, was too angry. I moderated my tone immediately. "You should know better than even to phrase such a question, Ded. The Pendragon are our allies and our friends."

Ded was unimpressed and undaunted. "Perhaps," he murmured, but his softly spoken words were clearly heard by everyone. "But it strikes me there are fifty lads from Camulod lying cold out there in Calibri who might think otherwise."

Before I could respond to that, Ambrose intervened. "That is true, Captain Dedalus," he drawled. "But there are also fifteen of King Uther's bowmen asleep at this moment, here beneath our roof. They came to us in friendship, offering us their skills to use until such time as order is restored in their home lands. And should you care to count, you would find, I am quite sure, well upward of a hundred more about and throughout our domain, living in amity among our people. Are we at war, so suddenly, with these? Or should we look at numbers only? A hundred living here, at least, and a hundred Celtic raiders, arguably Pendragon. Shall we then say we are at war with half the Pendragon, but that the other half are still our friends and allies and thus we will fight husbands and spare wives? Or kill fathers and recruit sons?"

Dedalus shrugged and grinned and spread his hands, dipping his head in unrepentant acceptance. "You are talking sense, Ambrose, and that is all I wanted to hear. From the moment I saw those cut-off arrow shafts, I've had a nasty feeling in my guts. Now I feel better, having heard you say I'm not the only one with doubts about the wisdom of reacting too soon and too thoughtlessly."

My sudden impatience had dissipated while both men spoke, and now I picked up the flask of mead again.

"We have much to discuss, gentlemen," I said to the assembly. "Normally, I would forbid drinking at a time like this, but this is far from normal and I have but the one small flask; a sip or two for each of us. Dedalus, break out the cups from the chest there and pour for everyone, and, Rufio, replenish the fire in the brazier there. It's almost out. In the meantime, we should all sit down. There are sufficient chairs and stools in the other rooms close by. Please make yourselves comfortable."

I used the interval while everyone was occupied with drinks and seating to arrange my thoughts.

By the time stillness had fallen in the Watch Room once again and all eyes had returned to me, I had taken up the severed arrow shafts from the table and held them fanned in front of me, examining their bloody points, to some of which dried, clotted matter still adhered. They were evil-looking things when viewed so closely, their points razor-sharp and their barbs wickedly fashioned so that, once lodged, they locked and could be withdrawn only by main force, torn out with great attendant tissue damage. Someone cleared his throat nervously, and I looked up from my examination.

"Young Maripo was right, my friends. The death of the first Camulodian trooper from one of these weapons signalled a drastic change in the way we must wage war from now on. This was the first time our men faced the Pendragon longbow, but it will not be the last. Weapons like these, in skillful hands in a concerted attack, could wreak havoc among us. They render us impotent. There is no safety, in our current tactics, against shafts like these." No one presumed to speak, so I continued. "The question facing us is whether or not the Pendragon people, allies and friends for more than fifty years, must now be considered otherwise." I waited, but still no one was willing to add his comment to my own.

"Pendragon longbows have been used against us. This evidence is unde-niable." I dropped the arrow shafts, letting them clatter on the tabletop. "But who used them, and how must we respond?" I looked around the room, catching each man's eye.

"We *must* respond, be very sure of that. Failure to do so would invite disastrous consequences. But *how* must we respond, and when, and in what strength?" I nodded my head, indicating Dedalus. "You all heard Ded's com-ments. He is unsure of how to proceed, as I am, but I have no doubt our basic feelings are alike. And you heard Ambrose speak of Huw Strongarm and his companions. As you all know, or should know, they left their homes to join us here because they have chosen not to live there any longer, with matters as they are. Uther's kingdom is torn by civil war. Contenders for his powers swarm everywhere and the common people know neither whom to trust, nor where to turn for succour. Strongarm himself, with his own force, was impotent in his own home, too new-arrived to be able to compete with already vested powers. He called his homeland a nest of rats, referring to the power-hungry who fight among themselves for domination. He said, too, that the pride his people have borne throughout their lives, of being Pendragon, has been blasted like a tree in a thunderstorm. I heard those very words from his own mouth."

During the pause that followed I was conscious of every eye in the group being fixed on mine.

"When I hear words like those being spoken by a man like Huw Strong-arm, I listen very carefully, and I think deeply on what caused them to be said. Now I really would appreciate some contribution to this monologue."

The only one to speak was Dedalus, again. "None of us can improve on what you have said so far, Merlyn, so speak on." The others grunted, or nodded, each in his own way supporting Dedalus.

"Very well then. It seems to me that we might simply have received a visitation from a single group of big Huw Strongarm's rats, ranging for a time far from their nest. We may never know what brought them to our lands or why they came, but they left with our horses, and those horses will destroy them, because where we find our horses we will have found our killers. And find them we will, by simply following their tracks into their hills, then searching farther.

"Tomorrow we will mend our own internal wounds and use the deaths of fifty of our own to make a poultice that will drain the poison from our military corpus, knitting its flesh into a whole, new body. The following day we will send out a force in strength, a thousand men, both horse and foot, to act in concert and avenge our fifty dead. Huw Strongarm and his men will ride with them. This force will be commanded either by me or by my brother Ambrose, and will serve a set of purposes, each of them hewn to fit a special need." I tallied them upon my fingers as I named them. "One, the most immediate and obvious, is to avenge our comrades and regain our missing horses. Two, it is time we showed our force in the north and west, reminding everyone up there that we are here and that we will accept no interference in our lives or in our welfare." I looked from Dedalus to Rufio. "Three, we will pass by Glevum, which is presently infested with another nest of rats, this time come recently from either Africa or the Berber Coast. Whichever, they are aliens and invaders and they constitute a threat to our domain. They must be cleaned out. Four, the expedition will enable us to glean current knowledge of the state of affairs in Cambria, particularly in the kingdom of Pendragon. We will seek no conflict there, other than with the group who raided us, but we will go there in sufficient strength to discourage any bibulous hothead who might seek to detain us. And five, the last but perhaps the most important, the expedition will give us the opportunity to put our new resolve for unity into effect. *The cavalry will ride as escort to the infantry.* They will not range ahead, save in emergency conditions."

I stopped again, awaiting comment, but there was none. I had a point to make, however. "Does anyone here object to any element of this proposal? You may speak out if you do. Dissent's permissible at this point, for your concerns may be valid and merit further discussion . . . Anyone?" I looked around me slowly, eyeing each man directly. None showed any concern. "Good! Then may I suggest we adjourn until the morning's scheduled meeting? There is nothing more to be done this night, and our troops should be arriving back throughout the morning. Goodnight, gentlemen." I stayed them with an upraised palm, however, before anyone could even begin to rise.

"Wait!" I had seen Dedalus grinning wickedly and shaking his head. Everyone stopped moving. "Captain Dedalus, you seem amused. Are you?"

His grin widened, but lost its ferocity and changed to one of good humour. "No, Commander, not at all; an errant thought occurred to me, that's all."

"Would you care to share it with us?" Ded knew as well as I did that the request was a command. He sniffed and grunted.

"Well, Commander, it occurred to me that an expeditionary force like the one you described might serve a more ambitious end, particularly were it even stronger than the thousand you decreed . . . With Uther's Cambria a nest of fighting rats and splintered factions, and the common people groaning for relief from civil war, it seemed to me they might be more than glad to welcome their allies from Camulod, and Camulod might quickly gain a new province at little cost . . ."

By the time he had said his opening words I was prepared for him. "A new province. To what end, Captain Dedalus?" I asked, governing my voice carefully to sound dismissive rather than patronising. "Simple conquest? Far from simple. And what would constitute your 'little cost'? Think about what you are saying, my friend. Conquest entails governance afterward; a garrison of occupation and the chronic risk of rebellion against our presence. As things stand, we barely have enough men under arms today to tend our own outposts. That is why we are here tonight, remember?" I laughed, shaking my head in what I hoped would pass as tolerant amazement. "By all the old gods, Ded, I sometimes wonder where your cynicism will lead you. This is Camulod! Do you truly believe, deep down inside yourself, that we could thrive on conquest, or might even wish to seek it? Unity is strength, Ded, and our unity is imperilled today by the rift within our own troops. Think how much worse it might be were half those troops—the disaffected half—ensconced in Cambria and fortified by mountains."

Dedalus grinned again and shrugged elaborately. "As I said, Commander, it was but an errant thought. I had dismissed it—for all those same reasons— when you noticed me smiling. Now I'm glad that you concur with me."

His outrageous impudence brought a storm of laughter and the meeting broke up immediately with good-natured muttering and smiles. I turned to thank Achmed Cato, who yet had several hours of duty ahead of him, and then found Ambrose by my elbow.

"What are you going to do now?" I asked him.

"I'm going back to my cot, what else? I'd been asleep for barely half an hour when I was summoned. What about you?"

I thought about that. I was not even slightly tired. "Records," I said. "I've been asleep for hours, ever since I got back, but I have not made an entry to my journal in weeks. An hour or two of that will make me tired again and bring me close to dawn. Is everything prepared for tomorrow's proceedings?"

"Aye. The camp on the plain has been prepared and everything is ready. Dedalus will speak to the troops."

"Dedalus? Are you serious, Ambrose?"

"Think of it, Cay; Ded is the perfect man for this task on this day, a well-known and respected veteran and one of our senior field commanders, popular with all the men, both cavalry and infantry, yet known for his ferocious discipline. When he talks, the men will listen, and they'll hear what he is saying more clearly than they would were it you or I addressing them. We are relative outsiders at this time, the two of us; I because I am a new arrival, and you because you've been so long 'away' in terms of your illness. Ded is one of them, and they love him."

It took me several long moments to accept and digest the truth, but I accepted it completely in the end. "So be it, then. I'll see you in the morning. Sleep well."

XXII

As I MADE my way back to my quarters my mind was filled with apprehension at how suddenly a potential war with the Pendragon had developed. It had seemed inconceivable to me, before that night, that enmity could spring up, for any reason, where such warmth had once prevailed between my own people here in Camulod and those others, equally my own, in my cousin Uther's kingdom. My single source of satisfaction from the experience of the past hour lay in my growing appreciation of my brother's perspicacity and natural leadership, and that had been an incidental, almost irrelevant awareness. I found myself praying that Ambrose would have no cause to demonstrate those skills in civil war.

I was crossing the torchlit entranceway of the Praesidium heading down into the darkened courtyard on the way to my own quarters, when I heard my name called and turned to see a heavily cloaked figure waving to me from the other side of the walkway. It was Lucanus, swathed in a long, black cloak like my own. He told me he was on his way to the Infirmary, where the wife of one of the Colonists was in labour and not expected to have an easy time. This would be the woman's third child, he told me, and each of the other two had been breech presentations, causing great difficulties for the mother and resulting in the deaths of both children. This time, Lucanus informed me, he was prepared to deliver the child the way Julius Caesar had been birthed, by cutting it alive from the mother's womb. I shuddered at the thought and for a spell we walked side by side in silence. It seemed to me that the night had grown colder while I was in the Watch Room with the others, and I said so to Lucanus. He agreed with me and muttered something about it being cold enough for snow, at which I scoffed, pointing out that we were only in November. We arranged to meet again later and spend some time together, and I left him at the entrance to the Infirmary, then hurried on to my own quarters, glad to find a brazier still glowing in the darkened room. It took me mere moments to blow on the coals and light a spill with which I lit an array of candles. I replenished the fire, and only then unfastened my cloak and hung it from a peg.

I lost track of time very quickly, caught up in the absorbing task of bringing my daily journal up to date from the brief notes I had written during the past few weeks. My Eirish recollections were exactly that—recollections. I had had neither writing materials nor time in Eire for recording events and ideas, even though I was aware at all times how important such a record might prove to be. Now, in the darkness of this single night, I emptied my mind of all my memories of the voyage, committing them to paper. Twice, I recall, I rose to throw more fuel on the fire, spurred in each instance by the chill that numbed the fingers of my writing hand.

Ambrose finally interrupted me, timing his arrival perfectly to coincide with my own decision to call an end to my efforts. The door burst open suddenly and he was there, admitting the pearly radiance of early day and a blast of cold air together.

"Thought you might still be here. It's time to eat," he said, by way of greeting. "Come and see this."

"This" was a scattering of snow upon the paving outside my door. I looked, and shivered, and went back inside, digesting the implications of this dusting of whiteness as I struggled to pull on my heavy cloak.

"That's wonderful, simply wonderful," I snarled in disgust. "All we really need, this day of all days, is snow! With an expedition to organize and a full parade to conduct in the meantime. Everyone is going to be enchanted."

Ambrose had been squinting up at the sky as I spoke, and now he began to stride towards the refectory. I fell into step beside him. "It was probably no more than an early flurry," he answered me, after a few moments. "It is only November, after all. Had it not been for this sudden cold snap, it would have fallen as rain. It'll pass over and clear up and what's here will melt, so there's no point in fretting about it. I'm hungry."

We turned a corner and a sudden blast of icy wind cut through me as though I were naked. I cursed aloud, feeling put upon and abused. "What if it doesn't?" I complained. "What if the damned snow stays?"

"Then there's no point in fretting about that either, is there? If it stays, it stays. We'll have a chilly parade this afternoon, in that case, but providing no more falls, the expedition can proceed as planned." He stopped walking suddenly and swung to face me, his face splitting into a giant smile. "But what if it really snows, eh? Think of that! What if it snows and snows and drifts and blows? Then we will all be stuck here until it thaws, save for the poor swine who must return to man the outposts before the storm really sets in. But we'll be safe, because our inability to move will be duplicated everywhere. The high hills and passes will be snowbound and blocked off, and the forest roads will be impassable."

I frowned at him, unable to grasp what he was saying, hearing only his evident delight about being walled within the fort by snow. "So what?" I asked him, finally. "Would you enjoy such enforced idleness?"

"Idleness? Opportunity, Cay! I won't go as far as to say I'd enjoy it, but by God, I could certainly put it to good use. A solid block of time, free of all outside threat, to solidify the changes we intend to make, and give all our people time to work together on the new order? Don't tell me you would not be grateful for such a godsend."

I would have been, of course, but I had not made the connection as quickly or as intuitively as he had. My admiration of the focused way his mind worked increased yet again. I glanced back to the sky, this time almost with regret. "Now that you point it out, I would. But as you say, it's still only November. This snow is two months early. I doubt that we could be so fortunate as to have it stay now, when we could use it so effectively. Let's hurry, I'm hungry now, too."

The refectory was chaotic that morning, a maelstrom of screaming cooks and running lackeys, all grossly overtaxed by the demands of having to feed so many people at one time and within hours. By the time we re-emerged from it, however, having exercised our privilege of rank and broken our fast on fresh-baked bread and tender, succulent meat cut for us by one of the

senior cooks from a spitted, broiling carcass that would be served cold later
that day, we were both feeling vastly improved. There was activity everywhere
and the evidence of the increased presence of our troops was unmistakable,
with work parties hurrying hither and yon under the watchful eyes of those
in charge, and an air of irrepressible gaiety widespread, in spite of the biting
cold. Great piles of fuel had been stacked close to every firepit on the summit
outside the walls and even, on this one auspicious occasion, against the interior surfaces of the walls themselves wherever there was space not yet occupied by buildings. They would be needed, too, for the day seemed to be
growing colder by the moment.

Most of the troops had long since returned from the outposts, but some
were still out there upon the roads, such as they were, and these would
continue to arrive throughout the morning. I had no doubt that every pile
of wood would feed a fire before the morning passed. The day's main activities were scheduled to begin after the noontime meal, which would be a
festive one, despite the fact that the individual units must remain together
and be ready to parade when summoned.

Ambrose and I had found ourselves in a unique situation that morning,
for we had done all that we could do in preparation for this day's events and
were now constrained to leave the final details in the hands of those to whom
we had delegated the tasks. We had agreed during our meal together that it
would be both unkind and unwise to let it appear now that we lacked trust
in anyone, and so for once we found ourselves at liberty to while away some
time in idleness while everyone about us worked with twice the normal intensity.

Amused by the thought, and by the novelty of this sensation of irrespon-
sibility, we set out to saunter at our leisure through the camp, but our progress was quickly retarded by the necessity of responding to an unending
series of deferential greetings, and the ensuing awkward small talk with harried men, which invariably interrupted the performance of some task. Both
of us quickly wearied of it and sought the silence of Aunt Luceiia's house,
where, to no one's surprise, we were attended by the Lady Ludmilla. She told
us she had been awake for the greater part of the night, assisting Master
Lucanus—she would never think of him as "Luke"; that was my privilege as
his friend—in his efforts to deliver a healthy child to the unfortunate woman
Lucanus had spoken of the previous night. I was surprised to learn that the
child had been born to Hector, one of our youngest and brightest Council
members, and his wife Julia, both of whom I knew and admired. Hector, in
particular, stood out among the councilors because he was a successful farmer
who had had no ties with the Farmers faction, having chosen instead to tend
to his own affairs and improve the quality of his arable land and his crops
consistently from year to year without significant input from any other farm.
I mentioned that I had met Luke on his way to the Infirmary for that purpose.
He had not named the woman, which I privately thought strange, since he
knew I was friendly with her and her husband. I said nothing of that to
Ludmilla, however, who reported that Julia and her newborn son were healthy
and well, and that the birth had occurred naturally and easily, with no need
for Luke's bright, shiny knives. In gratitude, she added, and this information
made me smile with pleasure, Julia had asked permission of Lucanus to name
the child after him, a request with which, according to Ludmilla, Lucanus

had seemed embarrassed and reluctant to comply, although he did not refuse. How could he, indeed? The child's name-granting lay within the parents' power alone, and the honour bestowed upon Lucanus was one he was powerless to refuse. From that topic, we moved on to discuss the rising number of children being born in Camulod. Fifteen had been birthed within the short months of the previous summer, as far as we could tally, and of those, twelve had survived, an extremely high number, attributable, we were sure, to the methods of Lucanus and his passion for cleanliness and meticulous postnatal care for both mothers and children.

Some time later, having exhausted the conversation, and aware that my presence had become a patiently borne burden to the others, besotted as they were with each other, I went into the Armoury where, to my surprise and delight, I found Shelagh contemplating an array of knives and daggers mounted to one side on the central wall. Her back was to me and she had not heard me enter—she had left the door ajar again—and so, having set out towards her, I stopped before she could notice me and indulged myself in the simple, but deliciously guilty pleasure of observing her. Even from behind, she was ravishingly lovely, her long, self-willed tresses sweeping in cascades across her shoulders and more than half-way down her back. She stood on tiptoe, peering upward, her hands braced on a table-top, and her stance threw the clean lines of hips and buttocks into relief beneath the softness of the single garment draped from her shoulders and circled with a loose-looped leather girdle. She moved once, reaching further, straining to touch the metal of a wicked, broad-leafed blade with one fingertip, and my heart leapt to see what the movement revealed to my prying eyes: taut slimness of waist and swell of half-glimpsed breast beneath her uplifted arm. I dared not stay a moment longer without announcing myself. So rapt was she in her scrutiny, however, that she remained unaware of me until I spoke.

"Good morning, Lady. You have an affinity for blades, I have observed."

She leapt backward and spun to face me, startled at the suddenness and closeness of my voice. "Oh, it's you, Commander Merlyn. Good morning. Knives, yes. Blades, only occasionally." She had regained her composure very quickly. "I should not be in here, should I?"

I smiled and shook my head. "No, you are welcome now. That rule—if rule it ever was—no longer applies. The only reason for my anger last time was the alarm I felt over my careless betrayal of my secret. Now you are privy to that secret, no secrecy applies."

She curtsied gracefully in the Roman fashion, holding her skirts out to her sides and dipping low, head bowed. "My thanks to you, Commander."

"Where did you learn to do that?" I asked, betraying my surprise. "I'll wager you would never do it at home in Eire."

Her eyes flashed and she tossed her head. "I never have, but who is to say I never will? I make my own rules of behaviour, Merlyn, and the man has not been born who can change any of them!"

I grinned, charmed by her scornful mettle. "Not even Donuil?"

"No, not even he." Then she relented, breaking into a smile. "Although he might *persuade* me in some things. He has a honeyed tongue, you know."

I grimaced. "Aye, I know. He has used it with me, too, although hardly in the way he must with you." I was suddenly and completely ill at ease with this conversation and my mind began to leap around, seeking alternative topics. Shelagh, however, was warming to her subject.

"He's a lovely man," she murmured, her thoughts evidently far from the Armoury. "I hope he comes back soon."

"He will," I assured her. "As soon as he can possibly make his way. Tell me about your knives."

If the abrupt change of direction surprised her, Shelagh gave no sign of it. "My knives," she said. "What would you like to know?"

"Anything, everything. Why do you have so many?"

"Well, they are throwing knives, and I have five of them. I suppose Donuil told you that?"

"No, not at all. He mentioned you had some skill with throwing them, that was all."

"Some skill? Is that what he said? *Some skill?* I'll show you some skill." She had begun looking about her, evidently searching for something. "Have you a piece of wood, a block of some kind?"

"A block? You mean like firewood? A log?"

"Aye, that would do, a big one. Have you?"

I shook my head, grinning. "No, but there are mountains of them outside in the courtyard."

"Good, then. Go you and fetch one here, and I'll get my knives. 'Some skill,' indeed!"

Suddenly I was alone, my eyes on the open door where she had vanished. Smiling still, and feeling strangely light-headed, I made my way outside, picked the largest log from the nearest pile and returned with it to the Armoury, where I set it down by the open fireplace. It was really large and heavy, as I had discovered carrying it into the building; the girth of a large man's chest and as long as the same man's torso. Moments later, Shelagh came striding back into the room, the blue, flowing fabric of her robe moulded to her thighs by the speed and length of her stride, her belt of knives suspended from her right shoulder, slanting down across her bosom and between her breasts. She was achingly beautiful and completely unaware of it, casting her eyes around the room from the moment she entered.

"May I move these books?"

"Of course. Here, let me move them over to this table."

"Good. Did you find a log?"

"I did. It's there, by the fireplace."

"It'll do. It looks heavy enough. Would you put it there for me, on the table?"

I did so, and she stood for several moments, looking at it.

"It's too low. Can we stand it on top of the books?"

I could not get rid of the smile on my lips, and was enjoying this thoroughly. "We can, but we'll have to put a cloth between the books and the log," I said. "It's filthy and the books are precious. How high would you like it to be?"

"About the height of your chest—the middle of the log, I mean."

Moments later, the heavy piece of wood sat atop four of Uncle Varrus's books, which were safe beneath a heavily embroidered covering cloth from the long table at the end of the room. The midpoint of its height came even with my breastbone and its top sat level with my chin. I stepped back and turned to her.

"There you are, Lady."

"My thanks. Now stand away." Her tone was fierce, her words clipped. I moved away, masking my smile behind my hand for the few remaining moments of its life.

With a speed I could scarcely credit, her right hand came up from her waist, unsheathing a knife in passing, then flashed downward, and a blurred streak passed my eyes and hammered into the raw wood with a solid *thunk*. Without waiting to see the result of her throw, Shelagh had spun on her heel and retreated two paces before spinning back and repeating the performance. Three times more she repeated this maneuvre, never pausing for an instant, so that by the time I had begun to come to terms with what I had witnessed, she stood ten paces farther down the room from the spot in which she had begun. My eyes had never even sought the target. I had been completely enthralled in watching her movements. Now she spoke to me, her tone still iron.

"Some skill, I think. Take a look!"

I stepped forward to the target, fully aware of it for the first time, and gazed, speechless, at what she had done. All five knives stood together, the buried tips of their blades touching, the thickness of their handles forcing them outwards into a wedge-shaped, solid bar.

"Good God, Shelagh," I gasped. "Where and when and how could you learn to throw like that? That seems impossible. I would have sworn no one could ever do that with accuracy, let alone at that speed!"

"When? I've spent my whole life learning how to do it, but I had a natural ability to start with," she answered, now sounding almost subdued.

"I know, Donuil told me you could kill a running rabbit with a knife as a mere child, but I thought he was exaggerating out of admiration and loyalty."

"No, it was true. But when I was older, though still a little girl—I was eleven at the time—and he was away with his brothers, something happened that Donuil knows nothing about. I was attacked in the woods while walking with a cousin. Her name was Rhona and she was older than I—much older. The man who did it leapt on Rhona and I ran away." Her voice had dropped almost to a whisper. "But before I ran, I threw my knife at him. It hit him in the throat, where I had aimed, but hilt first, and he laughed at me, then knocked my cousin down and chased after me. I escaped, terrified out of my wits, but he went back and raped and killed my cousin. I swore then that I would never miss with a thrown knife again, that the next man I aimed at would fall down and die with my blade in his throat and would never harm another woman. And so I learned my craft better than any other I have known. How did I learn? you asked. I learned by doing it. I threw, and threw and threw again until I learned to gauge the flight of any blade, once I had held it in my hand. I threw and threw until my arms—I throw with both—grew into wooden beams that moved down and through the same motion, exactly, every time. I threw until both my wrists became inured to endless throwing, and grew thicker than the wrists of any of my friends—you see?" She extended her arms to me, stretching them beyond the sleeves of her blue robe and, sure enough, the wrists, and her entire forearms, were thick, dense-looking and strongly muscled.

"That only leaves the 'where' of your questions, Master Merlyn. I learned wherever I happened to be at any time. I learned at home; I learned while working; I learned through endless hours and days and weeks of practising when other little girls and young women were learning women's skills, and yet I learned those, too. I learned while hunting and fighting with the men of our people, for among our folk there is no shame in being a woman and a warrior. You knew that, did you not?"

I nodded. "I did. It is the same among the Celts of this land. Women fight beside their men when danger threatens."

"Aye, and danger is never far afield." Her voice was now almost inaudible.

I turned once more to look at the five knives standing in the solid log. "You could do that again, right now," I murmured. It was an assertion, not a question.

"Aye, I could, but I'm no longer angry, and anger helps. I could do it again, nevertheless, and had you the nerve to blindfold me, then stand behind the log and speak to me, I could place all five blades into it from your throat to your breastbone before you had time to scream." She paused. "You would not do that, would you? Trust me that much?"

I hesitated, caught off balance by the suddenness of her challenge. Would I? I thought I might, but had to clear my throat before I could pronounce the words.

She smiled. "Then you would be a fool; a trusting fool worthy of gratitude, but none the less a fool for that. Accidents do happen, Caius."

I turned away again and began to prise the blades from the wood, finding it far from easy. When I had all five, I took them to where she stood and held them out to her, hilts forward, watching as she sheathed them, one after the other.

"Shelagh," I said, "you are magnificent."

She smiled at me, almost sadly. "No, but I know you mean that, so accept my thanks, for that, and for the other things."

"The other things?" I was puzzled, suddenly unsure of myself again. "What other things are those?"

"Your silence, and your reticence . . . respect, perhaps."

I felt my face grow red. "Forgive me, I don't know what you mean."

"Oh yes you do, Cay. I've seen you, felt you, watching me and known what your thoughts were. I am no maiden, to run blushing at such thoughts. But I am sworn to your friend, his wife in fact as well as name, and neither you nor I could ever deceive him or betray him in such manner."

I swung away, mortified at my own transparency, but she caught hold of my sleeve and turned me back to face her.

"Look at me, Caius Merlyn, look at me!"

I looked, cringing inwardly, and saw no sign of censure in her eyes, which gazed at me steadfastly. And then she smiled again, sweetly and gently, a smile of utter friendship.

"Here am I talking to you of maidens' blushes, and you outshine them all. Think of it thus, Cay: I am a woman, not a child, and aware that you perceive me as a woman. And I am flattered, as a woman, that I can attract the man you are. But I am a warrior, too. Never lose sight of that. I am a warrior, with a warrior's skills and depths. I have trained and hunted with men throughout my life, lived among them, fought with them and heard them speak of men's desires and lusts at all hours of the day and night through peace and war. I have killed men. And I have lain with some. No woman—and few men, for that matter—can survive a battle among comrades and not be physically drawn to some of them. You are a warrior, too, a soldier; you know the kind of fellowship shared peril breeds."

She paused again, staring at me keenly. "Do you understand what I am telling you, Caius Merlyn? These feelings you have, which you have been so painfully determined to conceal, are not one-sided. I feel them, too. That is why they persist; because I have allowed them to. Had they been unwelcome, I would have stamped upon them long before now, in any of a hundred ways that you would have accepted without ever knowing of my awareness. Do you hear me?"

I nodded, slowly, wonderstruck but still incapable of speech.

"Hmm," she said, smiling slightly. "Good. Do you feel any better? You look as though you've been hit on the head."

Dumbly, I shook my head. She laughed and grasped my wrist, pulling me with her towards the chairs that she and I had occupied a few days earlier. "Sit down, and let me put some wood upon the fire, then we will talk further. Is there anything to drink in here? Would you like some mead?"

I paused in the act of sitting, and straightened up again, forcing myself to swallow in the hope it might release my tongue. "No," I rasped, then cleared my throat loudly and captured a more natural tone of voice. "There's nothing in here, but I can call for some."

"Good, then do that, while I arrange this fire."

I cannot recall what thoughts went through my mind as I moved about the house thereafter. I know there were no servants to be found, and I ended up finding the mead myself and carrying it back to where she waited, and I know that as I entered, kicking the door shut behind me, and moved towards the fire, she sat watching me and smiling that small, friendly smile. I poured the mead and handed her a cup, then sat across from her, feeling the flames against my face and legs, and seeing the way her five, sheathed knives seemed to cling to her form, finding their own relaxed positions and each caressing her with intimate familiarity. She raised her cup to me and tipped it, spilling a small libation on the floor.

"Let us drink to ourselves, Caius Merlyn, to us and to our secrets: to the discussions we have had, the pair of us, and to our friendship, which will be permanent, I think, and spiced with innocent attraction and respect. I, too, may look, and lust inside with no harm done." She laughed, a lovely sound brim-full with mischief, then grew solemn. "We drink also to our friends and to our obligations, to the duties by which we are both *almost* gladly bound; and to your infant King, his destiny, and the families and lines from which he springs. What was it you called it? 'The great Dream of the Roman Eagles who founded Camulod.' Now *there* is a worthwhile litany of reasons why we should enjoy this mead. Will you not agree?"

"Aye," I said, feeling wondrously relieved. "And willingly, to all of them."

"And have you none to add? None of your own?"

I smiled easily now. "Aye, that I have, now you mention it. But we drink first to yours."

We touched the rims of our cups and sipped the fiery beverage they held, and I luxuriated in the honeyed glide of pleasure on my tongue.

She licked her lips and smacked them together. "Not as good as my own," she said. "But not trivial, either." She shifted in her seat and looked at me again. "Your turn; your list."

I took my time, enumerating and then refining the list of gratitudes I felt. Shelagh waited patiently.

"We will drink this time to us, once more, without constraint, and without regret: to this remarkable freedom from guilt you have granted me, and to the . . . obligation you have outlined in that granting. We drink to friendship, yours and mine, unorthodox as some might choose to see it, and that which we share with others. We drink also to Destiny and Duty, two fearsome taskmasters, as you have said, and to tomorrow . . . all tomorrows, in the hope and trust that they will bring fulfillment and contentment." I paused, and tipped the libation on the floor. "Will that suffice, think you?"

"For the gods, or for your list? I think both will be well." She raised her cup to mine again and we drank, then sat for a time in silence, gazing into the flames until I roused myself.

"What time of day is it, I wonder?"

"Around mid-morning." She spoke without looking at me. "Perhaps later, near the three-quarter point, but short of noon. Should you be elsewhere?"

"No, not until noon, but by then I must be dressed in formal parade gear. I still have time." I savoured the last mouthful of my mead.

"My sons—our sons, mine and Donuil's—will be companions to your infant King, you know. Had you thought of that?"

"No, I had not." I shook my head, ruefully. "But you may have daughters."

"Shame, Caius Merlyn! Do you doubt me now? I will have sons. I told you long ago when first we met; two of them, Gwin and Ghilleadh. And they will be companions to your ward, young Arthur . . . Cousins, too."

I shook my head, enjoying this sudden, novel feeling of relief from tension between myself and this delightful woman. "Come, Shelagh, you're not even yet with child."

She laughed. "Not even bedded, as a proper wife."

"No, but think what that means. Arthur is six months old and more, already. By the time your first son is born, even if Donuil were to come tonight and quicken you at once, there would be fifteen months between the two youngsters, and that means thirty months between your youngest and young Arthur. That is a vast gulf during childhood."

"Aye, but childhood is brief. Three years is nothing at all between young men. Look at yourself and Donuil; what is there, nine years between you? Besides, when two or three children grow up close together, age has little influence. Only when an elder child has other friends of his own age does difference emerge."

"But that will be the case, Shelagh! It seems there are children being born everywhere in Camulod today. Only last night, at dead of midnight, I met Lucanus on his way to a birthing. The child was born safely, to the young wife of one of our councilors. It was a boy. They'll call him Luke, Ludmilla told me earlier. So there's one more companion for the King."

"No, there will only be the three, Arthur and Gwin and Ghilleadh. Believe me." Her voice had altered somehow, and I felt a chill run over me, raising the small hairs on my neck and shoulders, but then she was speaking again in her normal tones, quite unaware, it seemed to me, of having said anything strange. "How long had you been standing there, behind me, before you spoke this morning?"

I looked at her then, remembering and smiling. "Not long. Why?"

"I don't know. I was wondering, but idly, if there is more to this 'attraction' than I had thought. It had been my intent to seek you out today, somehow, even though I was well aware of the demands upon your time."

"Why? Why seek me out? To what end?"

"To provoke this talk and deal with the things that had been troubling me. I dreamed of you last night."

My guts contracted as dismay expanded in my breast. "Oh . . . Was it . . ."

"No, not one of those." Her smile was fleeting but her headshake was emphatic. "No prophesy this time; mere fancies, vivid and very real, but disjointed and confusing, most of them erotic. I dreamed I lay with Donuil, and could feel him within me, but sometimes it was you—never for long; never sustained—but there, from time to time. I woke up at one point, in some distress, over what I can't recall, but I decided to do something, to speak to you of this. I wondered, lying there awake in the middle of the night, what effect your dreams might be having on you. If this fragmented chaos of sleeping images could distress me, safely asleep in all good conscience, what might yours be doing to your peace of mind, with all your strictures and your disciplines and loyalties? I've watched you, Cay, and I have seen your agonies of guilt, though the gods know no such guilt was ever less deserved." She shrugged. "And you came here, unexpected. Or were you unexpected? Had I guessed, though unaware of it, that you would come here? I don't know."

Before I could answer her, we heard the sound of studded boots approaching in the passageway outside, and then someone knocked on the door.

"Commander Merlyn?"

"Yes, Marcus, I'm here."

"You asked me to remind you when the time had come to dress, Commander. I have your parade uniform prepared."

"Thank you, Marcus. I'll come directly."

The footsteps receded again and I stood up and moved close to where Shelagh sat, her eyes once more upon the flickering flames in the big brazier. "Shelagh," I said, speaking to the top of her head, "I am leaving here a very different man from the one I was when I first walked in. I know not what this . . . thing, this feeling, this sense of inner freedom is, or whence it sprang, but I am full of it and I know it is your gift. For that . . . for all of it . . . for yesterday, today and all the tomorrows to which we drank together, I am too grateful ever to be able to find words to define my gratitude. But you will know it. You'll see it every time you see my face or hear my name. That is my promise."

She rose to her feet smoothly and with great speed, turning to face me in mid-motion and looking me directly in the eye. The belt of knives seemed natural across her front.

"I know that, Caius Merlyn, and it gladdens me. You have been too sad, too guilt-stricken in past days, but that's behind us." She grinned at me, her huge, wide eyes flashing with wicked humour. "Lust if you must, but keep your hands about yourself, my friend. Thus, we may both enjoy, without false guilt. Now go, before someone finds us and sets all our good work to naught with idle talk."

I left her there by the fire and strode out into the day with a lightened heart and the strength of twelve tall men.

I opted to exercise the privilege of rank again, for the second time that day, and avoided the festive midday meal, although there was no way to avoid the sound of it. I chose to spend that time alone, and had Marcus, my temporary adjutant—an assigned replacement for the absent Donuil—make alternative arrangements on my behalf. Then, nibbling at a platter of food he brought me in my quarters, and preparing myself mentally for the formal activities that lay ahead, I spent a half hour going over all the arrangements in my head for perhaps the hundredth time. Eventually, when I was sure of having done all that I should have done there in the fortress, I slipped quietly out through the postern gate and found my horse, saddled and ready, where I had told my man to leave it, prior to joining the general festivities. Unseen by anyone, I allowed my horse to pick his way down from the heights, and then I spurred him, galloping all the way round the hill of Camulod to the camp built at the bottom of the hill before, and again after, Lot's treacherous attack years earlier.

I have always found it stranger than merely strange that I should have difficulty recalling the events of that afternoon. "Strange" is a foolish and feeble word to use in describing the blankness of my mind regarding all that passed. I think of words like "ominous" instead, but even that would be misleading, for no ill came out of that day's gathering. The plain truth is, it led to great success on every front, in every way. The events and decisions and the sheer enthusiasm engendered in that single afternoon marked, clearly and undeniably, the beginning of Camulod's most truly potent years, a period that was to span three decades. At the end of the day itself, I was aware of all that had transpired—I must have been, for I was there, in charge, and in full health. But the time that came immediately thereafter absorbed me totally in other things, demanding all my skills and all my efforts, so that when I came to look back, eventually, on what had seemed at the time to be a momentous and portentous day, my mind was blank. The urgencies that had led up to it had been revealed by then, with the passing of time, as lacking stature, and had been replaced by greater urgencies and imperatives.

Dedalus distinguished himself that afternoon; no one had any doubt of that. His friends agreed his time had long been wasted as a soldier, and that he should have been upon a stage somewhere in Empire's headlands, stealing the hearts of emperors and languid women. There is no doubt he achieved what he set out to achieve: to win the hearts of all the Camulodian warriors and bind them into unity and amity again. He used me and Ambrose as his template, dwelling upon our startling similarities and on our different disciplines. He emphasized the difference of our births and boyhoods, one bred and raised right here in Camulod, the other in a distant part of Britain, yet both sprung, irrefutably, from Camulodian stock. Now we were joined as one,

Commanders of Camulod and individually indistinguishable one from the other and yet . . . and yet . . . one fought with cavalry, the other infantry. Together, using all our combined skills, he told them all, we could conquer the world! And would they quibble over which of us they followed?

It was heady stuff, presented with the flair and brilliance of a born actor who could charm tears from statuary. But, it appears, the true mark of his triumph was that he had them all convinced, swearing eternal comradeship, even before he introduced the new training schedule Ambrose had devised, to teach each discipline the tactics of the other and make it possible for those gifted one way or the other to transfer between commands. That was the binding ring that sealed the staves into a barrel. From the moment the new plans were announced, the schism had ended.

I do remember, with great clarity, that at one point shortly before the parade was dismissed, I saw a single snowflake drifting down to cling to the tail of Rufio's horsehair crest. I looked up to search for more, but saw nothing. The snow that had fallen before dawn had almost vanished beneath the trampling of so many feet, but the cold persisted. I continued to scan the faces ranked before me, filling every available space in the camp's parade ground. Some of them, many of them now, I knew by sight, and many more by name as well. But some were yet strangers to me, although they all knew me. Another flake came down, and then a third, large, fat and as light as thistledown. And then, as Ambrose gave the order to dismiss, the snow began to fall in earnest, hushing everything, it seemed, and obscuring the milling mass of men heading for shelter.

Ambrose was looking at me, smiling, his outstretched hand held upwards to the caressing snowflakes, which landed on his palm and disappeared. "Well, Brother, what think you? An omen?"

I attempted to catch some of the falling flakes in my right hand. "Perhaps," I said. "We will know tomorrow, if it snows all night. But I feel sorry for the outgoing troops. They'll not be too happy, slogging their way through this to the cold outposts. When do they leave?"

He threw his arm across my shoulders. "Within the hour. They'll reach the first line camps by dark and stay there overnight. In the morning, those who have to go to the outlying posts will make their way there, regardless of the weather, but the quartermasters have already issued winter gear. They won't be cold . . . or not too cold."

Because of the extraordinary numbers gathered for the parade, the Council Chamber had been allotted to the garrison officers for the remainder of that day and night, and I joined Ambrose and the others there for a celebration the like of which had never been known within the fortress. By the time I left to seek my cot, the entire courtyard was covered by a thick carpet of snow so that, on an impulse, I walked as far as the main gates and stepped out onto the bare hillside at the top of the hill road. The silence was absolute, and the falling snow seemed like a living thing. I went back in, bidding the guard a good night, and went to sleep. Ambrose, it seemed, might see his wish come true if the snow persisted for another day. It was still cold, and I threw my cloak on top of my blanket before I climbed into bed.

XXIII

IT SNOWED FOR seven days without respite, with intermittent, ferocious windstorms blowing and piling the drifting snow to incredible heights, death-filled depths and fantastical shapes. The eighth day dawned upon a motionless, utterly silent, white-shrouded emptiness beneath a solid mass of heavy, uniformly grey cloud. The snow had stopped and people began to emerge into daylight again, peering around them in stupefaction at the manner in which their universe had been altered. Before noon, the snow began to fall again, in a different form this time, the flakes much smaller now, and dense, like tiny chips of ice. In mid-afternoon the temperature plummeted within an hour, and remained at its lowest for nine more days and nights, immersing us in a frigid chaos of misery the like of which no one could remember. Exposed fingers, noses, ears and chins would freeze within moments, even out of the bitter wind. This cold was such that bare skin would adhere to metal, if one were foolish enough to permit such contact, and in the first few days many of us were.

No one had ever known such brutal cold, and soon it became lethal. Entire families living beyond the fortress wall, thinking the worst was over when the first snowfall ended, chose to remain in their homes rather than run the risk of attempting to make their way to safety in the fort, and froze to death when their supplies of fuel ran out during the days and nights that followed; many others, particularly the aged and infirm, starved to death, for neither fuel nor food could be obtained while the storm was raging, and both young and old, who went out into the storm to search for one or the other, lost their way in a trackless wilderness where only days before there had been pathways and clear landmarks to guide their steps. And as the cold killed people, so too it killed our stock; cattle and goats, swine and sheep and horses. Only those animals safely lodged and warm under roofs survived in any numbers. Most of our cavalry mounts remained safe. Of the remaining beasts, penned or abandoned under the skies without food, one in every three perished, a grim reminder of my own hubris in claiming, only months earlier, that we were rich enough, in the event of a poor harvest, to survive the winter months on meat alone.

Not until the first, most frightful phase had passed and life began to regain a form of normalcy did we in Camulod itself learn of the horrors that had stricken others less fortunate and more isolated than were we. We should have known, should have anticipated chaos. That was an opinion voiced by many who, armed with hindsight, could foretell that nothing so awful would ever occur again, were the matter left to them . . .

When first it broke upon us, that cataclysmic winter was a nightmare alien to everyone's experience. The oldest living in our lands, people like my own great-aunt and the Legates Flavius and Titus, each of whom had outlived seventy winters, had never known such weather, nor could they recall anyone from their early lives ever having spoken of such cold and ferocity. How, then, could any of the Council have been prepared for such a catastrophe, or anticipated the broad swathe of death those bleak November days would usher in?

December was nine days old by the time the vicious, killing cold abated the first time, although the snow had ceased to fall some days before. In Camulod, and in the camp beneath, we had been fortunate beyond our awareness, in that the mountainous supplies of firewood assembled for the convocation day had not all been consumed as intended because of the onset of the storm. By the latter days, however, all of it had gone, and even valuable, seasoned wood from the carpenters' stores had been exhausted. Large foraging parties were sent out to gather fuel as soon as the snow stopped, and they had painful, heavy, back-breaking work to find it and bring it back. Wheeled vehicles were useless, so our carpenters removed the wheels and fashioned skids and bound them to the axles of the wagons. Even so, the snow was too deep for the horses to plough through, and so our soldiers had to clear a path ahead of each team. Not since the days of the Emperor Claudius, more than four hundred years before, had soldiers worked so hard at building roads in Britain.

As they made their way through the wilderness, the forage parties began to find the dead. When the first news of such a discovery came back to Camulod, it was greeted with appalled anguish. Within the week, however, such grisly findings were all but commonplace and we had become inured to the new way of things. Many had died: the old, the weak and the unfortunate. Many more, however, had survived frightful deprivation under frequently incredible conditions. One family of seven had fed themselves for seven days on the body of an injured wolf that had died outside their hut. The father had fallen over it, hidden beneath the snow, as he ran out into the storm, in the vain, desperate hope of finding assistance for his starving children. They had boiled it, piece by piece, with melted snow to make a stew, and only the head was left when the soldiers came to rescue them.

It was inevitable that, having found the dead, we had no way of burying them. The frozen ground beneath its waistdeep robe of snow was impervious to mattock, pick or shovel. All we could do, it appeared, was store the bodies of our dead to await the thaw, and I awoke one night in a heavy sweat from a vivid dream of things to come. I had foreseen the thaw: the melting snow and dripping icicles; the warming air and the piles of stacked-up corpses; and the still-frozen earth, yielding its hardness only with painful slowness to the mild air above. I was unable to sleep again that night and sat huddled by a tiny fire in the Armoury, shuddering anew from time to time as the memory of the stink of the rotting carcasses of more than one hundred friends and neighbours came back to me.

Even now, from the distance of decades and destinies, I have difficulty in writing of that time and that awful night, for foremost in that dreadful dream had been the rotting face of my beloved Aunt Luceiia. Luceiia Britannicus Varrus died on the last night of the Great Storm, as it came to be known. She was unaffected by either cold or hunger. She died only because it was her allotted time, and she died as she had lived, with tranquillity and dignity, slipping away peacefully in her sleep to join her husband Publius

Varrus who, I had no doubt, stood waiting for her with her brother Caius, each of them leaning forward, stretching out a hand to help her from this sad world to their much brighter one. I was there, sitting by her bedside at the time, accompanied by Ambrose, Lucanus, Ludmilla and Shelagh, whom the old woman had grown to love as quickly as she had my wife Cassandra, my Deirdre of the Violet Eyes. One other had been present, a man called Enos, the last in the long progression of itinerant bishops who had been ever welcome in my great-aunt's home. Enos, who had arrived some days before the storm, had perforce remained for its duration. He had been praying constantly beside her bed for three entire days, unweakened in his vigil by any need for rest, it seemed to me—although perhaps he slept when I was absent—and consecrating bread and wine each day for her consumption in total certainty of her salvation. Ever a pragmatist, Auntie had known it was her time and was prepared. She had said all her farewells the previous day, and Lucanus had warned us that we should not expect her to survive another night. We sat grouped around her, watching her closely, and so gentle was her passing that none of us saw her final breath. There came a moment when I looked at Ambrose, questioning, and Lucanus stooped to touch her, and she had already gone.

The only tragic element in her departure lay in the timing of it; dead of peaceful and natural causes, she must now await burial with all the others killed by the storm. The knowledge of that haunted me, robbing me of sleep with visions of her high-cheeked, lovely face and fragile form stacked among others, stiff and frozen in an open-sided storage house, exposed to the icy wind. Our minds do strange things to us. I knew well she was not stacked like a piece of wood but lay alone and apart, where I myself had carried her, wrapped in a heavy shroud made from her own best bedspread and then swaddled in the dense-furred skins of bears, but the image persisted.

And then, sitting there before my tiny fire and staring into it, my mind took me among the flames, showing me things I had not known, and things I had forgotten lay therein: I saw once more the blue and white, lambent ferocity at the heart of the pyre that had consumed my father, searing my eyes and melting his flesh to ashes in the confines of his iron coffin; I saw the glowing, ill-shaped white-hot blade that would become Excalibur, as Publius Varrus pulled it from the red- and blue- and yellow-blazing charcoal of his forge; and I saw the blazing piles of fuel—bushes, trees and grass—that he had used years earlier to dry the muddy bed of a fresh-drained mountain lake, baking its viscous wetness into clay that he could break with pick and mattock until he reached mud again and then repeating the entire process until he found and could exhume his Skystone. And my heart began to pound as I discerned the meaning of such memories: Heat! Strong enough to melt flesh and bone; to smelt raw iron out of stone; to dry the liquid mud that lay beneath a lake. Heat, therefore, strong enough to melt the ice beneath it.

The following morning, I outlined my thoughts to Ambrose, who agreed that what I proposed might well be feasible. Our soldiers had already cleared broad pathways to the trees by then, felling and cutting to supply our fuel needs, then sledding the logs back to the base of the hill, where they were raised to the summit by an elaborate system of ropes and pulleys. This refuelling was a massive operation, involving the creation of common stockpiles

on the plain beneath for the use of our other Colonists—we had learned
that lesson quickly.

Now, with the adoption of the burial scheme, this drive took on a new
intensity. A great, rectangular space was selected on the plain below, beside
the military camp, and designated as the burial ground. It lay beside the
older common grave of the Camulodian soldiers killed in repulsing Lot's first,
treacherous attack long years before. Once designated, the space then had to
be cleared of snow, a task that took two days and involved every soldier not
assigned to other duty. An advance party had to dig its way forward from the
camp's north gate to the closest point on the margin of the selected area,
gauging their progress by signals from the engineers by the gates at the top
of the fortress hill. As that party made the initial penetration, others advanced behind it, widening the access, shovelling the displaced snow into
skid-mounted wagons, which shipped it back to where it could be piled out
of the way in dirty mountains that could be left to melt in their own time.

Once arrived at the perimeter of the burial area, the advance party doubled in strength and then branched right and left, beginning the arduous
process of clearing the borders of the rectangle, directed all the while by
signals from the hilltop. Eventually, that task complete, they turned inward
towards the centre, and as the working clearance grew, the number of workers
increased in proportion, so that by the morning of the second day the work
was running smoothly on all four sides and the project progressed with ever-
increasing speed. The snow was uniformly almost shoulder high across the
space selected, and dense-packed by the cold, incessant winds, so that it
broke beneath the shovels like dry clay and, although heavy, was simple to
handle.

As soon as the perimeter was wide enough to permit easy access, the
skidded wagons served a double purpose, hauling snow outward to the dis-
persal points and bringing back fuel for the burning, spreading it thickly on
the now-bare, hard soil of the northern end of the burial ground.

It had not escaped Ambrose that all this wood we gathered would be
green and difficult to burn, and he proposed a solution that I thought again
betrayed his brilliance. We had as many animal carcasses as human. Ambrose
proposed stripping them of all fat and rendering that to liquid, which would
then be poured upon the wood and itself used as fuel. The remaining meat,
inedible because the animals had died and lain intact, was kept aside to be
burned or buried later, after the main tasks were completed. The stench it
would create were we to attempt, as one man had suggested, to burn it in
the melting of the ground, would be unbearable to those on the hill above.
In consequence, another large operation was simultaneously under way at the
southern end of the site, where massive iron cauldrons, commandeered from
the quartermasters, were suspended over fires to render down the fat of oxen
and sheep, swine, goats and even horses. As each cauldron was filled, it was
lowered with great care from the tripod that supported it and carried on a
yoke between two men to where another team directed the disposal of the
fat, taking care that none should be wasted and no part of the fuel should
be untreated.

The fires at the north end of the area were lit the second night, long after
nightfall, and by dawn, our men were out there, digging down through the

warm ashes into the softened ground until the earth grew hard again beneath their picks.

The work was killing, but the task was completed as expected, and our dead were eventually interred with dignity and much solemnity, in the presence of the assembled populace of Camulod. It had taken ten long days to complete the task, and by the end of them everyone, and every animal in Camulod, stank from the omnipresent, cloying smoke. The bath houses on the hill and in the Villa Britannicus to the north of the burial ground operated throughout each night and day, and the furnaces and hypocausts never grew cool. And while all of this had been going on, a minor version of the same events occurred within the fort itself, where Luceiia Britannicus Varrus was laid to rest beside her husband and her brother, in new-turned earth that had been warmed to welcome her.

The cold abated finally, the temperature rising from the depths it had sustained for so long to the point at which it now seemed relatively warm, yet the cold was bitter still. The snow endured, too, although we had a period of three entire weeks without a fresh snowfall. And then the temperature soared, and the sound of running water was heard everywhere, and people wept for joy. For six sweet days it lasted, before the running water turned again to ice overnight and another storm swept in and held for four more days. This time there was to be no respite. And so it went on, with intermittent storms but always bitter cold, through January and into February.

By the time spring did arrive that year, early in March, people had begun to fear it might never appear at all. But come it did, and the snow and ice vanished gradually, and the grass grew beneath and new life appeared with shoots and buds and promise of green brightness. We were to discover, later, that a new phenomenon had touched our lands: large groves of trees, healthy the previous year, had died during that winter, killed, it would seem, by the appalling cold. Julia, the wife of Hector, our farmer Council member, had a pretty way of growing flowers outside her home, planting them each year in earthen pots, an oddity she had learned in her girlhood from an old nurse who had been raised in Greece. Hector and she had noticed that these flowers would die some years, if they were blighted early in their pots by a late frost, and he later attributed the same fate to the dead groves of trees, speculating that they might have suffered from the brief thaw that had come partway through the winter; that their roots might have stirred to life too soon and then been killed by the returning cold. It seemed reasonable to me at the time. I would never forget the ferocity of that searing cold.

In the earliest days of the final thaw, the aged Legate Titus, a dear-held fixture in my life since my seventh year, fell on a patch of ice and broke his pelvis. Lucanus did all in his power to assuage his pain, but the old man died within days of the accident. Within the month, his lifelong friend and companion, the Legate Flavius, who had sat steadfast by his friend's bedside throughout his final, painful days, had joined him in death, for no apparent reason other than that he had lost all will to live longer without his familiar. With him passed my last intimate contact with those who had known my own father, Picus Britannicus. I mourned both of them deeply.

If anything worthwhile emerged from that winter, it was the fulfillment of Ambrose's wish for unity among our men. Confined within the fort and equally within the outposts at the borders of our lands, the men of Camulod forgot the schism that had split them into jealous factions. Cavalry could not function amid snow that reached higher than the bellies of their horses, and so all the men of Camulod once more became mere soldiers, bunking together in cramped quarters, sharing the soldier's hardships and boredom, the sameness and the tedium. Yet there was a difference among their ranks: the foot-soldiers worked with the horses now, tending and feeding them; they learned the ways of horses, and they drilled with cavalry weapons, learning to sit on saddles and to ride with stirrups, to control a mount, even though they were confined to those small areas that had been cleared of surface snow.

Ambrose and I watched closely as the healing magic of propinquity and shared hardship welded our men together, and soon, one evening long before the final thaw arrived, we were discussing tactics and the order of our march to Cambria and Glevum. The winter must end soon, and we would be prepared. Our strikes on Glevum and on Cambria must come as quickly as the snows permitted us to move. Ambrose believed the harshness of the winter would aid us with Cambria, since the higher altitudes would remain snowbound long after we were free of snow. Glevum was a different matter, he believed, built as it was beside the river estuary, where fresh winds from the sea would have cut down the snow. What if the bireme had returned before our arrival, he wondered. Then we might face a force of five hundred or more men, fortified by the ruined town. What should we do then? Only the knowledge that the Berbers came from warmer climes made me feel sanguine. I felt sure that they would rather sit elsewhere and await the spring than voluntarily expose themselves to Britain's winter weather.

Lucanus had sat listening to us talk for some time, but had said nothing, and this unwonted silence finally made me aware that he was in the grip of some despondency. I interrupted Ambrose in mid-speech and asked Lucanus what was wrong, but he demurred, shaking his head and mumbling something that I did not hear. Ambrose, aware now, too, that something was ailing Luke, sat silent. Finally Luke admitted that he had been preoccupied with thoughts of Mordechai Emancipatus and his colony. If, as he suspected, the winter had been as savage there as we had known it, he feared greatly for their safety and welfare. As soon as he had named them, I myself became concerned, and feeling guilty that I had not thought of them before, I promised to visit Mordechai in passing, taking another wagonload of supplies to help them mend the ravages of the winter months. My promise allowed Lucanus to feel better, but I could see he would not be at ease until I had fulfilled it and brought back word that all was well with the lepers.

I had difficulty that winter, deep within myself, in dealing with the deaths of three companions, my great-aunt and the two Legates, yet somehow, for reasons I could not explain, I could weep for none of them. Winter had ended by the time old Flavius died, but there was still winter in my soul. Each night, in Auntie's family room, which now was mine alone since Ambrose would not hear of sharing it, I met for hours with Ambrose, Ludmilla, Shelagh and her father Liam. Lucanus was more times present than absent at these sessions, which followed no pattern but evolved steadily into what became my new family life. Less frequently we might be joined by others, among them Dedalus, Philip, Benedict and Rufio, and Hector and his wife Julia, who had formed close friendships with Ludmilla and Shelagh. To my great surprise one evening, I discovered that these two had decided, for some reason unquestioned by anyone, against calling their child Lucanus and had named him Bedwyr. On hearing that I turned to Luke, surprised, but he had frowned, shaking his head for me to hold my tongue, and I made my mind up to ask him another time what had led to this reversal.

I got my chance one day when we spent the afternoon together in one of the smithies, incidentally the warmest places in the fortress, where I had taken a whim to work on my own at fashioning a spearhead of the kind Donuil and I had talked about in Eire. We had been speaking of celibacy, with no great ease on either side, continuing a conversation begun and abandoned days before, when we had been interrupted. Laying aside my hammer, and thrusting the rough spearhead among the coals to heat again, I unburdened myself and told Lucanus of my lust for Shelagh, and of its resolution. Now that Shelagh and I had discussed it openly, I told him, exposing it for what it was, mere natural attraction and no cause for shame, the sullen burn of it had left me, but the knowledge of *my* knowledge, if he could follow the direction of my thoughts, was there, a constant, never wavering distraction. It made my earlier talk of celibacy, I told him, mere talk. Shelagh had now become a constant in my life, beneath my eyes, within my reach each day, and although I no longer felt the driving guilt and lustful yearnings I had had before, the fact remained that I admired her greatly and would take her to wife tomorrow if, God forbid, Donuil were to come to harm in Eire. How could I become truly celibate, living in such a condition, with mind and body in constant turmoil?

When I had finished speaking, Luke sighed and swung away from me, clasping his hands behind his back, and I felt my gut spasm in misgiving, thinking I had offended him. He remained that way for long moments, holding himself stiffly erect, then slumped and turned to face me. My eyes sought his as he turned, but there was no anger in his expression. Instead, there was something I could not identify. He unclasped his hands from behind his back and examined the palms minutely, peering at them closely, and when he spoke his words held no significance for me, seeming to have no bearing upon anything that I had said.

"Caius, why do you think Hector named his son Bedwyr?"

I blinked at him, bereft of a response to such a non sequitur. He smiled, a wan, sad smile, lowering his hands. "I have a reason for asking."

I shook my head. "I have no idea. I know Julia wished to name the child for you. Hector, evidently, had other notions and preferred Bedwyr. But what has that to do with Shelagh?"

"Nothing, yet perhaps everything. The child is Bedwyr because that is the name chosen for him by his mother. I suggested it to her."

"Very well, I accept that. Ludmilla told me at the time that you had seemed unwilling to have the child named in your honour. But was Julia not offended? Was she not hurt by your rejection? It appears rather cruel to me, hearing of it thus."

"Aye." Luke nodded. "At first she was, but I explained my reasons, and she accepted them with great courtesy. And then she asked me to propose another name. Bedwyr was in my mind, I know not why. I said it, she accepted it, and so the child was named."

I felt my own confusion upon my face. "But what has that to do with me and Shelagh?"

"Nothing, Caius, but it has everything to do with your condition . . ." He waited, smiling more naturally now, waiting for my reaction. When he saw that my confusion had merely increased, he spoke again. "The child's mother, Julia, is the only woman in more than thirty years who has come close to making me regret my celibacy. Her mere existence disturbs me deeply. I lust for her, asleep and awake, and I am an old man." My mouth fell open but he spoke on, now giving me no opportunity to respond. "The mere sight or recollection of her fills me with terror and with thoughts and sensations I would have sworn were dead within me. Aware of that, the prospect of having a child of hers named after me would have been unbearable, a living reminder of my weakness. So you see, Caius, you are not unique, and no one, ever, is impervious to lust."

"Good God, Luke! And you told her this?"

"Not entirely, but she understood."

"And now what? How does she behave towards you?"

He shrugged. "Entirely as she always has, with kindness and consideration. Only with a more marked avoidance of approaching me too closely."

"She avoids you?"

"Not at all. She is merely gracious enough not to tempt me more than she must by her presence."

"You did tell her!"

We were interrupted at that point by the arrival of Dedalus who sought to drag me off to speak with Achmed Cato on a disciplinary matter. I held up my hand to stay Ded and indicate that I would come directly, but I kept my eyes on Lucanus. He smiled again and shrugged his shoulders. "Some of it. As in your case, I benefited thereby. Confession is good for the soul."

I heaved a great sigh of relief, feeling enormously better. "Thank you for this, Luke," I said, turning to where Ded stood frowning at both of us, curious as he always was. "I know how difficult it must have been, but I appreciate your candour."

Later that evening, in the family room, I watched Julia closely, marvelling over what Luke had told me. She was a comely, wholesome, healthy young woman, generously fleshed, aged somewhere short of thirty I suspected, with a pleasant, happy nature and an ever-ready smile. She doted visibly upon her husband and upon the son she now held easily within the cradle of one arm. But I could see no reason for Luke's lust. She was no Siren, bearing more resemblance to Juno, with her double chin and ample, milk-swelled breasts, than to Venus. Lucanus ignored both her and me that night, until the bishop Enos wandered in and settled by the fire and the talk changed to churchly things for once. Enos was saying that the Church maintained its methods of communicating from one land to another, so that the word could go from bishops in Britain to others far afield, like my old friend Bishop Germanus in Gaul. That captured all my attention, and when I asked him if he was saying a letter could be sent from one land and delivered safely in another he seemed surprised that I might doubt it for a moment. From that moment

on, Germanus remained foremost in my thoughts, and that night I sat down
to write to him.

Germanus Pontifex
From Caius Merlyn Britannicus

Greetings:
*I write to you as bishop, though recalling you clearly as Legate, soldier
and friend, in complete uncertainty that you will ever read my words.*

*My father's aunt, Luceiia Britannicus Varrus, of whom we spoke
when first we met on the way to Verulamium, has recently died, as have
some other, aged friends, and my grief is still fresh and new. She was
old when I met you, as you may recall; too old to make the hundred-
mile journey to hear your judgment on the teachings of my father's friend
Pelagius. Seven years have passed since then, and she has finally expired.*

*Much has occurred in my life during those years, Master Germanus,
and I had met no other bishop since that time until my aunt lay dying.
She was devout, and faithful to the teachings of her gentle Christus,
and she took pleasure all her life in the sustenance of His labourers, the
bishops and the wandering men of God who keep this land of ours
enlightened.*

*One of these men, calling himself Enos, was present at her bedside
when she died, and consecrated bread and wine to her salvation. He has
no home today, no Seat to oversee, now that the towns in this fair land
of ours are fallen into ruin. You were correct in that, prophetic. Now
Enos wanders, as he says, "wherever Heaven bids him," and he tells me
that the Church is stronger here in Britain nowadays than it has ever
been. When there were towns, the Christians held the towns, but the
majority of rural folk were pagan pantheists. Now that has changed, he
tells me, and the Word of God is everywhere throughout the land.*

*I asked about your schools. In Verulamium you had decreed that
schools be founded to instruct the teachers in the ways of God. Where
are they? He answered that they are within the hearts and minds and
bodies of such as he; that their classrooms are the open glades and
riverbanks and village pastures; that their students are the people, all
the folk, including Saxons.*

*That disturbed me. It still does. Saxons are not "the folk." The folk
of Britain are the native Celts and the descendants of four hundred
years of Roman life and Roman occupation. Enos told me I am unchristian to deny God's wealth to any. I responded that God spread His
wealth with even-handedness and that I grudge no man God's wealth,
providing he enjoys it in his own homeland. So be it, I fear I may be
damned.*

*I transmit this with Enos, who has hopes that it may reach you,
somehow, in your home in Gaul. I hope it may, but were it lost forever,
the writing of it has eased a troubled mind.*
Farewell
Merlyn Britannicus

Post Scriptum:

I rejoice to tell you that I have heard nothing in years from that new breed of Roman priests whom you called the monastics. You, for your part, may take pleasure in the knowledge that the name Pelagius has faded from our tongues . . . and hence from the minds of all save errant fools like me.

The advent of spring revived imperatives that could no longer be neglected or denied. Before the last of the snow had melted from the ground, our horsemen were maneuvering again, the veteran cavalry once more forming the tight formations we had evolved through the years and sharpening the skills we had been unable to practice through the the long months that had passed. New cavalry troops had been created, too, during the winter, and now rode in groups and squadrons, though without the tightly disciplined sharpness of the others. These men had learned to ride in theory only, walking or trotting their horses on the frozen drilling plain, learning the basic features of control. None of them, however, had ridden at the canter, and none had known the elemental freedom and power born of being astride a running horse at full gallop. Now they began to learn, and many a flying rump learned painfully that the frost had not yet loosed its hold on the earth.

This training all took place in an atmosphere of good-natured raillery, but there was serious intent beneath the laughter. The thousand men dispatched this spring from Camulod would all be horsed. Five hundred would be seasoned cavalry, the other five experienced infantry, mounted for speed. When the time came to fight, as come it would, the two would act in unison, the infantry dismounted, in their own element, and the cavalry free to range widely, driving the enemy onto the spears awaiting in the infantry's serried ranks.

I sat my horse beside Ambrose and Dedalus one afternoon close to the drilling ground, on the road, some way above the wide-stretched plain, where I could watch the parties wheel and regroup. Beside me, Dedalus cleared his throat and growled, "Now there's a likely rider."

I turned and glanced to see who had attracted his attention and failed to recognize the rider who was galloping towards us, crouched low over the neck of a big black like my own that was running strongly. Only when the rider sat back, reining the horse into a sliding halt and pulling off the helmet did I recognize Shelagh, and such was my shock that I could not react beyond staring open-mouthed. She shook out her long hair, appearing extremely pleased with herself, and kneed her horse towards us, up the hill, and as she did so I heard my companions explode into howls of hilarity. Shelagh was dressed as a man, armoured from head to toe in my own black and silver colours. Heavy, ring-mail leggings covered her legs and a tunic of the same material hung beneath her cuirass. She came straight up to where I sat, and bowed from the saddle as deeply as her armour would allow.

"Are you surprised then, Merlyn Britannicus?" Her great, hawk eyes were flashing with pleasure and her teeth were alabaster white behind her crimson, wind-stung lips. I knew I must respond soon, and well. I could feel the eyes of my companions.

"Surprised?" I managed to say, forcing myself to drawl. "I am thunderstruck! I've watched your husband clutch one hand to his horse's mane and the other to his saddle for years, and had believed no Eirishman could ever ride a horse."

"Mayhap you're right, Commander, for I am a woman, though that might be hard to tell at this moment."

That brought another bark of laughter from my friends who, as they were quick to tell me now, had all conspired to keep me uninformed on this. Dedalus himself had been her teacher—a reluctant one at first, bound by the promise he had made her on the boat to Britain, to aid her in anything with which she might require assistance. Once begun, however, it had quickly become apparent to Ded that his tyro student had a natural seat upon a horse and was, in fact, a born equestrian. Excited by the discovery, but bound by a promise to say nothing to me, he had brought Rufio into the plot, and soon all eight companions of the Eirish expedition were taking turns to groom and train the prodigy. Ambrose, as joint Commander, had been admitted to the secret, too, since Shelagh's serious training could not go forward without the approval of either him or me. And so it was done. Of all the new recruits trained in the winter's exercise, Shelagh had been the most outstanding; the one spectacular success, adopted by the troopers to a man, so that they had combined to keep her presence hidden from my eyes.

At that point, I had turned to Shelagh. "Are these men telling me that you have ridden right before my eyes without my knowing?"

She grinned, completely unashamed. "Aye, and with your veterans, too! You've looked right through me, many times, though once you mentioned me to Ded for having performed well in a wheel sweep."

"Damnation," I said. "I need a drink of mead." I turned to the others. "I am not used to drinking with conspirators of any stripe, but all things change, it seems. Will you join me?" We rode uphill to the fort and retired to the family room, which Ludmilla and the other women of the household kept as pristine as it had been while its castellan yet lived there.

A week thereafter, to the day, our expedition left for Glevum and Shelagh rode with us, having earned her place. Even with the merit she had earned, however, I would have been loath to include her, had it not been for the fact that her father would ride with us, too, driving the wagon filled with goods for Mordechai, which he would unload before following us into Glevum, there to await the arrival of Donuil and Feargus's galleys bearing his livestock.

Her father's wagon would slow us down too much, I knew, even upon the great, straight Roman road that we would ride to Glevum, and so I seconded an escort of fifty men, under the command of Rufio, to ride with it and follow on our heels as quickly as they could. Shelagh stayed with her father, and I promised to rejoin them at the hostelry of the Red Dragon as soon as we had cleared the Berbers out of Glevum.

Huw Strongarm and his men went with us, too, but they remained on foot, serving as scouts. They left a day ahead of us and remained out of sight, save for a single man who came each evening, after we had camped, to tell us all was well and nothing moved ahead of us or around us.

We made excellent time, considering there were still large snowbanks on the great roadway among the deeper woods, and we came within sight of Glevum in the early afternoon of our fourth day out from Camulod. Huw sat on a milestone waiting for me two miles from the town. The Berbers were there, he reported, and had apparently wintered in one of the warehouses by the harbourside. They had grown careless and overconfident, doubtless through having remained undisturbed for months, and Strongarm's men had been able to penetrate the town itself in daylight without being discovered. He reported thirty-four Berbers present, all armed with bows and long, curving swords. No contact had been made with anyone, he said, so we might well surprise them if we proceeded cautiously.

His report caused me concern. I had thought to find more men than thirty-four, and said so. Huw shrugged and said nothing, since there was nothing he could say, and Dedalus proposed that the Berbers' numbers might have been severely depleted during the winter months. These people were not accustomed to cold, he pointed out. Their natural habitat was desert land, beneath the sun of Africa. I was unconvinced, but had no option but to concur. Huw now volunteered a plan.

His suggestion was based, he said, on the fact that all the Berbers were bowmen and afoot. My troopers, horsed or unhorsed, would be at a serious disadvantage among the streets and buildings. I nodded, telling him I knew exactly what he meant, for we had had precisely that problem on our previous visit. Now he suggested we permit him and his men to vanguard the attack. They were sixteen, all told, against odds of two to one, but if they were in difficulty they would fall back, their lesser numbers tempting the Berbers to pursue them beyond the town and into our grasp. I could not deny the logic involved, but the odds against Huw and his men depressed me. The compromise that immediately came to me, however, offered them a better edge. If our infantry were to penetrate the town under cover of darkness, accompanied by his bowmen, then we could arrange to split our forces into groups, arranged in open spaces, that would await the Berbers in pursuit of Huw's bowmen, who would lead them directly into our traps. The only obstacle anyone could find in that was that we had no way of knowing where these traps should be set up. None of us knew the town. Huw sat grinning, then offered to take me with him into Glevum, to see for myself and select my own spots.

The idea appealed to me immediately, and the inherent danger heightened its appeal. And so Dedalus and I, accompanied by Huw himself, the giant Powys, and Owain of the Caves, slipped into Glevum on foot in the light of day and made our dispositions *in situ*. We returned without having seen a sign of Berbers, though we could smell the smoke from their cooking fires.

That night, in the darkest hours before dawn, we made our way back again at the head of two hundred of our men, moving in stealth and silence, our arms and armour muffled against the slightest betraying clink of sound, and settled down to wait. We saw the dawn grow to day and the sun rise in the east in a clear blue sky before the first howls of outrage assailed our ears. We closed ranks immediately, four groups of fifty men, each assigned a specific location to which Huw's bowmen would lead their pursuers. It was over within the hour and our casualties were slight: two men killed and five wounded, none of those seriously. Of the two men killed, one was from Camulod, a veteran called Marc Mercus killed in the streetfighting, and one a Celt, the hairless Elfred Egghead, killed in the opening moments of the attack by an arrow in the back, shot by a guard who must have been asleep, since Elfred had passed him by without seeing him. The Berbers fought hard, to the last man, evidently preferring death to the prospect of captivity. I myself had not bloodied my sword throughout the entire affair, and I led the withdrawal from the town assailed by a sense of foreboding. What should have been a satisfying victory had been a stale, unwholesome business.

We assembled our entire force on the flats beyond the town, within sight of the estuary, established a camp and allowed the men to break their fast. I left Dedalus in charge there and rode alone to meet with Liam's party, after which I would ride to visit Mordechai as promised, and then rejoin the army. We would leave for Cambria as soon as I returned the following morning.

Not all bad days are born of ill beginnings. The bright blue sky that had come with the dawn yielded to heavy, sullen clouds by mid-morning, and I found myself testing the chilliness of the wind as I rode, in fear of yet more snow. It was too warm for snow, however, and the truth of that was shown when a heavy spattering of fat raindrops swept from the west and rattled audibly against my helmet. I wrapped my cloak more tightly about my shoulders and rode on, but the rain held off.

I arrived at the site of the Red Dragon hostelry well before noon, after a two-hour ride, to find Liam, Shelagh and their escort already awaiting me. Of the hostelry, however, all that remained was a black pile of charred and broken beams covered by icy, brittle-crusted snow. The fire that had destroyed it had obviously occurred before the onset of winter, and I assumed the Berbers had been responsible. Angry at being thus bereft of the few moments' rest and warmth I had anticipated, I controlled my ill-humour and issued my new orders. Since Rufio reported that his party's progress had been uneventful, I sent the escort on to Glevum, where they could camp with their companions and enjoy a break, no matter how short, from the tedium of the journey. I kept back only Rufio himself to ride with me in company with Shelagh and Liam's wagon. The ride to Mordechai's colony was short from here, less than ten miles, and I saw no reason to expose our men either to contagion or the fear of it. We four would arrive well before nightfall, I estimated, unload the wagon, eat and sleep, and be ready to return again at first light.

The rain began to fall as we sat by the ruined hostelry and watched our men march off to be concealed by the forest that encroached here to the edges of the road. I glanced down at the cobbles between my horse's feet, seeing the raindrops overpowering the shrinking gaps of dryness on the stones, and saw a tiny sapling growing there. I immediately remembered Benedict's prediction and agreed with it, knowing conclusively that this road on which we sat would be destroyed and vanish completely within a hundred years. Behind me, I heard Liam click his gums, stirring the wagon horse to movement, and then the iron tyres began their clamour over the cobbles.

We soon discovered that Lucanus's worst fears had been justified and exceeded. Mordechai's colony lay empty and abandoned, all signs of life extinguished. I knew from the first moment, looking down into the tiny dell from the hillside above through a driving downpour, that we were far, far too late. There is an aspect of emptiness that speaks eloquently of abandonment rather than temporary relocation, and it consists largely of an impression of neglect; it is a visual impression, difficult to define yet unmistakable. This place had lain untended for long weeks, perhaps even months.

I had told Shelagh and Liam the tale of Mordechai Emancipatus on the journey from the ruined hostelry, and now we sat at the top of the rise for a long time, ignoring the rain since we were long since drenched, each of us wordlessly inspecting the scene below. Finally, faced with the choice of simply riding off without a closer look, or making some attempt to discover the when and how of things, I kneed my horse forward, bidding Liam remain where he was with the wagon. Shelagh and Rufio accompanied me, but I alone dismounted when I reached the threshold of the longhouse, with its sagging, open door. Full of the fears that had all but overwhelmed me on my first visit to this place, I held my breath and leaned forward to look inside the long, low building. There was no one there. I called aloud, still making no attempt to enter, and my voice echoed back to me.

Sighing, but relieved of the fear of having to enter, I turned away and swept my eyes around the grassy bowl that formed the common ground. Nothing. And then I saw the pot, the new one we had brought from Camulod on our first visit. It sat where I had seen it last, amid the long-dead ashes of the cooking fire, and it was scaled with rust, accumulated over months. Rufio spoke from behind me.

"How sick were these people, Merlyn?"

"Very sick, some more than others. Why do you ask?" I looked up at him, to see him staring off along the far side of the longhouse. He nodded in the direction of his gaze and I moved to where I could see what he was looking at.

"There's still a lot of snow piled up in there, out of the sun," he said. "They must have had it even worse than us these past few months. Some of them must have died."

"Aye, that's a fair assumption." I was eyeing the pile of snow uneasily, wondering what might lie beneath it.

"Then where are they?" Rufio asked, reinforcing my dismay. "There's no bodies lying around. The ground would be as hard here as it was in Camulod."

"You think they're there, under the snow?"

Rufio shrugged as I turned back to him. "They could be. They must be somewhere. And some must have survived and moved away, otherwise there would be at least one corpse lying around. The last one to die. No one would have dragged him anywhere."

"Aye, you're right, Rufio." Feeling immensely relieved at that realisation, I went directly along the side of the longhouse to the piled-up snow, looking for some means of shovelling it aside, closing my mind resolutely against the fear of what might lie concealed therein. An old, broken shovel leaned against the wall and I seized it quickly, using it to scrape the surface snow aside and then digging carefully until I reached bare soil. There were no corpses there. I rejoined the others and swung myself up into my saddle.

"Nothing there at all, but you're right, they must be somewhere. Stay here, I'm going to look around."

I found nothing but the long-dead body of the horse we had left the lepers, but Rufio had ignored my order to stay where he was, and it was he who found the burial place. I heard his voice calling me from the woods opposite the longhouse, and arrived there to find him still astride his horse, a handful of his cloak held to his mouth. The pity of the scene was as overwhelming as the stench of it. A row of bodies lay arranged alongside each other, thirteen of them, each laid out in a semblance of decency and good order. Close by them someone, Mordechai, I had no doubt, had attempted to dig a pit large enough to inter them. It was wide and long, but less than a short-sword's length in depth, and its bottom yet retained the chipped, hard-broken look of frozen ground.

"Mordechai," I said. "He must have gone in search of help."

"Aye, but not long ago. Look at that one." The last body in the line closest to the unfinished pit looked different. We moved closer.

"This one's new dead, Merlyn," Rufio said, his eyes sharper than mine. "He's still fresh. Look, the skin's not even livid." I looked and it was true. This corpse could have been no more than eight or ten hours old, which meant that Mordechai could not be far away, since it must have been he who dragged the body here. As I sat there, feeling my heart accelerate, we heard Shelagh calling to us and kicked our horses to a trot, making directly for the sound of her voice. She was in front of the longhouse, in the act of swinging herself up into the saddle when we broke from the trees, and her excitement was clearly evident.

"Someone was here until this morning," she called as we approached. "Could it have been your friend Mordechai? I smelled fresh smoke inside the house, and sure enough, the ashes of the fire there are still warm. Whoever was here might still be close by, unless he had a horse."

"No, the only horse they had is dead," I answered her. "I found it over there, in the brush. It must have frozen in the storm. If this is Mordechai—and I would guess it is, for he's not among the dead—he'll be on foot, and probably extremely weak, since he'll be starving. Damnation! Where should we even begin to look?"

"That way and this." Shelagh swept her arm from left to right, indicating a faint, but clearly worn path that crossed the clearing in front of the long-house, disappearing into the woods on either side. "We know he didn't go towards Glevum or we would have seen him, and this path seems to be the only one leaving here. It has clearly been well used. If we split up and go both ways, one of us should find him."

"There's one more path," Rufio added. "I saw it when I found the bodies. It leads back into the forest, in that direction." He waved his arm towards the trees, at right angles to Shelagh's path. Three paths, three riders.

"Let's rejoin Liam and talk about this," I said, silently cursing the heavy rain, which seemed to be increasing.

When we had joined him, I explained the situation and Liam merely nodded and sat silent, waiting for me to tell them what to do.

"Very well then, we'll split up, one to each path. But let's be sensible in this. None of us needs to spend the night lost in the woods. We are on horseback, Mordechai's afoot. That means on a clear, unblocked path we should be able to move at least three times as fast as he can; probably four times faster. Let's assume he has been gone since early this morning, some time after daybreak, eight hours or so. I calculate we have four hours or more of daylight left to us. But in two hours, each of us should be able to cover the entire distance he might have made on foot, so be aware of time! Two hours, no more. At the end of that, turn back, no matter what, and let's hope one of us will have found him by then. Liam, you stay here and wait for us. Light a fire if you can, but don't try too hard or too long. Everything will soon be too soaked to burn. Don't drown yourself in the attempt. Let's go. We have no time to waste."

Rufio took the path that he had found and Shelagh and I went east and west along the main pathway that crossed the clearing. I turned one last time to wave to Liam Twistback, whose eyes were on his daughter's receding form, and as I did so the sky was sundered by a blast of searing blue light, followed by a deafening crack of thunder that brought Germanicus up in a screaming rear of fright. I fought him down grimly, and swung him back onto the path again, letting him feel my spurs as I put him towards the storm-lashed forest.

XXIV

THE DAY DARKENED rapidly as I rode along the narrow, twisting path among tall, close-packed, slender trees that bore delicate, pale leaves too small to impede the falling lancets of rain. The ground sloped upward steadily so that at times the pathway underneath my horse's hooves resembled a brook more than a footpath. About a mile from Mordechai's clearing, however, both the surrounding trees and the nature of the pathway changed for the better, giving way to a broader, drier path of needles carpeting the ground beneath soaring, heavy conifers. My mount responded quickly to the new ground underfoot, and for a time we made much better progress, increasing almost to a full gallop in places before the ground began to level out again and then slope downward. By this time I was riding through a craggy, rock-strewn landscape, where sudden cliffs, rearing up from the ground beneath and girt in places with the thick, gnarled roots of ancient trees, reminded me of the primeval forest we had traversed in Eire.

As we moved downward now, the slope increased and soon we dropped below the line at which the conifers began, finding ourselves again in a deciduous forest where the previous autumn's dead leaves, slick with the rain, made downward progress arduous and hazardous. At one point, the path became almost precipitous and I was thinking halfheartedly of dismounting and leading my mount down, when he made the choice for me, setting his hooves upon the slippery slope without a sign from me. Accepting that he knew what he was doing, I leaned back in the saddle, letting my reins go loose and trusting him to find his own way down. Avoiding the temptation to lean forward and see for myself where he was stepping, I looked about me instead, and saw the figure of a man hanging from a tree.

The sight terrified me for a moment, and the first thought that leapt into my mind was that I had found Mordechai. A second glance, however, told me I was wrong, because whoever the hanged man may have been, he had been swinging from that tree for months. Even in the semi-darkness of the hillside twilight, I could see the pallid glint of bones from where I was. In days, or weeks, now that the spring was here, nature would complete her reclamation and the last remains of this once-human thing would fall apart, dropping into the undergrowth beneath. Idly, and gauging only from the angle of the hillside beneath where he hung, I speculated that he had been bound on the ground beneath the tree, then hoisted into place by several others, higher up the hill. Sure enough, as I drew closer my eye picked out the other length of rope, stretching away beyond the gallows branch to the base of another tree farther up the hill.

I had reached the bottom of the descent safely and was riding on, eyeing the ghastly sight and idly wondering who the fellow could have been, when something else caught my eye. I could easily have missed it, gazing as I was at the rags and bones above, but that my horse shied and sidled, snorting nervously. I looked down and saw a tattered blanket lying on the path. Dismounting quickly, I gathered it up, saw it had been ripped apart and then saw bloodstains in the wool and the watery remnants of spilled blood beside where it had lain on the stony ground. Glancing backward, up along the slippery path we had just descended, I could now clearly see the marks where someone had fallen and slid down. Mordechai must be close by, I knew. Like me, he must have seen the hanging man and, distracted, had missed his footing and fallen, injuring himself.

I cupped my hands to my mouth and called his name several times, listening hard each time for a response, but I heard nothing other than the wind and rain. And then I saw fresh leaves and twigs in the mud, and beside them a deep mark gouged in the ground, and beyond that another, then another. It was plain that Mordechai had injured himself badly enough to have cut himself a crutch and padded the end with a piece of this torn blanket. I mounted quickly and set out to follow the marks he had left behind. Two hundred paces farther along, I came to a steep bank, which Mordechai had faced and failed to climb. His crutch marks, numerous and deep at the bottom of this clayey bank and deeply graven in the slick slope's surface, told the story eloquently. From there, accepting failure, he had veered aside and off the path, the marks of his crutch disappearing so steeply downward into the forest itself that I could not ride after him. Dismounting, I caught my horse's bridle and set out on foot, leading him, but quickly led him back up to the path again and tethered him. It would have been impossible to take him down into that wilderness and maintain anything approaching speed, and I knew that speed was vital. I knew, deep in my heart, that Mordechai was in deadly peril.

I found him a short time later, literally almost falling on top of him. The hillside was free of trees in this area; I had passed through the last of them some way above. The bushes that carpeted the hillside here, however, were so thick as to be almost impenetrable, and their very density permitted me to see where he had forced his way through them. And where he had gone I followed, almost to the end. I was saved from sharing his fate only by the fact that he, in falling, had grasped at a clump of shrubs on the edge of the abyss that had entrapped him, and from their condition it appeared that they had held him for some time, but he had been too weakened to pull himself back up and so had fallen. Using extreme caution, and aware of my heart thumping at my ribs from my close escape, I crept forward and peered over the edge.

Mordechai lay below me, much too far away for me to reach him, in the narrow, rubble-strewn bottom of a stark cleft in the hillside. The smooth rock face opposite me, at the foot of which he lay, seemed polished, stained with seepage and falling rain, and he lay sprawled at the foot of it, on his back, by the side of a strangely opaque, reflectionless pool that lay directly beneath my face as I peered down. His face was turned towards me and his crutch, identifiable by its padded end, lay lodged beneath his body. His left leg was obviously broken very badly, white bone splinters protruding from the shin, but I could see little blood. He was motionless, but I chose not to believe that he was dead. I called to him, but to no effect. Quickly I scanned the sides of the drop beneath me and saw that it, too, was sheer, like the other side, as though the rock had been cloven by a thunderbolt.

It was then, as I looked back towards him, that he moved, convulsing in a way that brought his right arm sweeping to hit a large splinter of stone that lay beside the edge of the dark pool I had noticed earlier. His arm hit the stone with sufficient strength to dislodge it and send it tumbling into the pool. My flesh crawled with horror, because I saw it fall and watched it disappear and there was no splash, no sound of any kind. What I had taken for a pool was a deep, black, bottomless hole in the floor of the crevice.

I rolled onto my back and sat upright, bracing myself on my straight arms and cursing the rain and my heavy armour. Mordechai needed help immediately, but I had no way of reaching him. He lay at least four times my own height beneath me, and even had I been able to climb down to where he lay, I could never climb up again, carrying him. My mind was filled with all the things I knew I could not do. I could not ride back for Rufio. By my reckoning, I had been riding for no more than an hour. One more hour to ride back would take me there just as the others were abandoning their search, with two hours yet to elapse before they won back to their starting point. By the time they arrived back it would be growing dark and we would still be one full hour away from here. Even were he still alive by then, it was clear to me that Mordechai would not survive the night, down in that hole in the cold and the rain. Even Liam Twistback was of no use to me. The path that lay between us was far too narrow, steep and dangerous for his large wagon. And then I remembered the rope from which the dead man hung, less than a mile away.

I scrambled back up the slope, mounted my horse and made my way back along the path to where I could climb up and cut the rope at the base of the tree that anchored it. The corpse fell to the hillside below me, disintegrating as it hit the ground, so that I had no worries about freeing the other end, and I began to coil the rope immediately, inspecting it as I brought it in. It appeared slightly worn at the point where it had lain across the tree limb for so long, but otherwise it seemed strong enough to do what I required of it. Another thunderclap rumbled away above as I finished the coils, satisfied with the weight and thickness of the rope. Looping it across my chest, I scrambled back down to my horse and made my way back to where Mordechai had left the track. There, remembering that there were few large trees below this point, I used my sword to chop down some strong saplings and cut them into lengths to use as splints. That done, I tore the remnants of his blanket into strips to bind the splints, then unrolled my saddle pack and removed my own thick, springy, waxed-wool blanket, wadding it tightly and securing it beneath my cloak where it would remain at least partially dry. I piled the remainder of my saddle pack's contents beside the path, and then removed my cloak again and divested myself of sword, helmet, shield and cuirass. They would be safe enough, I estimated, and I had no need of either their protection or their weight where I was going. I refastened the dry blanket against my ribs, secured my swordbelt, which now held only my dagger, and shrugged back into my heavy, wet cloak. Already the pleasure I had felt in freeing my head from my heavy helmet had gone, leaving me aware only of the runnels of icy rain trickling down my neck. Once I was certain I had everything that I might need, I slung the coils of rope across the saddle bow and led my patient horse once more into the wilderness of underbrush.

Mordechai had not moved, as far as I could tell, and was still unconscious. Wasting no time, I unloaded the coiled rope, the bundle of splints and the binding strips of blanket, then I went to tether my horse, looping his reins around a low-growing bush. Only then did I realize the true folly of what I was about. My horse, I knew, would remain where I tied him, no matter how loosely tethered. That was his training. But the rope by which I had thought to climb down to Mordechai required an anchor far stronger than a clump of low-lying shrubs, and I was already aware that there were no trees on this slope. The association, however, had escaped me until now! A hasty search revealed the full extent of my stupidity. There was nothing, not even an outcrop of rock that I could use as an anchor, and the rope was far too short to stretch uphill to the nearest tree. I was leaning against my saddle in despair, feeling the urge to weep with frustration, my face pressed against the leather, when my horse turned his head and nudged me with his muzzle. When I ignored him, he repeated the movement, this time nudging harder, pushing me. I stepped back and looked at him. "What? What is it?" He gazed at me and then tossed his head, whickering, as though trying to tell me something. Suddenly, and despite the seriousness of my situation, I felt the urge to laugh. Here I was, Caius Merlyn Britannicus, Legate Commander of the Forces of Camulod, talking with my horse, while a dreadfully injured man lay at the bottom of a hole in dire need of my help. And as I reflected on this, my gaze fastened on the pommel of my saddle and the horse whickered again, triumphantly, as though to say, "Finally! You see what I mean!"

My heart thudding now with excitement, I untethered him and led him slowly closer to the edge of the abyss, where I refastened his reins to another shrub. Then, carefully, I secured one end of the rope to the saddle horn, testing it firmly to make sure the knot would not slip. When I was sure it was trustworthy, I threw the end with the noose over the cliff, where it landed, with length to spare, close by Mordechai. I threw the splints and bindings after it, then turned to speak to my horse, calling him by his given name, a thing I did not often do, and one which he had come to know bespoke some special need.

"Germanicus," I said. "You are not the first Germanicus to serve a Britannicus, but today you have a chance to become the greatest. All you have to do is stand here, patiently as ever, and wait for me to come back to you. Can you do that?" He rolled an eye at me and I knew he could. I drew a deep breath, stepped to the edge of the abyss and sat on the edge, settling myself before taking a strong grip on the rope and rolling onto my belly. My horse stood gazing down at me with one great eye. "Remember," I grunted up to him. "Be patient. I will waste no time."

The rope was wet and hard, tearing at my hands which felt as though they were on fire before I was halfway down, but the rough hemp was far less harsh on me than was the cliff face beneath my knees and elbows. The descent seemed to take more time than I had thought possible, but I reached the bottom without injury, apart from scrapes and bruises to elbows and knees and one long, shallow cut on my right arm caused by a tiny snag of rock I had not noticed soon enough. Taking care to stay well clear of the frightening hole in the ground, I crossed to Mordechai, who was, as I had thought, deeply unconscious. When I placed my fingers beneath the points of his jaw, however, as Lucanus had taught me, I found his pulse strong and regular. Relieved, I turned to where the rope's end lay, and began to widen the noose. There was not as much rope to spare as I had thought, but there was enough. I grasped Mordechai by the shoulders and attempted to raise him up to where I could slip the noose over his head and secure it around his chest beneath his shoulders, but I must have twisted his shattered leg, because even in his deep sleep he moaned and heaved in protest. I knew then that I would have to splint that leg before doing anything else.

I diverted myself momentarily from the unpleasant task ahead of me by leaning forward and gazing down into the awful hole that gaped beside Mordechai. Fascinated, I picked up a large stone fragment and dropped it straight down, listening for the sound of its fall. I heard nothing, and remained there for long moments, contemplating what that meant before I turned, shuddering, back to my task. I worked quickly then, taking advantage of the fact that my companion was so deeply unconscious. I straightened the leg—a grim procedure marked by creaks and snapping, grinding sounds and much welling blood—by pulling on the ankle against the leverage of my own foot lodged in the side of Mordechai's crotch. He moaned again, three times, though still unconscious, and each time I felt sick. As soon as the leg was straight, I cleaned the worst of the blood from my hands before splinting the rough-set bones and binding everything tightly with the woollen strips I had prepared. Rainwater oozed from them as I tied the knots. That done, I reached again for the noose at the end of the rope, but the movement remained incomplete. As my hand stretched out, the air about me exploded in blinding light and I saw a ball of dazzling, unearthly brilliance flash down the cliff, pass in front of me and vanish upwards, streaking faster than my eyes could follow up the other face. Simultaneously, the walls of rock around me seemed to crack asunder, the sound, a solid, concussive impact, deafening me and throwing me aside so that I fell sprawling over Mordechai and into darkness.

I could not have been senseless for long, perhaps mere moments, for when I opened my eyes again, the daylight seemed as before, but my head was ringing with strange noises and my nostrils were filled with an alien scent. That something momentous had occurred I had no doubt, but I had no idea what it was. I touched my head and found that I had cut myself, in all probability when I had banged my head against the ground or the cliff wall. When I examined my fingers, they were coated with blood, but some of it, I knew, was Mordechai's, so how much was my own I had no way of telling. And then I saw the markings on the wall in front of me, a vertical black streak, a handspan wide, ascending with perfect regularity where the ball of fire had passed. Astonished, I turned my head to look behind me, but there was no similar marking on the other wall, down which the ball had flashed. Unknowing what to think, I turned to Mordechai. He had not moved. His leg lay flat, tightly splinted and bound. I had finished that, I thought, and was about to—

The rope had vanished.

I leapt to my feet and rushed to search for it, peering vainly up at the towering wall above me, and there, hanging down less than the height of a man from the edge above, I saw the noose, twisting slightly as it dangled. I knew what had happened now—my knees gave way and I slumped to the ground. A lightning strike had terrified my horse into running, and as he ran, the rope had travelled with him. He had not gone far, I could see, but far enough to condemn me to death with my injured companion. I felt tears mingle with the rain on my upturned face.

Some time in the course of the following hour, Germanicus returned to search for me, creeping forward daintily until he could look down, as greatly shamefaced as any horse could be, to where I sat huddled, looking up at him. Had he been smart enough, he might have kicked the rope back down to me, but he was no more than a horse, and soon he wandered off again in search of grazing.

It was growing dark when I heard and identified a tiny, alien sound as the chattering of Mordechai's teeth, and the recognition of it helped me pull my scattered wits together again. The others, I knew, would come seeking me at daybreak, and would have little trouble finding us. The sight of my armour piled at the side of the path would send them this way. I knew, too, that I would survive the night, but Mordechai's survival was another matter altogether, and I knew the achievement of it must become my primary concern. Gritting my teeth against the certain knowledge of his dreadful sickness, I dragged him closer to the cliff face, unfastened the warm blanket from against my ribs—I had forgotten its existence completely until then—and spread it over him. Miraculously, it was still dry, thanks mainly to the waterproofing wax scraped over both its surfaces, and the heat of my body. I then added my cloak on top of that and crept beneath both layers to lie beside him, so that we might share our bodies' warmth. Mordechai remained motionless throughout all of this, breathing deeply and regularly, and I felt some confidence that, if I could keep him warm through the night, he would live until morning.

Some time, long after dark, I fell asleep. When I awoke, hearing the caw of a crow somewhere above, my first conscious thought was that the rain had stopped, and my second was that Mordechai was dead. I could hear only my own breathing. I had no means of knowing when he died. I remember only that when I awoke, he was cold beside me.

Shelagh and Rufio found me as I had thought they would, less than two hours after daybreak. Germanicus was still above me on the hillside, and they threw the rope down to me. I stood with one foot in the noose and held on to the rope with both hands, my blanket and cloak slung over my shoulder, and they pulled me quickly from my prison, simply by making Germanicus walk forward. Before that, however, while Rufio and Shelagh looked on from above, I had tipped Mordechai's body into the abyss by which he had lain, saying a silent prayer as he tumbled over the edge. I did not hear him land, but as I rose up the cliff face I gained some comfort from the thought that it was unlikely, wherever he now lay, that his bones would be gnawed by animals.

When I reached the top of the cliff, Shelagh took one look at me and set Rufio to work gathering fuel higher up the hill. She would not let me ride, but bullied me into walking up the slope until we were among the trees again, where she produced a tinder box and soon had a fire going. As soon as she believed the flames healthy enough to feed themselves, she unloaded the pack roll behind her saddle and brought out dry, clean clothes. Knowing that I, and presumably Mordechai, had spent the night out in the rain, and the entire day, too, she had come prepared to find us dying of exposure.

I stripped naked, shivering too mightily even to think of being modest, let alone concupiscent, and dried myself with my own blanket, and then Shelagh threw another over me, after which she and Rufio took turns pummelling me and chafing me until I grew warm again. I had never thought, even in the midst of the terrible winter that had gone before, that I could be so deeply chilled as I was then. In the meantime, on two stones over the fire she had heated a clay bowl of meat and vegetable stew, made by Liam the day before. It was too hot to hold at first, and as I waited for the chill of the damp grass to cool it, the saliva filled my mouth with agonising pangs of hunger.

While I ate, I told them everything that had transpired, here on this cold hillside, and Rufio groomed my poor horse while I spoke. I noticed Shelagh looking at me strangely and asked her what was wrong. She sniffed and shook her head.

"You're covered in blood, all of it dried. You've a cut on your head, and another on your arm there. You are a mess, Commander."

"I know, Shelagh," I said. "But the blood is not all mine. The greater part of it belonged to poor Mordechai. I'll be fine."

"Aye." She looked far from convinced. "Well, do you feel strong enough to travel now? We told Ded we would be back by sunset and here we are, a whole night late and still four to six hours' ride away from Glevum. They'll be waiting for us, ready to go."

"True, they will, but they will wait."

"Aye, and they'll be fretting even now, and will have sent out searchers."

I heaved a great sigh. "You're right, they'll do all of those things, and it would be unfair to prolong their ignorance. But can we take this fire with us? This seems like the first time I've been warm since last summer."

Shelagh shook her head with a fleeting smile. "Not unless you would care to carry it in your helmet. You'll warm up again once we are on the road. Better for you to walk for a while, rather than ride. The exercise will loosen your bones and sinews. Later, when you reach Cambria and find your raiders, you can light a fire to burn the earth."

XXV

THOSE WORDS OF Shelagh's came back to me days later as I sat slouched in my saddle, staring at the prospect ahead of me. To light a fire that would burn the earth here in the high hills of Cambria would require the powers of Vulcan himself. Nothing would burn in this place, for the simple reason that there was nothing to burn. Winter maintained its icy grip and permitted nothing to be seen but rocky cliffs and snow-shrouded, shadowed, treacherous wastes of whiteness. Yet, beside this incontrovertible fact, there was a growing certainty in my mind that I had not the slightest wish to burn anything in Cambria, in spite of all I had said to the contrary in former days.

Dedalus had been sitting quietly beside me as I pondered the sight before me, and now his voice broke into my thoughts, confirming my own opinion of our location but scattering the other, nebulous thoughts I had been mulling over in my head.

"We are too high, here, Cay. They must be below us in another valley, and somehow we have missed them." I nodded, accepting the truth of that in silence as he continued. "Horses could not survive up here in winter. Even had these people been foolish enough to bring the beasts so high into the hills, and even had they done it before the snow fell, they would never be able to keep them alive in such deep drifts."

I turned my head to face him. "I know that, Ded. I came to the same conclusion some time ago. But I have had other, more troubling thoughts upon my mind."

He hawked and spat into the snow. "Aye?" he said eventually. "And you think the higher air up here will clear your head?"

I had to smile at his tone. "Something akin to that," I murmured.

"What's on your mind, then?"

I snatched a deep, slow breath and held it for a time before expelling it through pursed lips, blowing like a horse. "I really can't tell you that here and now, my friend. I've not yet thought the matter through. But I am working on it, and when I have decided what my problem is, and how to phrase it, I'll come to you for your advice." He said nothing, but pouted his own lips and dipped his head eloquently. "In the meantime," I continued, "there's no arguing with you. We are too high. We'll make our way back down into the valley where we left the commissary wagons and camp there tonight. Then we'll head south and west, keeping below the snow line if we can, and see if we can pick up any sign of our quarry in that direction."

"Good. I'll get the men turned around and moving."

I watched him ride away to where the others waited, and thought again how fortunate I was in my friends. Then, as the waiting ranks broke up in the apparent confusion of reversing their tracks without endangering their mounts either in the deep snow or on the precipitous slope that flanked the narrow ridge we had ascended, I returned to contemplating the unease that lay within me, finding it matched by the desolate yet magnificent panorama of snow-filled gorges and soaring peaks around us.

I had found, quite suddenly, that I had no wish to declare or prosecute any form of war on the Pendragon people, and the belated realisation, within the past few days, had caught me unprepared.

In the dying days of the previous autumn, faced with incontrovertible evidence of invasion and treachery on the part of at least one deviant faction of the Pendragon, my sense of outrage over the wanton slaughter of my men had made my resolution to avenge the attack upon Calibri seem straightforward and necessary. That conviction had remained ever present in me throughout the dreadful winter that followed and had governed my plans for the spring. It had burned bright and clear within my breast throughout the approach to Glevum and the engagement with the aliens quartered there. The change had occurred after that, after my night-long imprisonment with the dying Mordechai in the rain-soaked rock fissure and after my farewell to Shelagh.

I had experienced no epiphany; no sudden revulsion over my course. No new idea had sprung, full-bred, into my mind, nor had any chain of tangible events given rise to my change of heart, although several factors had contributed thereto. The transformation of my thoughts had simply occurred, slowly and unheralded, within my deepest feelings. And radical as it was, the thought had merely emerged within me, and grown with utter conviction over a period of days, that I had no wish to carry warfare into the Pendragon lands. Yet I was gravely troubled by this change of heart, because my reason, arguing in the persona of Commander of Camulod, told me that I must, imperatively, issue warning—clarion, stark and deadly, backed with dire example—of the draconian consequences that would attend any future sallies into Camulod from Cambria. I had spoken to no one of my thoughts, and had ridden silent and brooding ever since Glevum, aware that I provided but ill company to my friends.

"Commander Merlyn! Will you remain behind?"

I turned in the saddle and waved in acknowledgment of Ded's shout, kicking Germanicus into motion to follow my men, and as he ambled forward, picking his way with care, I attempted to focus my thoughts upon the amorphous reasons underlying my new frame of mind.

One common element was real enough and would, I somehow knew, eventually come to overpower all others: the child Arthur, my ward, was heir to Cambria, heir to Pendragon. While he was yet too young to be aware of anything, he would not always be so, and he would, I felt, have but scant cause to thank me later if I stirred enmity between his people and ourselves during his childhood. The fact that Pendragon had spilled first blood would bear little weight were the boy to emerge into manhood inheriting a legacy of hatred and fear where once there had been alliance and amity, generations in the making. That element I could accept without difficulty. There remained only the very real need for some form of retribution and example in this present case—a requirement that I feared might prove troublesome if I adhered to the logic plaguing me at present. I had, when all was said and done, led a force of a thousand men all the way from Camulod in the name of retribution.

Yet there were other influences to my thinking, some of them stark in their simplicity, others more obscure. Mordechai's death had affected me greatly, but not until long after I had been pulled up out of the cleft that was his grave. To be sure, I had felt sadness and pain and deep regret on awakening to find him stiff and cold beneath my blanket, but my physical discomfort and the arrival of Shelagh and Rufio and the need thereafter to win free of that stony sepulchre had kept my mind focused upon other things and dulled complete comprehension of the implications of his death.

Shelagh's commonsense advice to me had been wisely given. I had walked up the slope from the fire she had kindled to the path, hobbling in agony from my stiff and aching muscles. Once on the flatness of the path, however, my anguish had begun to abate. Hobbling along behind Rufio and ahead of Shelagh, who led my horse, I had begun to feel my muscles loosening again, but the ascent of the slippery slope beneath the spot where I had found the hanging man, which called for greater effort from a different set of muscles, had been a purgatory, unmitigated by the fact that my companions had to dismount, too, and lead their horses upward with care.

Once free of that killing slope, however, and on fairly level ground once more, warmth had begun to return to my muscles. I found what our runners call "the second wind," and my bone-weariness seemed to fall away from me within a short time. Even then, however, I did not mount my horse, but broke into a trot, instead, and soon found I could lengthen my stride into a full, clean run. Marvel that it seemed at the time, I felt my strength grow as I ran, rather than diminish, so that I was soon feeling euphoric, covering distance easily and covered by a sheen of hard-wrung sweat. Three miles and more I kept this up, up slope and down, before my legs began to falter, and then I called to the others to stop, beside an icy streamlet, where I washed in shocking, clear, cold water and then dried myself with a blanket before shrugging into fresh clothes from the store they had brought for Mordechai and me. Once dressed, I donned my armour and mounted Germanicus again.

A short time after that we regained the abandoned colony and found Liam Twistback waiting in his wagon for us, by a fire on the top of the little hill, with two rabbits spitted on sticks over the flames. All of us were hungry and the sounds and sight of broiling meat set our saliva flowing. Fresh bread Liam had, too, baked in the ashes of the fire he had kept burning all night long. When we had assuaged the fiercest of our hunger pangs, we told him of my misadventures and his face grew long in the listening.

"Poor people," he murmured, glancing around at the abandoned encampment beneath. "I feel great pity in my heart for all of them. Ill as they fell, through no fault of their own, they were abandoned by the entire world save this man Mordechai . . . How did you say his last name?"

"Emancipatus," I told him, noticing the way the clear, hard Latin sound sat ill in the fluid Eirish tongue I now spoke as well as my former hosts. "It means 'free man,' or rather, 'freed man.' "

"Aye, well, he's freed now, right enough, poor man. I should have liked to meet him, for all that we must leave his people rigid and unburied 'neath the open skies."

As I listened to him utter the words, I realized that Liam was right. We could not bury Mordechai's dead, for a number of reasons, the major of which was the one that had frustrated his own attempt: the hardness of the ground.

And so, in the end, we left them as they were, ranged neatly alongside the open, half-dug pit that should have been their grave, with the rough, barely remembered prayers I could recall as their sole benison.

Later, as I rode behind the wagon, idly watching father and daughter talking together on the driver's bench, I recalled the tenor of what Liam had said and thought about the fate of those sad folk who had been stricken with the leprosy. In my youth, I had heard tell of leprosy and its foulness and had, with shivering detachment, accepted its horrors as described to me. Why should I not? I had seen nothing of it; knew none who suffered from it; thought never to encounter it in my fair life. Some I had heard describe it as God's punishment on evildoers, His scourge on those whose sins were overweening, and in my youthful ignorance and folly I had had no thought to question what was said. Lepers were lepers. None thought of them as human folk. Now, however, I knew differently. Lepers were no more than ordinary people like ourselves who had contracted a dread, fell disease. And the one in ten thousand people who retained no fear of them, people like my friend Luke and his friend Mordechai, were helpless to assist them other than in giving solitary comfort and solace. But that comfort and that solace had a value beyond price to those who bore the brand of Leper.

Mordechai and his people had all died simply because, alone and unassisted, they lacked the means to sustain themselves through a hard winter. That such was a risk all people bore was true, and witnessed by the deaths in Camulod, but other, normal people had the opportunity, at least, of gaining help from neighbours and community. Had such communal help been offered—even from a distance and in fear and pity—to Mordechai's lepers, they might have survived. I knew now, beyond doubt, that there was moral wrong involved therein, but no means of redress would come to me. I had no one on whom to affix blame. There was no town nearby, no settlement whose people might have changed the outcome. The lepers here had fled normal community, some driven out, in fear of being killed, and others spurred by fears of passing on their contamination to friends and loved ones. The very nature of their illness demanded seclusion and sequestration, precluding normal human contact. But somehow, I felt, there had to be a means of alleviating the soul-searing pity of such things. I knew I was ill equipped to answer this by myself, but I resolved to take the matter up with Luke, once back in Camulod.

My drifting thoughts were interrupted at that point by a shout of warning from Rufio, who had seen movement ahead of us on the road. Our alarm was short-lived, however, for we quickly recognised our own men, a double squadron under the command of the taciturn Benedict, dispatched to look for us at dawn after the concern caused by our failure to arrive back at Glevum the previous night. They met us just short of the burned-out ruin of the Red Dragon hostelry, close to where the lesser road we followed joined the broader highway to Glevum itself, and thereafter we made better time.

Two hours later, deep in a conversation with Benedict, I was startled again by a loud, female shout from the wagon ahead of me as Shelagh leapt to her feet and then jumped down from the still-moving wagon to run forward, off the road to where my view was blocked by the vehicle itself. Startled into action, Benedict and I spurred our horses and cantered around the wagon just in time to see her launch herself upward towards the summit of the low hill we were traversing, climbing bent forward with her skirts already kilted and tucked between her knees, scrambling upward using hands and feet like a small boy fleeing from an angry farmer. Astonished, I turned to where her father sat smiling, watching her from the wagon.

"In God's name, Liam, what ails her?"

He grinned at me, waving his arm towards the sea. We had been climbing steadily for more than an hour, our path taking us parallel to the coast in a northeasterly direction, and at this point on the flank of the hill, no more than five miles from Glevum, the distant sea had come into view, off on our left. There, by some trick of height combined with clear morning light, a small fleet of vessels lay plain to see, some larger than others, all of them tiny and far distant, but one of them showing clearly the black galley outlined on its square, central sail. Shelagh had spied Donuil's return, or at least the return of her people. Now, with a shout of my own, I bade Benedict remain where he was and spurred my horse to the hillside in Shelagh's tracks, feeling the power of his mighty, bunching muscles as he thrust himself upward, overtaking her rapidly. I thought to catch her quickly, before she reached the crest of the hillside, but she was as agile as a deer and we gained the summit almost together, she mere paces ahead of me, leaping up and down in her excitement and waving with all her might towards the distant fleet. I drew rein and watched her, seeing the radiant joy that shone from her, a vision that rendered me momentarily incapable of looking towards the west and the galleys that lay there. Suddenly, then, she spun towards me and ran to grasp me by the ankle, tugging at me to alight.

"It's Donuil, Cay! He's here! My future husband comes to seek me!" As quickly as she had grasped me, she released me again and ran towards the edge of the summit, stopping only when she reached the highest point, there to begin waving again, although she must know as well as I that there was not the slightest hope of anyone aboard those craft seeing her. Grinning ruefully to myself, I swung down from my saddle to join her, looking carefully now for the first time towards the ships below. Clearly seen from this height, they were about a mile from shore, making great speed and proceeding directly towards the coastline under oar and sail. They made a stirring sight. Four great galleys, I counted, two of them larger than the others, and ten smaller craft, similar to the vessel Liam had built for Shelagh. These would be the vessels, birneys rather than galleys, built to transport Liam's livestock. I guessed that one of the two largest galleys would be Connor's—all four now clearly showed the black galley device on their sails. Feargus's craft, one of the smaller pair, I recognized by the colour of its sail, more reddish than the plain, dun brown of the others, and where Feargus sailed, Logan would be in consort, which marked his vessel plainly, too, since it was of a size with Feargus's. The fourth galley, though, was as big as Connor's, and I had no idea who might captain it.

As I reached her side, Shelagh reached out and drew my arm through hers, hugging it close so that I felt the cushioned softness of her breast against my elbow. She spoke no word, merely gazing, rapt, towards the distant spectacle.

"Feargus and Logan, certainly," I said. "And Connor, I would guess, but who is the other?"

"Brander," she replied.

"Brander? Come to Britain without his fleet? That makes no sense. Why would he come here alone?"

She looked up at me, as if to see whether or not I was making fun of her. "Alone? Brander goes nowhere alone. See yonder."

I looked where she pointed and saw nothing, but then my eyes adjusted to the distance and searched even farther and I felt my stomach turn over. All along the line of the horizon to the northwest the straightness of the sharp-lined join of sea and sky was marred by tiny imperfections which revealed themselves immediately as the shapes of distant vessels, score upon score of them, ten miles and more from shore.

"Sweet Jesus!" I breathed. "How many are there?"

Shelagh looked, without great interest. "Five or six score. Brander must be returning home to the northern isles. That means the war is won, for better or for worse. His galleys will be needed in the north."

"Won?" Even asking the question, I had to smile at her sanguinity, though I was grateful she remained unaware of my smile since the alternative to her assessment could not be thought of as amusing in any way.

"Aye, won or being won. Were it not won, there would be no livestock to bring over here, and Brander would not be sailing back to the north."

"Aye, I suppose . . . But—"

"But what?" She was looking at me now, gazing up at me with those hawk's eyes of hers.

"Shelagh, I thought I heard King Athol say the animals were to be removed for their protection. If the war is won, they would need no such protection. They would be safe."

"Aye, safe, but hungry." She clutched my hand now in her own right hand, keeping her left arm clamped close upon my forearm, so that when she pulled my hand towards her, my curling fingers came to rest between her breasts. I knew she had no thought in her of what she did or of what it did to me, so I gave no sign of being aware of what I touched.

"Before this war was thought upon, our biggest pains were overgrazing, Cay. We lack the space to feed our beasts, and our people grow more numerous all the time. That's why the king wished my father to bring the kine to Britain, with your assistance and permission. Here, in these open grasslands, they will thrive and prosper, grow and breed. In a few short years, we can transport them to the north and raise them there in safety. But not yet. Now they are come here, in safety. And escorted by Brander's whole fleet, ensuring safe passage. Such is their value, these animals of ours. Goats and swine and sheep and cattle. They mean prosperity and ongoing security for our folk. So I say the war is won. You wait, you'll see. Would you dare to wager with me?"

I smiled and shook my head. "No. A man would be a fool to wager against you, Lady."

"Hah! You think so? I see you are a man of wisdom." She broke off, frowning. "What's wrong? What are you thinking?"

I shook my head, but she would have none of it, insisting on an answer.

"Donuil," I muttered, eventually, hating to have the thought wrung from my unwilling mind that he might have died in the war.

"What of him?" She was smiling up at me. "Surely you are not jealous of his coming?"

"No," I said, refusing to be teased. "But what will you do if he is not aboard those galleys?"

She laughed gaily. "Then I shall marry you and be queen over Camulod."

Her levity shocked me profoundly. "Shelagh!" I gasped, feeling my face constrict with disapproval.

She became immediately contrite and pulled me down to where she could kiss my cheek and bathe me in the perfume of her hair. "Och, Cay," she said into my ear. "Do you take me for a foolish woman or a callous wretch? Of course he is there! Look at Logan's galley, at the mast, the cross spar. What's there?"

I looked and gasped again. "A hanging man!"

"Aye, but a hanging *wooden* man! Yon is my throwing target, brought for me by Logan, who made it for me when I was a lass. I made him promise to bring it to me here, and also that if all was well, he would suspend it from the spar where I could see it long before they came to land. Were it not there, I should have known my husband was not coming and would then have had time to prepare myself before they made landfall."

I was looking at her now with more respect than I had ever felt for her before. "When did you arrange that?"

"In Glevum, when we landed. You seized Feargus by the arm and wandered off to whisper with him, trading secret things. While you were gone, I had words of my own with Logan, who has been like another father to me since I was a babe. He it was who taught me how to throw a knife with consistency, you know. I had talent, and a true eye, but he showed me the knack of throwing true time after time. And one winter, he carved out a target man for me from a great log, and bound its breast in leather armour. I called it Mungo, out of dislike for Mungo Rohan who was even then a great black pig. Now it seems right that a hanging Mungo should announce my husband's safe return, do you not think so?"

I had been watching the galleys below as she spoke. They had come about and were now sailing swiftly to the left of us, southward, Brander's huge craft veering across the wakes of the other vessels to take up a station to seaward.

"Look at that! Where are they going now?"

"Southward, to where I shall find them, eight leagues south of Glevum."

Again she had surprised me. "How can you know that?"

She shrugged, gesturing with one hand to where the ships moved below. "Because it was so arranged. There is broad grassland there, and a banked shoreline, where the galleys can unload. Feargus and Logan found the spot the first time they came here in search of Donuil. They could not land at Glevum, you'll recall, because the other, alien vessel was there when they arrived, stealing the coloured stone, the marble. Eight leagues, Logan told me. How far are we from Glevum now?"

"No more than five miles. Under two leagues."

"Then we have six to travel. I had best collect my father and be on my way. We will meet again when you return from Cambria."

"But—"

"But what, Merlyn Britannicus? Your men await you in Glevum and your duty is clear. You must avenge your people soon, before the weather robs you of the chance to find your stolen horses."

"Damnation, Shelagh! I can't simply leave you here. I'll take you to Donuil."

Now she swung to face me, real surprise and concern in her face. "What nonsense is this? You were to leave me at Glevum! That would have left me with eight leagues to ride, instead of six. My father and I will be in no danger. We'll meet the others before you have time to lead your troops out of the town."

"But I want to see Donuil!"

She flashed a grin at me. "So do I! And so you shall, when you return. But in the meantime, my need is greater than yours, and I have no desire to spend the night waiting for Donuil to finish talking with you before he beds me."

"I would not deprive you in such a way, Shelagh."

Her grin became a laugh. "Not willingly, not intentionally, but you would; or he would. No, you may not come."

"But what about Brander? I would like to meet him."

"Brander won't land. He, too, has people awaiting his return. Look you there, already he veers off, his charges safely brought to shore."

Sure enough, Brander's distant galley was turning again, pointing its dragon beak towards the north and west.

"Connor, then. He will be there."

"He will, and will remain until you return. Come you here." She caught me by the chin strap of my helmet and pulled my face down towards her, and then she kissed me as she never had before, a long, sweet, aching kiss that filled my breast with joy and yearning, yet strangely stirred no passion in my loins, since I knew of its intent.

"Merlyn," she said softly, when she had broken contact lingeringly with my mouth. "That kiss was for your friendship and your love and your restraint. I wish it could be more, but we have said all that. Go now, and do what you must do, knowing that you hold a place within my breast that none will ever share, even my husband. I have two sons to bear, and you a child to rear and train to be a king. I cannot envy you that task, Merlyn Britannicus, but I know that you will excel in the doing of it and that the child, having you as tutor, will be taught the things a king must know, and a man must do . . . and I know that those are seldom the same things. Few men, few kings, excel at both. Even Athol, king among his Scots, was better king than father, for in the tending of his people he had not the time to tend his sons in fullness, and so bred ingrates and murderers among his own. Remember that, dear friend, when you turn to the teaching of your king. Governance, and equity, must be for all. Go you now, with my love, in spirit more than ever could be fleshly."

I stood mute, feeling my throat filled with a ball of grief and mixed emotions. Then I nodded, still silent, and led her down to where her father and my escort waited.

Long after she was gone to join Donuil, her words resonated in my breast, but presently the words she had whispered of her love for me faded into acceptance, leaving only the words she had said about my task, and kingship. Words that simmered in my breast and brought me to a change of mind and heart about the duty facing me in the days to follow.

XXVI

On the morning of the second day after we had turned around to descend beneath the snow line again, we found our horses. Huw Strongarm and his Celts had left our camp shortly after daybreak, heading directly southward from where we had spent the night on a quiet, well-watered upland plateau beyond which the ground sloped gently south towards another line of hills. There was no sign of winter anywhere that morning. The skies were clear, filled with the promise of a bright spring day, and the invigorating nip of the early morning air buoyed our spirits as we prepared to break camp and follow our scouts into the valleys to the south of us. I had just dismissed my ten troop commanders after the morning meeting and was checking the cinch on my horse's saddle when I heard my name called and looked up to see Philip waving to me from some distance away, where he had been watching his assembling troop. When he saw me look towards him he waved his arm southward, indicating something beyond my sight farther down the slope.

Curious, but not yet alarmed, I pulled myself up into the saddle and kicked Germanicus into motion, making my way to where Philip had been joined by Benedict and Rufio. Dedalus and two others joined them before I reached their side, and all of us stared off to the south. Three men, who could only be our own scouts, were running towards us and were soon close enough for the keen-eyed Dedalus to identify them as Menester, Gwern and Guidog, the inseparable trio. They were still more than a mile from where we sat watching them, and when Ded stated the obvious, that they had evidently found something, I cleared my throat.

"Aye, and there's little point in making them run all the way up here to tell us what it is, when they'll have to accompany us back down again. I'm going to meet them, gentlemen. Form up your troops and follow me, but hold them in check, if you please. Raise no alarm until we have discovered the truth of this."

I spurred forward and kicked my horse to a canter, breathing deeply and wondering at the calm that filled me. When the three men saw me approaching, they stopped as one, leaning forward, hands on their knees, to catch their breath. As I rode up to them, Guidog, the spokesman of the three, called out their news.

"Dead men, Commander. Thirty of 'em. Hanging from trees down there in the next vale. An' horse tracks everywhere. Shod tracks and horse shit. Looks like they been keepin' 'em there all winter long."

I drew rein, looking back over my shoulder to where my men were coming down the long slope behind me in five columns of two hundred men each, ten wide by twenty long. Already they had spread out to form a five-front advance, and they looked impressive.

"Where is Huw?" I asked Guidog.

"He stayed there, Commander. Sent us back for you. Sent the others on ahead to follow the tracks."

"Very well, let's go." I stood in my stirrups and circled my hand above my head, signing the others to follow me, and then I moved forward again at the canter. Wordlessly Guidog and Gwern placed themselves on either side of me, each grasping a stirrup leather. Menester ran ahead, loping easily, as though he had not already run for several miles uphill. We came soon to a place where the ground began to dip more steeply, swinging west, and we followed the natural fall of the land into a narrow pass that opened out soon afterwards into a wide, gently contoured valley floored with deep, rich grass. Below us, more than half a mile ahead, a copse of massive trees stood alone in the midst of the green bowl.

"Oak trees," Gwern grunted from beside my left knee. "That's where they're all hanging, some of 'em nine to a limb. There's Huw."

I saw Huw Strongarm emerge from the trees and stand awaiting us, but as we approached I paid more attention to the macabre fruit hanging from the oak branches than I did to my chief scout. Guidog had not exaggerated. I counted thirty swinging corpses. Huw stood watching us approach, and appeared to be leaning on his unstrung bow stave. I knew that was not so, however, since no Pendragon would endanger his own bow, his most prized possession, by treating it so carelessly. He said nothing until I spoke.

"Who are they, Huw?"

"Two Pendragon renegades. The others are landless."

"Landless? You mean Outlanders?"

"No, they're locals, but they're not of our folk. I recognize none of them. They're dirty, though. Long-time dirt, too. They stink from afar. That's what tells me they're landless. Folk who belong—anywhere—keep themselves clean."

I made no attempt to pursue that thought. "How long have they been hanging, and who would have done this?"

Huw hawked and spat. "Yesterday, I'd guess. They've been up there overnight. Soaked with dew, all of 'em. But who did it? Your guess is as good as mine there. But whoever it was, they took your horses. These people wintered here. You'll see that when you go around these trees. There's a stream there, a couple of huts and some well-used firepits. And they kept the horses there, strung from lines most of the time, it looks like." He broke off to gaze up at the man hanging closest to him. "Reckon that's where they got the rope to hang these from."

I could hear the noise of my men approaching behind me. "You sent the others on ahead to follow the horse tracks?"

"Aye. There's no trick to following them now, Merlyn. They'll leave a track like one of your Roman roads. They can't be far ahead."

"Good. Wait here."

I swung my horse around and rode back to join the others, who were in the process of forming their parade ranks while they waited for my next instructions. I waved the ten commanders forward and told them what had transpired here, and that we would ride on immediately. Rufio looked at Dedalus and raised one eyebrow, not knowing I was watching him do it.

"What does that mean, Rufio, that look? Have you something on your mind?"

"No, Commander!" The look he threw me was one of wide-eyed innocence. It was Dedalus who answered my question properly.

"We were talking on the way down here, Merlyn. About the lie of the land. It makes me itchy."

"Why, in God's name? It's perfect cavalry country, firm and dry."

"Aye, except up there." He gestured to the north and west, where the hillside sloped up above us on our right. I looked where he pointed and saw nothing but open grassland stretching to the horizon for more than a mile.

"What do you mean? There's nothing up there."

"Perhaps not, Merlyn, but we haven't looked, have we?"

"No, we have not." I was almost laughing at him, surprised by his unease. "You think there might be cavalry up there? Hidden beyond the crest?"

"No, I don't, since we have the only cavalry in the country, and there's a mile of open hillside there. But if we continue down this valley, beyond the trees there, for another half mile, the hillside on the right there grows steeper and shorter. That's where the cavalry could be behind the hilltop . . . Or the Celts and their longbows."

That wiped the smile from my face, as it was meant to. I had an instant vision of massed Pendragon bowmen shooting at us from a height as we rode uphill towards them and it was not a pleasant image. As few as a hundred bowmen, shooting from high ground, in massed volleys, could create havoc among a thousand horsemen.

"Aye . . . Foolish of me. You're right, Ded. We haven't looked yet. But now we will. As soon as we move out, send a squadron up to ride along the crest. Do it now. Any other questions?"

Benedict coughed and spoke. "How do you want us to proceed, Merlyn? The valley's wide here, but what if it narrows farther down? Two columns abreast?"

"Aye, perhaps. We're going downhill, so we'll be able to see once we're free of these trees. Be ready to deploy on my signal. Let's go."

We rode on for half an hour longer, following the clear sign left by our missing forty horses, and the track led us down and down to our left, ever southward, away from the hill crest that had so concerned Dedalus, until all threat of danger from that direction died away and I had him signal his men down from the heights to join us again.

And then, as we swung left once again, still advancing in five columns across open ground, a horn sounded from ahead of us, slightly to our right, where a low rise too small to be called a hill broke the smoothness of the valley floor. I stopped immediately, as did everyone behind me, our heads swivelling as one to the point from where the sound had come. A small knot of mounted men emerged from behind the rise, riding in single file, and sat there, facing us. I counted nine of them, too distant to identify, but clearly Celts mounted on the shaggy hill ponies on which I had learned to ride as a boy.

"Dergyll." The word came from Huw Strongarm who stood by my right knee.

"Who?"

"Dergyll ap Griffyd." He turned and looked up at me. "You know him. First cousin to Uther. Their fathers were brothers."

"Hmm. Friendly?"

"Friendly?" Big Huw grinned and made a harrumphing noise deep in his throat. "Perhaps, perhaps not. I sought to join him first, when we returned from Cornwall, but he was engaged elsewhere and did not return throughout our stay. Friend or foe, this I'll say for him, he's the best real warrior Pendragon has, now that Uther's dead."

"What's he doing here, think you?"

Huw swung his head around to look again towards the distant group. "Protecting his own, I should think. This is Pendragon ground."

"Aye. Of course." I held up my arm, fingers spread and palm twisted backward to still the sounds behind me, where some of the men and their mounts were growing restive. "Well," I asked, feeling peculiarly indecisive. "What should we do, think you?"

Huw kept his back to me, speaking over his shoulder. "Right now? Talk to the man, Merlyn. Thank him for hanging your thieves and saving you the trouble."

"Aye, indeed. It must have been he."

Now Huw turned again and glanced up at me, his face unreadable. "Who else? They tell me he commands two thousand men."

That made me think deeply, although only in terms of numbers, not of odds. I would have backed five hundred Camulodian troopers against two thousand unmounted Celts without thought a short time before. Now, however, Ded's strictures against the folly of pitting mounted men against massed bowmen gave me pause.

"I will ride forward alone and speak with him." I glanced at Huw for confirmation. "You think that is foolish?"

The big Celt shrugged. "No, not if he's the same man he was five years ago, but he might have changed since then."

"Changed in what way?"

"In any way. Perhaps he lost a wife or a son. He certainly lost a crown, for he should have been next in line for the kingship after Uther's death. You won't know until you approach him, Merlyn, and the only alternative is to attack him now. You want to risk that?"

"I have no wish to do that, Huw, risk or no, so I'll parley." I stood in my stirrups and signalled my commanders forward to me again. Dedalus, as usual, was first to reach me.

"What's up? Who are those people?"

"Pendragon chiefs. Huw recognizes the leader, a war chief called Dergyll, cousin to Uther. I'm going forward to talk with him."

"Then I'm coming with you."

I looked at Dedalus and decided not to remonstrate with him. "As you wish," I said. "But the others will hold their position here. Bring forward my standard to advance with us. The rest of you await our signal here. If we are attacked or molested in any way, you will attack immediately in a pincer move. Columns one and five under Philip and Benedict to take the right and left flanks, bypassing the rise before engaging; two and four under Rufio and Falvo will mount the frontal attack, and column three, yours, Quintus, to hold in reserve behind Rufio and Falvo."

Quintus had the only question. "What if they have bowmen?"

"Where would they have them? There's no place to conceal them, Quint."

He nodded. "Fine. Then why are those leaders exposing themselves like that, without protection? We could ride them down and kill all of them."

I shrugged my shoulders. "Perhaps they know we won't do that . . . Or they might have another thousand men hidden behind their little hill." I paused, remembering Uther's experience in Cornwall, when the enemy had concealed themselves in covered pits. "Still," I added. "Best to take no chances. You're right, Quint. If trouble does develop, warn your men to be on the alert for a trap. The same goes for all of you. At the first sight of bowmen in any numbers, spread your people out, but keep them moving. Don't let them group tightly against volleys of arrows or they will be slaughtered. But—" I broke off, eyeing the distant Celts again. "I have a feeling we will have no trouble, so let's find out if I am right or not."

Benedict leaned forward in his saddle and spat on the ground. "Well, we all know your feelings, Merlyn. Let's hope you're right again this time." He swung his horse around without further comment and made his way back to his men, followed by the others. My standardbearer passed them on his way towards us. When he had arrived, I nodded at him and spoke to Huw Strongarm, who had stood listening to all of this in silence. "Huw, I think you should stay here, too, since I don't know what kind of reception we will receive from these people. I see no point in endangering you."

Big Huw glowered up at me. "How would you endanger me?"

"By simply having you among us. If these warriors decide to fight, they might well decide your presence here with us is worth your death before any of ours. Humour me, my friend. Remain here with the others."

Huw shrugged, sniffed and turned to walk back to where the troopers were drawn up. I looked at Dedalus.

"Well. Shall we go?"

He sank his spurs into his horse's flanks, and the three of us cantered together towards the distant Celts on their low hilltop. They sat motionless and watched us approach until we were within a hundred paces of them, at which point their leader kicked his own horse into motion and came towards us, followed by two of his people. We stopped and awaited them now, and when less than twenty paces separated our two groups the Celtic leader stopped and dismounted by swinging his right leg completely over his horse's head and sliding to the ground. His two companions remained mounted.

"Very well, wait for me." I dismounted and walked towards this man, searching my mind for memories of him and examining him as closely as he was examining me. He was not a large man, but was strongly built, bareheaded, compact and wiry with broad, straight shoulders and a thick neck supporting a high-held, proud head. His long, black hair and long, flowing moustaches in the Celtic fashion on an otherwise clean-shaven face gave him an air of severity. His clothing was simple, yet strikingly barbaric to my Romanized eyes. An almost-knee-length, kilted tunic of dark green wool, with an embroidered border of yellow leaves around the hem and across the yoke of his chest provided the only strong colours. His legs were covered by sheepskin leggings, worn fleece inward, onto which had been sewn small, over-

lapping, rectangular metal plates that gave a metallic ring to his walk and he
wore a heavy breastplate of thickened bull hide, covered with the same plates,
two larger, thicker pieces covering his breasts. A heavy cloak, fastened with
a broad, silver clasp of interwoven snakes, had been thrown back over his
shoulders so that it hung behind him, leaving his arms free. The arms were
strong, heavily muscled and protected from wrist to elbow by thick leather
armlets. A broad belt, slung across his chest from right to left, supported a
heavy, much-used-looking sword, bare-bladed and slung simply through a ring
of metal, and a second belt, of plain leather, girdled his waist and held an
ornately hilted dagger in a jewelled leather sheath.

We stopped together, facing each other from a distance of a couple of
paces. He spoke first.

"Merlyn," he said, nodding in greeting, his face otherwise expressionless.
"It's been many years. What brings you to Pendragon lands? And with so
many followers?"

I still could not remember him, although I knew we must have met, since
he so evidently knew me. I returned his nod. "Dergyll, is it not?"

"Aye, that's right. Dergyll, son of Griffyd. My father was brother to Uric
Pendragon."

"So we are kin?"

He shrugged. "Aye, of some kind, but not close. You have not answered
me. What brings you here?"

"Horses."

He raised an eyebrow, looking beyond me to where my thousand men sat
ranked in their five divisions.

"Aye," he said. "I can see that. Many horses, and large." He looked back
at me and his mouth quirked slightly into what might have been a grin,
although I could not know for sure beneath the fullness of his moustache.
"There is one grand and tragic thing about horses, Merlyn. Do you know
what it is?"

I was unsure how to respond, unable to define his attitude as either
hostile or placatory. I decided to assume arrogance. "Aye," I said. "They are
invincible, particularly against men on foot, or on smaller horses."

He was definitely smiling now, but his smile had a hard edge. "That's
grand enough, I grant, but where is the tragedy in that?"

"Among the men on foot."

"Ah! I see. But no, you are wrong, Merlyn, and there's the right of it.
Against most men on foot, you may be right, but against Pendragon? No.
There you are sadly ill-advised. The tragedy of horses such as yours is that
they make such grand targets." He raised his left hand straight into the air,
holding it, with fingers spread, above his head, then turned his head slowly
to his left. I swung my head with his and felt my skin chill with gooseflesh
as the entire hillside above us, empty and bare until this moment, came to
life. Everywhere, men threw back the covers over pits dug in the ground and
came pouring into view, forming ranks rapidly, deploying into massed formations of bowmen, each nocking an arrow to his long bow and taking aim
at the packed mass of my formations on the slope below. A full two hundred
paces separated the closest of the bowmen from my men, but I knew that
distance was as nothing to the great longbows. Close on four hundred men,

I gauged, and likely more. Certainly more than sufficient, firing in massed volleys, to wipe out my cavalry before we could ever reach them. I fought to keep my own face expressionless, masking my dismay.

Now it was my turn to raise my arm, bidding my own men stand fast. I turned around to see Dedalus repeating my gesture. Behind him, my men remained immobile. I drew a deep breath, determined to allow my voice to show no tremor, and turned back to Dergyll.

"Very impressive," I told him. "But we expected no less. Uther used the same tactic frequently. I knew you would not expose yourself as you have done without good reason. I think, however, that you misunderstood what I said. I meant we came in search of horses, not mounted on them."

Again he raised an eyebrow. "Go on."

"One of our border outposts was attacked, before the winter set in. All our men there were killed and forty horses stolen. We found Pendragon arrows in our men. The horses we could live without, but we could not ignore the slaughter. Before the snow came on we followed the trail of the horses. It led here. Before we could mount a proper expedition to find them, the winter came."

"I see. And as soon as the snow melted, you set out again."

I nodded.

"So you bring war against us?"

"No, I think not." He eyed me in silence, waiting for me to continue. "I think we rode against the men whose bodies hang from the oak grove back there."

"Hmm." It was neither question nor comment. I hurried on.

"I think whoever hanged them did our work for us, and I think it was you. If I am correct, and it was you, then I believe there is no quarrel between Camulod and your people. The hanged men back there were not Pendragon, at least most of them were not."

"How do you know that?"

"Huw Strongarm told me. He said there were only two Pendragon faces among the corpses. The others were landless."

"Aye. Renegades all, human filth. They slaughtered as many of our people, probably more of them, than they did yours. How many did you lose?"

"Close to fifty."

"We count ours in hundreds, thanks to your contribution to our wars."

That confused me, as he saw by my immediate frown. "What do you mean, *my* contribution? Your wars are no concern of mine."

He shook his head slightly. "Not yours personally, Camulod's."

I still had no idea of what he meant. "That is nonsense," I said. "What possible contribution might Camulod have made to your wars? I command in Camulod, with my brother Ambrose, and I would know of any such interference. This force here is the first from Camulod ever to set foot in Pendragon country."

"The first armed force, aye. I was thinking of force of another kind." He paused, his head tilted to one side, and suddenly I remembered him from that gesture. We had been friends, one summer long ago, when we were both but boys, years short of man's estate. I remembered him swimming like a fish and springing up from the water onto a bank, shaking the water from his long hair and tilting his head that way to look at me.

"I remember you now," I said.

"Aye, as I said, it has been many years, but I did not know you had a brother."

"A half-brother, and I did not know, either, until a short time ago. For almost thirty years we lived apart, in ignorance each of the other's existence. Now we are close. But I still don't know what you are talking about. What kind of force can there be that is not armed?"

"Personality, Merlyn. Character. The force of one strong man who can control and dominate one weaker than himself."

I blew the breath from my mouth sharply, turning away impatiently, my mind racing over his words and seeking his meaning. Above me on the hillside, the serried ranks of Pendragon bowmen stood looking down, alert and menacing. I glanced towards my own men, then swung back to face Dergyll.

"Look here, Dergyll, are we to fight? I seek no quarrel with you, but I believe you have our horses. I do not believe you stole them, or that you were responsible for any of the deaths in Camulod. But they were back there, by the grove of oaks, no later than a day ago, and if indeed you hanged the renegades back there, then you must have taken the horses."

He chose not to answer me directly, his tone indicating nevertheless that fighting was not in the forefront of his thoughts at that moment. "Does the name Carthac mean anything to you?"

I frowned. "Carthac? It is familiar, but I don't know how. Didn't Uther have a cousin named Carthac? A strange boy, it seems to me, though it has been years since I thought of him. He was misshapen, was he not?"

Dergyll nodded. "Aye, he was, and is. Misshapen is a good word for him."

I was perplexed. "Why would you ask me about him, Carthac? Does he rule in Uther's place now?"

The answer to that was an abrupt bark of savage laughter. "Hah! Do you remember Mod?"

"Mod?" The non sequitur confused me yet again, but a face jumped into my mind immediately. "Yes, I knew a lad called Mod, apprenticed to my friend Daffyd, the Druid. Is that the Mod you mean?"

"Aye, and what of Ironhair?"

"Ironhair!" The name stunned me. "You mean Peter Ironhair? The smith?"

"Smith . . . Aye, I've heard it said he is a smith. But Peter Ironhair is what this fellow calls himself. He is from Camulod, no?"

"No! Or yes, he lived there for a time, until he deemed it wiser to move on. He was a newcomer, though, not one of our own. He made himself a power there, for a short time, while I lay ill. When I had recovered, he and I . . . disagreed . . . over some matters of policy and government. He tried to have me killed, but failed, then disappeared before he could be taken. How do you know Ironhair?"

"Because he fled from you to us. But he told us no tale of flight, or of murder attempted. He told us he was your friend, sent by you as a gesture of friendship, to work among us after the death of Uther, the king, your cousin."

"What? But—"

"Wait you." Now Dergyll raised his other arm, his right, and one of the men sitting on the knoll behind him produced a long horn and wound a low, ululating note from it. For long moments nothing happened, and then two things occurred at once. The bowmen positioned on the flank of the hillside broke into new movement, breaking ranks and beginning to move laterally, back in the direction of the hill at the chief's back, to where they would no longer constitute a threat to my own men. At the same time, a new surge of movement broke out from behind the low hill ahead of me, and our forty missing horses were brought forward, herded by five or six men mounted on the smaller mountain ponies of the Celts.

"We have a camp, a mile farther down the valley. And we have hunters out. Bring your men, and join us. Mod is there, in our camp. He has a tale for you."

"I will, but wait you now. You believe this Ironhair to be a friend of mine?"

He smiled, and the grimness of his features disappeared. "I did, but your own face gave the lie to it. Now I know different. That's why I called away my men. Come you ahead when you have spoken with your people. I'll see you in the camp. There is a stream, and ample water and grazing for your beasts."

He turned and ran lithely back to where he had left his horse, leaping fluidly up onto its back without hesitation, so that I remembered again what a wondrous rider he had been even as a boy. I walked back to my own horse, mulling over the entire confrontation.

Dedalus sat and watched me, making no move to speak until I was safely anchored in my saddle. When he did speak, it was in his usual sardonic manner.

"How are your bowels?"

"Remarkable, why do you ask?"

"I simply wondered if they spasmed as much as mine when those creatures up there threw off their coverings. Come now, admit they did."

I smiled at him, nodding ruefully. "A little, I must admit, but I had already foreseen the possibility, thanks to Quint's comment earlier. And I remembered how Uther had been caught in much the same way, by Lot's people hiding beneath nets, in a ravine. That was the time Lot's bowmen used the poisoned arrows, you recall?"

"Recall? Shit! I was there, right in the thick of it. One of those arrows hit my cuirass, smack between the nipples, knocked me back in my saddle and then skipped off, up over my shoulder. Must have missed my neck and jaw by a hair's width. That's why my bowels turn to water when I see bowmen. When those whoresons jumped up above us there, my sphincter clenched so tight I hurt my stomach muscles. So what's to happen now? We have the horses. Are we going home?"

"No. We're going to join Dergyll and his men at their camp. We'll eat with them, probably spend the night there, and perhaps head home tomorrow." I could see from Ded's frown that he was about to argue with me, so I cut him off before he could begin to speak. "He has a tale to tell me, and there's also an old friend of mine in his camp. And Ironhair is here, in Cambria, no friend of Dergyll's. That much I can tell you. The rest I'll learn later. Come, let's tell the others what we are about."

Ded's argument, whatever it might have been, remained unspoken as we joined the rest of our party and led them towards the low hill where Dergyll's party had sat. Once there, I ascended the hill to where I could see all my men, and then I told them all that had transpired, thanking them and congratulating them for their steadfastness under the threat of the massed bowmen on the hill. That done, I led them onwards, still in formation, to Dergyll's campsite, which contained, I estimated, somewhere in the region of six hundred men.

Dergyll's Pendragon men stood watching us in silence as we arrived, and although I sensed nothing inimical in their silence it was, at the very least, disconcerting. My own men, for their part, took the silence as their tutor and responded in kind, so that the meeting of the two hosts was one of the most unusual any present there had witnessed. I led our formation, riding alone in front, almost directly to the edge of the encampment and then sat there while my troops lined up formally behind me. Then, seemingly at the precise moment when the sounds of moving horses and harness behind me faded to silence, Dergyll himself came striding from one of the few tents at the centre of the Celtic gathering and bade us welcome in a great, stentorian, parade-ground voice. His shout, clearly heard by every man present, and his wide-armed signal for me to join him, were the signals for a general surge of noise and activity as his Celts relaxed all at once, breaking away to resume the activities interrupted by our arrival and speak among themselves as though nothing had happened. That was not strictly true, however, for I noticed many of his men move forward to address some of my own veterans, and I realized there were more than a few there who obviously knew each other from the days of the wars with Lot. Huw Strongarm and his group, I saw, were mingling easily among the others. I signalled to Dedalus to take over the dismounting and deployment of our troops and horses, and dismounted, waving casually to Dergyll to indicate that I would join him presently, then made my way to where big Huw stood among his own group and others who had joined them. Huw saw me approach and moved to join me, and I pulled him aside, turning my back to the main throng and keeping my voice low, so that he had to lean in towards me to hear what I said.

"This Dergyll," I began. "You said that when you came back home you went to offer your services to him before any other?"

"Aye, why?"

"Then you would trust him?"

"Trust him?" Huw twisted his face into a scowl that might have been a smile of some kind. "Trust's a chancy thing . . . Aye, I suppose I would trust him as soon as any other, and more than most. He was a good man when I knew him well, before these wars broke out."

"Could I trust him? That's what I'm asking you, Huw."

He sniffed and appeared to consider his next words carefully, then he nodded once, and then again.

"Aye. Aye, you may trust him, so be it you both make plain in what your trust lies vested."

"My thanks." I left him there and made my way directly to where Dergyll stood awaiting me. As soon as I had joined him, he turned away and led me to the large, leather tent from which he had earlier emerged, holding back the flap to give me access. I stooped and entered, anticipating darkness, but then was pleased to see that it was open to the sunlight, thanks to a folded-back flap in the roofing. There, on a pile of skins, I found my young friend Mod, now grown almost to full manhood, and the sight of him deprived me of the power to speak.

Mod had always been a pleasant lad, fresh-faced and enthusiastic about everything to which he turned his hand and his mind. At our first meeting, he had been no more than seven or eight years old, newly apprenticed to the Druid Daffyd, but already well versed in the first of the complex tales assigned to him, the tales that had always represented, to my pragmatic Uncle Varrus, a form of earthly magic.

The invading Roman legions had sought to stamp out the Druids in the course of their conquest of Britain, hundreds of years earlier during the reigns of the emperors Claudius and Nero. The reason for their persecutions lay in their accurate assessment of the ancient druidic priesthood as the lodestone of Celtic resistance to the Roman threat. Roman records of that time told of a great slaughter of Druids conducted as a meticulous military campaign, culminating in a massive, thoroughly coordinated drive under the command of Suetonius Paulinus to isolate the last surviving Druids and their supporters on the Isle of Anglesey, the traditional seat of Druidism, where, amid the destruction of their sacred groves of trees, the pestilential priests were finally, officially extirpated, once and for all time. After that, the druidic religion and its traditions had been decreed dead in Britain.

The facts of the matter were decidedly different. A living religion, with its entrenched beliefs and spiritual traditions, is among the most difficult things on earth to eradicate, and the Druids were the custodians not only of their people's theology, but of their history. In consequence, once the direction of the Romans' malice had been defined and the objective of their dire campaign had been identified, the people of Britain set out to protect, defend and conceal their Druids. A Druid could become an ordinary Celt by the simple expedient of changing his clothes, and hundreds did. By the same logic, ordinary people could appear as Druids by donning those same clothes, and once again, hundreds did. The peaceful, solitary Druids, depicted by the Roman invaders for their own purposes as ravening beasts who practised human sacrifice, emerged as doughty fighters in the course of that campaign because, through one of those anomalous upsurges of feeling that occur from time to time in every land and all societies given the proper stimuli, strong men took up the cause of the Druids and fought on their behalf, wearing their robes and dying fiercely, seeking to deny dominion and conquest to Rome. The difficulties faced by Suetonius in rooting out this troublesome priesthood were compounded by his need to deal with the concurrent mass revolt of Boudicca and her *Iceni* on the other side of the country, and he had withdrawn his legions from Anglesey in haste, their task incomplete, to lead them north and east across the heart of Britain. Many Druids died on Anglesey, but many more survived to carry out their tasks and teachings, quietly and in secrecy thereafter, throughout the hundreds of years of Roman occupation of their land.

The Roman overlords themselves, victorious eventually throughout Britain, remained vociferously exultant over their "conquest" of the Druids, an exultation dictated by their need to be perceived as invincible, and by their superstitious fear of what the Druids represented, for the Romans' understanding of what the Druids had been, and what they had stood for, had never been complete. Druids, thereafter, had been attributed magical, supernatural powers by the descendants of the Roman soldiers who had "destroyed" them.

Magic, Publius Varrus had written, the Druids assuredly had, but he saw it as the "magic" of trained memory, enabling them to carry in their minds, verbatim and intact, the history of their ancient people. Each Druid spent his life, from earliest boyhood, working to become the custodian of several lengthy tales, learning them scrupulously by rote from his own teachers, retelling them at length to his own people in his most active years for their pleasure, entertainment and enlightenment, and then passing them along in his late years to the next bearer of the Druid's burden, a young boy chosen, as he himself had been, for his mental agility, his observed characteristics and his demonstrated willingness to learn.

Mod had been such a boy, as had his fellow student Tumac, two years his junior, both of them given into the care of the Druid Daffyd, whose face had been familiar in Camulod throughout my youth. The Mod who faced me now, however, bore little resemblance to the sunny lad I had known for years. This one, wasted and gaunt, his eyes deep sunken in his skull, his skin grey with the pallour of mortal sickness, looked ancient, far beyond his years. I had no doubt, however, that he recognised me, for his face lit up and he attempted to smile and greet me, seeming to move at the same time to sit up. The effort was too much for him and he subsided backward, catching his breath with an audible hiss and losing consciousness even as I fell to my knees beside him, calling his name. Evident as it was to me that he was far beyond my reach, I tried nevertheless to revive him and bring him back to awareness, but was finally forced to accept that there was nothing I could do. I knelt there beside him, my cupped palm against his brow, feeling the fever that raged there, and gazed up at Dergyll in fury.

"What happened to him?"

Dergyll shrugged his shoulders eloquently. "He was stabbed through the chest and left for dead, more than a week ago. Two of my men found him by sheer accident. They were on their way to meet me. They knew him by sight, and they brought him with them. He hovered on the edge of death for a few days, then seemed to rally, growing stronger every day for the following four days. He was speaking coherently by that time and told us what had happened to him. Then, the day before yesterday, he began to cough up blood, almost as though something had broken or given way inside him. He is still lucid, but growing weaker, as you can see, with every hour that passes. I doubt now he will survive the day."

Unable to remain kneeling, I rose to my feet and stared out through the open flap in the tent's roof.

"He was a Druid, Dergyll. Who among your people kills a Druid?"

He cleared his throat. "There are a few who have no fear of being accursed, since they already are. He was not a Druid, though, Merlyn; merely an initiate, not yet fully trained. Not that it would have made a difference. Those who killed him killed his teacher, too."

"Daffyd?" I felt my head begin to spin and heard a roaring in my ears. Daffyd had nursed and tended my wife. "They killed Daffyd?"

"Aye. Him first. The boy there sought to stop it, and was struck down for it."

"Who? Who has done this?"

Dergyll fell to one knee and tucked some of the skins around Mod's body, which was shivering now. "Fever's what will kill him," he said, then brushed a lock of hair from the young man's forehead. Then he turned his eyes up towards me, where I stood over him.

"Carthac," he said, his voice barren of inflection. When I made no move to respond, he rose to his feet again. "Let's find some mead." Another man, who had been standing motionless in the tent since we arrived, unnoticed by me despite the smallness of the space, now stepped forward and took Dergyll's place beside the dying youth. Dergyll glanced at him and nodded, then motioned to me to leave. I turned and did as he bade me, casting one last, sad glance at Mod.

Outside, in the bustle of the busy encampment, Dergyll said, "That's Timor who's with him now. He's a Druid, too. He'll tend him well. Come."

I followed him in silence as he wended his way among the few tents that served his army, until we arrived by a blazing fire stacked over a clay oven. Several thick logs were grouped around the fire and Dergyll sat on one, pointing me to another. From the ground at his feet he picked up a leather-bound flask and uncorked it, tipping back his head to swallow a great draught, then handing it to me. It was mead, and I gulped it deeply, after which I sighed and stared into the fire.

"Tell me about this Carthac," I said.

"What is there to tell? You knew him, as a boy. He is demented."

"Demented? I did not know that, or I don't remember. I never knew him well. I knew he was misshapen but can remember no more of him, other than that he was generally disliked. Uther, I recall, could not abide him."

"No one could. We were all first cousins. Carthac's mother, my father and Uther's father were siblings. And we were all much of an age, too, less than two years between Uther, who was oldest, and Carthac, the youngest of us. I fell in the middle." He reached for the flask and took another deep drink. "Carthac was always . . . troublesome, even as a child. His mother died birthing him and his skull was crushed out of shape in the delivery. But then he was kicked in the head by a horse, when he was eight."

"I met him after that," I told him. "Two years after he had been kicked. I thought it was the horse's kick that had deformed him."

Dergyll shook his head. "No. That happened at birth. The kick merely completed his undoing, it seems. He was never well liked. Even you remember that, after meeting him only long years ago. He was a treacherous little whoreson even then. Would he had stayed that way. In his fourteenth year, Carthac began to grow prodigiously, and it seemed he might never stop. But as his body grew, and his strength multiplied, his mind degenerated. He was ungovernable—still is . . . He would fly into fantastic rages, often for no reason that anyone could see or understand, and in such rages he would kill anything or anyone that crossed his path. Killed several people before he attained manhood."

I shook my head. "Couldn't anyone restrain him?"

Dergyll pursed his lips and shook his head. "Nah. Finally they banished him, drove him out altogether. But he kept coming back, and because his father was who he was, Carthac was permitted to commit atrocities no one else would ever have dreamed of. Then he turned to violating women, and several of us, myself and a few others, decided to teach him a real lesson. We beat him badly; broke a few bones, then dragged him, tied and kicking in a cart, up to a cave in the hills, miles from the village. We left him there and told him that if he ever came back, we would kill him. We should have killed him there and then.

"Anyway." He heaved a great sigh and looked around him before continuing. "It seemed we had made the correct impression on him. He stayed away for years, and we forgot he was even there. But he was there, and over those years he attracted some followers, the gods alone know how. Then Uther went to war with you against the Cornishman and died there, and all a sudden we had wars of our own. Uther had been king but had no son, and there was never any settlement of the succession, although it should have come to me on Uther's death. But even before then that fire was beyond control. We had problems with invaders, people from the north of us, who thought they could take our lands because the major part of our manpower was away from home. And then Carthac emerged from hiding, backed by a rabble of landless filth and worse, far worse than he had ever been. But he fought craftily and well. We fought a pitched battle against him, and he almost beat us. He's crazed, of course, but he fights like a devil . . . Anyway, Ironhair had arrived in our lands just before that. I disliked him from the outset, but many others didn't particularly since he mantained he had been a friend to both you and Uther . . .

"He was there the day we fought against Carthac and he found out that Carthac had a claim to being king. Shortly after that he disappeared and now he is Carthac's closest friend and trusted adviser. It must be sorcery of some kind, but he seems to be able to control the animal sufficiently to make him do whatever Ironhair wishes to have done, and what Ironhair wishes to have done has caused me endless grief for months now. The end is coming, for all that. We almost had them, day before yesterday, but caught only their rearguard. Carthac and Ironhair evaded us by hours. We questioned the few people left alive after our fight and one of them told us about this camp, with its stolen horses. We were close by, so we came down, and then you came."

"But you knew we were coming. How?"

He dipped his head. "You were seen."

"Not so! We took great pains to remain unseen."

"Aye, but insufficient, nonetheless. You passed a solitary shepherd, lying hid on a hill slope. He saw a thousand horsemen led by one whose standard was a silver-metal bear, on black. That night, he told the Druid Daffyd what he'd seen, and Daffyd made his way direct to me—or would have, had he not unexpectedly encountered Carthac and his band. Brought face to face with Ironhair, Daffyd confronted him and denounced him, knowing the truth of his perfidy, Mod says, accusing him of having tried to murder you. Carthac cut Daffyd down and threw him on a fire for his daring. Mod tried to pull the old man from the fire, and Carthac skewered him with a hunting spear. They left him lying there, thinking him dead, when they rode on, and as I told you, two of my men found him when they passed by the same way that afternoon."

I sat and stared into the fire, losing myself in the leaping transparency of the daylight-dimmed flames. Dergyll left me to my thoughts, content to dwell

upon his own for the time being. Eventually, he leaned in front of me and
thrust a horn cup full of mead into my grasp. I took it with a nod, and sipped
at it, lost in thoughts that no longer primarily concerned Mod and Daffyd
or even Carthac and Peter Ironhair. My thoughts at that point, in the main,
had to do with Dergyll himself, and with the underlying reasons for my
presence here in Cambria.

After my return from Cornwall, late the previous summer, I had been
concerned about the attitude I might have provoked among the Pendragon
by my own apparent lack of gratitude for the sacrifices made on my behalf
by Uther's people, who were half my own people, too, through my mother's
blood. As recently as my return from Eire, when I had been concerned about
Liam's liberty to raise his breeding stock in safety on Pendragon land, these
thoughts had plagued me, and then the raid on our outpost had almost
crystallized the belief in my mind that we had forsworn the alliance between
Camulod and Pendragon. Now, it appeared, an opportunity had come to
hand to reassess the situation. Dergyll seemed to bear us no resentment over
the matter of Lot's wars or the losses his people had sustained because of
them. I knew, however, that I might be indulging in wishful thinking there.
For all I knew, he might be deeply angered over the whole affair and merely
be holding his peace for reasons of his own, as important to him as mine
were to me.

I snapped back to attention when I heard my name being called from
across the fire, and I looked up to see Dergyll approaching me from that
direction. I had been unaware of his having moved from beside me, and now
I made to rise to my feet, but he waved me back and came to join me,
seating himself on the log beside me and resuming his attack upon the flask
of mead.

"Your men are settled in," he grunted eventually, offering me the flask
again. Seeing my headshake, he dropped it to the ground beside his foot.
"Dedalus, your man in charge, says there is nothing for you to concern yourself over, and bids you take your ease."

I smiled. "Thank you for that," I said. "But take my ease?" I considered
that, then laughed aloud. "Why not, indeed? There's little else for me to do
right now. Ded's a good man. He really has no need of me at all, since it
was he who taught me the knowledge of command."

"You say so? He doesn't look that old."

"Nor is he . . . perhaps four or five years my senior . . . but Ded is old in
soldiering. He was a centurion when I was a raw recruit and my father named
him shepherd to me on my first command patrol."

"What will you do now, Merlyn? Now that you have your horses back?"

I looked at him squarely. "Go home, I suppose. But one thing troubles
me."

"Name it."

"My men, the ones killed in the raid last year. They were killed by Pendragon arrows, not by landless renegades like those you hanged back there
among the oaks. From all I know of Pendragon, you guard your longbows
closely."

"Hmm. That is true, we hold our bows close. True, too, that some of
your men might have died that way, but not all of them. That's not possible.
Others have bows, even these renegades we hanged." He turned away and

shouted to one of his lieutenants close by, and when the fellow came over, sent him off to bring the bows they had confiscated from the renegades. The man returned a short time later, followed by another. The first carried an armload of bow staves, all shorter by an arm's length than the great Pendragon longbows, and the other bore several quivers of arrows, similarly short by the full span of a hand. Together they dropped the weapons by the fire with a clatter. Dergyll eyed them and then spoke to me. "There were two of our bows there as well. Two of our men took those. The arrows are useless to us." He leaned forward and picked up one of the quivers, containing a dozen arrows or more, and tossed it onto the fire.

I shook my head, unconvinced. "The arrows that we found were all Pendragon arrows. We had to cut them out of our men's flesh."

"Aye, you would have. And were all the dead men full of arrows?"

"No, but they all bore arrow wounds."

"There you are then! Only our arrows hit heavily enough to pierce and lodge and defy recovery. They'll cut right into bone, if they're launched hard enough or close enough. These things—" He waved a hand in disgust at the remaining, shorter arrows. "These things are useless. They'll kill you, but so will a pebble if it's thrown properly and you're unlucky." He paused, then continued. "You can thank your friend Ironhair for the deaths of your men. I told you he disappeared from our camp and went to join Carthac. He took two score bows with him, and arrows for them, pulling them in a hand cart. Walked right through the line of my guards and not a man questioned him."

I smiled, slightly incredulous. "What did you do to the guards?"

"Hanged one of them. He was drunk and probably asleep. Didn't see a thing. The tracks of the cart passed by within paces of him. Anyway, since that time, we have been trying to win back those bows. They have a value far beyond any other thing to us."

"And how many have you recovered?"

"Seventeen, of two score, including the two we took back last night."

I stooped now and picked up one of the lesser bow staves, examining it. It was rectangular in section, unlike the round longbow, and made of ash, I guessed, undoubtedly less than one tenth as powerful as my own compound bow. "So you are telling me that my men were probably killed by bows like this, in the hands of renegades assisted by a few Pendragon from Carthac's following?"

"No, I am not, for any who follow Carthac have forfeited their claims to be Pendragon, but you are something right. The matter of the horses should confirm it. Horses like yours are of no use to us, high in our hills. Our own are more sure-footed, bred to the mountainsides. Only Carthac, influenced by such as Ironhair, would be fool enough to see it otherwise."

"Hmm. To lose one's name, especially the right to call oneself Pendragon, would be a potent punishment, I think. Not to be entered into lightly . . . Unless Carthac emerges victor in your war," I suggested, one eyebrow raised. Dergyll saw no humour in my suggestion.

"Hah!" Dergyll scoffed at the mere idea. "He might win a few fights, but Carthac will never be the victor here, for victory will mean that all the true Pendragon have been slain."

"I would like the opportunity to take Ironhair," I mused. I had completely accepted his explanation of the raid upon our outpost.

"Forget Ironhair, Merlyn. Leave him to Pendragon. He has much to answer for and I will see to his answering." He stopped, gazing into the fire and evidently thinking deeply, then turned his face to me again, his mind made up.

"Are we still allies, Merlyn?"

I was unable to mask my sudden gladness and relief.

"Still allies? Pendragon and Camulod? You doubt that? It had never crossed my mind that it might not be so." I felt like a hypocrite, mouthing the lie, yet was deeply grateful for the great draughts of mead that had lowered his guard and permitted me to overreact so shamelessly.

He frowned at that, however, betraying that he was not yet far gone in drink. "You say so here, with all your thousand troops?"

"Of course," I assured him. "Think of it, Dergyll, the sense of it! What kind of fool would I be to ride against all Pendragon with a thousand men? And if Pendragon were at war with us, would they have stopped short at one petty raid against one outpost? No, my friend, I rode against one band of murderers and thieves, and brought a thousand men to teach a lesson. That lesson, undelivered now and unrequired, is yet swiftly stated: war among yourselves if you must, but remain clear of Camulod."

He was still gazing at me. "You marched against but a band, then, unaware of who commanded it?"

"Aye. A band, not a people. We knew your people are at war among themselves. We also knew the waging of that war is no concern of ours, although the preservation of our alliance did concern us. Not knowing whose claim stood against whose, we had no other choice but to remain apart, unless sought out, and let you solve your problems by yourselves. But sought out we were. We were attacked, by people who, unchecked and unreproved, might return to do the same again."

"Aye." Deep in thought again, Dergyll leaned forward and threw several more of the short bow staves on the fire. Then he coughed, deep in his throat, and when he spoke again his voice was clear-edged and full of resolve. "You and I had better talk more then, of alliance."

Within half an hour, we had resolved that I would leave four squadrons behind when I returned to Camulod, under the overall command of Dedalus, with Philip as his deputy. Four mounted squadrons amounted to one hundred and twenty-eight men, plus half as many extra mounts. These forces would police the lower parts of Dergyll's territories, under the titular command of Camulod. Dergyll had convinced me that only he and Carthac remained active in the kingship dispute, all other claims having fallen under his own by various treaties. The campaign against Carthac was destined to be short-lived, he swore, and conducted mainly in the high hills of the northernmost Pendragon territories. The presence on the lower hills of a band of swift-moving cavalry would aid in this, keeping the hunted renegades penned up in the highlands, where Dergyll's bowmen could deal with them effectively.

For their side of the bargain, six score Pendragon bowmen would return with us to Camulod, under the command of Huw Strongarm, who was a kinsman to Dergyll and whom Dergyll trusted more than some of his own subordinates, to train with Ambrose in conjunction with the armies of Camulod. Dergyll would fight his war and win in his own way. Camulodian horsemen would protect his flanks within his own boundaries, and Camulod itself would guard the outer zone. It was more than I would have dared hope for days earlier, and the thought of facing the Council and explaining my precipitate decision to leave my men here held no terrors for me. I was returning with six score of Pendragon bows.

Most satisfying of all, however, was the thought of the smile that would appear on Shelagh's face when I told her the news that Dergyll, soon to be King of the Pendragon, had ratified Huw's gift of residence and safekeeping to her father and herself within Pendragon lands.

XXVII

THE QUIET, UNDEMONSTRATIVE joy that marked my reunion with Donuil and Shelagh and the peaceful establishment of Liam Twist-back's farm close by the western sea to the south of Glevum, after our safe return to Camulod, accompanied by the Pendragon bowmen, was crowned by the tidings of the renewed alliance with our friends in Cambria. So began a blessed, five-year period of peace within and without our Colony, a time of prosperity and renewal and rebuilding, of gathering and accumulating strength, aided by gentle winters followed by glorious summers and swelling, bountiful harvests.

It was a time of many events that enriched all our lives and only a few that impoverished any of us. My brother Ambrose wed his love Ludmilla on the Celtic feast of Beltane, amid the rites of Spring that first year, and Donuil and Shelagh joined with them to make a double celebration and to bind themselves more closely and more publicly to their new lives in Camulod. Within the ensuing ninety days, both wives grew quick with child, and their husbands walked with greater pride and more awareness in their gait. That awareness, in the case of Ambrose, brought him to a decision regarding his perceived duty to Vortigern in his northeastern kingdom, and his desire to return in person was supplanted by a more sedate determination to inform the king of his new life and marriage. Accordingly, he penned a lengthy letter, and dispatched it to Northumbria with several of his men who had expressed a desire to return to their families in Lindum. Thereafter, he made no more mention of riding eastward. Towards the year's end, however, in November, Ludmilla fell sick of a short-lived but virulent illness that was rife among our people for a spell. Thanks to the skills and ministrations of Lucanus, she survived the sickness, but her unborn child did not and Ludmilla miscarried. The entire Colony grieved with the young couple, for thanks to her healing skills and Lucanus's teaching, Ludmilla had become almost as beloved by the ordinary folk of Camulod as Ambrose was by his soldiers.

They bore their grief stoically, consoling each other privately and throwing themselves into their work thereafter, Ludmilla in the Infirmary with Luke and Ambrose in his self-appointed task of training a new army, cavalry, infantry and bowmen, to fight together as a whole in defense of our Colony. And their grief passed, so that by the time Shelagh birthed her first-born in late spring the following year, Ludmilla was with child again, three months into her term and blooming like a flower. Shelagh's baby was a lusty, strapping boy whom she named Gwin, first of her promised pair of sons.

Early that second summer, too, Connor of Eire came to Camulod to visit his brother and his nephew Arthur, now in his third year of rude and robust infancy, a bustling badger of a child incapable of walking, it appeared, since he must needs run everywhere, his densely muscled, solid little bulk rendering him an uncontrollable terror to his nurse Turga, who continued to regard him and to treat him as her own child. He was beautiful, as few male children can be beautiful. His hair had darkened since his birth, its yellow highlights muted to mere hints among the rich, brown chestnut of his curling locks. His eyes were lambent, startling in their tawny, yellowish golden irises, and when he laughed, which was most of the time, his laughter was a crowing gurgle of delight with overtones of the depth and sonority that were to come from his strong, broad chest in years ahead. Arthur, the child of Uther Pendragon, was a complete delight to all around him.

On the day before Connor's unexpected arrival, I had found Arthur in the stables, one of his favourite haunts, despite the fact that almost everyone did everything possible to keep him out of there. On this occasion, as I began to move towards him to pick him up and take him home to Turga, something in his attitude attracted my attention. He was standing in front of Germanicus's stall when I entered, and in the sudden dimness of the stable, blindingly dark after the bright sunshine outside, I had the distinct impression he was holding something up to my horse. Germanicus's head was high up in the air, as though straining away from the lad, and his great eye was rolling in his head. Frowning, I stepped towards them, aware of the tininess of the boy against the enormous size of my large horse, although the lad was outside the stall and therefore in no danger.

"Arthur, what are you doing?"

He turned to look at me, and his face broke into one of his great grins. "Mellin," he crowed, and came running towards me, his right hand outstretched. I crouched down and held out my own hand for whatever it was, and he deposited a large frog, bright green with yellow markings, into my open palm. I had seen what it was only moments before I found myself holding it, but it was already too late to withdraw my hand. I swallowed hard and reminded myself that I had held hundreds of the things before, in my own boyhood, and that none of them had ever bitten me or harmed me. Nevertheless, the sensation of the creature sitting there on my palm made my skin crawl.

"Big, Mellin," the boy said, smiling still, his eyes on the frog.

"Aye, it is, Arthur. Where did you catch it?" He blinked at me, plainly not understanding. I tried again.

"Where did it come from, Arthur?" He scratched himself with one fingertip, worrying at a spot below his ribs, his brows knit in fierce concentration, and I knew he was not going to answer me. "Arthur?" He continued to peer at the frog. So did I, and the frog peered back at me, its great, liquid eyes bright and shiny. Arthur reached out a pointing finger.

"Beast," he said.

I grinned. "No . . . well, yes, I suppose it is a beast. But it's a frog, Arthur. A frog."

He frowned. "Fwog." His two-and-a-half-year-old tongue could still not fit around the letter R.

"Yes, a frog. Were you showing him to Germanicus?" He nodded solemnly, his eyes still on the frog. "Where did you find him?"

"I caught it, Commander Merlyn, and gave it to the lad." I had not heard the stableman enter, and his voice, directly behind my shoulder, startled me so that I jerked, and the frog took a mighty leap from my hand, landing at least two paces from where I crouched. It paused there for a heartbeat or two, collecting itself, and then leaped again and again, bounding this time into an empty stall. With a startled hiss of surprise and excitement, the boy threw himself after his escaping prisoner, dropping to his hands and knees to scuttle beneath the stall door in hot pursuit. I stood up, glancing ruefully at the stableman.

"His aunt Shelagh's going to be really grateful to you if he finds that thing again and takes it home with him." The stableman—his name had completely escaped me—shrugged philosophically.

"Boys catch frogs, Commander. It's part of being a boy."

"Aye, but not at two-and-a-half. He shouldn't be in here, you know. It's too dangerous. He could be kicked, or trampled."

The big man grinned, shaking his head and contradicted me without malice, chewing his words and slurring them until they were barely discernible as Latin. "Not that 'un, Commander. Every 'orse in the place knows 'im, and they all seem to know just 'ow little 'e is. They step very carefully around 'im, almost as if they're taking extra care not to damage 'im."

I looked sharply at him, thinking he was gulling me, but his face held no hint of raillery. "That is ridiculous." He shrugged again.

"I know that's 'ow it seems, but it's the truth, Commander. They all knows 'im, an' 'e knows all of them—by name, although 'e can't pronounce your mount's full name. Jemans, 'e calls 'im. An' Jemans comes to 'im and eats out of 'is 'and. Lad climbs right up the rails, alongside the 'orse's 'ead, there. I never seen the like, an' 'im so little."

At that moment the boy emerged from the empty stall, covered in ends of straw and clotted horse manure and clutching his prize triumphantly, holding it gently but firmly with both hands around its abdomen. Its hind legs, extended now, seemed longer than his arms. "Fwog!" he announced, holding the hapless creature high.

"Frog," I repeated, looking from him to the grinning stableman. "Let's take it home and show it to your aunt Shelagh." I waited until he changed his grip, frowning with concentration until he held the frog securely in one hand, and then I took his other hand in my own and led him out of the stable.

When his Uncle Connor arrived the following day, he had to meet Fwog formally and gain his acceptance before he was allowed to hug Fwog's patron . . .

I had met with Connor briefly on my return from Cambria the previous year, when he had brought the breeding cattle to Liam and delivered his brother Donuil to his wife as part of the endeavour. He had been prepared to leave to return to Eire the day we arrived, but had waited an extra day to spend some time with me and tell the true, unembellished tale of "Donuil's War," Connor's own name for the rebellion his young brother had forestalled. He had had little choice in thus remaining, Connor had explained to me that evening, since one of two alternatives was certain to occur and he had no way of knowing which: either his brother would be overcome with unwonted modesty and would play down his own heroics, thereby shaming his wife, or he would take the other route and grasp all of the credit to himself, thereby shaming his wife. Better that Connor should remain an extra day

then, he reasoned with a wink at me, and see the median path of honesty
and the dignity of Donuil's wife both well served.

He had proceeded to relate the story of how Donuil, who had left home
a mere boy in a man's frame, returned from the sea alone and stood as a
man against treacherous brethren. Ignoring Mungo Rohan completely, since
Donuil himself had executed the fat man the night he arrived home, Rohan's
guilt in the death of their brother Kerry established by the dried blood-stains
on the clothing he had not yet contrived to burn, Connor told me that
Fingael had not been the only one of Athol's kin who had stooped to treachery, allying themselves with enemies in hopes of snatching up their king's
fallen coronet of gold. Another brother, Kewn, whom I had heard of but not
met, had treated with the MacNyalls of the west, and two of Athol's own
brothers had been close with the enemy, one of them liaising with the de-
praved clan who called themselves the Children of Garn, the other dealing
closely with the northeastern federation who called themselves the Sons of
Condran and were commanded by Condran's sons, Brian on land and Liam
at sea.

Donuil, sharing the leadership of the land armies with his father Athol,
had led his forces to three great victories, while his brothers Connor and
Brander, using their fleets in consort, had destroyed the shipping of the alliance, interdicting their supplies and inflicting a second, crushing defeat at
sea on Liam, the younger son of Condran and the old king's admiral.

Much mead had flowed during the retelling of this tale, which lost nothing in the rivalry of the two brothers in the reporting of it, and the night
had long grown dark before we went to sleep. Before we did, however, I
invited Connor to visit Camulod next time he came to Britain, since he had
said he would be returning regularly thenceforth, checking on the welfare
and the needs of Liam and his stock, now that permission to be there had
been clearly granted them by the Pendragon. He had mulled upon that in
silence for some time, and then admitted he would think on it. I had said
no more, other than to remind him of it the next morning before he left.

Now here he was, in Camulod itself, attempting to disguise the awe our
fortress stirred in him. He had arrived in comfort, in a wagon, with an escort
of three score of his "kerns," as these fierce Ersemen called themselves,
marching behind and around him. And their coming had stirred chaos. Fortunately Donuil, aware that Connor might arrive one day, had discussed such
an unheralded arrival with me and Ambrose, and standing orders had been
issued to our outposts to expect such a visit, and to supply an honour guard
to bring our guests to Camulod itself. We had also left word with Liam
Twistback that Connor, should he come, would be welcomed if he approached our outposts openly and named himself.

And so it had happened. Connor and his men had come to our outpost
at Acorn Lake and announced themselves, and the officer in charge there,
young Jacob Cato, had led them directly to the fortress, sending word on
ahead that they were coming.

I was acutely aware, from the first, of Connor's gratification at the high
esteem enjoyed in our Colony by his younger brother, since it echoed my
own satisfaction with Donuil's progress among us.

From the first day of Donuil's return to duty, I had marked a change in him. He had asked me that day if I would object were he to find himself armour like mine. Delighted that he should wish to do so, I gave him leave to find whatever he could unearth to cover his huge frame, and within two weeks he appeared one morning dressed from head to toe in a completely uniform set of burnished-bronze armour made especially for him and worn over a new, white woollen tunic bordered with my own favourite Greek key pattern. Upon my asking how he had achieved all this so quickly, he merely smiled and quietly reminded me that, early in our relationship when I held doubts about his capabilities, I had told him that the single most distinguishing characteristic of a good adjutant was the ability to get things *done*, without fanfare, without upheaval, without apparent effort and without crowing about his methods. Chastened, and subtly rebuked, I resisted the temptation to question him further.

From that day forward, Donuil had been at my side constantly, immaculately turned out in Roman splendour and capable, it seemed, of anticipating every need not only of mine, but of Ambrose, too, with whom he had developed a deep friendship. And when he was not with me, on duty, he went riding with his wife, as long as she was able, learning from her the equestrian skills he and I both had sworn would be beyond his reach forever.

Relieved of his concerns over his brother's function here among Outlanders, Connor relaxed and the remaining six days of his visit sped by, enlivened by long evenings when he and I, in company with Donuil, Shelagh, Ambrose and Ludmilla and assorted others, enjoyed each other's company increasingly, so that there was no longer any need to issue invitations to return. Return became a simple matter of arrangements.

When he and his kerns marched off northwest again, they marched accompanied by sixty of our troopers who went north to relieve half of Ded's contingent, which was still involved in Cambria after more than a year. Twice in the year elapsed we had made such changes, and still the war in Cambria dragged on, although the cost to us and ours was nil. Our forces in the low Pendragon lands had met with no resistance or, at least, had remained unchallenged. Dergyll had managed to maintain his campaign as he wished, high in the upper reaches of their hills. Only twice in all the time spent there had Dedalus led his men forward into action, and on both occasions, after the merest skirmish, he had led them back whence they came, unblooded and unbloodied.

The effect of the alliance in Camulod, however, had been salutary. We had had, at the outset, a total of one hundred and thirty-eight longbows, and two hundred bowmen, including the men Huw and his people had begun to train. Now, after a year, we had close on two hundred bows, a full thirty of them made by our own bowyers from the few yew trees we had been able to find locally. The source of the remaining score and more remained a mystery to me, although Huw Strongarm and his Celts seldom returned from visiting their homes without at least one extra bow among them. Thanks to our adoption of the laws laid down by Ullic Pendragon regarding bows—no man could own one, but each must serve as guardian and custodian of one for an entire year, responsible for its care and maintenance—we had no lack of caretakers for the new weapons, and indeed we had a glut of would-be bowmen, never less than four trainees for every bow available. An entire area on one side of the great drilling ground at the base of the fortress hill had been

set apart for practise, and permanent targets—"butts" the men called them—
had been set up at either end. Nowadays, too, there was no longer anything
noteworthy in the sight of ranks of bowmen, densely packed, lofting their
arrows over and ahead of ranks of charging horsemen, changing their stance
and aim so that each volley flew farther, landing ever ahead of the advancing
cavalry. Surprisingly few of these arrows were destroyed by the advancing
horses, but those that were were reckoned a small price to pay for the advantage gained. To this point, however, accuracy notwithstanding, all such
arrows flew with weighted but unpointed heads.

Thus passed the second year, with one more, golden harvest. Ludmilla
had a baby girl that autumn, a raven-haired beauty whom she named Luceiia,
and by Yuletide Shelagh was with child again.

In May the following year, again at the feast of Beltane, a stranger showed
up at our gates, escorted by a guard from our southernmost border. At first
glance, I did not recognize the stranger as a priest, yet when he raised his
hand to bless me, I was unsurprised. He had that air of sanctity about him.
He also had a heavy, weatherproofed package containing a letter from Germanus, a response to my epistle of two years before. I left him in the care
of Donuil and Ambrose, and took myself off to read what my friend had
written:

Auxerre, Gaul
436 Anno Domini
Caius Merlyn Britannicus

Dear Friend:
You can have no idea how pleasant was the surprise I felt when I received
your letter. I have read it many times since then, smiling each time as
I perceived your face, clear in my mind, reflecting the conviction of your
words.

I grieved for you, in reading of your loss. The brutal winter that
deprived you of your friends and of your much-beloved aunt afflicted
even us, here in the warmth of Gaul, but nowhere near as painfully as
it scourged your land of Britain.

Let me add, however, that I have never feared for the condition of
your great-aunt's soul. I have heard her spoken of by many of my breth-
ren, as you know, and all who knew her spoke of her as being among
God's blessed and chosen servants. She has passed into a life, Caius,
where winter is unknown. Convinced of that, my prayers have gone to
God on your behalf, that you might come to know the peace of mind
such certitude entails.

Your missive reached the Bishop, here in Gaul. The Legate whom
you remember retired from life long since, and has not even mounted a
horse since our return from Britain all those years ago. Despite that
flight of time, nevertheless, and without negating or regretting or ma-
ligning any of the duties and concerns that fill my life today and keep
me working long into each night, I will admit to you, between ourselves,
that I experienced some pangs of yearning when I read your words and
felt the tone of them.

I live in contemplation nowadays but not, alas, in quietude. All who address me now—and there are far too many such, each day and every day—do so with regard to my position and supposed sanctity, my position in and of itself alone, be it understood, entailing the supposed sanctity. How refreshing then, my friend, to be hailed simply as a man and a fellow-soldier by such as yourself! Humility, I find, becomes more difficult to attain from day to day when one is constantly besought by supplicants and must deal with abject entreaties and with the obsequious flattery of those who seek preferment.

I note your mention of the absence of monastics in your lands. They are there, my friend, nonetheless, and are proliferating here in Gaul. I find them, in the main, obedient, pious and devout—though quite culpable, I fear, in meriting your succinct revulsion over their personal habits of cleanliness. Thanks to my own early military training and a lifetime of assiduous ablutions, my feelings tend to lean towards yours in that aspect, I will admit to your eyes alone! And yet the Bishop that I am today must, and does, recognise the value of self-denial and of rededication and devotion to the principles of Our Lord, after the Godless excesses of the Empire. We must take care, however—and I am at pains to teach this viewpoint—to observe the median of moderation and avoid the temptation to excessiveness in bringing change. Fastidiousness aside, however, I find myself approving of the spirit underlying the development of this monastic application. I see the zealots within the movement plainly—their presence is impossible to miss—and I do what I may to obviate their intemperance, but the outcome lies with God, as it must in all things earthly, and in Him I am content to repose my trust.

And upon that thought, I took much heart from your report upon the spread of Our Lord's work in Britain. Others send such word to me, not least the British Bishops, but the ratification from you, unsolicited, is encouraging. It pleased me, too, to read that the name of Pelagius is no longer heard in Camulod, save in your own heart, loyal to its roots. Would that were true elsewhere! In many parts of Britain, it appears, his heresy is still being taught despite our Verulamium conclave, although my schools do prosper otherwise. I sent word to Bishop Enos of my gratitude for his service in this matter of your letter and asked him to assure himself from time to time of the good of you and yours.

I must observe, my friend, that Enos is correct to censure you, albeit mildly, for your attitude towards these Christian souls who bear the name of Saxon. I have thought long and deeply on this matter since reading of your difficulty in accepting the mere thought of such. Your ancestors, and mine, were once regarded in the self-same light by those who live in amity beside you now. Think upon that, and upon this: I speak of Christian souls, not of pagan raiders; of families now settled and secure on holdings that they nurture, with children who will know no other home. Consider it, my friend, in Christian charity.

I have sat hours here, writing by myself, and now grow tired. My prayers include you frequently, along with the quite selfish wish that we might meet again some day. Take care.

Your brother in God and friendship,
Germanus

It was to be another entire year, and I would receive a second letter from Germanus, before I would sit down to write to him again. At the time of reading that first letter, I had no thought of failing to respond immediately, nor did I procrastinate to any great extent. The intervening year quite simply vanished, eaten alive by the endless minutiae of tending a thriving, healthy community.

The recent intake of new troopers we had absorbed, for example, necessitated housing arrangements, since our barracks, built in the earliest years of our growth, had long been overcrowded. That crowding, reinforced by the fact that many of our former soldiery had lived outside the barracks with their families, forced us to take prompt steps to deal with the incursion of more than a thousand fresh men, a number of whom had families of their own in train. All required permanent, solid, new housing, for we could not simply dispossess the widows and children of our dead and missing veterans.

That task alone took months, involving every artisan and every set of muscles in the Colony, but eventually we had new, bright, modern quarters for our troops among the woodlands cleared of trees to build the houses that now filled the open spaces thus created.

Aunt Luceiia's Council of Women, led and inspired anew by fresh, young blood in the form of Ludmilla, Shelagh and their friend Julia, was of major assistance in this task, bringing pragmatic feminine common sense to a project that would otherwise have fallen to the lot of simple, stolid, military men. The result, achieved in a consensus of goodwill, was a system of quasi-hamlets, practical above all as they needs must be, yet built with a regard for simple aesthetics and for the realities of life—community, comfort and ease of access—beyond the barrack-room.

Our training program, needless to say, continued throughout this building phase, as did the daily life of Camulod itself. Children continued to be born in ever-growing numbers throughout our domain. Shelagh bore Donuil a second son, Ghilleadh, as she had sworn to do, and Ambrose and Ludmilla had another daughter, Octavia. Young Arthur, now aged four, began to disappear consistently, to be sought and found each time in one or other of the stables, among the horses of which he had not the slightest fear. He and young Bedwyr, the son of Hector and Julia and some six months his junior, had become inseparable, and that caused me more than once to think of Shelagh's gift of dreams and of my own. She had been adamant at one time, I recalled, that only her two sons would be important in Arthur's future, and had dismissed young Bedwyr completely. Now it was evident that she had been wrong, and that her gift was not infallible. Clearly, she could discern matters concerning her own life and family, but suffered from common human ignorance beyond such things. Prescient she might be, but her prescience had limits, and that gave me, perhaps unworthily, some comfort when examining the severe limitations of my own gift.

Dedalus returned that year, as well, with his entire contingent, having lost not one man in more than two whole years and having been finally released from duty by Dergyll, whose wars, it seemed, were over and who now bore the title King of the Pendragon. Carthac and Ironhair had eluded

Dergyll's vengeance at the last, but their force was spent, eroded and worn out by the incessant hammering of Dergyll's ever-growing army. Abandoned by their followers, the two, putative king and would-be king-maker, had disappeared from the Pendragon world months earlier, and Dedalus brought warning from Dergyll that we should watch for them within our boundaries. We discussed that warning, Ambrose, Donuil, Dedalus and I, and while we were prepared to discount such an incursion as most improbable, we yet took steps to warn our outposts and patrols to be on the watch for Ironhair. Then, in the summertime again, a second letter came from Germanus.

Auxerre, Gaul
437 Anno Domini
Caius Merlyn Britannicus

Greetings, my dear Friend:
It has but lately come to my attention that a condition of civil war exists among the race of Pendragon whence your mother came. The tidings disturbed me, for there is no worse disease than civil strife, and I thought immediately of you in the hope you might be uninvolved. The fact that you have not written since I last sent word to you, however, invites me to suppose that your own sense of duty might dictate that you defend yourself and those whom God has placed within your charge. I pray that need has not arisen, and so shall write as though it had not.

I thought of you some months ago, upon a day of pleasant duty, and recalled a tale you told me once about your uncle's saintly friend the bishop Alaric. The tale involved, for I recall it clearly, the sacred altar-stone he had prepared to grace your gathering place in Camulod. I know you are familiar with the stone, since stone can never perish and therefore must be there still, in Christian use. I wonder, however, if you recall the occasion when you told me of the stone? It was on the first day we met, in my camp there beneath the escarpment from which you loosed the arrows that delivered us from certain death. We spoke of many things that afternoon, you and I, but I recall with fondness how you spoke of Alaric, whose soul you feared for at my judgment, and your description, almost defiant, of his gift to Camulod.

"Concealed within its case," you said, "its sanctity intact, it lies inured against the profane speech of ordinary men. Revealed, however, and exposed to view, it sanctifies the premises it graces and makes an altar of the meanest table on which it may be laid." You had a point to make there, my friend, and I heard it clearly, enunciated in words other than your own, by Jesus Himself: "Render unto Caesar those things which are Caesar's, and unto God those things which are God's."

Let me now enlighten you as to why I should be writing thus, for I have no doubt in my mind you must be wondering if age has overtaken me. Not so. Not sufficiently, at least, to debilitate my thinking.

The pleasant duty to which I referred earlier herein was the dedication of an ecclesia, a building erected solely to serve the Will of God and to enhance the spreading of His Word. A house of God, in fact; not a mere basilica or any similar place of commerce capable of housing a religious gathering and service, but a permanent house of worship that will never be profaned by worldly functions. Think of that, my friend. A Christian temple, unlike any built before our time, since it will house, permanently and for all time henceforth, the Holy Spirit and the Living Essence of our eternal Saviour . . .

Of course, this was not the first such edifice to be built and consecrated to God's Truth. There are many such nowadays, throughout the world, and their use is spreading rapidly, for which we all give thanks. It was, however, the first such sacred place to be erected within my patrimony, and thus it prompted me to think of you.

How so? say you. Be patient yet awhile, for I have an answer, and it lies in this: The altar in our new ecclesia is built of hand-wrought stone, and in the upper slab, recessed and portable in case of sudden cataclysm, lies a holy, consecrated stone much like the one your Bishop Alaric bestowed on Camulod in gift. Now do you see my meaning?

When last I wrote to you, you were in mourning for your Aunt Luceiia who had been, throughout her life, a constant source of succour and a haven to those men of God who laboured in your land to spread His Word.

How fitting it would be, it seems to me, that you erect a small ecclesia within your lands in memory of her, and that it should contain, in permanent and public reverence, the very altar-stone bequeathed to you so long ago by one of God's great spirits on this earth. Picus Britannicus, your father, I know, would have had no objection to such a gesture of respect for loved ones and their God. What think you?

I shall await your response with patience and forbearance. But bear in mind, my friend, the man you know, who is less patient than the Bishop. Farewell, Merlyn. My thoughts and prayers are often filled with you and yours.

Your brother in God and friendship,
Germanus

A small *ecclesia*, built of stone. Two large horns on one dilemma, contained within a single phrase. With our current populace approaching the six thousand mark, four thousand and more of them Christian, smallness was not a fitting criterion for any place of worship we might use. Our communal religious ceremonies, few as they might be, were always held beneath the open skies and strongly attended. The very portability of Alaric's altar-stone was what made that possible. As for a stone edifice, the mere idea was ludicrous. Our fortress walls were made not of stone but of stones, painfully amassed, with great difficulty and single-minded obstinacy, over long years, by the combined and sustained efforts of an entire people inspired by visionary leaders. Stone walls, walls made of stone, suggested dressed and fitted blocks of quarried masonry in an edifice designed and constructed to withstand the ravages of time on the scale of centuries. Our walls were nowhere near so grand, for we had no quarries, no convenient source of stone. Germanus's idea appealed to me, nevertheless, in its aspect of forming a useful and decorative memorial to the Founders of our Colony, and I brought the matter up in Council some time later. The result, however, was as I expected. After lengthy discussion of the matter, pro and contra, the decision

of the Council, reluctant and regretful, was that here was an idea ahead of
its time. Such an *ecclesia* might well be built some day and should be planned
for, in the longer term, but the very grandeur of the notion dictated that the
site should be elsewhere, close to a source of stone, where the labours of
construction might be minimised. I wrote back to Germanus and explained,
at length and with compassion, how and why we could not accede to his
suggestion. Alaric's altar-stone, I assured him, would continue to be put to
frequent and respectful use, and would suffer no erosion, safe within its
carrying case. His response, received months later, was complacent, his enthusiasm undimmed by the prospect of "some day."

So time passed, and children grew, and Camulod prospered in peace, and
the world outside paid us no attention. And then, one day, reviewing our
parading troops on a special holiday created and deemed to mark the seventy-
fifth anniversary of the founding of our Colony, I looked at the seven-year-
old boy who rode between Ambrose and me, his head high and his wide-eyed
young face flushed with pride and excitement at being part of such a grand
occasion, and I realized that I had reached my fortieth year of life.

That night, in the celebration that followed the day's ceremonies, I mentioned the matter to our gathering at what had become our favourite spot,
around the first firepit outside the fortress walls. For some reason, that night
the women were not present, and I sat at ease among Lucanus, Ambrose,
Donuil, Hector, Dedalus, Rufio, Quintus and Benedict. Huw Strongarm had
been with us earlier, but had left to rejoin his own people whose voices we
could hear, raised high in song, some distance from us on the dark hillside.
Amid much raillery, I bewailed the fact that life had passed me by and soon
I would be forty. Ded, closer to fifty, and Luke, now beyond sixty, gave short
shrift to my complaint, and indeed it seemed, when we examined it, that I
was among the youngest of our group. Only Donuil, Benedict and Ambrose
were junior to me, and Ambrose by a matter of mere months. During a pause
in the conversation shortly after we had abandoned the topic of my age,
Lucanus changed the subject, addressing Ambrose.

"Do you ever regret, Ambrose, not having returned to visit Vortigern? I
recall that when you first came here you were insistent that you should return
to make your final severance with him face to face."

I found myself glowering fiercely at Lucanus, shaking my head urgently
to warn him to desist. It had been years since Ambrose spoke of going east,
and I had no wish to rekindle the ambition in his mind. Of course, I was far
too late to forestall Luke's words. Ambrose made no response for a long time
and when he did reply, his tone was musing.

"Yes, Luke," he said. "I do regret it. Not often, and for different reasons
than you might suppose. The bonds that bind me here, to Camulod, are far
more solid and enduring than those that once linked me to Vortigern, and
yet I would like to return, some day, to see how things progress there in
Northumbria without me."

"Then you should go, and soon."

I began to rise to my feet in protest, but Lucanus had my measure. He
swung to face me.

"Both of you should go. Together, and immediately." He held up one
hand to stop me from speaking. "Think of it, Merlyn, before you say you
cannot. You talked of it before, planned it indeed, to happen after your return

from Cambria. What has happened in the interim? We have had five years, almost six, of prosperity and peace. Our Colony is strong and secure, and no danger threatens anywhere. You have just been imposing on our collective goodwill as friends, weeping about how life has passed you by. Well, here is a chance to go out there and meet it, and arrest its too-swift progress. There is not one reason in this world why you may not go, not even if you were to leave tomorrow."

His eyes moved from me to Ambrose and back. No one else spoke.

"Is there?" He looked at each of us again. "Can you provide one? One solid reason why you should not take a furlough and enjoy yourselves away from home for a short space of months?" A pause generated no response from anyone present, and he continued speaking. "I thought not, for there is no good reason to the contrary, particularly when such a course would serve a useful purpose. By visiting Vortigern you could discuss alliance with him. There was a time you deemed that to be important, did you not? Nothing has changed in that, I think, save for the fact that you have done nothing to make it happen. Why don't you go now? Our affairs are in good hands and, though the hearing of it may surprise and dismay you, we can manage to live without you for at least a short time."

I looked at Ambrose, who returned my look and slowly began to smile.

"Brother," he said, "I think our friends have an eye to our welfare. I also think such an expedition would be fun. Why not do as Luke says, and simply up and go?"

I grinned back at him, already and quite suddenly convinced that we should, feeling excitement at the notion stirring in my breast.

"What about your wife? Will she allow you to leave? I have no such encumbrance."

"Hah! She will be glad to be rid of me for a spell, especially since I would be travelling with you, my saintly brother, and therefore likely to avoid temptation in the fleshpots of the world."

There are times when careful planning ensures success, and there are times when the most careful planning comes to naught. But there are also times when spontaneity brings benefits uncountable. This was one of those times.

XXVIII

ON A MORNING more than two weeks after that, deep within the borderless, alien territory known as the Saxon Shore, I knelt in wet grass beside my brother, peering through a screen of bushes at a man who had almost fatally surprised us. He was evidently the owner of a hay-filled barn where we had spent the night, exhausted after a long day's travel in heavy rain, and he was a Saxon. We had come upon his barn without warning the previous evening, just as night was falling and, soaked and tired and lulled by the torrential rain, we had succumbed to the temptation to shelter there, uncaring whether the owner was Briton or Saxon. In the last half hour of fading light, thankful for the solid roof over our heads, we had unsaddled and tended our horses, then dried ourselves and changed our soaked clothing before crawling into the fragrant piles of loose hay that filled the building and on which our horses were feeding placidly. Sleep overcame us quickly. I can remember only feeling grateful for the softness of the hay and listening to the gentle crunching of the eating beasts, then nothing.

The extent of our exhaustion became apparent in the dawn of the new day, when Ambrose shook me awake, his hand clasped over my mouth. I looked where he was looking, and saw the form of a large man approaching through the trees. Motionless, we watched him come, each of us wondering what was to happen here. As he drew closer, he loomed larger, and I began to feel an insane urge to laugh aloud, because he still had not looked up to see our four horses among his hay, clearly outlined as they were to us, against the morning light. We ourselves lay hidden in the hay. Yet he did not look up, seemingly intent upon his feet, so deep was he in thought. And then, as my searching fingers closed about the handle of my sword, a cry came from behind him and he stopped and turned away, listening intently. The cry came again, a woman's voice, and he called back, the tongue he used discordant and alien to my ears. Again the woman called, and then with a muttered curse he walked away, back whence he had come, until the trees concealed him.

Within moments, we had saddled our mounts and packhorses and Ambrose led them from the barn while I concealed the signs of our stay. I ran to join him immediately, thankful the rain had stopped during the night, and found him waiting just beyond the barn, holding the reins of all four animals, but making no attempt to mount. He held up one hand, wrapped about with reins, bidding me be still as he cocked his head to listen. I listened too. There was nothing to hear.

"He's gone," I said, my voice still low.

"Aye, but he might come back. What would you have done, had he seen us?"

I glanced at him, surprised that he need ask. "He was a dead man. Why?"

"You would have killed him, not knowing who or what he was?"

"He was a Saxon; what more need I know? Even before I heard him speak, I knew that."

Ambrose shook his head, pouting his lips. "No, he's no Saxon. At least, the language he spoke was no Saxon tongue I've ever heard, and I've heard several. Probably an Angle."

"A what?" I *felt* the blankness in my face.

"An Angle . . . some people, Vortigern's Danes among them, call them Anglians. Another race altogether from the Saxons. They come from farther north."

"Farther north of where?"

His teeth flashed in a quick grin. "Of where the Saxons come from. They are different peoples. Like Donuil's Celts and your Pendragons. The same in many things, perhaps, but from different places and speaking different tongues."

I shook my head. "Nah!" I said. "That can't be right. The Pendragon are Celts, too. I speak the Pendragon language, and though it sounds different from Donuil's tongue I could yet understand what Donuil said the first time I met him. You said this fellow here spoke unintelligibly."

"Exactly, so he cannot be a Saxon. Therefore he must be an Angle, or perhaps a Jute—" He smiled again, seeing my face. "Another race entirely. There are many of them."

"Aye." I said no more, allowing my tone to convey my disgust in the single syllable and reaching to grasp my saddle horn, preparing to mount. His hand on my arm stopped me.

"No, wait, Cay. I want to see what kind of place this is, what kind of farm they have. That barn is large, larger than I would have expected to find in a place like this." He stopped, looking me in the eye. "Will you wait for me? Or will you join me?"

I looked up at the sky and sniffed loudly. It was already almost full daylight, and the man might be returning even now, but I had already learned not to argue with my brother when his curiosity was stirring.

"What if we meet him in the woods?"

"Then we nod and pass by, what else? We won't meet him, Cay! How stupid do you think I am? I'm not suggesting we ride boldly forward here. We'll harness our horses back there in the woods behind the barn and make our way forward on foot, clear of the path. If someone comes, we'll drop flat. Come on, I'm curious to see what we have here."

We did as he suggested and moved forward carefully, and less than a hundred paces from the barn we came upon the main holding, an extensive farm yard containing a long, low, central building made of stone, with a thickly thatched roof, surrounded by a collection of smaller huts and shelters, some of them strongly built, the others a ragtag variety of lean-to sheds in various stages of repair. The strongest-looking outhouses, all walled byres, were for cattle. We could hear the sounds of them from where we crouched behind the screen of bushes separating us from the yard. Smoke billowed from a vent in the roof of the main building, but we could see neither door nor windows from where we crouched; nothing but stone walls. Muttering that these people had obviously lived here for some time, since the buildings had been carefully and strongly built, requiring years of effort, Ambrose beck-

oned me to follow him and cautiously, ready to drop at any sound, we made
our way laterally until the front of the longhouse came into view. It had one
wide, central door divided laterally into two sections, top and bottom, much
like those I had seen in Eire. The top section was open and we could hear
voices from inside, but then a woman's face appeared and she reached over,
raising the latch that held the bottom closed. She emerged as it swung open, a
tall, well-made, wholesome-looking woman in her early twenties, I surmised,
and was followed by a brood of brawling children, three of them, all boys, tugging and hauling at each other as they spilled into the light of day. She
snapped some words at them and crossed directly to a solid-looking table
close by the door, where she lowered the large wooden bowl she had been
holding in her right arm. One of the boys, the smallest, hit by one of his
brothers, ran to her in tears and clutched her skirts, burying his face against
her leg. She dropped one hand protectively to his bowed head and gave his
siblings the rough edge of her tongue, then raised her head and called out
again. Her man, the one who had almost stumbled on us, came from the
largest outhouse, evidently in answer to her summons. Seen thus, in full light,
he appeared even larger than he had before, an enormous, broad-shouldered,
blond-haired man with a handsome face almost completely covered by a
dense beard. The little skin I could see around his bright blue eyes looked
deeply tanned. The woman gestured to the wooden bowl, then knelt to
soothe the little boy, while her man approached and looked into the deep-
sided bowl. From it he took a jug, a wedge of bread and what appeared to
be a handful of dried grain, and then he leaned against the table's edge,
feeding from his closed fist and grinning as he watched his woman fussing
with the child. She bussed the boy, then cleaned his tear-streaked face with
her apron, just as a woman of our Colony would have, after which she
straightened and moved to stand beside her man. He raised the hand in
which he held the jug, and she came into the crook of his arm, leaning against
him. He lowered his head and nuzzled his bearded face against her hair, then
continued eating while she spoke to him.

I had no notion of what she was saying, but the domesticity of the scene
surprised me, although had I been asked how I might have expected such
people to behave towards each other I would have been unable to provide
an answer. The man turned his head slightly and called out something, and
a young girl appeared in the doorway. She was most evidently the daughter
or the sister of the first woman, and my mind immediately chose the former,
adjusting its estimate of the woman's age accordingly. The girl was laughing
at something her father had said as she turned and disappeared again into
the interior of the house.

I felt Ambrose's eyes upon my face and turned to look at him. He merely
raised an eyebrow, a half-smile upon his face, but then he froze, head cocked
to the side, and gestured urgently, a small, tight movement of one hand. The
sounds he had heard reached my ears immediately, and then a two-wheeled
cart, drawn by a horse and containing three more men, came creaking from
the woods on the other side of the farm yard and approached the house. The
driver was an older man, about equal in age to the farmer, and the other two
were younger, beardless youths. It was evident that they had been expected,
for the farmer, swigging a quick drink from the jug before setting it down,
hugged his wife one-armed, pinching a buttock fondly, and they moved to-

gether to greet the newcomers. One of the younger men was already handing down tools, shovels and mattocks, to his companion who had jumped to the ground.

Ambrose tugged at my sleeve and we backed away cautiously until we were sure we were in no danger of being seen, and then we headed back towards our horses.

"Well," he asked me as he walked. "Don't you feel glad you didn't have to kill him?" I shook my head, impatient with his tone, but he would not let be. "Come, Brother. Would you rather have left him dead, simply for being here, and her a widow with a brood to feed?"

I looked at him, tight-lipped, but he merely grinned and swung himself up into his saddle. And so we rode in silence for a spell. I was deeply disturbed, however, by the scene we had just witnessed, although I would have been at a loss for words had Ambrose asked me why. The word that came back to me, and refused to leave my mind, was "domesticity." That family on whom we had spied so briefly was long settled and its members were happy in their home and with each other. They fitted ill with my own long-held and jealously cherished notion of the invaders who were despoiling Britain, and yet they tallied precisely with the kind of people Germanus had described to me in his first letter, bidding me to be charitable. I found myself going over, time and again, the various other comments I had heard and with which I had vociferously disagreed, regarding the peaceful intentions of many of the new settlers and even desirable aspects of having such people as neighbours. Equus's son Lars and his family, isolated in their rundown hostelry near the abandoned town of Isca in the south, had told me they would rather treat with the settled Saxons they had come to know, who were quiet, orderly neighbours, than they would with their own island people who had consistently brought them warfare and disruption. The thought had horrified me when I first heard it stated. And months later, it had been reinforced by both Ambrose and Donuil.

All of my training, all I had been taught throughout my life, told me that they were wrong; they *must* be wrong. Were that not so, I told myself now for the twentieth time, then all our training, and Camulod's very existence, was the result of an error in judgment. These people were invaders, alien to our ways and to our life, as much as to our land. What did it matter that some of them were now peaceful farmers and "good neighbours," as I had been assured by their apologists? They had landed here as raiders in the very recent past and had remained as local conquerors. My mind reeled with the conviction that accepting their pacific behaviour now must entail, in logic, nothing less than total capitulation to the tide they represented; the abandonment of all reservations towards them would amount to the complete welcome of an inevitability. Within a decade of that acceptance, it seemed to me, we would be outnumbered, our Romano-Celtic roots overwhelmed and buried, stamped out forever. Britain would cease to be Britain and would become a Saxon province.

Shaken and disturbed by my own logic, I could not believe my friends, for all their own strong-mindedness, had thought this matter through in its entirety, and I told myself that someone, most probably me, had to do just that: examine the entire problem judiciously and logically, and then convince all of them of their error. I could see no alternative, although I knew I faced a thankless task. Survival—our own survival—depended on their being wrong. And so I rode in silence, and I was deeply troubled.

We had ridden for about a mile when I became aware that Ambrose, slightly ahead of me, had stopped and now stood upright in his stirrups, head cocked to the side, listening. I stopped my own mount and listened, too, but I could hear nothing. I had had ample evidence on this journey, however, that my brother's hearing was far more acute than my own, so I was ready when he put his fingers to his lips and waved us off the path. I kicked Germanicus forward and kept close as Ambrose spurred his horse through the bushes and up a slight rise that was crowned by a clump of large trees, their boles concealed by heavy brush. I reined in beside him and looked in the direction he was watching.

"What did you hear?"

"People coming towards us. More than a few. Listen."

I strained my ears for long moments, then finally heard the noises that had alerted him: voices, now below us, approaching along the path.

"We're pretty exposed up here, don't you think?"

"Come, we'll tether the horses behind the hilltop, out of sight, and then go forward again and find a place to watch from." As we swung down from our saddles, the sounds were already much closer, individual voices audible in the buzz of quiet conversation.

"Ach, too late," he said. "They'll be past here by the time we come back." He was looking around as he spoke, and suddenly he pulled the Pendragon longbow he had "adopted" from the saddle of his pack-horse. "Leave the horses and bring your bow, but take off your helmet and carry it. We'll watch from over there!" He nodded towards a trio of large trees some distance to our left; then, pulling a bowstring from his scrip, he quickly strung his bow and snatched a quiver of arrows that hung by the pack saddle while I did the same, and within moments we were crouching side by side between the two largest trees. Below us, less than thirty paces from where we crouched, a long line of men emerged from the forest, all of them armed and armoured, wearing conical helmets, some of which had horns, walking in a double file along the path. Ambrose slipped back, keeping his head low, and crossed to where I crouched.

"Now *those*," he whispered, "are Saxons."

As he said the words, one of the men in the lead stopped abruptly, holding up one arm so that the line of men behind him came to a halt, their voices dying away rapidly. For a space of heartbeats I thought he must have heard Ambrose's whisper, but he immediately began to speak to his people, his voice urgent and minatory. I glanced at Ambrose, but he shook his head at me, frowning with concentration as he listened to what was being said below. Whatever it was, it was briefly stated. Two men immediately moved up ahead of the leader and vanished along the pathway. Moments later, the train moved forward again, proceeding now in silence. We watched them leave, and I counted twenty-four of them, including the two who had gone ahead of the main party. When the sounds of their passage had diminished, I turned to Ambrose, who was still frowning.

"What was that about? Did you understand him?"

"Aye, I did," he replied, his face grim. His eyes moved restlessly from side

to side, looking from where the Saxons had disappeared along the track, to
the point at which they had come into view. Finally, my impatience took
over.

"Well? What did he say?"

Now his eyes moved to me. "He told them they must be quiet from here
on, to achieve surprise. Then he sent two scouts on ahead to make sure no
one on the road would be able to raise an alarm."

It took me several moments to absorb what he had said.

"You mean they're going to attack that farm? The Saxon farm?"

"Any time now," he answered. "The *Anglian* farm. I told you, they're a
different people, a different race altogether; an *enemy* race."

"Good God!" I had a vision, immediate and stark, of that tall, fair young
mother being raped, her husband and her young sons lying dead around her,
and my mind went back to the sight of young Arthur's nurse, Turga, when
I had first seen her, witless with despair, demented eyes gazing sightlessly at
the dead baby in front of her.

"We have to raise an alarm!"

Ambrose glanced at me again. "How? It's too late now. We're behind
them. To sound any kind of warning we would have to be ahead of them,
between them and the farm."

"Damnation! There must be something we can do," I retorted, but he
was right and I had seen the truth of it as soon as he had said the words.
The forest grew too densely here on either side to allow us to make any kind
of speedy progress away from the path, even on horseback.

"There may be." His voice was curt. "I have one idea and I think it may
be insane. Come, quickly!" He had snatched up his helmet and now turned,
running towards the horses. I was close behind him as he reached them, but
he was already mounted by the time I began to unhitch my reins.

"Quick," he snapped. "Leave the pack animals. We have no time."

I swung myself up into the saddle and then saw that he was standing in
his stirrups. He had unstrung his bow and was shrugging off his cloak and
wrapping it around his bow stave and quiver.

"Do the same as I'm doing."

Mystified, but making no attempt to argue, I slipped down from my
saddle again and quickly unstrung my bow, then used the string to tie the
bundle made by my bow stave and quiver wrapped in my cloak as securely
as I could before slinging it, as he had, from my saddle horn.

"Right," he said as I remounted. "Make sure your helmet's tight on your
head. Fasten your chin strap. And you'll need that." He was pointing to my
iron flail, which hung at its usual place by my right knee from the hook
mounted on my saddle. I reached for it and gripped its leather-bound wooden
handle tightly, feeling the weight of the heavy iron ball at the end of its
chain. Ambrose had unslung his long cavalry sword and now he kicked his
horse hard, angling it downhill to regain the path. I spurred Germanicus hard.

"What's the plan?" I called as I gained his side. Our horses were already
stretching to a full gallop, their shod hooves making surprisingly little noise
on the pathway, cushioned by a thick carpet of leaves sodden by the previous
day's rain.

"The first part is straightforward," he called back. "Surprise backed up by
impetus. We couldn't leave the path—they won't be able to, either. So we'll

catch them from behind, if we're fast enough, and smash through them. The people at the farm should hear the commotion and be able to prepare themselves. At least they won't be taken completely unawares."

"What if we don't catch them on the path?" I was bent forward now, head down to avoid the twigs and branches flailing at my head and face.

"Then we charge at them wherever we do find them, but in either case we ride clear through them and out the other side. Don't stop."

"Why not?" We were making no attempt to be quiet.

"That's the second part—*aha!*"

We had caught up with the rear part of the Saxon column, and I saw the surprise and fright on the faces that turned towards us in consternation. One fellow had time to throw up his shield and raise his sword, but then Germanicus was upon him, smashing the shield with his great shoulder and hurling the fellow aside, into his nearest companion and directly into the path of Ambrose's charging horse.

I was standing upright in my stirrups, swinging my lethal flail with all my strength, and whatever the iron ball struck it crushed and maimed. Germanicus bore me forward, his pace unflagging, adding his own bulk and momentum to the havoc we wreaked on that narrow pathway. A horse will normally attempt to avoid trampling a man, but a trained war-horse has no such scruples. Side by side, our charging mounts constituted an implacable and irresistible force, and the men on the ground ahead of us were too surprised, too tightly packed and too terror-stricken to offer anything in the way of resistance. In the sudden chaos, many threw themselves bodily into the dense brush on either side of the path to save themselves, and we were unopposed. For a long count of moments we were in utter turmoil, and then we were through the press and clear, with the barn where we had spent the night directly ahead of us. Ambrose had fallen slightly behind me on my left, but as I turned to see if all was well with him he drew level with me, leaning in to shout into my ear.

"Did you hear? They took us for Romans." I shook my head, concentrating on the tunnel of trees ahead of us, which led into the farm yard. "Ride straight through," he yelled again. "There's a small knoll to the north, at the far end of the farm yard. Some big trees on it. Keep going until we're over the brow and out of sight."

Suddenly we were in the yard itself, galloping past the rear of the farmhouse, our horses' hooves clattering over the hard-packed surface. The place seemed deserted, showing no sign of the people we had watched earlier.

"They won't be far behind us," Ambrose shouted. "Once they find we're not coming back at them, they'll come on hard and they'll be angry. I think I killed three of them . . . What about you?"

"Two, perhaps three," I yelled back. "If I hit them with this thing, they're as good as dead."

We were beyond the farm yard now, the sound of our hoofbeats changing as we surged up the tree-clad hill on the far side of it. As soon as we had cleared the summit, however, and dropped out of sight of the farm on the other side, Ambrose hauled back on his reins so that his horse halted in a skidding stop, almost on its haunches. He dismounted easily, stepping out of his stirrups and taking the cloak-wrapped bundle from where it hung by his saddle. I did the same.

When he had restrung his bow, Ambrose slung the quiver of arrows around his waist and shook out his cloak, reversing it so that its snowy white lining of fine wool was uppermost. He grinned at me, moving quickly, his teeth bared.

"Now, Brother, this is the insane part I mentioned. Take off your helmet. Did you notice the boulders?"

"What boulders?"

"Two of them, one to each side of the summit of the knoll. Listen!" He cocked his head, pointing his right ear in the direction of the farm beyond the hilltop. I could hear nothing, but he relaxed, his face breaking into a smile again.

"There are two large piles of rocks, one over yonder to our left, the other that way, on the right. I noticed them this morning. They are similar in size, and almost equidistant from the largest oak tree on the summit there." He nodded towards the massive tree that crowned the knoll above and behind us. "About sixty, perhaps seventy-five paces between them. Now, please don't ask me where the idea came from." His grin grew wider. "You wear the silver bear on your black cloak. Mine has no emblem. But both cloaks are white inside, so that, reversed, they are identical. And so are we, especially when we remove our helms and let our hair hang free. And even more when we do this." He had been looking down at the ground by his feet and now he stooped quickly to a small puddle that had been churned into mud by animal hooves, goats and sheep. The surplus water had soaked into the ground, and the remaining mud gleamed black and viscous. He scooped up a handful of the stuff and smeared it diagonally down the left side of his face, coating it from forehead to chin, so that the stuff caked in the hollow of his eye. He dug out the surplus with a fingertip before continuing.

"If you do the same thing now, carefully, we will be identical and indistinguishable from far less than a hundred paces. After that, as each of us steps from hiding, from behind his own pile of rock, in sequence, Brother, and never both at the same time, it will seem as though one and the same man is shooting, moving from rock to rock at magical speed, without being seen to move at all. What say you?"

I found my tongue at last. "What can I say? You're right, it is insane. Completely insane."

He laughed. "Aye, but it will work. These Saxons are a superstitious breed and for them, white is the colour of death, dread and mourning."

I expelled my breath in a gust and bent to scoop up my own handful of mud, which I then applied to my own face, taking care to do it exactly as he had, caking it thickly on my own forehead and in the hollow of my eye, between brow and cheekbone, before scooping it out again with a fingertip. As I completed the task, the sound of shouting reached us from behind the hill.

"It has begun," Ambrose said. "We should take our places now, while their attention is centred on the farm buildings. The most difficult part for us will be getting from here to the rocks without being seen from below, but if we move quickly and carefully, we should be able to manage it. After that, it's simply a question of staying out of sight once we're in place and hidden. Which side do you want?"

I shrugged. "Makes no difference. You realise our bows are completely

different? Mine curves one way, yours another. They don't look even faintly
similar."

"From the distance at which we'll be shooting? All they will see is a
yellow-haired man with a white cloak, a half-black face and a long bow, and
when they see how magically he moves from side to side they'll be too afraid
even to notice, let alone analyze, the difference in our bows.

"Let's go, and wait for me to shoot first. When I have loosed, give me a
count of five to hide myself again, then you step out and fire. I'll do the
same . . . a five count after you, I'll shoot again. I'm nowhere near as good a
marksman as you are, but let's hope they don't notice that down there."

It took me some time to work my way into position on the left flank of
the hill, and I had to crawl through high bracken for about a hundred paces
in order to reach the rock pile. Once there, however, I was able to observe
what was happening in the farm yard below, slightly more than a hundred
paces from where I crouched.

The inhabitants had evidently taken shelter in the main house, for the
shutters were closed over the windows, barred from the inside. At least one
of them, I saw, had a bow, because two helmeted corpses sprawled in the
open yard before the house, the arrows which had killed them clearly discernible from where I was.

A knot of eight or ten of the attackers—their positioning made it difficult
to see clearly—huddled in the lee of the outhouse closest to me, and I saw
smoke wisping up above them. The other attackers were scattered around
the farmhouse, keeping low and out of sight from the shuttered windows.
They must have been driven off by the defenders while I was making my way
down through the bracken on the hillside. Even as I looked, however, several
of them darted forward towards the house from different directions, one of
them swinging a great, two-headed axe at the door of the building and two
others battering at the shuttered windows. At the same time, under the cover
of these diversions, one of the main group broke away and ran towards the
house, whirling a smoking object round his head and plainly intent upon
firing the thatch of the building. I sensed, rather than saw movement to my
right, and then Ambrose loosed his first arrow.

His modest claim to poor marksmanship was set at naught immediately,
as the running man below went flying sideways, knocked off his feet by the
power of the missile that killed him. The swinging firebrand he had held
arced briefly and uselessly, falling to the ground several paces short of the
building. I began to count immediately.

For the first four of my counts, all movement was suspended below, and
then I saw faces turned upward to where Ambrose yet stood in plain view,
some seventy paces to my right. He allowed them to note him clearly, then
stepped back into safety behind his rocks as the first retaliatory arrow came
uphill, seeking him. I began my count again, and as I counted, the man at
the front door dropped his great axe and ran to recover the burning firebrand,
snatching it up and swinging it around his head as I stepped into view, an
arrow already nocked and partway drawn. I sighted and loosed in one movement and he, too, went down as though smitten by his own great axe. This
time, however, the firebrand landed on top of the dead man. A shout of
surprise came up to me clearly and, knowing now that Ambrose could see
me, I stood there a moment longer, then drew another arrow from my quiver,

sighted, and brought down a second man. Five bodies now lay sprawled in the yard. Unhurriedly, I stepped back and out of sight.

"Yours," I called to Ambrose.

"Glutton," he called back, his voice pitched so that I only could hear him. "Can you see me when I shoot?"

"Yes."

"Good. I can see you, too, so take what targets are offered. I'm up now. Two arrows."

He stepped into view again and the cries of consternation from below were immediate. The tongue was alien to me, but the content was unmistakable. *How did he do that? How did he get there so quickly?*

His next arrow took a man in the leg. The one after that missed altogether, smacking into a wall as its intended target threw himself flat and scurried into shelter on all fours behind a wooden cattle trough, unknowing that he had left himself exposed to me.

When Ambrose stepped back and I exposed myself mere moments later, easily killing the man who had escaped my brother's arrow, the shouts of the surviving Saxons turned to wails. And then I found myself searching in vain for another target, since the farm yard suddenly appeared to be deserted, not a living body, a limb, or even a fraction of a protruding limb in sight. I held my second arrow, unwilling to waste it, and stepped back behind my rock, leaving Ambrose to shoot at anything he might see, but he, too, lacked a target and we had reached a stalemate, although that condition could not last. I resigned myself to waiting until someone should move below, and then all at once the shutters on the farmhouse windows swung open and bowmen, at least two of them, began shooting from inside the house, striking death and confusion into the attackers trapped between the outhouses fronting the house. Ambrose and I had already established a crossfire, driving the attackers into the only shelter available to them, the spaces between the outhouses, protected from us, but exposed to the farmhouse itself. Now, encouraged by our assistance, the farm's defenders took advantage of the targets exposed to them, adding a third, triangulated angle of attack.

Ambrose was still in place, looking down on the scene, and as the remaining survivors of what had been the central knot of attackers scattered, panic-stricken, from this new assault, he fired again and I saw his arrow strike sparks from a flint as it struck the ground between the feet of a fleeing man.

"Yours," he called, ducking quickly out of sight. "Take what you can, now!"

I emerged immediately, as soon as he was out of sight, and I had two clear targets, both of whom I shot, although neither shot was fatal. The move, however, completed the demoralization of the raiders and their attack was over as first one, then all who could, began to flee back the way they had come. I stood and watched them run, waiting until they began to converge, inevitably, at the entrance to the pathway leading back to the distant barn. I estimated a dozen of them, at least one of whom was wounded, and sent two final arrows hissing among them as added encouragement to speed them on their way. One arrow, at least, found a mark and then suddenly, there was silence.

I stepped back then to lean against my rock, scanning the ground below. Six dead men lay in clear view, and I guessed that at least a couple of others, shot from the windows of the house, must be concealed from my view by the intervening buildings, byres and storage sheds between which they had been trapped when seeking shelter from our arrows. We had counted twenty-four in the original party. A dozen had fled back along the path; six lay dead in view. I had wounded several and Ambrose at least one. The count seemed accurate enough and I suspected several injured men might still be lying in concealment down there. I heard sounds approaching from my right and Ambrose joined me, still crouching low among the bracken.

"What now?" I asked him as he crept up. "Do we show ourselves?"

"Not yet, and don't look at me. There are still at least ten of them out there and they might be watching from the safety of the trees. If they see that we are two, instead of one with magic powers, they might not be amused, and might not be so easy to discourage next time. Don't forget there were two who came ahead of the others. I don't know if they joined the main attack, but they may have remained outside, watching from concealment to guard against surprises."

"You mean like the one we gave them? They were not very effective if they were there."

"No, but who can guard against magic?" Ambrose was smiling again, his eyes watching the farm yard.

"Well, if they were there, watching, they know there are two of us. They must have seen us ride up here. They'll know there is no magic involved."

"Nonsense." He did not look at me but continued watching the farmhouse closely. "Not at all. Remember the tales of Merlyn and his magic powers, Brother. The eyewitness accounts of the crippled girl in the guarded room, who disappeared in the night. That's what put the thought into my head. Men believe what they want to believe. Two ghostly, mounted Romans attacked them on the path, and everyone knows the Romans have been gone from here for two score years, and then one white-robed Druid savaged them from afar with a mighty bow the likes of which none of them has ever seen. We're far from Pendragon territory here, don't forget that. Our longbows are unheard of in these parts. But I think you're right. The two scouts must have joined the others in the attack." He drew back suddenly, lowering himself to where there was no danger of being seen. "There's someone coming out of the house."

The big farmer emerged first, followed by the man we had seen arriving with the wagon. The farmer stopped in the yard, peering about him cautiously for signs of danger, then turned to gaze up to where I stood in plain view. I raised my hand to him, palm outwards, indicating my lack of hostility and after a long moment he returned the gesture, then beckoned me to come down. I told Ambrose what was happening. He said nothing, content to allow me to represent both of us.

Now the farmer turned away and, followed by his companion, strode purposefully towards the row of buildings opposite the house, both men disappearing among the huts. Moments later they reappeared, cleaning the blades of their weapons, and then they split up, one of them going around each end of the farmhouse itself. I watched the big man until he vanished around the back of the gable end facing me, maintaining a running report on the activities for the benefit of Ambrose who remained hidden from view.

The two men eventually re-emerged from behind the house, their weapons now sheathed, and in response to their call, which came up to us clearly, the other occupants of the house came out into the yard. The two youths emerged first, each moving towards the huddled bodies on the ground. At their backs, the farmer's wife appeared, clutching her brood against her skirts, and last of all came the half-grown girl, her daughter, peering timidly about her as she stepped beyond the threshold.

The farmer looked my way again and his gaze directed the eyes of his companions to where I stood. Then, extending a half-raised arm to the others in a clear command to remain where they were, the big man set off purposefully towards me.

"He's coming up here," I said. "The farmer, alone."

"Aye, well, he must, mustn't he? What other choice does he have? Can't ignore you. Go to meet him. I'll stay here, out of sight for a while longer."

"Then what? Won't you come down with me? You can talk to them. I can't."

"No, I can't either, remember? I didn't understand a word of what they said, any more than you did. Go down to him, before he sees me. When you have their attention, and when I'm quite sure you're safe and they mean you no harm, I'll slip away unseen and collect the other horses. I'll bring them back and wait for you by the barn."

I was feeling increasingly foolish, having to speak without looking at him, and trying to do so without moving my lips, lest the approaching farmer thought me a madman, talking to myself.

"What will I say to them?"

"Tell them your name. Then collect our arrows, accept some food from them, enough for both of us, since they'll be grateful, and bid them farewell. They won't attempt to stop you. They'll think you're magic, too. Go down now, before he has a chance to see the two of us. You'll have no need of speech. A friendly smile will suffice, you'll see. You did save their lives, after all. Besides, you need to meet them, to see for yourself that they are ordinary people, just like our own in Camulod. Being Angles does not make them any less than human. Go, now, but don't stay long. I'll see you later."

Resigned to the strangeness of the situation, I set off down the slope towards the farmer, who stopped as soon as I began to move. He remained motionless, giving me ample opportunity to examine him as I drew near. He wore the same half-sleeved tunic he had worn earlier, but now it was covered by a one-piece, knee-length overcoat of heavy, toughened leather, embossed with bronze, rectangular lozenges of armour. His head was thrust through the single yoke-hole and the garment was cinched at his waist, protecting his sides with an overlapping, double thickness, by a thick leather belt with a silver, ornately carved buckle in the shape of a writhing serpent. He wore heavy, leather brogans on his feet, fastened by long ties that criss-crossed up his calves to his knees, binding his leggings in place. He wore neither cloak nor helmet, nor did he carry a shield. His entire weaponry consisted of a longish, heavy-looking sword in a sheath by his side, and a broad-bladed dagger thrust into his belt.

I halted when a distance of four paces separated us and he stood gazing at me for several moments more, his eyes narrowed almost to slits, wary and speculative. Somehow, I summoned up a smile and nodded to him, and he relaxed at once, although the slight sagging at his shoulders was the only sign he gave that he had been under any kind of tension.

The act of crinkling my face in a smile had reminded me of the mud that coated one side of my face, and now I reached up to pick at the tight coating beneath my left eye. A large flake came free and I rubbed at it, feeling it crumble between my fingers. It may have been the simple humanity of the gesture that finally convinced him that he was dealing with a man and not some alien woodland deity, for he suddenly spoke, in a deep, grave voice, laying the spread fingers of one hand upon his breast.

"Gethelrud," he rumbled, and I guessed he had named himself.

I repeated the sound as closely as I could, adding my own interrogative note. "Gethelrud?"

He nodded, apparently pleased, and repeated it. I touched my own breast in the same manner.

"Merlyn."

"Merlyn." Grave-faced, he repeated my name yet again and then broke into a flood of speech, of which I recognized no single sound. When he fell silent again, I shook my head, then spoke to him in Latin, asking him if he understood that tongue. His incomprehension was as complete as mine had been. I spoke then in our native Celtic tongue of the West, and then in Donuil's Erse tongue, and again made no impression.

Finally he grunted and shrugged eloquently, a gesture that required no translation, before following that with another movement, this one an obvious invitation to accompany him to his home. We walked side by side, and I was as conscious of his fascination with my huge African bow as I was of the awe with which his people watched my approach.

Face to face with all of them finally, in the farm yard, I was overwhelmed by the impossibility of communicating with them. The farmer had spoken to them as we approached, naming my name and evidently telling them I did not know their tongue, and now no one made any attempt to speak, all of them simply staring at me in silence. I could read gratitude and uncertainty in the eyes of the adults and sheer awe in the faces of the youngsters. It was the woman, however, who took the initiative to break the awkwardness of the moment. With a glance at her husband, she stepped towards me, reaching for my right hand. Taking it between her own, a tremulous half-smile on her handsome face, she raised it towards her forehead, bringing it eventually, palm downward, to touch the top of her head, which she lowered towards me in an unmistakable gesture of gratitude, friendship and submission. I saw, before she lowered her eyes, that they were grey and large. I now guessed her age to be somewhere in her mid to late twenties, but the smooth skin of her face was yet unmarked by the lines of hardship and age.

As I stood there feeling slightly foolish, the woman transferred her right hand gently to my wrist and turned slightly, waving her left hand towards the open door behind her. Removing my hand equally gently from her head, I smiled and nodded, first to her and then to her husband, and thereafter to each of the others in turn. Satisfied that she had succeeded in communicating her message, the woman turned away and moved quickly into the house, followed by her daughter. Gethelrud gestured with his hand, indicating that I should follow them, but as I nodded and began to turn that way, my eye fell upon one of our arrows—the one that had struck sparks from the stony ground—lying close by my feet. I bent and recovered it, checking its point, which seemed undamaged, before slipping it into my quiver and looking around for more. Three I could see protruding from the bodies of the men they had killed. Seeing my gaze and correctly guessing my intent, Gethelrud laid a detaining hand on my arm and began issuing instructions to the others who immediately moved away and set to work cleaning up the carnage in the farm yard. One of them, the other man of Gethelrud's age, whom I now took to be his brother, ripped an arrow audibly from the nearest corpse and held it out towards me, nodding plainly towards the nearby trough, mutely inquiring if I would like him to clean the missile and return it to me. I nodded and he moved to place the arrow point-downward in the water, leaving it to steep as he moved to collect another. The two youths had gone off some-where, dispatched by Gethelrud, presumably to warn their neighbours of the threat posed by the raiders.

A movement at the door caught my attention and the daughter came out again, carrying three pottery mugs with thick foam bubbling over their rims. My mouth immediately went dry with thirst and, on an impulse, I winked an eye at the one of the trio of small boys who still stood gaping at me. None of them had uttered a word since I appeared. Now, however, as I accepted a cool mug from their sister, this urchin, emboldened by my wink, stepped forward, his eyes on mine, and pointed to the bow I still held in my left hand. I have no idea what he asked me, but I realized immediately that what had held them silent all this time was mere shyness, and not superstitious dread and with that realisation it became suddenly apparent to me that none of the people in the farmhouse could have seen the effect engineered by Ambrose to astound and terrify their attackers. The shuttered windows of the house all faced the yard. These people all believed, quite clearly, that I had been alone upon the hill, shooting from one position. Amused now, and relieved, I decided to call Ambrose into view. Signalling open-handed to Gethelrud to alert him, I put down my mug, placed two fingers between my teeth, and whistled loudly.

Nothing happened. Ambrose had departed. Aware of the astonished looks on the faces of my hosts, I grinned sheepishly and shrugged, then picked up my mug again and moved towards the house.

The next hour or so passed pleasantly, despite the fact that we had to communicate by gestures. They fed me well, with roasted venison and fresh-baked bread, and their ale was excellent, foamier and more yeasty yet paler than our own beer, and when I indicated to them at last that I must leave, they packed more food and a large earthen jug of ale for me to take with me. I bade them farewell in the early afternoon and made my way back alone towards the barn where Ambrose and I had spent the previous night, waving back to all of them before I entered the long, tunnelled road that masked them finally from view.

Ambrose had found the pack-horses where we had left them, although both of us had privately suspected that they might have been found and either stolen or killed by the fleeing raiders. By the time I reached the barn he had unsaddled the poor brutes and was in the process of rubbing them down. I gave him the bag of food and the jug of beer I had brought with me, and while he was eating I completed the horses' grooming, then led

them to a nearby brook to drink, after which I fed each of them a small
amount of grain in their nosebags. As we waited for the beasts to finish
eating, I asked Ambrose whether he thought the raiders might have been
part of the mercenary force maintained by Vortigern. He shook his head
emphatically.

"No," he grunted. "All Vortigern's men, locals and mercenaries, wear his
colours—a square of red cloth bearing a yellow trefoil flower—sewn on their
left shoulders." He reached into his saddlebag and produced one of the
squares, handing it to me, and as soon as I saw it I recalled having seen the
device in Verulamium years earlier. "Besides," he went on, "we're still too far
south."

"How do you know that?" I handed the emblem back to him and he
replaced it in his saddlebag before standing up and stretching.

"I know it because Vortigern's Danes, under Hengist, are too efficient.
No raiders would dare intrude into their territories. They've been there for
years, remember, and Vortigern relies on their savagery to keep his borders
safe. The word went out long years ago: Stay clear of Northumbria! The
raiders do, all of them."

"Do you think, then, those people will come back this way again, in
force?"

"They might, but I doubt it." He began removing the nosebags, and I
stepped to help him as he continued speaking. "The whole countryside knows
they're about by this time, I should think. I imagine those two young lads
we saw at the farm would have been sent out to spread the word quickly
enough to the neighbouring farms. Now they're forewarned, our Saxon visitors will take little pleasure in seeking further adventure around here. We
bloodied them to good effect, don't forget. One man in two or three is a
high price to pay for an aborted raid. My guess is they'll move on and try
somewhere else."

I glanced up at the sky above the clearing. "How long till darkness falls,
do you think? Five hours? Six?"

"At least. Probably more. It's June. We've light enough to make ten miles
and more before we need to look for a place to camp. Finish this beer and
we'll leave the jug here in the barn."

We busied ourselves replacing our saddles and pack gear, and as he pulled
himself up into his stirrups Ambrose opined that we were still at least two
days south of Vortigern's borders. Nevertheless, by the campfire later that
evening, he took the precaution of attaching Vortigern's colours to his left
shoulder, sewing the patch of cloth securely to his cloak with large, looping
stitches of coarse yarn.

He had been exactly correct. In the middle of the morning of the third day
after his prediction, we were challenged as we emerged from a thicket and
entered a short-grassed clearing, and moments later we found ourselves surrounded by a ring of hard-faced men, all heavily armed and helmed, most of
them holding short, heavy-looking bows, drawn arrows pointing towards us.

The obvious leader of the group, a medium-sized fellow in a massively
horned helmet and a long tunic of heavy ring mail, did not know quite what
to make of us. His leader's colours were bright on my brother's shoulder, but
our Roman-style armour and our armoured cavalry mounts marked us as

aliens. The man clearly did not know whether to kill us out of hand, or to accept the evidence of amity on Ambrose's shoulder. Ambrose relieved him of the need to decide.

"Ambrose of Lindum," he shouted. "Seeking Vortigern." I recognised only the names.

The leader scowled. "Ambrose of Lindum is dead, years ago," he growled. Again, I recognised only the name but guessed at the rest from the tone of voice.

Ambrose reached up and removed his Roman helmet with its obscuring, protective flaps.

"Ranulf," he said, using Latin for my benefit. "Don't you know me?"

It was a pleasure to meet Vortigern once again, especially since he recalled me clearly despite the lapse of years since he and I had met. Moreover, his delight in Ambrose's return was total, spontaneous and unfeigned, although it faded slightly, to be sure, when he discovered that Ambrose had returned only to bid him hail and farewell again.

I found the king greatly changed since our first meeting. Still handsome and regal in his bearing, he had matured well during the years since Verulamium and the Great Debate convened by Germanus. His hair had turned from iron grey to silver, but he had retained all of it, so that it hung thickly to frame his noble face, and he now wore a full beard, carefully trimmed and groomed. His shoulders were unbowed by advancing years and he stood almost as tall as my brother and I, holding himself at all times in an erect, military posture, shoulders squared, so that he appeared to dominate every gathering. But it was in his manner that I thought to detect a change. When first we had met, I had been favourably impressed by the ease, the appearance of casual repose, that he had shown to everyone with whom he dealt, treating each man, bishop or man-at-arms, with an easygoing goodwill that spoke of confidence and boundless self-assurance. My admiration of his dignity and self-possession had been unstinting then, causing me to think of him as "regal," a word I would have applied to no man before that time. Outwardly, Vortigern the King seemed at first glance to be as he had been in Verulamium, urbane and gracious, good-humoured and at ease with all around him, yet I sensed undertones of something new in his demeanour, a reticence I had not marked before; a tendency to veer away from certain topics so effectively that they were never raised to prominence. I said nothing of these vague misgivings to my brother. I merely watched, and listened closely, and felt somehow disturbed.

We remained with Vortigern and his people for the first two weeks of June and he entertained us lavishly, demonstrating himself to be a gracious and noble host. As we talked, he came to appreciate the advantages of having Ambrose, a trusted friend, in charge of friendly forces, cavalry in particular, guarding the western and southwestern approaches to his lands. He had troubles enough to occupy him to the north and east and south, he told us, keeping his borders, sea and land, free from trespass by Picts, Anglians, Jutes and the ubiquitous Saxons.

He had seen our cavalry in Verulamium, of course, but like Ambrose, he had failed entirely to understand the power it represented. Now, impressed by Ambrose's radiant enthusiasm in speaking of our strength, Vortigern ex-

amined our horses and our equipment and accessories minutely, paying close
heed to our stirrups and how they were adjustable to each man's leg length
on our saddles. I showed him everything ungrudgingly, secure in the knowledge that he lacked the resources, if not the will, to develop similar powers
of his own.

On the seventh day of our visit, while Ambrose was elsewhere greeting
friends and renewing old acquaintances, I met Vortigern's friend and ally
Hengist the Dane. "Dane" was a term I had not heard before Ambrose used
it mere days earlier, but Hengist was insistent that such was his race. I, who
had but recently thought of all the invaders of our land generically as Saxons,
took note of this additional distinction and said nothing.

Hengist was an enormous man, more in the sense of bulk, be it said, than
mere height. He was tall enough, a handsbreadth taller than any of his fellows, but Vortigern stood taller than he did, as indeed did Ambrose and I.
In terms of sheer size, girth and physical power, however, Hengist stood
alone. Only two men I could recall rivalled him in sheer massiveness, one of
those being Huw Strongarm's factotum Powys, and the other Cullum, the
giant Hibernian Scot whose boar spear I had seized to fight the bear that
day in front of Athol's stronghold.

On that first occasion we met, Hengist had walked unannounced into the
private chamber Vortigern reserved for his personal use in his own Hall, pausing on the threshold as he realised that the king was not alone. Standing
there in the doorway, stooped over slightly to avoid scraping the lintel with
the massive helmet he had not removed, he appeared to fill the space completely, blocking the light from beyond.

"Oh," he growled, peering into the dark interior. "Your pardon, Vortigern.
I was unaware you had company. I'll come back." I realised that he had
spoken in Latin and sat straighter, showing my surprise, so that he cocked
his head to one side and narrowed his eyes, looking at me more closely now.
"Ambrose? Is that you?"

"No, Hengist, it is not. Come in." Vortigern rose to his feet quickly and
stepped to where the big man stood hesitating. The king took him by the
arm and drew him forward to where I now stood, having risen to my feet
with my host. "This is Merlyn Britannicus, Ambrose's brother. Remarkable
resemblance, is it not?"

Hengist stepped forward and his eyes grew wide as he scanned my face,
so that it occurred to me again that I might never grow accustomed to the
shock people betrayed on seeing the similarity between us two. Hengist recovered quickly, however, and greeted me affably, removing his helmet and
shaking out his thick, iron-grey hair as he explained that he had just returned
from an inspection tour of their coastal garrisons. I noted that word "garrisons" in silence, reflecting that I yet had much to learn of Vortigern's allies
and the extent of their duties and activities, as well as their strength. He
seated himself across the table from Vortigern and me and took the large
mug of ale proffered by a silent servant, drinking deeply before setting it
down and turning the full force of his personality upon me.

Reassured by his fluent mastery of my own Latin tongue, I allowed myself
to relax and enjoy his company, asking him openly after a time about his
evidently deep friendship with the king, who slouched easily in his high-

backed, armed chair and waved an open palm at the big man, giving him leave to tell me all he could.

It transpired that their fathers had been friends when both of them were very young, in the closing days of Rome's dominion here in Britain and elsewhere in the Western Empire. Vortigern's father, a powerful magistrate under Roman rule, although a king in name alone, had travelled into the Dane Merk, as Hengist called his homeland, on a diplomatic mission of some kind to Hengist's grandfather, and had remained there, with his family, for seven years. The two boys had become close friends at the outset of that mission, and by the end of the seven years each had been fluent in the other's tongue. During that time, Vortigern had formed a deep liking for the Danish folk among whom he lived, and a great admiration for their prowess in war. Theirs was an infertile land, its soil thin and sour and suited only to the conifers that covered it. In consequence, the Danes for centuries had sought a great part of their sustenance abroad, sailing in galley-style craft crewed by fighting men since, in addition to having to fight to obtain their plundered cargoes, they frequently had to fight to retain and defend them on the journey home.

In later years, after the Roman presence had been withdrawn from Britain, Vortigern had attained the titular kingship held by his father. By that time, however, with the Romans gone never to return, his people had looked to Vortigern himself for real leadership and protection. Soft and weakened by four hundred years of largely peaceful occupation by the Roman legions, they were incapable of defending themselves against the escalating depredations of the raiders who swarmed across the seas from the western coasts of the Germanic and northern lands in ever-growing numbers.

Faced with disaster sweeping in from the seas on great banks of oars, Vortigern remembered his boyhood friend and his warlike people, and travelled across the sea himself to seek out Hengist in the Dane Merk. He found him without difficulty, for Hengist himself had become a king of sorts in his own right: paramount war chief among his folk. Vortigern had then offered his friend a proposition: in return for their military support and active assistance in the defence of his lands, he offered Hengist and his people land in his own domain in Britain—sweet, rich farmland to replace their own thin, unprofitable fields in the Merk. Hengist had required little time for deliberation. He had put Vortigern's proposal to his people in their moot council and it had been accepted. Preparations for departure had begun immediately; five years had been required to effect their exodus completely.

At that time, Vortigern and Hengist had both been young men, not yet twenty years old and full of restless visions. Since then, more than thirty years had elapsed. Now Vortigern's territories were secure and unthreatened, and he and his Danish allies had begun to push their borders outward, embracing the lands to the south and west abandoned by their former inhabitants, who had either fled or been killed by the swarming raiders from the sea.

I had sat silent through Hengist's recital of this tale, but now he stopped, his gaze fixed on me.

"I can see from your face that something troubles you, my friend. Do you have a question to ask me?"

I glanced towards Vortigern, then cleared my throat.

"Well, yes, I do, but I fear it will merely show my ignorance of how things truly stand in this region. As you know, our lands of Camulod lie in the far west and we have problems of our own with raiders from the seas. But we have only Celts to deal with, mainly from Hibernia. The Picts from the far north come down our way but seldom, and we have had a few visitations, though none recently, from Gaul. Most recently, we have had incursions by African pirates, seeking marble stone." Both men watched me closely, nodding politely. I paused, collecting myself, then blurted my question straight out.

"If you and yours are the Danes, and the people we encountered some days ago to the south of here are Angles or Anglians as Ambrose says, then who, exactly, are the Saxons?"

Hengist let out a great, booming laugh.

"Who indeed?" He laughed again, then sobered abruptly. "The Saxons, my friend Merlyn, are similar to many other races in that they are a fiction: a creation of the arrogant Romans, who called themselves Masters of the World. There are Saxons out there, be sure of that, but they all come from one territory, in what Rome termed the Germanic lands. They are a blond people, warlike and not easily subdued, and they fought long and hard against the Roman Eagles. But in the end they were absorbed, as were we all. In the interim, however, so well had they defied the Roman conquest that their name became an eponym for savagery, so that all the Germanic peoples and their northern neighbours became known to Rome as Saxons. To us, however, the differences are clear. There are the Angles, or the Anglians, whichever you prefer, and the Jutes; there are the Friesians, who call themselves the Goths—the Romans, bureaucratic to the last, called them Visigoths and Ostrogoths. Then there are the Norsemen, from the lands abutting ours. North of those are the Sverigen, and to the east of them the Letts. And there are also Saxons. But even we, the Danes, the folk of the Dane Merk, were Saxons in the eyes of Rome."

When he fell silent I sat nodding, absorbing what he had said.

"So then," I observed eventually, "what you are telling me is that these other peoples, these 'Saxons,' are a mixture of many tribes and all of them are as alien to you, the Danes, as they are to us, the people of this land?"

He nodded slowly, a peculiar expression on his face, which might have been ironic amusement. "Precisely, Master Merlyn. Save for the minor point that we, my own people, now count ourselves among 'the people of this land.' But you are essentially correct. The Anglians are among the most prolific of these aliens, but the true Germanic tribes, the Saxons, are the most savage, and all of them seek a foothold here in Britain. They are determined, too— more so, perhaps, than we are. We can control our borders at this time, but they swarm everywhere around us like wasps. We fight them off, but like the wasps they resemble they are difficult to kill in sufficient numbers and they die hard, stinging even in death. And the survivors build new nests, far from the eyes of seekers."

I sat mute after that. Hengist's analogy was apt, and chilling.

XXIX

LATER THAT DAY, towards evening, we were summoned to a festive meal prepared to welcome Hengist home after his long absence. Vortigern's formal hospitality proved to be no less impressive than the informal welcome we had received. The meal was sumptuous and the courses startlingly varied, and tumblers, acrobats, musicians and mummers regaled the gathering throughout the event. The assembly broke up suddenly, however, in the wake of an incident of violence caused by some slight, real or imagined, offered by one drunken young man to an older, more sober warrior. It flared up quickly and was soon over, and it occurred at sufficient distance from where we sat at the dais table to ensure that we were unaware of it while it was going on. The first warning that anything was amiss was a sudden increase in the volume of men's voices, and then Hengist was on his feet, moving quickly, pushing his way determinedly and with great purpose through the crowd of men who suddenly thronged together, craning their necks to see what was going on.

Vortigern, who had sprung to his feet with the rest of us, sat down again and leaned sideways to speak to Ambrose, and I bent close to hear what he was saying. It was something about bad blood, but before I could ask for an explanation, the crowd parted and four men approached the dais from the far end of the Hall, carrying a fifth, his tunic drenched in blood. They carried him face upward and his head hung facing us, his eyes wide and sightless, already glazed in death.

Vortigern rose slowly to his feet again, his body tense, his face stony with rage. In a choking voice he asked who had done this and a man was named. Moving stiffly then, his limbs jerking almost like those of an automaton, the king stepped forward and reached out a rigid hand to the dead man's face, closing the sightless eyes with a gentleness that belied the tension in his stance. Then he closed his own eyes and flicked his hand sideways, indicating that they should take the dead man away. Over the heads of the others, thanks to my elevation on the king's dais, I saw a knot of grim-faced men hustling a prisoner—evidently the killer—from the Hall.

Order was quickly restored, and the din subsided as people resumed their seats and their interrupted activities. Hengist did not return to the dais, and shortly afterwards, muttering apologies to Ambrose and me, the king quit the table, too, and did not return. For the remainder of the time spent in the Hall, Ambrose spoke constantly with others, slipping easily from the local dialect into Danish, depending upon whom he was talking to. For my part, I sat silent, watching and listening, although most of the babble of voices was unintelligible to my ears, a mixture of the alien language of the Danes and the curiously broadened vowels and slurred consonants of the local Britons.

Not until long after the incident, when Ambrose and I were finally alone, did I have an opportunity to question him on what had happened. He thought for a while, and his eventual response seemed strangely elliptical at first.

"How much did you understand?"

"Nothing, or very little," I responded. "I saw the dead man, as you did, and I know the thing had flared up suddenly. But I don't understand why Hengist disappeared, or why the king went, too. I should have thought they would return, once assured that the culprit had been taken. This kind of thing must happen occasionally. It seems strange to me that it should require the attentions of the two most prominent men in the land, unless the dead man himself was also prominent, in which case he should have been on the dais and not out there among the general throng."

"Aye. Tell me, now that you have seen for yourself, what think you of Vortigern's allies? You still believe he courts disaster, nursing an adder in his bed?"

"Aye, I do," I said, speaking slowly. "But not quite as strongly as I did before. Not since meeting Hengist. I liked him far more than I expected to, and I can see now why Vortigern has placed such trust in him. Hengist is a man of honour. He would never betray that trust."

"Aye." Ambrose nodded his head deeply. "Hengist is an honourable man. But Hengist is growing old. When I left here to ride to Camulod his hair was black as night."

"So? All men grow old, Ambrose. Vortigern himself has aged greatly since I first saw him in Verulamium. So have we. What has that to do with what happened tonight?"

"Nothing, and everything. Your assessment of Hengist is completely accurate. He is honest, dependable, completely trustworthy and capable, and his friendship for Vortigern is unimpeachable. But he has a son who is not half the man his father is in such respects."

"Horsa? How is he different? I have not seen him since we arrived."

"Nor will you, for he is not here and will not come here. He is somewhere on the coast with his army—his own army. It was one of his captains who did the butchery tonight. That's why Hengist did not return to the dais. His son, or his son's supporters, have made sure that Hengist will be busy now for days, seeking to keep the peace."

"Among whom, his own people?"

"Aye, some of his own, but mainly Vortigern's folk. The dead man was a Briton."

"Bad blood," I said, feeling my own concerns about Vortigern grow stronger. "That's what Vortigern was talking about, isn't it?"

Ambrose nodded, his face solemn. "That's it. For thirty years the folk of both these races have existed peacefully, side by side, but all of that has changed since I've been away." He paused, considering that, then resumed. "It had started prior to that, now that I think of it, and all of it—or most of it—is Horsa's doing. He's an arrogant and overbearing young lout, intolerant and unbiddable, save to his father, Hengist. He was still a lad when I left here, well-nigh as big as his father, but yet young enough to be controlled by him. Now all of that has changed, it seems. Horsa has grown to manhood, and he controls the younger hotheads among the Danes.

"He is still in awe of his father, and to a lesser extent of Vortigern himself, but the day is coming when Hengist's age will permit Horsa to dominate him, or at least to flout his authority more openly than he dares attempt today."

"And his followers, Horsa's, I mean—are they from both camps?"

"No. His followers are Danes to a man. None of Vortigern's folk at all. That is Hengist's problem, and it will soon be Vortigern's. The older people, the established leaders, have complete faith in Hengist, but his son's behaviour is worrisome to everyone, and insupportable to some. Yet what can Hengist do? Horsa is his son and, to this point at least, he has done nothing overtly culpable, and nothing openly deserving of chastisement. His people, his supporters, are outrageous and insufferable in their behaviour from time to time, but that cannot, in conscience, be laid at Horsa's door." He sighed, a sudden, gusty sound of impatience. "But Horsa will assume his father's leadership in the course of time. As things stand, despite his grave concerns, Hengist cannot simply dispossess him, short of causing civil war, and things are too far gone already, even for that. Horsa is too strong and now he stays away from here, secure among an army of his own."

"And yet his people, his supporters, like this captain of his, move among the people here quite openly?"

"Oh aye, it has not come to open hostility. Not yet."

"But it's inevitable, you believe?"

Ambrose nodded. "It would seem so."

I sighed. "So it appears our father was correct, when all is said and done. Even despite the integrity of a friend such as Hengist, Vortigern courted death when first he brought the Danes into his land."

"Aye. I have no doubt of it now, although I've argued long and hard with you about it in the past. I've changed my mind within the past few days, after the conversations I have had with people whose opinions and judgment I long since learned to trust. Vortigern himself may not live to see it happen, and Hengist certainly will not, since he would and must die rather than permit it, but the day is coming when the Dane will rule alone in Northumbria and Vortigern's folk will be dispossessed and reduced to the status of servitors."

"Slaves."

He frowned quickly. "No, not slaves. I doubt it will come to that. But they will be reduced to servitude."

"Hmm. So what will happen to the man who killed tonight?"

Ambrose raised one eyebrow. "It already has, I should think. You'll see him hanging from a tree somewhere tomorrow, in plain view. I said Hengist is *growing* old. He's far from toothless yet. The first step towards placating those offended by the killing here tonight must be the public and immediate punishment of the offender. He was probably hanged as soon as they took him out of the gathering. What he did was indefensible. It was also political, and probably deliberately planned."

"What, for effect? Are you suggesting the man made a deliberate sacrifice of his own life for Horsa?"

"Aye, to make a point, stir up the other men, increase the tension. It's highly probable, and according to what I have heard today he's not the first to have done so."

"But why? What possible inducement could bring a man to give up his life merely to achieve a political effect? How could he think to benefit from such a course?"

Ambrose was regarding me with what I took to be wry amusement.

"There could be many reasons, Cay. These men are Danes. Their ways and customs, even their beliefs, are vastly different from ours. Perhaps he thought his sacrifice might be rewarded in some afterlife Elysium. Or he might have purchased some preferment for his family. Perhaps he died willingly in return for an extended time of pleasure with a group of courtesans. Who knows? Men have differing values, and to men like these Danes death is of little import. All we may be sure of is that he knew well before he did the deed that he would die for it."

My mind was racing, reviewing and reassessing my earlier conclusions about the stability of Vortigern and Hengist's situation. Ambrose sat watching me.

"What is it?" he asked eventually. "You look as though every gear in your mind is threatening to lock up."

"Camulod," I said. "I'm trying to assess the threat to Camulod; the timing of it."

"What threat? Horsa is no threat to us in Camulod. When Hengist dies, before or after Vortigern—it makes no difference—Horsa will have his hands full here. He will have no easy task imposing himself upon the structure left here by his father, and not all the Danes will follow him. Hengist and Vortigern, between them, have taken care of that with land grants and careful planning these past few years. The prime Danish lands, the most arable, are held by Hengist's most loyal veterans and are carefully distributed among the lands held by Vortigern's own people. The holdings are set out like a gaming board, in blocks, so that each Dane has a Briton north, south, east and west of his holdings and each Briton has Danes in the same positions. None of them will bend the knee or meekly give away his lands to Horsa and his people, so Horsa must accept the status quo and win new lands of his own for his people, or he must go to war against his own."

"How likely is he to do that, to go to war?"

Ambrose shrugged. "I have no idea, nor does anyone to whom I have spoken. There is great hope, naturally enough, that he will opt for the former course and settle his levies on outlying lands, keeping his father's holdings for himself as he's entitled to, but the final answer to that lies with Horsa, and he appears to like it that way. Hence his absence. He has not set foot here in Vortigern's enclosure for more than a year, ignoring his father's summonses. Hengist stopped sending them as soon as he discerned that Horsa would not obey them. Anyway, everyone is waiting now to see what happens at this summer's end. If the incoming raiders winter in Britain again this year, as they seem to do now every year, Horsa will stay out in the marshes, fighting through the winter."

"What about Vortigern's own sons? They are not here, either. There are two of them, you told me."

"Were. One of them is dead. Areltane, the younger of the brothers. He was killed in a raid, two years ago. The other, Cuthbert, is campaigning in the north, against the Picts and Anglians up there. He is expected daily, and he is, of course, the other element in this volatile mix—flint against Horsa's steel. Each time they meet, sparks fly, although they once were friends."

"Did you not tell me Areltane was the more able of the two?"

"That's right, I did, and he was. Had Areltane survived, no one would have concerns about Horsa. Areltane had his measure. But Areltane is dead."

"And Cuthbert is not strong enough?"

"No, he is not. Not that he lacks in strength *per se*, but he lacks wisdom and discretion. He's a hothead, and none too bright; brave to a fault, but headstrong, as I said, and as unbiddable as Horsa. In a confrontation between the two, I would wager on Horsa."

"Unfortunate. Have you talked to Vortigern about these things?"

Ambrose shook his head. "No. He's made no mention of it and it's not my place to bring it up without some indication that he is willing to discuss it."

"How can you say that? You are his friend."

"Because he is the king. Besides, your tense is wrong. I used to be one of his captains, but I'm no longer bound to him in any way. That makes me a mere guest here, just like you. No more than that, save that Vortigern has known me longer and once trusted me. Now he can no longer do that—trust me, I mean. As king, he can afford few friends, and friends may turn suddenly to enemies when kingdoms are at stake."

"Hmm. How long, then, must we remain here? We should return home, don't you agree? Vortigern has no need of guests, it seems to me, distracting him from his legitimate concerns."

My brother sat gazing at me for long moments then, gnawing the inside of his cheek, but then he nodded in agreement. On the fourth day after that, having made our farewells to Vortigern and Hengist and obtained their good-will and permission to travel once more across their lands, we set out again for Camulod.

We experienced no trouble on the road that was not caused by weather. Perhaps the sight of us, armoured as we were on our large horses, riding side by side with long, strung bows, was sufficient to discourage anyone who might have sought to hinder us, but we rode unmolested across the breast of Britain.

The weather through which we rode, however, was atrocious. It was the month of June and approaching July, and our expectation had been of high summer weather. That year, however, June was unique in its malevolence. We had had fine weather on our outward journey, in late May, with heavy rain at times, certainly, but for the most part we had ridden beneath sunny skies, enjoying the green lushness of the forest and the cleared farmlands we passed, and the singing of the birds that filled the air of Britain: skylark and blackbird, thrush and linnet and a hundred others.

As soon as we left Vortigern, turning our faces homeward, that changed. The days grew cold and the nights glacial, and the rain came down in torrents, driven by evil and malevolent winds that made a mockery of our woven travelling cloaks of thick, waxed wool. Our armour grew cold and heavy and began to chafe, and even our horses grew dispirited, walking head down and hunched against the bitter fury of what appeared to be a single, endless storm.

There were entire days when we found it impossible to light a fire, no matter how secure the shelter we had found. Everything that might conceivably have been induced to burn was soggy and waterlogged, and the feral wind howled about us incessantly, changing direction from gust to gust, whipping away the tinder that we tried to use and extinguishing each tiny flame we coaxed into life.

For eight consecutive days that storm held sway without abating, and we spent four of those days huddled in a cave, trying to keep ourselves warm. For the last two we had no food at all, although we had no lack of water. We sat or lay, huddled together for warmth, wrapped about with the blankets we had taken from our horses, who shared the cave with us at night. Ambrose made light of the conditions for the first few days, and I sought at first to match him, but I fell sick on the fourth day, overcome with chills and fever, and Ambrose became my nursemaid.

I have no recollections of that time beyond the point at which the end of my nose grew red and sore from sniffling and my ineffectual attempts to wipe away the constant streams of mucus that ran down from my nostrils to coat my lower face. I can recall feeling my teeth chattering painfully, and an ache in my bones from the jolting of my saddle, and then nothing. All knowledge of what passed thereafter came to me from Ambrose, upon whom I was as dependent as a babe in arms.

He it was who found the cave that sheltered us, coming upon it by sheer chance because, in his efforts to support me in my saddle, he allowed his horse to wander from the path and into a tiny clearing for some thirty paces beyond where he should have been. By the time he became aware of what had happened, the cave was directly in front of him—a cavern hollowed out by the stream of water that had poured through it for ages unimaginable. Above his head, the cliff from which the cavern had been carved reared high enough to block the screaming wind, and the floor of the sheltered clearing before the entrance to the cave was bare, thick-coated with the needles of the great evergreens that grew there.

Ambrose had lowered me to the sodden pine needles and gone into the cave. It was large, he found, and almost dry, though open to the sky in places. Its vaulted roof was formed by two great slabs of slanted stone that he suspected might once have been a single piece, sundered by some cataclysmic force in ages past. Rainwater trickled down each side of the cleft, and from time to time great gusts of wind would whistle down the narrow flue they formed, creating wondrous and frightening noises that set the horses stirring at night in fear. All in all, nevertheless, almost dry and almost warm and almost sheltered from the howling gales, the cavern was our salvation. There Ambrose had finally been able to make a fire from pine needles that he first spread out to dry for several hours, then slowly kindled and fed lovingly with tiny twigs and moss and small pine cones. He had fed his fire cautiously and with great skill, huddled over it to guard it from errant gusts of wind and adding strips of his own undertunic to augment its heat whenever it began to fail against the wetness of the other fuel. Eventually, after a long, long time, throughout which I lay shivering beneath a damp horse blanket, he had nurtured his tiny blaze to the point at which its own embers could generate sufficient heat to dry and then ignite each new piece of fuel. For the next four days, he kept a blazing pyre alight, feeding it constantly to keep up its heat, hoping to drive the fever from my bones in running sweat.

I found out, once I had regained consciousness and begun to rally, that he had spent the entire afternoon and evening of that first day gathering fuel, which he piled inside the entrance to the cave, taking no time to rest between trips and entering the cavern after each excursion only to check on me and throw more fuel on the fire.

He abandoned his search for firewood only when darkness fell, and by that time he had amassed enough to the keep the fire ablaze throughout the night, providing he awoke often enough to replenish it. I was of absolutely no assistance to him in any of that. I was, in fact, a grievous source of concern, for my breathing became heavy, laborious and irregular so that there were times, he told me later, when he lay straining to listen, holding his own breath while he waited for me to breathe again, all the time fearing I might not.

In the end, in the deepest part of the night, he abandoned his attempts to sleep and set to work to make me as dry, warm and comfortable as he could. Our heavy woollen cloaks, which he had hung stretched behind the fire, had dried by that time, as had our extra tunics and the other articles of clothing from our packs. Somehow, handling the solid deadweight of me, he had undressed me completely and then washed me with water heated on the fire, drying me afterward with a rough, dry cloth, chafing both heat and energy into my chilled limbs. That done, he had dressed me again in a dry tunic and wrapped me in my warm cloak before dragging me closer to the fire.

When he was sure there was no more he could do to increase my immediate, external comfort, he used the last of our provisions—dry, salted venison, dried fruit and roasted grain—to concoct a hot soup, which he fed to me with a bone spoon, until he could coax no more flavour or substance from what remained. The soup lasted for two days and he ate none of it. On the third day, by which time my poor brother was growing frantic, I recovered my senses, my fever dropped away and the wind subsided, although the rain continued to pour down.

All that day, too, driven by his relief that I had not yet died under his care, he hovered about me like a solicitous hen with a single, ailing chick, and even though neither of us ate that day, I had improved sufficiently by nightfall to convince him that I could survive now on my own and tend the fire for the length of time it might take him to go out into the woods and find us something more to eat. That night, he slept at last while I remained awake and fed the fire.

The following morning, satisfied that I was on the mend, Ambrose departed shortly after dawn and was back by mid-morning with the fruits of his hunt: a large hare, a small rabbit, wild garlic, onions, tender young nettles and a scrip full of fresh mushrooms. Within an hour of his return, the aroma from the leather boiling bag above the fire had set our saliva flowing and we were hard pressed to keep our hunger in abeyance until the meat was cooked sufficiently to eat. My contribution to the feast my brother set before us was a single twist of salt, the last I had, which had lain hidden in my saddlebag for weeks, but it was the crowning touch for an Epicurean stew.

My sickness, the debilitating fever and the ague in its train, had passed, but with its passing I inherited another malady, a maddening itch that consumed my entire body from my waist to the top of my crown. I quickly learned that I could not, or should not, scratch to relieve the discomfort it caused, for the mere act of scratching, while producing some slight relief, at the same time increased the burning itch surrounding the scratch marks. My skin bled in places, yet still I could not desist from clawing at myself.

I sought relief, eventually, by plunging my body into the cold stream in front of the cave—the rain had stopped some time that day—but then, chilled to the bone, I had to rub myself briskly to bring the warmth back to my skin, and with the friction and the returning warmth, the agony came back. I tried to dress myself, thinking that fully dressed I might feel better and we might be able to resume our interrupted journey, but the merest sensation of the clothes upon my skin was unbearable.

Two further days of that torment I bore before the itch abated, leaving me weak again and filled with nausea, and it was to be another three whole days before I felt strong enough to mount my horse and travel. From that day on, however, my recovery was swift and total, and we passed the intervening miles to Camulod without further hindrance or mishap.

We had been gone for almost three months and our eventual return was almost an anticlimax. Although our friends were glad to see us safely home again, and to make us welcome, none of them seemed to think we had been gone for any length of time. What had seemed an age to Ambrose and to me had passed in Camulod almost without notice.

Nothing of note had occurred during our absence. The weather had been fine, with no sign of the awful storms that had beset us on the road. The crops were ripening; children had been born; the Colony's cooperage had been expanded into a new building where more barrels could be fabricated at one time; our stonemasons had set themselves to building battlements upon the fortress walls, adding new crenellations to protect the sentries on the parapet walk; the last cantonment of new barrack-blocks had been completed; and a large new workshop had been built upon the hilltop to house the Colony's most hard-worked artisans, the weapons smiths, cobblers and carpenters who kept our soldiers and citizens dry-footed, well-equipped and adequately housed. Life had simply progressed in our absence, without alarums, and because of that our absence, while widely noted, had not been a matter of concern.

On our first night home, we dined with family and friends. Lucanus came to dinner, as did Donuil and Shelagh, and Hector and Julia. Ludmilla played hostess to us all. They made much of us then, so that we soon forgot the slight chagrin we had felt on our unheralded return. I had made Ambrose promise to say nothing of the strange sickness that had laid me low, and he kept his promise.

One change that had taken place during our absence was the remarkable growth that had occurred, in such a short space of time, in my young ward Arthur. In the space of one brief season, he appeared to have shot upward, so that the man he would become was suddenly quite startlingly apparent in the boy. I had left a child behind me in the month of May when we set out, but had returned in July to find a young man waiting to welcome me home.

I had made much of the boy at the time of our return, aware of the pleasure that had filled his face as he watched us arrive, although he had hung back on the fringes of the crowd gathered to welcome us, his expression radiant and his cheeks flushed with excitement as his eyes moved constantly from Ambrose to me and back again. As soon as he had seen me watching him, however, he had drawn back out of my sight, taking refuge behind the man in front of him. The gesture touched me, and I suddenly recalled the thrilling pleasure I had felt at his age, watching my father and his men returning from patrol. Then I had been desperately anxious not to miss a single word of what they would report, and frantic with fear that I might not be allowed to listen to the tales of their adventures, so I had always sought to hide, to obscure myself and become invisible, believing that only then would I be able to insinuate myself into their presence and listen from concealment in whatever hiding-place I could find.

Recalling that fevered anticipation with a poignant clarity, I made my way through the crowd and moved directly to the boy, where I squatted on one knee and greeted him as an equal, asking him how he had fared in our absence and then holding out my hand to him, inviting him to come with me. He had faced me squarely and with gravity, his gold-flecked eyes reflecting his amazement that I should seek him out directly. Then he had smiled his wonderful, open smile and placed his hand in mine before walking back with me, his shoulders proudly squared, to join the others.

Ambrose had watched this and now he stepped forward, too, grinning a welcome and winking fondly at the boy before ruffling his thick, brown, gold-streaked hair and drawing him into a quick embrace against his waist. Enjoying the boy's shy, embarrassed delight, I also saw the furtive glance he threw towards the crowd, and following the direction of his look, I saw his young companions Bedwyr and Gwin watching him with awe stamped plain upon their faces. Young Bedwyr, I noticed, was of a size with Arthur, a sturdy, strapping lad. The other boy, Gwin, Donuil and Shelagh's eldest, was smaller and younger, six years old to their seven.

As we filed in a small, informal procession from the main courtyard towards the quarters that had once accommodated the Varrus household and now were home to Ambrose and to me, we replied to the greetings of passing well-wishers, and young Arthur Pendragon walked between us, each of his hands in one of ours. Thereafter, ensconced comfortably against a wall in the family room, he listened closely, and no one sought, or thought, to question his presence.

Oddly enough, it was not until the arrival of Connor the following day, on what had become his annual visit, that I became aware of another, more important difference in the boy. Connor's arrival always stirred up a commotion, for he was a flamboyant figure who did nothing by halves, and the ease with which he coped with his infirmity invariably added to the wonder and excitement of his presence. This year, he came in grand style, quite different and more impressive than he had ever been before.

At sea, Connor was the master of his own movement, conning his galley confidently from the swinging chair built into the ship's structure to meet his needs. Ashore, he was scarcely less competent, covering the ground easily in his curious rolling gait, which took little notice of the eccentricities of the terrain. Only over long distances, like those that lay between Camulod and the distant shore, was he at a disadvantage, hampered by the sheer impossibility of crossing miles of rough country afoot, and so we had grown used to the sight of him arriving in a wagon, reclining like a Roman emperor surrounded by his bodyguard. This year, however, he arrived upright, driving

a brightly painted, two-wheeled chariot in the ancient style drawn by a
matched pair of sturdy Eirish garrons. From the first year of Liam Twistback's
coming, since which time his original three-year tenure had been indefinitely
extended, the transportation of animals from Eire in specially built galleys
had become almost commonplace, but the effect this gaudy chariot had upon
everyone was quite spectacular, and Ambrose and I had to push and elbow
our way through the dense crowd that gathered around the vehicle, exclaim-
ing in wonder at the cunningness of its construction. While Ambrose and
Connor were embracing each other, exchanging the usual friendly banter, I
examined the device and smiled in admiration, acknowledging the crafts-
manship and insight, and the good memory, that had gone into the building
of it.

On his previous visit, I had shown Connor the unique vehicle built years
before by Publius Varrus, a high-wheeled, single-axle cart, mounted on
springs of bowed iron. Varrus had called it his racing cart, and had used it
for travelling about the Colony's farm lands. Connor's new chariot had a
leather-covered iron seat, mounted upon a similar set of springs, more solidly
fashioned than the high cart's springs and evidently designed to be less resilient, yet far more comfortable than a solid wooden bar or bench. Connor
saw me looking at it as he turned to embrace me, and he matched my smile
with his own as he threw his arms about me.

"Yellow Head, good to see you, Brother," he said into my ear. "You like
my new chariot?"

"Aye," I said, returning his embrace. "It has some interesting features."

"It does, it does." He released me and leant sideways to slap the seat.
"Good ideas should be put to work, Merlyn. I told you that the first time I
saw your uncle's cart last year. A few adaptations along the lines of my galley
chair, and even a one-legged wreck like me may ride in comfort. Where's my
nephew?" He turned to look about him, ostentatiously pretending not to see
the boy who stood within arm's reach of him, peering up at him in worship.
"Arthur!" he roared. "Where's Arthur?"

"I'm here, Uncle Connor." The boy's voice was almost squeaking with
anxiety. Connor looked down towards the sound of it and pretended a great
leap of fright.

"By the light of Lud! Are you my nephew Arthur? No, you can't be! You're
much too big. Arthur Pendragon's just a little tad. I saw him but last summer
and he wasn't half the size of you."

The boy was bright pink with pleasure. "I grew up," he said shyly.

"Grew up? Grew up! You *soared*, lad, you exploded! Let's have a look at
you!" Connor bent quickly and picked him up, holding him effortlessly beneath the arms and swinging him with ease to the level of his eyes. "By the
gods," he said, holding him at arm's length, "I soon won't be able to lift you
at all if you keep growing this way. You're huge, boyo! Come here to me."

He clasped the lad to his breast, hugging him gently, his eyes closed, and
then he opened them again and winked at me before transferring his grip
and holding the boy out at arm's length again, his expression changing to
dismay.

"Ach, fool that I am, I never thought you would have grown so big so
quickly, and I brought you a wee, small gift, never thinking of the size of
you today."

Behind young Arthur's back, from the rear of Connor's train, two warriors came forward through the crowd, each leading a brace of ponies, all four animals virtually identical, piebald beauties with a grace and delicacy the like of which I had never seen. They were miniatures of our great war-horses, between one third and one half the size and perfectly proportioned, and they had been groomed until their black and white coats shone like burnished metal. Arthur's eyes were fixed on his uncle's, mirroring the dismay he saw there.

"What, Uncle?" he said, his voice almost quavering. "What is it?"

"Ach," Connor said, savouring the moment and drawing it out. "It's just a wee horse and three of its friends. You might not like it, now that you're so big. Look!"

He transferred the boy smoothly into the crook of his right arm and turned him to where he could see the animals. I moved, too, keeping my eyes on Arthur's. For several moments the boy stared at the four perfect little horses, failing to absorb what Connor had said, but then comprehension dawned and his face became suffused with joy and incredulity and a stillness fell upon the watching crowd.

The boy was unaware of it. His entire world was taken up with the entrancing little horses he was beginning to perceive as his. He turned from them to Connor, his mouth forming a question that his voice was incapable of generating. Connor grinned at him, squeezed him close again and then released him to slip smoothly to the ground.

"Aye, lad," he growled, his voice gruff with emotion at the boy's delight. "They're for you. Go now and look to them."

The crowd fell back, parting to clear the way for the boy, but he stood hesitant, not yet quite able to believe. He took one slow step, and then another, gazing at the sight before him, then turned back to face Connor.

"Four of them? For me?" Connor nodded, and the boy looked back at them and then again at Connor, his face betraying swift-moving thoughts and varying emotions. "Can I . . . ?" His voice trailed away.

"Can you what?"

The boy swallowed hard. "Give some away? I have friends." He stopped short, looking appalled, afraid his uncle might grow angry. But then his young face settled and he plunged on. "Can I give Bedwyr one? And Gwin?"

Connor laughed aloud. "Aye, you can, and Ghilleadh, too, if he's big enough to mount one. But pick out your own first. That's why there's four of them."

It was then, in that moment of courage, determination and unselfishness, that I marked the change in my young ward, and saw the future man within the boy.

XXX

"MERLYN, WHAT'S AN interregnum?"

It was an evening in early summer, and I was writing in my journal while Arthur, seated across from me, was reading one of his great grandfather's large, parchment books. I put down my pen and stretched, glad of the distraction.

"It's the name given to the time between the death of one ruler and the ascension of another. Where did you find that?"

"In here. Great grandfather Varrus was writing about something your grandfather said . . . That there had been so many emperors in power at one time for so long that there had been no interregnum in living memory." The boy's Latin was smooth and fluent, utterly colloquial, considering that he spoke the Celtic tongue most of the time.

"And how long d'you think that might have been?"

"Living memory? Simply what it says . . . No one alive could remember such a thing." He frowned slightly, watching my eyes. "Isn't that what it means?"

"So how long would it be?"

"Fifty years . . . sixty?"

I leaned back and locked my hands behind my head. "I think it's longer than that, if you consider the implications. Think about it."

He did, tilting his head slightly to one side, then dropping his eyes again to the page in front of him, a tiny frown of concentration between his brows. Finally he looked up, shaking his head in annoyance at himself. "I don't understand. Living memory is the memory of someone who is alive. Logic says it can't be anything else."

I smiled at his use of logic. "Perhaps so, but would you not expect a source of living memory to be someone very old, and might not his memories include the recollections of others who were old when he was young, and of their similar, stated memories of what others older than they had said?"

The boy's face cleared, and he nodded, beginning to smile. I prompted him gently.

"So, therefore, living memory means . . . ?"

". . . That the last time something like that happened was so long ago that no one can even recall hearing of such a thing."

"Precisely."

"So it really means for generations, or for ages unknown. But . . ."

"But what?"

"Interregnum. Isn't a *regnum* a king's lifetime? Rome had emperors, not kings. Shouldn't the word be interimperium?"

I grunted a laugh. "It should I suppose, but it's an ancient word, dating from the time when Rome had kings, before the Republic was founded. It means what it means—the time between rulers—I suppose no one ever thought it worth the effort to change it."

"What's the difference, the real difference I mean, between a king and an emperor?"

I pursed my lips and fingered the end of my nose, scratching at an itch. "You know the rules, Arthur. You tell me what you think the difference is . . . I correct you if I think you're wrong, and if we disagree, we find an arbitrator. So, tell me."

"Territory . . ." He was thinking deeply. "And power."

"How so?"

"Emperors have power over kings."

"Not always. Not if the kings wish to deny that power."

"Then there is war, and the Emperor always wins, because he has the power of Empire behind him."

"Always? Then where is the Empire today? Alaric and his Goths sacked Rome before you were born, and Alaric wasn't even a king, he was a warrior— a warlord. So what does *that* imply?"

The boy sat silent for a long time, and then raised his head to answer me, and I knew from the expression in his eyes that he was far from confident about what he would say.

"I thought Alaric was king of the Goths, but even so, his victory means that the Empire was weak, too weak to withstand his strength . . . and that implies . . . that the man, the leader . . . the man himself . . . contains the greatness or the weakness . . . the success or failure of . . . of . . ."

"Of his enterprise, Arthur, whether it be an empire, a kingdom, or a chieftain's sway over his people. Bravo! It is the leader who commands the times in which he lives. Alexander, Scipio Africanus, Gaius Marius, Julius Caesar, Caesar Augustus, Marcus Aurelius, Theodosius, Flavius Stilicho, and Alaric the Goth. Each stood against towering odds and fearsome enemies; enemies the likes of Pompey the Great, Darius and Xerxes and Hannibal— and Stilicho and Alaric were ranged against each other, until the emperor Honorius had Stilicho murdered and opened his own empire to defeat by Alaric."

"Hmm . . ." A long, contemplative silence followed that musing sound, and I made no attempt to break it. The boy was deep in thought. Finally he nodded his head gently. "So it's the leader who's important. It doesn't matter what he rules; empire, kingdom, town or fort. It's him, and the example that he sets, that inspires other men to fight for him and win."

"Aye, that's right, and the winning is very important. Never forget, Arthur, that in order to win, men must *want* to fight . . . And bear in mind, that doesn't necessarily hold true when you reverse it. It's not the same to say that to fight, men must want to win. Not at all the same. But to win, men must want to fight, they must be inspired, willing to follow their leader to the death. That willingness to die achieving victory for another man's purposes only results from great and inspiring leadership. No sane man will willingly follow someone he detests or disrespects. He might be constrained to do it, forced to fight, but then he'll never fight for any other purpose than to save his own life, and that means he'll never fight enthusiastically, to win a great victory for his leader. The lesson is ended. Out with you, now! I have work to finish here . . ." I paused, suddenly seeing the troubled expression on his face. "What? What is it?"

He shook his head, as though to dislodge an annoying thought. "Can't a bad man be a good leader, though? Not all victories have been won by great leaders, and some great leaders have been defeated. Isn't that true?"

"Yes, it is." His face remained clouded. "You seem perplexed. What's troubling you, Arthur?" There was a long silence.

"Was . . . was my father a good leader, Merlyn?"

The unexpectedness of the question, and the tremulous tone in which it was posed almost overwhelmed me, and I was suddenly and fully aware that this was an eight-year-old boy who spoke to me. Even as I write the words now, they appear fatuous in their presumption that I could have been unaware of such a thing, but in dealing with Arthur Pendragon, even in his extreme youth, it was impossible not to treat him as a perceptive and intuitive intellect, far older than his years. Now, with one question, he had reestablished his youthfulness and insecurity. The logical, analytical thinker was banished, and the tentative, unformed boy revealed. He had never known his father, Uther Pendragon, and we seldom spoke of him, simply, I believed, because he had never directly influenced the boy's life. Because of that, until this moment, had anyone asked me I would have opined that the boy seldom thought of the father he had never known. Now, with that one question, I knew otherwise, and I knew also that it was time to deal with my neglect. I leaned back and crossed my arms on my chest, considering my next words carefully. Arthur sat watching me tensely.

"Your father was not simply a good leader, Arthur, he was a superb leader. His men would have followed him anywhere—and they did. He was the best we had."

"Better than you, Merlyn?"

I smiled. "Aye, lad, far better me than me in many, many ways. He was bolder, more ferocious, more high-spirited and valorous. Uther Pendragon was a truly mighty warrior."

A beat of silence, then: "But was he a good man?"

"None finer. He might not have been good in the way bishops and other churchmen would like us to be good—always at prayer and full of piety— but your father was good in the way of simple nobility, justice and kindness. Some might have thought him wild and undisciplined, but he had a gentleness in him to match the wild rages that could sometimes sweep him, and his self-discipline was absolute, in its own fashion . . . And he harmed none who did not harm him." A very large portion of my mind was writhing in discomfort with my own memories of what I had once believed of Uther, but I dared show no discomfort here, and I knew well that the guilt causing these feelings was mine alone and had nothing to do with Uther as he was and had been.

"He was defeated and killed."

"He was killed in a skirmish, Arthur; struck down from behind in a wild scuffle in dense woods, and the man who killed him didn't know who he was. It was an accident of war, not a death in formal battle, defeated in the field."

"But he was defeated in battle, was he not? His armies were destroyed." This was growing difficult. I nodded to emphasize my words.

"Yes, he was defeated in a battle. His army was defeated on one occasion. But it was *one* army, and it was not large, and he had been in the field for long months without respite, and Lot of Cornwall caught him between three armies, two of those fresh and unblooded. There was no grand strategy involved, no contest between generals. Lot had more men, and they were fresh; your father had fewer and they were tired."

He sat staring at me, his face unreadable. To fill the silence, I began counting to myself. I had reached twenty before the boy spoke again.

"If he was a good leader, he should have known Lot was trying to entrap him. A leader's first responsibility is to the men under his command. You always say that."

"Well, yes, I do, and that's true . . ." I found myself trapped by my own lessons. "But—"

"There can be no buts, Merlyn. I've heard you say, many times, that command responsibility has no buts in it."

I silently cursed the exactness of his memory, but could not deny what he had said. I tried prevarication, not expecting it to be successful. "That is true, too, Arthur, but there are always exceptions to any rule. This occasion was one of those exceptions. Your father was concerned for you and your mother at the time. You were but new born and she was barely recovered from your birth, and still unfit to travel."

"Then he should have sent us away to safety with some of his men. He should have remained to command his army."

"No, Arthur, I cannot allow you to condemn your father this way. You were not there. I was, although I was too far away to be of assistance to him. Your father was dealing with Lot of Cornwall—a liar, a treacherous coward and a weakling. Lot hired alien mercenaries from beyond the seas to do his fighting for him. He won by deviousness and perfidy, and he made sure that he himself was never in the slightest danger. Someone killed him on the day your father died, for I found his body hanging from a tree, but I don't believe it was any of ours who brought about his death. I believe one of Lot's own killed him, perhaps for vengeance, since Lot was open-handed with his treachery, abusing friend and foe alike. Your father, had he not been killed the way he was, stabbed in the back in a petty woodland brawl, would have emerged the victor in Cornwall that very day. He had fought for that victory, and he had earned it. His untimely death in that woods was a tragedy."

"A tragedy that might have been avoided, had he not permitted my mother and me to divert him from his duty."

I blinked at the boy in disbelief, seeing the rigid, unyielding lines of pain in his young face. "Arthur, how can you even think such a thing? That is simply not true!"

He glared at me, pale faced. "Women and war do not mix. You told me that yourself, only last week. If Mark Antony had not become involved with Cleopatra of Egypt, you said, all history would have been different. That involvement was Antony's tragedy."

I had said exactly that, but now I denied it without the slightest hesitation. "Nothing of the kind," I snapped. "The Queen was the means of Antony's downfall, but Antony's true tragedy was that he was pitted against an even greater leader than himself, Octavius Caesar, who was destined to become Caesar Augustus, Caesar the Great, first Emperor of Rome."

The boy sat blinking at me now, his face less bleak looking, and I watched him review what I had said, absorbing the possibility that the tragedy I had mentioned might not be the tragedy he had understood. I spoke on, making my own point now, attempting to ameliorate his.

"It's the greatness that counts, Arthur. Pompey the Great, Caesar the Great, Alexander the Great, Xerxes the Great. There are hundreds of such names, and some of them will be remembered forever. Bad leaders may win battles, from time to time, through sheer numerical superiority, the way Lot did in his encounter with your father. They may even win wars, from time to time. But they never achieve true greatness, Arthur. Your father might have, had he lived. Greatness is an attribute bestowed upon a leader by those he leads, and those, being men, are loath to ascribe greatness to a man who has not earned it. But your father's men believed in Uther's greatness, and so must you. Believe me, a man may have the gift of leadership inborn in him, but greatness is something that he has to learn, and to earn, beneath the eyes of those who trust him and believe in what he represents. He must earn that faith through a lifetime of being trustworthy—no easy task, for there can be no lapses in his record—and if he ever should betray that trust, for one moment, and be discovered, as he must—then it is lost forever. Uther Pendragon was never false to any man. He was a terrible enemy, once angered, but he was never false and his integrity was never questioned, even by his enemies—with the sole exception of Lot of Cornwall, who was more of a mad dog than a man. I promise you, no man who deals in slyness or in treachery or duplicity can ever gain that pinnacle of greatness. He may succeed in some things, for a time, but he will fail and fall eventually.

"Integrity, on the other hand, was an attribute your father possessed in abundance, and integrity, entailing honesty and forthrightness, courage, bravery, honour and strict justice in dealing with all men—and women, too—contains the beginnings of greatness. You do know the difference between bravery and courage, don't you?"

As I had spoken my encomium to his father, the boy's face had changed, the tension and the harried look receding visibly as he evaluated and accepted what he heard me say. I had never lied to him and now I could see he believed my words completely, true as they were, and his resilient good nature was reasserting itself visibly. Now my last question, the tone of it, and my ironic look, had the effect I hoped to achieve. He smiled and stood up, closing the large, leather bound book he had been reading.

"Bravery is something you can experience on the spur of the moment, faced with danger. To have courage, you must think about the dangers in advance, then weigh the risks, and then do what you have to do, despite your fears." His face grew serious again. "Uncle Connor is that kind of leader, too, isn't he? With integrity, I mean. His men would follow him anywhere, and they don't care that he has a wooden leg."

"No, they don't, because it's not important. They follow what they love in him. The integrity. The fierceness and the courage, loyalty and honesty that make him who and what he is. That's what I mean when I talk to you of leadership—your Uncle Connor is another great leader. Observe him closely, and see if you can discern what it is about him that endears him most to his men. Then, when you have followers of your own, remember what you saw."

"I wonder when he'll come?"

"He'll come when he arrives, and not before. Now away with you before it grows too dark for me to see what I'm writing."

I didn't see him leave, and he closed the door silently behind him, but I could not return to my writing after that. I had too much on my mind, and none of it had to do with my diurnal notes. The lad had managed to surprise me yet again with the depth and scope of his thinking, and I allowed myself now to think about the progress he had made in everything we sought to teach him.

More than a year had passed since the day Connor delivered the four matched ponies, and he was now overdue to return again from Eire. In the intervening months, Arthur and his young friends had grown to be a familiar sight throughout the length and breadth of our estates, riding their startlingly coloured ponies everywhere in perfect freedom, thanks to the absence of any kind of threat to our well-being, and all four boys including Ghilleadh, the youngest, at barely six years old now rode like young centaurs.

Arthur, their uncontested leader in all things, was growing like a sapling starved for light, shooting upwards with a speed and vigour that, at times, made him appear to be too thin. Lucanus, however, dismissed my fears on that each time I mentioned it, which was quite frequently. The boy, he said, was healthy as a horse. His bones were good, his shoulders broad and likely to be massive, and his chest, though seeming to be frail, was deep and well-formed, with solid ribs. First, the boy must grow to his ordained height, Luke said, pointing out that we Britannici had never been a stunted family. Once his upward growth had been achieved, a matter of another count of years to match the eight he had attained so far, the rest would grow to match. In the meantime, he maintained, filling the lad's quick mind held more importance than the simple and self-sustaining development of his body.

That much I knew was true, and we were working hard in concert, and much to Arthur's dismay at times, on educating him for the task he would assume in time to come. Like all boys, Arthur himself would have preferred his schooling to be different. Given the choice, which I was careful to prevent, he would have opted for the parts he loved instinctively and consigned the other, less enthralling aspects of his training to some unspecified period called "later." But then, he had no notion he was being trained for anything more demanding than the life he knew today. He was aware that, as the ward of Ambrose and me, he would assume our tasks some day and work for the welfare and safety of the Colony that was his home, but he was eight years old and time meant nothing to him. We were immortal in his eyes, and boyhood was eternal, and so he lived a boy's life of constant challenge and adventure, taking it hard sometimes when there were days of brilliant sunshine that were lost to him because his lessons kept him within walls. All in all, however, he seemed well content to learn, no matter what the topic, and his mind was like a sponge, absorbing and retaining all we poured into it.

To make the process seem less personal and more palatable to the lad, we had decided, years before, that his close friends and cousins should be educated with Arthur, so that on days when he was made to fret indoors, he had at least the companionship of misery shared; Bedwyr and Gwin, and latterly Ghilleadh, suffered along with him, as did Ambrose and Ludmilla's daughters Luceiia and Octavia.

Their teaching was divided among six of us, with additional input from many others. Primarily, however, Ambrose, Lucanus, Donuil, Shelagh, Ludmilla and I myself had thought long and with gravity to devise a program that would meet the needs we had been able to define, all of us aware of the importance of the task we were delineating. The training must embrace two major elements, military and civil. Of that there was no doubt. Beyond that division, however, lay a country of bewildering diversities made the more difficult to traverse by the simple fact that none of us save Luke had any experience as teachers. Each of us had skills and knowledge to pass on, nevertheless, and some of those we shared with others of the group, so we had devised a program of instruction, hesitant and tentative at first, when Arthur was but four years old. That program had matured steadily since then, as we gained confidence and came to realize the nature, and the hunger, of the bright young minds with which we dealt.

In the range of what we termed "the civil studies" I was in charge of languages, although the task was shared by everyone. We taught the children patiently to read and then to write in Latin, eschewing Greek because it was not spoken in our land by then and we had few Greek texts. In spoken languages, the children worked in Latin but naturally spoke the local tongue, a liquid mixture born of Celtic and of Latin roots that had no name but flourished as a common, daily language known to all the people in our region. To keep the children's interest lively and alert, I also spoke with them much of the time in the Pendragon tongue, unsullied by Latin contaminations, and Donuil soon accustomed himself to speaking to them at all times in Erse, in which all six children could soon converse. Ambrose even attempted, at one point, to teach them the language used by Hengist's Danes, but that was a fruitless task, since his own knowledge of the tongue was rudimentary and there was no one near our lands who could assist him, and in any case young Bedwyr was the only one who showed the slightest interest in the alien sounds of that harsh language.

Lucanus soon emerged as the *magister* of the small room in his Infirmary that we converted to a schoolroom, and he throve on the responsibility. He it was who taught them basic logic and philosophy, and his keen mind was stretched further than it had ever been, he often said, when he approached the matter of how to interest such young people in simple debate and elementary polemics. He also taught them mathematics—principally the boys, although little Octavia was smartest of them all in this—and the principles of engineering based upon the geometry of Euclid, which he himself had mastered as a boy. And he recruited his own outstanding pupil Ludmilla to teach them the basics of skeletal anatomy and simple medicine.

Hector, Julia's husband and the father of Bedwyr, a councilor and an able administrator, worked with them one morning each alternate week to explain the elements of government, instructing them patiently, and with great success, on the way in which each of the various units and elements within our Colony—a working microcosm of all organised society—fed, and was in its turn dependent upon, the function of the others.

On reading what I have just written, it appears to me I might have conveyed the impression that the children were subjected to an endless litany of disciplines, but that was not the case at all. Their lives were open and enjoyable and the knowledge they acquired was gathered across the span of years. Few of the subjects they studied were ever covered simultaneously and they had ample time for laughter and for simply being children. The lessons I had learned in that regard from Aunt Luceiia and from the writings and example of Publius Varrus were yet vibrant memories.

Afternoons were for military studies and were the province of my brother Ambrose, assisted by me and by a wide range of willing volunteers. None of the boys was ever known to bewail that aspect of his learning and they learned all that we could teach them, which was much indeed.

They learned first to ride, of course, and part of that instruction was the care and maintenance of all on which their horsemanship relied: their animals, their saddlery and their equipment. They learned to groom and feed their horses, in that order, and how to mend, repair and even fashion saddlery. And as their bodies grew and strengthened, they learned weaponry, from the care and use of swords, daggers and shields to the techniques of spear handling and bow craft. They learned tracking; how to read the signs of passage left by men and animals. They learned to hunt and fish and forage, and to find dry kindling in the worst of weathers, even under snow. They learned, too, the basic elements of drill and discipline for infantry and cavalry, marching and counter-marching, forming up and deploying alongside our regular troops, both infantry and cavalry.

In years to come, Ambrose and I would teach them strategy and tactics, but in the meantime we fed their questing, eager minds with stories of adventure and of feats of arms and mighty victories. Arthur in particular was entranced by the tales of Alexander, whom men called The Great, and of his famed Companions, the noble warriors who campaigned, at their own expense, as bodyguards to the young Emperor from Macedonia seven hundred years ago and more. One day, enthralled by an account unheard before, he asked me how I came to know all this, and I told him of Uncle Varrus and his books. From that time on I would often find the boy, on rainy days, perched on a stool in the great Armoury where I had spent so much time in my youth, engrossed as I had been in Publius Varrus's accounts of days long past. And at such times I thought invariably about the gleaming sword that lay, its existence unsuspected, beneath the floor-boards at his feet. I was pleased, and more than pleased, with the boy's growth in every way. He was hungry, ravenous for knowledge, and he had the time to pursue it without disruption in his bright young life.

That thought by itself should have stirred me towards caution, but I was blind to its implications, allowing myself to be lulled by uneventful days and balmy summer evenings. I had completely lost sight of the fact that anyone familiar with the ways of hunting birds, the eagle or the hawk, should always be aware that death and destruction can come swooping from a cloudless sky with the speed and impact of a falling stone.

Never in my life, before or since that summer month of June in 440, have I been so unthinkingly careless of my duties for so long a time, and I have no excuse to offer for my dereliction other than that I was distracted by a haunting fear that peaked on the very day disaster struck. It was the most awful fear I have ever known, a crippling, dreadful burden of uncertainty and creeping terror against which I had fought so well and for so long that it was almost concealed from me in daylight, and I allowed myself to hide from it by the mere act of denying its existence. By night, however, the debilitating terror took on a life of its own that left me powerless to sleep or even to think with anything resembling clarity.

Lucanus had grown concerned for me, I know, for he had asked me several times what ailed me, and upon my protest that I felt quite well he had held up a bronze mirror to my eyes, bidding me see how haggard I had grown. My other friends knew, too, that something was amiss, but I temporized by claiming that I could not sleep at night owing to an injury, a twisted back I had sustained mounting a skittish horse. They accepted that, but I know they all watched me closely.

Then, on that terrible day, Lucanus held up another mirror to me, this time an abstract mirror of words, and all unknowing, forced me to confront my fears and make admission to myself.

It was a hot afternoon of blazing sunshine, unseasonably so for June, and he and I were seated in the shady courtyard of the Infirmary, sipping cool wine and talking about the children and how much Arthur was growing to resemble Uther, the father whom the boy had never known. That led to a discussion of men and their physiology, and how resemblances were passed from parents to their offspring, the most startling example being my own resemblance to my half-brother Ambrose; two different mothers, yet two sons like beans from the same pod.

"No." Lucanus shook his head then. "No," he repeated, quite clearly recalling something. "It's more than that, Caius, more than mere parentage, father to son. The most amazing likeness I have ever seen, apart from you and Ambrose, and one I had forgotten for many years until now, was between a young man and his mother's brother, who was much younger than she." He paused, remembering. "I said it was amazing, and it was. The son bore not the slightest resemblance to his father, for I met him, too, one time when he came visiting. It really was extraordinary, and I can hardly believe I had forgotten it. Phideas Arripas was the wife's brother's name, and he and I were students together in Alexandria, as was his nephew, who was no more than two years his junior. The two were as alike as you and Ambrose, and yet the resemblance sprang from Phideas's sister to her son. The son, by the way, was Mordechai Emancipatus."

When Lucanus spoke that name it was as though the air about me darkened. My breath caught in my throat and my heart began to hammer loudly, as though it beat against my eardrums. Abruptly, I found myself on my feet, gazing about me wildly, aware of Lucanus's expression as he stared at me in astonishment. Blindly, gasping to control the sudden nausea that racked me, I lurched away, gesturing savagely to Luke to stay where he was.

Somehow, probably because of the heat that kept most people in the coolness of their homes that afternoon, I made my way across the entire fort without attracting any more attention to myself, although I knew that I was reeling like a drunken man, and then I found myself inside the stables, where I sagged against a wall and removed my helmet. I felt better after that, but my guts were awash with churning fear. I sensed someone approaching, one of the duty troopers, and bent quickly to a trough, plunging my head beneath the cold water. The man, whoever he was, had passed on when I straightened again to gulp a breath, drenching my upper body with the water from my head. The single certainty within me was that I must leave this place at once and make my way to where I could be alone to scream aloud my grief and guilt and crawling horror. No thought was in my mind that I might fight, or ever overcome, the brutal, soul-destroying terror I could feel bludgeoning the crumbling edges of my sanity.

I have no memory of saddling my horse, but as I drew myself into the saddle, the training of years somehow took precedence even over my consuming panic, preventing me from setting out defenseless. I rode directly to my day quarters in the Praetorium, our headquarters, and collected my bow and quiver. Then, as I mounted my horse again, I heard Lucanus call my name and felt his hand grasping at my ankle. Blinking my eyes clear and swallowing hard, I made myself turn and look down at him. He was distraught, his face taut with anxiety, and I knew, even in my despair, that I must say something to him.

"Forgive me, old friend." One small, quite lucid part of me was amazed to hear how calm my voice sounded. "I am not myself. A sudden nausea. I thought a ride might clear my head. A long, hard ride. Don't be concerned for me. I'll come back soon, when I feel better, and you can try your magic arts on me."

I wheeled my mount away and left him standing there in front of the headquarters building as I made my way out of the fort and down the hill and thence across the great campus that lay beneath, riding without awareness or volition, yet guiding my horse surely on the shortest route to the hidden valley that had been mine alone since childhood. It had been months since I had last been there, but Germanicus knew the way and brought me safely down the narrow, winding, bush-lined track among the enfolding hills to where my dead wife waited by the tiny lake, and there, by her graveside, I fell face down and wept, allowing all the horror I felt to engulf me.

I had suspected my true condition for months, even while denying every sign of it and concealing it inside me from my very self. As soon as I had heard the name of Mordechai upon Lucanus's lips, however, all of my pretences and self-delusion had fallen away in the appalling recognition of what I had become. I was a leper! The certain knowledge filled me, making me want to scream my terror and revulsion and disgust to all the world. Leper! Unclean, condemned to banishment from all the world of men. Merlyn Britannicus, Leper!

My sickness of the previous June, the weakness and the dreadful, scourging itch, had come again that winter, and even then I had denied the fear in me, fleeing into isolation in order to avoid the analytical, physician's eyes of Lucanus. He had tended me throughout the first phase of the sickness, to be sure, the fever and the draining weakness it entailed, but as soon as the fever had passed I had removed myself to here, in secrecy made possible only by the fact that Ambrose and Donuil, the only two who knew this place, were both away from Camulod at that time. Here, alone in my Avalon, I had borne the itchy, scaling ugliness of red and angry skin for eight whole days. This time, however, when the itch abated, the scaliness it caused remained, in patches, clear upon the skin above my waist, and lasted for weeks. Even after it had faded, however, I found flakes and patches of discomfort, not painful, and with no itch, but persistent.

Now, as my tears dried, I sat erect and, talking distractedly all the time of slight, inconsequential things to my dead wife Cassandra, who lay beneath the ground close by my side, I unfastened and removed my armour and shrugged out of my tunic, stripping until I wore only my boots, and gazing down at myself almost abstractedly, searching my body for deliverance from the horror in my soul, hearing some tiny voice of sanity within my mind urging me to be calm and search with care, and to draw strength from what my eyes told me: my skin was clean and sound, my body whole, and the contagion that so threatened me lay in my mind alone, huddled among my other, twisted and obscene night fantasies. But my eyes went directly to the site of all my fears.

The hair on my chest was blond and soft, approaching whiteness in its downy goldenness, but there was one patch, slightly larger than the first joint of my thumb and roughly circular in shape, that was pure white. Beneath it, faint yet noticeable, the skin around the edges of the area was pink, approaching redness, and the central area of skin was as white as the hair it bore. It seemed hardly significant, a small anomaly, but I had seen such marks before, on Mordechai's own chest. They were the early lesions of the foulest sickness known to man, the awful, lingering death-in-life called leprosy.

I noticed some time later that my blood was still bright red and clean-looking as it oozed from the skin around my knife point, and only then did I realise what I had done. The wound in my breast was a fingersbreadth deep, the knife blade sharply angled to cut beneath the lesion and slip on between my ribs into my heart. And then I was on my feet again, throwing the dagger from me so that it splashed into the shallows of the lake, and I was drenched in chilling, icy sweat. So close had I come to ultimate despair! Terrified now with a different kind of fear, I sprang to my feet and shrugged into my tunic again, pulling it quickly over my head to cover my nakedness and ignoring the blood streaming from my chest. I then seized my bow and quiver without thought, and leapt up onto Germanicus. My feet found the stirrups by habit, and I sank my spurs cruelly into the horse, sending him surging forward in a bounding leap so that he took the pathway at the gallop, branches whipping wildly at my face and arms as we crashed up the hill. Once on the top, I rowelled him again, spurring him viciously as he thundered across the hillside, avoiding trees, bushes and scattered rocks at breakneck speed and keeping his feet beneath him only by the grace of God. For miles we rode that way, our pace unflagging, until I felt the great horse falter as he gained a crest and I knew that he would soon fall dead.

Ashamed, and panting with exhaustion myself, I reined him to a halt and stripped the saddle from him, making a penance of the strength I used to groom him and to wipe him down, and hugging his great neck against my face until his laboured breathing and the trembling in his limbs had subsided. Then, after an age, when he was calm and breathing normally again, I led him down to water at a brook, after which I turned him free to graze, seating myself upon a fallen log and watching him with an ache inside my breast.

Within the space of one short hour, I had come close to killing both myself and my horse. Self-loathing roiled inside me and I found myself despising my own weakness, for what was sickness, if not weakness?

The blood on my chest had dried. I pulled my tunic off again and examined the wound. It had scabbed over, but when I probed it with a fingertip I felt nothing, and I recalled what Lucanus had said about the lesions. They were numb, incapable of registering sensations. I sighed and replaced my tunic, feeling dead inside, then led Germanicus back to where his saddle lay and harnessed him again.

As I swung myself up to his back again, I heard the sound of distant hoofbeats, clear in the still air of the afternoon, drumming hard against the hillside far below, on the other side of the crest of the small hill on which I sat. I realised then that I had no idea where I was. I had paid no attention to the path we followed when we left the valley, riding blindly over hill and dale in my despair. Now, although I had no real interest other than dulled curiosity, and simply because it seemed the natural thing to do, I kicked Germanicus forward to the crest to see who had intruded upon my solitude.

I recognised Shelagh immediately, though she was far distant and riding towards me through a screen of low bushes and small saplings. All riders have a personal style that makes them instantly recognisable to those who know them, and there was no mistaking Shelagh's. She was flat out, bent forward almost over her mount's ears, her long hair flying free behind her. My first reaction was pleasant surprise, but that was quickly followed by alarm. She was alone, and she should not have been. She had set out much earlier that day with Julia and Ludmilla and the children to go swimming in the wide and shallow river hole that was a favourite spot with all the youth of Camulod.

The thought was not complete before I had put Germanicus to the slope, flying to intersect Shelagh's path. Then I saw her pursuers and reined him back again. There were two of them, on foot, bounding downwards towards her on an intersecting course from the crest of another hill, across from me. They had not yet seen me. My mind drew imaginary intersecting lines from them to her, and I realised that they would intercept her soon, before I could. Now I knew where I was, and how they could pursue her on foot, when she was mounted. The path on which she rode was almost circular, making its way almost entirely around a low but steep-sided and densely treed hill between Camulod and the river. If they had seen her from the top of it, they would have had time to cut across in front of her, even on foot.

As that thought occurred to me, one of the two stopped running and brought up a bow, and with a thrill of fright I recognised it as a Pendragon longbow. Even as I flung myself down from the saddle he loosed his shot and I watched it helplessly as it sped across the intervening distance and zipped between Shelagh's body and her horse's neck. Then, filled with flaring rage, I launched an arrow of my own and watched with satisfaction as it took the fellow squarely in the chest, sending him crashing on his back. His companion had seen none of this, intent upon reaching Shelagh's path and unaware that he was approaching me as well with every leaping step. I sighted on his chest and then, for no clear reason that I could define, shifted my aim and shot him in the groin, above and to the right of his genitals, piercing the socket where his thigh bone met his pelvis. He doubled over violently, crashing headlong downhill to land on his face, screaming in shock and pain. I shouted to Shelagh, calling her by name and jumping back up into my saddle. She reined in brutally, bringing her horse down onto his hindquarters and gaping at me in disbelief.

Our meeting was constrained by shock on her part and bewildered incomprehension on mine, for now I saw that Shelagh wore no clothes other than a long, light cloak that failed utterly to conceal her body. She seemed completely unaware of her nakedness, however, and sat gazing at me wide-eyed until I reined in my horse beside her.

"Merlyn," she said, her voice sounding very strange. "Where did you come from?"

I barely heard her words, my mind and eyes full of the bareness of her body beneath the long, light mantle. The white smoothness of her belly and the skin between her breasts was slashed diagonally by the broad, black band of her knife belt, its five sheathed knives forming a line of overlapping crosses on her flesh. I raised my eyes to hers and saw the blankness there, the emptiness, and all at once I felt my guts contract in fear, so that I had to struggle to find the words I needed to say.

"Shelagh, where are the others, the children? What has happened? Why are you here like this and who were these people?"

The harsh tone of my voice must have penetrated her dazed mind, for her eyes widened and grew more alert and she turned her head quickly towards the man I had crippled, who now squirmed, screaming, on the hillside just above her and to her left. She looked at him and shuddered, then dropped her reins, crossing her arms over her bare breasts.

"Safe," she whispered. Then her eyes quit the writhing wretch and turned back to me as her voice grew stronger. "The children are safe. I left them with Ludmilla and rode for help."

"Like that?" I nodded towards her nakedness.

She looked down at herself without interest or concern, then her hands moved again, drawing the edges of her mantle together so that they covered her thighs. "Aye, like this. There was no time."

"No time? In God's name, Shelagh, what happened?"

She shook her head, a terse, violent motion like a shudder.

"We were attacked. By strangers, like these." She indicated the two men I had shot. "Julia and the children were attacked. Ludmilla and I weren't there. We had moved away, out of sight, but we heard their screams. Arthur and Bedwyr were both hurt, but not killed. Julia is dead."

Julia's face flashed before my eyes and vanished, banished by the news that Arthur had been hurt. Shelagh's tone rang in my ears like a death knell. A thousand questions sprang into my mind, but I rejected all of them as they clamoured for my attention. There was no point in asking questions other than the most important one.

"Where are they now?"

Shelagh twisted around in her saddle to look back the way she had come, then faced me again, raising her hands to her face, which she squeezed and rubbed as though washing it. When she spoke again, I knew she had regained possession of herself.

"Not far. I had thought them safe, but now I see I could be wrong. If there were these two, whom I had not seen, there might easily be others." She stopped, eyeing my bow and the quiver of arrows that hung from my shoulders. "You only have your bow? Where is your sword?"

I jerked my head impatiently, hefting the bow. "This is enough to kill with."

She thrust her hands through the front of the mantle, seizing her reins again and pulling her horse around, kicking him into motion. "Come quickly. It's not far."

As I galloped behind her back along the narrow path, the light cloak fluttered high around her, fanned by the speed of our passage, but I saw nothing erotic in her naked loveliness. I was aware only of the vulnerability of her bare flesh and of my own unarmoured body, clad in a light tunic. And I wondered why she was unclothed and why the belt of knives that hung, as always, from her right shoulder did so beneath her cloak, rather than over it.

It was less than a curving mile from where our paths had crossed to where the river ran, slow and somnolent, through the grassy glade that had been a favourite summer spot in Camulod for generations. We reached it in a far shorter time than I would have expected, and as we broke from the screen of trees surrounding the meadow I was already looking around for signs of life. There were signs of death everywhere. I saw four or five men's bodies scattered on the grass and noted that the only blood in sight lay spilled around them. Shelagh ignored the bodies, standing in her stirrups, looking about her. As she saw me look at her, she wrenched her horse to the left and sent him bounding down the gently sloping gradient towards the water, to where a giant elm hung outward over the wide swimming pool. I pulled up when she did, and saw a flash of immobile whiteness against the bank. I swung down from my saddle and ran forward.

It was Julia. She lay face down in the water, bereft of all humanity and grace, her long hair drifting slowly about her head, one ankle caught in a snag of tree root on the bank. Her bare, white buttocks thrust obscenely upward above the surface of the water, stained with blood in the crease, and a great diagonal slash high on her back gaped open, ragged-edged, washed clean by its immersion and eloquently fatal. My chest ached with the pain of my discovery and I moved instinctively to rescue her, but I knew she was dead and that my first task must be to find the others. Grimly, I spun on my heel and ran back to remount.

Before I was upright, Shelagh had kicked her horse forward again, pulling it round to the right and heading uphill, back towards the fringe of the forest that surrounded the clearing. I stayed close behind her, urging Germanicus to greater speed as we bounded up the steepening slope and into the undergrowth, climbing steadily until we breasted the first hill and Shelagh stopped, holding up her hand. As I drew level with her she stood in her stirrups again, calling Ludmilla's name, and was answered immediately by a cry from farther down the hill, deep within a dense thicket. We rode forward slowly, picking our way among trees and saplings, and as we went, the three oldest boys, Arthur, Gwin and Bedwyr, came running to meet us, calling at the tops of their voices. They were all safe, although Arthur had a blood-filled lump the size of a goose egg on his right temple and Bedwyr's left arm was heavily bandaged in a blood-stained cloth. Gwin seemed to be unharmed. Ludmilla emerged from the brush behind them, holding little Luceiia and Octavia by the hands. Behind her came the youngest boy, Ghilleadh, his eyes wide and staring, his face streaked with dirt and tear tracks.

Once the initial storm of greetings had passed and I had ascertained that they had been in no other danger since Shelagh's departure, I turned to Shelagh herself. In deference to the children's presence, she had closed her cloak modestly, holding it tight around her, its edges twisted in one hand.

"Your clothes," I said. "Where are they?"

She tossed her head, indicating the slope behind us. "Up there some-where."

"Find them, and dress. I'm going to see to Julia."

As soon as I said his mother's name, young Bedwyr's face crumpled and he began to weep, moaning deep in his throat, and Ludmilla swept him into her arms, comforting him and making crooning sounds of grief and sympathy. Arthur stiffened, his shoulders hunched, then raised his hand to the huge lump on his forehead, covering it with his palm, and turned away from all of us.

"Arthur." He turned towards me. "Where are your horses?"

The boy swallowed hard, visibly fighting to keep from breaking into tears as had his friend. He shook his head. "I don't know, Merlyn. We tethered them where we always do, at the top of the meadow, but I don't know if they're still there. I didn't see them after the men came. They might have stolen them." His lip trembled.

"No," I said. "I doubt that. They're probably where you left them. Come back with me. You can collect them while I do what I have to do."

His crumpled features straightened when his body did and he stepped towards me, his hand falling away from the swelling on his brow now that he had something to do, but before he reached my side he stopped and turned back towards the others. "Bedwyr," he called, his voice firm now. "I'm going to get the horses, do you want to come?"

Bedwyr, who had been weeping inconsolably on Ludmilla's breast, raised his tear-streaked face and turned around but made no attempt to move away from his source of comfort.

"We're going to need some help," Arthur continued. "They may be scat-tered."

Gwin had not moved since I had spoken first to Arthur. Now he turned his head towards Bedwyr, saying nothing. Bedwyr looked from Arthur to him, wiping his runny nose on his sleeve, then knuckled his eyes and looked back at Arthur.

"You want me to?" he asked.

Arthur smiled, and I realised that I was watching him with awe, seeing an eight-year-old boy behaving like a seasoned commander. "Are you com-ing?" was all he said.

Bedwyr nodded and snuffled again, blinking his eyes clear of the last tears, then stepped away from Ludmilla and began to make his way up to where we waited. Arthur glanced at Gwin. "Good," he said. "Let's go."

As we re-entered the meadow, I took care to turn left and uphill, leading the boys up to the spot where they had tethered the horses and away from where the body of Bedwyr's mother floated in the sluggish stream. I spotted a flash of whiteness back among the trees and Arthur saw it, too, as soon as I did.

"There's one of them," he said, and I heard relief in his young voice.

"Aye, and the others will be close by," I answered. "Go you now and collect them, but be cautious. They were cut loose, perhaps injured, and may still be panicky. Take your time. I'll join you in a little while."

I sat and watched them until the woods swallowed them, then turned my horse around and went down to the river.

Julia was already cold with death, and with the chill of the water. I dragged her body gently to the bank and laid her on her back, concealing the huge wound that had killed her and the bloodied evidence of her violation. She bore no visible signs of violence in front, save for a split lower lip and single large bruise high up on her face. Any other evidence had been washed away by the river. I found her clothing scattered near by and covered her decently, fighting the urge to scream aloud in rage and grief as I closed the glazed, empty eyes that once had been so warm and lively, full of love and life and joy. Lucanus, I knew, would be as griefstricken as her husband Hector. Kneeling beside her, I bowed my head in a prayer, then stooped to kiss her cheek, after which I covered her face and made my way up to collect the boys, who had found all the horses.

Moments later, we were on our way back to Camulod, riding in silence, for the most part, since there was little merit in discussing what had happened at that time. The attackers had been strangers. The younger children were too young to know what had occurred, and the older boys, I believed, too fragile to listen to a discussion of death and rapine that had taken one of their mothers. Shelagh and Ludmilla had their own thoughts to occupy them and I, God knew, had mine.

Two hours had passed since our return to the fortress and I had done everything I could think to do. The frantic activity stirred up by our arrival and the news we carried had finally died down, to be replaced by a strained atmosphere of expectation as we waited for the first reports to begin coming in. The children, all six of them, were under the care of Lucanus and Ludmilla, safe in the Infirmary and confined to bed for observation, as Luke termed their quarantine. In fact, they were being isolated for their own protection from the rumours and speculation, now being embroidered upon and argued over by everyone who still remained in Camulod.

The garrison was out already, scouring the countryside for strangers, only a holding force remaining in the fortress. Ambrose had taken overall command of that operation, coordinating the search from the Praesidium. Dedalus, Quintus, Benedict and Rufio had each been assigned a quadrant of our lands to search, radiating outward from the fort, and their cavalry was supported by eight infantry contingents, two under the nominal command of each of these four but controlled by their own officers. Fast riders had also been dispatched to each of our perimeter outposts to spread the word to seal our borders, permitting no one to exit from our lands. If there were interlopers still alive in Camulod, they would be found.

Hector, the one most intimately injured by this day's events, had ridden out with Dedalus to the scene of the attack, to bring his wife's remains home, under guard. No one had been able to dissuade him from going. Dedalus, on the same sweep, would also seek the man whom I had wounded in the groin and if the wretch was still alive he, too, would be sent to Camulod for questioning.

Now there remained only the matter of Shelagh's account of the day's events. Two separate matters had vied within my mind for attention throughout all that I had done that afternoon, and I had kept them in check successfully only by a single-minded effort of sheer will. The first of these, by far the more pernicious, was that I might even now be passing on my sickness to my friends; the other was occasioned by the fact that there had been four, perhaps five slain men there in the glade by the river, and no explanation of their deaths.

I drew a deep breath before knocking on the door to the quarters occupied by Donuil and Shelagh, and moments later it swung open and Donuil stood looking at me, his face unreadable. He had taken Shelagh away shortly after the chaos of our arrival began to die down, both of them white-faced and badly shaken by the narrowness of her escape from death. Now there was silence in the room behind him.

"How is she, Donuil?"

He shrugged and stepped aside to allow me to enter. Behind him, his wife sprawled in a stuffed armchair, her legs spread and her head tilted back, eyes closed. There was colour in her cheeks now, nevertheless, and in one hand she held a cup containing what I had no doubt was her own fiery, homemade mead. Her belt of knives lay on a nearby table, dropped in a careless heap. I glanced at Donuil, who merely shook his head, then I moved closer to her.

"Shelagh?"

She opened her eyes and looked up at me, heaving a great, deep sigh before straightening up, blinking her eyes as though to clear them of sleep.

"Merlyn," she said, showing no surprise. "Is everything in hand?"

"Aye, for the time being."

She indicated the deep couch across from her, and I sat down. Donuil remained on his feet, merely resting his buttocks against the edge of the heavy table.

"You want to know what happened," she said, a statement rather than a question. I nodded, and she squeezed her temples between the thumb and fingers of her free hand.

"So do I, Merlyn, so do I . . . I knew you'd come, so I've said nothing yet to Donuil, for I knew I could only go through this once . . ." She shook her head, frowning slightly. "It was sudden, unexpected, and I had no time to think or plan; none of us did . . ." She glanced towards her husband. "Donuil, please sit down. I won't be able to think clearly with you looming over me like that."

Expressionless, Donuil moved quietly to sit beside me on the couch. Shelagh waited until he was settled, then spoke in a voice that made it seem as though she were talking to herself.

"From the beginning, then . . ." We sat in silence while she evidently marshalled her thoughts. Then, snatching another deep-drawn breath, she launched into her tale.

"We should all have been taken in the first attack. The only thing that saved us was the lazy indolence of a hot summer afternoon. It was peaceful, hot and beautiful, the slightest breeze imaginable coming once in a while to fan us. The boys were fishing and Julia was showing the girls how to knit, using straight twigs that I had cut for them. They had all been playing in the water earlier, but had grown tired of it . . .

"I was sitting against a tree, a little way from Julia and the girls, peeling a willow branch with a knife, and Ludmilla was lying beside me. I thought she was asleep, but she had been watching me, and suddenly she suggested that I might like to practise with my knives. She can never see enough of that. She has been fascinated by how I can throw them ever since the first time she saw me do it.

"The thought was already in my mind when she spoke, so I was willing, but I knew that as soon as I produced the knives the boys would be all over me, wanting to be allowed to throw them, too, and I had no patience to put up with all the fuss of that. It was too hot. And so I told Ludmilla that if she wanted a throwing lesson I would give her one, but we would have to slip away together to where we could have peace and quiet, safe from the boys. I strolled over to Julia and told her where we were going, and then Ludmilla and I simply wandered off, betraying no purpose until we were out of sight.

"There's a place I know of, where I've been before; a big, dead tree stump with heavy bark, about the height of a man and a perfect target. We went there. It's about a hundred and fifty paces from the riverbank, just over the brow of the hill . . .

"Anyway, once we were there, I showed Ludmilla how to hold a knife and throw it, but she found it more difficult to grasp the trick of it than either of us expected—some people simply aren't attuned to things like that, I suppose. Anyway, she ended up sitting close by, watching me as I practised, and an hour or so went by. And then we heard the screams."

She stopped, and her eyes changed colour, or intensity; I did not know which, only that they had changed. Donuil and I sat motionless. She sighed again, a ragged, uneven sound this time, then swallowed audibly.

"There were five of them, big, dirty-looking men. By the time we reached the edge of the meadow, still among the trees, there was nothing we could do without endangering ourselves and making matters worse. Arthur was lying on the ground, unmoving, and young Bedwyr knelt on the grass beside him, holding his own arm, blood streaming through his fingers. Two men were each holding two of the other children, one in each hand. The two little girls were screaming, and so was Ghilleadh. Gwin, the only one of the three older boys uninjured, was fighting to break free and as I looked, the man who held him let him go, then smashed him with his fist, behind the head. The boy went down and lay there as though dead."

I interrupted, unable to contain myself, since I knew the boys were well. "What about Julia?"

Shelagh looked at me, her face as cold as stone.

"She was fighting, down on her knees, her skirts over her head, muffling her cries. A naked man stood over her, his feet on either side of her head, holding her hands together by the wrists, behind her back, forcing her face against the ground. Another knelt behind her, gripping her by the waist, pulling her against him, violating her. A third was tearing off the remainder of his clothing, laughing like a demented thing, preparing to take over when his friend had done—"

"Dia!" Donuil leapt to his feet and stalked away, slamming one fist into his open hand, unable to endure such words without reaction. For my part, I grew cold, recalling another, similar account of death and rapine told to me by Shelagh in explanation of her skill with knives. I stared at her now, knowing what she had achieved, but at a loss over how she had been able to achieve it. She was looking at me directly, both of us aware that Donuil knew nothing of that first story or its consequences. She shrugged her shoulders.

"I killed all of them," she said, her voice expressionless.

Her words stopped Donuil in his agitated pacing. He turned to face her, his eyes wide with shock. "You *killed* them? Five men? All of them?"

Shelagh's eyes had not wavered from mine, and now I nodded.

"I know, but how?"

"With ease," she said, her face wooden. "I played the foolish, silly woman." She waited for me to respond, and when I said nothing she continued.

"My first concern was to ensure Ludmilla kept her mouth shut, for I knew what I must do and if she screamed, or panicked, we would both have been in the same cauldron with Julia. Fortunately, Ludmilla is nobody's fool. I told her what I meant to do—the only thing I could do—and sent her to hide and wait for whatever might pass. Then, as soon as she was on her way, I ran up the hill as far as I could without endangering my plan, for it had come into my mind full-born and I knew it would work.

"Once there, high above them, I threw off my clothes, then put my mantle on again, over my belt. I had to keep that hidden, so I tucked the fabric of the mantle up beneath the strap, concealing my knives and their scabbards but exposing myself. Then I began to scream and run downhill towards them, begging them to stop what they were doing and let the children go. They stopped, sure enough, thinking themselves attacked. Then, when they saw that I was all alone, and naked, they came after me, leaving poor Julia where she lay. She must have been already dead, for I saw no one stab her . . ."

Once again her voice died away and she sat silent for a time, before continuing in the same placid, unemphatic tone.

"I knew I had to make them run to me, and I knew they knew whoever caught me first would have me first, and so I ran to meet them, squealing in panic but swerving as I ran, keeping the distance I required from each of them. The fools saw only my skin beneath the mantle . . . white flesh and female hair. None of them thought to see a weapon, and they made a game of hunting me, forming a ring about me, just like sheep herding a dog, never seeing the foolishness of such a thing.

"At length, when they had me surrounded, closing in, I stopped and waited for them, whining and whimpering. Three of them wore nothing at all, and none of them had a weapon drawn. The two who carried knives sheathed them, to leave their hands free for the game to come. The fools were laughing, making great sport of it. When they came close enough, I killed all five of them. Even the last of them to die had not begun to understand what had happened by the time my knife took him beneath his ugly chin."

Donuil was staring at his wife in awe. I gazed at her in total admiration, envisioning the scene she had described and remembering the awe-inspiring speed with which she had planted her blades so close together in the block of wood that day in the Armoury.

"So," I said, eventually. "You finally took vengeance for your friend Rhona."

"Aye, I did, but it gave me little satisfaction." She sipped again now at her drink, draining the cup. "Ludmilla had been watching from the trees, and she came running, calling to the children. I went with her to check them, and as soon as I had seen that Arthur and the other boys were alive and all were well enough, I bade her look to Julia and then ran to summon help, in case there should be more of these people about. I thought I could make better time alone, rather than taking everyone with me, all of us virtually unarmed. I retrieved my knives, then caught my horse and left immediately. The rest you know."

I rose from the couch and crossed to fill her cup again with mead. Donuil moved, too, to sit on the arm of her chair, his hand touching her hair. He had barely spoken a word since my arrival, but I knew that he was fiercely proud of the tale his wife had told.

"Donuil," I said, raising my own cup in a salute to Shelagh, "I think your wife has earned a debt of gratitude today that all of Camulod will be forever helpless to repay." He nodded, still wordless, and I addressed myself to Shelagh.

"Shelagh," I said, "you are a warrior like no other I have known. Men flatter themselves, calling themselves warriors and boasting of their prowess under arms, and some have performed great feats. Few men, for all of that, have sought, or fought, such odds, five against one, naked and unafraid. And so I pay tribute, one soldier to another. Honour and fortitude and skills like those you showed today are truly rare, and I feel privileged to call you friend. There is none like you anywhere, I swear."

She gazed at me, half smiling, as I drank my mead, and when I had finished she spoke again.

"Fortitude, Merlyn? Naked and unafraid? I think not. Panic, certainly. I knew no other way to tempt those animals away from Julia. Had I known she was already dead, I never could have done it. Naked I was, of desperate necessity, but I was far from unafraid. I have never been more terrified in all my life."

I nodded and put down my cup. "I believe you. But fear is healthy and keeps warriors alive. The facing of it, however, and the conquest of it, is what men call courage. Now, if you will pardon me, I shall leave you two in peace. Good night."

XXXI

My definition of courage, intended as it was for Shelagh, became a goad for me, for I could not put it from my mind thereafter, and my mental anguish grew like a mushroom over the course of the days that followed, heightened by the terror writhing in my soul. I had no sound sleep during all that time, although I spent too much time lying in my bed, avoiding daylight and people. Cowardice was alien to me, and yet I knew myself to be a coward, not merely unwilling to face my fears and conquer them, but totally incapable of even contemplating the attempt.

On the morning of the fourth day following my meeting with Shelagh and Donuil, Lucanus entered my sleeping chamber uninvited and was pulling down the heavy curtains from the narrow window high up on the wall before I had time to absorb the fact that he was there. By the time I had risen to one elbow, squinting against the glare of the harsh morning light, he was standing above my cot, glowering down at me, ignoring my pathetic noises of complaint.

"Growing a beard, are you?" His voice was deep and angry. "And evidently making some attempt to discover just how badly one man can come to smell, to boot . . ."

I cringed beneath his merciless stare, only too well aware how poorly I must look. He spun away on one heel and walked out, leaving me alone to sit up and rub at my eyes. Moments later, I heard him return with someone else.

"Leave it there." I heard scuffling sounds beyond the curtain of my sleeping alcove, and then someone withdrew. I swung my legs over the side of the bed, feeling the floor tiles cold against my feet as the curtain was thrown open, admitting yet more light. Lucanus stepped inside the room and stopped.

"There's hot water here, and towels. I presume you have fresh clothes. You have an hour before the meeting I have urged Ambrose to call in your default. It will be a small gathering. Ambrose, myself and Dedalus, Rufio, Donuil and you. We need you there, so please *be* there. You might not suffer from a visit to the bath house between now and then. One hour."

The wind of his exit ruffled the curtain in the doorway and I quaked with shame, but then I bestirred myself and did as he suggested.

An hour later I walked into the Praesidium fully dressed, clean-shaven and armoured for the first time in almost a week. The guard on duty evidently expected me and told me that I was awaited in my own day room. As I entered, everyone stopped talking and looked at me, and I scanned their faces quickly, looking for scorn, or disdain, or anything from which I might infer a hint of disapproval. I saw nothing of the kind. Ambrose leapt to his feet and came to meet me with a smile of welcome, throwing an arm about my shoulders and asking after my health. Lucanus had informed them I was sick of something, and they were all glad to see me up and about again.

I glanced towards Lucanus and his eyes met mine without the slightest sign of anything but pleasure. Unsure of what to say, I said nothing and merely greeted each of them in turn, after which I sat down in the place reserved for me, with my back to the door. Ambrose faced me at the other end of the rectangular table and he proceeded to the matters in hand immediately, addressing himself to me and bringing me up to date on all that had transpired since the day of the attack. I listened closely, the seriousness of this affair enabling me to forget my own problem for the first time in many days.

"I'm glad you're back, Merlyn," Ambrose began. "There's much to talk about. All the reports are in now, our troops are all back in garrison, and I think we have been able to reconstruct the why and all the wherefores of what happened. What I do not know is how much you recall of what had been discovered before you fell sick."

Faced with his openness, I spoke the truth. "I don't know anything, and if I did, I have forgotten. Start at the beginning."

"Right." Ambrose glanced around the table, his gaze settling on Dedalus. "Ded. Tell us about the hunt."

Dedalus cleared his throat. "The hunt, aye." He spoke to me directly. "We found the man you shot, still alive but out of his mind with pain. Sent him back here right away, for Lucanus to see what he could do with him before we began to question him."

"You were able to question him?" I had not expected the man to live.

"Oh, aye, we were able to question him, and he was able to answer, too, with a little persuasion." I merely nodded, unwilling to pursue that any further, and he went on. "What he had to tell us will come later. It was Rufio he spoke to. For now, there's this: we recovered Julia's body and those of the slain men, five in the river meadow and another on the hillside by the wounded fellow. You said one of them had used a Pendragon bow. They were all Pendragon. We found five more longbows, with arrows, where they had been left before the attack, on the other side of the river, and then we found another by the dead man on the hill—that was the one you saw—and after that we found another on the hilltop, where it had been dropped by your wounded man when he went running down the hill. Seven men, seven bows, seven Pendragon corpses, but none of our Pendragon people knew any of them."

"Six," I said. "Six corpses."

"Seven. The wounded man died, too."

I glanced around the table. No one betrayed any concern.

"I see. Go on."

"We had alerted all the outposts, as you know. No one passed by them, at least no one was *seen*. We turned the territories upside down, apart from that, and found a total of twenty-seven people unknown to us, mainly in the southern quadrant, where Rufio was in charge. They were all harmless enough, but they were trespassers. We questioned them and found the same thing in all cases: they knew they were there unlawfully, and all of them had crossed our boundaries at night, evading our patrols in the darkness. Some of them had been there for months. We have to do something about that—

about our night defenses. If ordinary folk can walk across our lines in the dark with ease, so can our enemies." He broke off for a moment, then resumed. "We now know that young Arthur was the target of the attack, and that there were twelve attackers. Seven died, so five escaped, most probably at night."

"Who were they, and how do you know that?"

Dedalus flicked a hand at me, in a clear, yet unconscious signal to me not to interrupt his train of thought. "The prisoner," was all he said. Then, taking up where he left off, he spoke again. "The most disturbing piece of information we received came from one of the boys, young Bedwyr. He heard one of the men who held the children mention Peter Ironhair—not the first name, just Ironhair. There's no possibility of error, for the boy had never heard the name before and didn't know who Ironhair was, but the name stuck in his mind and he remembered it when Donuil here was questioning him about what happened. He hadn't heard much, distracted by his mother's screaming, but it appears that early on in the proceedings, after Arthur had been laid low, the men were arguing over what they ought to do. They didn't know which boy was Arthur. 'The Pendragon brat,' they called him. They asked the boys, but by then they were too late, and Bedwyr spat at them. One of them thought they should abduct all three of the oldest boys. Another was in favour of simply killing them all. A third remembered Ironhair had given exact instructions: 'Bring the Pendragon brat back if you can' had been his words, this fellow said. 'And if you can't bring him, then kill him. Just be sure you don't come back and leave the little swine alive.' "

My mind was seething now with a hundred questions, but I made myself sit still and listen. Dedalus had not finished.

"Anyway," he continued. "All of that arguing gave way to lust as soon as the others had started humping—" He broke off and glanced around guiltily. "I mean the business with the boy's mother, Julia. Young Arthur had been felled in the opening rush, struck down by a sword hilt. Now Bedwyr tried to help his mother, and broke free, but one of them caught him, backhanded, with his blade, below the elbow, and that put the boy out of things. A moment later, the other lad, Gwin, was knocked down, too, and the two remaining men left the other children there, the youngest ones, threatening to come back and kill them if they moved or tried to run away. They ran to join the others at their sport with Julia, but before they could get there they were interrupted by the sight of fresher game, when Shelagh arrived. All five then went for Shelagh, as you know. The last to leave poor Julia must have killed her, or perhaps they had killed her earlier. We'll never know." Dedalus looked from me to Ambrose then. "That's my end of it. Someone else can go on from there."

Ambrose looked at Rufio, who sat up straighter and took over immediately.

"I was responsible for questioning the prisoner, Commander," he told me. "And knowing what the boy had told us made the whole thing easier. The prisoner had been under the care of Master Lucanus for two whole days before we turned to him, and he was well enough to speak. He was . . ." Rufio paused, searching for a word. "He was surprised, to say the very least, when he discovered that we knew why he was there and who had sent him. That knowledge made him talkative . . .

"Ironhair, it appears, made his way to Cornwall after leaving Cambria ahead of Dergyll's vengeance."

I interrupted him. "What about Carthac, was he with Ironhair?"

Rufio shook his head. "I know nothing of that. No Carthac was mentioned."

"Very well, continue, please."

"Aye. Well, once in Cornwall, Ironhair made alliance with a fellow called Dumnoric, the war chief who came out on top of the dungheap of petty wars that sprang up after Lot was safely dead. This Dumnoric is now supreme in Cornwall, it seems, calling himself king there. Ironhair is no fool, we all know that, and he has no love in his heart for Camulod. He could not enlist support for his hatred of you, for your name means nothing in Cornwall, but he blamed all of the ills that had befallen Cornwall on Camulod and on Uther Pendragon, who waged war there and brought fire and sword to the whole region. 'Uther of Camulod' was the name he used most often, it appears, and he was successful. He forged some kind of treaty with this Dumnoric. In return for Cornish aid to conquer Cambria and 'win back' Ironhair's 'kingdom,' he would undertake to storm Camulod and kill the spawn of Uther, or of Lot, whichever Dumnoric preferred to think, thereby removing all threats, both to the Cornish king, since Arthur holds the seal of Gulrhys Lot, and to the Cambrian kingship he might seek to claim as Uther's alleged son.

"To hear this fellow tell it, it was very complicated, but the upshot was that Ironhair obtained a promise of this Dumnoric's support in Cambria, provided he could prove that 'the Pendragon brat' was dead. He returned to these parts, selected twelve specialists in murder, and promised them the world if they could do what he required of them. They failed, thanks to Julia and to Shelagh's knives. That's all."

For long moments, no one moved or spoke, and I gazed around the table. Donuil and Lucanus had sat silent through all that had been said. Now Donuil spoke.

"Everything we have learned, Commander, boils down to three questions. How did the word get out about Arthur's identity? I thought that was a secret. Then how did Ironhair learn of it? And what steps must we now take to protect the boy?"

At that moment, overwhelmed as I was by all I had heard, I was unprepared to answer any of those questions. Not so Ambrose.

"Well," he asserted, speaking forcefully. "One thing is certain. The boy will have to be placed under close guard from this time on."

"Close *guard?*" Lucanus sounded outraged. "What kind of solution is that? The boy is eight years old, Ambrose. Would you make him a prisoner for life? He is a *boy*, not a criminal!"

Ambrose drew back as though he had been slapped. "I meant no such thing. I merely said—"

"I heard what you said. There has to be some other way."

Dedalus intervened, cutting both of them off. "This of the secret, your first question, Donuil. It's ridiculous. There is no secret. I myself heard Connor call the boy Pendragon openly, last summer, before a throng of people when he brought the lad the ponies. It surprised me at the time, because I hadn't known and hadn't thought about it, but when I looked, I saw it. The boy's the image of his father Uther. If I could see that, anyone could. What concerns me is, who told Ironhair?"

"Aye, Ded, and you should be concerned, although the answer's partly obvious." I had not spoken for some time, and all eyes moved to me again. "It was one of our own, someone in Camulod. But the worst part is that Ironhair, from this same source, knew of the seal of Gulrhys Lot being here. That is truly disturbing, for that *is* a secret known, I thought, to me alone. Only my aunt knew of it, next to me, and she would never have mentioned it." I glanced around the faces watching me. "Were any of you aware of it?" It was plain that no one was. I nodded. "That is as I expected. I have the seal in my own quarters, in a leather bag with Uther's seal. I have never shown it to anyone else since that first day."

The silence that ensued was long and troubled. I sat slumped in my chair and completed my thoughts.

"That means, my friends, that someone close to us—close enough to enjoy access of some kind to my quarters—is in Ironhair's employ, and our chances of finding who it is are slight, at best. While Luceiia Britannicus was alive, visitors there were few and all close friends. Since then, things have changed. Ambrose and Ludmilla and their daughters live there now, with me, and Shelagh and Donuil and their boys share a portion of the rooms, so many people come and go every day. Peter Ironhair has an active sympathizer here, in Camulod, today." I looked at Ambrose. "And that, Brother, makes nonsense of your plan to guard young Arthur closely. How close could that guard be, when we do not know against whom we are guarding? Against outside attack, well, that's one thing, but what we have discovered here is something else entirely."

I stood up, feeling older than I ever had before. "I have heard enough," I said, "and now I have to think this through. I thank you for your time, but I would ask, if I may, for more assistance from each of you. Please think upon these matters, too, for all of you know what we have to solve, and meet me here tomorrow at the same time."

They all rose to leave, nodding in agreement and talking among themselves as they filed out. Ambrose was the last to go and he hesitated at the door, plainly on the point of asking me something, but then he shrugged and merely said, "Tomorrow," before leaving me alone.

My solitude was brief. The door had barely closed behind Ambrose before it swung open again and Lucanus re-entered, moving directly to the head of the table, where he stood eyeing me closely.

"You know the answer, don't you? It's as plain as your nose. You have to take the boy away somewhere far from here where he can be a boy for five more years. As long as he stays here in Camulod, his life will be at risk."

I lowered myself carefully into my chair again, feeling as though I bore the weight of the world.

"I can't do that, Luke."

His eyes went wide. "What do you mean, you can't do that? It's all you *can* do, Merlyn."

"No, it is not. I cannot do it. Don't ask me why, because I can't explain, but I can't take him with me."

"Take—?" Lucanus cut himself short, then looked around the room as though it were a strange place in which he had suddenly found himself. He moved directly then to the chest in which I always kept a flask of Shelagh's mead. Without looking at me, he produced two cups and poured an ample measure into each of them, measuring them carefully. When he was satisfied they held equal amounts, he reinserted the stopper and replaced the flask within the chest, then approached me, holding out one cup and tilting the other unmistakably in the ancient gesture which invited me to join him in a libation to the gods. Wondering what was in his mind, I tipped my cup and spilled the few obligatory drops. He did the same.

"To Aesculapius and Hippocrates," he said, with a smile. "The patrons of medicine: a manlike god and a godlike man." He sipped his drink and sat down in the chair Ambrose had occupied, at the opposite end of the table from me. I felt the honeyed fire of the mead at the roots of my tongue and fatigue swept over me again.

"When did you learn of it?"

I blinked at him, confused, unwilling to acknowledge what I had heard in his tone.

"What? When did I learn of what?" He gazed at me, then tilted his head slightly backward, jerking his chin towards me in a gesture similar to pointing a finger.

"The sickness."

My stomach turned over. "Sickness? What sickness do you mean? I don't know what you're talking about." I could hear my own bluster.

"The leprosy."

The whole room seemed to sway and the cup fell from my hand and rolled on the wooden floor. I moved my lips to speak, but no sound emerged. Lucanus was smiling at me, a smile filled with goodwill and friendship.

"Oh, come, Merlyn, do you really think me such a fool? You believe you have contracted leprosy, though how you could even think so baffles me. You grew distraught the other day, and at first I could find no reason, although I was much alarmed. But then, when I observed some other things, I recalled that you had leapt up and fled at the mention of Mordechai's name. Since then, in spite of all that has been going on about you, you have shunned us all. And now you say you cannot take young Arthur with you when you go ... to wherever you are fleeing. You, who have been telling me for years that you believe your destiny is to instruct this child and bring him into manhood whole, and fit to rule this land in law and justice. What else but the fear of leprosy could bring about such change so quickly and so devastatingly in Merlyn Britannicus? I know how the very name of it appalls you. The fear of thinking you may have it must be driving you to despair."

Slowly, my mind spinning in search for some means of denying what he said, I reached down and retrieved the fallen cup, which had remained intact on striking the floor. I placed it gently on the tabletop and looked directly into his eyes.

"It is not fear," I said, my voice a mere whisper. "It's certain knowledge, Luke. I have the lesions."

Lucanus straightened up in shock and it was clear to me that, of all the things I might have said to him, this was the one he could least have expected. I watched him take his lower lip between his teeth and bite down hard enough to whiten it.

"What lesions are these?" he asked me, finally, speaking slowly and quietly. "Show me."

I held up my hand. "Later." I closed my eyes then, and a great, explosive sigh shook me. The truth was out! And Lucanus had not yet fled the room. "Tell me about leprosy, Luke."

He was frowning now. "What, everything I have learned in a lifetime of study, here and now?" He shook his head, but when he spoke again, moments later, his voice was gentle. "It is a strange illness and little understood, even today. But some things we do know. It is extremely slow to propagate and progress and, with proper care and cleanliness it can be held at bay for years, almost indefinitely in some cases." His voice strengthened, becoming more hard-edged. "It is also extremely slow to spread, and infection only occurs after prolonged—and careless—exposure to contamination. You have not had such exposure, Merlyn. Your sickness is in your mind, born of your fear."

"What causes it—in new cases, I mean, lacking infection from another person?"

He shook his head, frowning anew. "We don't know, but it is probably bred of filth and squalor in some way. Most dire sickness is."

"And the lesions? Let me see if I can recall . . ." I felt almost light-headed, in being able thus to voice my fears. "White blemishes appear on the skin— or they may be sometimes yellowish, or pink, brownish, or even red—and are surrounded by a slight, reddish, rough-textured discoloration. The blemishes take on a circular appearance and the body hair within such spots turns white as well. The area grows numb, immune to pain or feeling. Am I not correct?"

"You are, and you know it, so you are using sophistry to make your point. You saw such lesions once, on Mordechai's chest, and you discussed them with him. I was there, you may recall."

"I recall clearly. But I've seen them twice, Luke. I have seen them twice . . . Once upon Mordechai's chest and once on my own."

Lucanus was smiling still, shaking his head. "That is not possible, Merlyn. You are mistaken. You were not exposed to Mordechai's disease. His sickness was not virulent."

"Perhaps, perhaps not, but I was exposed to him, the night he died."

He froze, frowning, and I realised he knew nothing of the details of that episode. I had omitted them at the time, merely reporting Mordechai's death with the end of his colony, not wishing to cause Luke unnecessary pain. I told him now, and as he listened to my account his face grew pale and he put down his cup. When I had finished he sat staring, groping for words.

"You say . . . You said his blood mixed with your own?"

"Aye, some of it. Both of us were bleeding freely, me from my arms and head, Mordechai from various places. Why? Is that important?"

He ignored my question, leaning forward. "These lesions you speak of, where are they sited?"

"On my chest, but there's only one of them."

"May I see it? You could be wrong . . ." I noticed he had lost the emphasis of his denial.

"I doubt I am, but I can't show you here. I'll have to strip, and there are too many people about."

He nodded and stood up and I led the way back to my own quarters, where I disrobed and showed him my breast. His face tightened and he touched one fingertip to the scab beside the whitened patch of hair and skin.

"What's that?"

"A cut . . . A stab wound. I stopped short, but I came close to ending it that first day."

He looked at me levelly. "I hope that phase is over?"

"It is."

"Good." He returned his inspection to the infected area of my chest, then turned away. "You may put your tunic on again."

"Well? Am I correct? Is it a leprous lesion?"

Lucanus faced me squarely. "It could be. It looks like one, but it is only one and I see no sign of others. It could also be another thousand, harmless things. I don't know, Merlyn. I simply do not know. My strongest inclination is to scepticism, but I confess this thing about the mingling of your blood with Mordechai's is worrisome. I have some texts I want to read before I reach any conclusions." He paused, continuing to look directly into my eyes, his own shifting slightly as his gaze switched from my right eye back to my left. "Bear this in mind, nevertheless: even should you be right, and I am wrong, this is no death sentence. I cannot tell you not to be concerned, for that would be sheer foolishness, but I can urge you to remember this: it is a sickness, a progressive, but very slow-moving, combatable sickness. Mordechai himself was sick with it for more than twelve years, as you know, and yet the signs of it were barely noticeable, and he worked hard and diligently throughout all that time. And he died of injuries, not leprosy. Above all, I believe implicitly that it is not communicable through casual, normal contact. You constitute no threat to anyone else's health, even if your fears have a solid foundation, which I doubt. Do you understand what I am telling you, Merlyn?" I nodded, and he nodded back. "Good. I would be even more emphatic were it not for this matter of the mixing of your blood with Mordechai's. That is the only matter that concerns me and, as I have said, I have some texts I wish to read on that subject before I make a judgment. I know I've read something about this somewhere, and I know I have the source in my possession. Now, when did you last sleep?"

I smiled, amazed at the ease with which I could do so now. "You woke me up a few hours ago. Don't you remember?"

"I remember that, but I meant when did you last enjoy an untroubled, restful sleep?"

I sobered. "A long time ago. The night before you mentioned Mordechai, I think."

"Hmm. I'm going to bring you back a sleeping draught, as quickly as I can go and return. You will drink it immediately, and you will sleep."

"But it's only a short time after noon!"

"It is bedtime for you, my friend. Lack of sleep is the better part of your problem. Wait here."

I said nothing as he left, merely staring at the swinging curtain after he passed through, and I had not moved when he returned a short time later. My mind was calm and the panic gone. I drank the draught he gave me, then I slept. And as I slept, I dreamed.

*   *   *

I slept for almost an entire day, awakening gently the following morning as from a normal night of restful sleep, to find my sleeping chamber brightly lit by the mid-morning sun because I had not replaced the curtains Luke had pulled down the previous day.

Wonderingly aware of the lightness of spirit that filled my mind and body, I made my way first to the bath house, where I found the steam room empty. Much relieved, for had it been occupied I would not have entered, I steamed luxuriously for a time, sweating the residual tiredness from my body, then dried myself with a thick towel, which I took with me when I left.

From there, I went to the kitchens to eat, returning the greetings of those who spoke to me and examining my thoughts and feelings with astonishment as I walked. I still believed that I had leprosy—no doubt of that existed in my mind—but the mere act of sharing my grim knowledge with Lucanus seemed to have released my soul, somehow, from the chains in which it had been bound up for so long. Lucanus's concern, upon hearing of this mixing of Mordechai's blood with mine, had been the final confirmation I required, although the reason for his fear escaped me. His first reaction to that information, however spontaneous as it had been, had quite convinced me that I was right. Why then, I wondered, did I feel so light, and so relieved? I had, within my body, the foulest sickness known to man, so when and how had my despair withdrawn into peace of mind? I decided that these questions had no answers, and resolved to continue as I always had, until the day my fears returned again, and I ate heartily at a table in the corner of the kitchens, exchanging normal, carefree banter with the bustling cooks.

When I arrived back in my day room in the Praetorium for the meeting with the others, Lucanus was absent. Ambrose noted my glance at the empty chair and explained that Luke had been detained and would come when he could. I found it easy to grin at Ambrose as I took my own seat opposite him as before, at the end of the table closest to the door.

"You look like death, Brother," I told him. "What's wrong? Too much to drink last night?" He flushed and looked away, and I heard him say something inaudible about not having slept all night. I assumed one of the children must have been sick and thought no more of it as Donuil approached me, holding out a large, earthen mug, its outside dewy with moisture.

"Here, Commander, a little luxury. Connor arrived late yesterday, and he brought ice down from the northern mountains, packed in straw." For the first time, I noticed similar mugs in front of every seat. I thanked him and gulped at the drink it contained, water, flavoured with the astringent juice of some strange, delicious fruit. It was cold and marvellous, making my throat ache with the chill of it.

Ambrose cut me off before I could inquire after Connor.

"Gentlemen, shall we begin? We have much to discuss."

Once again, as on the previous day, I found myself in audience, listening as one by one my friends laid out the possible solutions they had all devised to meet the problems and the questions we had taken from the table at the end of that meeting. I alone had failed to do what I had asked of them. As they spoke, however, I became aware of a formless tension within the room, although I remained unable to define it. I could sense, nevertheless, that something had changed here since the previous day. Rufio was the last to speak again, and when he finished everyone turned to Ambrose, who had been sitting rapt, his fingers clasped together, supporting his chin, his eyes fixed on the table-top as he digested every word.

"Our thanks, Rufio," he said, then turned to look at me. "Now, to sum up." Everyone sat straighter, and again I could discern the curious air of tension I had noted earlier. The thought occurred to me that this had all been said before, agreed upon, and was now being repeated for my benefit alone. I stirred and uncrossed my ankles, telling myself that the thought was ludicrous as Ambrose began to speak, counting his points off on the fingers of one hand.

He began by emphasising, for my benefit, that everything that had been done in this matter was predicated upon my own belief, which was fully shared by every person there, in the vital importance of the boy Arthur, not simply because of who he was, although that was significant enough, but even more because of what he stood for. Arthur Pendragon was the embodiment of a cherished vision; a dream first visualized by Camulod's founders, but shared since then by everyone in Camulod who dared to dream at all. The boy, and the Dream he embodied, represented freedom and survival in the face of chaos. Arthur Pendragon symbolized the future and the continuance of the way of life Camulod had been intended to preserve from its inception. He personified the hopes for the future for all, and the rule of law and reason; the simple dignities all free people required to remain free. No one around this table doubted that, Ambrose said, nor did anyone doubt that, lacking the hope symbolised by Arthur's presence and the promise he represented, the entire world of Britain, not merely Camulod, would dissolve into anarchy and ruin.

I listened, greatly moved by my brother's eloquence and the evident conviction radiating from his face, and my throat grew tight with emotion as I thought of the men and women who had made possible all that he spoke of, among them his and my own forebears Caius Britannicus, Publius and Luceiia Varrus, Ullic and Uric and Enid Pendragon and Picus Britannicus.

Ambrose was still speaking. "We have come to agree, generally, all voices except yours concurring, that the constant guarding of young Arthur is not a viable option, under the current circumstances. It might have been so, had we been able to guarantee that only outside forces would conspire against him, but we cannot do that. Camulod itself has been infiltrated and defiled by Ironhair's adherents. Apart from that, however, the lad could not develop normally, living under constant guard and scrutiny, and we have all agreed that if he is to grow to be the man this Colony and this land will need tomorrow, then he must be permitted to grow naturally, continuing exactly as he has begun already. So . . ." I waited.

"The remaining option facing us is to remove him to some other place where he will be safe and may grow into manhood properly, living a life of freedom and continuing to receive the same instruction and tuition he has known until this time."

I nodded in agreement, accepting what he said completely. All the people gathered here were Arthur's teachers, and they ratified the truth of what Ambrose was saying.

"I agree," I said, speaking for the first time. "But where can we send him?"

Ambrose grunted. "Well, as you have heard, we have identified the places where he can't go. He can't stay here, or anywhere close to our domain. Too many people know him and us.

"He can't go east, either, for along the Saxon Shore, by our own reports, the invaders spread farther inland every year, and the whole land is war-torn. Nor can he go to Vortigern's kingdom, up in Northumbria. The problem with the Danes there is too perilous. South and southeast of us, the situation is the same as on the Saxon Shore, heavily invested with aliens. Southwest and west are Cornwall and Cambria, Ironhair's domain, and in the north, below the Wall, the Picts swarm everywhere." He paused, looking around, and then continued in the same tone.

"That leaves two, or three, alternatives. We could send him to Gaul, to live with your friend Bishop Germanus in Auxerre, or we could send him to his mother's people in Eire, or even to their new holdings among the isles off Caledonia. All of those possibilities, however, safe as they may be, remove the boy from Britain, and that seems wrong. We all believe that if he is to be of any use to Britain as a man, he should remain in Britain as a boy." He stopped. "Your turn, Brother. What must we do?"

I sat for long moments, looking at no one as I sought to digest all I had heard, and then I spoke my mind, saying the words that had been forming there since the first man had spoken.

"Deadlock," I said. "There's nothing to be done. Your analysis is accurate and nothing can be gained by sending Arthur out of Britain. We will have to keep him here, in Camulod, and make the best of it. There's no alternative."

"Ah, but there is, one other, and we have agreed to adopt it." I looked at Ambrose now in surprise.

"I've missed it then. What is it?"

"We've been discussing regions, Merlyn; north, south, east and west. We don't require a region for this undertaking, simply a place to live, an isolated area; a place that's far enough from here to be secure, yet close enough to give us ease of access."

"That is a contradiction in terms."

Ambrose shook his head. "No, it is not; not if you have Connor's galleys at your command, and if the place you choose lies close to his waters and under his protection."

My mind gave a great leap, and fragmentary images of a fleet of galleys flashed behind my eyes.

"We believe you must take the boy, Merlyn, and go with him, under Connor's protection. Arthur is your ward, and you have jurisdiction over his upbringing. Go then, and raise him in peace and safety. Wait!" He held up a hand to stop me from interrupting him. "No one suggests you should do this alone. Some of us will go with you. Donuil and Shelagh and their boys, who are young Arthur's friends. Ded and Rufio will go, and Turga. I shall stay here and govern Camulod, for someone must, but I shall visit with you every year."

They were all staring at me. I blinked and shook my head. My tongue was dry. I swallowed thickly.

"I cannot do that, but someone must. Send someone else."

I had not heard the door open behind me, but now Lucanus spoke over my head.

"You can do it, Merlyn, and you must, for no one else is suited to the task as you are."

I swung in my seat to face him, but he was already passing me, followed by Connor, who grinned at me and nodded before taking a stool from its place against the wall and placing it beside the chair in which Lucanus now sat. I gazed from one to the other of them, my heart hammering, and suddenly identified the tension I had felt since entering the room. They knew! All of them knew.

"You told them."

Lucanus merely shrugged and raised a hand. "I told them you are troubled, yes. I told them of your skin condition and your groundless fears, and I assured them that the best thing you could do is leave here for a while until you are satisfied that you are well again. I told them also that I would go with you as your friend, since I am not really needed here at present. Camulod, I am pleased to say, has no lack of medical skills or personnel. Besides, by being with you, as your physician, I could ensure that, with the proper care and attention, we can clear up this condition of yours. It interests me. Skin ailments always have."

I listened in disbelief, hearing no mention of the dreaded name of my "condition" as he continued.

"So, it seemed reasonable to us all that since we two are the boy's principal instructors, we should take him with us, thus solving several problems at one time. Connor here offered us his galley for our journey, and then Donuil and Shelagh volunteered to come with us, and others followed their lead. We were here all night discussing the matter."

I licked my lips, moistening them before I spoke. "Come with us to where, and for how long?"

Lucanus smiled at me with open candour. "To Cumbria, not Cambria. It is far in the northwest, below Hadrian's Wall and sheltered by mountains. The Roman influence was strong up there, I recall, and the region was garrisoned until the final days of the withdrawals. There is a port there, Connor tells me, where he sometimes stops to buy fresh meat. It is called Glan, something . . ." His eyes crinkled as he sought the name.

"Ravenglass," I said and saw his eyes go wide in surprise. "The Romans called it Glannaventa, but to the local Celts it has always been Ravenglass, Yr-afon-glas, The Green Harbour."

I was conscious of a great and solemn stillness, somewhere deep inside my breast, and my dream of the previous night came flooding back. Arthur had been there in that dream, standing upon a headland with his back to me as he gazed out upon a sea dotted with Connor's galleys. The wind had stirred his cloak and he had turned to me, laughing a strong man's laugh, and I had seen his adult face before I saw the crimson dragon blazoned on his chest and was amazed to see he wore his father's armour. I had reached out to touch it, feeling the coldness of the metal plate beneath my outspread fingers.

"Arthur," I had asked him. "Where did you find this armour?"

He had laughed again, the same loud, rolling laugh, and I had looked up into the enigmatic, shrewd, but not unfriendly eyes of the man who had slain Uther: Derek, who called himself the King of Ravenglass.

EPILOGUE

SOME MEMORIES REMAIN forever in our consciousness, branded upon our minds in the moment of their creation without awareness on our part of how or why that moment should be momentous. I will never forget my first view of the former Roman port of Glannaventa.

I stood on the stern deck beside Connor's swinging chair, my right hand resting on Arthur's shoulder. The other boys, Bedwyr, Gwin and Ghilleadh, were on the fore-platform with the remainder of our group, peering landward into the low-lying morning fog that clung to the calm surface of the water. I felt Arthur stir uneasily, itching to join his friends, and tightened my grip to hold him still. Connor had been speaking to him moments before, describing the land we were approaching, but now sat silent, his eyes seeking to pierce the fog.

Somewhere ahead of us and above, a gull began to cry and soon was joined by others in a screeching cacophony of noise. To my left, Tearlach, Connor's Captain, stood with Sean the navigator, both men equally attentive.

We had dropped anchor in the pre-dawn of a crystal, starry night, to await the coming of day, in order not to cause alarm by approaching the harbour without being recognised. At dawn, after the calm of the night, Sean had told us, a sea fog would spring up, but would soon dissipate in the fresh day's offshore breeze and the heat of the sun. The sun had risen an hour before, the anchor had been raised, and now we waited, held in place by occasional gentle oar strokes on one side or the other, for the breeze to come from the shore.

"Wind," Sean said softly. As he spoke, I sensed a difference, saw an eddy in the wall of fog ahead of us, and then the clouds parted and seemed to roll away and an offshore wind revealed what lay ahead of us, gilded in the bright sunshine of an early autumn morning.

The first thing I saw was a hillside; a low, swelling bank of land rising directly from the waters ahead and to our left, and the unworthy thought occurred to me that Sean had been mistaken and there was no harbour here. But then the fog bank rolled farther off and showed the bank to be an island, low and wide, around which the water stretched into a shallow bay.

"Half oars," Connor murmured, and Tearlach leaned towards the well of the ship to bellow the order to the men below. Slowly, gathering way only gradually, Connor's long galley began to move towards shore, propelled gently by only half the oarsmen, the others holding their sweeps inboard, standing up vertically so that they formed a row of palisades along each side of the vessel. The great sail, with its black galley device, hung empty from the enormous spar that supported it; its purpose was identification this morning, not propulsion. Ahead of us, the entire western shoreline of the port was revealed to be the exterior wall of a Roman fort, built of stone, from which long wooden piers reached out on either side of the central western gate, into the deep water channel. Above our heads, the watchman at the masthead called out instructions to the pilot below, guiding him along the channel. Someone on the walls began to blow a horn, and within moments we could see figures running along the parapet walk behind the walls.

Arthur squirmed and looked up at me.

"Please, Merlyn, can I go to the prow?"

I released him and watched as he ran along the central spine of the galley like a cat, never once looking where he placed his feet, and then I turned my eyes beyond the fort, looking to either side. Low, densely treed hills stretched away, rising steeply as they receded from the sea. I received simultaneous impressions of peace, strength, wealth and stability, although I had little on which to base such responses and all might have been merely wishful thinking.

"They know us now. Take us in, Tearlach." Connor swung himself to face me, a half grin twisting the corner of his mouth. "Well, Yellow Head, so far I think everything is as planned. *Our* welcome is assured; are you quite sure of yours?"

I glanced at him, then back towards the prow, where my party stood, their excitement evident from their attitudes. Donuil and Shelagh were there, holding their two boys Gwin and Ghilleadh by the hand, restraining them, and Dedalus and Rufio stood one on either side of Lucanus. In front of them stood Turga, Arthur's nurse, and the recently bereaved Hector, who had insisted on accompanying us, unwilling to remain in Camulod when his son Bedwyr's only friends were leaving him. Bedwyr and Arthur, the two oldest boys, were screened from sight by the adults. Hearing the creak of Connor's chair, I turned back to follow his gaze and was in time to see Feargus's galley slipping into place beside Logan's, both of them waiting safely out of range of any danger from the shore.

Looking away again, I wondered what form, indeed, our welcome might take. For all I knew, Derek of Ravenglass might even refuse us right to land in his domain. We had been enemies, he and I, thrown together only twice in the past, by merest chance, although we had never fought and had maintained a wary truce between us. I felt myself smiling and Connor noticed it.

"What are you grinning at?"

"I am about to approach a man who knows me only as an enemy, seeking sanctuary, and I have no idea how he will react. Both times we have met, it has been as enemies. And now I come to him as a supplicant, seeking a life for the son of a man he killed, for which I should have killed him. And yet, outside of my own kin and closest friends, and without any sane reason, I believe I would trust him over any man I know. I can't explain it any better than that."

He smiled back. "Well," he said, his voice strangely gentle. "If he refuses you, you can come north with us. Up there, since it's isolation you are seeking, you should find much to please you. But we'll soon find out if you're sane or not, for I think that's him coming out onto the pier."

A group of people were hurrying to meet us, some of them taking positions to receive thrown ropes, and among them, in the very centre of them, I saw the enormous figure of Derek, their king. I felt a stirring in my gut and, wishing to hide my own uncertainty, quickly looked away, down into the body of the boat, to where a pile of wooden crates lay bound. Within them were the treasures I had brought with me, to sustain us in whatever kind of life might lie ahead: cases of books and parchments, written by my grandfather, my father and my Uncle Varrus; my own favourite selections from the ancient weaponry in Publius Varrus's Armoury; Lucanus's medicinal supplies; a stock of arms and armour for the horses and men now confined in the two galleys that rode behind us; and, in one large crate, the most sacred and the most mysterious things I owned—the oaken case containing Excalibur, and the two menace-filled, iron-bound boxes that had belonged to my father's murderers, the Egyptian sorcerers Caspar and Memnon. In the time ahead, I estimated, I would have ample time to explore those chests and catalogue their contents.

Camulod and Cornwall and Cambria and their dangers lay behind us for a spell. Ahead of us lay Cumbria.